If You Want Blood... You've Got It

The Hanging Chads Omnibus Vol. 2

Evan Clouse

COVER IMAGE ILLUSTRATED BY
Arpit Mehta

This book is dedicated to every person who cares about our personal freedom. To every person who cares about our democracy. To every person who shuns the politics of hate and division. To every person who accepts and embraces others for who they are. Thank you for your voices. Thank you for your caring. Thank you for your kind hearts. I love you all.

Acknowledgments

I would like to thank every person who has supported me and understands just how important this work is to me. Thank you for reading. Thank you for your input. Thank you for caring. You know who you are.

CONTENTS

SOUL TWO SOUL

PURPLE REIGN

TWINFINITY

SOUL TWO SOUL

Chapter 1

Greetings and Salutations

The grandfather clock chimed at exactly midnight to usher in September 1, 2034. At that moment, she was awoken with a start. Her tie-dyed T-shirt and red plaid boxer shorts were saturated with her own sweat. Her pupils expanded to allow what little light that there was into her deep hazel eyes. Her eyes continued expanding as a dark purple cloud formed at the foot of her bed. The eerie cloud continued its transformation into the loose form of a lanky female with glowing red eyes and what appeared to be a tight bun of copper hair upon its misty head. Her eyes widened as the gaseous form began a high-pitched cackle that sent shivers down her spine. She pinched herself. It was just a dream.

At that moment, she was awoken with a start. Her tie-dyed T-shirt and red plaid boxer shorts were saturated with her own sweat. Her pupils expanded to allow what little light that there was into her deep hazel eyes. Her eyes continued expanding as a dark purple cloud formed at the foot of her bed. The eerie cloud continued its transformation into the loose form of a lanky female with glowing red eyes and what appeared to be a tight bun of copper hair upon its misty head. Her eyes widened as the gaseous form began a high-pitched cackle that sent shivers down her spine. She pinched herself. It was just a dream.

At that moment, she was awoken with a start. Her tie-dyed T-shirt and red plaid boxer shorts were saturated with her own sweat. Her pupils expanded to allow what little light that there was into her deep hazel eyes. Her eyes continued expanding as a dark purple cloud formed at the foot of her bed. The eerie cloud continued its transformation into the loose form of a lanky female with glowing red eyes and what appeared to be a tight bun of copper hair upon its misty head. Her eyes widened as the gaseous form began a high-pitched cackle that sent shivers down her spine. She pinched herself. "Ow!" she exclaimed. This was not a dream.

The unearthly dark purple form continued its cackling as it floated slowly upon her bed. It continued its effortless path, leaving a pungent trail of sticky, purple residue upon the young woman's body. It peered down at her with her emblazoned crimson eyes and ceased its cackling. It frowned at the frozen young woman and screamed in a high-pitched, nasally voice, "Stay away from her! Stay out of this! She is mine! You will *not* be warned again!"

At that moment, she was awoken with a start. Her tie-dyed T-shirt and red plaid boxer shorts were saturated with her own sweat. Her entire body had a purple molasses-like residue on it. Her boxer shorts were soaked from having wet herself. She was trembling. She vigorously shook her head to shake the nightmarish encounter from her consciousness, went to the bathroom and looked at her bloodshot eyes in the mirror. *What the hell did they put in that stuff last night?* she wondered to herself as she was finally coming to grips that this experience had been nothing more than a really bad trip. And that the previous night's party must have been much messier than what she remembered.

"Eeeewwww"! she cried out as the hot water rinsed the purple slime from her five-foot seven full figured caramel skinned body. She scrubbed intensely in order to wash the ooze from her tight Rastafarian shoulder length braids.

She made her way down the rickety stairs of the three-bedroom New Orleans home that she shared with her three best friends. "Well good morning sweetheart! What is up with all the screaming?" Jamie Johnson beamed as she made her way into the living room and handed the still slightly trembling Arima Azan a steaming cup of jet-black coffee. Jamie's floral nightgown rode up to briefly expose her despised member as she sat on the couch next to her best friend since kindergarten. "Oopsie!" she declared through her laughter. "Better put *that* one away. *That* is *not* for you. And, hopefully not for *me* soon. So….tell me… what was with the screaming?"

Arima looked at her coffee with disinterest and said, "Ah, its nothin'. Just a bad trip, I guess. But it seemed so real. I don't even want to talk about it. It still creeps me out. I just need to lay off the weed for today. Y'know, get my system cleaned out or somethin'. Nope, *not* gonna smoke at all today".

Jamie looked at her best friend with a wide-eyed and bemused expression as she continued to listen to Arima. "Nope, none for me today, thanks. Well…at least not before dinner. I need to maybe just make that a nighttime activity or something. Or…well…*definitely* not before lunch. I already pig out enough *without* a case of the munchies. Save it up for the early afternoon, that's my new motto." Arima surveyed the coffee table that was littered with pizza boxes, beer cans, mail, magazines, and a *lot* of stems. Noticing the objects that she was looking for, she hazily said, "Hey…hand me that pipe and baggie wouldja? But I'm *definitely* gonna start that other thing tomorrow. Or maybe the next day. Well…we'll just see how it goes."

"What is going on?" came the desperate cry of a woman's voice from the downstairs bedroom. "Uh…I dunno baby, I'm really trying" came a male's response. "Well…try putting it in there!" the woman demanded. "You know that I already tried that! It doesn't fit there!" the man roared back.

Arima and Jamie stared at each other in shocked silence with gleeful smiles upon their faces as they continued to listen to this uncharacteristic marital squabble between Jessie and Cliff West. "C'mon baby," Jessie pleaded. "You *know* I need it first thing in the morning. Make it work!" "I'm telling you I'm trying but…its just dead. Its just lying there. Nothing is working! I can't get it up!" came the exasperated reply of her beloved husband Cliff. "Fine! I'll just use Jamie's then!"

The petite, pink camisole-clad blonde figure came into the living room with determination and stood in front of her bewildered trans friend. "Give it to me," Jessie demanded. "Um…um…um….give *what* to you?" came Jamie's hesitant inquiry. The impatient Jessie replied, "Your phone. Neither of ours is working and you know how I have to check my likes every morning. Give it to me. Where is it?"

"Oh…*that*…alrighty then, sweetie. *That* I can give to you. I'll just get it from my bedroom," a relieved Jamie responded as she wiped sweat from her brow.

"What's wrong with her?" Jessie asked Arima as Jamie ascended the staircase towards her bedroom.

"Um…well," Arima began as she attempted to think of how to put this delicately. "We weren't quite sure what you guys were doing and… well…it kinda sounded like you wanted to use Jamie's dick."

Jessie burst out in hysterical laughter as her husband entered the room, still in his pajamas. "She thought *what*? That I wanted to use her *dick*? I mean…I've *always* fantasized about maybe having an interracial thing with a Black dude, but if that happens, I'd prefer that I'm with somebody who is actually into me, y'know?"

"Wait…what?" a confused Cliff asked as his wife playfully patted his ass, looked up at him with a grin and said, "Don't worry, baby. It's just a fantasy. You are quite…adequate."

"Yeah, that's reassuring," Cliff replied as he made his way to the kitchen. "Do you want some eggs?"

"Sure, baby! Right after I feast on all of my likes!" Jessie hungrily replied as she grabbed the iPhone from Jamie's hand.

"What…the…*hell*?" Jessie screamed out once again. "I know that I paid the Internet. It comes right out of my account. Turn on the TV. Let's see if something's going on."

Arima dug into the couch cushions, found the remote mingled with lint and stale corn chips, and pressed the power button. The TV came on, but none of the streaming services were operational.

"This is *really* starting to piss me off!" Jessie roared as she flipped open her laptop and began searching the web for information. The computer would not connect. Jessie sat silently as tears began to form in her eyes. "Hey, baby?" she meekly stated to her husband. "Could you just hold me? Something's wrong. I can't get to my feeds. I can't post anything. I can't see my likes and my loves. I'm…I'm…lost."

Arima looked at her friend with no expression and stated flatly, "Y'know, maybe this is a good thing. You're becoming addicted to that shit."

"Addicted?" Jessie roared back. "Oh, that's *really* rich coming from the stoner of the year! Year? Hell, stoner of the *decade*! I'm *not* addicted.

But I have followers who hang on my *every word*. My every action. My every experience. They are *lost* without my guidance. What I do is provide advice and funny memes to help people through their day! Now, what are *they* going to do?"

"Um…I dunno," Arima replied. "Probably just find some other way to blow off their jobs and waste their time. Well, good luck with that. I've gotta get dressed and go over to Gram's. Then I've gotta go to that job interview at the morgue."

"And then, sweetie," Jamie gushed. "You will be meeting *us* for your twenty-third birthday celebration!"

"Oh yeah," Arima replied whimsically. "It's my birthday. I guess I forgot what day it was. Looking forward to the birthday brownies."

As Arima began up the stairs, she heard Jessie exclaim once again as she broke down into tears, "Why won't this *work*? What is going *on*? This is the worst thing that has *ever happened!*"

Jamie found and turned on a small radio. Out of the tiny speaker came static, then an announcer's voice declaring, "*Once again, all wireless internet services throughout the world have been compromised and taken offline. Repair crews are baffled as to the cause of the constant power overloads and are unable to restore the service for any period of time greater than five minutes. As of right now, it appears that the only way that internet service can be accessed is through outdated phone lines and landline modems. We will keep you updated as this tragic event unfolds. This emergency news break has been brought to you by NoSkids laundry detergent. Leave your mark by leaving NoSkids today!*"

"Oh…my….GAAAAAAWD!" Jessie wailed out as she flew out of the room and flung herself face-first onto her bed crying hysterically. "Well, shit," Jamie stated as she slowly shook her head. "There goes my internet porn". Cliff just looked at the floor and silently nodded.

———

Arima was nearly bowled over by the seven young school-children as they were hastily leaving her grandmother's house to begin their first day of school. Louise Azan's sixty-two-year-old tan face beamed with pride as she watched her well-fed neighbor children scurry down the block.

She then looked at the beautiful young woman standing in her doorway. Arima was her pride and joy. She had raised her since birth following the tragic loss of her daughter shortly after her granddaughter's emergence into the world. She chuckled to herself as she remembered holding her newly born granddaughter for the first time twenty-three years ago. She was then, as she was now. Mellow. Arima very rarely made a sound as an infant with the exception of some light cooing. Her caramel skin was the product of her all-Jamaican mother and western European... Her mind forced the thought of Arima's biological father out of her head. He was not worth even a second of consideration. She focused instead once again on her beautiful granddaughter.

As a child, Arima loved everybody and everything. She was a pure soul who was always eager to help others in need, although she would do so at her own pace and in her own time. Nothing was ever urgent to her, but when something important needed to be done, she possessed the quick intellect and ability to apply herself in order to complete the task at hand. Usually without too much grumbling. She adored nature, especially animals, and took it upon herself to shelter and feed as many neighborhood strays as she could.

As a teenager, she began volunteering at a local animal shelter. Upon graduation from high school- which was finally completed as her taskmaster grandmother stood over her shoulder to ensure that she completed all of her missed assignments- she became a full-time employee at the shelter.

She moved out of her house and moved in with her lifelong friends at the age of twenty-one. Louise was aware of the parties and of Arima's other more pungent interests. She was not at all surprised when Arima began smoking in her late teens. In fact, although Louise did not imbibe in this herself at this stage of her life, she tacitly approved of Arima's participation as long as it did not interfere with her being able to support herself.

There was really no difference between that and casual consumption of alcohol, she thought. And, this form of escape was much more in keeping with her nonchalant and low-key persona. Alcohol, Louise believed, was responsible for summoning the demons that reside in each of us. Marijuana served to keep them away.

At least this is what Louise hoped was the case as she continued to gaze upon her granddaughter on this, her fateful twenty-third birthday. It was on this day that every female Azan descendent had learned about the full extent of their special gift to the world. The type of energy that they possessed would reveal itself in its true form and the honing of that power would begin under the tutelage of her female elders. Louise felt that she knew what her beloved granddaughter's special feminine ability would be. It would be to communicate with the spirit world and to guide them onto the realm of Enlightenment where their souls could watch over and guide others who remained upon the earth.

She smiled and cupped Arima's cheeks in her hands. She gazed deeply into her granddaughter's hazel eyes. Her smile faded and she began trembling. Her beautiful granddaughter could indeed guide hapless spirits into Enlightenment. Tears formed in her eyes as she now realized that her granddaughter could also be used, inhabited by, and manipulated by the more maniacal spirits in this universe. The soulless. The demons. Louise could feel it in her very essence. It was one of *her* gifts. It would take more than a few tokes off of a joint to keep these demons away. It would take concerted effort and training to give her trusting granddaughter the tools that she needed in order to remain a pure soul. And it would require that she have the conversation with her beloved granddaughter that she had longed dreaded and prayed would never be necessary. She had to tell Arima the story of her father.

Chapter 2

Well, That's One Way to Start a Day

"Come inside this instant, my child," Louise stated with urgency as Arima replied, "Sure. What's the rush, Grams?"

"Oh, my child, sit with me. We need to have a talk." As Arima sat next to her grandmother on her floral couch in the main sitting room, she looked around at the walls which were adorned with paintings and sculptures from their native Jamaica. Arima had always been comforted by being surrounded by her heritage in this room. But today was different. As she looked upon the colorful artifacts today, she saw things in them that she had not noticed before. She saw things that were unsettling. Dark shadows and silhouettes swirled throughout the artwork that had not been there before. She thought about the urgency of her grandmother's demeanor, and she shuddered.

"Um…so what's up Grams? What's with all of the drama?"

"Give me your hands, child, and look into my eyes," came Louise's cordial demand. "Look deeply into my eyes, my lovely. Now…tell me what you saw last night."

"Uh…last night? Nothing really. Just a weird nightmare. I gotta stop getting my stuff from that guy. His quality control is really going downhill," came Arima's nonchalant reply.

"Tell me about it, child. Tell me about who you saw," Louise replied impatiently.

"Uh…I don't know. It was just, like, this weird purple ghost crazy bitch. She had red eyes and told me to stay out of something. That she was hers. I haven't a clue what it means. She was large and purple, so maybe just a weird Freudian penis envy thing in my subconscious. Plus, I had some weird purple yuck on me after the dream, so…yep…probably penis envy."

"She left a residue," Louise inquired hesitantly.

"Uh…no…it wasn't the *dream*," Arima replied through her light chuckles. "I musta just spilled something on myself. It was just a dream, Grams. Nothin' to get uptight about. I know you have your rituals and beliefs but I…well…I respect them, but I don't really believe in that stuff."

"Tell me, child, *exactly* what this apparition looked like," Louise demanded.

"Ummmm…I don't know. Like I said, just a weird purple mist or something. Tall, lanky, glowing red eyes. Y'know…the standard nightmare ghost stuff. Oh…this was a bit strange though. She had a tight bun of copper hair on her head. Kind of a weird detail in a dream, dontcha think?"

Louise began trembling. Her mind was immediately transported back to an evening three weeks prior when she was sitting and watching one of her stories on television. The screen had gone black just before the final reveal of who the killer was. Disgusted, Louise turned the TV off, then on again. Instead of the program, a dark purple static emerged from the screen, casting the entire room in its eerie regal glow. A pair of glowing red eyes appeared and a diabolically misty form began to emerge from the television. It was nine feet tall and impossibly lanky. It had a tight bun of copper hair upon its head, and it spoke in an evil, nasally voice.

"Your granddaughter is quite beautiful," the wicked specter began. "Yes, quite beautiful, indeed. And soon she will be quite gifted. She will be called to assist one of my own. She will be called to interfere. This *must* not happen. I am warning you now just as I will warn her upon her twenty-third birthday when *she* will be able to hear me. If she interferes with me, I will *destroy* her. I will destroy *you*. I will *destroy* everything that you both hold dear. She will listen to you. Tell her to never go to New York. *Ever*. Tell her to stay away. It is *not* her fight. Tell her…"

The floating grotesque figure bent down to look Louise directly into her fear-stricken eyes and concluded in a demonic growl, "Tell her or I will rip her from her insides out and hang her from the highest tree. Tell her or the ravens will feast upon her intestines as she desperately clings to life. Tell her or she *will die* a most gruesome death. *TELL HER!*" At that moment, the apparition dissipated and the television came back on. Louise just sat there trembling in shock.

Louise stared once again at her beloved granddaughter before getting up and taking a picture off of the mantle. She placed the photograph of a beautiful woman of Jamaican descent into Arima's hands. Arima gazed at the picture of the full-figured beauty, her smile beaming and her face glowing with happiness. She was holding her newborn child.

"Uh, yeah?" the perplexed Arima began. "So…why did you hand me this picture of my mother?"

"My dearest," Louise began with trepidation. "This picture was taken on the day your mother brought you home. This was your third day in this world and your mother was so happy. She was so proud. And she was so relieved. Relieved that your father was finally out of her life. The divorce proceedings were concluded just a few days prior to your birth. He signed away custody of you. And your mother was…free.

"I know that we have never spoken about your father, but we must do so today. You must understand who he truly was so that you may understand who you truly have become on this day. You must listen to me, my darling. You must *listen*. You must *understand*. And you must *accept* my guidance. Do you understand?"

"Uh…I guess so," Arima replied as she began feeling increasingly uncomfortable with her grandmother's demeanor and the path that the discussion was taking.

"I never wanted to discuss your father with you, but I knew that the day would come when I was forced to do so. Today is that day. Your father had been a pastor but became a traveling salesman. He was quite good at what he did. He was so charming. So charismatic. So handsome…except for his disfigured hands." Louise's voice then dropped as she continued. "So manipulative. So overbearing. So controlling. So sadistic. So evil. He was the con man's con man. He could sell Satan to the missionaries. And he did.

"He was a soldier for the demon Vetis, the Tempter of the Holy. He was one of many throughout the world who would lie to and manipulate the weak-minded. He would manipulate them into turning their backs on their holy beliefs, whether they be Christian, Jew, Muslim, Buddhist or any of the other great religious philosophies. He would manipulate them into believing that they had a God-given dominion over this earth. He would manipulate them into hating all of those that did not follow him. He would manipulate them into committing heinous acts of violence and bloodshed in his name.

"It was all in preparation for the arrival of Vetis. We have seen this play out over the last two decades in our country and all over the world. Horrendous populace uprisings that have attempted to overthrow our world's great democracies and replace them with tyrannical dictatorships. It was thought by many that the orange one was the embodiment of Vetis when he rose to power in 2016. He was not. He was just another hapless pawn put in place to continue to move the needle towards hell on earth. And that period was just another scene in a very long movie. A movie that has yet to play out. And one of your father's orders was to place someone upon this earth that could fight alongside him when Vetis made his final push for world domination. Someone with special abilities. That is why he sought out your mother. He knew that your mother would soon possess *her* special abilities and could give birth to his unholy seed. He seduced her, impregnated her and dominated her. But he miscalculated the strength of the Azar womanhood. We fought back. *She* fought back. And like all petty little bullies, he slinked back into his swamp at the first sign of fortitude. Although things seem to be stabilizing around the world at the moment, this is but the calm before the storm. And your father and all of the millions of knowing soldiers and unwitting followers of Vetis are continuing to prepare for the final battle. I do not know when this battle will be waged, but I know that you are a key part of your father's plans. I know that he will return for you. That is why I have nurtured and protected you. And I shall do so always, even beyond my parting breath."

"Okay. Grams?" Arima replied without knowing how exactly to respond. "Um…listen. Maybe we need to go see your doctor, huh? Maybe one of your heart pills is messing you up a little. Do you want me to maybe make an appointment? Besides, if Mom was away from this jerk and was so happy, then why did she run away? Why did she abandon me? I'm sorry, Grams, but this all seems a bit…far-fetched. And that's coming from someone who is *really* buzzed right now."

Louise looked up at the ceiling with a bemused expression on her face. With a tone of resolve she said as she continued to look upward, "Yes, I must tell her now. You are correct, my dear. She must know… everything."

"Ummm…Grams? Who are ya talkin' to?" a confused Arima inquired as she was beginning to think that she may need to reschedule her job interview at the city morgue in order to take her beloved grandmother to an appointment for a *different* kind of doctor.

"Yes, my darling," Louise began again as her gaze fell upon her granddaughter's perplexed face. "You were told that your mother abandoned you. That she was a free spirit who simply could not be tied down. That was the story. And that was a lie. And I am sorry that I had you believe that for all of these years. Look again at your mother's picture, my dear. Look deeply. Focus on the love that I know that you have for her. What do you see?"

Arima let out a deep sigh of disregard, rolled her eyes, and stared at the picture. She experienced her conflicted feelings of love and disdain for the woman who had given birth to her, then abandoned her three days later. She felt tears begin to well up in her slightly bloodshot eyes as her feelings began to overwhelm her psyche. And then, she saw it. Her mother's image began glowing and her smile began to widen. The woman in the picture gave her daughter a playful wink of her eye. And her daughter sat there transfixed on the beauty of her mother and her mother's love that she now could feel penetrate her soul.

"Wha…wha…what is happening?" is all that Arima could manage before her grandmother began once again.

"Listen to me. Your mother did not abandon you. A few hours after this picture was taken, your father called one final time. He told her that although he would not be involved with you, he still wanted to make arrangements for your future. Just one final meeting and then he would be out of her life forever. I pleaded with her not to go, but her youthful nineteen-year-old mind did not heed my warnings. Despite all of the treachery at that man's hands, he never was able to beat her carefree spirit and optimism out of her. Perhaps it should have been. She did not return that evening. She did not *ever* return. She was found three days later on an altar in the swamp. She had been cut open and her insides were splayed all over the dark grey granite. Her head was on a pike. And that was the last image that I ever had of your mother. My daughter. My lovely Abdalla."

Louise began a slight nervous chuckle as she lit a candle on top of the mantle. "He should have known. He should have seen that she would never completely submit to him. But I suppose he wanted a challenge. And he was assured that their offspring would be quite powerful. But still, he should have known. You see, 'Abdalla' means 'servant of God'.

"Um…um…um," was Arima's response as her mind began trying to wrap itself around what she had just been told. *What? My mother was to have special powers that she could pass on to me? So that I could fight at my sadistic father's side? My father who murdered my mother? So that some weird dick of a demon could take over the world? And now I'm seeing weird forms in the artwork and my mother's picture is winking at me? And to top it off…that creepy bitch last night was real? Oh man, this is too much. I need a hit.*

"Oh, my darling Arima," Louise began again in an understanding tone. "I know this is a lot to take in. And smoking dope is *not* going to help you process this right now. There are forces who have been waiting for you to come of age. And that has happened on this day. I had always hoped that it would only be the forces of the righteous who would be able to employ your special abilities. But I'm sorry to say, my dear, that you are a product of both your mother *and* your father. Your special ability is to be able to sense when spirits are trapped here. Spirits who have more work to do before they can move on to Enlightenment so that they may watch over and guide their earthbound loved ones. You will be able to sense them, let them into your soul, and assist them in completing their earthly work so that they may then move on.

"And if you are able to find another woman with special abilities, a woman who can harness and discharge spiritual energy, then it may be possible for the two of you to place that spirit into another living being. You have the ability to make the connection and bring it into our realm and into your soul. The other would be able to capture that spirit's energy and place it into another's body. Then, that spirit will be able to complete their work on this earth in a new human form.

"But there is a troubling side to your gift. A dangerous side. An evil side. If you are not careful, a maniacal spirit may be able to possess your soul and use you for their treacherous will. That is what your father has planned for you. And the evil spirit that came to you last night may possess that ability. She perhaps is a demonic force that is acting in concert with your father. She is very strong. I know. I, too, have been visited by her. I, too, was warned by her. I am pleading with you Arima. Take her warnings seriously. Whatever it is that she is involved in, it is not your battle. I do not know when, but it appears that at some point in your life you will be summoned to New York. *Do not go*! Ignore it. Live your life and *do not* be manipulated into someone else's battles. And I do not know why, but I find it very strange that all of this has happened on the day that the wireless internet has been knocked out by some unexplained force. I just get the feeling that that force may be the source of trouble for you. Heed that devil's warning, Arima. Heed *my* warning. If you do nothing else for me in your life, promise me this one thing: do *not* go to New York. Ever."

CHAPTER 3
ART GALLERY

"Not planning on it...especially now," came Arima's uninterested response. "So, anyway Grams, you got any tea made? My throats kinda dry from...well, heh, heh...you know."

"Of course, darling," Louise replied thoughtfully as she gave her beloved granddaughter a light kiss upon her tan forehead. "And perhaps some of my sugar cookies?"

"Yeah, that would be good," Arima replied. "I need something to help me calm my nerves. You just laid a ton on me, Grams, and...I mean... maybe my eyes are playing tricks on me. I could have sworn I saw my mother's picture wink at me. I dunno. This is pretty messed up, Grams."

"I know it is my dearest," Louise replied softly as she began making her way toward the kitchen. Louise was out of Arima's earshot when she concluded her thought with, "This is indeed quite messed up. And this, I fear, is just the calm before the storm."

Arima stared at her mother's picture. She picked it up and moved it to the left, to the right, and tipped it at every angle so as to try to recreate the shadow and light pattern that had created the earlier hallucination. The picture's image never changed. It remained a static photograph of her mother's angelic, smiling face.

Okay, okay. Just another weird experience left over from that batch of dope.

Nothin' to be concerned about Arima thought to herself as her anxiety began to subside. She began laughing out loud at the absurdity of what her grandmother had just told her. *Oh, Grams! You have always been good at practical jokes, but this one takes the cake! And on my birthday, no less. I wonder how long this crazy ol' broad has been cooking this up. Yep, nothing more than one of her jokes like she used to play with me as a child to get me up in the mornings or to get me to do my homework. She just wants me on edge so that I take this interview seriously. And I really do need this job since the animal shelter moved to its new location. All right, Grams, I guess I'll just play along and not disappoint you today.*

Arima then burst into laughter as she thought about the previous jokes that her grandmother had played on her throughout her life. Her poorly attempted homework that would mysteriously disappear so that she would have to do it all over again. But correctly this time. Turning the heat down in the winter and whipping her blankets off of her in order to force her to get up and start a new day. Replacing her junk food stash of candy and chips with fruit and granola bars. The list of jokes was endless. But they did serve to give Arima the required nudge in the right direction to keep her motivated and keep her proceeding through her life. And Arima never gave her grandmother the satisfaction of acknowledging her little pranks. She simply accepted the lesson and never mentioned it to her. *Nope, never gave her the satisfaction,* Arima thought to herself as she wiped amused tears from her eyes while continuing her laughter and looking up at a painting.

It was one of her favorites. A beautiful scene of the sun setting over a Jamaican harbor, the brilliant oranges and yellows being reflected off of the lush green of the palm trees and brilliant blue of the lapping waves. This painting had always calmed her as a child as she allowed her mind to bask in the warm glow of her motherland. This painting had always called to her.

As she stared at the artwork, it gradually became darker. Black clouds began to form which blotted out the brilliance of the setting sun. The grand leaves on the majestic palms began to dry and wither. The enchanting blue waves turned dark red.

Arima stared in disbelief and immediately ceased her laughter once a pair of dark grey eyes emerged at the top of the painting, and it began cackling. *What the hell are you laughing at, bitch?* the newly formed mouth stated as an evil-looking face began protruding beyond the wooden frame of the canvas. *I have been stuck in this damned picture for centuries! I've been waiting for you! Waiting for the time that you will be able to help me! And you* will *help me or else I will...*

Arima let out a ghastly shriek as Louise entered the room with the tea and cookies. The twisted face immediately receded and the painting returned to its initial beauty. Arima looked at her bemused grand-mother and stammered, "The painting...in the painting...there was a face...a *horrible* face demanding that I help him...what the *hell,* Grams? What the hell is *happening* to me? This isn't one of your practical jokes, is it? This shit is really *happening!*"

Louise set the tray of tea and cookies upon the worn coffee table as she chuckled and shook her head. "Oh, I see that you've met Howard. I was wondering when he might try to connect with you," she said to Arima's fearfully bewildered face.

"Who...the hell...is *Howard?*" Arima screamed out.

"Well, dear," Louise began calmly as she poured the tea into a flow-ered porcelain cup. "Howard was a dreadful man. He controlled the importing and exporting of African slaves through Jamaica to his home-land of Virginia. He was especially brutal, even for those times. His retribution against even the slightest of infractions was swift and merci-less. The removal of tongues. Vicious beatings. Even more vicious rapes of the poor slave women. He was a monster. But he had a vulnerability."

"He absolutely adored the darker complexion and beauty of Jamaican women. To say that he was a womanizer would be quite an understatement indeed. And, although impossibly brutal, he always longed for a beautiful Jamaican woman that he could wed and bring home with him. Now this was, of course, not only taboo but illegal at that time, so he met a woman and fell under her intoxicating spell. Following a short courtship, he wed her secretly in Jamaica and brought her to his plantation in Virginia under the guise of being his house servant. He truly did love her, I do believe.

"And I also believe that his bride loved murdering him at the first chance that she had upon her arrival in her new home. This woman had two things that she wanted to accomplish. The first was that she desired safe passage to the newly formed United States without fear of becoming enslaved herself. The second was that she wanted revenge against this vile man that she had witnessed committing the most abhorrent atrocities to other human beings.

"So, in 1789, three days after her twenty-third birthday, she wed Howard and was immediately brought to Virginia with him. As the story goes, they consummated their marriage that night as her impatient eyes gazed upon this very painting that she had brought with her. As he achieved…well…as he was finishing his business which would result in a daughter, she took a dagger from underneath her pillow and plunged it into the man's neck. It is said that no one in the house thought much of his shrieking as he was always quite loud when he was involved in such activities.

"As he lay there dying, she made connection with his…well…not his *soul*. Men like that do not have a *soul* to speak of. She made connection with his essence, drew it out of his body, and banished it into this painting for all of eternity. Since that fateful evening, Howard's essence has been trapped there, burning in the constantly setting sun and drowning in the cool water simultaneously. I suppose that he has had quite an unpleasant time of it. And deservingly so. And, if he has frightened you and is being demanding of you, then I am guessing…"

Louise's voice trailed off as she looked up at the painting and smirked. "I am guessing, Howard, that despite the years upon years that you have been trapped in there that you have not *learned* your *lesson*. I am guessing that you are *still* the same miserable son of a bitch as that night my namesake placed you in there. Have you learned nothing? Are you still the same brutally racist and sexist deplorable that you had always been? You can try to frighten Arima all you like. But you *need to learn* that she will *not* respond to your silly little threats or intimidation. *You need to learn* that you will catch many more flies with honey than vinegar. You need to learn that or there will be *nobody* to *ever* assist you in releasing you so that you may ascend to Enlightenment. Now…you just *sit* in that painting and *think about that* as you watch yet *another* generation slip out of your grasp. So there!"

"Wait, Grams," Arima inquired in the most animated cadence that she had ever uttered. "Your namesake? You said that this Jamaican woman was your namesake. Who was she? What happened to her?"

"She, my lovely, was the very first Louise Azan," Louise replied wistfully. "She left that house under the cover of night that very evening and went on a journey that finally ended in the land that would become Louisiana. She is your…let's see now…how many would there be? Ah, yes. She would be your great, great, great, great, great, great grandmother. She was the original Azan to live in this land. And she began the tradition of quite powerful and gifted Azan women. My mother saw *my* special gifts upon my birth and named me after her, which I have *always* considered to be the greatest of family honors.

"Although I never cared much for my family nickname. You see dear, that is why everyone in my family calls me 'Junior.' Because I am the second 'Louise' in this family. I have also been referred to as 'LJ' or 'Louise, Junior.' I suppose it doesn't matter much, but it did provide fuel for when I felt like placing snakes in my brother's bed, heh, heh, heh. He was such a nice boy, but so very gullible. I wish that you had been able to meet him. But he was taken from us at a young age. My destiny was to raise you, I have since learned. His destiny was to go to Enlightenment and watch over me. To guide me. To protect me from there. And he has. Every morning, I go to my window and say hello to his spirit. Then, the little chirping bird containing my brother's spirit will fly away, content that his sister still remembers and adores him. But that is a story for another time."

"So," Arima responded as her mind whirled through a slight veil of THC and a thick veil of confusion. "So this is all *real*? Everything that you have told me? About my *mother*? My *father*? A *demon* wanting to rise to power over the earth by lying to and manipulating those that profess to be holy? None of this is one of your practical jokes?"

"Everything that I have told you is real, my darling," Louise responded sincerely. "But I do not know what you mean by my practical jokes. What are you referring to, dear?"

"Oh! C'mon, Grams!" Arima exclaimed. "You know how you would hide my homework so that I would have to do it over. Or when you would replace my snacks with fruit and stuff. Or pull my blankets off of me so that I'd get cold and wake up in the morning. Listen, I never wanted to give you the satisfaction of knowing your little pranks worked, so I never talked to you about it. And it was a pretty clever way to get me going sometimes. But you can drop the ruse. Just admit that you used to pull those pranks on me. I believe everything that you've just told me, but just come clean on the pranks."

Louise burst out into a deep, guttural, booming laugh that bounced around the room and echoed off the artistically adorned walls. She finally gained her composure and wiped a joyful tear from her eye. She placed her hands upon the cheeks of her beloved granddaughter, stared into her brown eyes and said gleefully, "Oh, my darling. That wasn't *me*. That was your *mother*."

"Sure, sure. Of course it was," Arima replied with subdued resignation. "Yup. My dead mother's spirit played pranks on me. Sure. Makes perfect sense. Well, Grams, I think this is just about as much family time as I can deal with at the moment. I think I'll just head out to my interview and see how strange *that* gets. Then my birthday party. Yep. It's been a banner day".

"And your interview is at the morgue, dear?" Louise inquired.

"Yeah, it's just like an overnight security kind of a gig. All I have to do is watch over the stiffs and fill out some paperwork if a new one comes in. Should be just a lot of sitting around and playing on my phone. Should give me lots of time to send snarky replies to Jessie's self-absorbed posts, heh, heh, heh. I mean, if that's even a thing again. Wow, what a weird day".

"My lovely," Louise stated as the pair got up from their seats. "If you get a job at the morgue, I have a feeling that you may not have much time for playing on your silly little contraption. I have a feeling that there are a number of Howards out there that may vie for your attention. I have a feeling that this may be quite an interesting experience for you. But if you take this job, and you are contacted by souls who are unable to move on to Enlightenment, you must tell me about them before you allow them in. And if you are ever visited again by that copper-headed monstrosity…well…just tell me and do exactly as she says. I do not get frightened easily. I have seen many things in my sixty-two years. But I have never been in the presence of such evil in my life. So, please, darling. Be careful, all right?"

"Of course, Grams," Arima replied as she gave her grandmother a loving embrace.

As Arima and Louise departed the living room and began walking toward the front door, a painting on the opposite wall of Howard's began giggling. Howard's black eyes peered across the room at the three swirling dark silhouettes in the painting and said sinisterly, *You three leave her alone. She is mine!*

Chapter 4

Dorks, Spirits, and Bears...Oh, My!

Jeez, this place is creepy. Could it kill them to put up a couple pictures? Arima thought to herself as she stared at the grey concrete walls in the office of the morgue's manager. She sat there nervously shuffling her feet, causing her brightly-colored flowered dress to sway slightly. She felt beads of sweat begin to form on her forehead as she watched this middle-aged Caucasian man with a very bad comb over and thick glasses carefully review her resume.

"So," the man began in a dry, uninterested tone, "It seems as though you have no experience in this field then?"

"Uh, no, uh...Mr. Man...um...Manfren...um...," Arima stammered.

"Manfrengensen," the man replied. "It is quite a difficult name, so please, just call me 'Clyde.'"

"Um, okay then...um...Mr. Clyde. I don't really have experience working in a morgue. I have pretty much just worked at a no-kill animal shelter. But there are similarities, I think. There was a lot of paperwork to do, and I had to talk with people who were adopting pets to be in their forever homes, so...y'know...I can talk to people. Oh, and if this job requires any...um...clean-up...let me assure you that I have had to clean up pretty much anything you can think of. From vomit to piss to blood to...well, I guess you can imagine. Anyway, I'm pretty smart and I can pick up on stuff pretty quickly and I'm really excited to begin a new career if you could just give me a chance."

"I see, I see," Clyde began again. "And, please, let me ask you, since you are obviously quite fond of animals, why are you leaving that position and why have you applied to work here in our...heh, heh, heh... *warm* and *inviting* little corner of the world?"

Huh. This dude actually has a sense of humor. Dry as hell, but... Arima thought to herself before responding to the question. "Well, the animal shelter was forced to relocate from its current building. I guess it's being torn down to make way for condos or a shopping center or something. There are a lot of grand old historical buildings there that are going to be demolished, which I think is very sad. Anyway, the new location is too far away. I don't have a car because I've never really needed one and it would take over an hour on the bus, so I had to leave there. And why this job? Well, I'm not gonna lie to you. It pays way more than my previous one and my Grams- I mean, my grandmother- wanted me to find something that had benefits like health insurance and a retirement plan. Not that I need it right now. I'm only twenty-three. But she wanted me to have some financial stability, I guess. And as far as the actual job, y'know, I'm kinda a night owl, anyway, and I figured this was a job that I could learn without much...um...effort, I guess."

Arima then began hearing whispers in the furthest corner of her mind.

Come see! Come See!

What? What is it?

There is one! Right in there! One who can hear us!

Really? One that can help us move on and leave this horribly boring place? A chance to move on from sitting and watching other souls go to Enlightenment while we are stuck here?

Yes! Yes! We must make contact with her!

"Very good," Clyde began once again. "I suppose that answer is as good as any I have heard. And honest. I like that. Not many people dream of working overnight in a morgue. So, do you frighten easily? Some have said is it downright *creepy* down here in the...heh, heh, heh... dead of night, being surrounded by corpses."

Arima began sweating profusely as her eyes darted around at the bare concrete walls and she heard, *Oh! What a grand question.*

Yes, it will be quite interesting to see how she answers this. Just how easily are you to scare, deary?

"Uh…uh…uh…" Arima began stuttering before tightly closing her eyes for a moment in order to block out the formless voices and focus on her answer. "Uh…no, not usually. I'm really into horror movies, so it takes quite a bit to shock me. And there's no such thing as zombies…I think. But recently I…um…no, I think I'll be fine."

Fine! She says she will be fine!

Oh, she doesn't know what she has in store for her. We'll see if she can make it through a night. Then we'll see how fine she is, heh, heh, heh.

"Very well," Clyde replied. "One more question, and this is most important. Have you ever had or thought about having sex with a dead person?"

"Wha…wha…*what? Eeeewww!*" Arima exclaimed as her mind thought, *Although there was that guy a couple years ago who just laid there like a dead fish, but he did have a heartbeat…I think.*

Clyde looked up at Arima for the first time with a broad smile on his face. "Well, I shall take your reaction as a 'no.' Very good. You may be surprised if you knew just how many night staff I have had to fire because of such…um…activities. Oh, my, there was an incident several years ago where two college girls died of alcohol poisoning at the same party. The night watchman…um…let's just say he took advantage of the still-warm bodies and made quite a mess. It was quite disgusting and, of course, we had to involve the authorities. That is one of our little sayings around here… 'If it is a corpse you want to nail, then your ass is going to jail!' Oh, and another one is, 'You are not allowed to screw any body that is blue!' I thought that I would make rhymes of it, so that people would remember should they feel any…um…urges. You would be wise to keep this in mind."

I think she's kind of cute, Arima heard the male spirit's voice say. *I don't know that I would have minded if she had wanted to take a ride on my body. Y'know. Before it was buried.*

Oh, my lord! We may be dead, but we are still married. I am so tired of watching you ogle the living females that come in here!

C'mon honey. It's not like I can do anything with them. Lighten up.

It is the intention that matters, not the act. The intention itself is a betrayal to me and to our vows. Now, you just think about that!

Oh, I will! Right after I think about picking you up from that sleazy hotel the night we died!

"Uh…uh…uh…okay then," Arima stuttered. "So…will you get back to me, or…"

"Why yes!" Clyde replied with surprising excitement. "I'll get back to you right now! When can you start? I have a very good feeling about you."

"Uh…yeah. Great. I can start right away," Arima excitedly exclaimed. "And… you won't regret this. I'll show up every night and I'll always be on time, and I'll keep all of these spirits who are trapped here in line!"

Arima clasped her mouth as she realized what she had just blurted out. Clyde just stared at her for a moment before letting out a slight snorting snicker and said, "Oh…and a sense of humor to boot! Yes, you will fit in just fine here. We are focused on our business at hand, but… well, just between you and me, we *do* like to *cut up* every now and again, heh, heh, heh. Oh, dear. Where is that form? Excuse me for a moment, won't you? I need to go to another office and get a form. I swore I had made enough copies. Why do these things keep coming up missing?"

As soon as Clyde left the room, Arima looked upward at the ceiling and said quietly, "Listen, you two. We're going to have to co-exist with each other down here. And I'm telling you right now, that if you do *anything* to get me in trouble, I will…well… I'm not sure yet what I can do, but you will not like it. So, do not give me any shit, all right?"

Jeez, she's a bit moody, isn't she, dear? the female spirit stated.

Why, yes, she is. All right, Arima. We won't give you any trouble. But we will want your help to move on in return, deal?

"Uh…sure. Don't know how I can be of help, but…um…sure. What are your names?"

The female spirit replied, *You may address us as "Mr. and Mrs. Roper."*

———

"Sorry, folks, no karaoke tonight. We still can't connect to the Internet," the DJ announced from the stage as Jessie West broke down once again in uncontrollable sobbing. Her loving husband, Cliff, just held her as her blonde hair bounced with every exhalation of grief. His high school football jersey was saturated in her tears as he listened to the next announcement.

Louise Azar's voice came booming through the PA system. "Ladies and gentlemen! Please welcome my most beloved granddaughter and wish her a happy birthday!"

Arima was encased in smiles and hugs from her friends and family, and she was placed at a table in the middle of the dance floor. The plastic top was removed from the dish in the middle of the table and Arima began to drool. The candles were lit on the stack of brownies and the group burst out into a jovial version of "Happy Birthday To You." Arima stared at the stack of flickering brownies in anticipation of taking her first bite and procuring her first step toward a well-earned buzz when she heard two unfamiliar male voices singing much more loudly and with a much more pronounced slur than the rest of the group.

She looked up at them. They were two brawny, hairy men clinging to one another and their gold shirts were unbuttoned down to their protruding bellies. Both had finely trimmed beards. One had naturally silver-grey hair. The other probably did as well, but it was covered by a ghastly black dye job.

Arima blew out the candles and made a wish. *I wish to get the greatest buzz of my life tonight. And maybe get laid. But mainly the buzz. Thanks.* Only one of those wishes would come true on this particular evening. She took her first bite of a brownie, and her first wish was on its way to being fulfilled.

"Hey Jessie, Cliff," Arima said as she tentatively approached two of her best friends and housemates. "Sorry that the internet thing still isn't working. I'm sure they'll get it..." Arima was cut off as Jessie went screaming into the bathroom.

"Dammit, Arima. I know you meant well, but...I just got her out of there. Jessie! Sweetie! It'll all be okay! When we get home, you can write down all of your posts you want to send! I'll like them, I promise! I'll draw a bunch of little thumbs ups! Please sweetie! Please come out of the bathroom!"

Arima rolled her eyes and sighed as she went up to her closest friend and confidant, Jamie, who was loudly laughing with the brawny pair of overexaggerated singers. "Arima! My love! Come and meet my new friends!" Jamie declared as she embraced Arima, forcing her face between Jamie's recently acquired breasts.

"I...can't...breathe!" Arima cried out before releasing herself from Jamie's clutches. "Seriously, Jamie. I know you always wanted a great rack, but those things are ridiculous!"

"Oh, we'll see how ridiculous they are later tonight when I have that man's face covered with them!"

Arima looked over at the slightly built, plaid-shirt-and-blue-jeans-wearing cowboy in the corner. "Uh...I don't think so. He looks straight to me."

Jamie and her two new friends burst out laughing. "Oh, deary," the black-dyed-haired man gushed. "They may all *look* straight. But *trust* me. They most certainly are not *all* straight! Now just what do you think that a man that looks like *that* is looking for in a place like *this*? Well, sweetie, he is looking for someone like *me*. But his dirty little conscience thinks that that is wrong, so he will end up with someone like *her* and rationalize that it isn't wrong if he is with a woman that just *happens* to have the *real* equipment that he so desires!"

"Oh, my lord. Must you *always* be so vulgar?" the silver-haired man responded. "And I would remind the two of you to tread lightly with that man. He may become offended at too much of a flirtation, just as straight women are rightfully offended by too much of an overture from a straight man. It is no different. Do not assume that every buck you see is down for a...well, roll in the hay. It is pompous and arrogant of you just as it is in the straight world."

"Really? But I'm fabulous!" Jamie declared. "Yes, you are, girlfriend!" exclaimed the darker haired man.

"Yes, you are," came the moderating voice of the silver-haired man. "But not everyone will think so and not everyone desires you. We would all, straight, gay, or otherwise, do well to remember that. We make a pass. See if we catch their eye. If not, we move on. That is being respectful to another human being. That is all that I have to say on this matter."

The dark-haired man squealed out in delight and declared, "Oh, my god! You are *so* sexy when you lecture me! Now give Papa Bear a big kiss!"

"Okay," Arima replied with disinterest as she stared at these two embracing men through her increasingly bloodshot eyes. "So, who *are* you guys?"

"Oh, my dearies, I am *soooo* sorry!" Jamie exclaimed. "*This* dark haired brute is Paciano and *this* silver fox is Stellan! Aren't their names just wonderful and exotic? The name 'Stellan' is Swedish and means 'peaceful one.' And 'Paciano' is Spanish and means 'peace.' It was as though they were meant to find one another! Isn't it just so romantically delicious? And they have just been married and are here on their honeymoon! Oh, how *overjoyed* I am to have found you two. You are an inspiration. Tell me. When do you have to return to New York?"

Louise Azar interrupted at that moment and said, "Excuse me, gentlemen, but may I borrow my granddaughter for a moment?"

Louise took Arima by the hand and sat her at a corner booth at the far end of the bar. "Arima, please listen to me. Those two seem like fine men, but they are from New York. They may be the lure that will lead you to involvement with the copper-headed demon. I am asking you to please just steer clear of those two. Just to be safe, all right?"

"Awwww, Grams," Arima replied as she stared at her hands and contemplated the miracle that was the movement of her fingers. "They're just a couple of fun guys here on their honeymoon. I'll probably never see them again. Nothin' to get worked up over. Hey, are there any more brownies?"

"Yes, there are. But before that, I must know. Did anyone or… anything…try to make a connection with you today at the morgue?"

Arima burst out in a giggle and stated loudly, "Did anyone reach out to me? Oh, Grams! I'm gonna *love* this gig. Let me tell you about the Ropers!"

CHAPTER 5
WELL...HELLO, THERE, HANDSOME

Arima arrived one hour before her shift on her first night at the morgue for her mandatory training session. She entered the meeting room down the hall from the morgue and took her seat on a hard plastic chair behind a well-worn metal folding table. She looked around the room. *Wow. They really don't believe in decorating around here, do they?* she thought to herself as she read the Workplace Rules posters regarding harassment, safety, and emergency procedures that were clinging to the grey concrete walls with tape. *Man, this job is going to be so boring. I wonder if maybe I could just take a hit once in a while?* she mused before her eyes widened at the broad image coming through the door.

Her bored expression was immediately replaced by a wide smile as a tall, handsome-faced, somewhat portly Black man entered the room. The shirt tail of his light blue button-up shirt was halfway out of his faded blue jeans. He looked somewhat disheveled and slovenly. To Arima, he looked ideal. He took his place at the front of the room and smiled.

"Hey, there," he said. "Welcome to our little slice of heaven. My name is Marcus. Marcus Jefferson. I usually work the second shift and I'll be your trainer tonight. And if you have any questions, feel free to call me any time. My number's on the call list in the office."

Oh, I think I'm gonna have a lot *of questions*, Arima thought as she noticed the striking man's unencumbered left ring finger.

"So, please. What is your name?" Marcus asked with a tone of genuine interest.

"Me?" Arima immediately stammered, "I mean…of course, me. Heh. I'm the only one here. Sorry, um…I'm Arima Azan and I just want to say how thankful I am for this opportunity."

"Uh, yeah, cool," a slightly confused Marcus replied. "But you don't have to kiss my ass. I'm a working stiff just like you. Get it? Working *stiff*? Just one of our little jokes around here. And really, you don't have to kiss anybody's ass. Not even Clyde's. He's a pretty cool dude. He just wants us to show up, do our jobs, and not make waves. He's pretty low key. You don't even have to laugh at his jokes, although I've been here for three years now, and I have to admit, sometimes I kinda chuckle at them. Wow. That's pretty sad because his jokes are so awful. Maybe it's a sign that I need to move on, huh?"

No! No! No! You can't go anywhere! Arima's voice in her head screamed out at him. "Uh, no. I think that…um…you're where you belong right now. I mean…well, I mean…you have to get me trained up, right?"

"Oh, yeah!" Marcus yelled out. "That's why I'm in here tonight! Man, I gotta admit, this job is overall pretty boring. It's even worse now that the wireless Internet has been taken down by terrorists or somethin'. Can't even pass the time watching po-…I mean, playing on my phone. So, when I get really bored, I just kinda…y'know…take a puff. Not much. Just enough to, y'know, take the edge off. Then I eat a lot of candy and chips."

Arima's heart melted as she thought to herself, *Oh, my God. I'm in love*.

Marcus went into his training. He covered safety procedures, emergency procedures, delivery intake, miscellaneous forms and the corpse filing system. Arima clung to his every word while simultaneously not learning anything. The intended hour-long training took Marcus eighteen minutes before he said, "Well, just one more thing in here. You gotta watch this video on the legal shit around having sex with corpses. They take that pretty seriously. Then we'll tour the morgue, all right?"

"All right," Arima replied dreamily. Marcus turned out the buzzing fluorescent overhead lights and turned on the twenty-year-old flatscreen TV. As the nine-minute epic training video entitled *Digging Your Own Grave: An Introduction to the Legal Consequences of Having Intercourse with Expired Humans*, began flickering on the screen, Arima gazed over at her handsome trainer and began fantasizing about what she would like to do to- or with- him. She gazed back at the TV and thought, *If they don't want us to have sex in here, why did they make all of the corpses in this video so damn hot?*

The video ended and Marcus turned the lights back on. The overhead bulbs began buzzing once again as Marcus asked, "Okay, so that's about it, any questions?"

"Nope," Arima immediately replied. "I think I've got it. Don't play with the stiffs on the stiffs. Got it."

Marcus looked at Arima with bewildered eyes before bursting out laughing. "Oh, man! That was classic! You're gonna do just fine here. You gotta tell that one to Clyde in the morning!"

They entered the morgue and Arima immediately heard the spirit of Mr. Roper.

She's here! She's come back!

Who is here? Oh, your new little human fantasy. Isn't that nice?

Oh, like you don't dream about our Marcus there?

Well, of course I do! But I can't make contact with him. I can't interact with him the way you can with Arima, so it is completely different!

Wasn't so different the night we...

The Ropers bickering ceased when Arima said to them under her breath, "Would you two just pipe down?"

"Excuse me?" Marcus asked as he turned around from opening one of the morgue corpse drawers.

"Oh, um, nothin'," an embarrassed Arima hastily replied. "I was just sayin'...um...aren't you so wise now."

"Wise? Me?" Marcus replied with a chuckle. "Well, that's not somethin' I get accused of often. I don't know how wise I've been in my twenty-five years. It wasn't so wise to drop outta high school. Nope. That little trick got me kicked out of the house. Moms and Pops love me, but they were tired of me pullin' pranks and shit, so they decided to teach me a lesson. And they did. Kicked me out on my eighteenth birthday, right after I dropped out. So, I pretty much just couch- surfed for a few years and got fired from every job I had. They were just too boring, or the manager was a prick or somethin', y'know? But they always had me over for Sunday dinner after we all went to church together. They kept tryin' to get me to be responsible. To take life seriously. I just never really listened. I never did anything really *bad*, but I never did anything really *good* either. I was young and selfish. That all changed when…"

Marcus's voice trailed off and he looked away to hide the tears that were forming in his eyes. He had known Arima for less than an hour but felt as though she was a kindred soul that he could open up to. He looked back at her with his eyes filled with tears. Arima immediately wished to be able to embrace him and absorb whatever pain it was that he was experiencing at that moment.

"Sorry, I didn't mean to get all gushy and shit," Marcus stated sheepishly as he looked down at his well-worn canvas tennis shoes. "It's just that, a few years ago, I had to grow up. You see, my Moms got herself some cancer. It's pretty bad and she's so weak usually that she can't work anymore. And my Pops just couldn't keep up with all the bills and everything. So I buckled down and settled into this job. They let me move back home and most of my paycheck goes to keeping the household up. Y'know, the mortgage, bills, food. That way, Pops can afford to get the care that Moms needs, so…y'know…she can stay with us. I've learned that there are more important things in life than our own personal needs. I've learned that we all need to lean on one another sometimes to make this world work."

The urge to hug Marcus became overwhelming and Arima extended her arms and enveloped his frame with hers. She felt his body tense, then immediately relax as he accepted this emotional respite from his newfound friend. She concentrated and could feel his pain being absorbed into her soul. She focused harder and envisioned his pain being consumed by burning flames. She heard him let out a relieved exhalation and the hurtfulness dissipated for the both of them as she felt his pain turn to harmless ashes.

Arima relinquished her embrace and said reservedly, "Um…sorry, I guess that wasn't very professional of me. I just thought…I mean…I just wanted to…"

"No, no, no," Marcus immediately replied. "It's okay. Thank you. That was probably the best hug that I've ever had. Like, you made all my hurt go away. I guess I just needed a hug in that moment and you were there for me".

And I always will be, Arima thought to herself before hearing the Ropers say to her in a childish sing-song voice,

Arima's got a boyfriend, Arima's got a boyfriend, Arima's got a...

"Just shut up!" Arima yelled out.

"Uh, ok, sorry," a surprised Marcus responded.

"No, not you," Arima hastily replied. Her mind raced as she wondered whether she could confide in him about her newfound talents. After all, he had just opened up to her. They just had an intense emotional connection. Perhaps he wouldn't think that she was crazy. On the other hand...

Arima began chuckling and said, "Not *you*. I wasn't talking to *you*. It's just...um...sometimes when I get kinda emotional I get thoughts in my head, and I tell them to shut up. I just got caught up in the moment and forgot where I was. Sorry."

"Yeah, you got emotional?" Marcus asked tenderly as he gazed into Arima's mahogany eyes for the first time.

"Delivery time!" came the exclamation from the police officer who was wheeling in a newly deceased corpse. "Got a fresh one for ya straight from the autopsy. Real piece of work, this one. Had to be gunned down after a standoff with us. Was chanting all kinds of weird religious and racist shit. The world's better off, if ya ask me. Here, sign this".

Marcus showed her how to check in and "file" the corpse. They awkwardly chuckled to one another as Marcus said, "Well, I guess I should go now, but listen. If you need anything and I mean *anything*, I'm just a phone call away, okay? And Clyde will be in around seven. He'll probably come in a little early on your first few nights, just to check up on you, all right?"

"Yeah, all right," Arima dreamily replied.

Marcus left the room and Arima began skipping around in a large circle on the cold concrete floor while giggling.

So, Arima, Mrs. Roper's voice echoed in her head. *How does it feel to be in love?*

Yes, Arima. Pretty good first day on the job, I would say.

Yes, dear. Remember when we were first in love? Just look at her face. How I wish I had never allowed that look to go off of my face.

Me, too, dear, me, too. We both made so many mistakes all those years ago. And now, our children are devoid of love in their hearts. We must talk to them. We must...

Mr. Roper's voice was cut off by a dark eerie presence emerging from the recently closed drawer. The fluorescent lights remained on, but became encased in a dark purple shroud, causing the entire room to darken in a sinister purplish hue.

Arima began hyperventilating as she could feel the dark presence swirling around her soul, looking for an entrance.

Oh, no, Mr. Roper stated mournfully. *It's one of those. So many more of those here recently. Arima, stay away from him. Do not let him in. He is dangerous to you. To us. Just let him pull his pranks and stay out of it.*

Shut up, you two. The sinister spirit's low, gravelly voice came emanating from the dark purple mist that could only be seen by Arima and The Ropers.

I won't be trapped here forever. I will be sent for. I will rise again in another form and continue to do the bidding of the great Vetis, the Tempter of the Holy! Those mortals have no idea that they have made me stronger! More powerful! All I need is a vessel to consume. A weak-minded medium to absorb my spirit and transfer it into another.

Arima's hyperventilation continued, and her eyes rolled back into her head. She began violently shaking as she elevated off of the floor.

The demonic spirit began cackling as he gleefully watched Arima's seizing body floating helplessly.

*Ah, I see that I have found one already. Oh, you can hear me, can't you? Good. Well, listen up, bitch. If you want to survive. If you do not wish to perish, then you shall do exactly as I tell you. Because if you don't, I will shred your flesh from your body. I shall feast upon your organs. I will kill you so slowly that by the end, you will be begging for me to let you die. And then, once you finally do die, I will do the same thing to your soul. I shall murder you in the most violent ways over and over again for all eternity. Or...you can let me in and transfer me to the next human that walks through that door. The choice is yours. You got that- n****r?*

CHAPTER 6

YOU PROBABLY SHOULDN'T HAVE SAID THAT

"Oh! *Hell,* no! I am *not* putting up with any racist shit from some deplorable spirit!" Arima screamed out at the swirling smog. "You want in? You want me to take your soul in and transfer you into someone else so you can continue your racist bullshit on this earth? That really what you want? All right, then. C'mon in here, cracker".

The devilish spirit cackled in delight as Arima instinctively opened her soul to his.

No, Arima! Don't! Mrs. Roper's spirit pleaded.

Don't do it, Arima. He is too powerful. He will use you and your body for horrible things. Do not let him in! Mr. Roper added.

"Yeah?" a smirking Arima replied. "You think so? I think that this little worm doesn't know *what* he is going up against".

And then she felt it. She felt him penetrate her. She elevated off of the ground as her eyes rolled back into her head and she once again began violently seizing.

Heh, heh, heh. Thanks bitch, the sinister presence stated as he entered the warmth of Arima's being. *You think you can go up against me? Here. Let me show you a few things.*

Her mind began projecting images as though she were sitting in a movie theatre. They were blurry at first. Just a mix of disembodied colors mixing in with one another. Then the images began coming into focus until they were crystal clear. Arima was repulsed by them.

There were three white men with shaven heads. They were wearing tattered and stained blue jeans and brown short-sleeved shirts. Their arms and necks were scarred by tattoos of ignorant hate. They had a young Black girl surrounded. She could not have been more than twelve years old. She was pleading with them to stop. To let her go. Tears streamed down her innocent face as her anguished pleas continued.

With every begging sentence that she uttered, the sadistic men laughed harder. They tore at her clothes. They slapped her in the face. They brutally punched and kicked her in her abdomen, ribs, and back. The cackling trio circled her mercilessly as the child was forced to absorb the never-ending blows. She was thrown to the ground and her underpants were ripped from her flailing legs.

Arima's soul screamed out in anguish as she witnessed that which no human being, especially a child, should ever have to experience. It was the most depraved action that anyone could ever take against another. It was brutal. It was disgusting. It was sadistic. It was the vile actions of the small, weak-willed, and weak-minded. It was the actions of people who have no regard for the sanctity of another's rights or dignity. Who have no regard for the sanctity of life itself. Arima's soul began to warm and expand as she realized for the first time that those who hold no sanctity for life should carry no expectations of continuing theirs. They had waived that right through their brutality of others. They are, indeed, deplorable. And they should die.

The depraved spirit howled with laughter as he showed Arima the final scene. The young girl's corpse was hanging from a flashing stop sign. Her battered, naked body was morbidly illuminated by flashing red, revealing multiple bruises and deep lacerations. One of her broken ribs was protruding from her side. A small red flag with a swastika had been hung from it. Her innocent face was gashed open and her formerly brilliant eyes were swollen shut. Her lips had been bitten off. The "men's" vile semen slithered down her tender thighs.

Arima was a lover of all things horror. Movies, books, comics. She loved it all. She loved the thrill she got from a jump scare or the creepy vibes that caused goosebumps as she read about demonic possession. But that was fiction. That was she, as a viewer, safely expunging her darker thoughts through watching the fictional violence of others. She, and her horror-loving friends, could absolve themselves of feeling guilt about their darker impulses by living vicariously through the fabricated violence of others. It was nothing more than thrill-seeking entertainment in the comfort of her own home. No one was ever *really* injured in any way. The horror that she watched and read was fake. The screams were fake. The blood was fake. The trauma was fake. The death was fake.

This, however, was all too real, Arima realized. This had actually *happened.* This was *actually happening* at this very moment to some other innocent person. At this very moment, some innocent child was pleading for the pain to stop. This was the true horror of actual life for far too many of our sisters and brothers. This was the barbarous horror that even fiction writers dared not discuss, because it is too taboo, too dark, and too brutal for even the most desensitized viewer. But by our choosing to not shine a bright spotlight on the true horrors in our world, we allow it to grow. To continue. To thrive. For generation after generation after generation. Brutality of others cannot be swept under the rug. It cannot be wished away. It cannot be prayed away. It must be exposed in the same graphic way that it had been experienced in order for it to be truly understood and felt to our core. We must *see* the innocent school children whose bodies have been torn apart by the bullets of a coward. We must *see* the tortured bodies of murder victims. We must *see* the torn-apart bodies of the innocent civilian victims of our brutal wars. We must *hear* the stories of physical and mental trauma caused by sexual assault and harassment. Arima finally understood that we cannot allow ourselves to become complacent about the world's *true* horrors that seem so distant to most of us. For if we do, those *true* horrors very well may be inflicted upon us and our own loved ones. We must acknowledge the reality of it. The senselessness of it. The sadistic brutality of it. The inhumanity of it. We must shed a genuine empathetic tear. And then, the horror must be confronted. And it must be confronted with the same amount of force and brutality with which it was originally inflicted by soulless trash.

Heh, heh, heh. And that was all it took to rid an entire neighborhood of the Black infestation of vermin like you. You see now, don't you, bitch? the arrogant spirit whispered into Arima's soul. *You see what you're up against now, don't you? And if you do not place me in an another's able body, I will do to your soul what I did to that kid's body. You have seen how I can make your body convulse. And that is without much effort. Just imagine the pain that I can inflict if I put my mind to it. I will rape and torture you until you beg me to die. And once you die, I will simply wait for another like you to come along and force them to do my bidding. Now be the good slave girl that you were put here to be. Just walk outside onto the street. I'll tell you when the right one comes along. Do it...now!*

Arima's body stopped convulsing as she descended until her canvas-adorned feet touched the floor. Her eyes rolled back into their natural position and were opened. Her deep mahogany pupils were raging with a glimmering fire that she had never experienced before.

What...what are you...how did you do that? I didn't release you! the disheveled spirit stuttered out in confusion.

Arima furled her brow, wiped the drool from her lips and smiled devilishly before saying, "Now, asshole you are going to listen to *me*. I may be new to this game, but it's like I just instinctively now know what I can and can't do. And I know that you are *far* too weak and pathetic to have any control over me. I *allowed* you to do those things to my body, but I was in complete control of it the entire time. I *allowed* you to show me those horrendous images, but I could have stopped them at any time. I didn't because I needed to know. I needed to experience it. I needed to feel it. And I do now know. I now know that there is true evil in this world that must be vanquished. And I now know the name of that sweet girl. *And* the names of your accomplices."

"Now, let me correct you on a couple things. For starters, there are probably demonic spirits of the followers of Vetis who *can* control me if I allow them in. Who can take over my body and soul and force me to do terrible things. I guess that is the curse that I carry for being made of equal parts of my sweet mother *and* my sadistic father. But *you* do not possess that power. I could sense it from the first moment that I met you. How does it feel to have a girl of Jamaican descent with brown skin wield *far* more power than your impotent Aryan shell of a self?

"And another point of clarification. There may be some women who can transfer spirits from their bodies into another living body. I don't know about that. All that I know is that I can allow spirits in and allow them to use my body to try to redeem themselves so that they may move on to Enlightenment. And I can transfer those spirits. I can expel them from me back into the vast nothingness of their current hell that they are trapped in. Or I can transfer them into inanimate objects. And that is just what I will now do to you."

"Let's see here. Where to put a low-life scumbag like you? Heh, heh, heh. Oh, I know."

Where are we going? Where are you taking me? Talk to me, bitch! the demon screamed out at Arima as she walked out of the morgue, down the hallway, and into the meeting room where she had received her training.

"You are a part of the master race, huh?" Arima stated haughtily. "Yeah, I don't think so because *I* am now the master of *you*. Enjoy your reading for all of eternity, you sick bastard!"

Arima concentrated and began expunging the demonic one from her being. She could feel his brittle nails scraping against her soul as he attempted in vain to cling to her essence. She concentrated further and heard his anguished wail as his spirit was permanently placed into the Workplace Harassment poster.

She chuckled to herself as she read the parts of the poster that she felt were most fitting for this impotent worm of an entity.

HARRASSMENT WILL NOT BE TOLERATED!

It is our company policy to provide a safe workplace. We will not tolerate any form of harassment.

Examples of Harassment:

- Verbal abuse- shouting, yelling, swearing, name calling, and vulgarity.
- Threats or physical abuse.
- Intimidation or manipulation.
- Cruel comments, belittling, or insults.
- Aggressive behavior.
- Sexual harassment, unwanted touching, or stalking
- Unequal treatment due to race, gender, age, size, religion, sexual orientation, gender identity, or country of origin.

"I suggest you read that carefully," Arima stated boldly as she stood in front of the poster like a conquering hero. "I *will not* tolerate any harassment from *you*. But *you*, on the other hand, will be subjected to an *eternity* of harassment from *me*, so you better keep your damned filthy mouth shut!"

Arima returned to the morgue and flopped her frame upon the wheeled office chair in front of her desk. She lazily pulled a fresh joint from her breast pocket, lit it, and inhaled deeply. "Ahhh…that's the stuff," she stated in a quiet satisfied voice before picking up the receiver of the phone.

Who are you calling Arima? Mrs. Roper inquired.

"The cops. I gotta tell them who murdered that poor little girl," Arima replied flatly before explaining to the Ropers the horrendous images that she had been shown.

But what will you tell them Arima? Mr. Roper replied. *What will you tell them as to how you know all of this? Will you tell them the truth? Do you think that they will believe you? No, dear. Put the phone down. The others must be dealt with in another way.*

"But how?" Arima cried out.

You know how, dear, Mrs. Roper answered. *They must be dealt with in a much more permanent manner. And then, you can place them with their cowardly friend in the poster. That was quite clever my dear. To place the spirit of a misogynistic, xenophobic, racist into a Workplace Harassment poster to torment him for all of eternity. I am beginning to really like you, my dear.*

"What? *Kill them?*" Arima cried out to the seemingly blank walls. "I can't *kill them*! I would *never* be able to do that! It's just not in me! But you have a point. They need to be taken out by someone. Jeez. Knowing a vigilante serial killer right now sure would come in handy. But, like, someone like *that* really exists in this world. It's absurd. Any other ideas you two?"

Yes. I believe that I might have a solution to your little problem, Mrs. Roper answered.

No, dear, not him, Mr. Roper quickly responded.

Yes. Him. Arima, dear, there is another spirit who has been trapped here for some time that you have not yet met. He keeps to himself, and it may take some coaxing to draw him out, but I believe that he may be able to help you. He prefers to be known as the Botanist.

CHAPTER 7
I Picked These Just for You

Herbert Jenkins, who would later be known simply as "the Botanist," was a pathetically weak individual from the moment his meager cry emerged from his mother's body. As a child, he was always awkward around other people, especially other children who would ridicule him mercilessly for his gangly frame and beak-like hooked nose that protruded from between his constantly blinking, beady eyes.

Herbert had no friends, except for his doting mother. His father had been killed in action during World War I just prior to his birth and his mother, whose appearance was just as homely as her son's, never re-married. The pair would spend their evenings listening to their favorite radio programs or playing in their lavish garden behind their modest, but well-kept one-bedroom bungalow in New Orleans.

Herbert would spend hour upon blissful hour in their family garden, tending to his plants as though they were his own children. Over the years, he built the garden into a local showcase that traveling green thumbs would tour. They would gaze in amazement at the majesty of his creation. The various shades of green and textures of the leaves that would joyously blend together. The multiple colors and shapes of the delicate petals that overlapped one another as though their blooms were in loving embraces throughout the yard. The prisms that were created as the morning sun's rays penetrated the modest dew drops that clung to the flora. It was all quite spectacular and overwhelming for the throngs of visitors that arrived to tour on a nearly daily basis.

And standing in the middle of it all, as the amazed tourists made their way through the kaleidoscopic yard, was a beaming Herbert. This was his creation. This was his world. And it was the only place where he found acceptance, if not outright affection, from other people. In *his* world, he was not ugly. He was not ridiculed. He was enveloped with the love and adoration of others. This is where Herbert was home.

It was the exact opposite in his school. Herbert would frequently attempt to feign illness to skip school, but his mother usually saw through his ruse and would make him get up and get dressed, often in ill-fitting shirts and pants that had fit the rapidly growing boy just a few months prior.

He would be subjected to endless ridicule as his lanky frame, which was typically a foot taller than his classmates, strode down the school's hallways. He was called many names, including "honker," "flood," and "crane." The most hurtful to Herbert was when he was called "flower girl" as this was not just an attack upon his person, but also towards his beloved friends in his garden.

By junior high school, Herbert would frequently be caught dreamily gazing at a pretty classmate from across the room. The young lady would be all too happy to tell her boyfriend about the perceived slight. And the boyfriend, in turn, would be only too happy to pummel Herbert after school. Herbert would limp home with his shirt torn, dirty, and bloody. His face would carry multiple purplish bruises and his small eyes would be blackened and swollen. He would open the gate of the white picket fence and go around the house and be enveloped by his world. He would sit in the middle of his majestic garden and cry. He would then go to a certain area in the back of the garden near his tool shed. This area of his world was his most cherished as it housed plants that held the capability of healing. He would use the oils from his dearest friends to treat his wounds. Herbert had learned not only how to plant and tend for his flowers. He was now beginning to experiment and learn about the medicinal benefits that many flowers possessed. His flowers depended upon him for their survival. And he depended upon them for his.

By high school, Herbert had become conditioned to avoid any

contact with his female classmates. It was simply too painful for him. The pain would either be physical and come from a jealous boyfriend eager to show "his girl" his male dominance or, more frequently, would be emotional as he would see the mockingly cruel expression upon a young lady's face as he would give her an innocent smile. Although these female wonders looked as beautiful and delicate as his beloved flowers, he resigned himself to believing that females did not contain nectar or sweet-smelling pollen. To the contrary, to Herbert, women were poisonous.

Although brilliant in the sciences, especially chemistry and, of course, botany, he was emotionally insecure and immature and did not understand how gender played no role in personality type. And he did not understand how peer pressure affected his classmates. If a female were ever to be kind to him, then she would be met with the same cruel treatment that he was receiving. So even the most kindhearted of classmates would simply avoid him. Herbert also lacked the social skills to try to endear himself to others in other ways to counter his awkward appearance. He was not handsome. He had little to no personality. He had no physical strength or athletic aptitude. So, in the world of young romance, he had no chance.

Beginning in high school, Herbert firmly believed that most people were uncaring and cruel, and this was especially true of women. He would live his life alone and love and be loved by his cherished plants and his endearing mother. He would ironically use his intellectual prowess to harness the medicinal power of his friends to help other people recover from their assorted maladies. This would be his contribution to his species that contributed nothing to him.

This outlook dramatically changed in the spring of 1952. Herbert, now 34 and working in a pharmaceutical laboratory, saw the most beautiful vision that his constantly blinking, beady eyes had ever seen. The young woman was a recent graduate with a master's degree and had gained employment as Herbert's assistant. Her pale skin seemed to glow as the sun's rays beamed upon her through the laboratory's window. Her golden hair cascaded over her delicate shoulders and framed her brilliant blue eyes. Her smile was reminiscent of a brilliant red rose petal as it began to open. Her figure was slim and her hips and behind were tightly enveloped in a knee-length pencil skirt. Her calves were stretched and accentuated to perfection by her three-inch high black leather pumps and sheer stockings. And little was left to the imagination as her tight, short-sleeved light pink sweater clung to her shapely breasts. Herbert wondered to himself if God had ever created someone or something this perfect.

Herbert had his answer the moment the young woman opened her lips to introduce herself. The answer was "no." This was the most perfect creature that God had ever created. His heart opened and years of bitterness melted away as she smiled at him demurely. She spoke to him. She listened to him. There was never a trace of repulsion toward him upon her angelic face. She looked upon him as they spoke together as ideally and non-judgmentally as his cherished flowers in his garden. She responded to his meek attempts at humor with light giggles, a hair flip, and a light touch upon his boney shoulder. He felt goosebumps and slightly woozy as he experienced the first delicate touch of a woman in his life. She was intoxicating.

The pair quickly forged a strong and slightly flirtatious working relationship as Herbert educated her on the various experimental plant-based treatments that he was working on. Each morning he would bring her coffee exactly as she liked it. One cream, two sugars. They would eat lunch together in the facility cafeteria and she would lightly brush his foot with hers while ignoring the bewildered expressions of their on-looking co-workers.

Herbert began bringing her presents, especially after she would casually mention a certain piece of jewelry or dress or shoes that she had seen window shopping. She could never afford such extravagances, she would tell him, but she enjoyed dreaming about how she might have them some day. Herbert took it upon himself to make all of her dreams come true, so over the next few weeks the presents became increasingly expensive. And her response to the presents would become increasingly gracious as she began giving the love-stricken suitor a provocative peck on his pasty cheek.

He would beam with titillated pleasure as she would come to work wearing the dress, broach, earrings, or bejeweled ring that he had given her the day before. His bank account was dwindling, but his heart was exploding from the rapturous delight of his first love. He was convinced that this wondrous personification of perfection would be his bride someday.

Herbert felt that this was the one person in the world that he could open up to. He told her about his garden and how it was his most cherished place in all of the world. He told her how his garden made him feel accepted and loved. He told her how his garden made him feel whole. He then told her that she made him feel the same way and that he was falling in love with her. He handed her a voluminous bouquet of his most cherished flowers from his most cherished place on the earth. To him, it was the most loving and thoughtful gift that he could bestow upon her. The combination of the various scents of the flowers was overwhelmingly sweet and beautiful. She looked at his teary eyes and sincere expression with loving admiration as her blue eyes sparkled under the neon lights in the laboratory. She smiled sweetly, gave him a quick peck upon his cheek, took the flowers and excused herself. Before leaving the room, she looked back at him and gave him a not-so-subtle wink and shake of her rump.

She was gone for quite a while. He thought that he had heard her voice coming from outside of an open window. He could not make out what was being said until he went to the opened window and leaned his ear toward the screen. He heard another female co-worker ask what she had received from him that day. His love responded by saying "just these." He then heard two female voices along with that of a male co-worker burst into jeering laughter.

His heart metaphorically wilted, dried, and blew away into the unforgiving breeze as he listened to this most perfect creation speak about how she had manipulated him into buying her lavish gifts. The trio continued their deriding guffawing as they each called him names like "dope," "oaf," and… "flower girl." He listened to her say through her mocking laughter how he had a face that nobody could love. Probably not even his own mother. He then heard the male co-worker ask his love out for a date. Her response was an enthusiastic 'yes,' complete with an invitation back to her home after their dinner and movie.

Herbert wrote a note that said that he wasn't feeling well and that he was going home early for the day. As he exited the building, he looked down on the trash can that sat beside the exit door. There he found his bouquet of flowers that he had lovingly selected just for her. Just for this moment. They were just lying there, sadly mixed in with various papers, wrappers, cans, and bottles. They were crumpled and covered in cigarette butts, partially-eaten sandwiches, a banana peel, and sticky residue from discarded soda bottles.

What was to be the happiest day of his life had turned into the darkest. He went home and immediately went to his garden. He wept as he selected a new bouquet to give to his former love.

The following morning, he was greeted with an enthusiastic smile and light kiss on the cheek from her. He handed her coffee to her and presented her with his new bouquet. It did not escape him that she failed to inquire as to how he was feeling. He asked her to have a drink of the coffee, then breathe deeply the flowers' aroma. She did so, unsuspectingly. He explained to her how different plants and flowers have different effects upon people. He explained how the *combination* of certain flowers and plants, including coffee beans, can impact people. He explained how *some* of those impacts could result in the death of a person.

The young woman's eyes knowingly widened at his latest revelation. He watched as she began coughing. He watched as she began foaming at the mouth. He watched as her body began twitching. He watched as her eyes rolled back into her head. And he watched as her body slumped to the floor as she let out her final exhalation. His face held a solemn expression as he drank from her coffee cup and breathed deeply from her bouquet.

He looked down upon his lifeless, pathetic body before ascending further. He saw brilliant lights, then clouds, then silhouettes. They were dark silhouettes that did not become brighter as they approached. They remained black as they explained to him that he was not welcome in the Enlightenment. He had done an evil thing and he would not be allowed to ascend to the peace that is Enlightenment until he redeemed himself. He must right an evil, demonic wrong on the earth. Then and only then would he be considered for acceptance in Enlightenment. The dark forms then grabbed him and forced him to descend rapidly back to his body which was now placed in the city morgue.

And that is where Herbert Jenkins, the Botanist, has remained since 1952, Mrs. Roper concluded. *He has sat quietly in the corners of this morgue lamenting his lost love while looking over the various plants that are placed here. He rarely speaks to anyone. He does not believe in redemption for himself or for any other person. He believes that humans, including himself, are irredeemable and that he must suffer for all of eternity for what he has done.*

As Arima had been listening to Mrs. Roper's story, she had noticed that all of the plants that adorned the morgue's window sills had steadily begun to droop and wilt. She shook her head and wiped a tear from her eye before saying, "Wow, Herbert…or 'Mr. Botanist'…or whatever. That really sucks. I'm sorry that you went through all that. And I'm sorry for that woman, too. I mean, she sounds like she was a bitch, but she didn't deserve to die. Not for that. I mean, grow up. We all get a broken heart. Tell the bitch off and find someone new, but don't poison her! Sorry, but that's how I feel. Listen, I know you were treated badly by a lot of people, especially women, but we're not *all* bad. Hell, not even *most* of us are bad. Most people are actually *good*. We sometimes just make bad decisions and do bad things. You just got stuck with some bitches who were immature and shit and that warped your view of women. And believe me, I know some women who feel the *same way* about men. It's all so stupid how we prejudge people based on gender or anything else for that matter. But I'm telling you. We are *not* all bad! And that little girl wasn't bad. She didn't deserve to be raped and murdered. I don't know if helping me will get you to Enlightenment or not, but you sure as hell will take some sick bastards off the street and keep them from hurting others. C'mon, Herbert. I need you. That innocent girl's soul needs you. Please, help me just this once, okay?"

All of the plants on the windowsill began returning to their lush green hue. Their stems stood upright until they looked like a battalion of little soldiers waiting for their marching orders. In the middle of all of them, a large purple iris exploded into full bloom. Arima had her answer.

Chapter 8
Death by Bouquet

"Well, good morning sweetie," a beaming Jamie stated as she fluttered into the living room to greet her best friend. "How was your first night at work?"

"Uh…yeah…It was…um," Arima began as she searched for the proper words to use to describe her rather eventful first night at the morgue. She had fallen in love, communicated with the dead, banished an evil soul into a Workplace Harassment poster, and formed an alliance with another lost soul to murder racists. The only word that she could come up with was, "interesting."

"I just wanna get baked and fall into bed," she said to Jamie as she observed what was happening with the television set.

In the place of their high-tech, high-definition streaming television, there was a nineteen-inch black and white console that her other two housemates, Jessie and Cliff, were feverishly working on.

"So…what are *you* guys doing?" Arima inquired drowsily.

Cliff replied in a frustrated tone, "We're trying to get this damned dinosaur hooked up. One of the local TV stations has begun broadcasting from their old tower. But you have to have an old-fashioned TV set with an antenna. Right now, besides the radio or having a phone modem on your computer, this is the only way to get information. We found this old thing up in the attic and…"

At that moment, the television set began humming with black and white horizontal lines rolling on the screen. Cliff turned the channel knob until it rested on the appropriate number. He adjusted the antenna, and the rolling lines and static became a somewhat clear picture of a broadcaster, who was saying...

Again, ladies and gentlemen of our viewing audience, the wireless internet service throughout the world has been taken down by terrorists. The moment that it is repaired anywhere, it is overloaded and taken down again in about five minutes. Authorities and technicians are baffled by what might be the cause. In the meantime, the only way to get internet service is through old fashioned modems, if you happen to live in an area with phone lines, which is, of course, quite rare. And television streaming services are disabled as well. The management at this station is committed to bringing you the most up to date information and quality entertainment and that is why we have redeployed our broadcast tower. So tell your friends and neighbors to dust off their old antennae TV's and enjoy our programming until such time as this crisis is over. This news update has been brought to you by Sniffles *facial tissue. Wipe away your sniffles with* Sniffles. *Now, please enjoy this twelve-hour* Matlock *marathon. We will break in as the situation warrants.*

Jessie West stood in front of the television in morbid silence. Her lower lip began puckering and trembling. She then let out a tortured wail and ran into her bedroom in despair while screaming, "*Matlock?* What the hell is *Matlock?* My world has just ended! My online world that I have carefully cultivated! My online world where people can see me as I *want* them to see me! Now what am I supposed to do? Be *myself?* Who in the hell would ever be interested in the *real* me?"

Cliff hastily followed his wife as he tried to reassure her. "C'mon, baby, it'll be okay. *I* love the real you and other people will too. And... um...maybe we'll like *Matlock.* And Ooo! Ooo! I think they're playing *Car 54, Where Are You?* later. I think that I've heard of that. It'll all be okay baby. Please don't cry anymore."

"Wow," Arima replied flatly. "Now I *really* gotta get baked and then..."

No Arima, the Botanist's voice said to Arima's soul. *Please do not do that. I need to concentrate to complete my work and I'll be unable to do that if we are high. Please, just go to bed and go to sleep. I will take control of your body and do what needs to be done. All that I need to know is whether you want these men to die peacefully or...painfully.*

Arima thought back at the sadistic scene that she had witnessed of the dear child being brutally raped and murdered by this scum and said forcefully, "Painfully. Definitely painfully".

"What's that, sweetie?" Jamie inquired. "Did you say 'painfully?'"

"Oh...uh, yeah. Sorry," Arima replied as she thought, *I've gotta remember not to talk to these spirits out loud, dammit!* "I was just saying that this is definitely painful for poor Jessie. She's so wrapped up in her online personality, y'know? Anyway, I think I'll skip the hit. I'm just too tired. I'll see you later this evening before work."

"All right, dearie, nighty night!" Jamie cheerfully responded. "I've gotta go out for a bit, anyway, and show a house to a lovely couple. Now, where did I put my tape? My pantsuit for today is a bit...revealing in all the wrong areas, and I don't know how this cute little suburban family might...um...react. So many macho men out there who would just *die* to have a ten-inch penis and for me, it is a curse. Ah, well, nothing that my trusty tape can't handle."

Arima changed into her shorts and T-shirt, threw her work clothes on the floor of her closet, crashed face first onto her bed, and immediately fell into a deep slumber.

Seemingly five minutes later, Arima woke up. She wiped the sleep from her eyes and looked around. The sun was beginning to set outside of a filthy and cracked window. She was fully dressed and sitting on a stained and torn couch with a floral print. Sitting in front of her were two men who were wearing brown shirts and worn blue jeans with very visible urine stains. They had neo-Nazi tattoos and shaved heads. And they were bound by duct tape on two beat-up living room wooden chairs. They were the men that she had been shown. They were the last two murderers of that little girl.

They were struggling in vain to free themselves while saying, "Wh-wh-what the fuck, bitch? What the hell did you do to us? Let us go and maybe we won't kill you, you little bitch whore!"

Arima responded to the suffering pair with a simple, "Um...I don't know. I don't know *what* I have done to you".

It's all right, Arima, the Botanist said softly to her. *I'll explain it. Just let me regain control over your body and I will explain everything to these horrible men...and to you.*

"Um...all right, I'm pretty curious myself," Arima dryly replied out loud before her voice changed in its cadence slightly and the Botanist began explaining what he had done while in control of Arima's body.

"Well, you see, boys, I saw what you and your horrible friend did to that little girl. And we decided that you should not go on living so that you can do that to others. And once you die, Arima will take your souls and place them somewhere where you can never harm another person. Here is what I did. I went back to my old home and found the remnants of my beloved plants in the back yard. It was so sad to see my lovely garden in such a weed-infested state. Just as it is so sad to see how human weeds have infested our beautiful planet. I took the certain flowers that I needed for this and developed two different toxins."

"The first toxin I put into your sodas as you were gawking at and cat calling a woman at the convenience store. You called me such horrible names when I walked into the store. You whispered to me what you would do to me after I left the store. But by the time I found you outside waiting for me, you had already guzzled your sodas and you were both too woozy to care about me, so you went right to this hellhole of a home and you fell asleep."

"I followed you here and once you were asleep, I came in and obviously bound you to these chairs. *I* then waited for *you*. I waited for you to wake up so that I could tell you what *I* would do to *you*. What I would do to two spineless worms who get thrills by dominating others. Raping others. Murdering others. And all because they don't *look* like you or *love* like you or *believe* like you. You are all so sad and pathetic. I never thought much about humankind while I was alive, but I have learned that there are many good people out there. It's just that the *truly evil* people get all of the attention. You hear about such vile people over and over again until you get beaten down by it and you think horrible thoughts about everybody that you encounter. Instead of trusting others and believing in the goodness of others, you are always suspicious of others. You are always on the defense. What did that smile mean? Do they truly mean those words of support for me or are they just playing a cruel game? Do they truly like me or is it all just a manipulation? It all grows so tiresome. And we can *all* be cruel in our own ways. None of us are perfect. But most people's cruelty is unintentional. It is something that is said in the heat of the moment or something you do when you aren't thinking straight. It is cruelty that arises from an error in judgement. And then, the person feels remorse for their actions and tries not to repeat those hurtful actions.

"That is not true in your case. In your case, you *purposefully* hurt people. Your cruelty is *planned*. It is *calculated*. And it is acted upon with an unholy ferocity without any remorse. Without any sense of guilt or responsibility. *You* are the weeds that are infesting our beautiful garden. And in order for a garden to grow...to thrive...to reach its full beauty... well...the weeds must be pulled and discarded. Over and over and over. We must be ever vigilant in pulling the weeds. Otherwise, the constantly invading and growing weeds will take over and the garden will die. And the weeds will hold dominion over a dark and barren land that holds joy for no one.

"So it is now my duty...and my pleasure...to pull *these* weeds. To discard *you* so that you may never harm another soul ever again. You will want to hold your breath now."

Arima's spirit-controlled body got up from the beaten couch and picked up a beautiful bouquet of exotic flowers. Her body went up to the first bound man, grabbed him by the back of his head and thrust his face into the bouquet.

"Yes. Let's just see how long you can hold your breath before having to breathe deeply of my most deadly friends," the Botanist said through Arima's voice. The man's body shook as he attempted to hold his breath before finally succumbing and deeply breathing in the intoxicating fragrance of the flowers.

Arima's body then went to the second bound man and repeated the grave procedure. Her body sat back down on the beaten couch and waited.

"You see," the Botanist stated through Arima's voice. "What you have just inhaled is a quite potent combination of oils. The effect will be that the oils will combine in your system and begin attacking your internal organs. They will be ripped apart and will be torn from your body. It is an old Laotian recipe that I found a very long time ago. The most common forms of this toxin are as a lotion or a gas, but I found a way to combine the oils and scents of the plants themselves in a lovely bouquet to have the very same effect. It is really quite effective and really quite painful, as you are about to find out."

The men began violently convulsing. Their eyes rolled back into their heads and frothing blood mixed with saliva began drooling from their trembling mouths, oozing down the swastikas on their necks. They screamed in unholy agony as their brown shirts turned crimson. Their internal organs lumbered out of their torn abdomens and haphazardly fell to the floor with a discernible "plopping" sound.

Ah, very good, the Botanist said to Arima. *The weeds have been pulled from this earth. It is now up to you, Arima, to discard them for all time. To destroy their spirits so that they may never harm another in this or any other life again.*

"Uh, okay," a bewildered Arima replied. "Wow. That was really pretty cool. Okay, assholes, come on in. I'm taking you for a ride!"

Arima opened her soul once again and pulled the dark spirits into her essence. The Botanist then entwined the two vile souls in his spiritual vines of his own creation. The moment they began to speak, he covered their unearthly mouths tightly with his conjured leaves.

Arima left the shack and proceeded immediately to the morgue. She could feel the dark souls struggling to free themselves within her. As she was sneaking past the morgue toward the meeting room, she observed Marcus gazing in delight at an old magazine that was most certainly not intended for children…or some adults, for that matter. She chuckled to herself at the sight, then let out a boisterous internal laugh as The Botanist released his grip on the dark spirits and she expelled them into the Workplace Harassment poster.

She took the poster down, rolled it up to the muffled cries of the three entrapped demonic souls and went out the back exit. In the back alley, she placed the rolled-up poster into a burn barrel. She first lit a joint and inhaled with deep satisfaction. She then lit the poster. She did not know *how* she knew, but she knew that she could destroy these sadistic spirits if she destroyed the inanimate object that they had been trapped in. She watched with both sorrow and glee as the fire consumed the poster. She heard the anguished wails of the destroyed spirits float away with the spent ashes on the warm evening breeze.

Arima, I must leave you now, the Botanist said with slight regret. *I am being called to Enlightenment. I have redeemed myself. It has been a pleasure to get to know you. Thank you. Thank you for helping me move on. Perhaps now, I can find peace. But, before I go, let me tell you a little trick as to how to grow the most lovely marijuana plants. It will be like inhaling the nectar of the gods.*

As the Botanist whispered his secret into Arima's soul, she smiled more broadly than she had in her entire life.

Herbert Jenkins felt himself being lifted from Arima's body. He continued his ascension beyond the clouds until coming to a rest. He felt at peace and was surrounded by bright white light and a delicate mist. A silhouette approached him. It was dark at first, then became bright green as it came closer. Herbert once again looked upon the loveliest face he had ever seen. He had not fallen in love with her so many years ago just because of her physical beauty. He had also fallen in love with her name. It was her name that convinced him that they were meant to be together for all eternity.

"Hello, Herbert," the angelic green mouth stated.

"Um…hello, Iris Rose," Herbert bashfully replied. "It's been so long and…I am so sorry. I am so sorry for what I did to you. You did not deserve that. I wish that I could make it up to you."

"But you have, Herbert," Iris responded. "You *have* made it up to me. You have vanquished two demonic souls of Vetis. You have reduced his army. You have redeemed yourself. To me. And to the universe. And *I* am sorry for how I treated *you*. How I used you. And it wasn't just you. I manipulated many men in my time on earth. I certainly didn't deserve to be murdered for it, but it wasn't exactly nice of me. In fact, it was cruel. Because of how I died, I was allowed to join Enlightenment. But my punishment for all time is that I will forever be green. Green to match my jealous soul. That is why I manipulated men into buying me things. I was horribly jealous of others who had more than me. And that jealousy consumed me and compelled me to do cruel things. I was also made green by the powers of Enlightenment as a constant reminder of what I did to *you* and how I bastardized the love you had for your precious plants and flowers. I will always regret that, Herbert. And, I will always regret having to look this way."

A spiritual tear formed in Herbert's eye as he looked upon Iris and said, "You should never regret that. You are the most beautiful vision that I have ever seen in my life…or afterlife. To me, you are once again perfect."

"Come, then, Herbert," Iris sighed as she took his hand. "In Enlightenment, we can create our own world. We can surround ourselves with what makes us most happy. And I have used that ability to create something for *you*...for *us*." The mist lifted and they were standing in the middle of the most luxuriously beautiful garden. There was every type of plant from throughout the earth, and other worlds as well. The explosive array of scents, textures, and colors was overwhelming. For the first time in his existence, Herbert cried out with genuine rapture.

The spiritual form of a twelve-year-old Black girl emerged from a nearby forest and walked steadily toward the pair. Herbert looked down upon her with hopeful anticipation as the child said, "Thank you, sir. Thank you for avenging me. Thank you for ridding the world of those bad men. I can now rest peacefully here."

Tears once again began to form in Herbert's eyes as he said, "W-Would you like to rest peacefully *here*? With *us*? Would you like to join our family?"

The girl looked up at the couple and burst into tears as Herbert lifted her up. The new family embraced tightly as tears of peaceful joy poured out of their souls. The torrent of tears poured out of Enlightenment. The torrent of tears cascaded down towards the earth.

As an exhausted Arima was walking home, she was suddenly drenched by a downpour of warm rain. She looked up at the sky and instinctively understood that she was not being covered in rainfall. She smiled as she realized that she was being covered in the euphoria of a peaceful spirit.

CHAPTER 9
TODAY'S SERMON

Sweat was flying off of the seventy-one-year-old Pastor's flailing forearms, forehead, and hair as he reached into his soul and delivered his rapturous Sunday morning sermon to his noticeably dwindling congregation. His veins protruded from his neck and his face was bright purple as he barked out with an uproarious cadence the various scriptures that were meticulously selected for this week's lesson for his entranced congregation.

He passionately preached repeatedly about the kindness of Jesus Christ. His charity. His mercy. His sacrifice. The parishioners wept. They rejoiced. They threw their hands up into the air and screamed "Hallelujah" or "Amen" precisely on cue. The sermon was an overwhelming success for those in attendance.

It was successful in the further entrenchment of these pliable souls into the work of Vetis, the Tempter of the Holy. It was successful in twisting the kindness, generosity, and selflessness of the preaching of Jesus Christ into a self-serving hatred of the other. The other that did not look like them. The other that did not love like them. The other that did not vote like them. The other who was indoctrinating their children into sinful thoughts and deeds through their "woke" schools and libraries. The other who was taking their country away from them through nefarious means. The other who sacrificed babies to their demonic beliefs in the basement of a pizza parlor. The other who was their sworn enemy. The other who they must *vanquish* in order to reclaim *their* rightful dominion over this country and this earth.

Such fools, the Pastor would chuckle to himself as he witnessed the joyfully ignorant acceptance on his flock's faces. *They have no idea that we are the other. I am the other. I am the one who is indoctrinating them. I am the one who is taking their freedom away. I am the one who is leading them to an existence of subservience to our great Vetis. They will be subservient upon this earth, and they will be subservient in the after life once we have gathered enough of their dark souls to conquer Enlightenment. The earth shall be ours. The heavens will be ours! And these fools will be the willful participants of their own demise. And I shall be one of the chosen few to sit at the side of Vetis and witness this most glorious oppression.*

The Pastor was still wiping his brow with a saturated handkerchief as he flashed his serpentine smile and shook the hands of his departing congregation. The final woman's hands were still shaking in rapturous excitement as she took the Pastor's disfigured hands into hers and looked at them. "Pastor," she softly inquired. "How is it that your hands are so broken?"

The Pastor's expression grew dark as he replied remorsefully, "My hands. My hands, and my body were beaten mercilessly by one of the unholy ones in 2003. He was such a brutal, godless soul. But by God's mercy, he is no longer upon this earth with us. But there are others just like him my child. Others who would harm you and your children in the same manner."

The woman looked up into the Pastor's black eyes and said with a soft determination, "We must kill them all, Pastor. We must or else they will kill us."

"Yes, my child," the Pastor sneered in response. "We must. And it will be your time to be called to action soon. Thank you, my child. Thank you for your loyalty and...servitude. Peace be with you. God be with you."

He watched with arrogance as his flock proceeded to their vehicles, many still adorned with flags and banners celebrating Vetis's failed attempt at permanently installing one of his many dullard "Golden Calves" into the most prominent political position in the world. As he looked upon the faded, tattered, and nearly twenty-year old symbols of hatred, ignorance, and blind subservience flapping in the cool morning breeze, his own arrogance began to fade and tatter as well.

The waving symbols had represented their best chance to usher in the Age of Vetis. As a young man who was being groomed to be an earthly leader in the army of Vetis, he had been told of the ascension of an easily manipulated, narcissistic man who appeared charismatic to *other* easily manipulated and narcissistic people. Despite his diminished mental faculties, this man would hold the power to use his temperament, humor, and contrived conviction to tap into some people's fears and indoctrinate them into a cult of personality of hating anyone that was different from them and anything that they were not brainwashed to believe. Lies became truth and truth became "alternate facts" that would be quickly discarded by the logic-and informationally- impaired. They would be directed to march and dutifully shout simplistic three-syllable phrases. They would intimidate. They would bully. They would hate. This hatred would result in increasingly violent attacks upon civil society's most essential institutions of science, education and government. And this man *did* ascend to this most prestigious platform of power.

But not *permanently* as had been prognosticated. Pro-democracy forces battled this cult of usurpers at the election booth, airwaves, and neighborhoods that became literal battlefields. The autocratic movement of Vetis would strengthen and gain power in areas, only to be beaten back and fragmented once again. And now, in the year 2034, these freedom-fighters had apparently been successful in eliminating their most powerful tool to spread their deplorable lies and propaganda of insurgency: the wireless Internet.

As he watched the forces of his unholy movement become further degraded, he wondered if he would ever see the domination of Earth by Vetis in his lifetime. And if Earth was not conquered…if there could not be enough holy souls plunged into the blackness of their movement… then the conquest over Enlightenment would not be possible.

The Pastor had been placed upon this earth to recruit and indoctrinate others into the movement. He was one of many who would use people's fears to twist and bastardize their otherwise pure religious beliefs. It was from hundreds, if not thousands, of pulpits throughout the world that the earthly army of Vetis would be primarily built. His mission was to convince his unsuspecting sheep that they were doing the work of God, when in fact, they were doing the work of a power-hungry demon.

The Pastor mused to himself at how successful he had been in converting these otherwise kind people to wage war against others that they were *told* to wage war against. He thought about the hundreds of names that had been sent into battle. He laughed out loud as he thought about the hundreds of his followers whose blood had been shed and whose dark souls were now congregating in the netherworld, awaiting their orders to attack Enlightenment. He had been so successful at this aspect of the plan.

And the plan was a quite simple one. Convert otherwise good people to hate others. Indoctrinate them into believing violence against the hated others was God's work. Expand their ranks and dominate the earth with brutal, autocratic regimes. Sacrifice them on the earth's battlefields and re-construct them as an army of dark souls in the after-life. Attack and conquer Enlightenment. And then, welcome the glorious arrival and eternal dominion of Vetis.

The Pastor felt his arrogance re-emerge as he thought about his earthly manipulative victories. But his arrogance was once again short-lived as he witnessed the ceiling, floor, and walls of his modest church become encased in a thick, dark purple smog. And his heart sank as he heard an all-too-familiar, snide, nasally voice penetrate his very essence.

My, aren't we full of ourselves this morning, the sinister apparition stated as its tightly bound copper hair emerged from behind the pulpit and rose to full prominence through the dense purple fog. *I have been listening to your thoughts, Pastor. And yes, you have been quite successful in manipulating the weak into the service of our most glorious Vetis. But you have failed miserably at your most important commission.*

You have failed to produce a daughter with extraordinary power to fight and serve alongside us. It was through this daughter that we would have our most powerful ally. You failed in seducing your daughter to cower to our whims. You failed in seducing our daughter. And now, she has become one of the leading forces against our movement. Instead of recruiting her, you have turned her into our sworn enemy. And she is powerful. She is dangerous. And she must be eliminated.

"Me? What about you?" The Pastor yelled back incredulously. "I wasn't the one who allowed your husband's family to groom her. *I* wasn't the one who allowed those interlopers to give her a sense of righteous conviction and self-worth! She wasn't even biologically *related* to them and yet *they* succeeded at taking her from us! I tried to indoctrinate her. I tried to seduce her into our ways by any means necessary including sexual domination! And what did I get for it? Her bastard uncle beat me! Disfigured me for life! That is why I left Madison all those years ago and came to Louisiana. Our daughter was and still is a lost cause. But I have another daughter now. She just turned twenty-three and..."

The Pastor was abruptly interrupted by the ghastly spirit. *...And she has just become aware of her powers. Yes, I am quite aware of your Arima. I am quite aware at her ability to connect with and absorb the souls of those who are trapped here and unable to enter Enlightenment. I am quite aware of her ability to imprison those souls in inanimate objects and destroy them forever through the destruction of those inanimate objects. I am well aware of her great gift. And I am well aware at what an asset she could be for us...if you are able to re-enter her life and convince her to join you. But, she has too much of her mother and her grandmother in her. She must be indoctrinated, Pastor. With brutal force if necessary.*

I am also quite aware at just how dangerous she could be to us and our glorious movement. She must be convinced, or she must be destroyed. Just as I will personally destroy that little whore of a daughter that we darkened this earth with. I will take care of our daughter, and our granddaughter. I just need to find a soul who hates that little bitch as much as I do. Then, I will be able to entwine my soul with theirs and murder our little bundle of joy and her damned offspring! Yes, that little bitch is a lost cause as well. All peace and love with no thirst for violence or domination over others. But she could be dangerous as well. If she is able to tap into the attributes that she possesses from her whore mother and her damned father, then she could also be quite formidable. So my granddaughter must be sacrificed as well. And I will laugh as my husband and his family weep as they watch their beloved succumb to my icy grip of death.

But I am now warning you, just as I have already warned Arima. She must not become involved with our daughter. She must stay away from New York. I have spooked her and her grandmother enough, I believe, that it shouldn't be a problem. They aren't aware that I pose no real threat to them...yet.

Once I kill our daughter, she will not be allowed into Enlightenment. Not with all of the vengeful acts that she has committed in her forty-six years. Her soul will be trapped here. And the only being that will be able to make contact with her and allow her to re-emerge as a threat to us once again will be Arima. Your daughter. Our daughter's half-sister. If the two of them are allowed to join forces, either on Earth or in the spirit world, I fear that our dream of domination by our most glorious Vetis shall be vanquished. Yes, Pastor, consider that. As a unified force, they will be that powerful. They and their followers will have the power to defeat us.

So, Pastor...I'll take care of our *little mistake. You are to convert Arima. And, if you fail once again to bring one of your offspring into our fold, then you must do to her what you did to her mother. You must kill her. You must slice her open on a sacrificial altar. You must behead her and put her head on a spike as a tribute to our glorious Vetis. Do you understand?*

"Of course I understand!" The Pastor roared back. "I have no feelings for that girl. She is no more important to me than any of these other lemmings that we recruit to do our bidding. Except, in her case, she is quite powerful. And despite her upbringing by her damned Grand-mother, she still has a part of *me* in her as well. She has an ember of domination burning in her that I *will* exploit. I *will* succeed this time. And if I do not...then...Arima will die at my tortured hands."

Yes, she has a part of you in her. But may I remind you that our *daughter was made up of* both *of us and look at the disaster that she has become. I could almost sense it when she was growing in my womb. The way she would violently kick me. And once she was born and rejected my mother's milk, I instinctively knew that she was not destined to join us. As she grew from infant to toddler to child to young woman, she always had a rebellious streak against anything that did not seem right to her. I thought that I could beat her rebelliousness out of her. Perhaps I could have, if left alone, but I could only go so far with my husband's family watching over us. They were quite dangerous. But I don't really need to tell* you *that, now do I?*

I, too, was arrogant. I believed that I, along with the pathetic excuse of a man who thought he was her father, could mold her and brutally bend her to our will. But the more I beat her, the stronger she became. The more spiteful that little bitch became. That is when I sent her to you. To her true father. I believed that with my beating her body and soul and you raping her body and soul, that she would eventually succumb. That she would fall in line. And then, in her weakened state, we could rebuild her in our image. But it was never to be. My arrogance blinded me to the truth that she was a bad seed that should have been aborted. I had planned on doing just that when she was fifteen. I was planning on finally aborting that unwanted burden, but you convinced me to just let her go. You said that my husband's damned family finally had a complete grip on her and that they would destroy us if we harmed her. Perhaps you were right, but now look at the threat that she has grown into.

So do not depend too much on your genetic influence, Pastor. Genetics can only go so far against a person that holds true conviction and compassion for others of their kind. The question is...does Arima have any conviction towards anything or anyone besides her own selfish gratification? Because if not, you may have a chance at bringing her into our army. But if she is anything like her half-sister, then...we shall proceed without her.

Chapter 10
Youthful Indiscretions

"Awwww, yeah, man…this is the best pizza ever," a satisfied Arima stated hazily as she took the last bite of the last slice of pizza.

"Arima…what the hell!" Jessie exclaimed as she, her husband, Cliff, and fellow housemate Jamie entered the room with their drinks. "You ate the whole damn pizza? And you didn't even *pay* for it! I swear, you can be the most *selfish* person in the world!"

Cliff and Jamie could do nothing more than chuckle as Arima replied through her intoxicated haze, "Oh…hey, man…I'm sorry…but it's like…this is the best pizza ever. I just couldn't stop. Hey, are there any more of those cookies that you baked yesterday? Those were the best cookies ever."

"No," Jessie tersely replied with her arms folded and a look of disgust on her face. "No, you ate all of those yesterday while we were at work."

"Ahhhh, shit…Yeah," Arima replied. "How 'bout potato chips? We have some, right?"

Jessie sat next to her friend, took her hand and looked at her seriously. "Arima, we have been the best of friends since high school, and I love you. I truly do. You're totally chill and you are probably the least judgmental person that I know. You're fun to party with and have a great sense of humor. You are the greatest confidant and never spread gossip…probably because you don't remember any, but it's still a good quality. You are a fantastic person, and I am so grateful that you are in my life, but I want you to listen to me now."

Jessie's tone then immediately changed from irreverence to a roar. "When you are high, you are a damned pig! You eat *everything* in the house! You don't just get the munchies. You get the munchies on *steroids!* You are *literally* eating us out of house and home! So get off your ass and go to the grocery store! You've already eaten everything that Cliff and I have bought this week and it's not Jamie's turn yet. So, get up and get us some food!"

"Wait…what…now?" a confused Arima replied.

"Yes, now!" Jessie answered through her grinding teeth. "While you're gone, we'll just order another…oh never mind. I'm not telling you. You'll hide in the bushes and hijack it. Please, Arima. Just go and get us some food."

"Fine, I could use the exercise anyway," Arima replied in an uninterested tone as she got off of the couch, scratched her ass, brushed pizza crumbs from her top and put her jacket on over her pajamas.

An hour and a half later, Arima's three housemates were basking in the glow of post-pizza consumption.

"Wow," Jamie stated. "Arima was right. That may be the best pizza ever. And I'm not even high right now. That was almost better than sex."

"Almost?" Cliff chimed in. "That was *definitely* better than…"

Cliff thought it wise to not finish his statement once he saw his wife's brilliant blue eyes dart at him.

Arima entered the home, carrying two large grocery bags. "All right, here ya go. Can you guys put this stuff away for me? I gotta go see Grams before my shift tonight and I'm running a little late. I kinda got hung up at the store. Why are there so many types of cookies? I mean, there are so many, and they all look so good."

"Yeah, we can do that, sweetie," a chuckling Jamie replied as she took the bags from her friend and the trio entered the kitchen as Arima made her way up the stairs to get ready for work.

"Okay, we're not sending her to the store high *ever again!* I mean, how the hell did she eat three frozen burritos?" Jessie cried out as she looked at the contents of the grocery bags. There were three frozen burrito wrappers, a half-eaten bag of potato chips, an empty container of onion dip, a half-eaten box of peanut butter breakfast cereal, two candy bar wrappers, two empty packages of lemon cookies, and- for some unexplained reason- an onion.

———

Arima sauntered into her grandmother's home and announced her arrival. "Hey, Grams! I'm here! I brought you a 'nilla milkshake!"

Louise Azar came out of her kitchen in her flowing, brightly-colored robe and took the large paper cup from her beloved granddaughter. "Thank you, my child. That was so sweet of…"

Her thought trailed off as she realized that the milkshake was only about half-full. She shook her head, chuckled, and said, "Come, child, and tell me how your job is going. Have you had any…experiences?"

A now near-sober Arima relayed to her grandmother her violent exploits with the racists and The Botanist. Although Louise Azar had witnessed and participated in many incredible episodes in her life, she sat bewildered at the recounting of her granddaughter's adventures. She had sensed that Arima was powerful. But until this moment she had not realized just *how* powerful. She had not realized that Arima had the ability to completely control the spirits that she allowed into her soul. She had feared that a powerful dark soul might be able to consume and control her granddaughter, leaving Arima's body and soul helpless to defend herself against whatever the dark spirit may wish to do with it. This fear had now been mostly alleviated.

And she was apparently the first Azar woman who could permanently destroy the dark spirits that had been placed in inanimate objects through the destruction of those objects. Every Azar woman had tried to destroy Howard, whose darkened spirit was trapped in the beautiful painting of a Jamaican harbor. He, along with the painting, would be placed in a fireplace, or chopped to pieces with an axe or weighed down and drowned at the bottom of a lake.

It was all to no avail. The next morning, a completely restored painting would be hanging on the wall with evil chuckles emanating from it. They realized that the dark spirit had complete dominion over the object that it was imprisoned in. It could call upon its spiritual powers and restore these objects, thereby restoring their life in the afterlife. But they could not *leave* those objects. Not without being invited into the soul of someone such as Arima. So all of the Azar women resigned themselves to simply being the guardian of these haunted artifacts and ensure that the spirits that were trapped there were not allowed to escape.

This was not true of Arima. She held dominion over both the evil souls *and* their inanimate prison. She could take them into herself. She could place them into objects. She could manipulate them. And she could extinguish their essence for all time. She could destroy them through the simple act of setting them on fire or smashing them into pieces as nonchalantly as she could crumple up a wad of paper.

Louise realized that she was a more evolved version of herself and their Azan descendants. That she was a stronger warrior against pure evil than any of them had ever been. Louise allowed herself a moment of relaxation as relief replaced her great anxiety.

The relief was short-lived, however. Louise immediately thought that, although her strength was a blessing, it could also be a curse. That her strength might give Arima a false sense of invincibility and that, in turn, may lead her into battles that she would not be and could not be prepared for. This false sense of invincibility might lead her back to her despised father or whoever the copperhead was. Louise realized that it was her responsibility to temper her granddaughter's confidence in her gifts.

"Well, that is quite interesting, dear," Louise began casually. "Yes, quite interesting indeed. It is nice to know that you have that ability over…shall we say…*lesser* demonic forces. I mean, these puny little racists that you destroyed are, *of course,* at the *lowest* rung of the ladder as far as power and influence goes. You would do well to remember that. You sensed it, didn't you? You were able to sense just how powerful they were, or in this case, weren't. You could sense that you could easily overpower them."

"And that is the precise ability that we are going to have you hone. You must trust your feelings. Your sensations. If you sense that a spirit is more powerful than you, then you must leave it alone. Do not trifle with it. Whatever battle they are engaged in is *not* your battle. Do not, *under any circumstances,* let them in. They will overpower you. They will control you. And they will *destroy* you. Do you understand, my child?"

"Uh…sure, Grams," Arima replied dismissively. "Hey, you got any cookies?"

"Arima!" Louise barked out.

"What? Jeezus!" a shocked Arima responded.

"Arima, my dearest," Louise began again as she took Arima's delicate hands in hers. "Please listen to me. Please take this seriously. I have seen things, Arima. I have done things. I have gone up against very powerful forces of evil. There was a time when I thought that I could control any evil spirit that I allowed in. I would take them in and imprison them in a painting, plate, or vase. I would do this as easily as you have just done. I became conditioned to believe that my powers were far greater than any evil in this universe. I became arrogant. And I was wrong. My arrogance nearly killed me.

"Let me tell you a story of a time when I was not much older than you. When I was twenty-five years old, I had quite a bit of experience with my…abilities. Your mother was about five at the time and I left her with my younger brother, who was seventeen, as I had a date with someone that I was quite attracted to. It was as though he held a spell over me, and I was drawn to him. It was a magical evening until…he raped and nearly murdered me.

"As he was on top of me and strangling me, I was able to reach around, and I grabbed a large rock. I struck him fiercely in the head with it and he rolled off of me. I was enraged and struck him over and over with it until his head and face was bloody mush. It was then that I realized that it wasn't this young man who had done this to me. It may have been his body, but his body was being controlled by an evil spirit. I was so entranced by this young man and…well, I'm a bit ashamed to say…but I was a bit…aroused by him, so I ignored what my senses were telling me about him. I ignored the feelings of danger. I was so dismissive of it that I actually wondered to myself, *Why is it that good girls fall for bad boys?* Had I just left him alone and not gone out with him that night, this horrible event never would have happened. But my selfishness and libido overrode the danger that I was sensing. So, he raped and strangled me in the front yard of my home. And I, in turn, murdered that young man.

"Now you may be wondering how it was that this evil spirit came to control this young man. I was, and still am, involved in a group of women. We all have various skills and abilities, and we frequently meet to…well…that's another story for another time. Let's just say that we meet to look after our loved ones as best as our abilities will allow. There were three young women about my age in this group. I do not know why, but these three young women did not like me. Perhaps it was just petty jealousy or something more. Well…now that I think about it I did…how can I say this…steal one of their boyfriends away. So, this made this group of three best friends quite upset with me and they decided to eliminate me, which I felt was a bit of an overreaction on their part.

"One of the women had the same ability as us. She could absorb a soul into her or place it into an inanimate object, but nothing more. A second young woman possessed an amazing power. She was the only one that I have ever known. She had the power to control and manipulate energy, including that of souls. So she could take the energy of the soul that had been captured by the first woman and place it into another human being. And the third woman possessed the power of manipulating the spirit's actions. She could control the spirit that was controlling its human host.

"These three women found a human host in another town that they thought nobody would miss for a while. They found a spirit that was trapped here. They captured that spirit in the soul of one woman, then transferred that spirit's energy into the human host, then controlled the actions of that human host. And that human host that was being controlled by an evil spirit that was being controlled with the most vengeful of the women, seduced me.

"As I said, the moment I killed that young man, I knew that he had been possessed, because I saw and felt the evil spirit billow out of him, like some grey cloud of smog. At that very moment, my brother came running outside to see what was happening. The first woman absorbed the dark soul. The second woman transferred that soul's energy into my brother's body. And the third woman had that dark soul that was inhabiting my brother attack me. My brother's body lunged at me, and I reacted instinctively. I picked up a large log and struck him with it. He fell backward and he was impaled on the picket fence that surrounded our lovely flower garden in our front yard. Those three harlots took off into the night and the evil spirit left my brother's body and floated away as I stood there and watched my dear brother die. His blood was dripping down the wooden fence posts as he was gasping for air. He looked up at me and extended his hand. I was, of course, crying profusely and screaming how sorry I was. In his last breath, he said to me, *It's okay. It wasn't your fault. I love you and I will always be with you.* And he has been from that day forward."

Louise wiped a tear from her eye, got up from her sofa and stood in front of a scenic painting of three palm trees swaying in the breeze. She smiled briefly before continuing. "Now, those three women disappeared and hid from me. But another woman in our group had the ability to track down specific souls and she told me where they were. So, one by one, I snuck into the houses that they were hiding in, and I slit their throats. They, of course, were not allowed entry into Enlightenment upon their deaths, so I absorbed their souls and placed them into a painting. This painting. And now, my dearest Arima, I believe that I am tired of looking at this painting. Would you do your ol' Grams a favor and place it in the fire for me?"

The palm trees in the painting immediately wilted and three dark silhouettes began flying through the brush strokes in a frenzy as they pleaded with Louise and Arima for mercy. Their screams reached a fevered pitch as Arima threw the painting into the fire. The flames licked around the edges, then burst through the center and the women's dark souls were put to their final end in the ashes of oblivion.

Heh, heh, heh, you bitches are toast! Arima heard a sinister voice say from the painting on the opposite wall.

"Shut up, Howard or you're next," came Arima's terse reply. The painting did not make another sound.

As Louise and Arima watched the final flames recede from the wooden embers in the fireplace, Louise put her arm around Arima's shoulder and whispered into her ear, "My point of this story, my dear child, is trust your instincts. *Always* trust your instincts." A bewildered Arima could do nothing more than give a silent nod of understanding.

Chapter 11

Freudian and Other Unfortunate Slips

"So," Marcus began as he was avoiding eye contact with Arima by shuffling papers that had already been organized. "I…uh…well…I noticed that you're not on the schedule tomorrow night."

"Uh…nope," Arima replied as she could feel her anticipation building. "I have the next two nights off. Why do you ask?"

"Well," Marcus answered reservedly as he continued to avoid looking directly at Arima. "I have tomorrow evening off, too, and…well…I was just thinkin' that since *I* was off and *you* were off then maybe…um…maybe we could get off together…I mean, do something together on our night off…y'know…if ya want to."

Arima fought back the urge to giggle at Marcus's obvious Freudian slip as her heart began pounding. "Uh, yeah…sure. I would *love* to hang with you. What did you have in mind?"

Marcus's mind was whirring as he tried to think of the appropriate response. He hadn't actually thought about any sort of plan. He just knew that since her hug alleviated all of his pain a few nights earlier, that he couldn't stop thinking about her. And he knew precisely what he wanted to do with her. But he also knew that that was way too forward of a suggestion at this moment. So he summoned up all of his courage, took a big gulp, and said coolly, "Eat?"

Arima couldn't hold it in any longer. His fumbling attempts at asking her out were just too cute, so she burst out in laughter. "Eat? Um… okay," she managed to reply through her chuckles. "You mean dinner? Sure. That would be great. And then maybe we could go back to my place and hang for a while…like…up in my room…if ya want".

"Sure, sure, sure," a nearly hyperventilating Marcus replied quickly. "Um…um…um, where would you like to go? You know…to eat?"

"I want you to take me to your favorite place," Arima replied coyly.

Following making the arrangements for their first date, a smiling Marcus left the morgue with a proud strut and Arima began joyfully bouncing on the balls of her black canvass tennis shoes while squealing in delight.

Well, Arima…it looks like you do *have a boyfriend,* came Mrs. Roper's playful voice.

Yes, Arima. Congratulations, Mr. Roper replied. *Marcus is a fine young man. We're very happy for you, but…*

"But what," a fearfully intrigued Arima asked of the bodiless voices.

Well, Arima, Mrs. Roper answered, *we just want to give you a bit of advice. We do not want you to repeat our mistakes. We haven't had a chance to tell you why we are trapped here and now that you have a love interest, we believe that the time is right. Isn't that right, dear?*

Yes, of course, Mr. Roper responded. *Arima, we have been here for fourteen years. Since the year 2020. We had been married for seven years and had two small children. Our daughter was five and our son was three at the time of our death. For the last two years of our marriage…well…when we were living… we were just horrible to one another. We had allowed ourselves to grow apart. We did not consider our two small children. We became selfish. We both began having affairs. When we weren't out looking to get laid at some neighborhood bar, we were spying on one another. Our jealousy continued to grow and the more jealous we became of one another, the crueler we were to one another. And our children would be sitting at home with some babysitter, while we were out cavorting. All they ever learned from us was that we either weren't home to attend to their needs or we were constantly fighting. We provided a horrible upbringing for them. We provided a horrible example of how to be parents. Hell, we provided a horrible example of how to be decent human beings.*

The night that we died; I had drunk way too much. I followed my wife and some man to a seedy hotel. I burst into the room and found them together. In a fit of jealous rage, I took the bottle of vodka that I had and crushed the man's head with it. I killed him. He hadn't really done anything wrong. Just a typical guy carousing the streets for a good time. We were the ones that were wrong. Our infidelity towards one another and my violence. I killed that man that night.

We both killed him that night, dear, Mrs. Roper replied in a supportively somber tone.

Yes, perhaps, but I swung the bottle. He had a huge laceration from the top of his head to his throat. We just sat there and watched him bleed out. We were both drunk and in shock. We decided to leave and not tell anyone. And in my impaired state, I went the wrong way down a one-way street. I turned the corner and crashed headlong into an on-coming car. Both cars exploded. We were killed instantly.

And those teenagers in the other car were killed instantly too, Mrs. Roper added. *Four sixteen-year-old kids out on a double date coming home from bowling, we understand. They did not deserve that. Our selfishness. Our infidelity. Our damned drunken jealousy killed five innocent people that night. And not only that, but it also destroyed our children.*

Yes, Mr. Roper continued. *They are now nineteen and seventeen. They went to live with my sister's family, and they have been wonderful to them. But they have had to live with the fact that their parents are murderers. They have been picked on and ridiculed. They both have such a hard time making friends. And despite my sister's and her husband's best efforts, it seems as though they are doomed to not understanding how to have healthy relationships. They are introverted and distrustful. And that is our fault. And we have been told that we must make that right with them before we are allowed entry into Enlightenment. We have waited fourteen years for someone like you to come along, Arima. Someone that we could connect with who could perhaps help us. Fourteen years we have had to think about how to make amends. And we don't have a clue as to what to do.*

So, Arima, Mrs. Roper began again, *the reason why we are telling you this is, just be kind to other people, especially those that you love. We understand that this is your first date, but that look in both of your eyes is unmistakable. You were both so delighted when you first saw one another. Don't ever lose that. Don't ever forget what it was you first saw in that other person. Don't become complacent and don't allow yourselves to take each other for granted. Just be kind to one another and remember what it was that first attracted you to that other person. What it was that made your heart flutter. If you do that, all of the silly little things are just that.*

They won't seem important to you. They will just be silly little things that just a bit of kindness and understanding and honest expression can take care of. That is all it takes. But if you allow those toxic feelings to build, then your relationship will go down a dark path. And it will be your fault. Both of you. Just as it was our fault that we stopped communicating with one another. Stopped being thoughtful of one another. The end of your relationship may not hold the same deadly tragedy as our ending, but it will end tragically, nonetheless. Please take our advice Arima and cherish the love you have for this man and that he has for you. Because that type of love...that type of connection is hard to come by in this, or any, life.

And one other thing, Arima, Mr. Roper interjected. *We know this isn't your burden, but if you have any ideas as to how we can help our children and make up for the dastardly example that we set for them...well...we will always be in your debt.*

"Wow, um, yeah," a mournful Arima replied. "Wow. I'm so sorry, you guys. I'm sorry you did all that stuff and that those innocent people died. And I promise that I've listened to you. I'll try to be really cool to Marcus, even if he pisses me off. And I also promise that I will help you, somehow. I don't know how yet, but I'll think of something, or else my name isn't Arima Azan. And that's my name, so that's how it's going to be."

———

Arima arrived the following evening at seven o'clock at the address that Marcus had given her. Her heart leapt once again as she approached the dinery and saw him sitting outside waiting for her with tell-tale smoke tumbling from between his lips.

"Hey, uh...you want a drag?" Marcus offered as a greeting. "Oh, hell, yeah," Arima enthusiastically replied as she took the joint from his hand and savored the rich smoke coming from the spliff that had just been in her future lover's mouth. "This is, like...my favorite thing to do before coming here. This is *totally* my favorite restaurant, too! How 'bout we get it to go and go back to my place and put on a movie while we eat? I can dig out my old DVD's and find somethin' to watch."

Thirty minutes later, Arima sauntered through her front door with Marcus in tow. They were carrying seven take out bags. Jessie, Cliff, and

Jamie looked up in amazement as Arima said to them without breaking her stride, "Everybody, this my friend Marcus. Marcus, this is everybody. We're goin' up to my room to…um…eat and stuff. We'll be down later…probably."

Arima gleefully jumped on the bed with both knees and began unpacking their treasure. Within moments, the pair were staring at a culinary smörgåsbord that consisted of eight double cheeseburgers, two large fries, four fruit pies, four twenty-piece chicken nuggets, fifteen dipping sauces of every variety, two large onion rings, two large chocolate milkshakes, four chicken sandwiches, two diet sodas and for some unexplained reason, a packet of apple slices.

The engorged pair laid in the bed following their gluttonous endeavor with wide smiles of satisfaction as the images of their selected horror movie DVD flickered on the television. The bed was littered with crumbs, globs of ketchup, colorful junk food wrappers, empty drink cups and one unopened packet of apple slices. Arima looked over at Marcus and began laughing.

"Wh-what's so funny?" a nearly exhausted Marcus asked.

"Oh, my God, you have a pickle stuck to your face!" Arima cried out, nearly wetting herself from the uncontrolled laughter.

Marcus then began laughing and retorted playfully, "Oh yeah? Well, I sure as hell hope that's ranch dressing on your lips!"

"Why don't you taste it to find out?" Arima asked provocatively as she gazed into Marcus's eyes.

Thirty minutes and one set of broken bedsprings later, the pair descended the staircase and entered the living room to the knowing snickers of Arima's three housemates.

"Oh, sweetie," Jamie scolded. "Go upstairs and change your shirt. You have ranch dressing all over it."

"What?" Arima replied casually. "Oh, uh…yeah. That's what it is. I'll be right back."

While Arima was upstairs hastily going through her laundry hamper to find a "clean" shirt, Marcus was looking at the floor, nervously shuffling his feet.

"Oh, sweetie," Jamie began in order to reduce the awkwardness of the situation. "We have heard sooo much about you and we are sooo happy to finally meet you. Our Arima has been talking about you night and day, and…"

Jamie was then cut off by Jessie who interrupted with, "Yeah, she talks about you a lot. I mean, when she isn't eating everything in the house, that is. And from the…er…sounds that just came from her bedroom, I guess you make her pretty happy. So join us, won't you? We're just watching…what the hell *are* we watching, anyway?"

Cliff answered meekly, "It's a marathon of something called *Cheers*. It's actually kind of funny Jess. I actually know quite a bit about this show. For example, did you know that…"

"Shut up. No, you don't know *anything* about this show. You're just making stuff up again. And, no, it's really not funny," Jessie interrupted with a snotty attitude. "None of this old crap is any good. There wasn't anything worth watching since before the reboot of the reboot of the reboot of *Real Wives* in 2030. And that, my friends, is a *fact*. Those shows like *Real Wives* is *reality*. It is how the world actually *is*. *These* old shows from the stone age are just made-up stories by writers. They are fake. Fake characters, fake plots, fake stories. Fake! *Real Wives* is real. It's in the title! I guess the next thing you're going to tell me is that this next show that's coming on is funny, too. What or who the hell is *Seinfeld*, anyway? I can't stand this anymore. I need some reality in my life. I'm just going to go into the bedroom and read the *Inquirer*. Nice to meet you, Marcus. C'mon, Cliff!"

"So, that's Jessie and Cliff," came Arima's voice as she re-entered the living room. "They've been together since high school. He was a big-time jock, and she was the head cheerleader."

"With an emphasis on the *head*," Jamie squealed out in delight.

"Shut up! I can hear you!" Jessie yelled out from behind her closed bedroom door, eliciting even greater childish laughter from Jamie and Arima.

"Sorry, sweetie! Couldn't resist! We won't talk about you anymore!" Jamie yelled out before huddling between Arima and Marcus and dropping her voice to a whisper. "Now, just between us, Jessie is a peach. She was the only popular girl and he was the only popular guy in high school who would befriend a stoner slacker like Arima and a burgeoning drag queen such as myself. So they truly are wonderful people. Of course, it didn't hurt that Arima and I helped them quite a bit with their homework, but still, we all became the unlikeliest best of friends. It's just that...well...Jessie is a bit...informationally challenged and Cliff is a bit...um...how should I say this?"

"Cliff has no balls, is completely pussy-whipped, and allows Jess to lead him around by his nose," Arima blurted out. "But Jamie's right. They are both very nice. Plus, being with them helps us get into clubs that we wouldn't ordinarily be allowed into, so there's that benefit."

"Oh! That reminds me!" Jamie screamed out. "There's an underground drag show tonight. Do you kiddies wanna go? I just hate going out by myself. We need all the eyes we can get to keep a lookout for the cops and the deplorables. *Pleeeease?*"

Arima looked at Marcus with quiet trepidation. This was his first test. He was so nice. Certainly he couldn't be one of the oppressive haters, could he? Certainly he wasn't a homophobe or transphobe, right?

Arima did not have to wait long for her answer, as Marcus jumped up from the couch, hastily made his way to the door, and exclaimed, "Hell, yeah! That sounds fun! What are we waiting for? Let's go!"

As the gleeful trio made their way down the street, a lurking figure appeared from out of the evening fog. He heard a nasally voice in his head say, *Ah, your daughter has a new boyfriend. That will be her Achilles' heel. Manipulate him to manipulate her. And if he does not go along, then threaten him. Threaten his life. Imprison him and force her to do our bidding. And once we have Arima in the fold, I will be able to focus on ridding ourselves of our whore of a daughter. And then, the games can truly begin.*

Chapter 12

The Foreplay is Now Over

*Drip...Drip...Drip...*was all that Marcus could hear from a nearby leaky faucet. The dreaded sound had become almost as torturous as the seemingly endless waterboarding that he had been forced to endure for the previous two days. He could smell the dankness of the room from underneath his black hood. Blood, saliva, tears, and snot were trailing down his beaten face and congealing just above his shattered collarbone. He wondered why this was happening. He wondered why he had been chosen to be a victim of this brutality.

His mind raced to find a happier place. A place where the pain could dissipate for just a moment and give his tortured body and soul a brief reprieve. He thought of Arima. For the past three months, he and Arima had been nearly inseparable. They spent every waking, non-working moment together. Holding hands during long strolls to the convenience store for chocolate donuts, potato chips, or slushies. Gazing longingly into one another's eyes as they shared a milkshake. Laughing together as they rolled on Arima's bed following blissful lovemaking. She was the person that had become his best friend. His lover. His soul mate.

And the unbridled happiness did not come just from his new love. He also felt a renewed energy and zeal for life as his cancer-riddled mother had actually received some good news about her prognosis. There was a new drug that, although not a cure, could substantially improve the quality and length of her life. His father was beyond himself with joy as he embraced his life-long love following the consultation with the physician. They wanted to share the good news with their new pastor and invited him over for a Saturday evening dinner.

The pastor was a tall, lanky, seventy-one-year-old white man. He entered the Jeffersons's home with a confident charisma. He greeted Marcus's parents and delicately kissed his mother on the forehead before embracing her. The pastor was new to their church. He was introduced six weeks earlier, following the sudden disappearance of their previous clergy. The previous pastor had been found in the swamp, half-eaten by alligators and other assorted wildlife. There was no explanation. But the new pastor attempted to shine a light on what may have happened to him.

He explained that there were evil, anti-Christian forces that were attempting to divide people by race. That was why most churches were now segregated. The Make America Godly Again, ultra-radical, white Christian nationalist people had grown distrustful, if not outwardly hostile, of non-white people. And, non-white people were increasingly fearful of white people, regardless of their societal views. That was why he assumed this position of looking over a nearly all-Black flock to go along with his responsibilities at an all-white church. He stated that he wanted to be a bridge between the two groups and heal the wounds that this senseless murder at the hands of white fascists had re-opened. And this joyous dinner to celebrate Mrs. Jefferson's good news was the perfect opportunity for people from two very different cultures to celebrate with one another. To rejoice with one another. To cry with one another. And to laugh with one another.

The pastor had been subtly encouraging Marcus to invite his girlfriend to his Sunday evening service. Arima had been quite resistant as she did not believe that she needed to be preached to in order to be a good person, but because it seemed so important to Marcus, she finally agreed to attend. And she did attend, the following morning. What the pastor had not considered, however, was that Marcus's girlfriend would also bring her grandmother along.

Arima's grandmother, Louise, absolutely adored Marcus. He was obviously in love with her cherished granddaughter, but there was more to it than that. She loved his carefree attitude while also being a young man that took his responsibilities seriously. She admired the sacrifices that he was making in order to support his parents through their difficulties. And she found him to be hysterically funny. She would look at her granddaughter gazing into the eyes of her new boyfriend and could sense that this was a pairing that had been destined. And it made her heart swell with pride and joy.

Louise was introduced to Marcus's parents as they approached the front pew of the modest-looking church. Mrs. Jefferson was being embraced warmly by everyone in the congregation in a celebration of her hopeful prognosis. More than one parishioner wondered aloud if it was possible that her good news and the arrival of their new, magnetic pastor was more than a mere coincidence. The congregation adored him, and they believed him capable of anything. Even a miracle.

They shed visible tears of rapture as the pastor made his way up to the pulpit and gazed down upon his reverential flock. Louise looked at the man's face for the first time. She, too, immediately believed that this man was capable of anything. Her mahogany skin flushed ghostly white, and she felt a sharp chill go up her spine. Her trembling hands desperately reached for Arima's. She pulled her astonished and confused granddaughter to her feet and dragged her hastily to the front door. This was the last time that Marcus had been seen or heard from by them for the past two days. The pair disappeared through the white door and into the sultry evening air as the Pastor looked on knowingly.

The subtle approach isn't going to work, the Pastor thought to himself as he launched into his animated and uplifting sermon.

Marcus had not heard another person's voice for two days. Following the Sunday evening service, Marcus said goodbye to his parents and immediately began walking towards Arima's house in order to find out what may have been wrong with her grandmother. He turned a corner and was greeted by a white man who asked him for a light. He felt a sharp pain on the top of his head.

He woke up to the sensation of drowning and lay there gasping for his life. For the past two days, there had been no talking. There had been only constant waterboarding and beatings. He would be dragged from his chair, laid at an angle on a flat board, and have water poured over his face. This was done continuously until Marcus was praying for death. He would be taken back to his chair, strapped down, and beaten with clubs throughout his face and body. He could feel, then hear his bones crack with each subsequent blow. His fingers had been snapped, meticulously. His ankles had been broken. His ribs had been broken. His jaw had been broken. His nose had been broken. His spirit had been broken.

He sat there, bound to his chair, weeping, when he finally heard another person's voice. The voice caused him to feel both confusion and bone-chilling fear simultaneously. It was the slithery voice of the Pastor.

"Hello, Marcus," the Pastor began with a calm arrogance. "I'm so sorry about all of this, but it is quite necessary, as you shall soon see. I'm going to remove your hood now and you and I are going to come to an…agreement."

The Pastor removed the hood from Marcus's battered face and his swollen eyes stared in disbelief at the blurred, smug expression of the Pastor.

"Let me explain what is happening, Marcus," the Pastor began again. "From the moment that I was born, I knew that I was destined for great things. That I was *destined* to serve a great power. Following the, well, we'll say, tragic death of my parents, I was taken in by a group. This group worships the great Vetis, the Tempter of the Holy. They showed me the mark of Vetis on the top of my head and told me that I was destined to be a revered general in Vetis's army. That Vetis would one day come to Earth and hold dominion over all of his Earth-bound subjects. And that Vetis would also wage a glorious war against the afterlife, against Enlightenment, and hold dominion over that as well. That Vetis was destined to dominate *this* life *and* the afterlife. And that *I* was one of his most important disciples who was *destined* to rule by his side.

"I was told that I would have two most important tasks. One task was to convert those on this earth who believed themselves to be *holy* to become *unholy*. To take their *pure devotion* to their chosen deity and *twist it* into a blind devotion to hatred and violence towards others. I am one of many who have this task and this battle has been waging for centuries. We have been so close to victory in the past twenty years, only to be beaten back again and again. We do not yet have enough numbers. We have yet to convert enough *souls* from light to dark. We do not yet have enough *power* to topple the world's democracies and replace them with brutal dictators that are humbled servants of Vetis. But this battle wages on and the dream is still quite alive.

"Which brings me to my second most important task. I was to sire a daughter. A most powerful daughter who would fight alongside me. And our unholy union would tip the scales of power in favor of *us*, the disciples of Vetis. I have two daughters. The first was born in Wisconsin and she has been…a disappointment. In fact, she has become quite a formidable adversary against us. But her mother will take care of her… in due time.

"My second daughter just came of age and has recently become aware of her great powers. She has the ability to absorb dark souls who are trapped here and enable them to use her body to commit the most glorious crimes against humanity. Or she can destroy them. Of course, the second daughter that I speak of is Arima."

Marcus began weeping uncontrollably as he prayed for this nightmare to end. But his prayers were not answered, and he was forced to continue to listen to the Pastor's deplorable diatribe.

"I must bring Arima into our fold. I had wanted her mother as well, but her soul was too pure to corrupt, so I sacrificed her to Vetis. I split her open so that her blood would be absorbed by the altar of Vetis and then I beheaded her and placed her head on a spike. Not unlike what I did to your previous pastor of your church. I needed a way to get to you so that I could use you to get to Arima. Plus, it gives me the opportunity to corrupt an entirely different group of believers. They are all so easily influenced. They all want to believe so badly that they are deserving of a grand afterlife. Some are. Most aren't. Most are greedy and self-serving bastards who would sell their own daughter out just for a small taste of the good life. Most are exactly like me. So I murdered your former pastor. And that is what will happen to Arima as well if she does not join me by my side. And that is where you come in.

"I am indeed sorry for having put you through such an…inconvenience, but, you see, you needed to understand what we…what *I* am capable of. You *must* understand that what I am telling you is true. You *must* understand that if you fail me, then the fate of Arima's mother will also be yours. And that fate will be Arima's as well.

"So how can you be of assistance to me you may want to ask? She has fallen in love with you. You hold great influence over her. You will call her and your family and tell them that you are fine. Tell them that you have gone on a trip and that you won't be back for some time. During that time, I will nurture you. I will *nurture* and *heal* both your body and your soul. You will join me and you will work with me on bringing Arima to me. You will deliver her to where she belongs. Once both your body and soul are...*healed*...shall we say...you will *murder* Arima's grandmother. She must be eliminated in order to have any chance of success. I would like to do that old bitch in myself, but it is better this way. You are able to get close to her. I am not, as you may have noticed at Sunday evening's service.

"Then you will seduce Arima and bring her to me. Arima will be quite weakened by the loss of her dear, old grandmother and she will be easily influenced. You will bring her to me and then...well...*I* will do what *I* do best. I will turn her light into darkness. And then, together, we will re-engage in the war that is being fought. And with Arima's help, we shall be victorious in turning this damnable democracy into a mindless herd of followers of Vetis's chosen pawn of a dictator. And once this country falls, the other democracies throughout the world will easily fall as well. And then Vetis shall arrive, and we shall collect all of our fallen dark souls and destroy Enlightenment itself!

"So, Marcus...what do you say? Are you going to help me or...should I just slit your throat right now and do this on my own?"

Every cell in every part of Marcus's being was throbbing with pain. Physical pain. Mental pain. Emotional pain. Spiritual pain. He wanted to resist. He wanted to spit in the Pastor's eye. He wanted to break free from his chains and beat this arrogant, selfish, sadistic bully with his hands until he was nothing more than bloody pulp. But he knew that he could not do any of that at this moment. He could willingly sacrifice himself. What he could *not* allow was Arima to be sacrificed as well. He had to buy some time and reach deeply into his personal faith and pray that he would not be converted like the mindless others. He must accept this now and pray for strength and the opportunity to fight another day. He was disgusted with himself as he heard his beleaguered voice come out of his split and bloody lips. "Y-yes. I will help you."

———

"And that, my child, is your father," Louise stated solemnly through her tears to her astonished granddaughter. "That is your father and that is what he is capable of. I have prayed that we would never see his hideous face ever again. But he is here. He is here for *you*. You cannot help Marcus now. If that vile man has him, then he's already gone, one way or another. We must get you far away, my dearest. We must hide you from him. He will try to get you to join him. And, if you do, it may mean the end of humanity as we know it. And if you don't, he will destroy you. I have already lost my beloved daughter and I will be damned if I lose you, too. Please, Arima. Let us go to the bus station and get you far away from here. And *not* New York! Perhaps the West Coast. I know some people there that can protect you. Please, my child. Pack a bag and let us go now."

Arima wiped tears from her eyes. The fear that her grandmother's story had instilled in her was turning into burning rage. And that burning rage was joined by a steely resolve.

"No," Arima bluntly stated with a blazing determination. "No. I *will* find Marcus. I *will not* have that fine man that I love be sacrificed. I *will not* allow him to be harmed because of me. I must find him, and I must destroy my father. All I need is to know how. I just need to figure out a plan. I just need…"

Arima's sentence was interrupted by an evil voice coming from a darkened, protruding, demonic face that was oozing from out of the scenic harbor painting. *Heh, heh, heh…perhaps I could be of some assistance? For a price, of course. Heh, heh, heh.*

CHAPTER 13
WRONG ON MULTIPLE LEVELS

Howard had not felt so alive in centuries. It had been 245 years, to be exact, since he was able to feel movement of his legs. He relished the warm breeze that he could feel whisking through Arima's braids and gazed in wonder through her mahogany eyes at the sites that was 2034 New Orleans. The neon signs. The bustling people. The electric lights. The motorcars. He was in complete ecstasy and didn't believe he could ever be happier. He immediately realized he was wrong about that as he saw a local shop as Arima's body strolled by with purpose down the busy street.

Here. Stop here. It looks perfect, Howard stated lasciviously to Arima's soul. *Yes, this place is amazing* he said gleefully as they entered the building. He excitedly gazed around the store as though he were a child making his first visit to a candy store. Everywhere he looked there was black leather. He literally squealed with delight as he perused the cornucopia of whips, shackles, hoods, paddles, and other...accessories. *What is this?* Howard squealed out again as he gazed upon a large strap-on phallus.

Oh, my God, that is so pervy! Howard, calm the hell down, Arima silently said to him. *I can feel you getting...aroused...and it's really creepy. Although, I have to admit, there is some fun stuff in here.*

I can't help it, Howard immediately replied as he was barely able to control his excitement. *This shop is...my dream. Oh, how much fun I could have had in my day with my little slave playthings if I had all of this. Oh, my. All of the blood. The screaming. The tears. The cu...*

Howard! Arima screamed at him.

I mean, heh, heh, heh, Howard hastily responded in an attempt to back track from his sadistic fantasies. *Not that I would ever do anything like* that *again. No, I have learned over these centuries. I have learned that slavery is wrong. I have learned that beating innocent people and raping innocent women is wrong. I have learned that I must change my ways in order to get into Enlightenment and be released from that damned painting. I'm sorry, Arima. Please forgive me.*

Bullshit, Arima replied sternly. *I cannot only hear you, but I can feel your intentions and you're the same sadistic prick that you've always been and the only reason why I've allowed you into my soul is so you can help me get my boyfriend back. I love him so much and that is the only thing that could ever allow me to let someone as sleazy as you into me. We have a deal. I will let you help me, and the powers of Enlightenment will decide if you have redeemed yourself or not. In exchange, I have promised that I won't burn the painting with your soul in it. But if you try to completely overtake me or do anything out of line, I will banish you once again into that painting and fry your racist, sexist ass! Got it? Now pick out what you need for this and let's get Marcus back!*

Yeah, yeah, yeah, I got it, Howard replied in a defeated tone. *You are so much more powerful than your ancestors, that I would never dream of trying to completely control you. You will allow me to control your body so that I can have fun with your father, the Pastor. But you must be awake for this, Arima. You will see everything that I do. Do you understand? Oh, this looks fun,* Howard concluded as Arima's hand grasped the handle of a paddle with metal studs protruding from it.

Don't worry. I may not want to do this shit myself, but I'm starting to enjoy being a voyeur. You do what you want. I'll let you know if you're going too far. But in this case, I don't think that's possible. I think we need one of these, too, Arima finished as she picked up a multi-tasseled motorcycle whip.

Now you're getting the idea, heh, heh, heh, Howard sneered as he looked at the sizes of the black zippered hoods.

———

The hot soup stung Marcus's split lips as he eagerly took it in and swallowed. He had not eaten in three days, and he welcomed the sustenance despite from whom it came.

"There now, Marcus," the Pastor's voice stated with a sinister arrogance. "That's good. Very good. The healing has begun. First, your body will be nourished and healed. Then your soul will be nourished and healed. Soon you will see that what we are doing is right. It is just. Now, one of *your* kind certainly will never be able to sit alongside our glorious Vetis. But you will be rewarded for being such a loyal subject. You will be rewarded for bringing Arima to me. You will be allowed to live a comfortable life with your parents. And that, my dear friend, is as good as it could ever be for your kind. The rest of your people and many others will die…viciously. But you, my friend, will live to tell the tale. Here, how about another bite?"

Marcus swallowed hard. Partially to quell his starvation and partially to ward off the tears that were once again welling in his beaten eyes. He was still too broken physically and mentally to put up any sort of resistance. And he knew that he would be in that condition for some time. He said a silent prayer as another scalding bite of broth slid down his welcoming throat. He prayed for the strength to resist this vile man's indoctrination. He prayed that he would be able to join the fight against this deplorable movement. But mostly he prayed that Arima would remain safely out of her father's twisted grasp.

His prayers were suddenly vanquished as he heard his love's voice from behind the bed that he was lying in.

"Hey, there…um…Dad," Arima's smooth, casual voice was heard. But instead of being comforted by it, Marcus was filled with feelings of dread and remorse. She was alone and he was completely unable to assist her. Why had she come here? Why had she offered herself up as a sacrificial lamb? His heart sank even lower as he heard Arima's explanation.

"So, Dad…I know what you're up to. Grams told me everything. She told me about how you are a follower of Vetis and how you all plan on conquering the world's democracies by converting holy souls into unholy souls. She told me that once that is done, the unholy souls will then engage in a battle with Enlightenment. And she told me that once Enlightenment is conquered, Vetis will rule the world and the afterlife.

"I understand what is happening. I see it on the news. I now know that the international autocratic movement that has been trying to topple the world's democracies, including ours, is not being done in the name of God. It is being done in the name of Vetis. The people who believe themselves to be holy and patriotic have instead been duped into becoming the pawns of a power-hungry demon.

"I also understand that I am destined to engage in this battle alongside my father. I don't know that I agree with all of this, but I know that I'm simply not powerful enough to fight against you and your forces in this war. Not after what I see you've done to Marcus. So, what I'm saying is that I'm in. But on one condition. You leave Marcus and Grams and my friends alone. Just let them be. If you promise to do that, then I will do what you need me to do. Do we have a deal?"

"Why...yes," a pleasantly surprised Pastor responded as he looked upon his black leather-clad daughter. "Yes, my dear child, we have a deal. My, if I had known it would be that easy, I wouldn't have...well... we won't discuss that now. You can sit at my side, and we can tend to your Marcus together. You can even keep him if you wish. You and I shall heal him and then we shall re-engage in this war. Oh, Arima, you have made me so happy. Together, we will be quite powerful. Together, we will be able to tip the scales in favor of Vetis. Together, we will be able to take out the various freedom-fighting forces throughout the world. Oh, my dearest child, this may be the happiest day of my life."

"Yeah, for me, too," Arima replied affectionately. "I've always had this strange feeling that I was meant to be with my father. I am not my mother nor am I my grandmother. I realize that now. I was meant for bigger things. I was meant to be in the warm embrace of my father. I was meant to be a warrior."

"Yes, you were, my child," the Pastor stated confidently as he strode toward Arima and wrapped his arms around her figure in a seemingly pre-ordained embrace.

Arima's eyes glanced over at her immobilized and tearful Marcus. She gave him a slight smile and wink before taking a dagger from behind her waist. She lifted the dagger, then plunged it into the back of her father.

The Pastor screamed in agony and began flailing around as he attempted to pull the dagger from his upper back. "You little bitch!" he screamed at Arima who was taking items out of her black duffle bag. "I will rip you apart for this!"

"No, you won't," came a sinister voice from Arima's mouth. "Heh, heh, heh. Arima is not in control at the moment. Oh. she is here. She is watching quite intently. And she can stop me at any moment, can't you, dear"?

Yup, Arima's soul replied to that of Howard's. *But I won't. He disgusts me. Damn, Howard. I have to admit. You're pretty good at this. I never would have thought of all that stuff to say to him. I wouldn't be able to keep it together long enough. I wouldn't have been able to kiss his ass like that. I just don't have it in me to be so deceitful.*

"Which is why you have me, my dear," Howard said aloud through Arima's voice as he cracked a bullwhip around the Pastor's ankles and pulled, causing the Pastor to fall backwards. The Pastor shrieked in pain once again as the knife plunged further into his back.

"Oh, that felt good," Howard sneered as he paced around the Pastor's struggling body. "I see I haven't lost my touch with the whip. Or have I? Perhaps just a bit more practice. Just to be sure."

Arima's body began lashing at the Pastor's face with the whip. Deep lacerations immediately began oozing blood as the harsh leather sliced his face repeatedly. Arima's voice cackled with a sinister glee as she turned the Pastor over, dropped his pants and began beating his behind repeatedly with the metal studs of the paddle. Bloody pock marks covered his posterior as he was struck repeatedly. Specks of blood covered the paddle and Arima's joyfully sadistic face. Then, the beating suddenly stopped.

Arima's body went back to her black duffle bag. As Howard's attention was preoccupied with finding his greatest treasure, the Pastor reached up to a nearby table and pulled the tablecloth until a lit kerosene lamp fell next to him. Howard pulled the strap-on phallus from the duffle and exclaimed in delight, "Ah, here it is! Oh, what fun we shall now have, won't we, Pastor? Or shall I call you…Peggy? Heh, heh, heh".

The panicked Pastor looked at Arima's possessed body, triumphantly holding the strap-on above her head, then flung the kerosene lamp onto the immobile body of Marcus.

Marcus's shirt immediately caught fire and Arima screamed, "No!"

Having retaken control over her body, she flew towards the howling Marcus. She grabbed a blanket and began beating the flames until they were extinguished. Arima looked down upon the slightly burned chest of her love. She looked at his broken body. She looked at his tattered face. And she wept.

Dammit Arima! Howard's voice yelled to her soul. *He is gone! I was not done with him yet! You have let him escape!*

"I-I-I don't care," Arima tearfully replied. "I have my Marcus back. I'll deal with that old bastard later." A confused Marcus smiled up at his love and began weeping. Arima gently ran her hands over his tortured body so as not to cause him any more pain. She got down on her knees, laid her head tenderly upon his chest and wept along with him.

"C'mon," she said to Marcus after she had regained her composure. "Let's get you out of here and get you some cheeseburgers. And some fries. And some onion rings. And maybe a milkshake."

Marcus did not mind the stabbing pain in his ribs as he laughed for the first time in days.

Louise Azar arrived at the abandoned church with several of her colleagues. "Very nicely done, ladies," she said to the group. "Thank you for helping my granddaughter track down these souls. It is a shame that that bastard got away, but now we know what we are dealing with. And we know that we can wound him. We know that *you* can wound him, Arima. And if you can *wound* him, then you can *kill* him. And you shall, one day. All right, ladies, let's get this poor boy home. He has a long recovery ahead of him."

As Arima and the soul of Howard were leaving the old church, Howard said in a jealous tone, *What is all this about* you *can hurt him and* you *can kill him? I'm the one that did all of the work! You were just along for the ride!*

"Howard, have you noticed that despite your helping me that you have not been called to Enlightenment"? Arima said to Howard aloud so that all could hear. "Do you know why that is, Howard? It is because you don't get into Enlightenment solely because of your deeds. It is the intent *behind* the deeds that gets you in. It is the *purity* of the intention. You can *kill* someone and still get in if your intentions were good. If you committed murder because you were selflessly protecting someone else, for example. The murder isn't the point. It is the reason *behind* the murder that is the point. And you could donate ten million dollars to build a wing on a children's hospital and *not* get in. Why? Because if your intent for that donation was for your own personal fame or increased power or more money for yourself later, then the gesture doesn't count. It wasn't done out of *selflessness*. It was done out of *selfishness*. So, it isn't your *actions* that get you to Enlightenment. It is the intent *behind* your actions. You would do well to think about that if… and I *do* mean if…you ever get this chance again."

Louise burst out laughing as she heard her granddaughter conclude her lecture with, "Oh, and one more thing. I don't care *who* is in control. I am *not* going to screw my own father…or anyone *else* for that matter… up the ass. I will *not* have my body used for that. That's just wrong on soooo many levels. Man, I can't wait to get home and get baked. I wonder if Jess has made any more cookies."

CHAPTER 14

THE FURY OF REDEMPTION...OR IS THAT FURRY?

For the next two months, Arima had very little time to enjoy her favorite pastime, which resulted in each week's groceries lasting considerably longer. When she wasn't busy helping Marcus's Pops care for his son and his ever-strengthening wife, she was studying with her grandmother in honing her abilities. She was learning how to focus. She was learning how to control her emotions and impulses. She was learning how to trust her instincts. And she was learning what a great responsibility it was that she had inherited.

And then there were her responsibilities at the morgue. She was asked, along with other employees, to pull a few extra shifts by Clyde while Marcus was recovering, which Arima enthusiastically agreed to. She was working sixty to seventy hours per week and giving the extra income to Marcus so that he could continue to fulfill his financial responsibilities to his parents' household.

And, of course, there were the trapped souls. At least one recently departed soul would ask Arima for her assistance to move on to Enlightenment each week. The Ropers selflessly assisted Arima by becoming her assistants. They knew that with each soul that Arima helped, their turn to redeem themselves and be allowed into Enlightenment was being delayed. But the Ropers had grown to love Arima as if she were their own and they were resolute in helping her for as long as she needed and in whatever way that they could. They would screen the applicants vying for Arima's special abilities, prioritize them, then make their suggestions to Arima as to how she might be able to help them.

Mr. Roper would greet the newly trapped soul and say, *Thank you for coming in. You may refer to me as Mr. Roper and this is my beautiful wife, Mrs. Roper. We shall be conducting your interview today on behalf of Arima.* Then he would begin the standardized questions that had been developed by his wife, who would be taking copious mental notes during the interview.

What is your name?

How did you die?

Why are you being kept here?

What is it that you feel you need to do to redeem yourself in order to move on to Enlightenment?

If nothing, who is it that you are here to watch over or protect?

If no one, what evil deed do you believe you need to exact retribution for and to whom? What means would you like to use to exact this retribution?

If you were stranded on a desert island, what five albums would you take with you? (An answer including Kid Rock was an immediate disqualifier. An answer including Bruce Springsteen, REM, David Bowie, Southern Culture on the Skids or The Cramps shot the applicant to the top of the list.)

If Arima chooses you to inhabit her body, do you swear that you will not use her body for anything untoward outside of the assigned mission? Untoward acts may include but are not limited to racist comments or actions, sexist comments or actions, homophobic or transphobic comments or actions, any form of brutality against an innocent, eating fruit, or having her put on a strap-on phallus and having anal intercourse with another person.

The interview would conclude with, *Very well. Thank you for coming in and for your interest in Arima's services. We will be in touch. And remember, all further communication is to be done through us. She is quite busy, and you must not contact Arima directly or you will not be considered.*

The anxious spirit would then take its place somewhere in the limbo that was the city morgue and wait.

The Ropers would consult with Arima who would then decide who to assist. Mrs. Roper would announce the spirit's name, who would then be allowed to have a personal consultation with Arima. She would sit in her beaten leather office chair, twiddling her thumbs, as she listened intently to the spirit's emphatic pleas for assistance. She looked like a godfather who was holding court and would frequently conclude with, "But you must understand that there may come a time that I ask a favor of *you*, even if you have been allowed into Enlightenment. Do you agree?"

The appreciative spirit would always joyfully agree and Arima would begin her work. Most of the cases were rather easy to resolve.

There was the bank executive who had gotten himself into financial difficulties and framed a co-worker for his embezzlement. He inhabited Arima's body and through her hands typed out and sent a letter to the District Attorney that detailed all of the evidence that would clear the wrongfully accused and implicate himself. His smiling spirit wept as he elevated out of Arima's body and ascended to Enlightenment.

There was the man who was murdered by his wife out of self-defense as he once again lunged at her with the intention of beating her. Immediately upon feeling his soul lift from his body, he felt his wife's pain and anguish. He also felt genuine remorse for his dastardly actions against the woman that he professed to love. Based on his authentic contrition, Arima took on his case and assisted him in locating the evidence of his crimes that he had hidden from his wife. This evidence included hospital records, phone records, recordings of their arguments, and pictures of her battered body. The evidence was placed into an envelope and sent to the prosecuting attorney. All charges against his wife were dropped, and she was able to collect his life insurance. He was admitted into Enlightenment but was sentenced to feel the pain and fear that his wife had experienced for all of eternity.

There was the young man who was tragically stricken down by cancer. His husband was despondent over the loss and vowed to never love again. The spirit loved his husband so much that he knew that he could not ascend until he saw his husband smile and feel genuine joy again. He inhabited Arima's body and followed his husband around in order to see if he could locate someone that would make his grieving husband happy. Someone that he could love. He noticed a handsome barista and could feel his genuine concern and caring for his husband, so he had Arima purchase two tickets to a concert that he knew his husband would attend. One ticket was sent to his husband, with a letter of congratulations on winning the prize. The other ticket and letter were sent to the barista. The seats were located next to each other. As the spirit watched his husband through Arima's eyes leave the concert hall hand-in-hand with his new love, he blissfully wept, then ascended in peace.

Other cases were a bit more complicated and messier. There was a young woman who had become indoctrinated to hate other people that were not like her. She had been indoctrinated in these fanatically dangerous beliefs at a local church by a particular Pastor. She was assigned to a local regiment of neo-fascist Brownshirts. On the evening of her initiation, she watched in horror as three sadistic Brownshirts beat, raped, and murdered a twelve-year-old African-American girl. The revolting images shook her to her core, and she suddenly realized that what she was involved with was not the work of God. She believed it to be the work of Satan himself. She fled the scene as the girl's battered body was being hung from a flashing stop sign.

She immediately went to a bus station and was standing in line to purchase a ticket to anywhere but there when a man in a brown shirt came up from behind and thrust something hard and round into her back. "Just take it easy. We just need to talk," the man stated quietly as he led her out of the bus station and into his waiting car. He drove her to an abandoned lot. And then, she was forced to endure what the little girl had endured. For hours. She finally succumbed as she bled out from the final laceration that was purposefully inflicted between her legs.

She was taken to the morgue, and she sat quietly and watched as the three Brownshirts that had murdered the little girl were destroyed by Arima. It was then that she decided that it was safe to reveal herself. It was then that she realized that she had to have justice for her murder. Brutal justice.

"Oh yeah. I'll *definitely* help you. My body is yours. You do to that bastard anything that you want," Arima stated with resolve to the spirit named Lillian.

Lillian watched through Arima's eyes as her murderer staggered out of a local tavern. She watched him sway for three blocks before turning up on a gravel driveway. His hip caught the back end of an old, rusted car and he fell over, laughing. He looked up and saw the furious face of Arima and said through his drunken chuckles, "Bitch, don't you know where you're at? You'd better get along now, lil' piggy, or else I'm-a-gonna beat you. Your kind don't belong here, so if'n you ain't down the street before I get up, then you're gonna end up in the river. Y'know… after I have some fun with ya first."

The Brownshirt's threat was moot. He never had the chance to get up. Arima could feel the intensity of Lillian's rage as she took a hammer from behind her back and struck the man in the temple with it. Her murderer could only scream as Lillian used Arima's body to straddle him and beat him in the face repeatedly with the hammer until it looked like children's play dough that had melted in the unforgiving heat of the sun.

Too much? Lillian's smiling soul asked Arima as she began to elevate upwards.

"Nope," Arima immediately replied as she wiped the man's blood from her face. "Maybe not *enough* for a prick like him. It was nice to meet you, Lillian. I hope we will meet again someday."

Arima was unable to help everyone, however. There was a sleazy local politician who had lied and cheated in order to cover up his affair with an adult film actress. Following the in-depth consultation, Arima determined that his crimes and narcissistic intentions behind those crimes were so far-reaching and entrenched that she could not help him, so she banished his spirit into a men's urinal. "Well, since I have seen that you're into golden showers, this should make you happy for all eternity," she said, laughing to the tantrum-throwing spirit as she placed him in the urinal. She returned to the morgue and said to the Ropers, "Hey, guys, you're doing a really great job but how 'bout tightening up the interview process a bit? That dick was a complete waste of my time."

And finally, there was the easiest case of them all. Or so it initially seemed. There was an elderly lady who passed away following a sudden stroke. She had lived her life selflessly and graciously. She had ushered three loving and admirable children into the world and overseen the growth of five beautiful grandchildren. Everyone adored her, even those that found it difficult to love anyone. This included her one-year-old cat, LucyFur. No one would take LucyFur in and the poor soul had been abandoned at the no-kill animal shelter. The old lady could not move on until she found a loving home for her beloved pet.

"Well, this one's easy enough. I guess I just adopted a cat!" Arima declared. The old lady's spirit smiled and thanked Arima as she elevated to Enlightenment.

"Wow, guys," Arima said aloud to the Ropers. "I feel really good about myself. I've really done some good things with my powers. And now, the universe has rewarded me with a sweet-ass cat! Who says there's no such thing as karma?"

Arima took LucyFur home and soon realized three things. She realized that there was no such thing as karma. She realized why no one was willing to adopt this animal because she also realized why this energetic and seemingly demonic furball had been named "LucyFur."

Upon returning home with her purring bundle of joy, she placed the grey and white long-haired cat down on the living room floor and said, "Okay, baby. I gotta go outside and bring your stuff in that I ordered, okay? So, just sit here and be sweet and don't get into anything."

As Arima was retrieving a litter box, bag of cat litter, cat food, and an overstuffed bag of cat toys from her front porch, her housemates arrived home. "Hey, sweetie, what's all this, then?" an intrigued Jamie inquired.

"Okay, don't freak out, you guys," Arima defensively answered. "I just adopted a cat. But she's super sweet and super cute and super mellow. She just sat on my lap and purred the entire bus ride home. I'll totally take care of her, and she won't be any trouble, okay?"

"Oh, fine," a slightly annoyed Jessie replied. "Just keep that thing away from me. Me and cats don't exactly jive, all right?"

"Yup, not a problem," Arima enthusiastically declared. "C'mon! I want to introduce you to her! I just know that you're gonna love her!"

Arima excitedly opened the front door. Four human jaws dropped simultaneously as they saw LucyFur sitting innocently in the middle of…absolute carnage.

The few curtains that had been allowed to remain hanging were torn to shreds. One entire couch cushion had been disemboweled. There were ripped newspapers and magazines covering the coffee table, floor, and furniture as though there had been an explosive ticker-tape parade. Two lamps and three vases were shattered on the floor. The roll of toilet paper was no longer recognizable as toilet paper. And there was a trail of tattered underwear coming from Cliff and Jessie's bedroom.

Jessie said nothing as she bent over and picked up a pair of her now crotchless panties. Cliff tried to lighten the moment by saying, "y'know, I kinda like them that way." Her daggered gaze made him quickly realize that it would be wise not to utter another sound and he obediently dropped his head to the floor. She stared silently at the cat, then at Arima in furious disbelief.

Jessie calmed herself slightly and asked curtly through her gritted teeth, "So, what's the cat's name?"

Arima meekly responded without daring to look up at her friend, "Um…LucyFur."

"No shit, huh? Can I freak out *now*?" Jessie tersely replied before making her way to her bedroom and slamming the door.

CHAPTER 15

BLOOD IS AN ACQUIRED TASTE

"Shut up! Just shut up!" the Pastor screamed at the dark purple smog that was billowing in the corner of a run-down evangelical church in West Texas. "I'm just now able to walk upright without much pain! I barely escaped Arima's attack on me! So I don't need you to tell me that I have failed! I don't need you to tell me how strong she is! I don't need you to tell me that she must be destroyed! I know all of that! What about you? Where the hell have *you* been? I see that our daughter is still successfully battling our forces. What are you going to do about *that?*"

Yes, Pastor, the nasally sinister voice began emanating from the copper headed purple cloud. *I am well aware of your failures. You really are quite good at getting yourself beaten, aren't you? And I am well aware of our daughter's exploits. Getting to her is much more complicated for me in this form. I either have to be welcomed in by someone such as Arima and be allowed to take over their body or I must find someone who hates our daughter as much as I do. If I can find such a dark soul, then I can enter them without their knowing. My hate will combine with theirs and they will be completely unaware that I have possessed them and that I can take control of them at any time.*

So what have I been doing? Searching, you fool. Searching for someone with that same intense hatred for our little whore daughter. I had thought that it would be quite easy. She has made so many enemies. Unfortunately, she has succeeded in eliminating most of those enemies. And she has this unique quality to build support and loyalty from those around her. That is her *special ability. People grow to love her and will do anything for her, despite her rather crass demeanor. That is* her *gift...along with her unbridled tenacity. So, Pastor, I have been searching for a body and soul to inhabit.*

And I have found one. In a mental institution in New York. A former friend of hers. Our daughter betrayed her by stealing her precious children away and recruiting them into her army. She despises our daughter. But not yet as much as I do. Despite the betrayal, she still harbors feelings for our daughter. So, I must beat her down. I must invade her dreams every night and methodically extinguish any feelings of love or respect that she has for our daughter. I must then allow her hatred to grow. And once I have done that, I will be able to possess her soul and take control of her body. But this will take time. Years perhaps. But once I have accomplished this, it will be as simple as pulling a trigger with my host's finger. And our little bitch daughter will be no more. And her soul will float out into limbo where I can destroy her once again, for all time.

But Arima must be taken out before then. If she will not join us, then she must be destroyed. Our daughter's spirit will never be vanquished as long as Arima is here in human form. Arima can serve as our daughter's gateway back here. Back to the battle. Back to us. And they will be together. These half-sisters must never be allowed to join forces. With Arima's abilities and our daughter's loyal army and tenacity, all will be lost. So, Pastor, take your little bitch out!

"Oh, I plan to," the Pastor replied through a dark chuckle as he looked down at his disfigured hands while still feeling a sharp pain from the healing knife wound in his back. "Oh, I am *definitely* taking out that little bitch. But I'm going to make her *suffer* first. I'm going to beat her down emotionally before I kill her. I am going to cause her so much mental anguish that she will be too weak to fight me and will welcome her own death. I am going to violently murder every person that she loves. One by one. I'll start with her best friends. Then her lover. And finally, I will find a way to take out that bitch grandmother of hers. Then maybe I can leave this damned church. Maybe *then* I will be able to go outside and feel the sun on my face again. But not until her grandmother is gone.

"I had no idea that her grandmother and those other bitches in their little voodoo cult could track souls. That they could track *my* soul. And I know that they are searching for me. They are like a pack of psychic bloodhounds. I have had to be very careful so that they cannot find me. I have had to insulate myself in this damnable church and surround myself with the symbols of Vetis in order to conceal my whereabouts. But once I am outside, and away from the symbols' protection, I will be vulnerable, and they will be able to find me. So, as much as I would like to do these little bastards in myself, I will have to depend on my minions to do my bidding for me."

The Pastor motioned to one of his Brownshirts and said to the skin-headed, hate tattoo covered dullard, "Go after the little blonde first. Do whatever you want to her. Have as much fun as you like. Just make it… *messy*, heh, heh, heh."

———

"Dammit Arima!" an increasingly frustrated Jessie yelled out. "Would you *please* do something about this damned cat? Now it's eaten my slippers!"

"Sorry, Jess," Arima replied with an embarrassed tone. "C'mon, Lucy-Fur. Let's go upstairs and get you a snack. *Please* leave Jess's stuff alone, okay?"

Cliff, Jamie, and Marcus were sitting on the couch, attempting not to burst out laughing as Jessie came into the living room and yelled, "Why does that cat *hate* me so much? What the hell did I ever do to *her*? Why does she only destroy *my* stuff? Oh, forget it! I've gotta go to work! But I'm adding all this stuff up Arima! You're going to pay me back for everything that little menace has destroyed! Got it?"

"Yeah," Arima's beleaguered voice came from upstairs. "I'm sorry, Jess, I'll keep working with her."

Jessie and LucyFur did not have a love/hate relationship. Jessie and LucyFur had a hate/hate relationship. The pair would literally hiss at one another whenever their paths crossed. For some reason only known to her, LucyFur had decided to take her anger and unbridled energy out only on Jessie's person and belongings. Children's locks had to be placed on all of the kitchen cabinet doors to prevent LucyFur from getting in them and destroying Jessie's boxes of tea, crackers, or cereal. She would watch attentively as groceries were put away and would eat only Jessie's food when given the opportunity. She had figured out how to jump up and turn the doorknob on Jessie and Cliff's bedroom door. Jessie would arrive home to find her tops, jeans, and delicates strewn about the room in tatters. Cliff's items were never bothered. When Jessie arrived home, she would have to cautiously open the front door. She would reach her hand inside and turn on the living room light. With trepidation, she would dart her eyes around the room to see where the inevitable attack would come from. Seeing no imminent danger, she would exhale in relief, enter the living room, and take a few steps. From out of nowhere, Jessie would then feel LucyFur's sharp claws on her ankles, calves, or shoulder. Jessie was in a state of constant anxiety. LucyFur was in a state of constant bemusement, and she would sit on another housemate's lap, contently purring while staring Jessie down as if she were taunting her.

LucyFur may have been vicious to Jessie, but she was extremely protective of anyone else in the house. She would watch over Arima, in particular. She would give Arima a mew of warning if she were about to step on something that could make her trip. She would claw Marcus's back if she confused Arima's moans of pleasure for pleas for help. And she would intensely eye anyone who came to the door. If LucyFur sensed that the interloper was a threat in any way, she would leap up and attack their face. Within one month of LucyFur's residing there, the household was no longer able to get a pizza delivered.

Jessie arrived home from work. Realizing that no one else would be there except for the demonic cat, she once again cautiously unlocked and opened the front door. Her anxiety increased as she scanned the room for the furball of fury. She checked her pantlegs to ensure that they were completely over her heavy combat boots. She zipped up her heavy coat, put the hood over her head and sprinted toward her bedroom. She shrieked as LucyFur lunged at her from on top of the door frame. She made it into her bedroom and slammed the door.

As she was sitting on her bed, shaking, she heard the doorbell ring. Her heart was pounding as she wondered how she would be able to navigate the cat's ninja-esque attacks in order to answer the door. She then heard the person pounding on the door and Jessie decided that it just wasn't worth it. She wasn't expecting anyone, so it just wasn't her problem. She curled up on her bed and shut her eyes. Then, whoever was at the door *became* her problem.

She heard the front door open, then close. She heard heavy footsteps steadily approaching her room. She then saw an axe shatter her bedroom door. Jessie screamed and rolled off of her bed as splinters of wood exploded around her. A man with a shaved head, brown shirt, and Nazi tattoos was laughing as he picked Jessie up by her golden hair and threw her onto the bed. He took out a knife and slashed through her heavy coat.

Jessie instinctively kicked the man in his balls, rolled off of the bed and ran toward the front door. The man caught up to her, grabbed her once again by her hair and threw her across the room into a glass cabinet. A dazed Jessie looked up at the man with shards of glass protruding from her pleading and bloody face.

"Oh, I'm gonna have *fun* with you," the sadistic man said in a devilish voice as he lasciviously licked the blade of his knife. Jessie put her hands in front of her wounded face and clenched her eyes shut as the man lumbered toward her. Jessie then heard a deep, persistent growl coming from the top of the shattered cabinet. She heard a man screaming and looked up.

LucyFur had straddled the man's face. She was shrieking in an unholy high pitch as she slashed at the man with her machete-like claws. The man was wailing as he futilely attempted to pull the frenzied animal from off of him.

He was finally able to grab the cat by its back fur and throw it across the room. LucyFur bounced off of the floor and in one leap was back on the man's face. She bit into his right eye. Blood and pus began shooting out of the man's socket as LucyFur pulled his eye out and swallowed it in one bite. She then sliced the man's left ear nearly off with one graceful swipe of her right paw.

The tortured man fell to the floor and began rolling around as the furious feline continued its frantic onslaught. Streams of blood were spattering around the room, creating thin red streaks on the furniture, decorations and walls. The room looked like a scene from a massacre. LucyFur finally bit deeply into the man's jugular. He could only lay there and helplessly gurgle as the cat continued in its vampiric quest and feasted on the man's fresh blood.

"Aw, man, that supper was great, Grams," Arima said as she, Cliff, Jamie, and Louise made their way up the front steps of the home.

"Thanks so much for taking us out. That was the best steak I've ever had. Too bad we couldn't get ahold of Jess. I don't know why she didn't answer the phone. We just got the landline put in last week. Now all we have to do is track down a modem and she'll be back online. She'll have a lot fewer followers, but at least she'll be back online. Then all I have to do is get her and LucyFur to get along and everything will be back to normal. Maybe they could patch things up by sharing this medium rare steak that we brought home for her."

Cliff was the first to enter the house. He turned on the light as the other three made their way in. "Jess, you home?" Cliff yelled out before his eyes adjusted to the light. Everyone's jaws dropped as they surveyed the destruction. The cabinet was in shambles and there was glass everywhere. Newly bought lamps and vases were shattered on the floor. There were streaks of drying blood on every surface of the room, including the ceiling. The foursome walked around the couch and found a dead man with his throat ripped out. He was missing an eye and his face looked as though it had been through a shredding machine.

They then looked at the couch. Sitting silently and staring straight ahead with a shocked look on her face was Jessie. She still had shards of glass in her pretty face and was spattered with blood. LucyFur was sitting on her lap, purring and cleaning the blood from her saturated bushy tail with long strokes of her bright pink tongue.

"Jess…wh-what happened…are you all right?" a deeply concerned Arima asked.

LucyFur stopped cleaning and looked up at Arima. Jessie then looked up at Arima with bewildered eyes and simply said, "Okay. We can keep the cat."

Chapter 16

Seriously, How Many Family Secrets Do We Need?

Jamie, Cliff, and a rattled Jessie sat staring in amazement as they listened to Louise Azar explain why this violent attack had occurred. They listened about the demon, Vetis and how he was trying to conquer both the Earth and Enlightenment by converting the holy to do his sadistic bidding. They listened about how this was occurring in the United States through self-appointed fascist militias that were attempting to create a race war and systemically dominate local areas. They listened about how freedom fighters throughout the world were battling these anti-Christ, anti-patriots and, despite many recent victories, how this war was far from over. They listened about how the leaders of this demonic dictatorial movement were hand chosen servants of Vetis. They listened as Louise told them that Arima's father was one of them and that it was he who had sent Jessie's assailant.

Their eyes grew wider as Louise explained to them about Arima's abilities. Their jaws dropped further as they learned how Arima could not only communicate with souls who were trapped here but could allow them into her own soul and allow them to use her body to complete their earthly work so that they could move on to Enlightenment. They immediately started looking around the room in a panic as Louise concluded with, "And of course, this bastard's soul is still here, isn't it dear?"

"Yeah, that prick's still hanging around," Arima replied nonchalantly as she took the joint that she had been sharing from Marcus. "I'm too tired to mess with him right now, Grams. I just need to relax, have a snack, and get some rest. He isn't going anywhere, and he can't do any real harm except annoy the shit out of me. I'll destroy him in the morning."

At that moment, LucyFur sprang from Jessie's lap and lunged at the new curtain that was hanging in the living room front window. She shredded the curtain in a frenzy while growling deeply. She then bounced on top of the entertainment center and began wildly clawing at the air.

"Aw, dammit," Arima stated with resignation while exhaling a long plume of smoke. "LucyFur's picked up on that prick. If I don't do something tonight, she'll destroy the house…again." Arima got up from her chair, walked into the middle of the room, spread her arms, and said to her friends who were sitting behind her on the couch, "Okay, guys. Don't freak out. This shit's gonna get kinda freaky."

Arima's body began levitating off of the floor as she focused on connecting with the evil spirit and began drawing him in. She was the only one besides Louise who could hear him screaming. *Oh no, bitch! You're not going to suck me in! I'm going to stay here for eternity and haunt your Black ass! I'm going to taunt that cat and have her destroy this house over and over! And if you move, I'll do worse to whoever moves in here! You have no power over me! And I will find other souls like mine, and we will team up and we will destroy you! We will…*

Jamie, Cliff, and Jessie looked on with confused expressions as they heard Arima begin to chuckle and say to apparently no one, "That's the funny thing about you dark souls. You are all so overconfident. You have had so much success bullying others that you have never learned how to size up your opponents. You think that you can threaten and intimidate and rape and murder your way through any battle. You think that you're all-powerful. Even *after* you've just been taken out by a *cat*. But you *aren't* all-powerful. In fact, I can sense that you have no *real* power at all except a few haunting parlor tricks. *I* am the one that has the power over *you*! I do not need your permission to draw you in! I can suck you into my essence as easily as I can suck in another puff of smoke. And that's what I'm going to do. So be a good little fascist prick and come to Momma, heh, heh, heh."

The evil spirit was screaming as it was drawn into Arima's essence. It continued screaming until Arima conjured a metal clasp around its mouth and bound it by her envisioned metal shackles. Arima's body was convulsing violently in mid-air as she bound him within her essence. Her convulsing suddenly stopped, and her bare toes gently returned to the floor.

"Damn, baby," Marcus stated as he watched his love through his bloodshot eyes. "I don't know if I'm *ever* gonna get used to you doing that shit. But it's kinda cool that I have a girlfriend that has powers and shit."

"So, you aren't intimidated by me? It doesn't bother you that I'm the most powerful one in this relationship?" Arima stated playfully as she straddled Marcus's lap and smiled.

"Hell, no," Marcus replied through his chuckles. "What the hell do *I* care? You take care of these demons or whatever and I'll take care of the snacks. It's a match made in heaven…or Enlightenment…or whatever. Hey baby, this one's spent. You want me to roll another one?"

Arima beamed at her love and gave him a long kiss.

"What the hell is going on?" she heard Jamie ask quietly behind her.

Arima got off of Marcus's lap and said to her friends, "What is going on is that I now have this bastard trapped inside me. But he's like squirming around and shit and I can't relax, so I need to trap him somewhere else. Now, where to put you?"

Arima scanned the room looking for a suitable inanimate object to trap him in, then destroy. Finding nothing, her search led her to the coffee table. She smiled, relinquished the dark soul and banished him into a…rolling paper. "Yeah, baby," Arima stated light-heartedly to Marcus. "Let's roll another one. And use *that* paper. We're gonna all *smoke* this bastard."

Arima and Louise chuckled to one another as they passed the joint around the room while listening to the tormented screams of the trapped spirit who was being painfully destroyed with each successive drag. The spirit was near complete eradication as Arima handed the roach clip to Jessie and said, "Hey, Jess. Wanna do the final honors?"

Jessie looked at her friend and flashed her a devilish grin as she eagerly took the clip, lit the final remnants, and inhaled deeply. Arima heard one final anguished wail, leaned back on Marcus's chest, and smiled with deep satisfaction.

Following the most mellow, slow, and giggly house cleaning in the history of the world, there was a knock at the door. "Ah, they are here to remove the body," Louise stated as she floated towards the door. She opened it and gasped. "M-Mother Rhea! I was not expecting you! To what do we owe this honor?"

"Hello, Louise. It is so nice to see you again," the ninety-year-old Black woman stated as she was being supported by two other young women with a third directly behind them. "Well," Rhea continued while chuckling. "Perhaps 'see' isn't quite the right word. No, my eyes have never been able to see since I was born. But what my eyes can't see, my soul can. I can see people through their souls. I can tell whether a soul is filled with light or if it is filled with darkness. And I can see the potential that other women may possess. I can see their special gifts. I can see their power. And, since I failed your daughter so many years ago, Louise, I have vowed to not fail you again. So, it is time for me to meet your granddaughter. It is time for me to see *her*. It is time for me to see what this world has in store for her and what she has in store for it. So, may I please rest my weary bones and look upon this blessed child?"

"B-but of course, Mother Rhea! Please, won't you come in?" The young Black women, all in their late-teens escorted Rhea to a flowered chair. She placed her backside down and gave out an immediate yelp. "What is *this*, then?" she playfully asked as she reached under her rump and pulled out a cat claw. "Oh, my, you have a cat. Ah, yes, I see her there. So sweet. So protective. She will be of use to our cause."

As if on cue, LucyFur pounced upon Rhea's lap and began kneading her abdomen while purring. Rhea let out a delighted laugh as she pet the loveable feline before beginning. "Yes, as you know, Louise, I do not venture far from home much anymore. But there is a storm brewing. I can feel it. What we have experienced up to now is *nothing* compared to what we will all be confronted with in the coming years. There will be a period of relative calm before all hell breaks loose around us. It will be a hellacious battle upon this earth, and it will be a hellacious battle in the heavens. And these battles will be waged simultaneously. And we must all be prepared to play our part in this battle. All of us. Including your precious Arima. Come, dear. Come closer and take my hands. Let me look upon you."

"Ummm…okay," Arima calmly replied as she sauntered over to Rhea and took her hands. Rhea looked directly at Arima, and her milky-white eyes began weeping. After a few moments, Rhea composed herself and said, "Oh, my child. I knew that you would come one day, and I am so grateful that you have come in the form of an Azar. Your family has such a rich history. But you, my dear, are the most powerful one yet. I know that your grandmother wishes to protect you, but I am sorry. You cannot be protected. You are destined for greatness. Your hideous father knows this all too well. That is why he has tried to corrupt you. But he couldn't. You are too strong. Too powerful. And, you have too much of your mother's kindness in you. So now, he will try to destroy you. He *must* destroy you before you meet your…well…perhaps *that* is for another time.

"We must begin this by finding Arima's father and destroying him before he can destroy her." Rhea then looked up at the three identical women standing to the side of her chair. "My beautiful granddaughters have been searching for him. My darlings, Gwen, Rachel, and Kayla have the ability to track and locate souls. Especially demonic ones. But he is being hidden. His black soul is being cloaked by the power of his demonic overlord, Vetis. And there is another demon in the spirit realm that is assisting him. All that I can sense about her is that she is powerful, but not as powerful as she has been led to believe. She appears to me in a dark purple smog with a head of…"

"Copper!" Louise gasped out.

"Yes, copper," Rhea affirmed. "It is the copper one and Arima's damned father who are trying to keep Arima from engaging in this battle. They are trying to keep her away from…well…that won't happen for some time, so there's no point in speaking of it now."

"Speak about *what?*" Arima and Louise blurted out in unison. "C'mon Rhea," Arima began pleading, "What are you talking about? I have been through a lot of weird and painful shit for the past few months. I deserve to know everything. Plus, you tell me that I have to be prepared. So how am I supposed to be prepared if you're keeping secrets from me? C'mon, just tell me…*please?*"

"Oh, very well," Rhea conceded as Louise experienced a feeling of dread over what might be about to be revealed. "I actually do not know too much about this other one. She is nothing more than a sensation that I feel from time to time in my dreams. I do not know who she is or where she is or what she looks like, but what I *do* know is that she shouldn't exist. At least not as she is. She is the offspring of pure evil. She is the offspring of your father and another demon. Perhaps the copperhead, but I am not sure about that. She *also* should be pure evil. She should be waging war at her father's side and oppressing the downtrodden and brainwashing the gullible. But she isn't. Somehow, she has eluded his grasp. And somehow, she has become a great force against the very evil that spawned her. I can feel…I can *sense*…that there will come a time when she will need you, Arima. I can sense that there will be a time that you will be called to help her. That there will be a time that you are called to help your…half-sister."

Arima and Louise looked at one another in astonishment as Rhea continued. "But now is not the time to dwell upon that. It will do you no good to look for her. She is a needle in a million haystacks. She will reveal herself to you at the appropriate time. And when that time comes, I sense that the two of you will combine your great gifts and be most powerful. That is what I feel. That is what I sense. But on the other hand, what do I know? I'm just an old woman with too much time on my arthritic hands. So don't dwell on that now. What we must focus on is finding your father. We must find him so that you can destroy him. So that you can destroy him in both human and then spirit form. That must be our focus."

"But, Grandmother," Gwen, who was the leader of the Triplets, interjected. "We have tried. Even with our combined energy, we have not been able to locate him. We don't have a clue as to his whereabouts. How are we to find him?"

"I know, my darlings, I know," Rhea gently replied as she shook her head in frustration. "You three are such powerful hunters and yet this one has eluded you. Even with your combined might, you are unable to break through the defenses of Vetis. We must find someone who has an even *greater* gift than yours, my lovelies. We must find someone who has the gift to behold. The gift to behold both beauty and to behold great ugliness. This isn't a task for a tracker. This is a task for a Beholder and that, my dears, is simply something that you are not able to do."

Rhea's head then lifted, and her pure white eyes stared at the couch. She smiled and subtly nodded toward Jessie as she said eerily, "But *she* can".

CHAPTER 17
THE PITFALLS OF PEER PRESSURE

It had been two years since Jessie and Cliff had been home. They, along with Rachel, Gwen, Kayla, and…LucyFur, had been traveling the back-roads of several southern states in an RV, searching for Arima's father. It was believed that Jessie's abilities as a Beholder would enhance the Triplets' ability to hone their soul tracking in on the slippery Pastor. Jessie had the ability to feel or behold pure good or pure evil in people, regardless of whether that evil was being cloaked. She could determine the general direction the feeling was coming from, leaving the Trackers to focus their energies on the specific dark soul that they were looking for. As the months went by, Jessie was amazed at how rapidly her newfound ability was developing. She was also amazed at the amount of pure evil that was present in the world. The feelings were overwhelming. The feelings made her painfully nauseous.

The first time that Jessie felt pure evil was in a small town in East Texas. Although the Trackers confirmed that the evil was not emanating from the specific dark soul that they were searching for, they stopped, nonetheless. They were compelled to stop as Jessie was in such anguish from the intensely unholy feelings that it was determined that the only way to relieve the pain was to eliminate the source of it. So they did. Mercilessly.

Cliff was in the bathroom of a shabby one-bedroom apartment

vomiting as Rachel, Gwen, and Kayla stood over the body of a local child molester. There were disgusting pictures and trophies from his victims haphazardly hanging from the walls and lying on cluttered shelves. The television was playing a VHS tape that no one should ever witness, let alone experience. As the shrieks from young children screamed out of the television's speaker, the Triplets watched the man's blood flow from his slashed throat and begin to congeal around their matching black boots.

Jessie bound into the apartment holding a purring LucyFur. "Oh, man, I feel great!" she exclaimed. "What did you guys *do*? I was curled up in pain on the floor of the RV and then suddenly, it just stopped. All of the pain, like, just went away. And not only that, but I feel *rejuvenated*. Like this huge weight has been lifted off of me. I feel like I could just float into the clouds and..."

At that moment, the unobservant Jessie slipped in a pool of blood that had oozed toward the front door of the apartment. She fell backwards and landed solidly on her back as Cliff entered the room and yelled out to her. "Oh, my God, Jess! Are you all right?" Cliff exclaimed in a panicked voice as he rushed to his wife's side.

"Yeah, I'm okay," a slightly woozy Jessie replied as LucyFur began licking her face caringly. "What the hell *is* all of this? And, oh, my God! What did you guys *do?*"

Jessie sat up and saw the fresh corpse lying a few feet from her for the first time. Her bewildered brilliant blue eyes were wide open as Gwen replied.

"Well, y'know, we killed him. It was pretty easy. He answered the door, and we rushed him and pushed him back into his apartment. Kayla and I held his arms and Rachel slit his throat. And that was all there was to it. One more dick gone from the physical world. It's the only way, Jess. I talked to Grandmother last night and she said that once you have beheld pure evil, that it will hurt you, and that you won't be able to let go of it until the evil has been destroyed, so...y'know...we kinda did *this*. And it seemed to have worked. Are you upset?"

Jessie looked down at her blood-soaked dress as LucyFur began lapping up blood from around her. "Am I *upset*? Hell, *yes*, I'm upset! Look at my *dress*! Do you know how much this *cost*? And now it's *ruined*! How about a heads-up next time?"

That episode began a nearly two-year killing spree throughout Texas, Arkansas, and Oklahoma as the sextet traversed the highways and backroads searching earnestly for the Pastor. The regional news outlets dubbed the murderers the *Bayou Bloodletters,* which the Triplets found amusing. Cliff, on the other hand, did not.

Cliff had signed up for this mission for one reason and one reason only: to protect his cherished Jessie. His beloved wife had been attacked and the source of that attack was still at large. So, he would help in bringing down this demon. But he had not signed up for *this*. A week did not go by without the Triplets responding to Jessie's anguish with a brutal murder. And although he did not doubt the inherent evil of their victims, he also did not believe that they should be killed for it.

Cliff had been raised Catholic and was devout in his beliefs. He was incredibly popular in high school as he was the star quarterback on the football team. He was a kind soul who got along with all of the various cliques whether they be the goths, jocks, brains, or…stoners. He especially took a liking to one particular stoner of Jamaican descent and her best friend. They made him laugh. They helped him pass his classes through private tutoring. And they made him re-think some of what had been indoctrinated into him.

Although people like his new friends, Arima and Jamie, were proclaimed to be "sinners," with Arima's drug use and reputation for usually being up for a good time in someone's backseat and Jamie's flamboyance and flaunting of her transexual sexuality, he knew in his heart that they were good people. These were not people to be hated. They were nice and fun and generally non-judgmental. They did not believe all that *he* believed in, and he did not believe in everything that *they* did. And that was all right with him. That did not prevent the trio from enjoying going to the movies or out to dinner or bowling together. That did not prevent them from laughing together. That did not prevent them from crying together. And the three of them formed an unlikely bond of friendship.

A fourth member of this improbable group was added on the first day of football practice in August 2027. The sixteen-year old star hunched several feet behind the center and shouted out the cadence. The ball was snapped and at that moment, Cliff was blinded by a vision more beautiful than anything he had ever seen. Strutting across the field in her brand-new cheerleader outfit was a golden-haired, blue-eyed dream. The ball hit him in the facemask. Then what seemed to be the entire defensive unit hit him.

The impossible weight of the defensive players rolled off of him as the coach screamed at them in the background. He looked up and plummeted into two pools of intoxicating blue eyes. He smiled meekly as he awaited her expression of concern. And he received it.

The new transfer student, Jessie, scrunched up her petite nose and said forcefully, "*Wow*! If you play like that in a *real* game, then *I'm* not gonna have much to cheer about. And if I don't have much to *cheer* about, then the newspaper isn't going to take *my* picture. And if I don't get *publicity*, then I'm not going to attract *followers* to influence! So, how 'bout you get your shit together, huh, champ?"

As he watched her perfectly petite frame bounce back to her squad, he vowed that one day he would marry her. Which, as it turned out, was the only way that Jessie was going to get any action from him. As a devout Catholic, Cliff had sworn off of any sort of overly amorous pursuits until his wedding night. This was *not* an oath that Jessie was fond of, and she was continuously frustrated by nothing more than light petting and kissing. Jessie would consult with her new friends, Arima and Jamie, about how to get her beau into bed. Their reply was always the same. Marry him. This was always followed by loud guffawing at the sincere young man's expense.

Although frustrated by his rejection of her frequent enticements, Jessie grew to love her boyfriend, in her own self-serving way. He was sweet and kind. He was devastatingly handsome. And most importantly, he was loyal. Plus, it didn't hurt her reputation that the head cheerleader was seen dating the captain of the football team. She just wished that there was more accuracy in her title of head cheerleader.

During his senior season, Cliff proposed to Jessie in the middle of the football field following yet another victory. The team was to go to the playoffs. Jessie had been accepted at Tulane, which was where her boyfriend had received a scholarship, although certainly not for his academic prowess. The pair would be married following their freshman year. And then, all of Jessie's dreams would come true. She would be married to a high-profile future pro athlete. She would be a high-profile influencer. There would be money and houses and cars and gala events and shoes and shoes and shoes and fame. And finally, there would be sex. And maybe kids, who knows, we'll see.

All of those dreams came crashing down in the second quarter of the state championship game. Cliff dropped back to pass, trailing by three points. He spotted an open receiver jetting toward the corner of the end zone. He pulled back his arm to launch the ball and was viciously hit by a defender. He fell awkwardly onto his shoulder and ruptured his rotator cuff. The entire crowd gasped as they watched the medical cart pull onto the field toward the writhing young gladiator. Cliff's football career had come to a shattering end. Jessie's dreams had come to a shattering end.

There was a picture of Jessie in the next morning's newspaper. Her hands were clenched around her shocked pretty face. There were tears welling in her deep blues eyes. The photograph was the perfect representation of great loss, caring, and sweetness and the picture went viral. Well-wishers from all over the world began frequenting her social media platforms. From the ashes of Cliff's future rose Jessie, the Influencer.

But that was not the only thing that had been born for Jessie on that fateful evening. For the first time in her life, as she watched her fiancé screaming in pain, she felt something for someone other than herself. She was not crying because she believed that her dreams had just been vanquished. She was crying because she actually cared about the man that she had committed herself to. She realized at that tragic moment that she was completely and totally in love with her Cliff, and she vowed that she would follow through with their wedding. Enthusiastically. And soon.

That evening, Jessie crept into Cliff's private hospital room. She was wearing a short nurse's outfit. She gently laid on top of him and kissed him. She professed her love for him. And they made plans to wed the next April when both of them would be eighteen. He smiled and cried genuine tears of joy. There was a slight crumpling sound as the nurse's outfit fell to the cold linoleum floor. No one ever determined what Jesus Christ felt about the couple's passionate exploits that evening, but Cliff finally had something interesting to confess.

Cliff smiled to himself as he thought about the last seven years with his Jessie. Unable to play football and not having the exact academic qualities that colleges were looking for, Cliff worked as a laborer directly out of high school. He became quite skilled at building and could fix almost anything. He worked on construction sites and free-lanced to build decks, remodel rooms, pour driveways or landscape. He had a well-earned reputation as an honest, hardworking young man and he was in constant demand. Cliff had never been ambitious. He just wanted to make enough money to keep his Jessie happy.

Unfortunately for Cliff, Jessie's spending habits were slightly more upscale than what he could afford. Especially when it came to shoes… and dresses…and jackets…and purses. Fortunately for him, however, Jessie had embarked on her own career as a successful and somewhat sought after influencer. She posted multiple times a day to turn her followers on to a new restaurant, perfume, vacation spot, exercise fad or, on some occasions, "massagers."

They moved in with Jamie shortly after they wed. Arima would join their household three years later, although nobody could really tell the difference as Arima was typically passed out on the couch most mornings as they were getting ready for work. They would look down at her crumb-encased frame and chuckle as they quietly would shut and lock the front door.

Cliff and Jessie weren't wealthy, but they were comfortable. And they were happy. Cliff never feared anything from Jessie, and he never feared *for* her. After all, he was always there to protect her. Until the night of the attack. And then, the revelation of her abilities as a Beholder which led to episodes of excruciating pain for her. Cliff felt helpless. He wanted so badly to be able to protect his beloved wife once again, but did not know how. He witnessed what killing the dark souls did for his wife but lamented the fact that the Triplets never tried anything else. He vowed that the next time Jessie had one of her episodes that he would talk the Triplets into capturing the evil-doer and taking them to the police for whatever dastardly deeds they were responsible for. He could not bear to be a witness to this bloodshed any longer. Not without trying something more humane, at least.

Then he thought about their mission. After two months on the road, it had become obvious to them that the Pastor was moving around and able to stay just out of their reach. As soon as Jessie felt his unique sensation of evil, it would dissipate. They knew that it was him. They knew that he could somehow sense that they were coming. They knew that he was on the run from them. And his elusiveness increased the frustration of the entire group with each passing day. But, although they had not cornered or captured him so that he may experience Arima's final judgement, they were successful in keeping him from implementing any sadistic plans through the indoctrination of a newly brainwashed congregation. He was simply too busy fleeing and trying to stay alive to focus on the bidding of Vetis.

Let's just get back to New Orleans without another one of Jess's episodes, Cliff thought to himself. *Lord, it will be so nice to see Arima and Jamie and everyone else again. It will be so nice to get a reprieve from this awful killing. It will be so nice to be normal again.*

At that moment, Jessie began shrieking and doubled over in pain. "Where is it, Jess?" Gwen shouted out. "Go that way!" Jessie yelled back through her gritted teeth. "Yes, that way! It's getting stronger!"

The RV pulled next to a barn. The Triplets poured out of the RV and opened the barn doors. There, they found fourteen corpses hanging from meat hooks. All of the corpses were non-white, and their blood was dripping off of them and pooling on the floor. They were all in various stages of dismemberment or disembowelment. The stench of the rotting flesh nearly bowled the young women over. They didn't believe that the scene could be any more gruesome. They were wrong. They looked to their right and saw the meat grinder.

A dark silhouette ran out of the back entrance of the barn. The Triplets unsheathed their knives and followed. Cliff was sitting in the driver's seat preparing for a fast getaway with the hopefully captured and not killed evildoer. He saw the dark silhouette from the rear-view mirror. It was approaching the RV with the Triplets following. Jessie was sobbing on the floor of the RV constricted in pain. He looked at his wife and his heart was pounding. He looked at the fast-approaching silhouette and his heart pounded faster. He acted. He sprung from the driver's seat and opened the side panel door of the RV just as the silhouette was about to pass. He tackled the man sending a sharp pain through his previously repaired rotator cuff. He picked the man up by his shaved head and placed him on his knees.

"Please, Cliff, do something! He's too close! I can't stand the pain!" Jessie cried out.

He looked once again at his tortured wife and his heart pounded. He looked into the barn and saw the hanging bodies and his heart pounded faster. He looked at the three ominous black-clad women surrounding him with their knives drawn. They slowly nodded at him in unison. He drew in a deep breath and his heartbeat relaxed as he snapped the man's neck.

"Oh, my God, that was worse than the others. Thank you, baby. Thank you for taking care of him," a tearful Jessie cried out as she threw herself around his neck, sobbing.

"You're welcome, baby. It's okay. I'll never let anybody hurt you again. I don't care *what* I have to do. Nobody will *ever* hurt you again."

He looked at the wry smiles on the faces of Rachel, Gwen, and Kayla and said softly, "C'mon. Let's get back on the road. We have an engagement party to get to."

CHAPTER 18

DEAD BEAT DADS

As Marcus walked toward Clyde's office, he was smiling at the thought of the most romantic conversation that he had ever had just a few weeks prior. As he and Arima were lying in her bed surrounded by the crumbs and wrapper remnants of their most recent gluttonous orgy, Marcus said nonchalantly, "So, we've been goin' out now for around two years".

"Uh, huh," Arima replied followed by a soft belch.

"Well," Marcus continued, "You wanna maybe get married or something?"

"Yeah, sure," came Arima's reserved response. "Why not? We get along okay, and we have similar interests and…hey do you want the last bite of this pizza?"

"Naw, you can have it," Marcus answered. "So, when do ya wanna get married?"

"I dunno," Arima replied with her mouth full of pizza crust and marinara dipping sauce dripping down her chin. "How about in a couple years? Knowing us, it'll take us that long to figure out what we want to do. Cool?"

"Yeah, cool," Marcus answered before asking, "So I suppose you'll want a ring, right?"

"Yeah, that would be nice, I guess," Arima replied before concluding with, "And a party. This will be a good excuse to have a party and get Cliff and Jess back here for a while."

Marcus wiped a tear from his overjoyed eyes and entered Clyde's office.

"Marcus!" Clyde enthusiastically exclaimed. "Come in, my lad, come in! You're here a bit early for your shift. What is it that I can do for you? Oh, I know. It *has* been a while since your last raise, hasn't it? Well, son, the budget is a bit tight right now, but you do such a *wonderful* job. I'll tell you what I'll do. I'll speak with some of the muckety-mucks and see if I can't squeeze out another twenty-five cents an hour, hmmm? Will that keep you in our happy little family?"

"Uh, yeah, thanks," Marcus awkwardly replied. "Yeah, that would be great, but that's not really why I'm here. You see, Arima and I just got engaged and we're throwing this party and, well, I was just wondering if you knew where I could get a nice suit for…y'know…kinda cheap."

Clyde squealed in delight in response. "Engaged? To Arima? Oh, how exciting! We haven't had such exciting news around here since the Peterson family deaths of '27! Oh, that was a sad sight. Speaking of which, do you have an engagement ring yet?"

"Uh, no," Marcus answered. "That was another question I was gonna ask you".

Clyde bounced from his creaky and worn office chair and said excitedly, "Come, come, come my lad. I have a little something to show you." Marcus followed Clyde down the hallway. He unlocked a heavy metal door and they entered another hallway. Marcus got chills as the temperature seemed to plummet in the dark corridor. They approached another metal door and Clyde looked up at Marcus with the flashlight lit under his face wearing a macabre smile.

Marcus shuddered as Clyde said in a cartoonish, dark tone, "Spoooooky isn't it? MWAHAHAHAHAAAA!" Seeing the shocked look on Marcus's face, Clyde quickly retreated. "Oh, my lad, I'm so sorry. I didn't mean to frighten you. You know how I love my little jokes. Here, step inside and feast your eyes upon this!"

Clyde opened the door and turned on the light. The overhead neon began flickering and buzzing as Marcus saw a large room filled with clothing. There were dresses and suits and casual wear all organized and hung neatly on racks.

Marcus had a sinking feeling as he asked the question that he was afraid to hear the answer to. "Wh-wh-what the hell *is* all of this, Clyde?"

"Oh, just my little stockpile, hee, hee, hee," Clyde gleefully responded. "You see, oftentimes our guests' clothing has been...um... stained or damaged in some way and their family does not want to keep them. So I have them cleaned and repaired as best I can, and I store them here for just such an occasion! Where do you think that I get all of *my* fine clothes?"

Marcus looked at Clyde's light blue shirt and noticed the slight red stain on the chest and felt nauseous. "Now, let's just find your size," Clyde continued as he pranced to a rack in the middle of the room. "Oh, my. We have some fine options for you here. Lucky for you, most of the connected men in the city are a bit...well...big-boned. Yes, those men do like to eat. And their fashion sense is impeccable! Look at these designer brands. You just need to overlook the few bullet holes and they are absolutely perfect! Here's one! Come, come! Try it on! I'll look for some shoes! You look to be size...hmmm...Arima is a lucky girl."

Marcus hesitantly took the suit and went into a small closet, disrobed and put the "new" suit on. *Awww damn, this is creepy. I don't wanna wear some dead dude's clothes. I'll have to find a way to let Clyde down easy*, Marcus thought to himself as he zipped up his slacks and tucked in the white shirt that had a few brownish-red embellishments around repaired holes. He looked at himself in the mirror and then thought, *Awww damn! I look sharp! Arima's gonna be all over me in this!*

Marcus emerged and Clyde squealed in delight once again as he looked upon this tall, handsome man whose somewhat portly features were concealed by a light grey with dark grey pinstripe double-breasted suit. The white shirt gleamed behind the designer silver tie. Clyde smiled up at him and handed Marcus a pair of black socks and shiny black Italian boots. Marcus beamed and quickly accepted the generous offering.

"Now for the ring," Clyde snickered as he opened a drawer and dug deep under a cornucopia of women's delicates. "Aw, here it is. We, of course, do not...um...inherit very many valuables. The family always takes those. But this ring was never claimed. And it is absolutely stunning!"

Clyde handed the ring to Marcus who marveled at it. The center diamond was at least three karats and fit inside a wedding band that wrapped around it in a diamond-encrusted orbit. "Clyde," Marcus began stammering. "I, I can't afford anything like this. I mean, it's absolutely beautiful, but I just can't swing it. Thanks for showing it to me, though."

"Afford?" Clyde gasped in response. "Why, my lad, who said anything about *money*? No, you may have this. It's not like I can sell it or pawn it. I just kept it here for safekeeping, hoping some lovely couple might cherish it as much as its original owner did. Yes, this was what gave me the idea to bring you in here. This ring belonged to Becky Peterson. It was said that she was a sweet young woman. She had two lovely little daughters. And she had a husband. One night, when their girls were around five and three, Mr. Peterson was away on business. There was a gas leak in the home and Becky and her darling daughters all asphyxiated. It was so sad and tragic. The husband was so remorseful that he didn't want to keep the ring. He just couldn't bear the sight of any reminders of his lost love. So this delightful little item has been sitting here for the past nine years waiting. Waiting for someone to come along and cherish it. It has been waiting for you and Arima. Please take it, my lad. Take it and put a wonderful smile on Arima's face. All that I ask in return is that...well...perhaps I could be invited to your little gathering?"

Marcus screamed in delight, picked Clyde up, and spun him around. Clyde's combed-over, greasy black hair looked like streamers on a kite as they flew in the breeze. "Okay, okay, put me down, now," Clyde stated through his giggles. "And one more thing. Well, this is such good news. Perhaps I can squeeze a bit *more* out of those muckety-mucks for both you *and* Arima."

Jamie clasped her hands over her mouth and let out a high-pitched shriek as Arima walked into her bedroom wearing a traditional Jamaican dress that was covered in yellow and green hibiscus flowers. Jamie's tears began flowing as she embraced her best friend on the evening of Arima's engagement party.

Jamie was overcome with joy. Arima was not only her best friend.

Arima was her savior. Arima was her hero. From the time they had met in junior high, Arima was the one person that Jamie could tell her secrets to. All of them. When she told Arima in eighth grade that, although she was born a boy, she felt as though she was a girl, Arima's response was, "Yeah, alright. So, you gonna finish that last cookie or what?"

"You mean you don't care?" an astonished Jamie inquired of her best friend and confidant.

"Well, yes and no," Arima replied casually. "I mean, on the one hand, I personally don't care at all. I mean, why would I? We're all made differ-ent. You were born a boy and you like boys, but you feel like you're a girl. Okay. What the hell do I care? All I know is that you're Jamie. You're my friend. You're kind and sweet and smart and I love you. What more do I need to know?"

"On the other hand, I care a lot. I care that other people care so much about something that there's nothing to care about. No...wait. They don't *care* so much as they *hate* other people just for being who they are. Whether it's a trans person, or a Black person, or a woman, or...hey. I just thought of something. Man, you are so *screwed*. You are a Black young man who wants to be with other young men and who wants to be a woman. Man, all of the fascist religious freaks are going to come after *your* ass. And not in the good way. That's why I care. I care because there are hateful people in our world who hate you just for who you are. You could be the nicest person in the world. You could save them from death, and they would still hate you. So I personally don't give a shit, but I *do* care about how many people are going to hate you for it. And I'll tell you this much. I will never leave you, no matter what, okay?"

Jamie had tears flowing from her eyes as she embraced her best friend. Several years later, Jamie decided that she was tired of hiding who she truly was and began wearing women's clothing. But only in her bedroom. When she was sixteen, she was standing in her bedroom looking in the mirror at her beautiful reflection. She looked dazzling in full makeup, silver hoop earrings, a short afro, and a glistening silver gown that she had found at a secondhand shop. She turned and twirled and posed and giggled as she looked at herself from every angle. For the first time in her life, she felt like herself. For the first time in her life, she saw Jamie.

Her father approached her bedroom door wishing to speak to his son, James. He opened the door and discovered that he had a daughter named Jamie. "I knew you were a goddamn fruit!" her father bellowed as he removed the belt from around his waist. Jamie screamed in physical, emotional, and mental agony as her father beat her. And beat her. And beat her. And beat her. The last words that she ever heard her father say were, "Get the hell out of my house and never come back, you freak. I have no son. And I sure as hell don't have a daughter."

Jamie limped the two miles to Arima's house through back alleys so as not to be discovered by the local hoodlums, racists, and homophobes. She meekly knocked upon Arima's door. Louise Azar answered the door and took one look at the tragic sight that stood before her. Jamie's lips were split open. Both eyes were battered and swelling. Black mascara and bright blue eye shadow streamed down her bruised face. Her silver gown was tattered and did nothing to cover the multiple purple welts that were forming upon her back, legs and chest.

Louise opened her arms and embraced Jamie's beaten body. Louise opened her heart and embraced Jamie's beaten soul. And Louise opened her home and embraced Jamie with the love, understanding, respect, and support that she so richly deserved. Jamie spent the rest of the night lying in Arima's caring embrace as both friends wept uncontrollably. And Jamie and Arima had never left each other's side from that tragically joyful moment on.

Jamie wiped the celebratory tears from her eyes and said with an apologetic laugh, "Oh, my darling, heh...I may have gotten some makeup on your lovely dress."

"Well," Arima softly replied. "It wouldn't be the first time and I'm sure it won't be the last. C'mon, I think our guests are arriving."

The pair went downstairs and let out an exuberant shriek as they saw their best friends, Jessie and Cliff, for the first time in nearly two years. LucyFur purred as she circled Arima's ankles as the quartet embraced. The Triplets made themselves drinks and began discussing their findings, or lack thereof, to Louise, who sat pensively and nodded. Clyde arrived with a bouquet of flowers and several bottles of alcohol.

"Clyde!" Arima exclaimed as she hugged her boss. "Thanks so much for coming! What's with all the booze?"

"Oh, well," Clyde responded mischievously. "What I hold here, my dear, is all of the ingredients for my specialty drink. So would you like me to make you a zombie? Heh, heh, heh."

The entire group jumped with a start as they heard a high-pitched squeal from Jamie. They then relaxed as they saw the sharp-dressed, lumbering, hairy reasons for the shriek. "Stellan! Paciano! You made it! Oh, come here, my lovelies!"

The entire room was in awe as they listened to Stellan and Paciano's exploits from the past two years. They told everybody how excited they were because they may get to move back to their home county. The group recoiled as they spoke about how they, and many others, had been driven from their homes by the local fascists. The beatings. The rapes. The murders. Anyone who did not succumb to their White Christian nationalist rule was a victim of it. The silver-haired Stellan's cadence became excited, however, when he began speaking about how a group of freedom fighters from Brooklyn had begun beating back the fascists. "And *these* are people," the black-dyed-haired Paciano interjected, "that are good to know. They are *brutal* in what they do. But no more brutal than what the fascists have been doing to all of us. It's just that what *they* do is beat down those that are beating down the innocent. The oppressed. We have heard such amazing stories of their exploits. They primarily work to keep the fascists and other undesirables out of Brooklyn, but we have heard that they have done things internationally as well. *We*, of course, aren't involved with *them*, but..."

Paciano was then cut off by Stellan. "That we *know* of. There are rumors, but nobody outside of their little group *really* knows who they are. Oh, darling! Remember that rumor about the cute little family who may hire us to care for their estate in our county once it is cleared of fascists? Oh, my, how hysterical! That is how *crazy* some of these rumors are. To think that such a cute little hum-drum family with the most *adorable* copper-headed little twelve-year-old girl could be involved with such...brutality. Well, we all had a big laugh over that one!"

Louise's spine stiffened upon hearing this last sentence. She shot a look at her beloved granddaughter who looked back and just rolled her eyes and shrugged. The tension was immediately broken between the two as the front door opened once again. Marcus and his proud parents entered the living room and were greeted immediately with joyful embraces.

Marcus looked at Arima in her smart hibiscus Jamaican dress. Arima looked at Marcus in his grey pinstripe double-breasted suit. They stared at each other for thirty seconds before Arima grabbed Marcus by the hand and said, "Come on!" The pair returned downstairs to their party eighteen minutes later, wearing lasciviously ornery smiles.

The revelry of drinks, food, stories and laughter flowed nonstop until everyone noticed Marcus take Arima by the hand and lead her to the center of the living room. He looked at her and smiled sheepishly as he said, "Well, I know I've already asked you this, but…um…well…I, like, got a ring, so I thought maybe we could make it official."

Although Arima already knew what he was about to ask, again, she couldn't keep her heart from beating through her chest. She watched in anticipation as Marcus went to one knee, looked up at her with tears forming in his eyes, and said, "Arima, will you marry me?"

This was a moment that would become one of Arima's most cherished memories. She did not want to mess this moment up. Arima messed the moment up.

"Uh, yeah, well, *maaaaybe*, heh, heh, heh," she replied mischievously.

"Arima!" Louise bellowed out. "You say, 'yes' this moment, young lady!"

"Fine! Whatevs. Just tryin' to be funny. Y'know…lighten the mood a little? Jeez! Fine! Yes, I will marry you!"

The entire room burst into laughter and tears as Marcus placed the extravagantly elegant ring upon Arima's finger. "What the *hell*, dude?" Arima cried out upon seeing the impossibly large engagement ring. "You win the lottery or something?"

"Naw," Marcus replied modestly as he looked over at a prideful Clyde. "I just had a little help, that's all. I hope you like it."

"Like it?" Arima cried out. "I love it! It's the most beautiful thing that…"

Arima stopped her sentence abruptly as she heard a voice say through her soul, *Who the hell are you that's wearing my ring?*

"Um…Marcus?" a concerned Arima whispered. "Where the hell did you get this ring?"

"Uh…listen, everybody," Arima then stated to her guests. "Listen, it's been a helluva night. It's been so great. I just need to go for a walk with my…y'know…fiancé and cool down a bit, okay? Just keep the party going. Oh, and you've got to try those brownies. I made them myself with my secret herb recipe. They'll knock you on your ass! Okay, we'll be back in a bit."

As the pair walked down the sidewalk, Arima said to Marcus, "Okay, I don't know where you got this ring, but there's a spirit in here, so if I'm gonna wear this, I need to get her outta here. I don't really want to walk around with spirits on my finger 'til death do us part, okay?"

"Yeah, okay," Marcus replied flatly. "So what else is new? I knew I shouldn't have used a ring from the morgue."

"The…*what?*" a shocked Arima yelled out. "The *morgue?* You got it from the *morgue?* Okay, we'll deal with that later. I've gotta straighten this shit out. Okay, spirit. You've got my attention. Just tell me how we can work this out, okay?"

All right, Arima, the spirit spoke to her. *I'm sorry to have frightened you. It really is so nice to be connected with you. And I think it's lovely that you are wearing my ring. You two make such a lovely couple. But I cannot move on, Arima. Not without your help. Will you help me? Will you help us?*

"Us? Who else is in there with you?" Marcus heard Arima say to no one.

My daughters, Arima. My daughters, the spirit replied. *My name is Becky Peterson. We died in 2027. There was a gas leak in our house. It was ruled an accident. But it wasn't. My husband and their father…murdered us. Oh, he thought he was so clever. The fake alibi. The award-winning acting. Oh, he was so smooth as he played the part of the grieving husband and father. No one suspected him. But it was him. I saw him do it. I saw him sneak back into our house after saying he would be away on business. I saw him sabotage the gas line. He grabbed me and put something over my mouth. That was my final living memory. He murdered me and his two daughters. My lord, Arima, they were only five and three at the time.*

Arima then heard two more voices. They were the voices of innocent little girls that said, *Our daddy is a bad man. He hurt us. Can you help us? Mommy says that there's a playground in the sky. Can you help us find it?*

So, Arima, Becky's voice began once again. *What will it be? Will you help us? Or are you going to wear trapped spirits on your left hand for the rest of your life?*

"Okay, I'll help you," Arima replied with resignation. "But it's gotta be quick. I gotta get back to my party before they eat all of the brownies. But before we do whatever it is that you need me to do, tell me one thing. Why did he do it?"

Oh, Arima, Becky responded with a sigh. *Why do brutal men do anything? Power? Money? Sex? I don't know. He was a sociopath, I suppose, and just got off on it. He got off on holding our lives in his hands and then destroying us. And don't worry about your party. We will get you back real soon. I know just where he is. Let us take over your body. We will take care of the rest.*

Becky Peterson used Arima's body to climb onto the deck of the yacht. Arima could see and feel everything as Becky scanned the deck. She found what she was looking for. She picked the fisherman's knife up and descended the stairs to the main cabin. There he was. Half-drunk with yet another drink in his hand.

Girls, you know what to do, was all that Arima heard before her body pounced upon the shocked man.

"Hi Daddy! We're back!" one of the girls cried out as Arima's right hand began plunging the knife into the gasping man's chest. "Yes, we're back! Die Daddy! Die Daddy! Die Daddy"! The three-year-old spirit repeated as she punctured the screaming man over and over again.

Blood was spraying throughout the cabin and all over Arima's dress as Marcus looked on with quiet reservation. He looked down at his watch and said calmly, "Listen. We've been gone nearly two hours. We need to get back. I know this is your big moment and everything, but what else is there to do?"

"Oh, there's one more thing to do," a sinister voice rolled off of Arima's tongue. "Now, it's *my* turn girls!" The dying man could do nothing but gurgle and spit up frothy blood as Becky used Arima's body to meticulously saw the man's head off with the serrated knife. Arima's body was cackling in three different pitches as she placed the head in the microwave and pressed '*High*'. Arima's body then sat on the adjacent sofa and watched the microwave intensely until she heard a loud 'pop.'

Marcus watched as three blue streaks of light floated majestically out of Arima's body. *Thank you, Arima. Perhaps there will be a time when we can help you. Enjoy my ring,* Becky stated sincerely.

Yes! Thank you, Arima! We're going to go play now! Oh, look, mommy!

Look at how silly Daddy's head looks! It's all mushy and gooey like our play dough! Arima wiped a tear from her eye as the little girls' giggling voices faded away with their souls.

As the pair were preparing to leave the yacht, Marcus said, "Hey, aren't you forgetting something?"

"Uh, I don't think so, why?" Arima replied.

"Well, isn't that bad dude's spirit still hanging around here? Don't you think you should finish him off so he can't ever cause any more problems?" Marcus elaborated.

"Oh, yeah. Thanks for reminding me, baby," an appreciative Arima responded. "Now, where are you? It won't do you any good to hide from me. I've got like evil spirit radar and shit so, oh…there you are. C'mon in."

Arima extended her arms and elevated briefly off of the floor before returning back down. "Okay, I've got him. And, man, he's scared as shit. As well he should be. Damn murdering prick. And his own wife and kids, too. Sometimes I still get shocked at the level of evil some people are possessed with. Now, where should I put you?"

Marcus smiled and handed Arima a half-full bottle of rum, a rolled-up bar towel, and a lighter.

As Arima and Marcus were walking hand in hand off of the pier there was a tremendous explosion from behind them. They didn't bother to look back. They didn't even break their stride.

The entire group gasped as Arima and Marcus re-entered their home. "Uh, sorry. We just went for a snack," Arima tried to explain. "I guess I spilled some ketchup on your dress, Grams. Sorry."

"That's all right my dear. Accidents happen," a smirking Louise answered as she watched LucyFur begin to lick the "ketchup" from off of Arima's dress.

Chapter 19

Aloha

How was your engagement party, Arima? Mrs. Roper playfully inquired before making over-exaggerated kissing noises and laughing.

"Man," Arima replied, "You know what? I think the older that you two get, the more immature you get. The party was great. I'm still kinda hung over and it was two days ago. You happy now? Now, just grow up!"

Oh, what fun would that be, dear? a laughing Mr. Roper interjected. *If we have to be stuck in this godforsaken morgue, the least we can do is have a bit of fun. Besides, watching you and Marcus keeps us young. Oh, how we wish we could have been there to see the celebration.*

"Yeah, me too," Arima responded with a genuine tone of regret. "You guys have kinda become like parental figures to me. You've done so much for me. You've sacrificed for me. You have put off going to Enlightenment just to stay here and help me. But, as it turns out, there probably wasn't enough room in my soul to have brought you two along."

What do you mean, dear? Mrs. Roper inquired.

"Well," Arima began through a light chuckle and said with a hint of sarcasm, "My *romantic* fiancé went *all out* and got me a ring from the *morgue*. Which is okay, I guess, because it's *absolutely gorgeous*. It's just that...well..."

At that moment Mr. Roper looked at the ring for the first time. *Oh, my!* he exclaimed. *Why, that is the ring that Becky Peterson was wearing when she was brought in here. Oh, she was so protective of her darling little girls that she hid them in that ring. And then, once the husband showed no interest in it, Clyde took it and locked it away. It must have been a dark existence for them. Were you able to help them, dear?*

"Yeah," Arima answered as she began sorting through that evening's paperwork to be filed. "It turns out her husband murdered them all, so, well, y'know. Her and her little girls used me to stab him, decapitate him and then put his head in the microwave to…well…kersplode it. Man, those little girls were…creepy as hell. But I guess being murdered by your father will do that to a spirit. Anyway, I took his dark soul, put it in a rum bottle with a rag for a fuse, lit it, and left that bastard to be blown up for all time. We did, however, leave a bit of a mess. Three other yachts in the marina got burned pretty badly. Oh well. It's not like those rich bastards don't have insurance. I guess they'll just have to rough it with their five vacation homes and two other yachts, heh, heh, heh. And maybe they won't have much money to buy off corrupt politicians, either. I saw where one of the yachts was owned by the CEO of a gun manufacturer. Man, I wish I could have the chance to mess up *his* greedy, rotten soul."

You know, dear, Mrs. Roper broke in. *I believe Clyde put* our *clothes from the night of our death back there.*

Yes, I believe you are right, Mr. Roper agreed.

"Hey! That gives me an idea!" Arima shouted out. "I think I know how you can make amends to your kids and then move on!"

No, Arima, Mr. Roper resisted, *We are needed here. We will go when the time is right.*

"The time *is* right," Arima argued back. "You two have been patient long enough. You have watched for the past two years as I've helped other trapped souls move on. You have patiently and selflessly helped me. Now it's *your* turn. I will always love you and I will miss you, but *now* is the time. Just listen. Do you think maybe *this* might work?"

The following morning, Clyde came into the morgue, whistling. "Gooooood morning, Arima!" he exclaimed as he entered the room. "Oh, what a lovely party you two threw last Saturday! To watch two young lovers commit to one another. It…well…it warmed my heart. Thank you so much for inviting me. I had such a wonderful time meeting your family and friends."

"Yeah, you're welcome and thanks for coming. Those drinks you made were…um…strong," Arima replied. "Say, Clyde? Do you remember a couple named Roper?"

"Oh, yes," Clyde answered. "But they passed some time ago. Oh, what a sight! Those two got drunk and plowed head-on into a car of teenagers. And they left two young children behind. I don't say this often, but if there is a hell, then those two are certainly in it!"

Well, maybe it wouldn't be so much of a hell if you would put up some damned decorations! Arima could hear Mrs. Roper angrily declare. *And who are you to judge? You don't know us! You don't know all that we have done to…to…* Mrs. Roper ended her sentence as she broke down into tears.

"Yeah, um, so do you still have their clothes? Um, their kids called… yeah, that's it! Their kids called and wanted them back. I don't know why, but I figured that if we still have them that it wouldn't hurt anything to give them back. I guess they still live together. Neither one of them has ever really dated or gotten married or anything. Their daughter is twenty-one and their son is nineteen now. They just work and come home to each other. They're afraid to fall in love, I guess, so they've kinda shut down their hearts to it."

"I…see," a suspicious Clyde responded. "Tell me, Arima. Just how do you know all of this about their children?"

"Oh, just something that I heard from a little birdie. So, do you have the clothes?"

"Why, yes, I do! I will go retrieve them at once!" Clyde answered enthusiastically. "Can you call them and tell them that they're ready for pick-up?"

"Uh, actually," Arima replied, "I was going to just drop them off at their house, if that's okay."

The children of Mr. and Mrs. Roper opened their front door to leave their home for another day of office-based drudgery. They looked down and saw a large box that was wrapped in paper that had their favorite animated mouse on it from when they were children. They both wore perplexed expressions as they looked at one another. The sister picked up the box and re-entered their home with her younger brother directly behind her.

The Ropers looked on with anticipation through Arima's eyes as they peered through a living room window. They saw their beloved children carefully unwrap the package and open the box. They let out a gasp as they took out their mother's dress and their father's shirt and slacks from the evening of their deaths. They began crying as they retrieved an envelope from the bottom of the box and opened it with quiet trepidation.

The children's eyes widened as they looked upon the letter that was written first in their mother's hand, then their father's. Their widened eyes continued to weep as they put their heads together and silently read.

Mr. and Mrs. Roper were sobbing as well as they watched their children read what they had written to them.

Oh, our darlings. We are so sorry to shock you like this and we know that this is hard to believe, but this letter is truly from us, your deceased parents. These are the clothes that we were wearing on the night that we made so many mistakes. We wanted you to have them to remind you of the foolish mistakes that we made. Our selfishness and misguided jealousy led us to kill those four innocent teenagers. And it led us to leaving you. Leaving you without truly knowing us. Leaving you without giving you better guidance about how to be good, kind, loving people. We have been watching you and have chosen now to say hello...and good-bye one final time. Please know that the example that we set for you is not how relationships are supposed to work. We allowed ourselves to take each other for granted. We allowed ourselves to become bored with one another. This led us to selfish acts that were nothing more than a betrayal to one another. And then, the jealousy. And the anger. And the intentionally hurting one another. We were so stupid, my dears. We know that we have left you with callous hearts, but please know that we are not the example that you should follow. Please, my dears, allow yourself to open up your hearts to others. Please allow yourself to love and be loved. It doesn't always work out. There will be ups and downs. But there is nothing in this world like finding the one that you were meant to be with. I found that man. I had forgotten how much I loved him for a time. But I remember now. I remember who it was that I first fell in love with. And I am pleased to say that I will be with that man for all of eternity.

Yes, you will dear. And I am pleased to spend eternity with you as well. Hi, kids. This is your father. You know that I'm not really great with words, but I, too, want to tell you that your parents were stupid, silly people. Life is short and can be extinguished at any moment. I think that I have a bit of expertise on the subject. Take advantage of every moment of your life. Every breath. Find that special someone and share those moments with them. Laugh together. Cry together. Love together. Please let go of your bitterness and allow yourself to feel the joy of being cherished by another. Allow yourself the joy of cherishing someone else. Be honest with and trust that other person. But, most importantly, be kind to that other person and allow them to be kind to you. That's really all that it takes. I just wish that it hadn't taken this tragedy for us to learn that. We have to go now. We are moving on. But we will say hello to you each morning. Just look in the tree in your front yard. You will see two birds chirping. That will be us saying that we love you.

The brother and sister carefully folded the letter and placed it back into the envelope. The envelope was placed back into the box and the clothes were delicately folded and placed back on top of the letter. They tenderly re-wrapped the package and placed it under their family portrait. It seemed to them that their parents' smiles were wider and more sincere. More loving. They laughed, wiped their tears from their eyes and embraced. "What do you say we skip work today?" the sister asked.

"Yeah, let's just enjoy our lives today. For Mom and Dad," the brother responded with sentimentality.

The Ropers continued to watch from the bushes as they saw their children leave the house together. There was a young man arriving across the street to tend to the landscaping. He saw the daughter, waved, and smiled. The daughter blushed, waved back and said, "Hey! We'll be back in a couple of hours! Why don't you come by after you're done working? I'll make you some lemonade!" The man smiled more widely and eagerly nodded.

A young woman then came jogging past their front yard. She flashed the son a flirtatious smile, then stopped. "Hey, I've seen you around before," she said playfully. "You know, I jog by here every morning trying to get your attention and you have not *once* even glanced at me. Listen, it's cool if I'm not your type or...y'know... gender. But I'm just gonna offer this once. You wanna go out sometime?"

"Uh...uh...uh," the son began stammering to his father's glee as he watched on. "S-sure. Um, do you wanna grab a bite to eat? Maybe tonight?"

The young woman chuckled and said, "Yeah, you're cute. I'll be by around six. See ya then!"

The pair of siblings looked at one another, laughed, and proceeded down the sidewalk.

They were unable to hear their mother's voice say, *Thank you, Arima. We can rest peacefully now.*

Yes, Mr. Roper added. *Thank you, my dear. We will love you always. We will love you as much as we love our own children.*

Arima felt the two souls detach and lift out of hers. She looked up at the sky at the two floating blue and white streaks of light. And she wept out of joyful loss.

"Aw, shit," she said aloud to herself. "I don't know how much of this I can take today. Now I gotta go to Grams and say good-bye to Jess and Cliff. Okay, baby, do your stuff," she concluded before lighting a fresh joint and inhaling deeply the intoxicating smoke from her own personally grown stash. "Wow!" she exclaimed. "Damn, Herbert. I don't know if you can hear me, but this stuff truly is amazing. Thanks again. This will help me get through my day."

As Arima turned to begin her walk to the bus stop, she did not notice the cluster of bright pink tulips that suddenly grew out of the ground and bloomed.

———

Arima opened the door and said flatly, "Hey, Grams," before looking up and seeing Rhea who was there to once again say good-bye to her granddaughters. And to do one other thing.

"Oh, my dear Jessie," Rhea was saying as Arima casually sauntered into the room and took a seat next to Cliff and Louise. "I know your gift has caused you such pain. I have known only one other Beholder in my time and she…well…wasn't terribly interested in using her gift. I truly did not know that it would be so hard on you my dear. I knew that there would be discomfort until you vanquished the evil that you were feeling, but I did not know just how debilitating that it would be. For the last two years, I have been trying to find some help for you. And I believe that I have. There is an ancient incantation that I have found. It was buried deep in one of my very old books and is reserved just for Beholders. Here is the incantation, my dear. When you behold true evil, you will still experience intense pain. But if a *pure* soul who is also a Beholder recites this incantation that pain can be transformed into… strength. Pure, unbridled, physical strength. You will have the strength of ten women combined and will have that strength for as long you are trying to vanquish the dark soul. Then, upon their death, you will return to normal. You'll be a bit tired, probably, but normal."

Arima burst out laughing and said through her herb-induced chortles, "Hey, Rhea! She has to be a *pure* soul? I've heard what she and Cliff do in their bedroom! There ain't *nothing* pure about *her* soul or anything else for that matter. I guess you two need to go back to strict missionary or you're screwed! And not in the good way!"

Jessie flashed her friend a look that could kill. Rhea shook her head in wonderment. Cliff blushed and looked towards the floor. Louise clasped her hand over her mouth in an attempt to not burst out laughing. And for the very first time, LucyFur growled at Arima.

"I mean," Arima immediately stated in an attempt to back-track, "I'm just, y'know, jokin'. That's really great news Jess. You'll be like a short-term superhero or somethin'. That's totally great and I just *know* it'll work on you because you are the *purest* soul I know…right, LucyFur?"

LucyFur stopped growling and pounced upon Arima's chest. Arima began sweating as the cat glared directly into her eyes. She then began kneading Arima's chest, laid down, and began purring.

Heh, heh, heh, came the sinister voice of Howard from the scenic Jamaican painting. *You had better not mess with that cat, girl. That cat has bonded with Jessie and will do anything to protect her. And I, Arima, will do anything to protect you. Really. When it comes time to battle your father, I want you to let me in. Let me help you again. I can help organize the others.*

"What others?" Arima said aloud to the perplexed looks of her friends.

The others, Arima. The other spirits that you have helped. They are connected to you. They are as protective of you as that demon cat is of Jessie. And they will be able to help you. They do not need to enter your body. Not any longer. They can now come to Earth and aid you directly while in spirit form. All that they need from you is a prayer for help. And they will be there. And I can help you organize an attack. And I want to say that I am not doing this just to get into Enlightenment and out of this damned painting. I am taking a risk, too. If you die while I'm in you, then I die, too. I'm truly not doing this for myself. I am offering this to help you. So, kid. What do ya say? Partners?

The entire room burst out laughing as Arima exclaimed for some unknown reason. "Fine! We'll give it a shot! But I'm gonna say this again! No pegging, and I mean it!"

You really aren't much fun, Howard replied with disappointment.

Chapter 20

Queen High Flush

August in East Texas had always been hot. But August in East Texas in the year 2037 was nearly unbearable with high temperatures consistently averaging near one-hundred and ten degrees. Even along the Gulf Coast with its "cool" breeze.

"You see the end of that pier?" Jessie asked Cliff, Rachel, Gwen, and Kayla as LucyFur eagerly lapped up vanilla ice cream that was melting down from Jessie's cone. "Remember that one time, Cliff when we came here in high school? I had that cheerleading competition?"

"Yeah, what about it?" Cliff answered.

"Well, remember that cute little burger joint we ate at?" Jessie continued. "The one where I bought that little tank top, hoping to get some action from you? That's where it used to be. Now it's the end of the pier. That's how much of the beachfront the ocean has swallowed up in the last several years. I mean, this is crazy at how fast this shit's moving. Coastlines getting flooded by the oceans. Extreme droughts in the Midwest. Off the scales hurricanes and tornados. Mother Earth is *really* pissed. And *now* it's payback time. If only our parents' generation had had enough balls to do something about it when there was still time. But nooooo. They had to fight just to keep our democracy from falling to the autocratic fascists. They were too busy trying to protect people's right to vote and trying to keep military weapons off of the streets and trying to protect individual liberties from the White Christian Nationalists.

"And that battle still wages. Here we are in the middle of it, trying to find Arima's evil father. But there is one thing that's good so far on this leg of the trip, I suppose. I have yet to feel any pure evil. Oh, sure, I get little twinges every now and then of people who may be sympathetic to those who are pure evil. Their pawns. But *they* aren't *inherently* pure evil. They're just easily brainwashed dullards that don't have the capacity to reason their way out of a paper bag. They just act on impulse and emotion and do whatever they think will get them what they want in that moment. They are ignorant and they are greedy. But they aren't pure evil. And dammit, I'm itching to try out this incantation. I really want to find out if it works".

"Yeah," Cliff interjected. "They're kinda like *your* followers used to be. Just mindlessly taking your advice. Of course, your advice wasn't to try to overthrow the government or oppress other people or anything like that, but I bet a certain percentage of them would have jumped on that bandwagon if you had told them to".

Jessie glared at Cliff at the suggestion. Then her expression softened, and tears formed in her blue eyes as she absorbed his revelation. "Wow, you're right. It was so *easy* to get those people to buy *anything*. Even stuff that I knew sucked. It didn't matter to my hardcore followers. You're right. I could have told them *anything* and they would have done it, without thinking about it. Jesus, when did so many of the people in this country become so simple? So self-absorbed? Or maybe they always have been. Maybe there have *always* been a bunch of people who would sell out to anyone and anything just to get what they want. And I kinda played a part in that. I played a part in brainwashing people to believe in me just because of an act I was playing on my platforms. It was all an act. The make-up. The hair. The bubbly personality. I was just performing for them. And they ate it up. I *knew* that I was manipulating them, and I *loved* that I was manipulating them. And I didn't think about how I was contributing to the brainwashing of the masses. I feel really ashamed right now."

Cliff sat next to his beloved wife and placed his arm gently around her shoulder. "Hey, it's okay. We *all* have played a part in this madness one way or another. Maybe we didn't vote. Maybe we didn't march.

Maybe we allowed ourselves to become indoctrinated into some mindless cult, like, well…I guess I've just been thinking about *my* upbringing. *My* religion. I've been questioning about how my entire religion just sat there as children were being raped by priests. They were raping children and creating more and more rapists from their congregations. For generation after generation after generation, so many of these innocent victims were so messed up that they became molesters as well. And what did my church do? Pope after Pope after Pope? They just moved the rapists around. Moved them to a new hunting ground, so they could rape a new batch of kids. They intimidated the victims and did everything they could to not take any responsibility. The congregation would just pray that it would stop. Well, how did that work out? How many kids were being raped by their priests at the *very moment* that congregations all over the world just sat on their hands and prayed. I don't know, Jess. If that's what it means to be a Christian, then…I guess I'm not one. But I *do* believe in Jesus Christ. I believe in the inherent goodness and acceptance of others in his teachings. I just don't think that *any* religion that would allow those horrible things to happen is very Christ-like. Something changed in me that night that I snapped that guy's neck. It's all fine and good to turn the other cheek. It's all fine and good to pray. But I think that Jesus wants us to actually *take action* when we need to. He wants us to *take action* to protect the vulnerable from the truly evil in this world. My church should have turned those horrible priests over to the authorities as soon as they found out about what they were doing. But they didn't. They tried to cover it up. And why? For their own self-interest. So that they wouldn't lose any of their flock. So that the collection plates would continue to fill up so that they could buy more priceless artifacts and build fancy churches. It's disgusting, and I'm pretty ashamed of myself, too. So I've also played *my* part in this madness. That's all that I'm saying. C'mon, the Triplets are getting impatient."

"C'mon you guys!" Gwen yelled out to them from the open window of their RV. "We're almost out of dough! We gotta get to the casino and restock the coffers!"

It is said that there are two absolutes in life: death and taxes. Actually, there is a third absolute. Vices. Regardless of the economic times, political upheaval, or personal situations that may be happening, people will always find a way to search for satisfaction within their own

personal vice whether that be junk food, tobacco, drugs, liquor, sex, or...
gambling.

As LucyFur was purring next to a battery-operated air conditioner
in the RV, Jessie, Cliff, Rachel, Gwen and Kayla were strutting into the
casino located in Galveston. They approached an elderly woman of
Japanese descent who was sitting at a slot machine pressing buttons.
She pressed one more button on the machine and red lights went off.
"Jackpot!" the woman exclaimed as she pressed *"Cash Out"*, took her
receipt, and turned to leave.

She pivoted from the operant conditioning device and saw five
smirking faces. "Oh, my darlings! It is soooo nice to see you!" she
exclaimed as she was enveloped in hugs. "Well, I've just about tapped
this place out. I'll hit two more slots, then shoot some craps for a while,
then retire to my comped suite. Oh, won't you stay the night? My suite
has plenty of room and there's an Eighties hair metal tribute band
playing in the lounge tonight. It will be sooooo fun, and I haven't seen
you all in soooo long!"

"We would be honored," Gwen replied as Kaneko squealed in delight,
"Wha-wha-whaaaat? You'll stay? Oh, how marvelous! Come, let's play a
bit of poker then. Let me show you my magic touch!"

Kaneko's family name meant "Golden Child." Her parents could not
have predicted the future impact of her given name. Once she was given
the name Kiaria, the dye for her future abilities had been cast. Together,
the name Kaneko Kiaria meant "Golden Child that is Fortunate." And
she was. In spades. And hearts. And clubs. And diamonds.

Kaneko had been lucky for all of her life. When she was a child, she
never lost a board game or game of cards. Ever. She would always draw
the exact card or roll the exact number on the dice that she needed to
win a contest. As a teenager, she slipped and took an unfortunate spill
off of a diving board only to land directly into the outstretched arms of
a handsome lifeguard. He became her first love. When she was of age,
she began buying lottery tickets. It was as though she could sense
exactly which ticket in the spool held the greatest payout, whether it
was within the first ten, fifty or hundred tickets. She would purchase
the required number of tickets, take them home and scratch them off.
Inevitably, there would be a jackpot. Then, there were the state lotteries.
She would wait until a particular lottery was built up, then buy one

ticket. She could imagine the winning numbers in her head. And she would win in state after state after state. She became a multi-millionaire and invested much of her winnings in stocks and bonds. Her portfolio never lost a dime. When she was in her thirties, she met Louise Azar, who was one year younger. The pair became the best of friends, and Louise marveled at Kaneko's gambling prowess. It also didn't hurt their friendship that Louise never had to pay for dinner or entertainment. Money was no object to Kaneko. Anything that she might need at any given moment was only a casino away.

Louise asked Kaneko if she would like to be introduced to the other members of her sosyete, to which Koneko replied, "What in the hell is a *sosyete?*"

Louise, answering through her chuckles, responded. "Well, the literal definition of a sosyete is a voodoo congregation. Now, our little group of ladies isn't so much about voodoo, although there are some that dabble in it. We adopted the name because we are a congregation of women with special abilities, and we combine our strength to protect ourselves and those that we care about. And I care about you and with your special golden touch, I believe that you would fit in wonderfully."

Kaneko was introduced and felt immediately loved and welcomed by the diverse group of powerful women. They taught her that her special ability was not just for her own use but could be used to help others as well. Although all of the ladies in the group were financially self-suffi-cient, it did not hurt to have a fortunate benefactor in their mix to bankroll the costs of special assignments. Special assignments like finding a purely evil pastor who was trying to usher in the Age of Vetis, for example.

Kaneko began accumulating wealth not just for her own purposes. She began to distribute that wealth to others who were less fortunate than her. She would donate money to help victims of a violent storm re-build or re-locate. She paid for numerous expensive medical procedures for those who were shut out of the American capitalistic health care system. She bought presents for the less fortunate at Christmas and school supplies for all of the area schools each September. She found that she loved to give even more than she loved to win, and this provided even more motivation to continue. She was not investing or gambling out of personal greed any longer. She was investing and gambling out of altruism. She was investing in and gambling for humankind.

And what she found to be *most* altruistic was to assist those who had been battered and abused by horrible men. She would listen with grave seriousness to the plight of a woman who was being abused and had no way out. She grieved with the women as they told her how they were simply unable to leave their abusive partners out of fear for the safety of themselves, their children or their friends and family. These were men who were so vile and consumed with power, that they would threaten death upon the women's loved ones in order to keep them under their sadistic thumbs. So the beatings continued. The bruises continued. The rapes continued. The lacerations continued. And the women found themselves in helpless and hopeless situations.

Until they would cross paths with a member of the sosyete, who would refer the woman to Kaneko. As Kaneko would look upon this sobbing, pitiful soul, she would ask quietly, "What do you want to have happen to this impotent worm?" The woman would respond forcefully in a deep, determined voice through her tears and gritted teeth, "I want him to die."

Within a week's time, the problem would be eliminated. Kaneko had become associated with a powerful hitman syndicate who had taken it upon themselves to be freed from the shackles of their organized crime overlords and use their skills to benefit the less fortunate. The down-trodden. Their services were quite expensive, but they had developed a network of benefactors to assist in payment for those who truly needed them. Although the group was based in Brooklyn, they performed their services throughout the world. And they were very effective.

She would place a call with a name, description, and address and the problem would be taken care of. She became a quiet, behind-the-scenes referral source and benefactor for the group and gained great stature in their eyes. Because of this, she was the only person outside of the group to ever know their true name. In the hushed circles of New York's underworld, they were known simply as Murder, Inc. Kaneko held the high honor of knowing them as *vendetta degli oppressi,* or *revenge of the downtrodden.*

Kaneko began leading her friends towards the high roller poker table in the rear of the casino. She looked like a mother leading her eager ducklings to a fresh pool of water. "The trick, my dears," Kaneko began explaining, "is to not stay at any one table or machine for *too* long and not win *too* much. You will see me fold many hands at this table. You will see me lose a number of times, but if I were to play every hand, I would win every hand. Then the big fish will swim away. I will have scared them off. And I don't know about you, but *I'm* in the mood for a grand prime rib dinner and perhaps six bottles of Dom tonight."

True to form, Kaneko folded multiple times. Frequently, she folded a pair of aces. The cigar- puffing men would chortle with greed as they would enthusiastically rake in the chips, hand after hand. They would whisper to each other and wonder why this Asian grandmotherly type was sitting here with her ever-present purse on her lap. Being men, they did not notice that her purse was a designer brand worth nearly $5000.00.

Kaneko would fold yet another hand, then say as she put the next ante in, "Oh, well. Maybe I'll get lucky this time, huh fellas?"

The men would roll their eyes and laugh at her dismissively. About an hour into her arrival at the table, the men's laughing abruptly stopped as Kaneko hit on a bit of a lucky streak. A queen- high flush that beat the ten-high flush. The four eights that beat the four threes. The jack-high full house that beat the four-high full house. The small straight that beat three of a kind. Within ninety minutes, Kaneko had turned $500.00 into $10,000.

"Well, *that* certainly was fun, wasn't it?" she said to the visibly shocked men. "I don't know what got into me. I guess Lady Luck is on my side tonight. You gentlemen have a lovely evening. Oh, and if you're going to go see the band tonight, please come and say 'hello'. I just love to dance! Toodles."

As the party began moving toward the elevators, Jessie said, "I'm going to go out to the RV and get LucyFur. Cliff, could you come along and help with the bags?"

"Of course," Cliff responded as he jumped to attention and followed his wife out the exit and toward the back parking lot.

As the loving pair approached the RV arm in arm, Jessie suddenly buckled over and exclaimed, "Oh Christ, Cliff! There's pure evil here! It hurts!"

In order to try to comfort her, Cliff bent by his wife's side as two dark figures rapidly emerged from the side of the RV and clubbed them in the head.

Cliff and Jessie woke up a few minutes later. Cliff had blood dripping down the side of his head as he looked at Jessie, who was shaking her head violently and attempting to free herself from the ropes around her arms and legs.

"Well, mornin'," one of the skinheads said while wearing a lascivious grin. "So you've been trackin' our boss, huh? Well, now *we're* trackin' *you*. And we're gonna send a little message to our boss's daughter. Yep, it's time that she come out and play. On *our* field. Damn, baby. You are cuyute! Why don't we just start by puttin' that purty lil' mouth of yours to work, huh? While your husband *watches*, heh, heh, heh."

Jessie looked up at the disgusting man as he began unbuttoning his filthy jeans. "Oh, I'll put my mouth to work, all right," Jessie replied in a dark determination. "Malum tuum dolorem facit. et dolor meus es fortitudo mea."

"What the hell did this bitch just say?" the other skinhead laughed out. "Hell, I thought she was American! I guess she's just another foreigner from one a-them shithole countries!"

"What I *said*," Jessie replied tersely, "is in Latin. "And what it *means* is...'your evil causes pain. my pain is my strength.' And what it means for *you* is that you both are *screwed*!"

Jessie tore out of her ropes with one movement, jumped to her feet, grabbed the nearest skinhead with both hands by his greasy skull, and pulled upward. The man shrieked in agony as his head and spinal column were ripped from his body, creating a geyser of blood that LucyFur drooled over from the RV window. She took the spinal column and impaled the other skinhead from under his chin through the top of his skull. An astounded Cliff sat there in silence as he was showered with pieces of brain, skull, and blood.

"Oh, baby, are you okay?" Jessie stated frantically as she bent over her husband and began straining against his ropes. "Oh, dammit!" she cried out. "I should have left one of them alive for a bit longer. As soon as they both died, I lost all of my strength. Sorry, baby. I'll go get a knife."

Cliff sat in shocked silence and nodded as LucyFur jumped out of the opened RV door and pounced upon the headless body. She began purring contently as she gluttonously lapped up the blood.

"Where have *you* two been? Kaneko asked as Jessie and Cliff approached their friends who were seated at a corner table of the buffet. Seeing that the pair had changed their clothes, she began chuckling and said, "Oh, I think that I know. Well, it took you awhile. Good for you, young man."

"No...it wasn't...um...*that* exactly," an embarrassed Cliff replied.

"Uh, no," Jessie interjected. "Let's just say we ran into a bit of trouble, and I think that it's in our best interest to miss the band tonight. I'll explain in the RV. But before we go, I've gotta find a manicurist."

"Why?" a confused Cliff asked.

An exasperated Jessie looked at him and replied, "Because! Just look at this! I've broken one of my nails! I can't go out in public looking like this! C'mon, Cliff! Let's find that manicurist. You guys finish your dinner, and we'll meet you back in the RV."

"Um, okay," was all that Cliff could say as he trailed behind his determined wife.

CHAPTER 21
HEY! YOU DIDN'T RSVP!

"This shade of pink does *nothing* for me!" Jessie bellowed out as Louise was helping to fix her hair on Valentine's Day 2038. "And I'm pushing thirty! I'm practically ancient! I can't afford to waste a day looking like… like…*this*! And, oh, my God! I'm going to be *photographed* in this pink nightmare!"

Louise and Jamie chuckled and shook their heads at the still youthful and perpetually vain twenty-seven-year-old former cheerleader. "Dearie," Jamie replied as she shimmied into an identical hot pink dress that had a plunging neckline and clung to her body just above her knee. "I picked these bridesmaids' dresses out myself! As you know, Arima really had no interest in making the wedding plans. She just told me to tell her when and where to show up. She *did* take charge of the reception buffet, however. But other than that, I have been *frantically* planning this! Booking Marcus's church! The florist! The photographer! The DJ! The guest list! The wedding invitations! And, yes, the bridesmaids' dresses and shoes. I am *telling* you, girlie, I am just about at my wit's end, so *do not* mess with me! It would *not* take much to make me violent today! You *will* wear that dress. You *will* smile, you *will* be pleasant, and you *will* stop your bitching! Do you understand?"

"Yeah, fine…Sorry," Jessie retreated before asking her friend, "So, are Stellan and Paciano gonna make it for this shindig?"

"Oh, I invited them, and it really isn't like them to miss such a gala event," Jamie began explaining with restored joviality. "But they have *finally* been hired by that sweet family from Brooklyn to restore an old country estate that they have purchased. It had been used as a compound by the local fascists there, but now that the fascists have been…well…*taken care of* in that county, they have purchased it and hired my lovely bears to restore it and be its caretakers. They are *soooo* excited to be back in their home county and to be able to live in such a grand estate. But they said the fascists tore the hell out of the place and they have only two years to get it ready. That is when the couple plan on retiring and showing it to their teenage daughter. Two years from today, in fact. On their wedding anniversary and their daughter's sixteenth birthday. Strange that Arima is getting married on the same day, isn't it?"

Louise stopped curling Jessie's hair for a brief moment as a slight unexplained chill ran up her spine. She then abruptly changed the subject and asked the Triplets, who were doing each other's hair and giggling, "So you have not been able to locate the reviled Pastor, hmmmm? It has been four years. I would have thought that with Jamie's Beholding ability to sense evil and your three's ability to hone in on a particular dark soul, that we would have located him by now. It has been nearly a year since his little piss ants ambushed you at the casino. What do you think is going on?"

"Louise, I'm so sorry, but I honestly don't know," the "eldest" triplet Gwen began explaining in a frustrated voice. "We know that he is able to shroud our tracking ability by hiding behind the symbol of Vetis. That the demonic symbol of Vetis can somehow shroud him. But it *can't* shroud him from Jessie Beholding his true evil. His sadistic essence. She has consistently been able to pick up on that, and we then were able to focus all of our tracking energy upon his soul. But he was always gone by the time we arrived at his latest hiding spot. He always was able to stay one step ahead of us. We had him on the run, at least. We were able to track his movements. That all changed several months ago, right after the ambush. We can think of only two explanations. He either has died and now is in spirit form, which may make him even *more* formidable, or he somehow has learned how to shroud himself from Jessie's

Beholding ability as well. To be honest with you, this wedding is a nice break for us. We've been doing this nearly non-stop for four years. We understand its importance, but it's really getting us down. So, we welcome this opportunity to let our hair down, get drunk and get laid! Right, girls?"

Rachel and Kayla began giggling in response, before Kayla said, "You know the type I wanna screw tonight? I don't know why, but I've always kinda been turned on by tall, pale dudes. Don't get me wrong, I love rolling around with a brother, but there's just something about those pasty skinny white boys that turns me on. And if they're blond, so much the better."

"Oh, *me, too*," Rachel purred. "It's almost like we have a white nerd fetish or something. Especially if they have a bit of *bad boy* in them. Respectful to us, of course, but…a bit of a mean streak and not afraid to get their hands dirty. That would be totally hot!"

"You two are *freaks*," Gwen shot back in a playfully disapproving tone before a laughing Louise said, "Well, I'm not aware of anyone that meets that…um…*criteria* being invited to the wedding. I think the closest thing to that would be Clyde, so I suppose you two could fight over him."

Rachel and Kayla looked at each other as they pondered the suggestion before bursting out laughing. "Um…I don't think so," Rachel stated before Kayla included, "Naw…I mean he's a *really* nice guy, especially for a white dude, but he's a bit too old and his hair's a bit too…um…not very much, so…yeah…nope."

———

"Come, my lad, let me get a good look at you!" Clyde excitedly ordered as Marcus came down the stairs of Arima's home to greet his wedding party. Marcus beamed with pride as he looked down upon Clyde, Cliff, and his Moms and Pops. "Oh, my! That gangster's black tuxedo looks just *wonderful* on you!" Clyde exclaimed. "And look! You can barely see the fifteen bullet holes on the chest and the blood stains are practically non-existent! Oh, how dashing you look, my lad."

"Thanks, Clyde," Marcus replied. "And thanks again for finding this suit. Wow, that was really great timing, wasn't it? You know how nervous I was about finding something nice to wear for my wedding that I could afford. I couldn't find anything, anywhere. And then, two weeks ago, this mobster who is *exactly* my size just buys it outside of the opening of his restaurant. He was a real dick, too. Racist. Womanizer. Woman beater. Scam artist. Arima had no idea where to put his spirit."

Marcus then let out a roaring laugh as he continued his story. "So... oh, man, I can't tell this with a straight face...Arima knew that he would never get into Enlightenment, and she didn't want his spirit hanging around, so she wanted to get rid of him. This dude hated Mexican folks, right? So she put his dark spirit into a pound of hamburger, cooked him up, and put him in tacos. She ate *all twelve* tacos, then...well...let's just say that several hours later, she flushed him away."

"Well," an astonished Marcus's Moms replied as his Pops was bent over in laughter. "Your new bride is certainly getting...um...*creative*, isn't she? Well, she is your perfect match, it would seem, and she has been so good for you. We absolutely love her, Marcus, and we are *so* proud of you today. We are proud of you *every* day, but *especially* today. There aren't a lot of men like you and your father around. Men who treat women with respect. Men who don't see women as subservient to them, but as equals. Men who aren't running around chasing everything in a skirt. There aren't many of you and I am *so* proud to be the wife of one and the mother of another. And we just *love* Arima. As if she were one of our own and we will be *so proud* to call her our daughter-in-law in just a few hours. Come here my son and give your parents a hug."

Following his emotional embrace with his parents, Cliff approached Marcus and placed a purple iris boutonniere on his lapel. "Congratulations," Cliff said with a slight tear in his eye. "I am so happy for you today. And I am so happy for my friend. I've known her for so long and she is such a kind soul. It just warms my heart to know that two of my favorite people in the world will be united today. I love you both. And I've seen Arima's dress. You're going to be blown away, dude."

———

"Oh, my God! Why aren't you *dressed* yet?" Jamie screamed at Arima who was lying on her bed in her stained pajamas while watching an old *Twilight Zone* and eating glazed donuts.

"What's the big deal?" Arima responded casually. "I just gotta put on my dress. We don't have to be there for, like, I dunno, two hours or something."

"Arima," Jamie coolly responded through gritted teeth as she folded her arms. "Are you *baked* right now?"

"Well, y'know…um…not much. Hey. Have you tried these donuts? They are like the greatest donuts in the history of the world. *Soooo good…*" Arima's thought trailed off as she took another large bite and slowly began chewing with a look of pure ecstasy on her face.

Jamie took in and then let out a deep breath before continuing. "Arima, I love you. But I have worked and worked on planning this wedding. For you. For my best friend. And *not only* do you need to put on the dress, but we have to do your *hair*. And your *make-up*. And I think you *might* just want to shower, seeing as how this is your *wedding day*. And no, we do *not* have two hours. We have *forty-five minutes* before your ass is to march down that aisle. So you will please forgive me when I say to you…put the donuts *down*, get off of the *goddamn* bed, get in the *shower* and get *dressed!*"

As Arima and her wedding party were about to depart for the church, a sobering Arima heard a sing-song voice in her soul. *Arima… Oh, Arimaaa….Aren't you forgetting something?*

"Ah, shit," Arima said out loud as she approached the painting of the Jamaican harbor. "Yeah, sorry, Howard. Okay, you can come along. Come on into my soul. But be on your best behavior or I'll put your old ass into the cake and eat you! Got it?"

Yeah, yeah, I got it, a disappointed Howard replied. *And have you invited the others? Will they be there?*

"Yeah," Arima answered. I've prayed for the attendance of Becky Peterson and her two daughters, Lillian, Herbert, and Iris, and their little adopted spirit daughter, and of course, the Ropers. They'll all be there."

Good, Howard replied with satisfaction. *I have a feeling that their presence will be important today.*

Marcus nearly passed out from a sudden rush of blood from his head to his other head as he saw the most beautiful vision of beauty being escorted down the aisle by Louise. Arima looked absolutely radiant in her dark purple strapless wedding dress. Her breasts were fighting against the soft fabric to remain in place as her long, flowing ruffled train followed behind each step that she took to the cadence of the wedding march. Light purple Zinnia petals appeared from nowhere and gracefully landed upon the carpeted aisle in front of her as Arima and Louise heard Lillian giving quiet instructions to two giggling young white sisters and a twelve-year-old Black girl.

Arima looked down upon her ring and saw the hazy image of a smiling Becky. As she approached the altar, all of the perfectly bloomed bouquets of purple iris stood perfectly upright, and their sweet scent filled the room.

The congregation observed a joyous Louise give her beloved grand-daughter a long embrace. She held Arima's tender face in both of her hands and said quietly, "I don't know how long that I will be with you on this earth, but I am so happy that I have lived to see this day. Today is the day that you will truly take your place in our long line of strong Azar women. Today is the day that you will grow up and completely see your destiny. Today is *your* day. And *nobody* can take this from you. I will always love you, my dearest child." Louise then took her seat next to Marcus's parents in the front pew. The congregation was unable to see what Arima then felt. They were not able to see Mr. and Mrs. Roper give Arima a light kiss upon her forehead before floating to the back of the church.

Arima's tear-filled eyes looked up and met those of Marcus. They stared at each other as they lovingly took each other's hands. Their hearts were pounding with pure joy as the pastor began.

"Dearly beloved," the pastor began with a soft sneer. Arima looked up at the face of their pastor. She then watched in horror as she saw his two disfigured hands grab the bottom of his face and lift upwards. Their pastor's face was removed to reveal the bloody face of her father...the Pastor.

The Pastor began cackling as everyone heard the church's doors being slammed and locked. Standing behind them were eight skin-headed, brown-shirted, fascist hooligans carrying assault rifles.

"Just calm down, everyone," the Pastor said haughtily to the now-panicked crowd. "Just take your seats and maybe, just *maybe*, *some* of you will make it out of this alive. Oh, my darling daughter. You didn't forget to invite your dear old dad now, *did you*? Oh, I wouldn't miss *this* blessed event for *anything* in the world. Oh…well…perhaps world *domination*, but this is a step towards that now, isn't it? I'll tell you what. You just come along with me now, and I'll spare everyone else in this damnable church. Even your bitch grandmother. Or you can try to fight me, and they will all experience a horrible death at your side. Your choice. Tick-tock, my little bundle of joy, *heh, heh, heh.*"

"Wh-why can I not sense you? Why can I not sense your evil?" Jessie blurted out.

"Oh…*that*," the Pastor responded arrogantly. "You see, I grew tired of our little cat and mouse game. And I grew tired of painting the symbols of our glorious Vetis all over the walls of whatever shack that I was forced to hide out in. They didn't stop *you*, anyway. So I needed something stronger. I needed to physically sacrifice for Vetis so that he would shield me from you. So…*heh, heh, heh*…I did *this!*"

The Pastor cackled wickedly as he removed his robe. There was a collective gasp as ever-widening eyes viewed the seventy-five-year-old lanky, naked frame of the Pastor that was covered in deep scars. Every inch of his body was covered by the carved marks of Vetis. Every inch except for his bloody face and disfigured hands.

"I am now *invincible!* There is *nothing* you can do to me! My *marks* will protect me! But there is *nothing* that can protect *you* my darling daughter! *Nothing!* And I will now *prove* it to you!"

The Pastor reached behind the altar, retrieved a long sword and impaled the heart of…Louise Azar, who had instinctively jumped to her feet, rushed the altar, and absorbed the lethal thrust.

"Grams!" an anguished Arima screamed. She heard the Pastor yell out, "Now!" Then the *rat-a-tat* of horrid guns launching their deadly projectiles. Nobody but Arima could hear the voice of Howard also yelling out *Now!* And the congregation, both living and spiritual, leapt into action.

The iris blossoms suddenly extended and began enveloping the marauders in their blooms, stems and leaves. The spirits of the three young girls were saying, *Die! Die! Die!* over and over as they used their energy to physically pick up candlesticks from around the church and plunge them into the eye sockets of three of the attackers. Lillian and Becky streaked from assassin to assassin, spinning them around and making them disoriented as Mr. and Mrs. Roper lifted various crucifixes and drove them into their blackened hearts.

Jessie softly uttered her incantation and rushed into the hailstorm of bullets alongside the knife-wielding Gwen, Rachel, and Kayla, as Cliff and Marcus grabbed as many of the members of the congregation as they could and led them out a side exit to safety before quickly returning to the battle. Jamie ran up to one of the iris-bound men and thrust her hot pink, spiked stiletto heel repeatedly into his groin while shouting, "Am I woman enough for you *now*, Father? Well, *am I?* Is this *macho* enough for you? Are you proud of me *now*, you bastard?" She looked the man in his dead eyes, took the weaponized shoe off, and flung it across the room, spraying the deplorable's blood and semen on its journey to the far wall.

Arima's tears were falling into the wide-open eyes of her deceased grandmother as she heard the voice of Louise say, *It's all right, my dearest.* A brilliant blue light slowly lifted from Louise's deceased frame and grabbed the Pastor by his left wrist. Another brilliant blue light emerged from inside the stained-glass window and grabbed him by his right wrist. Arima's mother, Abdalla, smiled at her as she and Louise lifted the Pastor three feet off of the ground. The Pastor began screaming, "What are you *doing?* You can't *do* this to me! I am *invincible!* Oh, glorious Vetis! Why have you *forsaken* me? Why have you…"

Arima then saw a third brilliant blue streak stand in front of the man and begin chuckling.

"Who…Who are *you?*" Arima asked the spirit, who turned his ethereal and brawny frame towards her and said in a mischievous voice, *Let's just say I'm a friend. I'll let you take care of this douchebag, and I know that I wasn't invited, but I just couldn't resist having a little bit of fun, heh, heh, heh.*

The Pastor began screaming out, "No! Not *you!*" as his fingers were meticulously snapped one at a time for the second time in his life. Following the final cracking sound from the Pastor's pinky, the third blue streak turned to Arima and winked. *Have fun, kid. I have a feeling we'll meet again sometime.* Then, he floated away as quickly as he had arrived.

The Pastor struggled in vain to free himself from the tight frigid grasp of Louise and Abdalla as they placed him on a large crucifix at the front of the church. The Ropers each grabbed a hammer and nails and pounded his re-disfigured hands and scarred feet to the cross as he screamed in agony.

Arima turned around and viewed the carnage that this demon...her father...had wrought. She saw the blood-soaked forms of Jessie, Cliff and Jamie holding each other while sobbing uncontrollably.

She saw Kayla and Rachel holding the head of Gwen between them in their laps. Gwen's brains were oozing out of her exploded skull and saturating their hot pink bridesmaids' gowns. She saw Clyde. His suit was beyond repair. As was his riddled face. And she saw Marcus with his fists clenched standing over the mutilated bodies of his parents. She then knelt down by her grandmother's body, gently closed her eyes and righted herself.

She glared directly at the Pastor and said with a deep resolve, "You son of a bitch. *Why?* What is *wrong* with you? All of this *pain.* All of this *suffering.* All of this *death.* For *what? Money? Power?* What *is* it that you hoped to *get* out of all of this? What goes on in your head to get such a *thrill* out of oppressing others? *Manipulating* others. *Murdering* others. *Raping* others. *Destroying* others. Destroying them *physically.* Destroying them *mentally.* Destroying them *emotionally. Why?* Because someone *looks* different than you? They don't believe *exactly* like you do? They don't *love* like you do? Anything that is *slightly different* from you has to be *destroyed? Why?* And how do *you* know that you are the one that is right? Maybe it's the Jamaicans who are the master race! Maybe it's the Hispanics! Or the Asians! Or the Buddhists, or Muslims! Maybe it's just women in general. Or maybe it's the transsexuals or lesbians or gay guys! Maybe it is. You don't know! You just use your white, faux-Christian, male privilege to convince others like you that *they* should be dominant over others. That they have the *right* to destroy others. Well, you don't. None of us do. None of those groups are any better or any worse than any other. We just want to live a happy, normal life without being *exploited* by corporations or politicians or clergy or pundits. Without being *gunned down* in our schools or churches. Without being *abused* and *assaulted* and *raped* and *murdered*. Is that too much to ask? To just treat each other with respect? To support one another and help one another to be happy? And not *despite* our differences, either. To support one another *because* of our differences. To support one another because we embrace and love other people because they *are* different from us. Look at you, writhing in pain, nailed to that cross like some sort of holy martyr. *You*, and *everyone* like you who uses religion to brainwash people into hating others are not Christ-like. *You* are the exact opposite. *You* are the anti-Christ. Spin this bastard!"

The spirits of Louise and Abdalla spun the cross so that the Pastor and crucifix were now inverted. Arima took the sword from her grandmother's still heart with certainty and turned toward the anguished Pastor whose blood was rushing to his face from his upside-down frame.

He began pleading using his most convincing slithery voice. "Please, Arima. Y-y-you are right. Of course, you are. But you are too *good* to do this. I *know* that now. *You* are not a killer. You are *good* and *kind* and..."

The Pastor's words were cut off as Arima said in a frigidly calm voice, "Oh, shut up, you manipulative, con-artist, slimy piece of shit." The Pastor's head was removed from his body with one violently smooth swing of Arima's arms. His head rolled and landed on the outstretched hand of Louise's body. A waterfall of blood flowed out of the Pastor's lifeless body, creating a crimson river that flowed down the carpeted stairs through the center aisle and seeped out of the bottom of the closed front door.

A dark purple, cackling plume emerged from his decapitated body. *Oh, you think that you have won now, do you? I will be even more powerful now! I have made the ultimate sacrifice and am sure to be in the favor of our glorious Vetis! I shall still see you destroyed, my darling daughter! Only this time, I shall find my way into your soul! I shall...*"

The Pastor's threats were silenced as his mouth was covered tightly by a large fig leaf. Then his essence was enveloped by that of Lillith. And the twelve-year old spirit that Lillith had avenged. And Becky. And Becky's young daughters. And the Ropers. And the Botanist. And Iris Rose. They encircled and bound the Pastor before being joined by the spirits of Clyde, Gwen, and Marcus's parents. The Pastor's muffled screams could be heard as his dark form was lifted up and out of the church.

Arima looked upon the final two spirits. She looked into the angelic eyes of her mother and grandmother. She smiled at them. They smiled back. The spirit of Louise then said, *It is my time, my dearest. My time to go to Enlightenment with my daughter. And we, along with the others, will keep that heinous man from you. We will protect you from him. We will leave these others for you. They are weak and you will be able to dispose of them as you please. Your father, however, is very powerful. We must protect you from him. But you must play your part. There is only so much we can do. If you get too close to him again, he may be able to penetrate you. He may be able to control you. Especially if he is in league with the copperhead. Please, my dearest. Stay here and protect your loved ones. Stay out of New York. C'mon, Howard, let's go.*

M-me? Do I get to go with you? an emotional Howard stated as he emerged from Arima's body. *Thank you, Arima. We will all be looking over you. Maybe there truly can be redemption for even the most darkened soul. If we allow ourselves to let go of our hatred towards others. Our pride. Our greed. Our lust. Maybe we can all be saved someday. Thank you for showing me that Arima. Thank you for giving me the opportunity to be someone decent. Good-bye.*

Arima watched with mournful ease as the final three brilliant blue streaks ascended out of the church toward Enlightenment.

Everyone in the room remained silent as Arima sploshed through the blood and collected each of the remaining eight dark souls that were attempting to hide from her. One by one she would capture them, then place them in the holy water font at the front of the church. She heard their desperate cries as their essence were being burned by the blessed liquid. Once the final dark soul was in its place, she lifted the font to her lips and drank deeply. Every drop. She wiped her mouth, belched, and said, "Well, it worked with the tacos, so I suppose this should work, too. I'll be right back. I gotta take a piss." She opened the bathroom stall and found the body of the church's true pastor. His throat was slit, and his face had been peeled from the skull.

Arima returned from the restroom and looked at the man who remained her fiancé. She broke down in tears once again as the weight of this tragic day fell upon her bloody, bare shoulders. Marcus wrapped her in his massive arms. He concentrated with all of his might. He concentrated on absorbing her pain. Her loss. And she concentrated on absorbing his. And at that moment, they realized that they did not need to have a ceremony to be wedded to one another. At that moment, their two souls became one.

Chapter 22

Woo Girls and Nuptials

On the morning of February 14, 2039, Marcus and Arima simultaneously woke up with a start. They wiped the drool from their respective chins, looked at one another and said in unison, "Do you wanna get married today?"

"Whoa," a startled Marcus stated. "What the hell is going on? I mean, I just had this dream where my Moms and my Pops were telling me… well…telling me…"

Arima completed his sentence. "Telling you *and* me that we needed to get married today. Officially. That this day can't be about mourning their loss. They want it to be a celebration of their lives. And the lives of the *others* that we lost that day. Clyde. Gwen. My Grams. That it is to be a celebration of their lives through being a celebration of our love for one another. And a celebration of defeating an evil man, whose sprit they have locked in confinement somewhere in the darkest corners of Enlightenment. Yeah, they said the same thing to me. I can connect with them directly when they allow me to. Apparently, they can come to you in your dreams. Kinda like that copperheaded bitch, I suppose. And I haven't heard from her in years, so I think I'm all clear on that front. Maybe she's been locked away, too. Or destroyed. I dunno. All that I know is that I think that I'm rid of her and my dick of a dad. So I think that I agree with your Moms and Pops. Let's do it. And let's do it right!

You're the manager of the morgue now, so you can take off whenever you want. And as your employee, I would like to request the next two days off, all right? Let's get the gang together, fly to Vegas, get drunk, get stoned, and get hitched!"

Marcus burst into joyous laughter as he rolled on top of his beloved and began kissing her passionately. Twenty-three minutes later, they picked up the receiver of their avocado green rotary phone and began making their plans.

"Fine!" Jessie yelled into the receiver. "But I am *not* wearing that pink nightmare again! It's got blood and shit all over it, anyway. Cliff! Call the folks that you're working with and tell them that you need a couple days off! Family emergency! We're going to Vegas! And go upstairs and get Kayla and Rachel up! They're coming too! And LucyFur…get off the counter! Um…or don't. It's okay. I guess you can be up there. Good kitty. Just be cool. Okay, Arima, we'll see you in a while."

Arima shook her head and chuckled as she placed the receiver back in its place. "Okay, let's go tell Jamie."

Since the passing of her grandmother, Arima had inherited her home and the group's living arrangements had changed. Marcus and Arima lived in her grandmother's home along with Jamie. Jessie and Cliff moved into the home of Marcus's parents that he now owned, and they opened up their new house to Kayla and Rachel.

Through their tragedies, the seven friends had become inseparable. This was partially due to their mutual enjoyment of each other's company and partially out of survival. They dubbed themselves, jokingly, *The Seven Saints*, as none of them were *really* very saint-like in their various extracurricular activities. But they *were* quite serious about their motto. They would gather, lift their glasses for their first drink of the evening, and declare, "Strength in numbers!" They vowed to look over one another and protect one another. They vowed to never leave anyone behind. And they vowed that none of them would ever be taken down by the hands of evil.

As Jamie was rushing around the house frantically packing and repeating, "Oh, what will I wear? What will I wear? What will I wear?" Arima was staring at the beautiful painting of the Jamaican harbor with Marcus standing behind her.

"Y'know," Arima stated with a hint of sorrow, "I miss everyone so much. Your Moms and Pops. Gwen. Clyde. My Grams, of course. And I even miss Howard. He was such a big dick, but he became a part of my life, y'know?"

"Yeah, I know," Marcus softly replied as he wrapped his arms around her from behind. "But just look at what you did with him. You took a miserable soul who had committed the most horrendous atrocities and, over time, showed him how to care about others. You gave him the chance to redeem himself. And that's really special. *You're* really special."

"Yeah, well," Arima replied as she began to snicker. "Grams visits me from time to time in my dreams. So does my mother. Anyway, they told me that Howard's life, if you can call it that, in Enlightenment isn't *exactly* what he had hoped. They said that he was there on the condition that he is the eternal servant of all of the souls that he had abused when he was alive. So he spends all of his time running around from soul to soul getting them drinks, rubbing their feet, and pretty much anything that they want him to do. He did find some chick's spirit that is into pegging though, so I guess he has *that* going for him."

"Man," Marcus stated as he physically recoiled from his love. "Why didja have to mention *that*? I don't wanna picture some female spirit giving it to Howard up the ass! Next time you hear something like that, just keep it to yourself, okay?"

"Okay," the laughing Arima replied as they heard the honk of a car horn outside. Jamie rushed out the door with her three suitcases, followed by Arima and Marcus who were sharing a small carry-on. Arima locked the front door, turned around and saw a thirty-foot white stretch limousine. Rachel and Kayla were hanging out of the sunroof with bottles of champagne and yelling, 'Wooo!' repeatedly for no known reason. Jessie was yelling at a nervous-looking Cliff outside of the car and saying, "What do you *mean* you didn't pack it? Why wouldn't you *pack* it? Do I have to tell you *everything*?"

And Kaneko was raising her glass while exclaiming, "C'mon, bitches! We've got a wedding to get to! Get your asses in the car and let's go party!"

"Hey, driver, turn here please," Arima instructed a short while later. "We have one stop to make before we go to the airport."

The Seven Saints and Kaneko delicately placed vibrant bouquets of flowers upon each grave of their departed loved ones. They all said a silent prayer at Clyde's grave before Marcus placed a motion-detector dancing skeleton upon his headstone. They began walking away, and the skeleton began laughing and dancing. "That's how I will always remember him," Marcus stated quietly. "Laughing. He was dry as hell and his jokes were so bad, but the man loved to laugh."

They placed another bouquet at the base of Gwen's black marble headstone. Rachel and Kayla, who were now referred to as *The Twins*, embraced and told a brief story about their fallen sister. "Y'know, Gwen was so funny," Rachel began. "She was always so protective of us. She was like a mother hen. Always scolding us. Always beating up anyone who bullied us in school. She appointed herself as our leader. And why?"

Kayla then answered while chuckling. "Because she was our *older* sister, heh, heh, heh. *By thirty seconds*! She popped out first and from that moment on she took it upon herself to mother us, I guess. I mean, she wasn't any smarter than us, right?"

"Well," Rachel quietly replied, "She *was* always the one that had the coolest head. She was more calculating than us. Less likely to act on pure emotion. We need to learn that from her, sis."

They moved on and were enveloped by the shadow of an eight-foot-tall granite sculpture of a Jamaican woman with an angel's wings. Her soft face peered down at her granddaughter as Arima placed the large bouquet of color in the sculpture's outstretched hand. Arima looked up into her eyes and swore that she saw a single tear fall from the granite. The entire party held hands as Arima said, while fighting back her tears, "Awww, shit, Grams. The things that you d-did for me. My entire life. You taught me how to be a good p-p-person. You never gave up on me. You guided me without y-yelling at me. You protected me from evil. You helped me learn how to use m-m-my abilities. Y-y-you truly loved me. Hell, you even d-died for me. I l-love you Grams, and I just cherish your visits with me in my d-dreams. But it's not the s-same, y'know? You're n-not there anymore to bake me your delicious c-c-cookies or to scold me when I'm b-being irresponsible. It's just not the s-same. But it is special. I l-love you, Grams, and I always will. I will t-try to make you p-proud. Thank you." A single bird flew to a nearby tree and began singing. Arima looked lovingly at it, smiled, and winked away a final tear.

"Why don't you all go back to the limo," Marcus suggested as the group made their way toward two modest headstones. "I kinda want to do this one myself, if that's okay."

"Of course, it's okay," Arima replied with a soft understanding before placing a light peck on her love's lips.

From the nearby limo, Arima watched her love kneel between the rose-colored granite headstones. He placed the bouquet between them, then a picture of his proud parents holding their infant son. He lowered his head and began sobbing. He then began laughing loudly, looked up to the sky and said, "Yeah, okay. I won't. I understand. I'll make ya proud of me. I love you both and, yeah, I'll visit."

Marcus entered the limo and looked upon the other seven grief-stricken faces. "Man, I don't know about all of you, but I *really* need to get baked."

The limo pulled up to the curb of the airport. The chauffeur got out, went around the lengthy vehicle and opened the side door. Billowing smoke came tumbling out, as did Kaneko, who landed on her side, then rolled over to sit on the sidewalk with her legs splayed open. She was laughing hysterically, as were the other seven revelers.

"Man, are they even gonna let us on the flight like this?' the ever-worried Cliff asked to a response of renewed laughter.

"Just be cool. Just be cool. Just be cool," was all Arima said repeatedly as they stood in the airport security line. The security guard looked at each member of the party, their ID's, and their boarding passes. He giggled slightly and said, "Vegas, huh? Well, that seems appropriate for you folks. I'm not sure you need a plane to get there, though. Looks to me like you all could fly there yourselves. Well, have a good flight. And remember! No smoking in the terminal or on the plane!"

"We won't, officer!" Kayla playfully replied before saying, "Hey. You're kinda *cute*. You wanna come with us?"

The tall, blond, pale young man stammered, "Ummm..yeah. I mean… um, no, ma'am. I have to work and stuff. But maybe when you get back…um…maybe…"

The disheveled young man was cut off by Rachel who said, "Nope. You had your chance. C'mon, sis. See ya!"

The young man had difficulty holding his attention on the next passenger as he heard one of the identical twins saying, "I *know* he's cute, but we can't *both* have him. I don't think. Don't worry. We'll find a pair of pasty-faced albinos to play games with at some point. I can feel it in my...well...let's just say that I've got this feeling."

The eight slightly sober friends followed Kaneko to their luxury suite. She opened the doors and exclaimed, "Welcome to paradise, kids! Marcus, you and Arima have that bedroom over there and your suit is waiting for you. Arima, I have your dress in my room, over here. Cliff and Jessie, you two take that room. And, sorry, folks, but Jamie, Rachel and Kayla will have to share. But if any of you need a little more...um... *privacy*, here are keys to three regular rooms on the twenty-third floor. Order what you want! Eat what you want! Drink what you want! You want a stripper? Get one. You want a massage? Get one. You want a full lobster dinner just to take one bite of? Get it! Who cares! Money is no object! Tonight, you are with Kaneko!"

"Wow," Jessie stated in wonder. "We *really* need to hang out with her more often." She then sheepishly inquired, "Soooo, what if one of us - and I'm not saying *who* - but one of us sees a pair of designer shoes?"

Kaneko burst out in laughter, embraced Jessie, and whispered into her ear, "Tonight, my dear, you will live like a queen. Get whatever you want. There are no limits."

Jessie's knees began quivering as she breathily ordered, "C'mon, Cliff. Let's check out the bed!"

"Uh, okay," Cliff dutifully replied. "But I'm sure it's fine. This is a *really* swanky place and I'm not really all that tired and..."

He was abruptly cut off by his wife who screamed, "Oh my God! You are so *dense* sometimes! Just get in here and screw me!" So, he did.

For the second time in his life, Marcus nearly passed out from the vision of beauty that was his Arima. He stood there in his brand new black designer tuxedo and watched his bride-to-be glide down the aisle in her full-length purple gown that was covered in beautiful green hibiscus blossoms. He took her hands and shed a tear as he peered upon her lovely face. They then looked intensely at the face of the wedding official. Arima could sense that others were doing the exact same thing at that moment. The Ropers. Lillian. Becky and her giggling daughters. Herbert, Iris and their adopted daughter. Louise. Gwen. Clyde. Abdalla. Marcus's parents. And...Howard.

Pull on his face Arima! I don't trust him! Howard bellowed out. *And make this quick. Don't take any chances this time. Just say your 'I Do's' and get the hell out of here!*

"Why are you in such a rush?" Arima's soul said to Howard's. "You got a hot date or something?"

Yeah, I actually do, Howard replied mischievously. *You know that woman spirit that's into pegging? Well, she just conjured up a new toy that she wants to use on me, so…*

"Howard! Shut the hell up!" Arima's soul yelled out as she could hear the laughter of all of the other spirits, with the exception of one. *Mommy, what is pegging?* Arima heard the voice of a young girl inquiring. *Never you mind, dear. Arima, let's get this thing going,* came Becky's terse reply.

"Okay, just a standard Elvis," Arima stated, following her intense inspection. "Let's go. Marcus, this was supposed to happen one year ago, and although that was…um…interrupted, that doesn't make this moment any less special. I love you and I want to spend my life eating with you, getting baked with you and rolling around in bed with you. You cool with that?"

"Yeah, sure am. Ditto," came Marcus's enthusiastic, albeit short response.

"*Ditto?* Is that *it?*" a slightly annoyed Arima asked.

"Yup, ditto," came Marcus's playful response. "What else do you need me to say? I mean, I'm starving, so what else is left?"

"Yeah, nothin', I guess," Arima answered through her chuckles. "And I'm starvin', too. Okay Padre or King, or whatever. Let's make this shit official!"

The rest of the evening was taken up by visits to two buffets, one fast food taco joint, a dispensary for another kind of joint and twelve bars, four of which they were *very* overdressed for. Their intoxicated heads and staggering bodies made their way back to their suite. Except for Rachel, Kayla and Jamie, who took new "friends" to private rooms on the twenty-third floor. As they were waiting for their limo to take them to the airport the following mid-morning, they recounted some of the previous evening's highlights. The specific names that are attributable to these quotes have been redacted based upon the "laws" of Las Vegas and shall always remain in Las Vegas.

"Worst wedding vows ever!"

"You did *what* in the bathroom?"

"I really didn't think that it would fit! But you know what? It did! Wooooo!"

"Then I opened my mouth and I…"

"Oh, my dearies! The look on that man's face when he looked up my skirt! It was a look of sheer delight!"

"Cliff! Hurry up with those bags! And don't drop the one with my new shoes!" (Okay- that one is Jessie)

"So then I said to him, why don't you stop talking and do something *else* with your pretty little mouth? So he went under the table and he…"

"I really didn't think that he would be that flexible. But you know what? He was! Wooooo!"

"No, I swear! I didn't get…um…y'know…hard when she was doing that on my lap! I swear, Jess!" (Okay- that one is Cliff)

"Hey, I think you got some sour cream on your shirt."

"That isn't sour cream, dearie."

"So, once I was able to talk again, I said to him, 'Fine. You can stick it in there. But if you're not done in five minutes, I'm calling it a night!"

"That might have been the most beautiful evening that I've ever spent with anyone."

"Yeah, me too. Those were the greatest buffets in the world. And the pot was pretty good. Not as good as mine, but it was okay. Oh, and our wedding night. That was great, too, baby."

Marcus and Arima flopped down on the sofa in their living room, looked at each other's exhausted faces and began laughing.

"Damn, baby!" Marcus stated through his chortles. "Now *that's* how to get married! Maybe we should do that again *next* year for our anniversary! And, man, those twins are wild! Get a few drinks in 'em and they're like ravenous tigers or something! I mean, how many dudes did they bang anyway?"

At that moment, Arima noticed the flashing red light on their answering machine. She pried herself off of her cushion and dragged her feet across the room as she said through her laughter, "Yeah, that was great, and those chicks are super fun. But if I hear 'wooooo!' one more time. Hold on a sec. I gotta check this."

Arima pushed *Play* on the answering machine and heard the panicked voice of Stellan. "Oh, Arima. This is Stellan and Paciano.

Could you please call us back as soon as you get this? Thank you, sweetheart."

"Huh," Arima stated. "I wonder what that's all about?"

She dialed the phone and heard Paciano's mournful voice say, "Yes, hello?"

"Hey Paciano. It's Arima. Sorry I missed your call, but we've been in Vegas. What's up?"

"Oh, sweetie, only the *worst* thing *imaginable* has happened!" Paciano began through his tears. "That *sweet man* who has hired us has been *murdered*! *Just last night*! *Stabbed in the back*! His poor wife is just *beside* herself I have heard. Oh, and their *poor* daughter. To lose her daddy at *only* the age of fifteen. And on her *birthday*, no less! We haven't met the darling yet, but I just *so* want to go to the city and give her a big bear hug! I'm sorry to bother you like this. I don't know why I called *you* right away. It was like I had this little voice in my head that said 'Call Arima. She can help'. Oh, my sweet, I don't know how you can help, and this sounds all so silly, but I just think that if you came to New York, then…well…maybe things would be better somehow."

"Oh, man, Paciano, I'm so sorry," Arima sincerely replied. "I would *love* to come to New York to help, but I just *can't* right now. I just took two days off to get married and I've got tons of other stuff going on. I'm so sorry. But how about this? Marcus and I were just talking about what to do for our one-year wedding anniversary. How about we lock it in? We will be in New York exactly one year from now to celebrate our anniversary and to meet your friends that you've been talking about. Okay?'

"Yes, yes, of course that would be wonderful," an understanding Paciano replied. "Just wonderful. One year from today. It will be so lovely to have something to celebrate rather than mourn. One year from now. February 14, 2040. It is a date."

Arima hung up the phone, turned to Marcus, and said, "Well. I guess we have anniversary plans. We'd better tell everyone to see if they want to go. Right after I get baked and take a nap. Then, maybe a snack. But I'm *definitely* calling everyone after that."

Chapter 23
Sister Act

There was a noticeable strut as the seven friends walked towards the baggage claim at LaGuardia, and with good cause. It had been a good year. The number of evil souls that they had all encountered, battled, and destroyed continued to dwindle. Their deceased loved ones kept them apprised of the Pastor's continued confinement. And there was no sign of the sinister copper headed demon. The forces of fascism continued to be beaten back in county after county in the United States, and they were playing their part in defeating the deplorable minions of Vetis. They had cause to be confident. They had cause to be happy. And once Kaneko arrived with Stellan and Paciano, there would *definitely* be cause to party on this Valentine's Day of 2040.

Upon reaching the baggage claim, Cliff dutifully watched for their bags as Jessie and Jamie went to the restroom to fix their faces. Kayla and Rachel giggled and scanned the crowd for potential love interests while periodically shouting 'wooo' for some unexplained reason. And Marcus and Arima stepped outside for a much needed "break."

As they were passing their joint between them and snickering, a large stretch limo pulled up to the curb. "Well, hello bitches!" Kaneko yelled out from her perch in the sunroof. "Get the other bitches and let's go shopping!"

Stellan and Paciano tumbled out of the limo, rushed up to Arima and

Marcus, and gave them tight bear hugs. "I…can't…breathe," was all that Arima could utter through her crushed diaphragm.

"Oh, I'm *soooo* sorry, sweetie!" Paciano declared. "It's just so *good* to see you both! Welcome to New York! It is gonna be hot in the city tonight!"

"Yes, it is!" Stellan enthusiastically agreed. "Once everyone gets assembled in the limo, we'll go over the plans for the day…and the night. And, Kaneko, it is so wonderful to meet you. Thank you *so much* for picking us up at the estate."

"Oh, you're welcome, fellas!" Kaneko shouted out. "And thanks for the tour of the place. That mother and daughter will be so happy there. And you've both done such a wonderful job restoring it. And it is so cool that your friends are the same people that are my associates here in New York. What an incredibly small world! I was just so shocked when I saw the family portrait hanging above their fireplace."

The remaining revelers jumped in the limo as Cliff helped the chauffeur load the bags. Once everyone was present, Kaneko began. "Okay, kids, so here's the plan. We're going to go get checked in at our hotel and drop this shit off. Then I've got a little…um…business to conduct with some associates that I have in Brooklyn. It shouldn't take too long. They have an IT whiz there that has been doing some…um…research for me and I just need to check in with him, and the boss of the joint, if she's around. But if not, I'll see her tonight, as it very pleasantly turns out. Gee, it must be my lucky day…ha! So, you kids are all going to be dropped off in a shopping district in Brooklyn. Here's a credit card. Buy whatever you want."

Jessie began trembling and said breathily, "Oh, Kaneko. I don't know that I've ever loved *anyone* as much as I love you right now." Jamie was visibly amused. Cliff was visibly displeased.

"Yeah, yeah, yeah, it's okay kiddo, my pleasure," Kaneko laughed in response. "So, we'll get together at six o'clock for dinner and drinks and then the main event. We will all be going to a fancy nightclub for a huge blowout. And finally, the *Seven Saints* from New Orleans and Murder, Inc. from Brooklyn will come together at last for a night of unified frivolity!"

Kayla and Rachel looked at each other, smiled, jumped up through the open sunroof, and began yelling "Wooooooooo!".

"Here, hold this bong and these rolling papers. Oh, and these donuts," Arima ordered Marcus, who was standing outside with Cliff, watching the blur of activity from shop to shop of their female counterparts. "Hey, man. Look at this sweet new coat I got. Isn't it just the most beautiful shade of purple? Here, hold my old one. I wanna wear this new one. It makes me feel regal or some shit."

"Cliff!" Jessie then commanded. "Here. Hold these shoes. And *these* shoes. And *these* shoes. And these dresses. And this purse. And *these* shoes. Thanks, honey!" Following a quick peck on the cheek, Jessie was once again a blur.

Marcus and Cliff just looked at each other and shrugged. "Decent weather today," Cliff suggested.

"Yeah, pretty normal February day in the mid-forties in New York, I guess," Marcus replied as he shook his head. "Man, I remember not that long ago when there would be *blizzards* in New York in February. And now, it's like early Spring. Yeah, but there's no such thing as climate change, now is there? Dumbasses." Marcus then saw the ride of his dreams come screeching around the corner and pull up to a very abrupt stop near the local pet store.

"Hey, Arima!" Marcus yelled to his wife who was across the street. "Check out this sweet ride!"

Arima looked to where Marcus was pointing and began drooling. Arima had possessed no interest in owning a car in her life, but the vision in front of her was a hippie's wet dream. It was also the wet dream of Kayla and Rachel, who saw two tall, pale young men emerge from the back. They were identical twins and had long blond hair and wore matching all-white suits.

"Oh, *hello*…" Kayla purred before Rachel added, "Oh, *yes*…come to Momma. Or come *on* momma. Whatever you *want*." Their excitement subsided when they saw a young blonde woman and a young African-American man emerge next. "Eh, *she's* probably not with them. And *he* isn't, either. I'm pretty sure they're single. And if not…well…they wouldn't be the *first* entangled guys that we've seduced," Rachel said confidently to a nodding Kayla.

Arima walked toward the vehicle as if in a trance. It was a completely restored 1976 VW bus. Its bright yellow paint glistened in the sunshine. There were randomly placed seventies-style flowers of multiple colors and sizes painted on the body. The passenger windows had multicol-ored beaded curtains that could be closed when the bus was not being driven. It was the epitome of utopian hippie freedom. It was the epitome of a symbol of peace. To Arima, it represented hope and friend-ship and love. She also thought that it would be the absolute best vehicle in the history of the world to get baked and laid in.

Two nearly identical women then emerged from the front of the van. The only discernible difference between the two was that the driver was at least twenty years older, and her copper-auburn hair was straight while the younger of the two had curly copper-auburn strands. But they were both short, had the exact same facial features and blazing green eyes.

The younger one got out of the passenger door, slammed it and yelled, "Mom, I *love* you, but sometimes you drive me *crazy*!"

The driver began laughing and said, "I love you too, sweetie. I *know* that I drive you crazy because I'm the one *driving*! Get it? Get the play on words? Hey! How come you're not laughing? That was *gold*! Pure fuckin' go—"

And then…all hell broke loose. Arima heard Jessie behind her scream in anguish, "Oh, my God! The pain! I've never felt such pain! Such evil!" There was a hail of gunfire, and the driver of the van was struck multiple times. Her petite body was flung eight feet backwards from the torrent of lead and she landed harshly on the cracked concrete.

From her peripheral vision, Arima saw Marcus and Cliff on one side of the street and Jamie, Kayla and Rachel on the other begin directing innocent bystanders to safety.

"Mom!" the younger woman cried out as she rushed to her mother's side and took her hand.

As did Arima. She ran as fast as she could, with her dark purple coat flying behind her like a cape. She reached the woman and held her other hand. She looked into the sobbing green eyes of the daughter, then down at the fading green eyes of the mother, who was gasping for air and spitting up blood as iron-scented, crimson molasses began pooling around them all.

Arima then heard the voice of the blonde female assassin. "I *told* you, bitch! I fucking *told* you that I'd get you back!" Arima looked up and saw the woman standing fifteen feet away, holding a smoking assault rifle with an expression of absolute glee on her face. "Oh, they all said that I was *crazy*! But they were *wrong*! Could a *crazy* person manipulate an attendant in a psych hospital into helping her escape? Could a *crazy* person frame him for the murder that she herself committed? That's *right*, bitch! *I'm* the one who stabbed your fucking husband in the back! Just like you *both* stabbed *me* in the back! I took him from you, and *now* I'm taking your worthless life!"

Arima became frozen in absolute fear as she heard the assassin's voice change. It changed to something even darker and more sinister. It changed to the voice that she had heard on her twenty-third birthday. *And we're going to take the life of your precious daughter, too. Hello, Madeline, I should thank you for waking me by desecrating my grave. You awoke me, and now I have come for my revenge. You were always such an ungrateful little whore. And now, I am sending you where you belong. All I needed to do was find a human vessel who hated you as much as I did. And I found her. And I entered her body. And I can live here forever and emerge whenever I choose. And now, before you die, I want you to watch as I send your daughter to Hell with you.*

Arima screamed at her body to move. To do something. But her psyche was too absorbed by absolute terror to do anything but watch as she continued to hold the hand of the fallen woman. She watched two pale, blond young men approach the assassin, say something to her emotionlessly, then calmly snap her neck.

A dark, shadowy cloud of filthy, purplish smog emerged from the assassin's warm corpse and looked down upon the carnage that it had created. It began to chuckle before a bright white cloud enveloped it. The two forms were swirling in and around each other in a billowy blur of entanglement. They looked like two curtains being whipped against one another in a violent windstorm as brilliant flashes of dark purple and brilliant light blue flashed in an epic war. The two forms savagely collided one final time and merged into one. There was an impossibly high-pitched, tormented shriek, and the battling shrouds dissipated as quickly as they had arrived.

The dying woman gave her daughter a slight smile as her eyes faded from green to grey. The daughter cried out in tortured loss. She was lifted from the blood-soaked pavement by the pale twins, a young African-American man and a young blonde woman. They escorted the inconsolable young woman away. Arima did not know why she felt such a bond to this particular woman. She had seen others die in front of her. She was always filled with remorse for the needless loss of an innocent life. But she had never felt it like this. This sense of loss and remorse penetrated her to her bones. This sense of loss and remorse penetrated her very soul.

And then she felt something else. Something much more familiar and comforting. She felt the dead woman's spirit. She was not gone. She had not been allowed to enter Enlightenment. Arima began silently reaching out to the woman. *Please, spirit. Tell me your name. Please. I am here to help you.*

The spirit seemed to Arima to either be too shy or too frightened to reveal herself to her.

Arima continued to try to make contact. For nearly five minutes, she continued to hold the corpse's hand and repeat over and over again, *Please spirit. Please tell me your name.*

Arima then learned that the spirit was neither shy nor frightened as she felt the spirit's soul connect with hers. The pair were facing each other soul to soul and were now two souls in one. Arima then heard the annoyed voice of the spirit say forcefully, *My name? My name's Maddy* fuckin' *Sommers! Who the fuck are* you, bitch?

TO BE CONTINUED IN *PURPLE REIGN: HANGING CHADS BOOK IV*

"Hey! Hold up a minute! Don't stop reading yet! Sorry for the interruption, but my name's Maddy Sommers. You just met me and…"

"Um…hey…Maddy? What're you doin'? I mean, the book's over and I think that I've earned a little down time after this. I just want my husband, a bong, and some potato chips. And donuts. And maybe a frozen burrito. Or two. Oh, and a pizza. Since I'm in New York, I *have* to try their pizza and…"

"Yeah, yeah, yeah, the fuckin' pizza's great here, Arima. But I've gotta talk to these readers for a minute. I mean, you have totally bogarted this *entire* fuckin' book! I got what…maybe *three fuckin' lines* in this whole thing? And I'm the fuckin' *star*! So, if you would *pleeeease* allow me to continue without interruption? Thank you for your cooperation in this matter. It is truly appreciated."

"Anywhoooo…as I was saying before I was so *rudely* interrupted, if you thought that this was just a one-off story that was not connected to a series, well…SURPRISE! It *is* connected to a series! My author thought that this might be a fun way to reach out to new readers and attract them to the series, but he doesn't know what the fuck he's doing, so what does he know?"

"Anyway, we all hope you enjoyed this little story. Not sure how you could, seeing as how I'm *barely* in it, but I digress. If you liked this, then the story will be continued in *Purple Reign: Hanging Chads Book IV*. But if you haven't read the first three in the series, you will have no idea *what* the fuck is going on. So, I encourage you to pick up *Hanging Chads, Lineage: Hanging Chads Book II* and *Ascension: Hanging Chads Book III*. Then, you'll be all caught up. And those three books are *waaaaay* better because they're all about lil' ol' me. Y'know, my upbringing and what drove me to be a vigilante serial killer, then falling in love and getting involved in a hit man syndicate, then having a kid and becoming a freedom fighting serial killer. Then there's all the stuff about my parents. That shit's pretty fucked up. It is packed full of violence, blood, gore, profanity, humor, societal discussion, and romance. Y'know. Typical stuff. So pick 'em up and I'll see ya in those pages! What do you have to lose, *heh, heh, heh*. Lata, Gatas! Maddy out!"

Purple Reign

Hanging Chads Book IV

PREFACE

It entered our world with a high-pitched demonic shriek on Christmas Day, 1963. Its anger was on full display as its tiny, emaciated looking and nearly translucent body writhed underneath the grotesque coating of red blood and puke green afterbirth. Its presence on this most majestic globe was blasphemous enough, but for It to have been born on the day of celebration of the birth of Jesus Christ was additional salt in the now wounded universe.

As Its high-pitched shrieks continued, a young nurse took It to another room to be cleansed. The nurse looked down and gave the vile infant a knowing smirk as she whisked it into the other room, Its mother lying on her blood-soaked sheets clinging to life after the thirteen hour laborious torture that resulted in its birth.

The nurse cleaned the gelatinous goo from the child, then immediately surveyed its scalp. Feverishly parting the brittle copper strands upon Its head, the nurse finally smiled, then cackled with glee. As a single tear fell upon the black birthmark in the shape of the sign of Vetis, the nurse spoke in a hushed yet rapturous voice.

"I have found her my lord, just as you had prognosticated. A new soldier for your army. A new soldier who will trick others into your ranks. The righteous. The holy. So many of them will fall under her spell and the spells of all the others that you are placing upon this earth.

The weak-minded and naive will march for you, kill for you, and lift you to your glorious ascension to this world's most powerful throne. Only to find that they have been tricked and oppressed once again. And this time, their oppression will be much more cruel and will be at the hands of their perceived savior. And she shall give birth to another. Another who shall transcend mere sadistic trickery and use her powers to vanquish the holy upon her blood-soaked blades. She shall be your true champion on this earth, my lord. And I accept this most glorious responsibility of grooming both the mother and the daughter until you call for them.

"Oh, most glorious Vetis, The Tempter of the Holy, she will be one of your most loved and special ones. And I shall protect her so that she and her most powerful daughter will one day sit at your side in the glow of absolute victory over the virtuous." The nurse cackled one final time as the squirming, unholy form in her arms finally settled.

It was placed into the arms of her waiting mother. The mother's sweat covered face looked down upon the dark eyes of her daughter and a deep chill ran up her spine as It grimaced up at her then plunged itself into her engorged bosom, gluttonously feeding upon its mother's milk.

It was taken home and raised by doting parents who attempted to be as patient as they could with their temperamental and emotionally distant daughter. As It grew, It rarely played with other children unless there was something that It wanted. It delighted in manipulating other children and sometimes Its teachers into doing Its bidding whether that was taking another child's toy, milk carton or crayons. It especially enjoyed manipulating the boys in Its class into performing outrageously dangerous stunts on the playground equipment. It would watch in silence with a dry smile as an ambulance would take the suffering boy away with a broken arm, broken leg, or severe head injury. It would go over to the spot on the playground that the boy had been taken from, place Its bony fingers in the blood that lay on the ground and then lasciviously lick the blood from itself while cackling. This was Its amusement through the first grade until It began being homeschooled.

Its parents were quite aware that their daughter was not at all like other children. It was selfish. It was arrogant. It was controlling. It would admonish adults in a dry, nasally condescending tone that led its parents to lose a number of friends and become largely isolated from their family. The parents realized that It was their responsibility. But they had no true love for It for they knew in their souls that *It* was incapable of love for *them*.

Shortly after Its sixth birthday, Its mother gave birth once again, this time to a son. The parents were delighted as their newborn infant would coo and beam a smile up to them. By the age of four months, the ever-engaging child had learned to illicit laughter from the adults in the room by sticking his tongue out from the corner of his mouth while crossing his brilliant green eyes. It did not care for this. It did not care for Its brother's spirit. It did not care for how he monopolized Its parents' attention. It did not care for this interloper.

The parents were mindful to not leave It alone with their baby. It would look through Its blackened pupils at the perpetually happy and spirited newborn with its curly copper locks bouncing. It would ask to hold the child. It would always be rebuffed by Its parents. It was always denied the opportunity to mold Its younger brother. It was always denied the opportunity to injure Its younger brother. It needed to do something about this.

In late May 1970, It was invited to a first grade graduation party that was being hosted by the school nurse. Its parents beamed with joy as their daughter was expressing interest in going outside of the house and socializing for the first time. As It embarked upon Its three-block trek to the party, It looked back and waved Its skeletal fingers while giving a wry smile. As the parents watched the tight copper-bunned adorned head of their daughter retreating down the street, they thought that this may be the turning point for their daughter. This may be the turning point for their family. Their family could now come together and live as one. They were correct. Up to a point. Their true family had indeed come together. They re-entered their cozy home and took their places upon the sofa as their bubbly infant fed. They felt drowsy. They fell asleep. They had not detected the faint smell of natural gas that was emanating from the kitchen. The true family had indeed come together, but not in life. They had come together in unceremonious death.

It returned home to the brilliant strobes of emergency vehicles. It glared with anticipation as each body bag was retrieved from the home and placed into an awaiting hearse. It experienced a shiver of delight as a two-foot-long grey body bag was placed alongside that of his parents.

It gave a dry smile and returned to the house that had hosted the graduation party.

It knocked on the door. The door was answered by the school nurse who was wearing a flowing, hooded crimson robe. Neither of them said a word as It entered Its new home with the sounds of ominous chanting coming from the basement. It was sat at the dining room table. It was handed a book. The cover of the book said, "Holy Bible". The opening page of the book said, "The Munich Manual of Demonic Magic."

Adoption papers would soon be signed. There would be no family custody battles over It. Nobody in Its family wanted anything to do with It. It would leave public school and become immersed in Its home-schooled studies. Of particular interest to It were studies in manipulation, coercion, and oppression of others' emotions. It excelled in its studies.

In 1984, It met a man. A man that was perfect for It. He was weak-minded, weak spirited and completely subservient to anyone that held the slightest indication of a spine. He was known as "Freddie the Fool." It and Its congregation would call him "Frederick". They began dating and he catered to Its every whim. He attended Its evangelical church. It would frequently speak privately to the pastor following services. The congregation vehemently preached their interpretation of the teachings of Jesus Christ. But the teachings were twisted and bastardized into vile testaments of hatred towards anyone who was different from themselves. Those that looked different, prayed differently, believed different or loved differently. The congregation was being groomed. Groomed into a false belief system that they were being oppressed. That *they* were the downtrodden. That they had divine dominion over the earth and all its creatures, including their fellow citizens. The congregation would swoon during every church service and swoon once again as they listened to more prominent servants of Vetis being broadcast through their radios and later through their televisions, computers, and phones. During each service, It would sit in between Frederick and Its adopted mother and smile wryly at the fire and brimstone pastor. The pastor and It would frequently lick their respective serpentine lips lasciviously.

It was introduced to Frederick's family. It did not care for them. It did not care for their care-free nature. Their unconditional love for one another. Their sense of fairness and justice. Their unwavering support for those that they loved. Their love and support of their community. Their fortitude. They were the antithesis to It. And they needed to be destroyed. But It inherently knew that It was incapable of their destruction by itself. It would need to bide Its time and await the great ascension of Vetis before she had the necessary forces to assure their destruction. It had to wait until the ascension of Its preordained daughter, for it would be one from their own family that would strike them down. It was assured of this by Its pastor and adopted mother.

Upon holding Its daughter for the first time, It knew instinctively that Its daughter was going to need her undying and brutal tutelage in order to fulfill her destiny. The daughter looked up into the cold, dead eyes of her mother and let out an anguished wail while refusing to feed from the mother's bosom.

It was faced with yet another barrier when Its husband told It that their daughter's extended family were planning on taking her away. He wasn't sure when or how, but he knew it. He impressed upon It the danger that his sisters and brother-in-law posed to them. He impressed upon her the advantages of using their lifestyle as an example to their daughter of everything that was wrong in the world. He impressed upon It the need to share custody in order to hold some sway over their daughter's development. The insipid fool was never aware of the demonic intentions that It had for Its daughter, but he instinctively knew that if they did not strike a deal then they would never see their daughter again. It reluctantly agreed to the conditions.

The nurse who was also Its adopted mother and the child's adopted grandmother entered the waiting room to survey the situation with the interloping family members. What she witnessed sent a sharp chill down her spine. As she stood there with a look of frozen horror, she peered into the determined eyes of the infant's uncle. He was holding the content, cooing, and blue blanketed infant in his massive arms. Their eyes locked in an intense stare. And he smiled at her. It was a twisted, maniacal smile that said, "Don't fuck with me". The nurse composed herself and quickly retreated to Its hospital room. What the nurse and It did not realize was that the infant's raven-haired aunt was standing outside of the door, listening. And she heard everything. And she conveyed that discussion to her adored husband who was continuing to bounce his most cherished bundle in his arms. There was a knowing glance between the husband and the wife.

Three evenings later, Frederick answered the door of their modest home. There was an eighteen inch by eighteen-inch package lying on the porch. The package was addressed to It. It opened the package with Its three-day-old's effervescent eyes looking up at her with infantile dread. It opened the note that said, "just in case you're thinking of backing out of our deal." She removed the crumpled newspaper at the top of the box to reveal the severed head of Its adopted mother which was frozen in an expression of pure terror. It stood silently for a moment, told the husband that It was a prank and took the box outside to the burn barrel. It lit a match. It now fully understood the forces that It was going up against. This was a battle that would wage past Its lifetime. This was a battle that would wage for eternity. It also knew that it either had to recruit Its daughter into Its abhorrent cause or...It had to destroy her.

PROLOGUE

As her body convulsed and desperately gasped for life affirming oxygen, her soul was being encased. Her fading emerald eyes peered into those of a kind stranger who was clutching her hand, and she could feel the pools of blood enveloping her very essence. But not just the blood. The bone fragments. The cartilage. The intestines. The fallen appendages. And yes, the blood.

The blood of every 'Chad' that she had ever sent to hell. The blood of the murderers, rapists, wife beaters, gay bashers, pedophiles, tyrants, terrorists, and traitors. It was all slowly oozing and congealing around her soul.

She tried to remain there. She tried to focus on the earthly here and now. She heard the anguished cries of her beloved daughter. She heard the cackling of her former friend as she gloated about her murder. She then heard the dry, condescending and nasal voice of her despised mother, mimicking the outrageous glee of her former friend. She tried to find her ember. She dug as deeply into her soul as she could to tap into her rage. Her fury. Her sense of justice.

But she was too weak. Blood was pouring out of the fourteen bullet holes that had cut her down. Her heart was slowing. The weight of her past murderous acts was encasing her soul with their remains until it was entrapped by an unholy cocoon of gore. She stared blankly upward.

Her brilliant effervescent eyes faded into a dull grey as she exhaled one final time and thought to herself *Erick, I'm coming home.*

She was lifted several feet into the air. She looked down upon her stiff body being held by the stranger and her adored Josie. She wept as she witnessed her sixteen-year-old daughter plead for her to stay. She briefly allowed herself a sly grin as she watched The Twins approach their maniacally insane mother, say something to her and unceremoniously snap her neck.

Then, a dark purple cloud emerged from her fallen former friend's body. It had deep red eyes that penetrated her very being. The cloud smiled then cackled insidiously just before it rushed her. Just before the evil apparition could reach her trembling form, a brilliant white and blue light cut it off and engaged it in a fierce battle. *My hero, my prince,* she thought to herself as the swirling manifestations collided with one another repeatedly until finally...they were both gone. They simply disappeared.

"Noooooo!" she cried out. "Erick! Come back! She isn't worth it! Come back to me!" She was lifted higher. Beyond the clouds. As she gazed at the brilliance of the universe, her mind raced with thoughts of betrayal and feelings of anguish, loss, and fear.

Her ascension stopped. She was enveloped in a bright, white light. She saw dark silhouettes coming toward her. She prepared herself for battle, *whatever the hell that looks like in* this *form*, she thought to herself. A hulking dark figure approached. His majestic white wings extended as his golden halo began glowing. He continued his lumbering approach as he said, "Well hello there Buttacup! Damn, I've missed you! Wanna go get some fuckin' ice cream?"

CHAPTER 70

HELLO THERE

"Please, please stop…please…stop," Rosa Alvarez was saying over and over for the third night in a row as her convulsing, sleeping body lay on her sweat-soaked sheets. "Rosa…Rosa, wake up!" Gregory Davenport pleaded repeatedly as he gently shook his beloved wife's body. Rosa let in a deep gasp of oxygen. She opened her eyes and saw her love's panicked face. She wiped the sweat from her brow with the delicate palm of her hand and smiled up at him.

Gregory had seen his love smile at him many times in the years that they had been together. But never a smile like this. This was a smile of confidence. It was a smile of fortitude. It was a smile that conveyed a deep understanding. A deep knowledge.

"Baby," Rosa stated through her knowing grin, "call Josie. Tell her that I now know what we're going up against. Tell her that I know everything. And tell her to get out of her damned bed! The time for mourning and feeling sorry for ourselves is over. We must prepare for battle. Tell her that it's time to get the band back together again."

"Yes, you are quite accurate," Adam Peterson stated flatly as he and his twin brother peered into the bedroom. "Yes, quite accurate indeed. It is time for Josie to play some games. Oh, how we love to play games with Josie," his brother Aaron added. "Yes…quite accurate my dears," came Vai Denhart's chilled voice as she entered the room with her newly dyed jet-black hair with a single silver streak down one side cascading around her shoulders. "It is time. Thank you, Rosa. I know that this has been painful for you for the past three nights, but I just knew that if you focused on the evil energy that spewed out of Kristy's dead body that you could figure this out. We must know *exactly* what we're going up against in order to prepare ourselves for the battle. We know that it is bigger...*much* bigger...than just the evil spirit of Josie's grandmother seeking revenge. There's way more to it than that. And you have tapped into that energy and unlocked the puzzle. You guys make the call. We'll go get Lionnel and Josie and we'll meet at the Brooklyn house."

"What about the new ones, Vai?" Adam asked. "Yes, Vai," Aaron added. "What about the new ones? The one that held Aunt Maddy's hand as she was passing from us. And her friends. They were quite helpful in keeping others safe that day, Vai. I believe that they too can help us. We have seen it."

"I'll go get them," the twenty-year-old Alexa enthusiastically stated as she came bounding into the room wearing her pink footie pajamas and plopped upon the bed. "I know where they're staying. And they're connected to that Kaneko woman somehow. You know, that rich old Japanese lady that hangs around sometimes? She took me shopping once for art supplies. She's *really* cool."

"Ok, great. We have a plan," Gregory agreed. "Now, would you people *please* get the fuck out of our bedroom so we can get ready? And stop lurking outside of our door! It's creepy as hell!"

———

Everyone in the room rose in reverence as the sixteen-year-old Josie entered. She was flanked by her closest confidants, Lionnel and Rod. The nineteen-year-old Lionnel was her true love. Her soulmate. She looked upon his handsome dark ebony face as they entered. And Rod was not only their resident introverted tech wizard but had been her frequent babysitter since her infancy. She chuckled to herself briefly as she recalled making him laugh as she would wear his pop-bottle glasses, stick her tongue out from one side of her mouth and cross her eyes while smiling.

Her bodyguards, Vai and The Twins entered immediately behind her. Vai had become the reserved and calculating embodiment of her Great-Aunt Blair. And The Twins were…the Twins. Their tall, pale twenty-four-year-old bodies covered, as always, by matching all-white suits. Their love for games, both the customary kind and the deadly kind had become addictive to her. She loved them as brothers, although she was not sure if they were capable of feeling that, or any, emotion themselves.

Josie's five-foot-four-and-a-half-inch petite frame was covered in a skintight faux-leather green catsuit of her own design. Her eyes were shielded by the curly copper strands that bowed down over her lowered youthful face. Her size six feet were adorned by green boots that had three-inch metal arrows protruding from them from every angle. The deadly heads of the projectiles created a strobe effect on the walls and ceiling as she entered the room.

This congregation was not sure whether this young woman was prepared for this challenge. Despite her brilliance, they were unsure that she possessed the same fortitude, tenacity, and killer instinct of their previous leader. Their leader who had just been gunned down three days prior. They just were not sure that Josie could fill her mother's figurative shoes.

There was an audible gasp from everyone in the room as their worries were alleviated. They saw Josie lift her head. They saw the same burning ember in her emerald green eyes that her mother had possessed. They saw compassion for the innocent mixed with a deadly determination against the bullying oppressors. In her eyes, the members of Vendetta Degli Oppressi, better known as Murder, Inc., saw their new leader. And they were immediately comforted by her presence.

Josie looked around the room that was now her domain. The room that she had been told had not changed in generations. The walls were papered in red velour, with gold accents. Multiple priceless paintings from some of the world's artistic masters adorned the walls. The furniture was all deep brown heavy oak with cushions that matched the walls. And there were portraits of all the previous leaders of this deadly organization. Despite his betrayals, the portrait of Detective Edmund Simmons was still in place, only now was being used as a dart board. She looked to the portrait immediately to its right and saw the ornery and beaming face of her mother. Her mischievous smile nearly outshining her penetrating green eyes. She then looked at the latest portrait which had just been hung. It was nearly identical to the previous portrait except the pretty face was several years younger and had curly hair. She wiped a slight tear from her eye as she looked upon her congregation.

There were all the members of the elite hit-man task force along with the various department heads of the organization. There was Sam sitting in her customized lethal wheelchair next to her beloved husband and dangerous sniper, Henri. His brawny dark brown arm was wrapped around her delicate caramel shoulders. A disinterested Jules was looking up at the ceiling next to her tattoo-adorned husband Jerry. Josie knew that her seeming disinterest was no more than an act to keep her from crying as her long, curly brown hair covered her eyes. Lucy's pretty, Laotian eyes were staring at Josie with intense anticipation as though she were a cobra ready to strike. *I really gotta keep a watch on her,* Josie thought to herself. *She can be so sweet. And she's so effective with her lethal potions and bombs, but man can she be unpredictable.* Josie looked at Lucy's girlfriend, Jennifer sitting at her side. Her blonde hair glistened as she whispered something to Lucy in her sweet British accent. *I gotta work with her girlfriend, Jennifer, on helping me with that. She can help me stabilize her.*

Josie forced a smile to ty to appear confident and said, "Thank you everyone. Thank you for your sentiments. Thank you for your love for my mother and my father. And thank you for your confidence in me. I know that I'm young, but I've been learning from my parents and from all of you for some time now. And, I have the greatest team assembled in the history of the world." She looked around the room once again at the reverentially mournful faces and let out a slight chuckle as she said, "man, would mom eat this shit up. She always loved attention. And she always found a way to get it. Of all the lethal characters in this room, she was the deadliest. But, together, we will succeed. We have every lethal character that we need right here. Thank you for embarking on this odyssey with me."

"Ummm…Josie," the ever-diplomatic Gregory interrupted. "We have a few others who wish to join us. We think that they can help. Alexa… Rosa…would you please show our new friends and allies in?"

"Sure!" the bubbly Alexa squealed as she bounced to the door with Rosa. The door opened and there was another gasp as Kaneko Kiaria came marching into the room with several people behind her. "Hiya, folks!" Kaneko exclaimed. "I'm so sorry that this isn't under better circumstances. I think I know several of you. I've been associated with this group for a number of years now, but for those of you who don't know me, well, I'm Kaneko Kiaria. My name in Japanese means Golden Child of Fortune and I'm…well…I'm just damned lucky. I never lose at anything. And I've been helping to bankroll this group for some time now. And these are my friends from New Orleans."

Kaneko grabbed a twenty-nine-year-old married couple by the shoulders and pushed them to the front. "This is Cliff West and his lovely wife Jessie. As many of you know, there are many women in the world who have evolved into having special powers. Special gifts. Mine is that I'm lucky. Your Rosa can connect with and manipulate any kind of energy. This young lady *here* is a Beholder. She can sense pure good. Or she can sense pure evil. Now, that pure evil makes her experience excruciating pain. But there is an incantation that she can recite that turns her intense pain into incredible physical strength. And, once she has used her strength to vanquish the evil, she returns to normal. Cliff is…well…not really *special*, like all men. Sorry gents. It's just how we're evolving as a species. You might wanna get used to it if you wanna keep getting laid. Anyhow, Cliff is very athletic and strong and can be a formidable opponent in his own right. And he loves his Jessie. Whipped? Sure. But he loves her."

"Which brings me to *these* two lovely ladies," Kaneko stated as she thrust two twenty-five-year-old African American identical twins in front of the group. "This one is Rachel and this one is Kayla…or maybe…this one's Kayla and this one's…oh who cares. They used to be triplets, but they lost their sister Gwen in a battle. Anyway, they are trackers. If there's a dark soul out there that you're looking for, then these two can find them. Then you all can gang up on them and take their asses out. Oh, and they're pretty good with knives too, aren'tcha sweethearts?"

Kayla and Rachel looked at the pair of tall, pale twins standing behind Josie, licked their lips seductively and then squealed "Woooooooo!" at an impossibly high decibel.

"Ok, ok," Kaneko continued. "I don't know what *that* was all about, but whatever. Now, this next lady is Jamie." Kaneko wrapped her arms around the waste of a tall, slender ebony woman who was dressed in a form-fitting pants suit. "Now Jamie here was born James, but then blossomed into who she was *truly* born to be. A kick-ass broad! Although she *does* still have a little James…uh…hanging around, if you know what I mean and I think that you do."

"Now, this rather…um…largish black god here is Marcus. He's really good at…well…he's really good at supply acquisition. Yeah, *that's* it! He's really good at getting stuff that we need. Plus, he keeps *this one* here happy."

The final person stepped forward. The twenty-nine-year-old had a five-foot seven-inch full-figured caramel skinned body that was wrapped in a deep purple dress with hibiscus flowers adorning it. Her tight Rastafarian shoulder length braids tumbled on either side of her pretty face. She giggled slightly and gazed at the group through her bloodshot eyes before introducing herself.

"Hey, all. I'm Arima. Arima Azar. Nice to meet you. Say, do any of you have any brownies? Y'know. The good kind? And how 'bout some 'tato chips? Man, I could go for a bag of those right now."

Kaneko gave Arima a slight pinch on her triceps and loudly cleared her throat before beginning once again. "Yes, this is our Arima. She's married to Marcus, and they came here on the invitation of Stellan and Paciano to celebrate their one-year anniversary. Since your horrible tragedy, I understand that Stellan and Paciano have been deployed back to the country estate to fortify it in case we need a refuge. But I digress. Marcus and Arima were married last Valentine's Day. Isn't that sweet? Anyway, she is *very* special. Well…when she's not baked. Arima can sense souls who have not been allowed to enter Enlightenment for one reason or another. And she can take those souls into her and help them finish their business so that they can move on. Or, for those who are undeserving, she can banish those evil souls into inanimate objects, then vanquish them forever by destroying the objects. Pretty cool, huh?"

Josie looked upon this new friend and felt a strange connection with her before saying pleadingly, "You can sense *souls*? You *can*? Is my *mother* here? Has she moved on? And my *father*? Can you find them? *Please.* I just need to know if they are okay. I just need to know if they are here with me. *Please!*"

Rosa stared at Arima suspiciously before Arima began stammering, "Ummm….well…you see…um…I think that I…" Arima ended her sentence as she heard a demanding voice from within her soul say, *not one fuckin' word Arima. Don't say a fuckin' thing. Not until I have found her father. Then, she can know. Hey! Can I take control over your body for a bit so I can have some 'tato chips too, hmmmmm?*

CHAPTER 71
SABOTAGE

"Um…ok Josie," Arima answered meekly. "I promise. I'll see what I can do. I'll…um…I promise that I'll find your mom, okay?"

"Yeah, thanks," Josie replied as she wiped a tear from her green eye and smiled. "I'm sorry to lay that shit on you. But thanks for any help you can give me. That you can give *us*. And welcome all of you. It's so weird that you guys met Stellan and Paciano and that they brought you to us. It's almost as though…as though…" Josie's thought trailed off for a moment as she shot a quick knowing glance over to a smirking Rosa. "It's almost as though they were used to summon you or something. But it doesn't matter. You're here now and we welcome you into our family. But we must make it official. Mom was a real stickler on making things official, so if you all would please join me at the desk."

Fuck yeah, I was, Arima heard an arrogant voice say in her soul. *She'd better not fuck this up, either.* Arima bellowed back internally, *Will you please be quiet? This shit's weird enough without you constantly interrupting. I'm trying to concentrate!* She was greeted with a snide response. *Yeah, yeah, yeah. What fuckin' ever. Just go sign the fuckin' book and let's move this shit along.*

Each member of the self-proclaimed *Seven Saints* approached the desk. Cliff was the first to be given the pen to sign his name in the register. Upon picking up the ink pen he inquired, "Um…do we need to sign in blood or something?" No," came Josie's bored response, "We're not a satanic cult. Just sign it in pen please." "Okay," Cliff responded, "But is there going to be some sort of an initiation or something?" "No," an increasingly annoyed Josie replied. "We're not a fraternity. Just your signature will do." "Okay...just askin'" Cliff replied as he grinned and signed the book emphatically large as though he were John Hancock signing the *Declaration of Independence.*

Kayla was next to sign the book followed in turn by Rachel, Jamie, Marcus, Arima and finally Jessie. The seven best friends and warriors were then ushered to a small table where Rod was sitting. Displayed in front of him were needles, syringes, and test tubes.

He took Cliff's arm and rubbed alcohol over a vein. His pasty face was inches away from Cliff's arm as he squinted through his pop bottle lenses and said in a dry staccato voice, "Um, this will just pinch a bit."

"Wait a minute!" Cliff yelled out. "What are you *doing*? Why do you need to take our blood? And are you even capable of doing this? Can you see?"

"Well," Rod began to answer before being cut off by Josie. "Yes, Rod is fully capable of doing this. He's done it a million times. And the reason that we need your blood is that we collect the DNA of every member of this organization. Just in case of...um...I don't know. Science or something."

"Oh, I know," Rod answered confidently. "This DNA holds a great deal of potential...I think. I have some theories. Now, please be still," Rod concluded before hearing Cliff yell out "Ow!"

As the blood began flowing into the tube, there was violent rustling in Jessie's backpack. She took the pink sequined backpack off, placed it on the floor and unzipped its upper compartment. Out of the opening came a cute little face with long grey fur and whiskers.

"Oh! A kitty!" Josie squealed in delight until the energetic feline jumped out of the bag and onto the table. The medical supplies were destroyed in an instant as the cat ferociously ripped the tube from Cliff's arm and began lapping up the spilled blood.

"Well, now I've got to start over," Rod stated flatly as he began cleaning up the mess.

"Sooooo," a shocked Josie began asking as she watched the cat ravenously licking up the blood, "what's the cat's name?"

"LucyFur," an embarrassed Jessie replied. "No shit, huh?" was all that Josie could utter.

Holy fuck! Arima heard her new soulmate say while laughing. *That cat's fuckin' nuts! Maybe it'll break Josie of her fuckin' stray animal fetish!*

The voice's hopes were immediately dashed as Josie went up to the growling animal, gently picked her up and began cradling her in her arms. LucyFur immediately began purring and giving a giggling Josie blood stained "kisses" on her lips.

Once the blood samples were drawn, Josie resumed her place in the front of the room and said, "Okay, Rosa. You're up. What the hell are we dealing with here?"

Rosa stood in front of the group. She took a deep breath, opened her eyes, and began. "Okay everybody. This is going to be *really weird*, but just listen. I'm going to go through this step by step. There's a demon named Vetis. He is known as The Tempter of the Holy and he has a plan for overtaking the Earth and then Enlightenment afterwards. Enlightenment is where the souls of the deceased go after they…y'know…are no longer here. If they can. Good souls who have no further work to do go to Enlightenment and live in bliss for eternity. Good souls who still have work to do on the Earth or are taken before their time remain here and wait for someone like…well…Arima to help them complete their business so that they can then move on. Then, there are the dark souls. Souls that are pure evil and will never get into Enlightenment, so they are trapped here until they are destroyed by someone like…well…Arima again.

"Vetis has a two-stage plan that he has been cultivating for centuries. The first stage is to use inherently evil and usually charismatic dullards on the Earth to convert the holy into the unholy. His minions seek out self-absorbed followers and use their patriotic and religious beliefs against them. They twist their genuine beliefs into hating others that are not like themselves. They use their religious and political sermons to intensify this hate until they do not view the other people as people anymore. They are viewed as less than human and are viewed as a threat. This then causes these followers to become violent. They oppress the others. They beat them. Rape them. Murder them. And, once they have been indoctrinated into this cult to that level, their souls have become dark. Pitch black, in fact. There is no longer any redemption for them. These human dark souls are trying to sabotage the world's great democracies and turn them into brutal dictatorships that would be led by evildoers that Vetis handpicks himself. This is what has been happening in *our* country for the past twenty-four years. That is who the fascist militias are. They are the brainwashed cult servants of Vetis."

"Uh…we kinda already know all of this," Arima whispered to her Marcus. "I mean, where the hell have *these* guys been? They've been battling these forces and didn't even know who they were *truly* fighting? Really?" "Shhhhh," Marcus whispered back. "This is for people who didn't read the last book. Just be quiet."

"Okay, everybody still with me?" Rosa inquired to the group who silently nodded in a bewildered response. "Good. Okay, so if Vetis is successful, he will then come to Earth and lord over a population of his created dark souls and the people oppressed by the dark souls. Then, once the dark souls pass away here on Earth, they will all congregate. For generations, Vetis has been collecting these dark souls. He is building an army. And once he has amassed enough dark souls, he intends to wage war against Enlightenment. He will wage war against the peaceful, good souls who exist there. His army will destroy them. He will then rule Enlightenment as well and then…well…the game is over. He will control both the Earth and the heavens and there will be no hope for resisting him. Ever. For all of eternity.

"Now, there are two dark souls in particular who are very powerful and in league with one another. One is Josie's grandmother. She is the one who took over the body of Alexa, Adam and Aaron's mother and used her to…um…y'know. She's the one that killed our Maddy. And Erick the year before. We need to find her. The last we saw of her was three days ago at the murder scene. There was a brilliant flash of blue light that seemed to be battling her then they both disappeared. We need to find them. Then, we need to destroy Josie's grandmother."

Yes, we do, the voice said to Arima's soul. *That blue light was my Erick. He fought her to keep her away from our Josie. And then, they just disappeared. We have to find them Arima. If we find my bitch of a mother, we will find Erick.*

"Yes, we do," Adam stated flatly followed by Aaron's, "Yes. We must destroy her. We have seen it, Rosa. We have seen what will happen if we fail. It was so sad that we had to kill our birth mother, but she had become dark. There was no other option. It was the first step toward the destruction of Josie's grandmother. Oh, how I will enjoy playing games with her." "In due time, my friends," came Vai's calm response to her adopted brothers. "In due time. You have seen Josie's ascension to this position. And you have seen the great battle that lies before us. What you have been unable to see is the end result of that battle. That, my brothers, is what we will be writing from this point forward. This is now *our* story to tell. It is now *our* responsibility to protect democracy. To protect humanity. To protect decency. And, at this moment, no one knows how it will turn out."

"Thank you, boys...Vai," Rosa replied. "Now, there is another. As I connected to the energy that was generated by Josie's grandmother, I had a vision of another. He is just as evil. Just as sadistic. And just as powerful. He is known as the Pastor and..."

A giggling Arima then interrupted. "The *Pastor*? Oh, you don't have to worry about him. He's actually...um...ah shit. I hate to say this, but he's my father...y'know...biologically speaking. Anyway, I killed him and the spirits of my mother and grandmother, who I call "Grams," well...they took his dark soul away and they have him locked up in like spirit prison or something. So, it's cool on that front. That dick's been taken care of and is out of the picture."

"Thank you, Arima," Rosa sincerely replied. "But I fear you may be mistaken. As long as his soul still exists, there is always the risk that he will be reunited with Josie's grandmother. I saw them together when they were living. I have seen them create...well...I think that we don't need to go into *that* now."

Go into what? The voice in Arima's soul screamed out. *Ask her Arima! Ask her what the fuck she is talking about. I know that she's talking about my bitch mother and I'm guessing that your father is also the fuckin' douche preacher of my mother's church who wanted to molest me and shit when I was a teenager! But my Uncle Joe took care of that fucker. Beat him to a fuckin' pulp then snapped all of his fingers, heh, heh, heh. Man, Uncle Joe is so cool.*

Snapped his fingers? Arima silently inquired to her new soul mate. *Huh. I think that maybe I've met your uncle Joe.*

"So, that's it," Rosa began again in conclusion. "The key to winning this war both here and in Enlightenment is to find and destroy both the

Pastor and Josie's grandmother. If we can do that, then the rest of Vetis's forces will be easier to eliminate. So, Josie. What's the plan?"

Hey. Watch this shit, the voice said to Arima's soul. *Watch what my little genius comes up with.*

Josie sat in bewilderment as she listened to Rosa's presentation. Once she had accepted that what Rosa was saying was true, her mind went from bewilderment to planning. She sat in silence for a few more moments as her 153 IQ brain absorbed and sorted through all the information. She then sprang to her feet and took her place at the front of the room.

"Okay, gang! First off, if there is anyone here that doesn't want to participate in this, then now is the time to excuse yourself. I understand that this is dangerous, and I understand that you all have loved ones. So, it's alright if you want out. You will not be judged."

The entire room burst into laughter as one of the lead hit-men said, "Aw, shit Josie. We were built for this. You're not gonna keep us from having some more fun against these fascist pricks and evil demons and shit. We're here. We're with you."

"And don't worry about losing any revenue folks!" Kaneko blurted out. "Just focus on *this* shit and I'll bankroll ya. If we run low, just get me to a casino. I'll take care of ya! You bitches are running with Kaneko!"

"Well, alrighty then!" Josie responded cheerfully. "Ok, then here's my plan!"

Josie then began reading from a notebook that she had furiously been scribbling on throughout Rosa's speech.

JOSIE PARKER'S PLAN TO SAVE THE EARTH AND ENLIGHTENMENT

BY JOSIE PARKER

"Numero-Uno: We find my parents. I think that's the key. If we find them, then I think that we will find my bitch grandmother. So, here's the team in charge of that.

"Jessie- You are a Beholder and can sense pure good or evil spirits.

"Rosa- You are able to tap into energy sources.

"Rachel and Kayla- you two are trackers and can home in on them once their general location is found.

"Rod- You are a genius and can find a way to amplify their powers, just as you did when the entire Coven took down the wireless internet."

"Wait! You did *what?*" a furious Jessie exploded. "It was *you* bitches that did that? *You* are responsible for me losing all my followers, all of my likes, all of my..."

Her sentence was cut off as Cliff put his arm around his beloved wife's shoulder and said, "And we have all agreed that the world is a better place for it. Right, honey?"

"Ok, sorry about that," Josie continued. "Kind of a sore subject, I guess."

I'll say it's a fuckin' sore subject! The voice roared in Arima's soul. *Because of these fuckers karaoke sucked! And I couldn't shop online anymore! And I lost all my followers too! Yeah, sure, the radical right-wing propogandists lost an important tool for spreading their cult bullshit and kids' suicide rates went way down because they weren't trying to live up to these fake expectations of them or be bullied on-line. And yeah, there weren't nearly as many online predators or scammers. But still, it fuckin' sucked for me!*

"Would you please just *shut up!*" Arima yelled out.

"Um...excuse me?" Josie inquired as The Twins straightened their spines and glared at Arima.

"Oh...*heh, heh, heh*...not *you,*" Arima attempted to backpedal. "No, not *you.* I was talking to...um...Jessie. Yeah, *that's* it! Jessie, please just shut up about it, okay? Sorry for the interruption Josie. Please continue." *Nice fuckin' save. Now don't you ever tell me to shut up again,* the voice stated sternly. *Yeah, whatever,* was Arima's disinterested, silent response.

"Okeedokeethen," Josie began again cautiously. "Now back to my plan. So, we have Jessie, Rosa, Rachel, Kayla, Rod and finally...

Arima- Once the souls are found, you can absorb them. You can help me communicate with my parents. They will help us find my bitch grandmother and The Pastor. Then, you can absorb them, place them into an inanimate object and...destroy them. Once and for all.

Numero-Two-O: We will have teams who will work with our international syndicate of hit men to continue our earthly battle against

CHARLIE and the rest of the Underground Autocratic Movement. We will take out their foot soldiers, yes. But the focus needs to be the *truly* evil souls who hold positions of influence in the world and who are in direct line with Vetis. We need to focus on the propogandists. The business leaders. The political leaders. The religious leaders. We chop the head off of each snake then either destroy their minions or watch them go slithering back into their holes. Either way, we win.

Here are the teams. Each of you will be leading a team of ten hitmen. Oh, and women. We *finally* have a few of those. It is 2040, after all:

Lucy and Sam will focus on the political leaders.

Jules and Jerry will focus on the business leaders.

Henri and Jamie will focus on the religious leaders.

And Lionnel, Vai, The Twins, Alexa and I will focus on the propogandists. We won't need any of the hitmen. We can take these bastards out ourselves.

The rest of Rosa's *Coven* will be responsible for holding down the fort here and looking after our pets and loved ones while we're off on missions. And finally, Jennifer. You will be responsible for coordinating transportation and flying everybody around the world.

Numero-Three-O: Gregory, Marcus and Cliff will go around the world and try to convince the good souls who have influence that this shit is real. Convince them that this is about more than democracy versus dictatorial fascism. Convince them that this is a battle that is an existential threat to humanity here and in the heavens for all of eternity. Convince them so that they will join us. Or at least stay out of our way.

Numero-Four-O: We all get back together, and we *all* fuck up these motherfuckin' douchebag evil spirits once and for all and save Enlightenment. Then, we're going to LOHAD and party like the world is going to end. Because it almost did."

Oooooh, this sounds fun, a male soul's voice was heard by Arima. *I will be invited to play as well, won't I, Arima? And the others?*

Who the fuck are you? *Where did* you *come from?* The female spirit's voice shouted out. *Get the fuck out of here! And watch your fuckin' ghostly hands! Arima, get this fuckin' creep out of here!*

Yeah Howard, an embarrassed Arima answered silently. *I'll pray for you and the others when I need you. Just go now, okay?*

The male's soul departed, and the female spirit said angrily, *well,* that *was fuckin' rude! Didn't even knock. And do you know what he whispered to me before he left? He asked if I was into pegging! What...the...fuck, Arima! And I'm a married spirit. But even if I weren't, I still wouldn't be into that weird shit...I don't think. I mean, maybe a little bondage and shit but...nope. Too fucked up for me.*

The entire group applauded as Josie finished. They raised their glasses and proclaimed, "Strength in numbers and long live Vendetta Degli Oppressi!"

As hands were being shaken and hugs were being exchanged a giggling Rachel and Kayla came bouncing up to Adam and Aaron and said flirtatiously, "So, do you fellas wanna get a drink or...maybe play a *game* with us?"

"Oh, we love playing games," Adam answered with a stoic enthusiasm. "Oh, my yes," Aaron added. "We love games, in fact. We are always looking for new people to play our games with."

Kayla and Rachel looked at each other, smiled broadly and yelled out "Wooooooo!"

CHAPTER 72
LET'S GET TOGETHER

"So, fellas, what's your *favorite* game to play?" Kayla asked flirtatiously as her twin sister Rachel licked her lips.

"Well, we do enjoy operation," came Adam's response followed by Aaron's, "Oh, yes. Operation is perhaps our favorite game to play. In fact, we are in the middle of a game right now. Would you like to play with us?"

"Sure would," a slightly confused but intrigued Rachel purred.

"Josie, Vai," Adam announced to his friends. "May we go and play a game with our new friends?" "Yes, they seem quite nice," Aaron added.

"Uh…yeah…okay," Vai answered with a hint of suspicion. "But just play *normal* games with them, okay? Nothing too…um…just play something *normal.*"

As the quartet made their way down the creaking basement stairs of LOHAD, Rachel asked cautiously, "So, hey guys. Where exactly are you taking us?"

"Yeah, that's a good question," Kayla whispered into her sister's ear. "This is getting kinda creepy. Maybe we should rethink this."

"Oh, this is the basement of LOHAD," Adam began explaining. "Yes," Aaron added. "LOHAD stands for Land of Hope and Dreams, and it was a nightclub that was owned by Josie's Great-Aunt Patty and her wife. It was to be a place for peace. But there was a terrible massacre here and everyone was gunned down by very bad men. Josie has restored it and it is now a…what does she call it again, brother?"

"She calls it a cool hangout for the kids," Adam answered. "It is to be a place where kids can eat dinner and listen to music and talk with one another in peace. There is to be no trouble at LOHAD. We are here to see to it."

"Yes," Aaron began again. "We oversee the security when Josie is here. We have looked over Josie since her birth, along with Vai. And we shall do so for all time. We have seen it."

"Yes," Adam contributed. "And we are allowed to use the basement here to play our games. Just see our latest gameboard!"

Adam turned on the basement light switch and the overhead neon began humming. The lights flickered three times before finally casting an eerie off-white throughout the concrete basement that was adorned with brownish-red stained pictures of peace signs, smiley faces, and various psychedelic prints. Hanging from a bedroom door in the front of the basement, was also the back of a man's torso that had a perfect rendition of the New York skyline painted upon it.

Rachel and Kayla's eyes darted around the room rapidly as they attempted to orient themselves to their morbid surroundings. They then gasped when they saw what was lying on the large metal table. There was a large assortment of blood-soaked hammers, knives, saws, scalpels, and other weaponized medical tools. And there was a gurgling, paralyzed man who looked at them pleadingly through his tear-filled sunken eyes. He was cut open from his chest to his groin and his nazi-inked skin was pulled apart and fastened to the table, leaving his internal organs completely exposed.

What the fuck? Rachel mouthed to her sister whose brown eyes were as wide as saucers. They started to carefully walk backwards towards the stairs when Adam said, "In order to play this game you must wear this." "Yes," Aaron added. "This game tends to be a bit messy, and we wouldn't want to stain our white suits or your pretty black dresses."

Rachel and Kayla took the plastic hazard material suits, looked at them and immediately tossed them onto the red vinyl couch.

"We have a *better* idea," Kayla stated. "How about if we play this game…um…*naked?*"

"Oh! What a marvelous idea!" Adam exclaimed followed by Aaron's,

"Yes! We have never played naked before. That way we can keep our suits clean and not have to buy so many plastic suits. We do go through so many plastic suits."

Rachel and Kayla began quivering slightly as they rapidly disrobed. Adam and Aaron removed their white suit coats, ties, and shirts. They then removed their shoes, socks, and slacks. They then removed their underpants.

Rachel and Kayla's eyes widened once again as a slight trail of drool dripped down their chins. They looked at each other, then looked back at the Twins, although *not* in their brilliant blue eyes. They smiled lasciviously before yelling out an unbridled "Wooooooo!" at an impossibly high decibel.

"Okay, that was really hot," Rachel stated breathily as she leaned her blood-soaked naked body against the metal table that was now adorned with various bodily organs.

"Yeah, that was fun," the quivering Kayla answered softly as she wrapped the man's slimy intestines around her shoulders and neck like a demented boa.

"Okay, boys," Rachel stated tersely as she began regaining her composure. "*You* got to pick a game. Now it's *our* turn."

"Oh joy!" Adam exclaimed. "Yes!" Aaron added. "We are not yet done playing games! Oh, do tell us what game you would like to play next!"

"We want to play something that's called...hide the sausage," Kayla answered with a twisted little smile upon her brown lips.

"Oh, my. That does sound fun!" Adam answered enthusiastically followed by Aaron's, "Yes! Quite fun! We have never played that game before. But, we haven't any sausages."

"Oh, *yeah* you do. You've *definitely* got sausages," Rachel responded as she sauntered over to the corpse and lifted the man's limp phallus. "*This* is the sausage that you will hide. Well, not *this* one, but the one that you have on your...incredibly beautiful, pale, tall, skinny blood-spattered bodies. This is *your* game piece and...well...*this* is mine. Now, this is a game that is played one-on-one...um...*usually* so we need to split up. Kayla, why don't you take Aaron into that back room and teach *him* how to play. And I'll stay in here and play on the couch with Adam."

"Oh, *hell* yes!" Kayla yelled out as she grabbed Aaron's blood covered hand and began hastily leading him to the back room. There was a thick trail of blood and crimson footprints left behind their naked frames as the door was slammed shut.

Following a brief explanation, Adam kneeled in between Rachel's opened legs and said, "So, if I understand the rules correctly, I insert my game piece into your game piece like this, then I move back and forth and then…oh my. I'm sorry. I seem to have made a mess in your game piece. Does that mean I win the game?"

"Nope," a visibly frustrated Rachel stated bluntly. "Nope. You definitely did *not* win the game. The object of the game is to move back and forth for as long as you can *before* you make a mess."

"Oh, I believe I understand now," Adam replied gleefully. "Oh brother! I have lost the game! But we are going to play again!"

"Yes, me too!" Aaron's voice came through the thin drywall. "We are about to play again as well. Oh, this game is such fun. I do hope I win this time!"

Rachel's shaking body lay on the couch. The dried blood had turned into liquid once again as it dripped down her muscular ebony frame along with her sweat. Adam looked down upon her and said, "Did I win the game?"

"Yeah," the nearly hyperventilating Rachel replied. "Yeah…you *definitely* won the game. Yeah. You're *really good* at this game. And your game piece is…perfect. Yeah…you won."

"Oh joy!" Adam yelled out. "I won the game brother!"

"Yes!" Aaron replied with the same enthusiasm. "I did too! This game was such fun. We should play again sometime!"

"Oh…we will," Kayla's exhausted voice was heard from behind the wall. "We're *definitely* playing this game again."

Later that evening, the Twins returned to the Parker-Sommers residence that they shared with Josie, Lionnel, and Vai.

"What the hell are *you two* so happy about?" Josie inquired as she saw the broad smiles on Adam and Aaron's faces.

"Oh, we had such fun playing games with Kayla and Rachel!" Adam declared, followed by Aaron's, "Oh yes! They were such fun to play with."

"Uh, huh," a suspicious Vai interjected. "So…what game did you play with them?"

"Well, we played operation!" Adam stated followed by Aaron's, "Yes! We played operation with them. They are quite good at it."

"*Operation?*" Vai yelled out. "*Operation?* You were *supposed* to play something *normal* like cards or a board game or something. You played *operation* with them? Wait…are they still alive?"

"Well, of course they are alive, Vai," Adam answered followed by Aaron. "Yes, they are quite fun. And since we picked out the first game then they got to pick out the second game."

"Aw, shit. If those chicks were into operation, I can only imagine what the next game might be. What was the second game?" Josie inquired hesitantly as Ziggy and Stardust curled up on her lap and began purring. Lionnel entered the room with a curious look on his face as he took a bite of his hot dog.

"Well," Adam began. "They introduced us to a new game called 'Hide the Sausage.'" Aaron then added, "Yes! It is quite fun. We did not win at first but then we understood the rules better and then we won the second time we played. Kayla and Rachel said that we were very good at playing and that they enjoyed our game pieces."

Lionnel burst out laughing. Partially chewed pieces of hot dog and bun went flying across the room as he fought to clear his throat so that he could breathe.

"Wait!" Josie blurted out. "Did you two *fuck* those girls?"

"We don't believe so," a confused Adam replied followed by Aaron. "No, that is not a word that they used before, during or after the game. I do not believe that we played that game. And perhaps it is that we do not know exactly what that word means. Uncle Erick and Aunt Maddy used to use it quite often and in a variety of ways. And now you are using it much more often as well, Josie."

"Okay," a slightly relieved Josie replied. "Okay, good. If you had… y'know…done that…well… it's just best that you didn't. So, tell me what the rules of 'Hide the Sausage' are."

Lionnel ran up the stairs in a fit of laughter following an unnecessarily vivid description of the rules of the game and a blow by blow, as it were, of how the game had been played. Josie and Vai could only sit together on the couch while holding their shaking heads in their hands.

"And in order to win the game," Adam concluded, "you must do that

with your game piece for as long as you can before you make a mess."
"Yes!" Aaron added. "That is what we were told. Is that correct, Josie?"

"Yup," Josie answered in a bewildered tone as she stared directly up at the ceiling to avoid eye contact with the Twins. "Yup, they're right. That's how you win the game."

"But listen to me my dears," Vai interjected. "You must *never* play that game against someone's will. Do you understand? You may ask a woman to play that game, but if she says 'no', which is more likely than not, then you *do not* try to play that game with them ever again. That is a very personal game that *both* people must agree to play. And *do not* go showing off your…um…game pieces either! Women hate that! Do you understand?"

"Why, of course, Vai," Adam replied followed by Aaron. "Yes, we understand. We never force anyone to play games with us. Except for the bad men, but you said that we can play any game we like to with them. We would never play hide the sausage with a woman who did not wish to play with us. That would be rude."

"Okay," Josie replied. "They have a bit of a moral compass when it comes to this. Good. It's a moral compass that's *twisted as fuck*, but still a moral compass. Listen. Let's continue this conversation later. Vai, we've got to get the next year's worth of assignments ready for the assassination groups. By my birthday next year, I want this planet to be *strewn* with the bodies of these evil, fascist fucks. Then Arima can destroy their dark souls for eternity. And I want to know where my parents are and that their souls are alright. C'mon, let's get to work."

Chapter 73
Ghosts

"C'mon! It'll be funny!" Maddy urged her husband as he stood there looking at her in disbelief. "No…it won't," Erick tersely replied. "Our daughter has been through *enough* this past year and *now* you want to put on *sheets* and walk around making ghost sounds? It's *totally* fucked up! Besides, she's going to end up shooting me with an arrow!"

"Oh, who fucking cares? She can't kill us," Maddy replied dismissively. "Maybe not," Erick countered, "but *that* shit is *still* going to hurt. Let's just find a more…sensitive way to make our appearance to her, ok?" Erick could tell by the ornery look on his beloved wife's face that this was a debate that he had no hope of winning.

Ten minutes later, Josie woke up in her bed and shook Lionnel. "Hey! Baby! Wake up!" she implored as she witnessed two eerie, white shrouded figures at the foot of her bed moaning and saying in ghostly falsetto wails, *"They tooooold us to coooome here!"* *"Yeees, we were toooold to coooome here! We were toooold to cooome for Joooosie Paaaarker!"*

As Lionnel wiped the sleep from his eyes and his mind was beginning to process the scene he heard his beloved girlfriend say, "Oh, fuck this!"

Josie grabbed her bow from beside the bed and launched an arrow into the taller of the "ghosts". "Ow!" He surprising yelled out. "Goddammit! I fucking *told* you that she'd do that!"

The smaller "ghost" was bent over laughing hysterically. "Oh, my fucking God! That was so fucking *funny*! Okay…I'm sorry. Are you alright baby?"

The taller ghost took off the sheet and Josie shrieked in surprise as she saw the animated body of her deceased father. "Yeah, I'll heal up. But it *hurts* like a motherfucker!"

Maddy took her sheet off and Josie shrieked once again. "What the fuck are you guys *doing* here? You're fucking *dead*!" She cried out in disbelief. "And why are you dressed like ghosts and scaring us?"

"Okay sweetie…a couple of things here," Maddy replied calmly. "Numero-Uno, it's fucking nice to see you too. Numero-Two-o, we thought it would be funny to scare you. And it fucking was. Numero-Three-O, your first question is a really good one and we'll circle back to that in a bit. It's kind of a long story. And, most importantly, Numero-Four-O…what's with the *fucking language*? We raised you *better* than to talk like that!"

"Mom!" Josie barked back. "No, you didn't! Neither *one* of you did! My first words were *fucking fascists*! You both talked like sailors for my entire fucking childhood!"

"Yeah, that's true, I guess," Maddy conceded. "Well, I have a simple explanation for that. I've always been fond of *seamen*. Hey, baby. Get it? I said *seamen* because it sounds like *semen*. You know like cum or jizz. Get it?"

Erick rolled his eyes at his beloved wife and replied in an exasperated tone, "Yeah…I get it. I got it the other *bajillion* times that I've heard that too! You *really* need some original material."

Maddy stood there with her arms folded while tapping her size six left foot and glaring at her husband from under her straight, auburn bangs with an annoyed expression. "Y'know? I *really* thought that you *dying* might lighten you up a little bit. That *maybe*, just *maybe* the universe would finally give you an appreciation for great humor. But nope. I guess I'm going to have to spend eternity with a fucking wet blanket!"

"Well," Erick responded as he looked at his wife from the corner of his eye with a mischievous grin. "Now that we have bodies and…*everything*…I know something that we could do to make *these* sheets wet."

"Oh…my…God…*gross*!" Josie cried out in embarrassment. "It's bad enough thinking about my *parents* having sex! It's even worse thinking of my *dead* parents having sex!"

"Sweetie," Erick began compassionately. "First of all, please don't think of us as dead. Think of us as…oh…I don't know…living impaired."

Maddy burst out laughing and chimed in. "Yeah! We're *living impaired* and we think it's really fucking *not cool* of you to stereotype us because of our non-living status! The living impaired have needs *too* and it's *really* fucked up of you to try to oppress us under your living human fascist regime!"

Lionnel laid in the bed with a bewildered face holding the covers tightly to his chin. He gulped hard as he watched Erick pull the arrow from his heart while staring right at him without blinking.

"So…. Lionnel," Erick began as he glared at the slightly trembling young man. "So, just how old *are* you now?"

"Dad!" Josie yelled out.

"Not right now sweetie," Erick replied with a determined softness in his voice. "I'm getting reacquainted with your Lionnel here. It's been such a long time. Now, Lionnel, please answer my question. How *old* are you?"

"Well, uh, sir," Lionnel answered with a quivering voice, "I-I'm nineteen."

"I see, I see," Erick calmly replied as he pushed the arrow through the palm of his left hand in a display of "manliness." Maddy rolled her eyes and placed her hand over her mouth to try to conceal her laughter at her love's obviously over-the-top display of testosterone.

"Dad! Stop it!" Josie yelled out again.

"Just a moment, sweetie," Erick replied softly to his beloved daughter without dropping his glare from Lionnel's flushed ebony face. "So, you are above the age of consent for certain…um…mature activities then, aren't you?"

"Uh, uh, yeah. Yeah, I am." Lionnel hastily replied.

"Yes, good for you, young man, good for you," Erick continued as he pulled the arrow from his hand and watched the wound heal before his eyes. He gave Lionnel a slight smile as he showed his healed palm to his young adversary. "And you must forgive me. My having been murdered seems to have affected my memory a bit. Please, could you remind me what the age of consent is in this state?"

Beads of sweat began pouring down Lionnel's forehead as he realized where this inquisition was going. "Uh…listen sir…I didn't…I mean…I wouldn't…like *ever*…unless…"

Lionnel was cut off by Erick's cold, calm voice. "Please, please young man. Just answer the question for me. What is the age of consent for such adult activities?"

"Dad, please," Josie began pleading. "C'mon. Just leave him alone."

"Yeah," Maddy interjected. "Leave the fuckin' kid alone. He hasn't done anything wrong."

Erick smiled first at his wife then at his daughter before saying, "Please ladies. This is a talk between Lionnel and me. This is a *man-to-man* talk, isn't it Lionnel? Because you are nineteen, and you are officially an adult. You are *officially* a man. Whereas my *daughter* just turned *seventeen* today. Why, that would make my daughter a child now wouldn't it. And I believe my memory is coming back. Yes. I believe the age of consent is *eighteen*. So, *that* means she has *one year left* before she reaches adulthood and the age of consent. Now, as you were trying to answer me, you said you wouldn't do something. Just what is it that you wouldn't do…Lionnel?"

"I…I would never..," Lionnel blurted out, "never, *ever* do anything like that unless Josie agreed to it. I swear! I wouldn't do *anything* that she didn't want to do!"

"I see," Erick responded coolly. "So, you are saying that my daughter *wants* to do this? Is *that* what you are saying? Are you saying that my daughter is a slut? Well, *are you*, Lionnel?"

"Ok, that's fuckin' it!" Josie yelled out as she bounced upon her knees on her mattress directly in front of her father. Her glaring emerald green eyes burned into the pupils of her father as she shouted, "Lionnel! Go change your shorts! I could tell that you just pissed yourself! And Dad, I may be seventeen, but I am now the head of an international freedom fighting hit man syndicate. Plus, it's not like I've had any parental guidance for the last year, so I think that I'm *completely capable* of making my *own* decisions about my *own* body and that includes when and with whom I have *sex!*"

"Oh my God! Gross!" Erick cried out. "Don't say it like that! Okay, okay. This conversation is over. You're right, of course. You are mature beyond your years. Always have been. I just wanted Lionnel to understand that I've got your back. That your dad is here to protect you, okay? Can we just drop it now and never, ever, *ever* talk about your personal life again, okay?"

Josie looked into the panicked eyes of her father. She looked over at her grinning mother. Tears began flowing from her green eyes as the weight of the moment finally hit her. "Oh...my...*God*! You are both *here*! You are *alive*!"

The entire *Family of Fury* embraced for the first time in two years. Their joyful sobbing was saturating their tops until the group burst into uncontrolled laughter after Maddy exclaimed, "That's right bitches! We're *aliiiiiiiiive*! MWAHAHAHAHAAAAAAA!"

Lionnel emerged from the bathroom wearing a fresh set of clothes. He sheepishly looked at Erick who said, "Come here Lionnel. I'm sorry. I just tend to be a bit...um...overprotective of my Josie. I know that you love her and that you will treat her right. Please, join us. Please, join our family."

As the foursome descended the metal staircase that led to the living room, Maddy whispered to her husband, "Nice save, mister. I'm very proud of you right now."

They entered the living room and their mouths dropped as they looked upon the carnage that was on their couch.

A giggling Arima Azar and Marcus Jefferson were sitting on the couch passing a joint to each other. There was an empty pizza box on the floor that Ziggy and Stardust were eagerly eating discarded cheese and sausage from. Littering the coffee table were crumpled up cheeseburger wrappers, empty french fry containers and milk shake cups that were melting all over the rich mahogany table. The jovial pair were covered in crumbs, ranch dip, ketchup and what appeared to be the remnants of carrot sticks, for some unexplained reason.

"Arima! Marcus!" Josie yelled out. "What are *you* guys doing here?"

"Oh, yeah, hey Josie," Arima replied as her bloodshot eyes squinted the newly arrived family into focus. "Yeah, wow man, you have some great food places in this neighborhood. Pizza place. Burger place. Minimart. You people live like kings. And this pizza is like the best pizza in the history of the world, man."

"Yeah, yeah, yeah," a slightly annoyed Maddy retorted. "That's what you said about the pizza place *last* night. *And* the night before that. Jesus, you guys. You really should start watching your diets."

Marcus looked up at Maddy with a confused expression and said, "Why?" before he and Arima once again burst into laughter. "Yeah, that's a good question, baby," Arima replied through her chuckles. "Hey, pass me that bag of chips. These are the best 'tato chips in the history of the world, man."

"Okay," Josie replied coolly in an attempt to calm herself. "How about we all just have a seat. Lionnel and I have just a *few* little questions at this point. Y'know, questions like, oh I don't know…how is it that my *dead parents* are *alive* and walking around in bodies *younger* than when I knew them? *Where* have my parents *been* for the last year? If they *were* around, why did my parents not try to contact me? Y'know. Just little questions like that. I think that maybe we can discuss Arima and Marcus's diet at some *other* point. That really doesn't seem to be the *most* pressing issue at this moment. Okay?"

Arima then blurted out, "Hey, Josie. You forgot one. You forgot a question."

"Oh yeah?" a suspicious Josie countered as her copper curly locks hung just above her glimmering emerald eyes. "And just what might *that* be, Arima?"

Arima began chuckling as she answered, "Well, you might want to ask how it is that I'm your *aunt*!"

Chapter 74
Feeling Gravity's Pull

"Aw, fuck," Maddy stated under her breath before saying to the group, "okay, let's not lead with that. There's a whole lot of ground to cover before we get to that. Everybody, just take a seat and get comfortable. This is going to take a while and...Arima! Where the fuck are you going?"

"Well," Arima answered as she began floating toward the kitchen area of the home, "I thought I'd heat up some of this left over lasagna that I saw in the fridge. Or maybe I can just eat it cold. And...ooooooh, cold cuts. And cheese."

"Okay, whatevs," Maddy dismissively replied before adding, "but make me a gin and tonic while you're up. I haven't had one of those for over a year!"

"Oh yeah, me too!" Josie added. She then looked over at her father's disapproving face and said meekly, "I mean, maybe just bring me a soda, okay?"

"Yeah, sure man. I'm on it," Arima agreed.

"Okay gang," Maddy began. "This shit all started exactly one year ago on Josie's sixteenth birthday. You all know that I was gunned down by my former friend, Kristy who had been possessed by my evil cunt of a mother. You all saw me die. Josie was holding one hand and Arima, who

I did not know at the time, was holding the other as I passed away. Now, for the part that you *don't* know from this past year. Once I died…"

————

As her body convulsed and desperately gasped for life affirming oxygen, her soul was being encased. Her fading emerald eyes peered into those of a kind stranger who was clutching her hand, and she could feel the pools of blood enveloping her very essence. But not just the blood. The bone fragments. The cartilage. The intestines. The fallen appendages. And yes, the blood.

The blood of every 'Chad' that she had ever sent to hell. The blood of the murderers, rapists, wife beaters, gay bashers, pedophiles, tyrants, terrorists, and traitors. It was all slowly oozing and congealing around her soul.

She tried to remain there. She tried to focus on the earthly here and now. She heard the anguished cries of her beloved daughter. She heard the cackling of her former friend as she gloated about her murder. She then heard the dry, condescending, and nasal voice of her despised mother, mimicking the outrageous glee of her former friend. She tried to find her ember. She dug as deeply into her soul as she could to tap into her rage. Her fury. Her sense of justice.

But she was too weak. Blood was pouring out of the fourteen bullet holes that had cut her down. Her heart was slowing. The weight of her past murderous acts was encasing her soul with their remains until it was entrapped by an unholy cocoon of gore. She stared blankly upward. Her brilliant effervescent eyes faded into a dull grey as she exhaled one final time and thought to herself *Erick, I'm coming home.*

She was lifted several feet into the air. She looked down upon her stiff body being held by the stranger and her adored Josie. She wept as she witnessed her sixteen-year-old daughter plead for her to stay. She briefly allowed herself a sly grin as she watched the Twins approach their maniacally insane mother, say something to her and unceremoniously snap her neck.

Then, a dark purple cloud emerged from her fallen former friend's body. It had deep red eyes that penetrated her very being. The cloud smiled then cackled insidiously just before it rushed her. Just before the evil apparition could reach her trembling form, a brilliant white and blue light cut it off and engaged it in a fierce battle. *My hero, my prince,* she thought to herself as the swirling manifestations collided with one another repeatedly until finally…they were both gone. They simply disappeared.

"Noooooo!" she cried out. "Erick! Come back! She isn't worth it! Come back to me!" She was lifted higher. Beyond the clouds. As she gazed at the brilliance of the universe, her mind raced with thoughts of betrayal and feelings of anguish, loss, and fear.

Her ascension stopped. She was enveloped in a bright, white light. She saw dark silhouettes coming toward her. She prepared herself for battle, *whatever the hell that looks like in* this *form,* she thought to herself. A hulking dark figure approached. His majestic white wings extended as his golden halo began glowing. He continued his lumbering approach as he said, "Well hello there Buttacup! Damn, I've missed you! Wanna go get some fuckin' ice cream?"

"U-u-uncle Joe!" Maddy exclaimed as she rushed into her beloved uncle's brawny arms. "Y-you're here! I am s-so happy to see you!"

"Yes, dear. We're all here," came the calm voice of her Aunt Blair. "Yeah, we are!" came the gruff, yet cracking voice of her Aunt Patty. "Now get your fuckin' ass over here and give us a hug!"

"Oh my God!" Maddy cried out as she was enveloped by the love of her spiritual family members. Her tears flowed onto their celestial white gowns and angel's wings as she sobbed uncontrollably. She sobbed out of the joy of being reunited with her beloved family. She sobbed out of the fear of realizing that she was no longer living on Earth. She sobbed out of worry for her adored husband's spirit who she knew was locked in an existential battle with her reviled mother. And she sobbed out of no longer being able to be with her cherished daughter and other earthly friends. She sobbed for what seemed like an eternity before composing herself, wiping her tears from her glowing green eyes and saying, "So, I guess I'm fuckin' dead, huh? I was so stupid. So arrogant. I didn't even check my surroundings. Fuck, man. *Now,* what do I do?"

"Well, dear," Blair's soothing voice surrounded her like a warm baby blanket. "Yes, you have passed away. And yes, you are here with us…for the moment. But it is much more complicated than that. There is a war that is being waged on the Earth. It is the same war that we all were engaged in. The war against the narcissistic fascists who are attempting to overthrow the world's democracies. But what we did not know until our passing was that *that* war was simply a prelude to an even larger battle. That once the Earth has been conquered, the war will come here. It will come to Enlightenment. All the dark souls that remain upon the Earth will be summoned here and they will engage us in battle. They will attempt to conquer us and turn the heavens black. As black as their demonic souls. Our work is far from over, my dear. *Your* work is far from over. Both *here* and upon the Earth."

What is your name spirit? Maddy heard a soft voice within her very essence.

"What? Who the fuck is that"? Maddy asked as she looked around for the source of the question.

"That, my darling," came the reply from Maddy's father, Freddie who had emerged from the white mist to join the reunion. "That, I am both happy and sad to say is the voice of your…half-sister."

"My, *what?*" What the fuck are you talking about Dad? Oh, and great to see you. I've missed you so much too!" Maddy yelled out. "I don't have a half-sister! I mean unless you…oh my God…Dad! Did you fuck some waitress or something? Oh, that would be classic! I mean, I'm not into the whole infidelity thing, but given who you were married to, who could blame you?"

"Yeah, it's not quite *that*, Mads," Patty chimed in as she rolled her spiritual eyes, "I once said that it would be impossible for my brother to jizz into that glacier that was your mother. And sadly, well, I was right."

Freddie began to weep as he continued meekly, "Yes. I would never have had the backbone to ever violate my marriage vows. No matter how justified I might have been. Your mother, on the other hand, did not have such…reservations. I did not know until my passing that your mother was a hand-picked demon upon the Earth. She was a servant of the demon, Vetis. And she was destined to consort with another servant of this demon. He was to sire a daughter. A very powerful daughter who would wage war and rule the Earth at his side. *He* is your true father. Your true, biological father is…the Pastor."

"*Whathefuckyousay!*" Maddy screamed out. Her ember began burning anew as she shrieked, "You mean that motherfuckin' *douchebag* pastor?

He is my *father*? I mean…Jesus Christ! He tried to *molest* me! What type of sick fucks are we *dealing* with here?"

"The sickest, buttacup," Uncle Joe answered in a deepened voice. "The absolute worst. These are dark people and dark forces with dark souls, if you can call them that. They want what they want when they want it. And they have no regard for anyone other than themselves. They don't care about *who* they hurt or *how* they hurt them. As long as they achieve ultimate power. And that included you. He was going to *groom* you. He was going to *rape* you into submission. Then, you would battle by his side. But you were too strong for them. That is your special gift. All of the women of the world have a special gift. Rosa, being a prime example. It's just that many women have yet to evolve enough to be able to recognize it. Your special gift is your fortitude. Your special gift is your undying servitude towards justice. That is your…"

Please, spirit, tell me your name, came the voice again.

"Jesus! There she is again! Kind of a persistent bitch, isn't she?" Maddy declared.

Maddy turned back towards her family and said with tears forming once again in her eyes, "So, this means that you guys…none of you…are my *real* family?"

"Aw fuck, Buttacup," Joe replied as he wiped a tear from his majestic eye. "Yes, we *are* your real family. Family isn't defined by some biological connection. Family is defined by the *love* that we hold for one another in our hearts. They say that blood is thicker than water. But do you know what's thicker than blood? *Ice cream*! C'mon, we still have a little bit of time before…well…we have a little bit of time. Let's go get some fuckin' ice cream!"

"Yeah, time's really fucked up, up here," Patty added. "What seems like a long time up here may be only a few minutes on Earth. And sometimes just a few minutes up here is like a whole year on Earth. It all depends. It all depends on our needs at the moment."

Maddy, Freddie, Blair, Patty, and Joe went into the mist arm in arm. The dense shroud lifted, and they found themselves in a perfect rendition of the Argento home in Madison.

"Oh my God!" Maddy cried out in disbelief. "It's *exactly* the same! The pictures! The furniture! And…and Rascal!" The small dog came running up to Maddy and began yipping and jumping until she picked him up and cradled him like a baby as he licked her overjoyed face.

"Yes," Blair began explaining. "We can create our own paradise up here. And our celestial paradise is the same as our Earthly one. This house. This home. Oh, and we have taken in Erick's cats, Hunky and Dory as well. Although, Rascal's spirit doesn't seem to care for them much."

Maddy burst out laughing as Hunky began waddling in behind his sister Dory. Joe entered the room with five bowls of the greatest butter ripple ice cream in the history of the world…er…universe and they silently began eating while looking reverentially at one another.

Please spirit, tell me your name, came the disembodied voice once again.

"Okay, this is starting to really piss me off," Maddy stated with an annoyed tone. "Hey! Bitch voice! Leave me the fuck alone! I'm trying to have some quality family time here!" She then looked at the smiling faces of her beloved family and said softly, "Yeah, quality time with my family. I don't care who fucked that bitch in order to create me. *This* is my family. You always have been, and you always will be. And Dad. You *are* my father. I know we didn't get much time together when we were… um…alive, I guess. But I am *so proud* to be your daughter."

"Th-thank you Madeline," Freddie replied through his choked-up voice. "A-and I am *most* proud to *have* you as my daughter. Now, and for always".

Maddy gave a slight chuckle as she wiped yet another tear from her shimmering green eye and said, "Okay, c'mon. Enough with the mushy shit. Now, what is this bullshit about a half-sister?"

What is your name spirit?

"Oh, for fuck sakes! Shut the fuck up bitch!" Maddy yelled out once again.

"Well dear," Blair began explaining, "Your demonic mother and father failed with you. So, the Pastor moved on to sire another. He moved to the New Orleans area and impregnated a young woman of Jamaican descent. Three days after the birth of his second daughter, he murdered her mother. He sliced her open on an altar in the swamp and placed her head on a spike. Your half-sister's grandmother is quite powerful in her own right as is the group of women that she belongs to.

So, the Pastor decided to bide his time and wait until your half-sister realized her special gift. He then tried to bring her under his spell. There was a fierce battle, and her grandmother perished."

"Yeah," Joe added while chuckling deeply. "And I went back and snapped that motherfucker's fingers again. In fact, I do that *every fucking day*. Your half-sister's mother and grandmother have imprisoned him up here. We all take turns watching over him. He can only be released by his soul mate. And that, unfortunately is your cold-ass bitch of a mother. We don't know where she is. All we know is that she was locked in a battle with your Erick and then they disappeared. That's why you need to go back, Buttacup. You have to use your friends on Earth to help you find Erick. Help him win that battle. Help him destroy her and the Pastor. They are the key to this whole thing. If they can be destroyed, then the Earth will be free to fight for their *own* freedom without the influence of demonic powers. And then Enlightenment will be safe once again as well. You have to go back now. You have work to do on the Earth before you join us. But you *will* join us."

"Yeah!" Patty yelled out excitedly. "And then we are gonna have a *fuckin' party*! Oh Mads! Just wait until you see the lineup that I'm putting together! It's gonna be a concert for the ages! We're talkin' Hendrix, Lennon, Holly, Prince, Joplin both Scott *and* Janis, Benny Goodman, Bon Scott, Lux Interior, Lou Reed oh…and Bowie! I got fuckin' *Bowie* to do "Life on Mars!" With fuckin' *Gershwin* accompanying him on piano! How fuckin' cool is *that* going to be?"

"But first, my dear sister," Blair interrupted. "There is much work to do. Maddy. I'm so sorry dear, but you must go now. You must join your half-sister and all of the others. You must join them in the battle for the Earth. And then, you will join us in the battle for Enlightenment. And then, my dearest Patty…then we can fuckin' party."

Please spirit, tell me your name.

"Ah, fuck. I really don't want to go. Please, can't I stay longer? I've missed you all so much. Please?" Maddy pleaded.

"No dear," Blair answered coolly. "You must go. Go to your daughter. And most importantly, go to your half-sister."

"Fine, fuck it, whatevs!" Maddy replied incredulously. "So, what is this bitches name anyway?"

"Her name, my darling daughter," Freddie answered, "is Arima."

What is your name spirit?

"Just hold the fuck on, *Arima* or *whoever* the fuck you are!" Maddy yelled out once again. "Arima, huh? That's a stupid fuckin' name, but whatevs. Okay, but before I go, I have to ask you guys something. So, you guys *really* have angel wings and halos and white robes and shit?"

Joseph began laughing out loud as he replied, "Nah. We just put this shit on to freak out the newbies. Your Aunt Patty nearly *shit* herself the first time she saw me!"

Maddy's spiritual form began descending. She looked up and saw the smiling faces of her loved ones disappear into the cosmos. She felt the full force of destiny's gravity as she fell through the clouds until she was hovering over a young woman wearing a purple coat. Her Rastafarian braids partially covered her brown pretty face. She wondered for a moment how it was that she was supposed to answer her.

Then, she felt another form of gravity. The young woman's soul was pulling her inside of her. Welcoming her. Maddy's soul became entwined with that of her host. Maddy felt a comforting warmth of familiarity, let out a deep sigh and said forcefully, *My name? My name's Maddy* fuckin' *Sommers! Who the fuck are* you, *bitch?*

Oh, hey, Arima replied. *Yeah, I'm Arima. It's like, really nice to meet you. Sorry it's not under better circumstances, but, hey, you wanna go with me to get baked? This has been a really screwed up day.*

Oh, you think it's been a screwed up day? Maddy roared back. *Really? Gee, I didn't notice. I've only been gunned down in the fuckin' street, went to something called Enlightenment and chatted with my dead fuckin' relatives and found out that I have a half-sister! Which is* you *by the way! Yeah, I think calling this a screwed-up day is kinda downplaying it a bit there, Arima!*

Yeah, I know. Really screwed up, huh? Arima casually replied. *So, how 'bout we get my husband and friends and get baked, then? Oh, and* you're *the one that's my half-sister. That's really cool. My Grams told me that I'd meet you someday, so...um...nice to meet you. And feel free to hang out with me as much as you want. I have plenty of room in my soul. Hey, do you want me to tell your daughter that you're...um...y'know...here with me?*

Maddy watched through Arima's eyes as her shocked and grieving daughter was being led away by Lionnel, Vai, and the Twins. She shook her spiritual head vigorously in order to clear it then said softly, *No. Not just yet. Not until I figure some shit out. She'll be okay. I need to find her father first. Then, I'll let her know that I'm...um...still around or some shit.*

Yeah, ok, cool, totally understand, Arima hazily replied. *So, how 'bout that whole plan of getting baked and then maybe getting a little snack. Y'know, maybe some burgers. And fries. And donuts. And maybe a pizza. I'll even let you take over my body every other bite so you can enjoy it too. What do you say?*

An amazed Maddy replied, *Burgers? Fries? Donuts? Fuckin' pizza? That's your response to this shit? Well, if that's your response then mine is... fuck yeah! This whole dying thing has made me famished. C'mon! I know just the block to go to. Grab your friends and let's get busy! Y'know, maybe being joined with my sister's soul won't be so bad after all.*

CHAPTER 75
HEY YOU

Maddy was seated in Arima's body alongside Cliff, Jessie, Jamie, Marcus, Rachel, Kayla, and Kaneko in the furthest pew in Pastor Tim's church observing her own funeral service.

Hey! She screamed out at Arima's soul. *I can't see a fuckin' thing back here! Why don't we move up a few pews, hmmmm? Kick those bastards out five rows ahead of us. I barely even knew those fuckers. It was nice of them to show up though.*

Maddy, Arima responded. *We are pretty much strangers here. They don't know us very well yet. The only reason why we were invited was because we know Stellan and Paciano. Please just be quiet and enjoy, um, I mean, y'know... just watch the service, okay?*

Yeah, fuck whatever, Maddy barked back. Her heart then sank as she watched her beautiful sixteen-year-old daughter climb the steps and take her place behind the pulpit. As her beloved daughter began to speak, Arima could feel the overwhelming anguish that her half-sister was experiencing. She could feel her pain. She could feel her loss. She could feel Maddy's desire to rush to the front of the church and embrace her daughter. She could also feel Maddy realize that that would be an unwise move at this heavily armed gathering.

Just be cool, okay? Arima advised. The only response that she received were the sobs of a grief-stricken spirit.

"Well," Josie began with a forced chuckle, "Mom was the one who was good with a joke, so I'm not even going to try. Oh, who am I kidding? We were both just horrible at jokes, and Dad was always quick to point that out to us. Then Mom would say something like, 'Why aren't you laughing, mister? That was pure gold!' And my dad would just roll his eyes at her. And then they would hug and laugh."

Maddy stopped sobbing for a moment and laughed out loud through her spiritual tears. *Yeah, that motherfucker always loved to roll his eyes at me. He never thought that my jokes were funny. But you know what it was? Jealousy! Pure fuckin' jealousy! His jokes always sucked so he had to make fun of mine. Man, I'm gonna lay into him when I see him again!*

Shhhhhh! Arima scolded. *Please! We'll miss the entire thing!*

They both listened intently as Josie continued while wiping a tear from her youthful eye. "I am here today to lay both of my parents in everlasting peace. I am here to give their souls back to the universe. I am here to remember their spirits. I am here to say goodbye to them.

"And I am here to say hello to the future. I am here to look forward to a future where we are all able to come together as one. A future where we don't hate one another for our petty differences. A future where we love and embrace one another *because* of those differences. A future where we do not have to live in fear of the bullying bastards who oppress us. Abuse us. Rape us. Murder us."

Yeah! You tell them baby! Maddy yelled out as Josie paused.

"That is the world that my parents were trying to build. For me. For you. And they, along with millions of other people throughout the world, took a step toward that. Christ knows they weren't perfect— none of us are. But they tried. They, alongside so many others, fought against the fascist forces of oppression. They fought against the forces of pure evil. And they taught me to do that as well. It's just that—"

Maddy's heart began to wilt once more as she heard Josie's voice begin to crack. "It's just that . . . I don't know if I have the strength to do this anymore. I've lost *so much* in these wars. We have *all* lost so much in these wars. I just don't know if I can—"

Aw shit, she's losing it. Maddy stated to Arima in a mournful voice. *She's losing her mojo. She's losing her will to fight.* She watched as her daughter's curly copper locks descended behind the tall, oak podium.

She watched as her daughter tried to conceal her anguish and hide away from her tortured reality.

Maddy noticed a window that had been left cracked open. *I gotta go, Arima! I gotta do something about this. She needs me. She needs my strength. She needs to feel hope. I'll be right back!*

Arima felt her half-sister leave her being. A few moments later, she heard the incessant chirping of a small bird from outside the cracked window. Maddy sat on the branch and looked through the window at her grieving daughter as she sang to her. She watched as her Josie began to rise once again. She watched with pride as her daughter nodded to the musical director with fortitude.

Maddy's soul began laughing and clapping as a thunderous AC/DC song came blasting out of the church's speakers and her daughter strutted down the center aisle as she tore off her conservative black dress to reveal a skintight green faux leather catsuit. She watched as Josie kicked open the church's doors and screamed to the universe, "Here I am, motherfuckers! Time to fuck some shit up!"

Maddy re-entered Arima's soul in a flash and said triumphantly, *Fuck yeah, Boyeeee! That's my fuckin' daughter! She's going to be okay. But Jeezus! That painted on green suit doesn't leave much to the imagination. That's* really *gonna piss Erick off if she ever wears that shit around him!*

The teams had been assigned and the missions had been handed out a day earlier by Josie. The team that was responsible for tracking and finding Maddy and Erick's souls began their first meeting. The participants looked at each other with unease and uncertainty about how to proceed, until Rosa began to speak.

"Okay, everybody. I know that what we're trying to do is *really strange*. And I know that none of us have tried this before. What we have to do is track two lost souls throughout the cosmos. We have to track them from another dimension of existence. But we can do this. With Rod's technical expertise I can amplify Jessie's Beholding ability. Once she has sensed the general area where the spirits are, we can then amplify Rachel and Kayla's ability to track them down. Then it will be Arima's turn to call out to them and bring them home. Simple, right?"

The entire group let out a nervous chuckle before they heard a familiar voice bellow from out of Arima's mouth.

"Okay, I can't stand this fuckin' shit anymore!"

"Maddy, um, what are you doin'? I thought that you wanted to stay hidden for right now," Arima's normal voice stated through the same parted lips.

"Yeah, yeah, yeah," Maddy replied dismissively after taking control over Arima's body once again and continuing. "But I can't just sit here and watch these amateurs try to run this fuckin' meeting, so I'm gonna have to take charge. Um, no offense everyone, but…"

Arima's body got up from her chair and began excitedly flailing her arms as Maddy began her declaration. "Here ye! Here ye! Here ye! We are officially calling this spirit location and acquisition meeting to order! That's right bitches, I'm back! I'm kinda in a spirit form hanging out in Arima, but I'm still back! So *obviously* you don't have to waste any time looking for lil' ol' me."

Shocked faces began shedding tears of joy as Maddy continued.

"Okay, okay, enough of the blubbering. Rosa and Rod, it's so nice to see both of you. And it is so nice to meet the friends of Arima, my half-sister. So, Rachel, Kayla, and Jessie, welcome. But Jessie, keep that fuckin' cat away from me! That fuckin' thing is nuts!"

Lucyfur let out a low growl from Jessie's lap as Jessie stated meekly, "Yeah, I know. I'll try to keep her in check."

"And yes, I *did* say half-sister," Maddy continued. "You see, apparently that freak fuck of a Pastor fucked my bitch cunt of a mother and made *me* so that I could battle alongside them and help this fucknut Vetis take over the world and Enlightenment. But I was like, '*fuck that.* I'm going to use my abilities to battle you and your soldiers.' So that pissed them off and the dick Pastor seduced Arima's mother and tried to make her do the same thing. But Arima said, '*fuck that.* I'm going to use *my* abilities to battle you and your soldiers.' So that pissed them off again, so they tried to kill Arima, and they did kill me. But that just brought us together. We are now two souls in one, and once I get my Erick back, we're going to join with Josie and everybody else and fuck them and their douchebag overlord up! Oh, and one more thing. Please. Not a word of this to Josie, okay? I'm not ready to reveal myself to her yet. Not until I have brought her father back to her, all right?"

The shocked group nodded obediently before Maddy yelled out of Arima's mouth, "Now let's say our new cool cheer! *Fuck* Vetis! *Fuck* the oppressors! And long live Vendetta Degli Oppressi!"

Everyone embraced Arima's smiling body as they yelled out at the top of their lungs, "*Fuck* Vetis! *Fuck* the oppressors! And long live Vendetta Degli Oppressi!"

Days passed. Then weeks. Then months. Day after day Rosa sat holding hands with Rachel, Kayla, Arima and Jessie as electronic circuits that they were connected to buzzed. Every day began with hope. Every evening ended with futility.

"Rod," Rosa inquired after month three. "Can we turn up the intensity? Can we turn up the amplification? We aren't getting anywhere with this."

"Yeah," Maddy yelled out of Arima's mouth. "This shit's getting old! I'm fuckin' bored and I need to find my husband. Rod, I love you, but can't we do something more? And stop staring at Arima's chest!"

"Um, I'm sorry Arima, er um, Maddy," Rod replied as he began sweating and adjusting his pop-bottle lensed glasses. "We really can't turn up the amplification anymore. Not without frying everybody. I mean, well perhaps we could for a *short* period of time. Yes, if we turn it up in short thirty second increments every ten minutes or so, then maybe -it *might* just be possible. I'm not sure. Please let me do some calculations and we'll start fresh tomorrow, okay?"

"Sure, sure," Maddy replied. "You go do your fancy math shit. Arima and I have a date with a joint and large pizza tonight, anyway, *don't* we sis?"

Arima replied out loud so that everyone could hear the conversation. "Well, um, Maddy, I was kinda thinkin'."

"Kinda thinkin' *what*, sis?" Maddy inquired in a suspicious tone.

"Well, I mean," Arima replied through forced chuckles. "Y'know, this trip was *supposed* to be a celebration of my one-year wedding anniversary. And, well, *now* we've all moved to New York to help in this battle. And, well, Marcus just got back from one of his missions. And, well, it's been a while since he and I have been able to, y'know, *do* stuff together. So, I was just thinkin' that maybe for tonight I could put you in something that you'd really like, and I could hang with Marcus. Alone."

"Oh, I see," came Maddy's hurt voice from Arima's mouth. "I see.

Your newfound sister…your flesh and blood…well, maybe not flesh and blood *anymore* but you know what I mean…is a *third wheel* and I'm not *welcome* with you anymore."

"Maddy, please don't be that way. Just for tonight, okay?" Arima pleaded.

"Sure, sure," Maddy replied again with fake sincerity and more than a hint of martyrdom. "No, it's okay. I understand. You have needs. Man, I sure do envy you. I'm sure it's nice to have an actual *body* and be able to *satisfy* those needs. But that's okay. I can just hang out in a picture or something all night. Don't worry about me. I'm sure that I can find some way to pass the time while you're having your fun. It's okay. I understand…Sis."

Several hours later, Arima and Marcus were lying in their bed that was covered in fast food wrappers, an almost empty pizza box, two empty containers of ice cream and assorted loose candies that kept rolling underneath their asses.

Soooooo, Arima heard a familiar voice in her soul. *Anyone gonna finish that last piece of pizza? Maybe you'd allow your dear ol' sis to have some, hmmmmm?*

"Oh, whatever. Just take it. We're going to sleep anyway," a frustrated Arima replied as her face beamed a wide smile and reached for the pizza.

The following morning, the group was back at work. Rod increased the amplification of Jessie's Beholding abilities every ten minutes for thirty seconds, until all the women cried out for him to turn it down.

Three hours had passed when Rosa suddenly said, "Wait! I sense something. Actually, I sense nothing. There's a dark space that is completely devoid of any form of energy. It is unlike anything that we've explored in this dimension. Rod, try to turn up the amplification as I focus Jessie's powers on that area."

"All right, Rosa," Rod dutifully replied as he turned a dial slightly.

"Oh, Jeezus this hurts." Jessie stated. Then she screamed out, "Don't touch that dial! I feel…I feel…absolute *peace* and absolute *evil* in one form! It's like they are intertwined or something! How can that *be*? How can *both* extremes exist in one form?"

"I'll tell you how!" Maddy yelled out through Arima. "It's *both* of them! My bitch mother *and* my prince! They're entangled or something! Jesus Christ, Jessie! You've *found* them!"

"Okay, okay," Rosa began through her near hyperventilation. "Ok, Rod, leave the amplification up for a bit longer. Maddy, I'm going to connect your energy with Rachel and Kayla's, okay? Girls, just focus! Maddy, do you see it? Do you see the path?"

"Oh, fuck. Yeah, I see it!" Maddy responded with dismay. "It's nothing but black. But he's in there. He *has* to be. Okay, kids, thanks and see ya in the funny pages!"

Arima felt Maddy's soul disconnect from hers and leave in an instant. The group sat there in a sweaty, exhausted dismay while wondering if they would ever be with their friend again.

———

"Oh fuck, it's dark," Maddy's freed spirit stated aloud as she entered the black void. Even in her lifeless state, Maddy could sense the plummeting temperatures as she ventured further into the blackness. She could feel Rachel and Kayla leading her through the void as though they were creating an other-worldly lighthouse through the densest of fog.

Then, she saw something. It was a mass of faint light blue and purple. She floated towards it and looked upon the emaciated forms of Erick and her mother. The mother was completely encased by Erick's spiritual form. Both shrouds' faces were drawn in and looked as though all their spiritual nutrients had been sucked from their being.

"Hey you!" Maddy yelled out.

Erick's beleaguered and withered face looked upon his love for the first time in three months. He managed a slight smile and said in a raspy whisper, "Go away Maddy. Go away, my love. Leave me here."

"Fuck that!" Maddy yelled out. "Just let her go and I'm taking you home, mister! We have shit to do!"

"No, Maddy," Erick responded sadly. "This is my contribution to the battle. I must hold on to this…this…thing. I must hold it for eternity, so it doesn't escape. So it doesn't release the Pastor. So it doesn't come after you. I took it from the Earth and brought it to this remote void so that I could hold it and imprison it for all time. I must hold onto this for all of eternity so that you and our loved ones throughout the Earth and

Enlightenment can remain out of their grasp. Please, just go now. I do not want you to see me like this. Please tell Josie that I think of her every moment of my existence. I love you both so. Please, baby. Just go now."

"Fuck this!" Maddy yelled out as she rushed the entangled form and began furiously pulling Erick's essence from that of her reviled mother.

The mother began cackling with glee as she said through her weakened nasally voice, "Yes, take this bastard away from me, you little whore. Take him away you foolish little tramp. Release me so that I can once again regain my strength. Release me so that I can find your father and we can *both* finish your little ass off once and for all. Release me so that the wars against the Earth and Enlightenment can start anew. That's right, you selfish little bitch. Don't think of anyone else. Just think about your own needs. Make your bastard of a husband release me."

Erick was clinging to the mother's demonic essence as hard as he could, but he no longer had nearly the strength of his wife's spirit as she tore him from her mother's vile essence. "No, Maddy. Please just let us be. Let me protect you and Josie and everyone else. Please," Erick stated through pleading tears.

"Fuck that baby," Maddy responded through her own tears. "Fuck *that* and fuck *her*. We'll find her again and we'll *destroy* her fucking ass!" Maddy gave one final vicious pull and the cackling mother's purplish smog of a form went flying away into the black abyss.

Maddy's spirit was holding that of her existentially wounded husband. "I, I can't go back like this Maddy. I need to stay here. I need to…"

Erick's soul faded into unconsciousness as he and his beloved wife were suddenly wrapped up in delicate leaves, stems and blossoms of a giant purple iris. They were being gently taken towards a bright, white light.

Maddy heard a booming voice say from within the brilliance, "Thanks Herbert! I owe ya one! Helluva job Buttacup! It'll all be okay! We'll get him fixed up as good as new!" Maddy wept as she realized that they were being gently taken back to Enlightenment. They were being taken back into the bosom of her family. They were being taken home.

"What the *fuck* do you *mean* we've been here for almost *nine months,*

Earth time?" Maddy screamed out at her beloved Uncle Joe and Aunt Blair. "We just got here like, *yesterday!*"

"We told you dear," Blair responded through her chuckles. "We told you that time works differently up here. What seemed like just a day or two to us was nearly nine months upon the Earth. But in that time, your Erick has been nurtured back to health. It is time for you to go back now. It is time for you to call out to Arima and for you both to re-enter her soul and re-enter the battle upon the Earth."

"Well, *that* fuckin' sucks," an incredulous Maddy retorted. "I mean, I want to get back to see Josie and everything, but fuck! We hardly had any time together and she's now nearly seventeen! I've missed so much!"

"Yeah, yeah, yeah," Maddy's Aunt Patty stated gruffly as she entered the room in a huff. "Yeah, you think *you've* got problems? Do you know how hard it is to get a *whole fucking concert* organized with a bunch of prima donna spirits? I mean, who *knows* how much time that we have to get this shit together. Jacklyn and I have been working our *asses* off in getting these fuckers rounded up, just in case this war comes to an abrupt end. This is going to be the concert of all fucking time! And it has to start as soon as victory is achieved! And we don't even have an *opener* yet! Why? Because Prince is being a *fucking tool*, that's why! He's insisting on opening the show, but I already promised Jerry Lee that he could open with "Great Balls of Fire." I mean, what's a better opener than *that* after an epic war? So now, he's all pissed off and won't come out of his corner of paradise! Yeah, cry me a fuckin' river sister! Just take your husband and his pussy music back to Earth and get this shit straightened out. I've got larger problems to fix up here!"

Erick and Maddy embraced Joe, Blair, and Patty for what seemed like an eternity. Joe turned to Erick and said, "Hey buddy. It was nice to finally meet you. It was nice to meet the man that is deserving of my niece. It was nice to meet the man who would do anything to protect her and your lovely daughter. And it will be nice to get to know you more once this shit's all over."

"The pleasure sir," Erick replied as he was failing to match the firmness of Joe's handshake, "Is all mine. We'll see you all soon. And we're going to have that bitch's head on a fucking platter."

"Okay, well here we go," Maddy stated with a mixture of remorse and hopefulness. "I'm going to call out to Arima now and have her lead us back into her soul. Erick, just stay next to me. And don't go *wandering off* and getting your ass lost again! Okay, let's just see what she's up to."

Maddy peered down upon the Earth and found her half-sister. She shook her head and said, "Yeah, we're going to have to wait for just a bit."

"Why, dear," Aunt Blair inquired.

Maddy replied in an exasperated tone, "Well, she's *kinda* fucking her husband right now. How the fuck do they do that on top of all of those *crumbs*? Don't they get shit in their um, crevasses and shit? *Jeezus!*"

Chapter 76
So Alive

"So that's where we've been for the last year," Maddy stated matter-of-factly as she munched on a ham and cheese sandwich that was drenched in mustard. "Y'know. The same old, same old. What's new with you?"

"Well," Josie answered as she looked at Lionnel's bewildered face then back to those of her parents. "That's all very *interesting*, but aren't you leaving out one small detail?"

"Uh, I don't think so, sweetie," Maddy replied with a confused expression as she looked at her beloved Erick. "Baby, do you know anything that we left out?"

"Nope," Erick replied as his eyelids were beginning to droop. "I think that pretty much covers it. At least for tonight. How about we just get a good night's rest, and we can answer any questions you might have tomorrow, okay?"

"Uh, no. Not okay." Josie replied sternly. "You ended the story with the two of you about to re-enter Arima's, well I guess, *Aunt* Arima's soul, right?"

"Yeah, what's your fucking point?" Maddy asked in an annoyed tone.

"Well," Josie answered as she attempted to maintain her composure. "Do you want to *maybe* explain *how the fuck* you are sitting here in human form and looking younger than I can remember? Do you think that maybe *that* would be a little detail to share with your fucking daughter?"

"Oh yeah," Erick replied with a chuckle. "We probably should explain that. But sweetie, I have to say that I really don't care for your newfound use of profanity. It just isn't ladylike."

"Yeah, act like a fuckin' lady, wouldja?" Maddy exclaimed in agreement before catching herself and saying, "Hey! Wait a minute! Are you saying that *I'm* not a lady?"

Erick felt sweat upon his brow for the first time in two years and looked down at his twiddling fingers as he began stammering, "Um, no. Of course not, dear. I was just *saying* that, um, well, I was just *saying* that…"

Erick was granted a reprieve by his daughter's booming voice shouting, "Oh my *GAAAAAWD*! Would you two *please* stop bickering and just tell me *how the fuck* it is that you're alive?"

"Well, it is a good question," Maddy playfully responded as she tussled Josie's curly locks. "Look at you. Just look at our little genius asking brilliant questions."

"Mother," Josie replied through gritted teeth. "It is very late. This has been quite a shock. It is an incredibly *pleasant* shock, but it is still a shock, nonetheless. So please. Please just explain this to me. Okay?"

"Wow, man, I mean, like, um, Niece Josie," Arima chimed in. "You seem pretty uptight. You maybe wanna take a hit off this and, y'know, chill out a bit? It's really good stuff. My own harvest. Well, I can't take *all* the credit. You see, there was this spirit named Herbert, but he liked to be called the Botanist. So, he helped me off some murdering fascists and I helped him get into Enlightenment. Anyway, he was a wiz at anything with plants and before he left the Earth, he gave me his secret to growing *killer* dope. Anyway, where was I? Oh yeah! Do you want some?"

Josie looked at her aunt, cocked her head, and gave Arima a patient smile beneath her burning green eyes before saying in an annoyed, lilted voice, "No thank you, Auntie Arima. I think that I would like to be in complete control of my faculties as my parents explain their reanimation to me. I think that this is a conversation that I would like to be *completely* alert for. But thank you very much for your offer. Perhaps *Marcus* would like to have another hit."

"Oh, hell yeah, gimme that spliff baby," Marcus replied with the enthusiasm and energy of a sloth.

Josie turned her glowering emerald green eyes to her parents and said with a determined softness, "Okay Mother. Father. Would you *please* begin?"

"Yeah, yeah, yeah," Maddy began as she rolled her eyes at her daughter and wiped mustard from her chin. "Y'know you're getting a little overbearing."

"Mother, *please!*" Josie shouted back causing her copper curls to bounce above her reddening face.

"Okay, okay," Maddy replied in an exasperated tone. "I *kinda* wanted to finish my sammich first, but whatevs. So, we were watching Marcus and Arima fucking and…"

———

"Finally! They're done! C'mon, let's go!" Maddy stated to her apprehensive husband's spirit.

"Um, can we wait for them to, um, cleanup a bit first? I mean, it just seems rude to enter her soul as they're, um, wiping themselves down."

Thirty-seven Earth minutes later, Arima jumped up out of bed and yelled, "Jesus Christ! Could you *at least* give me a bit of warning? I know I told you that that my soul was open to you whenever you need it, but a little heads-up would have been nice!"

Happy to see you too, Sis! Maddy's soul said to her half-sister. *Surprise! We're back! And by 'we' I mean me and my prince of a husband Erick! Erick, this is Arima. Arima this is Erick.*"

Hello Arima," Erick's soul stated. *It's so nice to meet you. It's much roomier here than I thought. Thanks so much for letting us…*

Erick's voice was cut off by his yelling wife. *Yeah, it's roomy* now, *but this bitch has* all kinds *of fuckin' spirits invading our territory! There's this one dick named Howard. Do you know what he asked me? He asked me if I was into pegging! Are you fucking kidding me? Who the fuck says that to a spirit that you've just met? Or anyone, for that matter! So, if that mother-fuckin' douchebag shows up again uninvited, I want you to kick his ass, okay?*

Well, maybe. Erick cautiously stated. *I mean, like, how big is he?*

A frustrated Maddy replied, *You know what? Don't worry about it. I'll take care of him, you big pussy.*

Pussy? Erick roared back. *Where the fuck do you think that I've been for the last year? Sacrificing myself by holding onto your bitch demonic mother, that's where! Pussy? Are you fucking kidding me?*

Okay, okay, I'm sorry baby, Maddy responded contritely. *Now Arima, what's the fuckin' plan? We want to go see Josie now.*

"Um, not quite yet," Arima stated out loud so that Marcus could hear her side of the conversation. "A couple months ago, I was told to bring you two to Rosa and Rod as soon as you returned. They have something to tell you. They've kept whatever it is from the rest of our team. Y'know. Jess, Rachel, and Kayla. But we'll all find out tomorrow. I'm too messed up to drive tonight."

Tomorrow? Maddy yelled back. *Fuck that! Let me take over your body. I'll drive.*

Why do you get to drive? Erick inquired. *Why can't I take over her body and drive?*

Because, Maddy replied in a condescending voice. *You, my dear, are directionally impaired and will get us fucking lost. I want to hear what the fuck these people have planned. And I want to hear it now.*

*Yeah, but…*Erick tried to interject before looking at the glowing green eyes of his beloved wife's spirit. Realizing the futility of the situation, he concluded with, *Yeah, all right. You can drive.*

I know I fucking can, Maddy stated arrogantly as she took control over Arima's body and made her way to the white telephone that was hanging from the kitchen wall.

"They are here!" Jessie, Kayla, and Rachel said in unison as Arima and Marcus entered the room.

"Both of them," Jessie continued. "I can feel them inside of Arima."

"Yeah, yeah, yeah, we're fuckin' here!" Maddy said through Arima's mouth. "Hello everybody. Um, Erick. These are Jessie, Rachel, and Kayla. You know Rod and Rosa, of course. He says it's nice to meet you. What's that baby? What's that growl?" Maddy inquired before LucyFur made her way from under a table, jumped into Arima's arms and stared at her intensely.

"Just chill the fuck out, cat," Maddy stated through Arima's trembling voice. "It's me. It's Maddy. Remember? We met. Don't worry. Your friend is in here too and she's safe. You can retract your claws now, okay?"

LucyFur took one last deep look into Arima's eyes, let out a mew, jumped down and went to her food dish.

"That cat's fuckin' nuts," Maddy said under Arima's breath before saying to Rod and Rosa, "Okay troops. Boy, do we have a story to tell you! But first, what's the plan? Why can't we go see Josie yet? It's her seventeenth birthday in four days and I want her to be able to actually celebrate this year. So, tick-tock motherfuckers. What's the plan?"

"Well," Rod replied in his nasal voice and staccato cadence. "How would you like to present yourself in your original human form? Or would you prefer to be ghosts?"

Whatthefuckyousay? Maddy yelled out. "Yeah, that's a good question baby. How is that possible?"

"Well," Rod replied through a rare chuckle. "First, we need to obtain two bodies. Two bodies that are still alive. Gender doesn't really matter, but the transformation will be easier if they are, um, hormonally similar to you both. So, we need one male and one female. And we have several candidates. This isn't necessary for what we're going to do, but from an ethical point of view, they need to be people who won't be missed and preferably at the end of their life. Now, there is an elderly husband and wife who are both on life support. They don't have any other family. No one will miss them. All we have to do is go to the hospice where they are living their final moments and retrieve them. But they do not have long. A day or two at the most before the decision is made to let them pass. Time is of the essence."

"Well," Kayla chimed in with a playfulness in her voice. "*We* know a couple of pale studs who are pretty good with, *tee hee, everything* to do with bodies."

"Yeah," Rachel added. "Let's send in the Twins.

"Yeah," Maddy stated with a deep determination in Arima's voice. "I don't know what all of your fucking tittering is about but go get the Twins."

Fuck. That shit's gonna get old, Maddy stated internally to Arima's soul as she heard Rachel and Kayla yell out, "Woooooooooo!"

———

What the fuck is this? Erick said internally to his wife as he looked down upon the pair of barely alive octogenarians.

"Yeah, you're right baby," Maddy replied through Arima. "Nope. Not gonna happen. Find another pair. Listen, we don't mean to be ageist and shit, but *how the fuck* are we supposed to battle demonic forces of evil in *these* fuckin' prunes? Oh, yeah, that's a good point too, baby. And *how the fuck* are we supposed to *fuck*? We'll break our fuckin' *hips* just getting out of our pajamas!"

"Maddy, Erick," Rosa's calm voice responded. "Please just be patient for a moment and allow us to explain. You will not be in these bodies. I mean, well, they will start out as these bodies, but they will be transformed into your own bodies. And your bodies will be, um, what age will their bodies be, Rod?"

"Well, let me just look at the date on this vile," Rod responded as he lifted two glass tubes from a tray. Yes, Erick's age when we extracted his DNA in 2023 was, let me see here. Oh yes, his body will be forty-seven! And Maddy's DNA was extracted the same year which would make the age of her body thirty-five!"

"Oh yeah *boyeeeee!*" Maddy yelled out through Arima. "I'm *still* fuckin' younger than you! I don't know. I'll ask. Erick would like to know if he could be closer to my age. Even though I never considered it a problem, he always felt a little creepy about being twelve-years older than me. So whaddayasay Rod? How about making him around forty? That way, he's happy but I'm *still* younger than him and can give him shit about it. Okay? Cool. I'm glad that's settled."

"Yeah, that's not quite how this works," Rosa began again. "Just bear with me here and I'll try to explain. As you know, I am able to control and enhance energy. All forms of energy including energy from souls. Arima can bring souls into her essence or place them in inanimate objects, but she can't place a soul into another living being. But I can. Arima will release your souls. I will capture their energy and place each of your souls into these respective bodies. Rod will then inject their brains with your DNA from 2023. Then, the magic happens.

"With Rod amplifying your DNA through electricity and my amplifying the energy generated by your souls, the combination will overtake that of the original hosts. Their souls will be released and yours will take over. Then your DNA will begin to dominate theirs and the bodies will begin to transform at the molecular level. The central nervous system will be transformed first. Then the bones, tissues, cartilage, and muscles. Then the organs. Then the blood-type, and so on until your exact body from 2023 exists once again."

"How about my tits?" Maddy blurted out. "I mean, I'm sure she was probably a looker in her day, but this is some saggy shit right here."

"*Everything* will transform," Rosa replied following an eye roll and deep sigh. "After three days of intense, non-stop concentration by me, your souls will be in your bodies from 2023. And they will remain that way. Your DNA from 2023 will not allow you to age. It will kill off any disease or virus. It will regenerate wounded body parts. The only way that you will be able to die is if the body's nervous system is detached. So, um, don't get decapitated."

"Well, that's not *entirely* true," Marcus added. "My Moms and Pops came to me one night in a dream and told me the rest of it. I mean, it's true that your bodies will live forever but only as long as your souls are in them. Once your work is done on Earth, then your souls will be recalled to Enlightenment. When that happens, your bodies will turn to dust. You will be purely in spirit form from that point on and will only be able to visit Earth through someone like Arima. Or birds. Or something. I actually don't know. It feels like I'm just making this shit up as I go along."

"Well, let's get this shit over with then," Maddy stated excitedly. "What's that baby? Yeah, I know. I tried. But it doesn't really matter now. As long as we're in human form we're, like, immortal or something, so our age doesn't matter. And it sure as hell won't matter once we're spirits again. Oh, just quit your whining and get your misty ass into this old coot you big baby! Jesus fucking Christ!"

"Jesus fucking Christ!" Maddy yelled out as her born-again bare torso rose from the cold metal table following her three-day transformation. "And what the fuck am I *covered* in?" she exclaimed as her astonished green eyes looked at her thirty-five-year-old body that was encased in an oozing greenish, reddish, whitish, brownish, gelatinous goo.

"Wassupbuttacup?" Erick stated as he entered the room wearing a plush, white robe and carrying a steaming cup of coffee.

"Hey you!" Maddy yelled out. "Oh my God! It's *you*! It's really *you*! Like, your *face*! Your *body*! Your – hey open your robe really quick."

Erick turned his back to the observation window and did as he was instructed.

"Yep! It's totally *you*!" Maddy cried out as she began clapping which sent streams of the thick goo flying across the room. "When did you wake up?"

"Oh, just about a half hour ago. And to answer your question, you are covered in all the remnants of the poor soul whose body you took over. It's like their leftovers get put into a blender and kinda ooze out of the skin. It does not look…or *smell* very pleasant. So, you might want to take a shower. And Arima said that she saw the smiling faces of the elderly couple moving on toward Enlightenment. So, all's well that ends well, I guess. So, are you gonna take that shower or what? I mean, it's great to see you but you're *really* fucking ripe and gross right now. But before you jump in the shower, go ahead, and say it."

"Uh, say what?" a confused Maddy asked.

"You know. Just say it. It'll be *really* funny this time," Erick answered as he flashed his beloved wife his mischievous grin.

An understanding Maddy mirrored his grin, lifted her head, and screamed out, "*I'm Aliiiiiiiiive! MWAHAHAHAHAAAA!*"

She then jumped off the table and began approaching her Erick. She made sloshing sounds with each step as the thick ooze from her size six feet met the concrete floor.

"What the fuck are you doing," Erick asked with trepidation as he began slowly walking backwards away from his approaching, well marinated wife.

"Oh, I'm *ripe* and *gross* now, am I?" Maddy stated through an evil little chuckle while wearing a playfully demented expression on her thirty-five-year-old face. "Well baby. We took a vow to share everything. And I mean *everything*. Through sickness and health. Through good times and bad times. 'Til death do us part. And since *that* shit's not happening, like ever, I have something to share with *you*."

"You wouldn't," Erick responded in a pitifully pleading tone. "C'mon. I just got that shit off of me. Maddy, I'm serious. Maddy, I'm *warning* you!

"Noooooo!" Erick cried out as his mischievous wife leapt upon him, covering him in her afterlife, after-birth. "This is fucking gross!" He kept crying out as his wife covered his face with gooey, smelly kisses.

"Oh, fuck it," he finally said with loving resignation. He took his disgustingly slimy wife into his arms, looked deeply into her emerald green eyes, wiped some thick mucus from her auburn bangs and gave her the most tender kiss in the history of the world.

Maddy and Erick emerged from their unnecessarily long shower wearing beaming smiles and white bath robes. As they entered the room, they heard applause from Rod, an exhausted Rosa, Arima, Marcus and Jessie. They then heard two familiar, yet creepy voices.

"Oh my, Uncle Erick and Aunt Maddy are back!" Adam stated with a giggling Rachel draped around him. "Yes, indeed!" Aaron added as Kayla tittered next to him. "Oh, how joyous! Now we will be able to play more games. Games that are even more fun than we have ever played before. Uncle Erick and Aunt Maddy are indeed back. Everything is coming to fruition just as we have seen, brother."

"Well," the snickering Kayla added. That's not the *only* thing that's *cumming* to fruition. Get it, boys?"

"No," is all that Adam said as he looked at his brother. "No, we do not get it," Aaron added. "Perhaps you will need to explain that to us."

"What the fuck is going on?" Maddy yelled out. "Did we fuck up the space-time continuum or some shit? How the *fuck* did *those two* ever get laid? Oh, fuck it. I'll deal with that shit later. C'mon, baby. There are only a few hours left of Josie's birthday and I want us to surprise her. I've got an idea that'll be *really* funny. Hey, are there any white sheets around here?"

"And that's where we've been for the last few days. We went through all kinds of shit just to surprise you before your birthday ended. Happy now, little miss thing? Now, I heard you give out assignments to the various teams. So, I'll ask again. What the fuck has been happening with you guys this past year?"

"And, *more* importantly," Erick added in a deep growl as his face began to twist into a sadistic glee. "When do *we* get to play?"

Chapter 77

Living Dead Girl

"Well Dad," Josie began with a sly grin upon her slightly befreckled seventeen-year-old face. "We've actually made a lot of progress this past year. Mom probably heard me hand out the assignments a year ago and heard me say that I wanted the world to be strewn with the bodies of these demonic fucks. And that is *just* what we've done. Each group is led by members of our inner circle, including one of our primary hit men. And the primary hit men lead a *group* of hit men…oh and women…we really need to change that title. Anyway, there are fifteen hit…um… *persons* in each group and there are seven primary hit men. Fuck. They really *are* all men. Another little tweak that I've gotta make. Anyway, that means we have one hundred and twelve hit…um…experts. No wait. *Assassination* experts. No wait. Assassination *technicians*! Yep, that's the term.

"So, each group had their assignments, and they went after the top people…well…they're not so much *people* as they are *demonic servants* of Vetis. Anyway, they went after some of the top ones that held influence over the weak-minded and the weak-willed. We really didn't go after any of the layperson members of their flock. They aren't demonic. They're just self-centered and stupid and self-serving. Most of them piss their pants, drop their stupid guns, and go running for the hills as soon as we or any type of resistance shows up.

"And it has been working. With each high-profile assassination, their ranks become increasingly splintered and have less conviction in their endeavors. We have assassinated hundreds of these motherfuckers and their followers are beginning to go back into their little racist, sexist, homophobic, transphobic closets. They're still little pricks. But they aren't *nearly* as dangerous as they were because they are fragmented and lack leadership. And since they have no original thoughts of their own, they are practically immobilized without some higher power telling them what to think and what to do.

"And we think that the higher power that was ultimately mobilizing these forces on the Earth were none other than the Pastor and my... *yech*! Grandmother. They seem to be the hand-picked servants of Vetis who have been charged with influencing and leading Vetis's puppets. They are the ones who have been whispering in their ears and giving them instructions."

"Wait just a fuckin' minute!" Maddy exclaimed. "Now it all makes sense! I remember the *one time* that I was in that dick Pastor's office. The time he was going to begin grooming me by raping me and shit. Before he came in, I was looking at his wall of pictures. Hundreds of pictures with him and some of the most influential business leaders, politicians, religious leaders, and radical right-wing media types. All smiling and shaking hands. And I remember thinking to myself, 'how is it that this fuckin' podunk preacher knows all these high-profile douchebags?' Then I felt his slithery fucking hands on my shoulders and all I could think about was getting the fuck out of there. And how much I hated my bitch mother. I haven't thought about that moment for years. It was just too creepy and painful. I had shut it out. Until now."

"Yes, Mom," Josie began again. "We think that you're right. And since those two haven't been around for some time, these *other* demonic servants have been pretty easy to pick off. One by one. A bomb here. A bullet through the brain there. Hundreds of them left lying in their own blood. Hundreds of shredded corpses to send a message. Hundreds of pretty pink roses left on their lifeless frames to send the message that Murder, Inc. is *not* fucking around!"

"Whoa!" Maddy yelled out. "You're still using your cool calling card? That's so cool sweetie."

"Yeah, it is pretty cool, I guess," Josie replied as her face slightly blushed, and she let out a light chuckle. "You can take the girl out of her hippie utopia, but you just can't take the hippie utopia completely out of the girl, I guess, *tee hee.*"

"Well," Erick chimed in with a sarcastic tone as he stared at Lionnel. "At least there's still *some* innocence left in our daughter."

Josie and Maddy stared at him silently and slowly shook their heads. Josie then let out a deep sigh and rolled her eyes before continuing.

"So, you can read all the reports of everybody our *Assassination Technicians*, heh, heh, heh-have taken out if you want. But let me just tell you about a few of the highlights."

"Okay, but before you do," Erick interjected. "Does that mean that we don't have anything to do? That it's all been taken care of? That we don't get to have any fun? Well fuck this! I didn't *die* then hold onto your bitch grandmother for a *fucking year* which nearly extinguished my soul then get *re-animated* just to hang out and twiddle my thumbs! I want some action *goddammit* and I want it *now!*"

"Jeezus," Maddy replied condescendingly while shaking her head at her beloved husband. "You are such a fucking baby sometimes. *Of course,* there's more to do, otherwise we wouldn't even *be* here. We'd be in Enlightenment hanging at one of Aunt Patty's cool parties. Remember what we were told? That we'd be called back to Earth when we were needed. It seemed to us that we were in Enlightenment for only a few days. But we were up there for nearly a year, Earth time. We've been called back at this point in time for a reason. Isn't that right, sweetie?"

"Yes, Mom. You are correct." Josie answered as Maddy looked at her husband with a haughty expression. "You *are* needed. What we have been told is that Vetis must conquer the Earth before he can engage in battle with Enlightenment. That his demonic anti-democracy forces will take over the Earth. They will then collect all their fallen dark souls and wage war against Enlightenment. That is what we have been told. But we have been wondering. What if that isn't *necessarily* the case? What if this Earthly war is nothing more than a ruse? What if conquering the Earth is nothing more than icing on the cake? That it isn't really that important? What if this Earthly battle is being waged not for domination of the Earth but to simply collect more and more dark souls for the *ultimate* goal of conquering Enlightenment? That his followers aren't the only ones that are pawns here. Maybe we are too.

We have sent a lot of evil fucks to their Earthly grave. And we have created a helluva lot of dark souls who are just hanging around waiting for their final marching orders. We now believe that is why you are here. We need to focus not just on getting rid of the Earthly threat but the threat in the afterlife as well. And we believe that the key to that is your union with Aunt Arima. That the two of you will be able to lead our forces against both the *living* and the *dead*. That the two of you can lead our forces to protect both the *Earth* and *Enlightenment*. From this point on, we need to focus on continuing to rid the Earth of the demonic pawns and then rid the cosmos of their dark souls for all eternity. Make sense?"

"Fuck, my heads hurts," Erick replied as he held his newly generated face in his hands. "I'm really sorry I asked. So, we kill their bodies then Maddy and Arima destroy their souls? Is that basically it?"

"Uh, yeah," Josie answered. "That's much more – um- simple. Yeah, that's basically it."

Arima's mellow voice then entered the conversation. "So, hey- um – like Niece Josie. So how is it that we're supposed to destroy all these dark souls? I mean, I can only do, like, one at a time. There's gotta be thousands of them."

"Yeah, there's the rub," Josie sheepishly responded. "We're not sure yet. We're working on it. It's like we need to create a huge dark soul vacuum or something that you can suck them into. Then we need something *really big* that you can send their souls into for their final destruction. We have Rod, Rosa and Lucy working on it. Oh. And speaking of Lucy, let me start telling you about the exploits of each group. Mom, as you may remember, Lucy and Sam were put in charge of taking out some of the top political leaders who were actually demonic pawns throughout the world. There have been so many at all levels of government. Local. State or Province or whatever. Federal. Most taken out by the Assassination Technicians under the leadership of Sam and Lucy. But there was *one* hit that stood out from the rest. Mom, you may want to put down that second sandwich. This is some twisted shit."

———

"This isn't just a hit," Sam lamented as Lucy assisted her in placing her fifty-two-year-old paralyzed legs into a pair of black faux leather slacks. "This is primarily a rescue mission."

"Yeah," Lucy replied, echoing Sam's subdued tone. "This is going to complicate things. It's so much easier to find out where a bunch of them are going to be congregating and plant a bomb or unleash one of my toxins. Just hit a button and watch their organs spill out. It's just so… hot. We don't have to worry about innocent bystanders in those situations. But this one is different. There are so many innocent people in this complex. And we're so isolated in this remote part of this Eastern European country. It won't be easy to get them out. And it won't be easy to get them two hundred miles to the airport where Jennifer is waiting with the plane. The hit men can take out the outside security. But how in the hell are we going to get in there? And how much security is on the inside? We need a better way to get in. We need someone on the inside. Any thoughts?"

"Yeah," Sam answered reservedly. "But I really don't like it. Here's my plan. And Lucy, just in case I don't make it, well, I love you."

The beautiful African American woman rolled her wheelchair into a neighborhood pub on the outskirts of the remote village. She feigned not understanding the language that was being spoken. She also feigned not understanding the meaning behind the guttural laughter of a small group of filthy men at a corner table.

The men approached her wearing broad smiles. Everyone in the bar looked away or down at their respective drinks. A rag was placed over her mouth. She breathed in deeply and allowed herself to succumb to the blackness.

Sam woke up and began coughing as a thick plume of smoke rolled from a large man's cigar and into her lungs. She lifted her head slightly to take note of her surroundings. She was in a small concrete cell with iron bars and still in her wheelchair. Most importantly, she was not bound. She looked up at the broad man who was wearing a devilish grin as he puffed away. He was well over six feet tall and nearly four feet wide. His thinning black hair was trimmed short, and he had stubble on his upper lip and chin. He was dressed in an all-black double-breasted suit. Sam looked down at her still legs and smiled. He was their primary target. He and the skinny white man who was standing next to him wearing a white coat.

He was an influential member of this country's Parliament. He was being groomed to be its next President. He was being groomed by Vetis.

To demonstrate his loyalty, ingenuity, and worthiness of being one of Vetis's hand-picked pawns he had begun experiments. Experiments to build the ultimate human fighting machines. To literally piece together an army made up of human parts of the highest quality. This had been done in fiction. It had never been accomplished in reality. Until now.

This wretched man and his more than willing scientist brother had succeeded in harvesting parts from multiple people and combining them to build the perfect fighting machine. They were so close to its completion. A fighting machine that could not feel pain. One with no feelings. One that was completely obedient to its overlord.

A fighting machine that was large. And fast. And strong. And…intelligent. A fighting machine that could process information. That could plan attacks. And counterattacks. A fighting machine that could travel with their orders and complete their mission anywhere in the world without being supervised. A fighting machine that, when completed, would be assigned to complete its first experimental mission in Brooklyn. Sam was aware of this. Rod had shown her the plans.

"Wh-what happened?" Sam asked as she tried to appear confused. "Where am I? I just got lost and was looking for directions to my hostel. What am I doing here?"

The large man laughed deeply then said in English with a thick accent, "You my dear are the final piece. The final piece of my most glorious puzzle. Do not fret, my dear. You won't be harmed…much. You will actually come to thank me as *you* are going to make history. You will be the first of your kind. The first of our super-soldiers.

"We have constructed the perfect fighting specimen. The heart and lungs of a former swimmer. The arms of a former weightlifter. The legs of a former gymnast. And so on. Why former, you might ask? Well, we take the parts from those who have been met with some… misfortune. Usually because of some accident. Usually, heh, heh, heh. They have become disabled. They are of no use to our world any longer. So, we have given them purpose. We have taken their beaten bodies and transformed them into something magnificent. Something that will aid our glorious Vetis in taking over this world. We have many of them here just waiting for their blessed transformation. Their blessed destiny.

"Yes, we have now created one. Our first. All that we need is…the right brain." The large man then looked at his quivering brother who stated, "I-I'm sorry. The jar just slipped, and I didn't think that the brain was damaged."

"Well, it was!" the large man roared back. "It *was* damaged! It too would have been the perfect brain. But now it is too damaged. Too unpredictable. Too emotional. But it has at least given us an opportunity to test some of our indoctrination techniques until we could find the right one. And you, my dear, are perfect. My men took you from the bar when they saw your damaged legs. They are to take anyone that we might be able to…harvest. But imagine our surprise and glee when we ran a scan of your brain. Your beautiful brain. So analytical. So unemotional. So compliant with rules. So transactional. It is perfect. *You* are perfect. So, let us celebrate! What would you like to dine on tonight, my special pet? You may have anything. For tomorrow, you will be dining in the greatest body that has ever been created. Then, we will begin your…conditioning, heh, heh, heh."

Sam looked up at the pompous man and said with a condescending arrogance, "Very well then. I will have vegetable lasagna. Not too much sauce and not runny. And *do not* use frozen vegetables. A small side salad with no cheese. Just greens and vegetables with a light vinaigrette dressing. And two slices of garlic toast. Lightly toasted. If they are too hard, then I'm sending the whole meal back and you can start over."

The large man stared at Sam's stoic face and burst into laughter. "Why yes indeed, princess! Coming right up! It's the least that we can do for our most honored guest!"

The pair left as Sam thought, *Well, that should keep them busy for a while. Let's start with the cameras.*

Sam reached under the right arm of her wheelchair, dislodged a small cover, and pressed a button. All the security cameras were still completely operational except that they were now frozen on a static image. Anyone who was not paying close attention would never notice the lack of movement from behind the multiple iron-barred doors. Or on the outside of the complex.

Lucy's transmitter began flashing green and she flashed a devilish smile to the nearest hitman. There was a nod of understanding followed by sixteen soft pops from the surrounding forest. Lucy and her sixteen partners exited the brush and quickly traversed the perimeter of the small concrete complex to ensure there were no survivors. There were none. Just ten men lying in their own blood and brains with bullet holes displayed perfectly between their eyes.

Sam took three small metal picks from inside of the left arm of the wheelchair. Reaching between the bars and with a slight flick of her wrist, her door swung open with a rusty creak.

She wheeled herself into the aisle with her toned and powerful arms. She looked around at the other nine cages with desperate eyes peering back at her. She looked to the back of the room and saw metal tables that were covered in bloody surgical tools. Beneath the tables were rusty metal bins that contained various body parts from the innocent victims. Sam wheeled her chair in a full circle and took in the entirety of this travesty. Her mind was immediately triggered back to her time, not so long ago, when she was brutally beaten and raped by men exactly like these. She looked down upon her shapely but immovable legs. And she wept.

Her tears of rage flowed down her caramel cheeks as she began barking orders. "Okay everybody. Listen up! If you want to get out of here alive, just listen to me. If you are able to fight, then join me in getting some weapons. If you aren't able to fight for any reason, just stay in your cell until I come and get you. And I would appreciate it if you would keep the profanity to a minimum. Everybody understand?"

"Oh, we understand," a middle eastern man with removed arms answered from a dark corner of his cell. "We understand *completely*. And we most *definitely* are going to fight."

As each metal door swung open, its occupant walked, limped, or wheeled themselves to the back table where they retrieved any weapon they could find. Three of the downtrodden had no arms. They were placed upon the lap of three people in wheelchairs and held long knives between their feet. The other three had disfigured features but full bodies. They picked up saws and cleavers and waited anxiously beside the heavy metal door.

Sam approached the door with a mixture of trepidation and fury.

She placed the picks into the locks and turned her wrist. There was a slight *click*.

The red lights and sirens that began blaring upon the door being swung open were quickly joined by screams of anguish as Sam launched four-inch metal projectiles from the arms of her wheelchair into the reacting guards. The three full-bodied persons launched themselves into the hallway and began hacking and slicing at anything that was approximately their height. The other three wheelchairs shot themselves down the hallway where their passengers planted the long knives into fleshy abdomens.

From behind the carnage there were light 'popping' sounds and little red dots. One of the red dots rested upon Sam's forehead.

"The Calvary's here," Lucy stated flatly as she surveyed the bloodbath that laid beneath their feet. Twelve sadistic men were lying on the concrete floor. Their blood was oozing from their skewered bodies. Only three had been killed by a gunshot. The rest had been disposed of in a gloriously messy fashion by those who had been called 'worthless.'

"Wow," Lucy stated with admiration. "Nice work. Remind me to never park in a handicapped spot again."

"Yeah, that's not really the term anymore," Sam admonished just before there was the booming sound of repeated banging from behind a large metal door to their left.

As Sam approached the door and took out her picks, a female in a wheelchair said, "Um. I don't know if you want to open that. She's… um…she's not very friendly."

The warning had come too late. The lock clicked open, and Sam was knocked backwards by the force of the swinging metal door.

"Who or *what* is that?" one of the hitmen yelled out.

Standing in the doorway was a six-foot-seven-inch behemoth. Her muscular arms clung to her toned torso that presented large perfectly shaped bosoms. Her front presented an equally impressive male member that dangled between a pair of impossibly muscled legs. Her stitched frame slowly approached, and the entire group was greeted by a beautiful, feminine face that was encased in platinum blonde shoulder-length hair. She smiled with a demure rage and said in a soft, childlike voice, "So where are they? You know. That politician and his twisted fucking brother. Where are they?"

"You mean these two?" One of the hitmen answered as he led the large man and his scientist brother into the hallway.

"Hey, hey, now," the large man began stammering. "P-please. You want money? I have lots of money. Jewels? Anything that you want. A-and, oh! Your lasagna is just about done miss! Just how you ordered it!"

The powerful transexual stood menacingly over the quivering pair. She flashed a devilish grin and said in a breathy, Monroe-esque voice, "No. We don't need anything from you. We are just going to take your lives. Just like you took ours. The torture you put us all through. And we're the lucky ones. So many didn't make it. So many who didn't live to see our revenge against you. You called us worthless. Because we didn't look like you. We didn't have the same body parts as you. You thought us to be weak. But we're not. We are strong. Stronger than you, in fact. We have been made strong because we have had to put up with the painful glances in our direction and the discrimination. The pitiful looks on others' faces as they look at our missing limbs. We are just people. We are not experiments. We are not objects of ridicule. And we are *not* objects of pity. We are just people. *You* are the ones that are worthless. *You* are the ones that oppress us. Belittle us. Use us. We are *not* freaks. *You* are the freaks. Anyone who abuses others for their own gain is a freak. A completely worthless freak. But maybe I can do you both a favor. Let me show you how it feels to be us. Let me free you from your freakishness."

The giant transexual reached down and grasped the large man's arms. He screamed in agony as she strained and pulled at the immobilized appendages. There was a loud 'pop' followed by two geysers of blood as the man's arms were ripped from his body. He collapsed upon the floor whimpering as he bled out.

She then picked up the skinny scientist and cracked his back over her steely knee. She tossed him onto the concrete floor with a thud. She smiled at him as though she were posing on a red carpet. She watched his lips tremble as he tried to move his paralyzed appendages with futility. She blew him a kiss then crushed his face and skull with her size sixteen foot.

"Ew," she said softly as she tried to shake the blood, skull fragments and brain matter from her right foot. "So. Does anyone have a cigarette? And maybe some tequila? I'm just *dying* for a drink right now. Oh, and you can call me...*Dragenstein*. And I am the transphobes *worst fucking nightmare.*"

———

"What the fuck!" Maddy cried out in dismay as Arima and Marcus sat on the couch giggling at the scene. "Are you telling me that we have a fucking Amazonian *Drag Queen* on our team? Really? Where the fuck is she? I gotta meet this bitch!"

"Uh, yeah," Josie replied nonchalantly. "She's on our team. I don't know where she's at tonight. She might be performing. She's really popular at this little place in Soho. Anywhooo, so that's *that* story. Now Jerry and Jules and *their* team had quite a different experience."

Chapter 78

Moneytalks

"Lucyfur! There you are!" Jessie exclaimed as she entered Rod's electronic lair. "C'mon, baby. It's time for your nummy-num-nums. I have fresh blood from a fascist for you!"

Lucyfur looked up from her comfortable perch on Jules's lap and looked up at her with slight confusion in her green eyes.

"Yeah, it's okay," Jules responded dryly to her feline companion. "Go get your nummy-oh Jesus Christ I can't say that. Go get your meal."

Lucyfur got up, stretched, and let out a soft mew of understanding before jumping from Jules's lap and making her way over to the welcoming Jessie.

Jessie picked the grey and white furball up and flashed her a broad smile. She then turned around and glared at Jules. "Hey! Bitch! Don't be stealing my cat!"

Jerry and Rod immediately looked away from the scene and toward the computer screen that was between the trio. This was not a confrontation that either of them had a desire to participate in.

"Yeah," Jules replied in a dismissive tone. "A couple of things here. For starters, LucyFur isn't *your* cat. She isn't *anybody's* cat. Cats aren't owned by *anybody*. They exist for their own pleasure and are dismissive of anyone and anything that does not bring them that pleasure. Or entertainment. Or food. When they want to eat, they'll find someone to feed them. When they want to fuck, then they'll find a temporary mate. There are no feelings. No emotional connection. Unless it serves their purpose. They love those that *they* choose, and they love them on their *own* terms. LucyFur loves you. And she loves Arima. And she loves me. You don't have anything to worry about. Well, from her. But if you ever call me a 'bitch' again, I will rip out your fucking throat with a fork. Or have you *not* heard the story about Maddy's hand? And just like LucyFur and all other cats, I won't feel a fucking thing for you. You got that... bitch?"

Jessie stared into Jules's eyes, which glowed with a detached intensity. Realizing that this was a battle that was best left alone, she gulped and said meekly, "Okay. Listen. I'm sorry. I shouldn't have said that. We're all on the same team, right? Friends?"

Jules gazed at her with disinterest and replied, "Yeah, whatever. I forgive you, I guess. Now leave us alone. We've got work to do. Okay Rod, what have you found for us?"

"Well," Rod began in his staccato, nasal voice as he began typing on his keyboard. "You wanted to find a gathering of multiple influential business leaders that are, in fact, earthly servants of Vetis. You wanted the worst of the worst. I believe that I may have found them."

He clicked his mouse and the image of two brothers popped up on the screen. They displayed broad, arrogant smiles and were wearing generic hunting garb, complete with matching cute little gun and ammo purses. They were two of the children of Vetis's failed hope to overthrow America's democracy. But although their father turned out to be a failure at everything that he touched, the brothers were still able to indoctrinate his gullible followers into believing that he was a prophet sent directly from God. And that they, in turn, were conceived to continue their dullard father's work to rid the world of the "unholy" democracies and replace them with "holy" and "patriotic" dictatorial autocracies that placed White Christians in dominion. All for a price, of course.

"I found this on the darkest site on the web. It is quite hard to find and quite expensive to join," Rod began explaining as he peered at the brothers' image through his pop-bottle lenses. "Only the wealthiest can join this site that peddles the most horrific lies and propaganda. And, of course, only the wealthiest would even have access to it since there is no wireless internet. Most people are still blocked from the web and only a few have the equipment to access it. It costs $50,000 a month to belong. It costs even more for what these two are offering."

Rod clicked 'play' and the image began to move. The brothers' sleezy smiles became broader before the dark haired one said gleefully, "Greetings fellow patriots! As you know, our great father was on a lifelong mission to rid the world of the scum of this Earth. The Non-believers. The N*****s. The K**kes. The Sp***s. The G**ks. The Fa*s. His glorious policies were working until the damned libs intervened and *sacrificed* our father at their unholy altar of 'wokeness.' They say that what they want is to promote understanding and acceptance. But that is a socialist lie. What they *actually* are doing is denying *you* your rightful place of dominion over our Earth. Denying *you* your God-given *right* to harvest Earth's bounty without government intervention. Denying *you* your God-given *right* to use the scum as your laborers. Denying *you* your God-given *right* to reap your entitled rewards of money and fame and women as has been pre-ordained. *They* have denied *you* your God-given right to own whatever it is that you want to own whether that's jewels or property or...people."

The lighter-haired brother then spoke with a noticeable slur of intoxication. "That's right brother! And now we are offering *you* the chance to join our battle to reclaim this Earth in a more exciting way than your corporate influence. You can now own a part of this movement! For the low, low price of *One-hundred-million-dollars* you have the opportunity to join us on a once in a lifetime experience. You have the opportunity to join us at our undisclosed private big game hunting grounds. We have rounded up some of the most prominent libs from around the country. We have stripped them naked and sent them out into the woods. The entire complex is surrounded by armed guards and electric fencing. They cannot escape. They cannot escape being hunted. They cannot escape being hunted by *you*. That's right fellow patriots! Join us on July 4! Join us so that you can now literally *Own the Libs*!"

The beaming dark-haired brother then concluded with, "Yes! You can now own your *very own* lib trophy. You think your friends are impressed by that elephant tusk or lion's head hanging from the wall of your den? Just imagine how impressed they will be when they see the head of a lib politician or clergy or industry leader hanging prominently in the middle of your showcase. And, as an added bonus, we will include a complete mounting and lighting kit that will allow your servant to hang your prized trophy upon your wall with ease! So, join us for this once in a lifetime event, won't you? Join us in *Owning the Libs!*"

Jerry wiped a tear from his eye with his tattooed and brawny right hand before saying, "Yeah. This is perfect. But how the hell are we supposed to get in there? I'm sure our hit-squad can take out the guards around the complex, but we still need to get inside. How the hell are we gonna break in? How the hell are we gonna do *that*?

"Oh, that is quite easy," Rod answered as his gaze rested unfortunately upon Jerry's chest. "You won't be breaking in. You both will be participants in the hunting party."

"C'mon, Rod," Jules dismissively countered. "I know Murder, Inc. is rich as fuck but we're talking two-hundred-million-dollars! Plus, the fee to join this twisted website. It won't work. We need to find another way."

Rod let out a slight and uncharacteristic snort before answering. "You have already joined the website. For the past two months, both of you have paid your dues. And I have constructed the perfect identities for you both so that you will be above suspicion. And, as far as the two-hundred-million-dollars goes…"

A delighted cackle came from a dark corner of the room before an enthusiastic voice proclaimed, "That's where *I* come in bitches! *I'm* going to bankroll this little adventure and *I'm* going to join you. I think that you will need all the luck you can get. Oh sure, they don't like my kind *either*, but money talks! I'm a member of this site too already. So, strap yourself in because on July 4 you're going hunting with Kaneko!"

"And one other thing," Rod added. "Once you have…um…eliminated the businessmen, you will need to be careful to navigate around the big cats that they have there. They have two lions, two tigers, two panthers and two cougars that they keep as living trophies. They have been hardly feeding them so that they are quite hungry and can be released if there is any trouble. You need to be mindful of that."

"Big *cats*, you say?" Jules replied with a sly smile. "Well, let's get the hit squad together then and start making our plans. And Rod, I think you miscounted."

"What is it that you mean, Jules?" a perplexed Rod inquired.

"There's about to be *three* cougars in that fucking place," Jules answered through a malicious grin.

———

"I look fucking ridiculous," Jerry whispered to his wife as he looked at himself in the mirror wearing his khaki hunting outfit.

Jules rolled her mahogany eyes and shook her brown curly mop as she slid her taught middle-aged frame out of her jeans. As the seven other male hunters ogled her female form, they did not notice the ignored figure of Kaneko floating around the room and dropping small acid pellets into the barrels of their guns, rendering them useless.

Jules tersely replied to her husband, "Just be cool. It'll look much better once it's covered with the blood of these rich fucks and...oh! Hey! Nice to meet you!"

"Yeah, nice to meet you too!" the bulbous gun manufacturer stated through an enthusiastic grin. "I'm just going around introducing myself and inviting everyone to a little post-hunt party I'm throwing at my resort. It's just twenty miles away outside of Little Rock. We're going to have some great laughs talking about our hunt today. A few drinks. A few jokes. Maybe a little...strip poker?"

Jules fought the urge to rip the lascivious man's throat out as she watched his eyes traverse her body and wipe drool from his mouth. Luckily, she was saved from another voice.

"Poker, you say? Well, I'm a bit of a novice, but what the hell? If I can afford to own a lib, I sure as hell can afford a new pair of panties!" Kaneko stated as she slapped the man's back-fat then fat ass.

"Uh, sure, maybe," the man replied as he calculated his next move to get into Jules's pants. "Hey, listen you three. There's a little catch to all of this. There's ten of us on this hunting trip but only nine libs. One of us is going home empty-handed. So, just stick with me, alright sweetheart? I've paid extra to find out where the libs have been hiding in the trees. Don't worry about it. Just stick with me and I'll get you your head. And that way, I'm pretty sure to get a little head *too*, huh sweetie?"

As luck would have it, a voice came over the intercom before an enraged Jerry could react. "Welcome everybody! My brother and I hope that you all have a wonderfully patriotic time today! Now, we put some tampered food out last night, so if your prey ate it, they should be really slow and easy to sneak up on. Hey! We're sportsmen after all, right? Some of you more than others. I see that some of you are choosing to use knives and swords and shit instead of guns. Cool with us. Whatever gets you off. It's your money. And there are nine of those lib assholes lurking somewhere in the woods. So just one head per hunter, understand? Don't be greedy. Or do! That's what this shit is all about! And if you do *not* get a trophy today, don't worry about it. You will be comped to an hour with one of our slave concubines. Believe me, these women will *not* disappoint you. And if they do, well, then just kill them and take *her* head home. No extra charge! Alright everybody. Get ready! Get Set! Go own those fucking libs!"

A large metal garage door on the side of the dressing room lifted to reveal a small pasture that was surrounded by dense forest. The brothers sat on golden thrones on a golden stage as gold-bikini clad young women brought them drinks and fed them grapes. They laughed with sadistic glee as they watched one-billion dollars' worth of "hunters" fan out with their guns and ridiculous matching costumes.

"This way!" the bulbous man yelled out to Jules and her companions. They entered the dense forest and cautiously walked twenty yards before the man held his hand up signaling them to stop. "There's one now. Up in that tree. Now everybody just be quiet. We wouldn't want our little snowflake to melt away now." He lifted his gun and put his right eye up to the telescopic gunsight.

He then silently fell into the brush. His gun was attached to his face by a metal rod that had been thrust through the sight, into his right eye and out the back of his head.

"That wasn't enough," Jules dryly stated.

"Enough for what," the slightly calming Jerry asked.

"Enough blood to make that silly fucking outfit look cool." Jules answered. "C'mon. One down, eight to go. You know what to do."

Kaneko looked up at the shivering figure hiding in the tree and said, "Go to the west gate. Tell any of the others to do the same. The outside guards and electric fence have been taken care of. There will be men and women in black suits waiting behind a hole in the fence. They will take you to safety. Now go."

Jerry ran frantically back into the pasture, flailing his arms. "What the hell are you two pulling here?" he screamed at the two confused brothers. "The quarry! They're fucking armed! Call the hunters back now! We have to get out of here!"

The shocked dark-haired brother held the microphone up to his mouth and announced, "Uh, listen up everybody! There's some sort of an...um...issue. Just come back to the pasture so that we can work it out. We'll get this shit straight then continue the hunt."

From inside the dense woods Jules could hear voices exclaiming, "Goddamit!"

"I knew that this was too good to be true!"

"Fuckups, just like their father!"

"Hey! My gun's jammed!"

"What should we have expected from a couple of con men?"

"Those bitch slave girls *better* be real!"

"I'm gonna have *someone's* head on my wall tonight! And I don't care whose!"

Jules could also hear scurrying feet from behind her heading towards the west gate. As soon as she heard a voice, Jules crept toward that area of the woods and hid behind a tree. She heard a "hunter" approach. As the disappointed body passed by her with his gun slumping at his side, she wrapped serrated razor wire around his throat and began sawing. She was showered with the blood that was spewing from the gurgling man's throat as she continued her frantic motion. She grunted one last time until the severed head dropped pathetically into the lush shrubbery.

The next one received a hatchet to the forehead the moment she jumped out in front of him. Then a knife to a man's temple. Then a machete was buried in the back of another man's head. Ten people went into the woods. Only five re-entered the pasture.

A blood-soaked Jules strode into the pasture and joined Jerry, Kaneko and the final two hunters.

"How do I look?" Jules asked her husband as blood dripped off her petite nose.

"You never looked better, baby. Damn, I love you," Jerry replied reverentially.

"Don't get all mushy and shit," Jules answered as her blushing face was concealed under coagulating blood. "Take care of these other two. My arms are tired."

As the brothers descended their golden staircase they were yelling, "Okay. What the hell is going on? What do you mean they're armed? That's impossible! Why is she covered with blood? Where are the rest of the hunters?"

"The same place as these two," Jerry replied sinisterly as he stood behind the confused final two "sportsmen." "In fucking hell!" Jerry unsheathed his broadsword and decapitated the two men with one furious swing. He continued to stand directly behind the men's torsos that were spraying blood into the air and upon his strapping frame. He smiled contently as he realized that his khaki hunting costume finally looked cool.

The brothers let out a panicked squeal and turned to make their retreat. They were blocked by twelve scantily clad young women. They grabbed the shrieking brothers by their arms and forced them to their knees.

"Thanks for the assist, ladies," Jules stated as she looked at the caged pairs of majestic cats looking at her with pleading eyes. She walked up to the large confinement and said something quietly to them before turning the lock.

The noble creatures sprang from their cage and immediately pounced upon the cowardly, piss-stained brothers. Their legs, arms and torsos were being ripped apart by gnashing teeth and flying claws as the brothers begged for their daddy. Their pathetic whimpering finally ceased while the mammoth cats continued to chew upon their intestines.

"What did you say to them?" an intrigued Jerry asked of his beloved wife.

Jules responded coldly, "I told them to leave their heads for me."

———

"Okay, a few questions here sweetie," Erick asked his daughter once she had concluded her tale. "Firstly, did Jules and Jerry keep their outfits? If so, did they launder them? And if so, how did they get the blood stains out? I have always had a helluva time getting blood stains out of my clothes, so if they've stumbled on a good detergent, I'd really like to know."

Maddy looked at her husband in shocked disbelief before roaring, "*That's* your brilliant fucking question? *That's* the first thing that popped into your head? *That's* what you took from this story? Seriously, man. What the fuck is *wrong* with you?"

"Yes," a defiant Erick yelled back. "That is *exactly* what popped into my head. You know that I'm the one who does *all* of the laundry around here and if we're going to war then there's going to be a lot of it! So, yes! I am looking for a detergent that is *really good* with blood stains! What's wrong with *that*? What brilliant question do *you* have?"

A dismayed Maddy responded as she tried to calm herself, "Well. How about if we ask about Jules who can now *apparently* talk to animals or some shit. Might *that* be of interest to you?"

"Yeah, I guess," Erick replied with a hint of an attitude. "But it doesn't do anything to help me with my laundry problem."

An unblinking Maddy could only stare at her husband with a look of dismay as Josie re-entered the discussion.

"Wow. You guys really haven't changed a bit, have you? And to answer your questions, I do not know Dad about the status of their outfits. And I do not know of any better detergents. And Mom, Jules can't talk to just any animal. She can only communicate with cats. She has the same detached 'fuck you' attitude that they do, I guess. Oh, but she brought them all back and they are now living on our estate with Stellan and Paciano. And we have built a climate-controlled barn that they can go into if they get too hot or cold. And my other cats and dogs just adore them, because no predator, human or otherwise, *dares* to set foot on our land with *them* lurking about. We now call the estate the Cool Cat Club. Isn't that great?"

"Uh, no," Maddy answered. "That *isn't* fucking great. How the fuck are we supposed to visit our own home with giant fucking cats waiting to eat us?"

"That's not a problem, Mom," Josie replied through her light chuckles. "Lucy has developed a perfume that is made of Jules's scent. Just a spritz behind the ears and those lovely animals will leave you alone."

"No, they don't!" Lionnel bellowed out. "They *do not* leave you alone!

They jump on you and lick you all over your face! Or rub up against you and knock you over! Those cats are a *real* pain in the ass!"

"Yeah?" Josie replied to her boyfriend with a cocked head. "Well, they weren't so much of a pain in the ass when we fed those radical religious fucks to them now were they? Oh! That reminds me of my next story. So, Henri and Jamie were tasked to head up a group to take down demonic religious leaders. Little did we know that we'd need to get Pastor Tim involved in this one. But before I tell that one, come to the basement. I have something to show you."

Josie led her family down the basement stairs and flicked on the light. The jaws of Maddy, Erick, Lionnel, Arima, and Marcus dropped as they saw the severed heads of the traitorous brothers mounted on the wall, bathing in a white-hot spotlight.

Josie stood triumphantly in front of the pitiable faces that were frozen in the moment that they had let out their final high-pitched squeal. She firmly placed her hands on her pajama-adorned hips, flashed a devilish grin and shouted out, "As the saying goes, two heads are better than one! Hey, get it? Why isn't anybody laughing?"

"Shit, that really *isn't* very funny, is it?" Maddy whispered to her exasperated husband who was holding his head in his hands.

Chapter 79
Dear God

"Henri, do you think that there is a God?" Jamie inquired of her friend and teammate as she applied dark blue eyeshadow on her eyelids. She looked at herself in the mirror as she awaited his answer. It had been many years since her reflection cast the image of James Johnson. In his place was now Jamie Johnson, an attractive African American transexual whose full afro was reminiscent of female activists from the Black Panther movement in the 1970's. Her full bosom was draped in a black and blue flowered gown that rested just above her knees to conceal the one remaining part of the time when she was known as 'James.' She gazed upon the colors in her gown and was briefly transported back to the evening when her father made her skin as black and blue as her elegant gown. Ever since that brutally tragic night, she had wondered why a benevolent God would make her the way that she was. Why would a benevolent God trap her feminine spirit in the prison of a male's body. Why would this God make someone in a way that made them the subject of harassment, ridicule, discrimination, and merciless beatings. Beatings from classmates, hooligans, and her very own father. Was this truly some form of spiritual or intelligent design? Or was it simply biological happenstance.

"Well, I honestly don't know," Henri replied in his thick Cameroonian accent. "I would like to think that there is a God. I have seen so much pure evil in this world. The beatings. The rapes. The oppression. The murders, including that of my beautiful first wife, Abana."

Henri wiped a tear away with the rag that he was using to clean his sniper's rifle before continuing. "But I have also seen absolute goodness as well. I have witnessed miracles. I truly have. My Sam's being able to survive the brutality that she was subjected to. I believe that to be a miracle. My son, Lionnel. To me, he is *my* miracle. The powers that so many women possess and are beginning to tap into. Your best friend Arima. Rosa. Now Jules. Those, to me, are miracles. And the way that people have banded together over these past two decades to beat back these forces of evil. That, too, I believe to be a miracle. I think that there is a never-ending battle between pure good and pure evil. We understand that better than ever now. We now know that there are demons in our midst. We are battling the forces of one right now. And if there are demons, there must be a Satan, right? And if there are demons, then there must be angels to serve as a counterbalance. And if there are angels, then there must be a God, right?

"That is what I think, anyway. I do not know if God and Satan are individual beings that hold dominion over their respective planes of existence or whether they are the combination of souls that creates a good or evil movement and leads each of us on our respective paths. Every time that we make the decision to act in a way that is purely self-serving, are we feeding into the entity commonly known as Satan? And every time that we act in a way that is selfless, are we not contributing to the power of God?

"That is *my* faith, anyway. We know there is pure evil, so therefore there must be *something* that is Satanic. And if there is pure evil, then I believe that there must be pure good as well. And that pure good is God-like. But what I pray that I am wrong about today is how the demons project their own greedy and sometimes sadistic deeds upon those that are unlike them. They have been doing that for decades. If there is something that they, themselves, are guilty of, then they project those sins upon others in order to further divide people and stoke hatred. There are many examples of this.

"They rail against the "socialist takers" and "welfare queens" while taking government money for themselves. But when the government gives *them* money, they are entitled to it. When it is given to someone else, they are accused of being takers. They yell about us 'cancelling' things that we disapprove of. They then 'cancel' everything from movies to candy to cereal to amusement parks. Hell, they even cancel types of beer. They have spoken for decades about being the victims of the liberal "deep state," when it was in fact *their* leader who tried to install subservient dullards into positions of power at all levels of government in order to turn our country into a dictatorship. They were correct. There *was* the beginning of a deep state. But it was a deep state that *they themselves* were creating. And are still trying to.

"But this is one projection that I pray is not happening. All of their other projections carry at least some truth to them. There *are* people who take advantage of government programs. There *are* people who overreact to a joke or use of the wrong pronoun and try to 'cancel' the offender. To humiliate them. To shame them. To ruin their careers and livelihoods. All for a joke that was not intended to harm and did not age well. But there is *nobody* that we would embrace who are doing what the most extreme of their voices say that we are doing. There is *nobody* that is sacrificing infants and drinking their blood. And I pray that *they* aren't either. But I won't be surprised. They are pure evil, after all."

The pair left their room and strode down the hallway of their Boston hotel. They knocked upon the door. They waited a few moments then saw the door open slightly to reveal a mahogany eye peering out from behind the security chain. The chain was unlocked, and the door was opened.

"Hello, my friends," Jeremy stated as he welcomed Henri and Jamie into the room. "He is almost ready."

Sitting cross-legged on the king-sized bed wearing a black suit was Pastor Tim. He was in a trance-like state and chanting something in Latin while clutching onto children's squirt guns. He was surrounded on the bed by various Holy texts of every major religion. His chanting stopped and he opened his blue eyes. He smiled upon his friends and said, "Well, I've done what I can do. I've never blessed this much before. Nor have I done it in so many languages and using so many religious philosophies. If this works, then we may have found a way to rid both the Earth and Enlightenment of these dark souls for all of eternity. And, if not, well- then I guess it's back to the drawing board."

Henri and Jamie wore long overcoats that swayed with each step as they entered the grand marble church. They looked up in awe at the prism of color that was being generated by the sunlight beaming through the priceless stained-glass windows. A member of the clergy entered the room and dark clouds immediately blotted out the sun. The room's vibrant colors were replaced by somber, grey shadows.

"Huh," Jamie whispered into Henri's ear. "Well, I don't know if that's a *good* sign or a *bad* sign."

Henri replied, "It is a *very* bad sign. And it is a sign that we are in the right place."

"Hello, my children," the clergyman began with an assumed kindness. "How may we be of service to you today?"

The pair looked upon the man's serpentine smile and knew that they had found their target. Ever since this clergyman's arrival, multiple infants had been reported taken from hospitals and from their warm cribs in their homes. Anguished parents feverishly made pleas to the local authorities and to the public for assistance in finding their precious children. Flyers were posted and phone banks were created. None of their efforts were fruitful in stopping the frantic parents' endless tears.

Rod had done an analysis comparing the arrival of new residents to the Boston neighborhood to the times and proximity of the disappearances. Once he had identified a prime suspect, Jessie was brought in to look at his image. Jessie did not even have to be in the vile man's presence to use her Beholding ability. "Yeah, that's him. I can feel his evil just by looking at his picture. Tell Jamie and Henri that we've found him. And tell them to be careful. He's powerful. I pray that I'm wrong about what the source of his power might be."

Jamie smiled demurely at the clergyman and said, "Yes, hello. I am Jamie and this is my handsome fiancé Henri. We are looking for the *perfect* church to hold our ceremony and the *perfect* clergyman to help us prepare for the day that we take our vows. Would you be interested?"

The pale clergyman licked his lips slightly as he looked upon the dark complexions of his guests. He was also momentarily fixated by the size of Jamie's adam's apple before he responded. "Why yes, we would *love* to serve as your gateway to eternal happiness. And I would be *honored* to be your personal spiritual guide as you walk together into heavenly marital bliss. Please, come to my office, won't you?"

The three entered the clergyman's plush office. Jamie looked around the room at the various pictures on the wall. One in particular sent a chill down her spine.

"That picture, there," she whispered to Henri. "That is the Pastor. That is Arima's demonic father."

Henri gave her a nod of understanding before being struck on the back of the head. When Henri and Jamie woke up in their chairs, they saw two men standing over their bound bodies with the smiling clergyman between them.

"Well, *that* wasn't so bad, now, was it?" the clergyman began arrogantly. "You've only been out for about ten minutes. And I am *so sorry* to inform you that you *will not* be able to be married in this church, or *anywhere*, for that matter. You see, we do not perform services for…*your* kind. You are both *definitely* the wrong color and *you*," his voice trailed off as he glared at Jamie. "Well, I'm not really sure *what* you are. So, we will be unable to perform your blasphemous ceremony. Oh, but we *can* perform experiments upon you. Yes, yes. That is something that we are *quite* fond of."

He then took two items from behind his back and said, "I really don't understand why you were concealing these toys under your coats. I shot them both onto a chair. It is nothing but water. Perhaps you were trying to intimidate me in some way, hmmmm? Regardless, let me tell you about my experiments. I think that you both will find it fascinating.

"The Pastor told me long ago that in order to get into the good graces of our glorious Vetis, that I must find ways to enhance myself. To enhance my influence over others. To enhance my power. And I believe that I may have found the perfect thing. And it is so wonderfully simple. Blood. Human blood. There is a vibrancy to human blood that, once ingested can enhance our-let's just say *darker* side, shall we? Yes, by drinking the blood of innocents I have been able to be more powerful. More convincing. My flock has grown tremendously since I began this practice. Some of the blood, as you will both soon find out, comes from relatively innocent adults. That is how it began a few months ago. But then I started wondering. What blood would be the *most* innocent? What blood would be the *most* powerful? What blood would offer me the best opportunity to sit at the side of the Pastor and of our glorious Vetis? Yes, you may have already guessed. The blood of infants. They are so unsullied by the world. Unjaded. Innocent. Pure. And, I might add, *quite* delicious, heh, heh, heh. Since I have been consuming the blood of infants, I have felt my power grow exponentially! They are now my main source of nutrition! But that doesn't mean that I can't be a bit *naughty* and have a little snack between meals, now does it?" he concluded as a slight trail of drool leaked from between his slithery lips.

"That's it! I've heard enough!" Henri yelled out as two thin, red laser beams came from outside of the office window. They rested upon the foreheads of the two guards. Then, the guards' brains rested upon the face and suit of the clergyman.

The office door opened, and two more Assassination Technicians entered the room with their guns drawn and pointed directly at the clergyman. Henri and Jamie were unbound, and they retrieved their squirt guns from off the desk.

"Take us to where you do your "experiments," Jamie commanded to the shivering clergyman. He stood there staring at the foursome in disbelief as blood, brain and skull fragments dripped slovenly off his face.

"Take us now, you sick fuck!" Henri ordered before grabbing the clergyman by the arm and marching him out of the room.

They went toward the back of the bastardized church. The pleading clergyman pulled a secret lever on a mantle. A door ominously creaked open. Henri roughly shoved the clergyman in front of him and commanded that he lead the way. Halfway down the ancient, winding stone staircase, Henri and Jamie could hear the sounds of men and women gagging and vomiting. They knew that it was the sounds of their associates who had used another secret entrance that Rod had located by analyzing blueprints that were centuries old. And they knew that any remaining guards had been taken care of.

Another of the Assassination Technicians came running up the staircase to greet Jamie and Henri. "Stop," the black-clad ninja-esque woman stated pleadingly through her black mask. "Please, just stop. We are highly trained. We are highly trained and have been desensitized to be able to confront *anything*. But *nothing* that we have encountered could have prepared us for…for…" The assassin's sentence was cut off as she lifted her black mask and vomited all over the face of the clergyman.

"No, we must see," Henri responded with pain and trepidation as they continued to descend the staircase. "We must confront this evil before we pass judgment onto…" Henri would never be able to cleanse his memory of the image that he had allowed himself just a glimpse of before the entire party turned their backs in disgust on the grisly scene.

"Back upstairs, now!" Jamie commanded. Henri shoved the clergyman repeatedly up the stairs and down the hall until they were once again in his office.

"Strap this motherfucker down!" Henri ordered as he began circling the pathetic clergyman. "Yes, you are correct. Blood is our lifeforce. And your demonic kind are correct when you preach about protecting innocent children. They deserve to live a childhood that is safe and innocent. But you are *wrong* about what they need to be protected *from*! They do *not* need to be protected from understanding who they truly are! They do *not* need to be protected from age-appropriate books! They do *not* need to be protected from beautiful drag queens who read to them! They do *not* need to be protected from learning their actual history and actual heritage!

"No! They *don't* need protection from *any* of that! What they *do* need to be protected from is being indoctrinated into hating others that don't look or love or worship like them! What they *do* need to be protected from is *bigots* who try to whitewash their education! What they *do* need to be protected from is the scourge of gun violence! What they *do* need to be protected from is autocratic tyrants who will strip away their rights! And what they *do* need protection from are monsters like you! Oh, you may take this shit to a *whole new*, twisted level, but there are *so* many more of you out there. Pathetic little worms who have no self esteem who abuse and rape and murder children just for their own feelings of power. It is pathetic. *You* are pathetic. I cannot give those poor babies their blood or lives back, but I sure as hell can take it from *you*!"

Jamie then twisted two knobs on an electric pump that began humming slightly. The bound clergyman was frantically trying to free himself from his bindings as he watched his crimson life force move down the four plastic tubes that had been inserted into veins in his arms and legs. He screamed in agony as he could feel himself weakening from the loss of blood. Once the blood reached the end of the plastic tubing it was sprayed throughout the room by attached lawn sprinklers.

Jamie and Henri's blood-soaked faces looked on with maniacal glee as the repugnant man began meekly gasping for air. Just before he exhaled for the final time, Jamie and Henri pointed their squirt guns at the emaciated near-corpse and began firing the blessed holy water. There was a dark purple smog that billowed from the perverted man's mouth with a high-pitched squeal. Henri and Jamie continued to spray the holy water at the floundering apparition until its shrieks ended in one final brilliant flash of dark purple light.

Henri and Jamie looked at one another with tearful eyes before falling into each other's arms in a release of pent-up anger, grief, and revulsion.

An assassin came up from the morbid basement and entered the room with a small bundle. "We-we're so sorry. We should have been earlier. Maybe we could have…could have saved more. But there is one. He is alive and unharmed."

Henri took the bundle and opened the blanket. Inside was a lightly cooing six-week-old infant of Persian descent. Henri enveloped the child in his hulking frame and re-entered the chapel. He looked down again and the infant flashed a slight smile of contentment. Henri laughed through his tears and declared, "He is a miracle!"

The dark shadows receded from the chapel as Jamie, Henri and the assassins all looked up once again in awe at the prism of color that was being generated by the sunlight beaming through the priceless stained-glass windows.

———

Maddy, Erick, Arima and Marcus sat expressionless in a stunned silence before Maddy yelled out, "Oh fuck! I shouldn't have eaten that second sammich!" She then ran to the kitchen and vomited in the sink.

"Yep, that's what we're dealing with," Josie said in a remorsefully controlled tone as she was being lovingly held by her Lionnel. "There is no bottom to this. There are no limits to their depravity. There is *nothing* that they won't do to assume power. Just like the Nazis. They were an earlier form of this evil. And now, we have *these* heartless, morbid fuckers. The cycle just continues.

"There are a lot of families in Boston who will never be able to have a restful night ever again. But that little boy survived. And maybe Henri was right. Maybe his still being with us *is* a miracle. His dead parents were found in the basement of that church too by the police after we tipped them off. A number of the cops that responded to the scene are still receiving some pretty heavy therapy. No one should ever witness something so horrid, let alone experience it."

Josie wiped tears from her remorseful green eyes and looked up while forcing a smile. "But, by the grace of God, or whatever, we have that child. He is about one year old now. We took him to the estate, and he was adopted by Stellan and Paciano. They break down crying every time they lift him from his crib. They love him so much and the baby loves them. The baby also loves to smile and laugh and play. He loves to play with toy trains and loves to play with the big cats. They just adore him. Stellan and Paciano will lay him down on a blanket near the apiary and play a Cat Stevens CD. The pairs of big cats then come from the surrounding woods and lay around the blanket forming a formidable feline shield. It is as if they sense that this child is special and needs to be protected."

Josie let out a slight chuckle of emotional release as she concluded in a cracking voice, "They named him Zihad. It is Muslim for 'fighting for peace.'

"Okay gang," Josie segued as she let out a deep exhale and returned to her normal lilted tone. "There's only so long that I can dwell on that shit before I feel like it's dragging me down permanently. Jesus, the Twins had to be pretty much locked up for a week after they heard about that. Fortunately, Rachel and Kayla agreed to spend several days just playing 'Hide the Sausage' with them, so they were able to kinda fuck out their aggression. And once we got them past *that*, it was then time for them to join Vai, Alexa, Lionnel, and myself for one of *our* little missions against the on-air demonic propogandists that are spreading the gospel of Vetis. So, lets lighten the mood up and have a little fun, shall we?"

Chapter 80

Liar

"I'm telling you Josie; I just don't like it!" Lionnel yelled out as Josie was applying a generous amount of makeup to her befreckled face. "I didn't like watching you kiss your first boyfriend, or whatever that dick was to you. I don't like it when you use yourself as bait to lure creeps to the basement of LOHAD for one of your slash dances. And I *sure as hell* do not like what you, Vai and Alexa are planning for tonight!"

Josie placed a pink rose over her left ear in her curly auburn locks, got up from her vanity and strode toward her love. Her black mini-dress clung to her seventeen-year-old, five-foot-four-and-a-half-inch frame as she sauntered closer to him wearing a broad smile on her face and black pumps on her size-six feet. She opened her arms and embraced him tenderly. She could feel his heart beating rapidly over concern for her well-being. She opened her petite, mauve lips and whispered into his ear, "I understand my love. And I truly appreciate your concern for me. I love you for wanting to protect me. To protect my safety and my innocence. You are much like my father in that respect. But what you don't understand is…"

Her voice trailed off as she pulled back from him revealing an even broader smile. She tussled her fingers through his black, curly hair and exclaimed playfully, "That this is gonna be *fuckin' funny*! Are you *kidding* me? We get these perverted propogandists all heated up and then…and then...Oh my *God*! It's going to be *so cool*! So just *lighten the fuck up* wouldja? You and the Twins will be around if we need you. But we won't. Tonight, my darling, the sisters are doing it for themselves. MWAHAHAHAHAAA! Now just chill out. I've gotta go see if the other two are ready. But first, we really need to play some appropriate prep music."

Josie strode over to the forty-year-old portable CD player and mused to herself as she began surveying her musical choices, "Let's see here. What would be a good song to get ready to? Something that *really* captures the moment. Oh! I know!" She took a CD out of its case and placed it into the player. She pushed 'play' and gave Lionnel a not-so-subtle wink as she strutted out of the room.

Lionnel settled into his oversized chair in the corner of his hotel suite as Bob Dylan's "The Times They are A-Changin'" came floating from the speakers. He shook his head and chuckled as he picked up a printout of the invitation that Rod had sent the three propogandist servants of Vetis on the darkest corner of the dark web. All three had replied immediately and enthusiastically. *Wow*, Lionnel thought to himself as he began reading the invitation. *This shit is really going down tonight. And she's becoming more like her mother every day.*

Greetings friends and fellow servants of Vetis,

As a small token of our undying gratitude for your decades-long service to our Glorious Vetis, you are hereby invited to join us for a private party where you will partake in any and all of the mortal pleasures that you desire. We will be providing you with the most exotic drinks ever created. We will be providing you with the most succulent cuisine that will be freshly prepared by the world's greatest chefs. And we will provide you with three of the most delectable virgins for you to play with, keep and mold as you see fit. Please RSVP to this private channel upon your receipt. This is a one-time opportunity to celebrate your undying loyalty to our cause.

Date: August 28, 2040

Time: 8:00PM SHARP!

Location: Upstage International Hotel, Penthouse Suite, Las Vegas

Weaponry: But of course! Feel free! We want you to feel safe and comfortable.

Security: Provided by us. No one besides your driver is allowed to know your location on this evening and the driver must remain with his vehicle. The event will be immediately cancelled upon detection of any person that was not personally invited. This is for both your safety and ours.

Lionnel's anger began to swell as he thought about what he was about to witness his love and the other two women on their team do this evening. He took out another piece of paper and began reading. His anger swelled further as he read a small sample of the hate-filled, treasonous lies that this trio had been spreading for decades through personal appearances, print, web, radio, and television. His eyes skimmed the headlines of the conspiratorial garbage that were intended to stoke fear in the White population. Then stoke hatred. Then stoke violence. Until the nation would be submerged in a cataclysmic race and culture war that would ultimately upend America's great Constitutional democracy and all the others throughout the world. Then, the dark souls would be summoned to Enlightenment for the ultimate battle for the control of people's souls throughout the cosmos.

Lib Demons Feast on Blood of Infants in Basement of D.C. Pizza Parlor!

Patriotic Freedom Fighters Incarcerated for Defending America's Only True President!

Twenty-three Adult Actors and Seventeen Child Actors Fake Own Deaths! Stage False-Flag Mass Shooting at Amusement Park for Gay Pedophiles!

Jews Control Everything! Even Space! Secret Jew Space Lasers Discovered!

Lib Books Teach Our Children to Hate Themselves! Suicide Rates Among White Children Explodes!

Fact! The End of Our Democracy Started When Women Got the Vote!

Freak Teachers Allowed Employment! They are Turning our Children Gay!

Innocent White Teen Defends Himself Against BLM Terrorists!

Gun Advocates Rejoice as Madison Man Protects Girlfriend!

Patriotic Motorist is Forced to Drive Through Violent Antifa Crowd in Self-Defense!

Kung-Flu Alert! Avoid All Asians!

Government Microchips Found in Vaccines! Deep State Using AI to Control Your Thoughts!

And so on and so on and so on, Lionnel somberly thought to himself. *How is it that so many people are susceptible to this indoctrination? This is shit that a five-year-old would laugh at. How can millions of people fall for this? Some are just stupid, I guess. But that can't be the whole thing. There were plenty of highly intelligent, accomplished people who knowingly gave their children poison at Jonestown. So, it isn't intelligence. It is personality. Anyone who gets indoctrinated into a cult of any type seems to share many of the same person-ality traits. Eccentricity. Narcissism. Paranoia of anything that is different from them. Grandiosity. A belief in self-entitlement. Distrustful. All of this adds up to an inability to process information and draw reasonable conclusions. They believe what they want to believe, despite actual facts that are staring them in the face.*

And it is these types of people that these three servants of Vetis, and thou-sands of others, prey upon. They use their additional personality trait of charis-matic manipulation to draw these people in and brainwash them. The foot-soldiers aren't the ones who are evil. If anything, they are pitiful. But those that wield influence over them are truly evil. Like these three that have been know-

ingly spreading outrageous lies for their own personal benefit and power. They know what they are saying. They know what they are doing. They know that they are creating millions of violent people. And they do it while sipping their wine and getting a blowjob from their mistress. They love it. They love the power that they wield over the feeble-minded. And that is pure evil. I may not like how Josie is going to do this tonight, but there is a part of me that is going to enjoy watching this.

Josie bounced into the room and yelled out, "Hey! I've been trying to get your attention for like five minutes! What the fuck are you thinking about? Never mind. We're ready. Let's go take these traitorous fucks off the air!"

"Good evening gentlemen," the tall, thin pale man with long, light blond hair stated before his identical twin immediately added, "Yes. Good evening. We are so pleased that you have joined us."

"Yes, quite pleased," the original twin agreed. "We are so pleased that you have agreed to play games with us this evening. We do enjoy games. Please, won't you come in?"

The Twins opened the door of the suite, and the three men were greeted by the sight of a long dark oak table that was covered in bottles of libations and a vast array of finely presented culinary delights.

"Please, have a seat, won't you?" Adam said followed by Aaron's, "Yes. Please make yourselves comfortable. You may place your guns over there if you wish. I believe that you will find that they may get in the way of some of the games you will be playing tonight. Especially 'Hide the Sausage.' Your guns will most definitely be in the way should you choose to play that game. But you must have someone to play with. It is time for you to select your dinner companions. We believe you will enjoy dining and playing with them. They enjoy playing games as well."

The three men sat in large red velour chairs that could easily seat two people. Aaron presented the first man with a purple bowl and said, "Won't you please select a key from the bowl? That will tell us which room to unlock in order to bring in your new playmate."

The obese man who was slovenly dressed looked up from under his long, feathered silver hair. He wore a misogynistic grin upon his stubbled face as he reached into the bowl and withdrew a key.

"Oh, Number three!" Adam exclaimed. "That is a very fine choice."
"Yes, very fine indeed," Aaron echoed. "She is quite fond of games. Our

houseboy Lionnel will now go and retrieve her. Lionnel! Please come in here!"

Lionnel entered the room wearing a sharp black suit on his body and an annoyed expression on his face.

"Please bring the occupant of Door Number Three to this fine man," Adam ordered.

Houseboy! An infuriated Lionnel thought to himself as he approached the door. *I'll show them fuckin' houseboy. Those two are enjoying this too much.* The door opened and Lionnel said in a flat tone, "Okay, you're up. You got one of the fat ones."

"Cool," the room's occupant replied casually as she sauntered past Lionnel and entered the main room of the suite.

The man's blood rushed from his head to his much, much, much smaller head as he witnessed the twenty-eight-year-old Vai Denhart come strutting in wearing six-inch pumps and black stockings over her toned legs. Her long, black hair contained a two-inch-wide silver streak down one side which cascaded down upon her shoulders, just above the bustline of her black-sequined mini-dress.

"W-well," the disgusting man began stammering. "Yeah, you'll do. But you look a bit too old to be a virgin."

"Well," Vai responded breathily. "I was raised by a *very* strict father, and I was never allowed to play with *boys*. But *men* are a different story. I *do so want* you to teach me games to play. And to spank me if I don't play them right. You'll teach me...won't you?" She concluded with a slight pout of her ruby lips.

"Very nice, Vai. Welcome to the party," Adam stated before Aaron took the purple bowl and presented it to the second man. His bulbous belly was covered in an ill-fitting blue striped oxford that did little to hide a pair of fleshy breasts. There was noticeable drool on his manicured black beard as he reached into the bowl greedily and pulled out a key.

"Room number One," Adam stated. "Another very fine selection. Lionnel, if you would please retrieve the occupant from Room One?"

"Of course, 'master,'" Lionnel replied bitterly as he took the key and went to Room One. "Okay, your turn. You got the other fat one."

"Oh, how fun!" the young lady squealed out as she bounced past Lionnel and into the main room.

The twenty-two-year-old Alexa came bounding into the room wearing the identical black sequined dress, only her blonde hair did not reach her dress. She had placed her hair in pigtails to accentuate her seeming innocence.

"Oh, well, you look fun!" the man boomed in his deep, boisterous voice.

"Well, I certainly *hope* so," Alexa replied with a youthful exhuberance. "I will do *anything* that I can to help *you* have fun. I think that you'll find me to be a *very good* student. And *very* enthusiastic."

"That only leaves Door Number Two," Adam stated followed by Aaron's, "Yes. Lionnel would you please retrieve the occupant from Door Number Two?"

Lionnel said nothing as he took the key from Aaron's pale hand and trudged his way to Door Two. He opened the door and said, "You got the one that wears bow ties."

"That's perfect. That reminds me of a story Mom told me one time about this insurance company fuck that she strangled with his own ties, heh, heh, heh." Josie then kissed her love passionately, gave him a slight wink and strutted into the main room.

"Fuck, this sucks," Lionnel said to himself under his breath as he watched his lover seductively saunter over to the man, smile and sensually undo his bowtie. She then let out a light giggle and said, "Okay boys. Here we are. We are all so ready to play games with you. Would you like to eat your main course first, or..." Her voice trailed off suggestively before staring at the third man with a devious little smile upon her mauve lips. "Or should we start with a little dessert?"

"Dessert! Dessert! Dessert!" the overstimulated pigs yelled out as their members stood as upright as they could manage.

"Very well, then," Josie said through a playful giggle as Lionnel's ebony face darkened with rage. "But we have something *very special* planned for you boys tonight. We thought it might be fun to start with a game that *we* picked. We just need to go back to our rooms for a moment and put on something a bit more...*revealing* as to who we truly are. Something that we don't mind getting a bit...*sticky*. Strap yourselves in boys, we're going to take you all for a fun ride."

The three tittering women left the room arm in arm. The three men sat there chortling with lustful, sexist anticipation. Lionnel re-entered the room and begrudgingly nodded at the Twins.

"Oh my, the games are about to begin!" Adam stated, followed by Aaron's, "Yes! This game will be quite fun. Let us begin!"

Aaron pressed a button, and the lights began to dim. The synth-heavy industrial beat of "Sex on Wheelz" by My Life With the Thrill Kill Kult began pulsing through a set of speakers and bright multi-colored strobe lights began illuminating the enraptured men's faces. Their expressions of delight immediately changed to confusion as thick, metal belts came from the sides of their chairs and began constricting their bloated abdomens.

"Wh-what the hell is going on?" One of the men cried out as three distinctly feminine forms emerged into the frenzied kaleidoscope of colors. They all wore skintight black vinyl body suits that were adorned with two-inch golden spikes, placed every inch around the entire garment. The only part of their actual bodies that were visible were their smiling, lush lips, and penetrating eyes. Two pairs of eyes gleamed in an electric blue. The third pair glowed in an intense emerald green.

Vai strutted up to the first bound man. His long, silver hair was now a mop of sweat as she said to him sternly, "I see you like looking at my tits. Here. Have a closer look." With that she grabbed the struggling man by the back of his head and plunged the two spikes that were directly over her nipples into his eyes. The man screamed in agony as blood from his eye sockets flowed down the spikes and onto the black vinyl. Vai laughed maniacally as she ground the man's face deeper onto the spikes until his pathetic gasps ceased.

Alexa then bounced to the second quivering man and enthusiastically yelled out, "Hey! You wanna lap dance? And believe me, this is *really* happening! This isn't some sort of false-flag!" She then straddled the man's lap and began bouncing up and down like a child playing on a trampoline. She squealed in delight as she plunged the golden spikes into his groin, legs, and thighs repeatedly in a fit of pure pleasure. She launched her torso upon his and began writhing up and down on his chest and abdomen. The sadistic man mercifully stopped his wails of angst and Alexa looked down upon her new piece of art. Her gyrations had slashed his flesh into a nearly perfect rendition of a Jackson Pollock painting.

"Your turn, baby," Josie stated menacingly as she approached the final traitorous provocateur.

"P-please. N-n-no. P-please. Stop," he pleaded as his face appeared as wilted as his now flaccid penis.

Josie stood over him and flashed her wicked little smile before saying softly, "Hey, hey. It's all going to be okay. It's all going to be okay because we are ridding the world of scum like *you*. Scum who twists people's devotion to their God and their country into something sinister. Scum who preys upon those who *you know* are vulnerable to your lies and manipulations. Scum who preaches hate over peace. Fiction over fact. Violence over love. We are sending a message. We are sending the message that you cannot hide behind the First Amendment any longer to spew your radical ideologies. You can't yell 'fire' in a movie theatre and incite panic, right? Well, our message is that if you incite a violent uprising, then that is *exactly* what you will get. A violent uprising. Against *you,* motherfucker. Now, how about a little kiss?"

The man shrieked with morbid torment as Josie straddled his lap and tightly hugged his torso. The golden spikes planted themselves effortlessly into his quivering flesh. Josie could feel the free flow of his blood dripping down her vinyl clad body. And she liked it. Her vibrant green eyes looked deeply into his. They were eyes that were filled with fearful tears and were pleading for mercy. She smiled demurely, slowly moved her spiked, vinyl face towards his and tenderly kissed his lips. His head struggled for release as the golden spikes slid into his face and eyes. He squealed in torturous muffled wails as his lips were encased in a death grip with hers. And then, he was still.

Josie began grunting as she tried to remove herself from the impaled traitor. She heard chuckling from behind her before yelling out from the side of her mouth, "Hey! Fuckers! I'm stuck on this little prick! How about a little help here!"

The next morning, the entertainment coordinator for the hotel turned on the stage lights in the auditorium to begin preparations for that evening's musical act. She shrieked, then fainted as she found three bloody heads covered in small craters planted upon microphone stands. The polished wooden stage was awash in a demented dark crimson. Each of the faces had a pink rose sticking out of one of the many holes.

There was a note nailed to the head of the silver-haired man that read, *You've Just Been Upstaged, Fuckers*!

———

Erick and Lionnel shook their heads disapprovingly while Arima and Marcus giggled with delight.

"Well, that *was* more fun!" Maddy yelled out. "Way to take the 'Slash-dance' thing to a whole new level! And I'm still lovin' the calling card, sweetie." She then beamed at her husband and exclaimed, "Hey, baby! We need one of those! We can't have our daughter being all cooler and shit than us!"

Erick looked into the green eyes of his beloved wife and said with a slight tone of exasperation, "Haven't you learned *anything*? Not *every-thing* is a competition. It is *okay* for other people to have things that we don't. It is *okay* for other people to have successes that are uniquely theirs. Let other people have their victories. In fact, *celebrate* their victories *with* them. It causes you *no harm* for others to have something that you don't. It costs you *nothing* to be genuinely happy for someone else. Celebrate the unique gifts that *you* bring to the world and be thankful for the unique contributions that *others* bring to this world. That is what makes this world an interesting place to live in. And it is what makes us humane. Don't you understand, dear?"

Maddy stared at her husband with a perplexed expression upon her slightly befreckled face before roaring back, "Well, I don't know what *that* fucking diatribe was all about, but it did *nothing* to help me think up a cool calling card! Whatevs. I'll think of it later by myself, *like always*. Okay sweetie, so how about Gregory, Marcus, and Cliff. Did they convince the world leaders to join us or stay the fuck out of our way, or what?"

Chapter 81

I Think I Smell a Rat

Cliff bowed his head and clutched onto Marcus's sweaty hand as they both said a silent prayer together before the international dignitaries were shown into the conference room in one of the New York buildings owned by Murder, Inc.

Seven Assassination Technicians dressed in their customary all-black suits entered the room silently as they ushered in fourteen diplomats from countries representing every region of the world. The diplomats took their place in plush white swivel chairs surrounding a large, black marble, oval meeting room table while looking at each other wearing confused expressions.

"Why the hell are *we* here?" the twenty-nine-year-old Cliff whispered to his thirty-one-year-old dear friend, Marcus. "We don't know *anything* about diplomacy. That's Gregory's deal, I guess. What are *we* supposed to do? What if we blow it?"

Marcus gave his friend a nod of understanding before replying in a hushed voice, "Because Josie wants only those within her inner circle to lead these efforts. She trusts us, man. We may not have all the skills needed, but those can be taught. You can't learn to be trustworthy. You must *earn* people's trust through your deeds. And that is what we have done. We have earned her trust and everyone else in Murder, Inc. So, we'll just stand here, and we'll take Gregory's lead. And we will not blow it or do *anything* to violate her trust. And, I don't know about you, but then I've got a date with a huge spliff and an even larger pizza."

Cliff let out a nervous chuckle, before a dignitary from a Central African nation broke the room's silence by saying, "Okay. You have succeeded in getting us here. After months of reaching out to us and telling us that you have information regarding an existential threat to humanity, we are here. We are some of the most trusted ambassadors for our respective nations. We hold a great deal of sway with our governments. So, getting us all together is no small feat. There are many existential threats to humanity. So, which one are you here to talk to us about? Climate change? Nuclear war? Famine? Drought? Economic upheaval? Culture wars between the various ideological tribes? Pandemics?"

"Yes," the forty-three-year-old Chadwick Gregory Davenport III stated bluntly as he stood at the head of the table. His black business suit was perfectly fit upon his taught frame and there was not a single drop of sweat upon his forehead as he continued. "Yes. All of that. And then some.

"Ladies and gentlemen, it is with the deepest respect and humility that I thank you all for joining us today. We truly understand the value of your time and we are honored by your presence. I will try to be succinct with my comments. But, again with the deepest respect, if you do not listen to our heeds today, you may be singularly responsible for the destruction of humanity as we know it. As well as the heavens."

Gregory's last comment initiated a round of loud guffawing by the dignitaries. "Oh, we not only have to protect *mankind*, but we must also now protect the *heavens*?" a Middle Eastern dignitary proclaimed sarcastically. "Well, now *this* I must hear! How is it that we can *save mankind* and the *heavens* young man? Please. Just tell us. We will do *whatever* you may need. But please make it fast. We all have dinner engagements."

Gregory looked upon the laughing group with a calm steadiness upon his face before stating, "Yes, I quite understand how this must sound to you all. If you please, just allow me to show you this brief presentation. We would be happy to answer any questions that you may have upon its conclusion. Marcus, would you please dim the lights? Cliff would you please start the show?"

The lights dimmed and a white screen descended from the ceiling. The projector that was placed in the middle of the table lit up and the screen became filled with a rapidly edited array of images of atrocities from the previous century. Images of starving children. Images of mass graves. Images of the victims of murderers. Of rapists. Of pedophiles. Of war crimes. Images of horrendous human experiments. Over and over and over the dignitaries' eyes were bombarded with images of the most grotesque carnage ever created by the human race. Sunken eyes. Terrorized faces. Bruises. Lacerations. Disembodied limbs. Entrails. Corpses. Blood. It was an explosion of morbidity which caused some of the dignitaries to begin to weep. Then suddenly, they were granted a reprieve as the monstrous bombardment mercifully ended. Gregory's relaxed voice could then be heard as a dark red blur replaced the butchery on the screen.

"Ladies and gentlemen. There is one common thread that holds together all the horrendous images that you have just witnessed. And that singular thread is that these atrocities were committed by human beings in name only. They may be biologically 'homo-sapien,' but they are not truly *human*. Because they aren't *humane*. Those that commit these atrocities are *incapable* of being humane because they lack a *soul*. Or, if they *do* possess a soul, it is as black as the darkest of nights.

"Yes, ladies and gentlemen, there truly is *pure evil* that walks amongst us in our world. And what you have just witnessed is but a small fraction of what they have done to us over time. It is but a small fraction of what they *intend* to do to every living person and every enlightened soul that has departed from our Earth. These images do not represent the end. They represent the *beginning*. The beginning of the suffering and torture and destruction and death. *This* is just the beginning.

"So, what is the end to all of this you may ask? The end for these soulless demonic servants is the toppling of our great democracies, replacing them with brutal dictatorships. The end is the creation of more and more dark souls that they can use and then sacrifice. The end is these sacrificed dark souls being summoned from their Earthly existence to wage war against the enlightened souls who reside peacefully in the heavens. The end is to rule every plane of existence where humanity resides. The end is the complete elimination of both Earth and Enlightenment.

"And that, my most esteemed friends, is the greatest existential threat that we have ever faced. All the threats that you listed are nothing more than tools for them. They will use them all, and then some, in order to breed distrust amongst us. Then hatred. Then violence. Then mass murder until Earth finally succumbs and the battle is engaged with our loved ones in Enlightenment.

"This battle is being overseen and waged by a *true* demon. A demon named Vetis. He is known as the 'Tempter of the Holy' and he creates then recruits human dark souls to build an army to fulfill what he believes is his ultimate destiny. Domination over the Earth is step one. Domination over Enlightenment is step two. Then, nothing will be able to stop his ultimate goal of his barbaric rule over the cosmos."

As Gregory concluded his final sentence, the image on the screen came into focus. It was the image of a devilish-looking beast sitting upon a throne of fire. He wore a sinister smile upon his dark red face and his forehead had protruding horns that twisted upward. His muscular torso had four arms, the scarred hands of which were squeezing blood from a screaming human being. He looked like a demented child that was gleefully torturing his toys. There was an audible gasp from the group as they were transfixed by this most nefarious sight.

"Poppycock!" the British dignitary exclaimed as he hastily got up from his chair. "What insanity! What rubbish! A demon is taking over the world and heavens? It is laughable and this has been an utter waste of our time! Come, my friends. Let us not waste one more moment listening to these…these…heretics!"

"I thought that you might react that way, Mr. Ambassador," Gregory responded calmly. "Marcus, Cliff, would you please bring in the isolation chamber and our special guests?"

"I will not stay for one more moment!" the British dignitary bellowed as he turned around and began his march toward the exit. He was stopped in his tracks as seven red dots converged upon his forehead.

Marcus and Jefferson wheeled in a plexiglass box that was six feet tall and three feet wide. In the center of the box was a metal chair with straps. And they were each carrying metal boxes that were shaking violently.

Gregory began approaching the frozen dignitary with ease as he stated, "I am sorry for this shocking development. I truly am. I want to assure the rest of you that you are completely safe. All that we ask is that you stay until the end of the presentation. Then, you will be allowed to leave completely unharmed. None of you have anything to fear because *your* souls are intact. *You*, on the other hand..."

Gregory's voice trailed off as he glared at the British ambassador with an intense serenity. "*You* do not possess a soul. *You* are a traitor to your mission. *You* are a traitor to your country. *You* are a traitor to your colleagues. And *you* are a traitor to all of humanity. So, won't you please take your seat in our chamber? We have a few questions to ask of you. Or would you prefer to have my friends blow your fucking brains out?"

The British dignitary dropped his hat and began trembling as Gregory led him into the chamber and bound his arms and legs to the metal chair.

"Good," Gregory stated in a satisfied tone. "Now we can begin the *true* presentation. This can go quite easily on you, or we can introduce you to our special guests. All you must do is answer one simple question for all of us. Is what I have just presented true or false?"

The dignitary began stammering as spittle flew from his pasty lips. "I-I have no idea what you are talking about! Release me this instant! I-I-I shall have you executed for this outrage!"

"Ah, the hard way," Gregory replied as he calmly circled the increasingly frightened man. "Very well, then. Marcus. Cliff. Would you please give our esteemed guest something sweet?"

Cliff climbed a small stepstool on the side of the chamber and opened a four-inch door at the top. Marcus handed him a gallon container containing a thick, golden substance. Cliff smiled, unscrewed the lid, and began pouring the substance over the quivering and confused man's head. The heavy stickiness flowed down his face, upon his shoulders and down his torso like oozing lava. Its golden hue glistened in the lights as it slid down his quivering body and pooled ominously upon the plexiglass floor.

"What you have just been covered in," Gregory began explaining, "is honey. Wonderfully sweet honey. In fact, it is some of the finest honey in all the world. It comes from the apiary of our friend and leader who owns an estate just a short drive from here. She is quite proud of her apiary. It was a gift from her father. Her father who was stabbed in the back by one of your demons. And she does love her bees. In fact, she loves *all* living things. Well, except for traitors, bigots and all the other dark souls that prey upon the innocent. She doesn't really care for *them* much. But she *does* love her honey. And she loves *feeding* her honey to her precious pets."

Cliff and Marcus then took off the metal encasing of each box, revealing a cage with four snarling white rats who were anxiously trying to escape their prison.

"Now," Gregory continued as he tried to contain his sadistic grin, "What will it be? Answer time? Or feeding time?"

"Fine! Fine!" the nearly hysterical dignitary screamed out as he struggled with his bindings. "Fine! I'll tell you! Just-just-keep those things away from me! I'll tell you! Yes! It is all true! Our most glorious Vetis is taking over the Earth. And Enlightenment. He is using the truly evil souls of this Earth to twist other people's faith and sense of patriotism into something hateful. Something violent. He is building an army of these dark souls and once they are done being used upon this Earth, they will be sacrificed, and their dark essence will be used to wage war against the hapless spirits of Enlightenment! They will be called to action by the two most demonic spirits who have ever existed upon this Earth. They are somewhere in the cosmos, searching for each other. And once they find each other they will use their combined will to summon all the Earth-bound dark souls into battle. And then our most Glorious Vetis shall join us *all* in holy domination over those who do not bow at his feet!"

The dignitary's body convulsed violently as he completed his descent into madness and let out non-stop maniacal cackles from his twisted mouth.

The man's insane giggles continued as Gregory turned to the remaining dignitaries. "So, you see that what we have said is true. We represent a group who has been battling these dark forces for some time now. Until recently, we thought that we were just battling traitorous anti-democratic forces in our respective countries. And we have been quite successful, which has resulted in these movements becoming increasingly fragmented and disorganized. But they still exist in large numbers and remain an existential threat. That is because we have now learned that our battle extends into the heavens. We have now learned that it isn't enough to rid the Earth of this vermin. We must destroy their very essence even after their human form has been vanquished. We are working on several fronts. We are taking out as many of the truly evil souls on the Earth as we can. And we are now working on a way to round up the dark spirits that remain here and then destroy them before they can be summoned for their final battle. But this is a task that is too large even for an organization as formidable as ours and we need your assistance. But first, let us show you what we do to those who aspire to oppress us all."

Gregory nodded at Cliff and Marcus who opened small doors at the bottom of the plexiglass tomb. They placed the snarling cages against the openings and released their locks. The hungry beasts lunged at the still cackling dignitary. His deranged laughter changed into agonizing screams as the rats began ravenously chewing on his honey-covered body. The rats' feeding increased to a frenzy as they began tasting the anguished man's blood that was now being mixed with the golden sweetness. The carnivorous creatures tore through his flesh beginning with his legs. They then moved up to his torso. One rat chewed a hole in the tortured man's abdomen, then tore its way through his body until its gore-soaked furry face emerged from his back. Another rat pounced upon the screaming man's face and began gnawing at his flesh. It ripped off his lips and swallowed them in one gluttonous bite. Then, it ate his nose as greedily as a child eating gummy candy. It paused briefly and stared into the dying man's eyes with an inquisitive look upon its bloody, furry face. Its whiskers began twitching playfully as it decided upon its next action. It took one last long look into the man's pleading eyes before deciding what it wanted for dessert.

The man let out one final wretched squeal as what was left of his body went limp. He now resembled a half-carved rack of lamb that had been shaved to make gyros. Cliff and Marcus kneeled beside the cages and made kissing sounds. The rats dutifully turned around, entered their cages, and settled into a satisfied slumber.

The room then darkened as a thick purple smog emerged from the man's carved frame. It cackled at the shocked group as it began to ascend out of the hole in the top of the plexiglass confinement. Its cackling stopped the moment that Cliff and Marcus began spraying it with holy water from harmless-looking squirt guns. The dense purple mist began shrieking and writhing until it dissipated into nothingness.

The dignitaries' faces held looks of horrified satisfaction as Gregory asked, "Okay then. Any questions?"

A female ambassador from Central Asia stood and looked at her colleagues in a respectful silence. She then inquired sincerely, "And just what is it that *we* can do to help in this endeavor?"

Marcus and Cliff each let out a deep sigh of relief and wiped sweat from their brows as Gregory allowed himself to smile for the first time in days.

———

"Oh, for fuck sakes Josie!" Maddy cried out. "This is totally *not cool*! Y'know, I'm really starting to think that you have problem. We need to take you to a shrink or somethin'!"

"What the fuck is wrong with *you*, Mom?" Josie yelled back.

"Rats? You're now keeping fucking *rats* as pets? Gross!" A disgusted Maddy retorted at the top of her voice.

"Oh, hey. Listen Maddy," Marcus slurred from his slouched position on the couch. "They're, like, really cool. They like to watch TV and shit and eat cheese crackers."

"Yeah. And pizza crust. They really like that," Arima chimed in as she loaded her bowl with a fresh hit. "They're really cool. They just like, hang out and shit. They sit really close to our faces when we're smoking and inhale the extra smoke. Then they get really mellow and chew on pizza or cheese or whatever we're having. There's nothing to worry about, sis."

"Wait just a fuckin' minute!" Maddy yelled. "Where the fuck *are* these things?"

"I dunno," Marcus answered calmly. "They're around here some-where. They don't really like strangers so maybe they're hiding from you."

As if on cue, a large white rat pounced upon Maddy's chest and stared at her with inquisitive pink eyes.

"Get-this-fucking-thing-off-of-me," Maddy ordered with a trembling voice.

Josie let out a deep sigh and rolled her eyes before going over to her mother. She picked the curious rat from Maddy's chest, giggled, and cradled it in her arms like an infant.

Erick just shrugged at his wife as she stared at him in bewilderment. He then said, "Okay, that's not really the point of the story. But kudos to you, Marcus, and your team. What an interesting way to rid the world of a dark soul. And I really enjoyed the traitor's descent into madness as he was being consumed. It's really an interesting analogy. He is a human 'rat' who betrayed his own kind. That is what human rats do. They consume one another. It was really a very creative way to send the message about how rats consume other rats. Bravo to you all."

"Um," Marcus began as his foggy mind searched for a response. "Thanks for that. But I don't think that's why Gregory did that. He just said that he thought it would be cool."

"What the fuck is it with you and your book reports?" Maddy asked her beloved husband with an annoyed tone. "Who gives a *fuck* about imagery and shit? The fucker's dead and that's all that matters. So, are these governments gonna help us or what?"

"Oh yeah, that!" Josie squealed out. "That's the best part! So, the world's democracies have banded together, and they are providing us with intelligence and logistical support. Jessie identifies the truly evil souls in their respective countries through her Beholding ability, and then they help us locate them. We pretty much do the rest. And not only that, but there are several countries that are run by dictators and other fascist scum that have resistance forces that are starting to help too. So not only are we making strides in saving the Earth's democracies, but we're starting to gain footholds in more oppressive countries to set the stage for the people regaining the power over their own destinies. Isn't that great?"

"Well, that's just wonderful sweetie!" Erick beamed. "We are so proud of you! Look at what you've accomplished in the past year! Look at our daughter, Buttacup. Aren't you proud of her?"

"Well, *of course* I'm proud, but..." Maddy's childlike 'hurt' voice trailed off briefly before continuing. "I'm just kind of *wondering* that if Josie could do all of *this*, then what does the group think about *my* time as leader? I mean, its *really cool* and shit, but *I* accomplished a lot too y'know?"

"Of course, you did, my love," Erick responded tenderly as he realized that his beloved wife's fragile ego needed his reassurance in this moment. "Josie *never* would have been able to accomplish *any* of this if *you* had not laid the foundation in *your* time as leader. And, if *you* had been in charge this past year, I'm *sure* that you would have accomplished just as much *if not more*."

"Yep! That's fuckin' true!" a rejuvenated Maddy arrogantly declared. "No question about it. Josie, you've done great and I'm *totally* proud of you. But your bragging about this shit is getting a little annoying so don't get a big fuckin' head, alright? Now, somebody get the message out that we're going to have a meeting tomorrow night. It's time that the rest of the group find out that I'm back. And *this* time, I'm not playing fucking games! This time I mean *fuckin' business*!"

"When *haven't* you meant…" Erick's voice trailed off as he stared into his wife's intense, green eyes. "Oh, never mind," he concluded as he looked at his daughter and gave her a knowing smirk.

CHAPTER 82

IF I KNEW YOU WERE COMIN' I'D'VE BAKED A CAKE

A hushed anxiety hovered over the meeting room as Murder, Inc's. top brass sat nervously awaiting the arrival of their leader. Darting glances at one another all communicated the same thing. *What is this meeting about? What is the urgency? Why was the message simply 'Meeting tomorrow night in the conference room 8PM SHARP. Your attendance is mandatory. Thank you.'*

The large oak door opened, and Josie's inner circle entered the room and began taking their seats at the head of the long table in the front. Arima, Marcus, Jessie (with LucyFur), Cliff, Kaneko, Jamie, Kayla, and Rachel took their designated places stage left. Lucy, Jennifer, Jules, Jerry, Sam, Henri, Rod, a still weakened Rosa, and Gregory took their designated places stage right.

Josie then entered the room arm-in-arm with her Lionnel. She wore a beaming smile upon her befreckled face as her curly copper locks bounced with each step that she took. Her brightly flowered minidress was hidden from view as her five-foot-four-and-a-half-inch frame was overtaken behind the large wooden podium. Her ever-present and ever-white-clad Adam, Aaron, Alexa, and Vai stood directly behind her. Their brilliant blue eyes darted constantly as they surveyed the room for signs of trouble.

The large gathering's anxiety increased as they watched Josie wipe a single tear from her effervescent eye before she began speaking. Their anxiety increased further as two black cloaked and hooded figures joined Josie on either side of her.

"Hello, my friends. Thank you all so much for joining us this evening," Josie began. "I am so sorry that it was on such short notice, but what I have to say tonight simply cannot wait. What I have to say tonight is nothing short of a miracle. What I have to say tonight is…"

Josie's attempt at a heartfelt introduction was unceremoniously cut off by the smaller of the black hooded figures muttering impatiently, "Oh, for fuck sakes. This is taking too long."

There was an audible gasp by the entire congregation as the shorter figure threw off her hood and cloak. Maddy's green eyes were glowing with a fiery intensity, and she had a wicked smile upon her youthful-looking face. She realized the importance of this moment. She realized that her words would have to be chosen carefully. She realized that she could not fuck this up. Maddy fucked it up as she exuberantly bellowed out, "Here ye! Here ye! Here ye! That's right, bitches! I'm back!"

Erick sheepishly took off his robe and quietly shook his head in embarrassment as he heard his beloved wife continue her arrogant diatribe.

"Yep, *I'm* back, my loving husband *Erick* is back and now we're all gonna have some fuckin' fun! I can see by the shocked looks on all your faces just how *thrilled* you all are to have me back. And I just want to say, that just like before, I shall rule this group with an iron fist or a velvet glove. The choice is yours. So, how about we just go around the room quick so that everybody can talk about just how *delighted* they are to have me back, hmmmmm?"

"Mother!" Josie yelled out. "What the fuck are you doing?"

Maddy looked at her daughter. The pair could easily have passed for nearly identical sisters. She delicately placed her hand upon Josie's cheek and said sweetly, "It's all okay, sweetie. Mommy's here now to make everything better. Why don't you just take a seat and I'll take it from here. I think there's a chair open third row from the back. Thank you very much for your cooperation in this matter."

Josie glared at her mother with a seething intensity as she said through gritted teeth, "Mom. I love you. And I love that you are here. But *I* am now the leader of this organization. *I* am the one that will be conducting this meeting. *I* am the one who is in charge here. And *you...you...you...*are the one that will sit your fucking ass down *now!*"

"Well, isn't *this* just a fine howdoyado?" Maddy responded in her 'wounded' voice. "Of all the disrespectful and hurtful things that you could have said to me. To your own mother. I just don't have the words to express how damaged I feel right now."

Erick stood behind his beloved wife and placed his hands upon her petite shoulders. He leaned his face forward so that his disheveled black hair was tickling her right ear. He then whispered to her, "My love. I know how excited you are right now. But this is Josie's organization. So, I'm sorry to say this to you and I realize that there will be a drought in your wearing sexy outfits for a while but shut the fuck up and let's sit down. This is what she was raised to do."

Maddy let out a shocked gasp. She looked around the room at the confused faces. She looked once again into the glowering eyes of her daughter. She sighed deeply and said with as much hubris that she could muster, "Well, *of course* I will take my seat. That was a test fuckers! I just wanted to make sure that you were all as loyal to our Josie as you were to me. *Of course*, it is your group, sweetie. Please continue. We shall just sit beside you and guide you as your consiglieres."

Maddy then leaned into her daughter's ear and whispered, "It's okay that we're still your consiglieres, isn't it?"

Josie's face softened, making her look once again like an innocent child as she whispered back, "It would be my honor. Thank you, Mom. Thank you, Dad. I love you both so much." The congregation began openly crying tears of joy as they witnessed 'The Family of Fury' lovingly embrace for the first time in over a year.

Maddy wiped a tear from her eye then looked at the two people who were seated on either side of Josie. "Arima! Lionnel! Move your fucking asses! *We* sit to the side of our daughter!" Maddy ordered.

"That's really kinda not cool, sis," Arima casually replied as she and Lionnel got up and stood to either side of the Twins. As Maddy was taking her seat, she heard someone comment from the back of the room, "Wow. I have no idea how she's here, but she sure as hell hasn't changed much."

"Hey!" Maddy screamed as her emerald eyes scanned the back of the room for the culprit. "Who said that? I'll put your head on a fuckin' pike!"

Erick placed his arm around his wife's shoulders and coaxed her body down upon her chair as he said, "It's all okay dear. It was meant as a compliment. Everybody adores and respects you here."

"Yeah, well it had *better* have been a compliment," Maddy retorted loudly.

Josie rolled her eyes and chuckled lightly before regaining control over her meeting. "So, I hope you all enjoyed our little production. We thought that a few of you might have doubted that my parents have been brought back to life, so we thought we'd just put on this little show. I mean, could *anyone* doubt that these are my parents after *that* little scene?"

The entire room let out their pent-up laughter and stood in applause. Maddy also stood and began taking exaggerated bows. Erick placed his head in his hands and shook it in disbelief. And Josie let out her largest laugh since before she had found out just who her parents truly were. Her laugh echoed a cherished time of innocence before she knew that her parents were freedom-fighting serial killers. A time before many of her closest friends and family had been slaughtered by the anti-democracy forces. A time when her biggest worry was finding loving forever homes for her beloved stray puppies and kittens. A time before she herself ascended to this throne of gory retribution. A time before she had literal blood on her hands. And her face. And her body.

"Yep, we're really something, aren't we," Josie stated as she concluded her laughter and motioned for people to take their seats once again. "Okay gang. The complete details of my presentation are contained in the packets that are being handed out to you but let me give you a brief update as to what is going on. As you know, Arima can connect with spirits who have not left our plane of existence and bring them into her soul. My mother still has work to do here, so her soul returned to us. She went looking for my father and she found him clinging to the dark spirit of my grandmother. My mother brought my father back here and they entered my Aunt Arima. Yes, my aunt. My mother and Aunt Arima are half-sisters. The evil Pastor fathered both of them. He is being held somewhere in Enlightenment. My grandmother, on the other hand, is unaccounted for. Anyway, Rod and Rosa developed a way to take my parents' souls, place them into another body and re-animate them. So, here they are until they are called back to Enlightenment.

"But that won't be until their work here is done. Their work to fight alongside all of us to finally take down the evil forces of the demon Vetis. We have done a great job of destroying much of the infrastructure and leadership of the *Underground Autocratic Movement*. We have assassinated many of their leaders. But in doing so, we have created more dark souls who will willingly serve Vetis in his battle against Enlightenment. So, what we are doing now is trying to come up with a way to collect as many of those dark souls that remain here and destroy them. We must destroy as many of them as we can before they are summoned to the next plane to engage in battle against Enlightenment. We must weaken their army as much as we can to give the pure souls of Enlightenment a fighting chance for victory. And we must do so before my grandmother has a chance to re-unite with the Pastor. Because it is through *their* union that the dark souls will be summoned and called into battle. It is *their* unholy union that still presents an existential threat to all of humankind. It is *their* unholy union which we must stop. Any questions? Everybody up to speed? Pretty simple, right? Okay, now moving on to this month's assignments! And please don't forget, that with each traitorous bigot dick that you kill, you get a free puppy or kitten. Plus, I'll even throw in a month's worth of food! Okay, when I call your name, please raise your hand."

One of the Assassination Technicians in the back of the room whispered to her colleague, "I really gotta get less efficient at killing people. I've run out of people that I can get to take all the puppies and kittens that I earn." Her colleague simply gave her a solemn nod of understanding.

———

"Okay, you motherfuckin' douchebag," the spirit of Joseph Angelo Argento stated with his customary surliness. "You know the drill. Gimme your fuckin' hands. Or do we need to do this the hard way like we did last week? Or was it last month? Fuck, there's no time up here."

The Pastor's dark spirit emerged from a blackened corner of his conjured cell and approached the barred door. He began weeping tears of black bile in painful anticipation as he hesitantly placed his newly healed hands between the bars. His hands were immediately bound to the cell's bars by thick, green vines.

"Thanks Botanist, or Herbert, or whatever," Joseph stated to a tall, gangly spirit sitting in the corner next to his green wife, Iris, and their adopted daughter whose twelve-year-old mortal body had been raped and murdered by members of a CHARLIE unit in New Orleans.

"May we watch, Uncle Joe?" a pair of giggling little girls' spirits inquired. "Now, girls," their mother, Becky Peterson scolded. "Please leave Joe alone. He has work to do."

"Ah, it's all right!" Joseph gleefully responded. "It's good for them to see what we do to pricks who are pure evil. And I'll tell you what girls! When we're done with this douchebag, we'll go get some ice cream, okay?"

"Yay!" the girls' spirits squealed with delight.

"We would *all* like to watch. Time is running short, Joseph. I can feel it," Blair Aubrey Sommers-Argento said with a delicate urgency to her beloved husband.

"Yeah! Let's get this show on the road!" Patricia Mercy Sommers cried out. "I've got a rehearsal coming up! I've got George Harrison and John Lennon to close the 'Victoryfuckinpalooza' show with "My Sweet Lord" then "Imagine." And *that* shit wasn't easy to pull off! How fuckin' cool is *that* gonna be? I'm nearly cumming just thinking about it!"

"Yes, we *all* want to watch," stated Howard who was surrounded by Arima's spiritual family and friends. Howard had found redemption through assisting Arima following an eternity of deserved hell while imprisoned in a painting. He was now the leader of this ragtag group of spirits who were completely devoted to Arima's safety and happiness. There were Mr. and Mrs. Roper, who assisted Arima in identifying worthy souls that she could then help to find their way into Enlightenment. Their selfless service was rewarded by Arima as she helped them heal their children before they ascended into the heavens as well. There was Arima and Marcus's supervisor from the morgue, Clyde Manfrengensen, who had been one of many mercilessly gunned down by the Pastor's henchmen on what was to be Arima's wedding day. There was the former CHARLIE member, Lillian, whose disgust at their sadistic actions led her to the same tragic fate as their other victims. Arima's mother, Abdalla Azar was also present as was her loving grandmother, Louise Azar. Louise glared into the Pastor's black eyes while holding the spiritual hands of two of his other victims, Marcus's Moms, and Pops. Her voice cracked slightly as she said in a deep voice, "I can *never* get enough of this. I can *never* get enough of watching the torture of the man who murdered my daughter, Abdalla and tried to destroy my granddaughter Arima. I will *never* get enough of this."

"Nor can I," came the uncharacteristically bold voice of Freddie Sommers's spirit. "In fact, Joe, I was wondering if I might have a bit of fun today as well? Oh, I could care less that he fucked my wife. If they weren't such an existential threat, I would wish that they would spend eternity together. These bastards deserve each other. But to take away my true fatherhood of my beloved Madeline. Well, that I shall never forgive."

"Uh, sure," Joseph replied as he surveyed the slight frame of his deceased brother-in-law. "Yeah, maybe you could do his pinkies or something. Come on over."

"Okay, let's get started," Joseph stated with enthusiasm as he showed Freddie where to place his hands on the Pastor's quivering right pinkie.

"I can call all of this off right now," the spirit of Gwen stated calmly to the Pastor's pleading eyes. "I can make all your pain go away. We will stop the torture and just let you spend eternity jailed here. It will be boring, but there will be no more pain. We will not continue to break your hands and body repeatedly after they are healed. All you must do is help us. Just tell us where she is. We know that you can sense her. We know that you know where she will be coming from. All you must do is tell us, so that I can track her. Then, we will summon her daughter to destroy her once and for all. And all of this will be over. For us. For you. Vetis will not be able to use the two of you to summon his Earthbound dark souls. There will be no war in Enlightenment. And there will be no more war upon the Earth after our mortal friends clean up the rest of the truly evil souls there. Just tell us where she is, and the pain will go away. Forever."

The Pastor let out a maniacal laugh as he tossed his marked head backwards. All the carved symbols of Vetis convulsed upon his dark purple flesh as his sadistic tittering echoed throughout the cavernous inner sanctum of Enlightenment. He stared deeply with his black eyes into the pure-white souls of each of the witnesses that surrounded him before saying sinisterly, "Go ahead. Do your worst. The pain that I experience today will be *nothing* compared to the pain that you all will feel when I am reunited with her. The pain that you will feel when we summon all the dark souls from the Earth. The pain that you will feel as we slaughter you. But you, Joe. You, I'm going to take my time with. I am going to beat you and tear you apart until your soul is in complete submission. And as you lay there wishing for an end to your agony, I am going to make you watch me drink the blood of your beloved niece and my regretted offspring from her shattered skull. I will floss my teeth with what remains of her copper hair, and I will plop her damnable green eyes into a fresh martini and suck it down in joyous triumph! Now get on with it. I have preparations to make."

Chapter 83
Candy Everybody Wants

"Hey, whatcha doin'?" Erick inquired of his wife as he entered the bedroom draped in a white towel while drying his hair.

Maddy was laid out on the bed wearing her pink shorts and tank top. Her size six bare feet were crossed as she looked up from the book she was reading.

"Oh, I've decided to write a book, so that's what I'm doin,'" she replied casually. "Since you pricks took out the wireless internet, it's difficult for me to get my ideas out there into the world. Plus, I don't know how much time I'll be down here on Earth before I get called back to Enlightenment. So, I decided to become an author so that I can get my cool ideas out into the world while I have the chance."

"Oh, cool. Are you doing some sort of research? Is that why you're reading the book?" Erick inquired.

"No...well...*sorta*," Maddy replied. "I know it *looks* like I'm reading a book right now, but I'm *actually* writing it. I have to read a bunch of *these* before I can write my own."

Erick, noticing the book's cover and title for the first time replied in a lecturing tone, "Why the fuck are you reading a bunch of romance novels? You hate that shit! And why are the covers always the same? It's always some bosomy woman and some shirtless stud, and they are almost always *white* if you haven't noticed. And then they fuck as humans and then become wolves and fuck as wolves or some shit. So, if you're writing a book, why are you reading *that*?"

An exasperated Maddy looked up at her husband and said haughtily, "Ok, listen, mister. You know *nothing* about being an author. This is how you write books. In order to write books, you have to do something called 'writing to market.' First, you figure out what genre is really *hot* right now. And believe me, people *really* like to read about fucking. Then, you read a whole bunch of popular books in that genre, and you read the reviews to figure out what readers like about them. Then, you put all those popular themes, tropes, styles, plot devices, and character-istics of the characters into a formula. And then you can write your own original book! Once I get the formula down, I figure I can crank out about twelve of these fuckers in the next year."

Erick shook his head in bewilderment and said with a hint of sarcasm, "Okay, let me get this straight. So, you read other people's work, take out the popular parts and rip them off. Wow. How artistic of you. Gee, human A.I. much? Why don't you just write what is in your *head*? Why don't you write what is in your *heart*? If all that you are doing is writing based upon a formula of other people's work, then you aren't adding anything to the human experience. You are depriving the reader of your uniqueness. Sure, it's impossible to be *completely* original in everything that is produced, but there's a difference between being *influenced* by other works and intentionally ripping them off. For exam-ple, what do you think about the song "Ice, Ice, Baby?"

"Uh, I hate that fuckin' song," Maddy replied bluntly.

"And just why is that?" Erick inquired further.

"Um," Maddy responded, "because the entire main riff was completely ripped off from "Under Pressure" by Bowie and Queen, but...hey...this is different!"

Erick began chuckling as he asked, "Oh, really? How so? How is ripping off the main musical riff in a song any different than ripping off the main themes and styles in a book? Both are the foundation of the work. And if there are tons of people out there doing that, then the marketplace is saturated by regurgitated drivel and artists who are at least *trying* to be original are drowned out. Maybe they're good. Maybe they suck. But they are at least *trying* to be true to who they are as a person and artist and trying new things."

"But...but...," Maddy stammered while attempting to salvage her dignity. "But that is how you make *money* at this shit! You *have* to give the audience what it wants! Otherwise, you'll *never* find a market, and there sure as shit isn't a market for the fucked-up shit that's in *my* head. So, I must produce something that is *tried and true* so that I can have *tons* of people read my work!"

Erick paused for a moment while calculating his response. He realized that his beloved wife was passionate about this. He realized that he needed to measure his words carefully to make his point without bruising Maddy's tender ego. He could not fuck this up. Erick did *not* fuck it up as he replied with a soft sincerity, "First, my love, it really isn't *your* work. It is your interpretation of *somebody else's* work. It is a caricature. It is an impersonation.

"Secondly, why can't something that is not directly stolen from someone else's work be popular? Why *can't* your fucked up shit find a market? I mean if it's any good at all, it will probably get noticed eventually. And if it isn't any good...well... then at least you've provided the world with some fireplace kindling and doorstops.

"And how do you know *exactly* what people want anyway? Why was "Ice, Ice, Baby" a huge hit? Because that riff was already popular. But it *wasn't* popular when Bowie and Queen came up with it. Someone had to come up with it first. People didn't know that they liked that riff until it was invented, and they had the opportunity to hear it. In music, there are only so many notes. So many keys. So many rhythms. None of that is original. But there *are* original ways to combine those notes, keys, and rhythms to create something that nobody has heard before. The same is true in literature. There are only so many original ideas. There are only so many character-types or plots or settings. But there *are* original ways of *presenting* those ideas. And it is that new combination that is creative. It is that new combination that some might consider to be art.

"So, if you are just stealing from other authors then all you are doing is supplying the market with the same stuff over and over and over with a different bare-chested dude and set of tits on the cover. The market is never *challenged* because they are never presented with any challenging *ideas*. All that I'm saying is that you have more to give than that. You have original ideas or at least an original way to present those ideas. I suppose if all that you are seeking is money and attention, then just churn out the same tired stories, plots, and characters. But true art doesn't come off the back of *other* people's work. True art comes from within *you*. Art connects with people emotionally. If you can get someone to shed a tear or burst out laughing at something that you created, then you have contributed to humanity. And contributions to humanity are art. Cheap knockoffs contribute nothing but a mindless passage of time. It just gets the reader a few hours closer to death, with nothing of substance to show for having had the experience. Originality inspires. Even if it's shit, it still inspires. It inspires criticism. It inspires the creator of the work to try to do better. To be better. And, at its best, true art, true originality inspires people to aspire themselves. To aspire that they *too* can be a writer. Or an actor. Or a musician. Or perhaps just a decent person. That type of inspiration comes from within the creator of the work. There is nothing inspirational about ripping off other people. And if people can't appreciate that, then fuck 'em."

"Wow," Maddy replied softly. "You really don't give a *shit* about biting the hand that feeds you, do you?"

"Nope," Erick proudly replied as he cranked the volume on the stereo which began blaring "Radio, Radio" by Elvis Costello. "Now, do ya wanna join us tonight?"

"Uh, maybe. What are you doing?" Maddy asked.

"Well, we found those three date-rapist frat boys that Josie wants us to use to get back into shape and for a little family bonding time. They've rented a cabin in the woods. It's the same cabin that people say had that old demonic book or some shit. Probably just a myth, but who knows after what we've been through. Anyway, Josie and I were going to go up there, put on hockey masks and cut them up with chainsaws. Wanna come?"

"Fuck yeah, I do!" Maddy squealed out. "Y'know, I've gotta hand it to you. You really are good at coming up with original ideas."

———

Three pairs of eyes peered at the run-down cabin from their hiding place in the dense woods. A thick fog had settled around the teetering structure as loud music was heard booming from its interior. They saw flashes of three laughing young men frequently darting from behind the cracked front window as they danced with a young woman who appeared to be unsteady on her feet. Erick then heard a soft, breathy voice behind his left ear.

"Ch-ch-ch-ha-ha-ha. Ch-ch-ch-ha-ha-ha. Ch-ch-ch-ha-ha-ha."

"Would you please stop that?" Erick shout-whispered to his wife. "It's annoying as fuck and your breath is tickling my ear!"

"Hey!" Maddy barked back with the same hushed intensity. "I'm trying to set the mood. This little caper is *already* ruined by us having to wear these fucking kitten masks! And where the fuck are the chainsaws that I was promised?"

"I'm sorry," Erick answered in an embarrassed tone. "I don't know what happened to the hockey masks. I looked all over for them. And these masks are the only ones Josie had in her van. I guess we *are* kinda out of practice for this shit."

Josie then responded to her parents in an apologetic whisper, "Um, I don't know what happened to the hockey masks either. I used to keep some in the van, but now they're gone. And I think Jules borrowed the chainsaws a couple of weeks ago. There were some 'chads' that were terrorizing some elderly folks in an apartment complex and it pissed her off, so she and Jerry took them to the basement of LOHAD and… well…you know. It did give the Twins some new parts to play with though and aren't these kitten masks just adorable?"

"I think that they're really cute, sweetie!" Erick replied enthusiastically. He then looked to his left and saw the face of a kitten sadly shaking its head at him.

"Hey! Here comes one now! He's mine!" Josie announced as one of the frat boys staggered down the front wooden steps and made his way to a tree. He leaned his back up against the tall maple, unzipped his pants and let out a satisfied sigh as a stream of pungent urine fell upon the crumpled leaves on this mid-February evening. He chuckled to himself just before feeling a leather strap being wrapped around his mouth. Then he felt increased pressure as the strap began tightening.

His confused screams were muffled by the constricting leather as he desperately attempted to pry the strap from his now-bleeding mouth. The pressure increased. He could feel his teeth begin to crack then snap off. He gagged as his jagged teeth slid down his throat. The pressure increased. He could feel the strap pushing his tongue backwards into his throat, cutting off his windpipe. The pressure increased. He could feel the strap binding the hinges of his jaw. He then felt someone's fingers pinch his nose. He violently writhed against the tree as he gasped for breath. Then, he became still. His corpse hung from the tree by the tight leather strap around his mouth. A pink rose was inserted into the top of his pants before his giggling assailant could be heard skipping through the brush.

"Wow!" Erick declared. "That was pretty cool!"

"Yeah, it was alright, I guess. Kinda amateurish if ya ask me, but whatevs," Maddy dismissively replied. "Hey! They're dragging that girl into the bathroom. We need to get in there before they do something to her that she didn't sign up for!"

"She clean yet?" one of the frat boys inquired as he drunkenly flopped upon a stained mattress. The creaking of the metal springs harmonized with the boy's evil chuckles as he waited for the arrival of his co-conspirators and latest conquest. *It is just so easy.* He arrogantly thought to himself. *Separate them from their pack. Put a little something in their drink. Drag them off somewhere. Then have all the fun you want. These stupid bitches. All they have to do is give it up. But noooooo. They make us work for it. They sit there and tease us with their tight sweaters and short skirts. They're all little sluts. We're just proving it to them. We're just taking what is rightfully ours. Don't they understand that we men have the right to take whatever we want? To have power and control over them? All they have to do is give us what is ours. And if they don't, well, I guess this little bitch is going to find out what happens, heh, heh, heh.*

He laid there smiling to himself in sadistic anticipation and his foot began tapping as "Footloose" by Kenny Loggins came on the radio. His smile turned to shocked terror as he felt the head of an arrow protrude out of the mattress, into the bottom of his neck and out of his trachea. His blood flowed freely down around his neck and began saturating the mattress with a new crimson stain.

He laid there trembling and let out his final gurgles as the third frat boy came bounding into the room and announced, "Here she is! Time to have some fun!" He did not have time to react to the sight of his dead friend as he was immediately struck on the back of his head by a blunt object. The drugged, scantily clad young woman watched her near-assailant crumple to the floor. She cautiously peered over her left shoulder and looked into a pair of brown eyes staring at her from behind a kitten mask. She let out a blood-curdling scream and passed out into the man's arms.

Erick gently laid the young woman on a tattered couch in the living room and tenderly covered her with a blanket. He then grabbed a sleeping bag and stuffed the unconscious rapist into it. He tied a thick chain around the sleeping bag. There was an ominous 'click' as a padlock was clasped shut on the chain, bringing the bound man back to consciousness. Erick unceremoniously dragged the now screaming and struggling rapist down the front steps of the cabin, picked him up and tossed him onto a neatly stacked pile of logs. The frantically struggling man screamed louder as he could feel something wet being poured upon him. His screams intensified as the scent of gasoline hit his olfactory nerves. His screams then transformed into tortured wails as his entire body burst into hellish flames.

"Fuckin' cool!" One of the 'kittens' excitedly yelled out as she began skipping back toward Josie's hippie-power VW bus. "I'll go get the hot dogs and marshmallows! Best fuckin' family vacation ever!"

"Mom!" another 'kitten' shouted out after her. "Don't forget to grab the ketchup!"

"I will *not* grab the ketchup!" the 'kitten' yelled back. "When are you going to grow up? Ketchup on hot dogs is *doing it wrong!*"

———

The giggling 'Family of Fury' came bouncing into their living room while loudly singing "Footloose." Maddy's sweatshirt was covered in mustard and relish. Josie's sweatshirt was covered in ketchup. And Erick's sweatshirt was covered in nothing as he had used a napkin.

They turned on the living room lights and were greeted by the dark figure of a man wearing tattered grey overalls and holding a machete. He was also wearing a hockey mask. Maddy surveyed the eyes of the man behind the mask and instantly recognized him. As did Erick.

"Well, there's one of the masks!" Erick yelled out as the hulking figure began approaching him.

The figure continued his menacing approach as Erick said, "Jason, I let you sucker punch me once, and I deserved it. But I'm tellin' ya *right now*, that I'm coming off of a thrill kill high so that shit's not gonna fly. So, take a step back or your toes will be pointing to the sky."

"Holy Fuck! You're like a Gangsta Rapper baby! That was great!" Maddy yelled out through her chuckles as the approaching form continued to approach them.

As Erick was being mentally self-congratulatory over his rapping "prowess", Maddy stood upright, looked the form in his eyes and said in a demanding voice, "Jason! Maddy is talking to you! Just knock it the fuck off! And why are you alive? We were told you were dead!"

The menacing figure stopped his advance and allowed the machete to fall pathetically to his side. He looked down sadly, revealing a completely bald head and said in a meek voice, "I'm sorry you guys. I just wanted to scare you. I thought I owed you that. I found the hockey masks in Josie's van and thought I'd freak you guys out. I just wanted to see you scared. Scared of *me*. I guess I fucked that up too."

"Hey, hey," Erick gently said as he approached Jason, placed his hand upon his shoulder and led him to the couch. "It's all okay. It's really good to see you. And listen. You really *did* frighten us. It's just that we're kinda used to having weird shit happen to us. We just had our game faces on, but deep inside we were trembling, right dear?"

Maddy looked at her husband, rolled her eyes and said incredulously, "Nope. I knew who this pussy fucker was as soon as I saw him and…"

Her thoughts were cut off by her husband's glaring brown eyes. "Okay, I'm just so used to acting tough. Yup. You got us Jason. We were all *really scared* of you." She then looked at her husband and mouthed to him as she folded her arms defiantly, *Happy now?*

"Really?" Jason said as he looked up at the pair. "Thanks, you guys. That really helps a lot."

Josie then blurted out impatiently, "Okay everybody! Who the fuck is this that's going around impersonating Jason?"

"I'm not *impersonating* Jason," Jason answered sincerely. He then removed his hockey mask and said, "I *am* Jason. Jason Anderson. I was married to Kristy before she went insane or got possessed or whatever and murdered your mother. I am the biological father of Aaron, Adam, and Alexa. I am the adopted father of Vai. And I've lost everything. My family. My job. Even my fucking hair. I crawled into a bottle a number of years ago and Alexa just couldn't take it anymore. I was an embarrassment to her. So, she came here and told you all that I had died. But she's stayed in touch, and she has always told me that when I'm ready to get help with my problem that I should come here. That you all would help me. That my former friends would embrace me again. And that is why I'm here. To ask for your help. I just wanted to get a little taste of revenge first. I know that was stupid but I'm half in the bag right now. I don't make the best decisions when I'm drunk, which is most of my waking hours. So, can you help me get clean and be a father that my children can respect again?"

"Oh, fuck Jason," Maddy answered sweetly with tears forming in her emerald eyes. "Of course, we will help you. We have connections at a really good rehab place. Our friend Jerry was there too. He can take you. You have always been such a sweet man. It was the absolute lowest point of my life when we took your children away. I'm so sorry about what that did to your life. And to Kristy's."

"You didn't take our children away," Jason replied. "They are different. They are special. You didn't take them away. They ran away to be with you. To help you. To help the world. They told me all about it a few days ago when I arrived back in town. Alexa was excited to see me, and the Twins were…well, they just said that they had seen this day coming so they weren't all that surprised. They then showed me their playroom and introduced me to their girlfriends. I've always wanted grandkids, but I pray that those two girls are…um…taking precautions. The four of *them* raising children? That would be trouble, I fear."

A sharp chill ran down Josie's spine as she simply said, "Yeah. That would totally suck. I'd better tell them to double-bag that shit."

Chapter 84

Jailbreak

The spiritual body of Blair Sommers-Argento lay in tatters in a dark purple ooze. Her arms had been ripped from her torso and were lying helplessly in opposite corners of the penitentiary in Enlightenment. One leg had been removed and had been snapped in four different sections. Her other leg was still attached to the torso but was left hanging from glowing white ghostly tendons. The shocked expression on the face of her decapitated head reflected the sudden savagery of the attack. Her pained bright-white soul crouched quivering in the corner as it looked frightfully upon her ravaged, conjured body parts. Blair's soul knew that she was weakened. She knew that she was defeated. She knew that she was helpless. She knew that she was dying for all eternity.

Her soul looked through the thick cloud of mixed purple and white haze and saw a copper, slithery figure. It cackled with glee as its serpentine form conjured spindly arms. Then legs. Then bulbous, sagging breasts upon its chest. Its scaled hood began wrapping around the top of its head until it formed a tight copper bun of hair. It looked at her with glimmering red eyes and cackled mercilessly once again.

Blair Argento recognized this face. This body. This frail-looking, corpse-like monstrosity. This was Maddy's biological mother, now reunited with her biological father. It had been Blair's turn to guard the Pastor. To keep her away from him. To sound the alarm should her presence be detected. She never had the chance as a copper blur suddenly invaded the bright-white incarceration unit and tore her conjured body apart in seconds. Now, all she could do was look upon this hideous form as she released her demonic love from his confinement. All she could do was watch helplessly as the pair embraced. Then laugh maniacally. All she could do was watch as the sadistic pair approached her shaking essence. All she could do was say one final prayer before they extinguished her soul forever.

"Well, it is quite nice to see you my dear," the Pastor stated to his dark-soul mate. "But you could have arrived a bit sooner. I have been brutalized by these…these…forms. Over and over again. They meticulously snapped my bones, one at a time, starting with my fingers. All to get information from me. Information about you. But I never wavered. I never flinched. I knew that you would come for me. I knew that we would be reunited so that we may now survey the number of dark souls that remain upon the Earth. And once there are enough of them created by these self-professed "patriots," we shall consummate our love once again and call them all here. They will be my ultimate congregation. They shall tear each and every enlightened soul that resides here apart. And then, our most glorious Vetis shall arrive to claim his dominion over the cosmos. So, I am quite grateful to see you, my love. But what took you so fucking long?"

"Well," It began in its nasal, condescending tone. "I may have made a bit of a mistake. It was a mistake to take out our little whore's husband first. To allow his spirit to remain upon the Earth to watch over her. To protect her. And when I used Kristy Anderson's body to murder that wretched little bitch, I had not anticipated that his soul would be there. As her confused soul emerged from her body, I lunged at her to extinguish her for all time. But he intercepted me. He flailed at me, wrapped me up in his essence and took me into a corner of the cosmos. Someplace cold and dark. It was actually quite peaceful in a way.

"And I underestimated the power of his love for her. It gave him strength. Through his pure love he clung onto me. Our souls battled each other for what seemed an eternity. Just clinging to one another, trying to absorb one another's energy. Trying to kill the other. He nearly succeeded. But our impetuous daughter found us and ripped me from his death grip. I was so weakened that all that I could do was fly away and hide out. I hid in the Realm of Perdition and our glorious Vetis ordered all the damned, sinful souls there to care for me. To rebuild me. And they did. It took quite some time for my black soul to regain all its strength. It took longer to satisfy Vetis's wishes and brutalize any damned soul who did not bow to my will. I had to prove myself to him. And I did. Many wretched souls were sacrificed at my hands. And my fangs. I conquered it and now that realm is ours. I am now the appointed ruler of the Realm of Perdition. And it is from there that we will stage our final attack.

"Now, I must admit, that was some time ago. I suppose I could have arrived earlier and released you from your personal hell. But I thought you might benefit from having a bit of tortured time to reflect. Time to reflect upon your failure to rape our daughter into submission. Your failure to bring your other daughter, Arima, into our fold. Your failure to escape the clutches of the souls of Enlightenment. Your failure to keep the half-sisters apart. I sincerely hope that you have used that time of reflection wisely. Because one more failure from you will bring swift and brutal retribution from our glorious Vetis. And it will be done by my hands."

The devilish pair then turned their attention to the quivering bright white orb that was Blair's soul in its most pure form.

"Hello, Blair," It began with an insincere sweetness. "So nice to see you once again. Yes, it is quite nice to see my despised sister-in-law in such a state. Can you feel your life being drained from you? Are you scared? Are you frightened to be nothing? Are you frightened to not be able to be here to protect your loved ones? Are you frightened about what we are going to do to them? Yes, I can see that you are. It fills me with great joy.

"But I am feeling a bit merciful at the moment. Would you like for me to allow your soul to live just long enough to bear witness to the godless atrocities that I am going to commit against your friends, both living and dead? What I am going to do to your beast of a husband? Your freak of a sister? Your little bitch of a daughter?"

It cackled maniacally before continuing. "Yes. I can feel your confusion at that last comment. Your daughter, Madeline. Allow me to explain. The Pastor and I were placed upon the Earth to convert holy souls into unholy ones. And it was through this proselytization that we would form an army. An army first made up of humans, then, upon their death, dark souls. And it was prognosticated that we would do so with a powerful female warrior of our own making at our side.

"So, we prayed and searched for a soul that I could raise and mold as my own. A soul that was capable of inhuman violence and brutality. A soul that held no empathy for her victims. A soul that had unequalled tenacity and delighted in her gory escapades. A soul that could smile at you sweetly one moment and rip out your throat the next without so much as a bat of her eye. A soul that was beyond redemption. And we found one. And she was perfect.

"But *you* stole her from us. For some reason, this soul was attracted to the family Sommers. And since Patty never engaged in activities that would lead to a child and your brother was such a pathetic worm that he would never get laid, her soul was attracted to you. Her soul was attracted to your strength. And to the strength of your vile husband. You became pregnant. You became pregnant with *our soul*! So, the Pastor placed a call so that your Joseph would be dispatched on a bogus service call. He hired two men to then go to your apartment and beat that soul's life out of you. And to ensure that your womb would never pose a threat to us again. You see, bitch. It was *Madeline's* soul that you miscarried on that night. We took her soul from you the same way you had taken her from us. Her soul was taken from you so that it would be once again free to belong to me. To us.

"But the soul was still attracted to your loathsome family. It was quite easy to manipulate and seduce your dullard of a brother and get him to marry me. The Pastor and I poured the blood that we had saved from your miscarriage over each other. And we fucked. We fucked like two beasts in the most rapturous of heat. And Madeline was conceived. And that child's soul was attracted once again to someone named Sommers. Her soul was attracted to me through my marriage to Freddie the Fool. I allowed you to keep her on the weekends. I found it quite delightful that you had to send her back to me every week. I laughed so hard every week that you sent your *own daughter* back to the one person that you most despised. And I thought that I would have the last laugh when I watched *your own daughter* rip you to shreds after she had been fully indoctrinated. But I was mistaken. Your family's influence was much greater than mine or the Pastor's. And she went down a dark path. She still became a brutal killer. But she killed not in the name of selfish domination. She killed in the name of what she felt was justice. I should have murdered that little bitch when she was a toddler. It would have been so easy. Just stick her little copper head into the bath water and hold it until her little gurgles stopped. But I didn't. And so now here we all are.

"Yes, Blair, you stupid bitch. I may have been Madeline's biological parent. But *you and Joseph* are her eternal *spiritual* parents. And it will be *our pleasure* to rip that little whore apart in front of you and force the parts of her body down your fucking throats! And *that* is why I am allowing you to live! I am allowing you to live because ultimately, I am going to *force you to consume your own daughter!*"

The purple and white mist changed into an ominous dark red as a slow clapping sound was heard. A tall, hulking red figure approached as he said, "You think that you've seen a demon? You haven't seen *anything* you motherfuckin' douchebags!"

The glowing red figure of Joseph Argento lunged and struck the Pastor firmly under his chin, sending his scarred, ghostly form across the space. It looked at him with deep red eyes, screeched and immediately transformed into a fifteen-foot copper serpent with two arms protruding from its side. It wrapped its tail around Joseph's spiritual body and lifted it up to its cavernous mouth.

"Oh my, I bet you're a kinky one, aren't you?" Howard's spirit gleefully exclaimed as he joined the battle, launched himself onto the beast's back and held its mouth open. The venom from its fangs was dripping down upon Joseph's face just before it broke free from Howard's grip and bit down.

There was a shriek of agony from Freddie Sommers as the vile serpent's fangs plunged into his ghostly form and penetrated his very soul. Joseph stared at Freddie's agonized face that was impaled by the two long fangs. It was the face of the man that he had previously found to be pathetic. It was the face of the man that he now held nothing but admiration. It was the face of the man who had just sacrificed himself to save him.

It reared up and violently shook its head in an attempt to dislodge the fallen soul of her husband from its fangs. It loosened its grip on Joseph just enough for him to break free. Joseph fell upon his side. His entire body glowed red from the intense hatred that he had always harbored towards this unholy succubus. He looked at the glowing orb that was his beaten wife's soul. It was just the two of them silently communicating with one another before he stood and grabbed it by its scaly tail. He whipped it around the room in a violent whirl. With each passing It knocked Its head and the lodged body of Freddie into the Pastor over and over until the evil spirits were gasping for soul-affirming breath.

The disheveled serpent-demon fell upon its side and squealed in agony. Joseph began prying open its mouth and two strong green vines emerged from the blood-red fog and wrapped around the fangs. Joseph pulled on the vines with all his spiritual strength until the fangs broke loose, dislodging Freddie's impaled head and causing his body to fly into Joseph's. Joseph lay on his back and stared into the dying eyes of his brother-in-law. A tear fell from his eye as Freddie uttered his last words. "Take care of my sisters, Joseph. And take care of *our* daughter. Tell Madeline that I will always love…"

Pitch black forms emerged from the red fog near the fallen body of the Pastor. The bright white forms of Patty, The Ropers, Lillian, Marcus's Moms and Pops, Herbert, Iris, and Becky Peterson emerged on the opposite side behind Joseph and Howard. The ethereal figures stared at each other with cautious disdain. They glared at one another, daring their opponents to make a move. The pitch-black forms solemnly picked up the bodies of the Pastor and the copper serpent and regressed back into the nothingness to begin their journey to the Realm of Perdition. Just before its scaly tail disappeared, its nasal voice was heard saying, "This is far from over you fools. We will be back. And we will feast upon you."

"J-Joseph?" Blair's weak voice inquired as her eyes opened for the first time since the battle. She looked down upon her reconstituted spiritual form and smiled meekly. Her smile broadened as she recognized the grip of the hand that was holding hers.

"Yeah, baby, I'm here," Joseph's gruffly tender voice responded. "You've been out for a while. Who knows how long. There's no time up here. But you're going to be fine. Your body is completely restored, and your spirit is strengthening by the day. You had me scared there for a while, but I knew you'd pull through. You were always the strong one in our family. I'm so sorry about your brother's soul. He's gone forever. But here. I brought you a present."

Joseph laid two fifteen-inch fangs upon her bosom. His beloved wife smiled and let out a pained laugh. "You always did know what to get me," she said through her tentative chuckles.

"But Joseph. You and I both know that this time, teeth aren't enough. Blood isn't enough. Body parts aren't enough. This time, you will not rest until you have brought me the black heart of that fucking bitch. Do you understand?"

"Of course, I understand," Joseph replied with a confident bluntness. "You just tell me what to do, my love. I'll bring home whatever you want for dinner. Just like always."

The pair embraced as they conjured their song in their respective heads. They swayed together to the sweet melody of "Groovy Kind of Love" while looking lovingly into one another's eyes. Blair broke the silence when she whispered into her Joseph's ear, "And I am not the strongest one in our family any longer. Our daughter is."

CHAPTER 85
OUR LOVE WILL CHANGE THE WORLD

"Awwww, fuck," Josie and Maddy said with dread simultaneously just after they had heard the latest high-pitched "Wooooo!" from a pair of ecstatic twin sisters. Fifteen minutes prior, a giggling Rachel and Kayla had entered the room wrapped around their respective beaus, Adam, and Aaron. Rachel and Kayla's expressions were typical of them. They had carefree looks upon their pretty brown faces as they loudly chewed and popped their bubble gum. Vai took one look at the unusually pleased expressions on the faces of her adopted brothers and instinctively knew that something was a-miss.

"Hello, everyone," Adam began followed, as always, by his identical twin brother Aaron. "Yes, greetings. It is quite nice to see you all."

"Uh, yeah, Hi," Josie replied as she was clearing the table of the breakfast dishes. Making their way from the dining room table into the living room of the Parker-Sommers home were Lionnel, Maddy, Erick, Arima, Marcus, Alexa, and Vai. Each one of them felt a strange sensation in the pits of their stomachs as they looked upon the unusually serene quartet.

"What the fuck are *you* four so happy about?" Maddy bellowed out as she plopped onto the couch. "And why are you late? You're *never* late."

"Well," Kayla giggled in response as she looked mischievously at her twin sister. "We're sorry we're late. But we have a good reason to be late."

"Uh, yeah," Rachel interjected. "But we're not just late for the meeting, *tee, hee*. Boys, would you like to explain why we're…um…late?"

"But of course!" Adam responded to his girlfriend. "Yes! We would be delighted!" Aaron added before explaining. "As you know, Rachel and Kayla have introduced us to the most fun game, 'Hide the Sausage.' And we have become quite good at it. We have been practicing for months now."

"Yes, we have," Adam contributed. "We have been practicing night and day. It is the most fun game that we have ever played, but we learned that we could not win using the game pieces that Josie told us to use."

The entire group turned to look at Josie with perplexed looks of revulsion. "Hey!" A defensive Josie yelled. "What are you talking about? I've *never* been involved in helping you with that-er-game!"

"Yes, you have, Josie," Aaron answered. "You told us that we needed to, and I quote, double bag it. But Rachel and Kayla said that we did not need those game pieces and that it was much more fun without the bags over the sausages and that we would never win the game if we did that. So, we stopped double-bagging the sausage several weeks ago."

"Yes!" Adam exclaimed. "And it did not take us long to win the game after that!"

Vai got up from her seat and cautiously walked over to her younger brothers. She took them both by the hand and led them a few feet away from their girlfriends. She looked into their piercing blue eyes and asked softly, "Okay boys. I need you to be quite clear with me. What do you mean you've 'won the game'?"

"Well, of course we will be quite clear," Adam replied followed by Aaron's, "Yes. Quite clear indeed. We won the game by impregnating both Rachel and Kayla."

"That's right!" Rachel yelled out excitedly. "We're knocked up bitches!" Rachel and Kayla then grinned at each other before releasing their customary, high-pitched, "Wooooooo!"

"Awwww, fuck," was all that could be heard following the announcement. Lionnel rushed out of the room to hide his laughter. Erick took his head in his hands and slowly began shaking it. Arima and Marcus loaded a bowl in their pipe, completely unaware of what was going on. There was what seemed to be an eternal silence until Alexa squealed, "You guys are *pregnant*? Yay! I'm going to be an aunt!"

"Well, well, well," Vai began stammering as she searched for the most appropriate words.

"Uh, yeah, you see Alexa-um-well..." Josie attempted to add until her genius-level brain ran out of responses.

"Oh, for fuck sakes! I'll handle this shit!" Maddy yelled out as she bounded up off the couch and marched toward the four glowing parents-to-be. She looked at each of them in their joyful eyes. She could see how delighted they each were at this moment. She knew that she had to be very careful with the words that she chose so as not to offend or hurt any of them. Maddy knew that she could *not* fuck this up.

Maddy fucked it up. "Pregnant? Are you fucking *kidding me*? This is what you're going to do. You're going to wipe those *fucking smirks* off of your faces and listen to me! Pregnant? This is the most *fucked up thing* that you could've done! First off, you're all what, twenty-five, twenty-six? That's waaaaay too fuckin' young to have a family. Um, I think. That's not the main point. Boys! You have *no idea* how to function in this world without our guidance! How the fuck are you going to raise kids? I mean, you call 'fucking' 'Hide the Sausage' for fuck sakes! You think this is a game! Well, let me tell you, raising children is *no game*! No. This is *not* going to happen. We will take Rachel and Kayla to a doctor and we'll, um, y'know, just take care of it. And you are *fucking banned* from playing 'Hide the Sausage' from this point on. You got that?"

"Yes, we understand, Aunt Maddy," Adam replied followed by Aaron's, "Yes. We believe that we understand quite well. We understand that we have been supportive of you and our extended family for our entire lives. We have done everything that you have asked of us. We have celebrated your achievements and we have mourned with you in your grief. We now understand that our support for you will not be reciprocated. We have achieved something that we are quite proud of. We have fallen in love with these two wonderful women. And we are going to have a family with them. We are going to produce something that is beautiful. Something that is important. It is quite hurtful to us to learn that the people that we have loved and supported do not love and support us back. If you do not support what we love and what we are passionate about, then you do not truly love *us*. And it is *that* level of support that *we* must now reciprocate. We wish you all well. It is time for us to take our leave. And we will do so with the women and unborn children that we love."

"Yeah! Fuck you bitch! How *dare* you shit on what was to be the happiest day of our lives!" Kayla screamed into Maddy's face as the quartet angrily made their way to the front door and exited.

"Nice job, Ace," Erick sarcastically stated to his wife. "You'd better apologize to them, and you'd better make it good. Those are four people that I do *not* want to be on the wrong side of. Oh, and while you're thinking up your apology, you might *also* want to be thinking about the wedding arrangements. I think the best way for all of us to apologize is to throw them a kick-ass wedding. And baby shower. Like it or not, people, this shit is happening. And they're right. They have always been with us. Hell, they murdered their *own mother* for us. I think the *least* that we can do is support them in this. Plus, they are going to need us to help raise their kids. Who the hell knows *what* type of hellions they're going to bring into the world. With the four of *them*, the product of *their* love could change the world. I think we might want to be involved in seeing just *how* they change the world."

"Fuck, alright," Maddy replied quietly with rare contrition. "I'll call Pastor Tim and see when we can get these little fuckers hitched. And I'll call them back here and apologize. But I'm not *wrong* am I? This is really going to be *fucked up*, isn't it?"

Erick went over to his wounded, beloved wife and kissed her on the top of her copper strands before saying, "No. You are not wrong. They are the *last* two people on this Earth that should be reproducing. But some people would have said that about us, too. Just look at how *our* love has changed the world." The pair shed a tear and smiled as their gaze fell upon their own daughter's brilliant green eyes.

Maddy called Pastor Tim. Erick could only smirk as he listened to his wife's side of the conversation. "Uh, hey there Pastor Tim. Listen, so the Twins have knocked up the-um-twins and we need to get them hitched. No, I'm *not* fucking joking. Yeah, I know. I have no idea how those little fuckers got laid either. Nope. Not an option. They're hell-bent on having these little bastards. Okay. Tomorrow night, then. Could you maybe get some flowers and shit? I don't know! Just get someone to throw up some wedding shit! I'll pay you back tomorrow night. And, I promise, we will *not* make a mess of your church this time."

Maddy's next call did not go as well. "Hey, guys! Why don't you just get your little asses back over here and…" her sentence was interrupted by the sound of the phone's receiver being slammed down.

The next call was not successful either. "Okay guys, I know you're pissed at me but…" SLAM!

The third time was not the charm. "Alright you four! You're *really* starting to piss me off! Get your asses over here so that I can apologi…" SLAM!

Erick sighed and took the receiver of the harvest gold rotary phone from his wife before saying, "Its okay. I'll call in the big guns."

Following a brief, polite phone call from Gregory, Kayla and Rachel were sitting on the couch in the Parker-Sommers home. They had their arms folded and were rapidly kicking their crossed legs. Their irritated expressions stared straight up to the ceiling, as they refused to make eye contact with the five-foot-four-and-a-half-inch waif that stood demurely in front of them. Adam and Aaron were sitting next to their girlfriends, holding their delicate tan hands. The colors of the Twin's pale white fingers intertwined with the dark tan fingers of their lovers resembled a vanilla-chocolate ice cream swirl.

"Sooooo," Maddy began cautiously. "What's new? Just jokin'!" Her attempt at humor at this tenuous moment resulted in dead silence.

"Okay, not in the mood for my great jokes, hmmmm? Well, let's just get on with it, shall we?" Maddy began again. "So, I think that I *may* have overreacted just a *little bit*, but if you *think* about it, I was *totally right* in…"

Maddy's attempt at contrition was interrupted by the sound of her husband loudly clearing his throat.

"No. I'm sorry. I *wasn't* right. I was-um-wr…wr…wr…wrong. There. I said it. I *never* should have reacted that way. I was just-um-surprised. And, hey! You know me! I can kinda fly off the handle sometimes. Not my best quality. So, I was-um-wr…,wr…oh, fuck it. I wasn't *exactly correct*, okay? Listen. We love you guys. All of you. I'm *so sorry* about what I said and I'm *so sorry* that I ever even thought about harming your unborn bundles of joy. We love you and we love your unborn children. Okay? Please? Adam. Aaron. You know me. You know this shit isn't easy for me. And you know that I wouldn't be saying this shit if I didn't mean it. Please. Just forgive me, okay?"

"Well, it really isn't up to us," Adam replied followed by Aaron. "No. We cannot forgive you unless Rachel and Kayla forgive you. They are a part of us. In fact, the four of us, along with our children will become a family unit. We love you Aunt Maddy, but it is *their* forgiveness that you must seek."

Maddy sheepishly peered from under her copper bangs at the still-annoyed sisters as she slightly puckered her lower lip and softly shuffled her left foot. *Well, this innocence shit used to work with Uncle Joe. And it sure as fuck works on Erick. Let's see if I can't get* these *bitches to bite, heh, heh, heh,* Maddy thought to herself.

Without looking at her adopted in-law, Kayla asked, "So. Are you truly sorry, or are you just saying that?"

"Yes," Maddy replied in as innocent of a voice that she could manage. "I *truuuuly* mean it. I'm *so, so, so* sorry."

Rachel then inquired, "And there will be no more judgement or interference from you?"

"Oh, *my* no," Maddy once again responded. "This is *your* family. I will *only* get involved if you *ask* me to. I just think that it is *wonderful* that you are all having babies. And it would be *my honor* to babysit whenever you need-um-assuming I'm still on Earth. Otherwise, I volunteer Arima."

"What?" Arima inquired before her Marcus said, "Don't worry about it, baby. I'll help ya. We'll teach these kids about the good things in life, just like we do the rats. Hey. Pass me that bag of chips, wouldja?"

"Plus," Maddy continued, "We are *sooooo* overjoyed and supportive that we would be *honored* if you would allow us to throw you a wedding tomorrow night, followed by a baby shower. And one final thing. If it's okay with you, we're going to take you off the battlefield for a while. We can handle this shit. We want you four to go to our estate and live there with Stellan and Paciano. We want you all to be safe. We want you to stay safe so that you can raise your children, hopefully in a much more peaceful world. Hopefully *your* children will never be needed to fight what *we* are all fighting right now. No. Fuck hopefully. The world that you raise them in *will* be peaceful. It *will* be welcoming. It *will* be supportive. That's just how its going to be or else my name's not Maddy fuckin' Sommers. And that's my name, so that's how it's going to be. That is my personal promise to you and to your children."

Kayla and Rachel dropped their annoyed gaze from the ceiling and looked at one another. They then smiled and yelled "Woooooo!" before bounding up from the couch and enveloping Maddy in a tight three-way hug.

"Of course, we forgive you, Aunt Maddy!" Rachel exclaimed. "C'mon! Let's Woo to the occasion!"

Maddy looked at her husband with dread before opening her mouth and belting out "Wooooo!"

"I'm never fucking doing that again," she said to a smirking Erick as the pair ascended the staircase, leaving the jovial party to their toasts and wedding plans.

CHAPTER 86

IF I WAS THE PRIEST

"I don't know why *I* wasn't asked to stand up there with them. *I'm* the one that arranged all this shit," Maddy angrily whispered to her husband from her seat in the front pew as she looked at Adam and Aaron standing at the altar with Alexa, Vai and Josie.

"Shhhhh," Erick whispered back as he gently squeezed her hand. "Today is not about you. Or me. Or anyone else but them. Today is about them and their future. Let's just enjoy the moment."

"Yeah, whatever," Maddy replied dismissively. "It wouldn't have killed you to wear something other than jeans, *by the way.*"

"There are very few things that *can* kill me at this point," Erick snapped back. "But wearing uncomfortable pants all fucking day is *certainly* one of them."

The congregation fell into silence, and they all turned to look to the back of Pastor Tim's church as David Bowie's "The Wedding Song" began to play. The song's effortless rhythm matched the cool glides of Rachel and Kayla as they strode arm in arm with their best friends, Arima and Marcus. Their white sequined wedding mini-dresses left very little to the imagination causing the Twins to immediately contemplate the game they would like to play with their wives once the formalities were over.

Rachel and Kayla smiled at their "bridesmaids," Jessie, Cliff, and

Jamie and took their places next to their respective husbands-to-be. They held each other's hands and gazed into each other's eyes. Two pairs of fierce cobalt connected with two pairs of majestic hazel. Rosa squirmed in her seat as she felt the outpouring of energy that these unions were generating. And the growing energy from the unborn fetuses.

"Hello friends," Pastor Tim began as his husband Jeremy stood to his side. "Welcome to this most wonderful day. A day where Rachel and Adam *and* Kayla and Aaron shall enter holy matrimony. A day that will serve as the foundation for their future and the future for their blessed children. And perhaps the foundation for the future of us all. I understand that the four of you have vows that you would like to share."

"We sure do!" Rachel cried out before taking the gum out of her mouth, handing it to Jeremy and saying, "Hey, hold onto this for a sec, will ya?"

A surprised Jeremy took his handkerchief out of his pocket and placed the gum into it as he smiled awkwardly and nodded at Rachel. He then presented the handkerchief to Kayla.

"Oh yeah, thanks!" Kayla replied as she took her saliva-coated gum out of her mouth and placed it in the handkerchief next to Kayla's. The well-chewed pieces of gum looked identical. It would be impossible to know which was whose. This was also true of their respective husbands-to-be, so they had their names tattooed on each of the Twin's inner thighs, to avoid any embarrassing, drunken mix-ups. Adam's inner thigh now said 'Kayla's' in an exotic script meaning Aaron's inner thigh naturally now said, 'Rachel's.'

"Okay guys," Kayla began. "I'm just going to do our vows for both Rachel and me, okay? We both worked *really hard* on this, like, for twenty minutes or something, so here it goes. So, here's the deal. We love you guys and shit. You are both so strong and brave and fun and um-*really* well hung. Plus, you knocked us up, so we want to spend the rest of our lives with you and shit. Cool?"

"Why yes, of course," Adam stated followed by Aaron's, "Yes. That is why we are here isn't it? We are a bit confused by the question."

The entire congregation let out a light chuckle as Rachel motioned for Stellan and Paciano to bring their adopted baby, Zihad, toward them. She took the rings from the infant's left breast suit pocket and gave them to the Twins. "Yeah, cool. Good enough. Just put these on."

"Very well, then," Adam stated followed by Aaron's, "Yes. Of course, we will put them on. Oh brother, aren't they marvelous? They are made entirely of Bloodstone which will help us face our challenges with courage!"

"Uh, yeah," Kayla sheepishly replied. "We actually just thought the name was cool, but glad you like them. Okay, boys. Your turn."

The Twins once again gazed into the eyes of their respective loves before they both said in unison with the exact same tenderly monotonous tone, "Kayla and Rachel. You have made us feel things that we have never felt before. You have made us feel things that we did not know that we *could* feel. We have seen things as children which have now come to pass. But we did not see this. You have been a surprise to us. A quite pleasant surprise. And we are surprised yet again by knowing that we are to be fathers. We are quite excited to think about all the games that we can teach our children. And the games that they will teach us. It will be quite fun. So, won't you please take these rings and be our wives?"

Adam and Aaron then reached into the opposite breast suit pocket of the sleeping Zihad and retrieved two rings. Rachel and Kayla marveled at the bands that were made from ground Amethyst for spiritual protection against evil and Angelite to assist in connecting with spirit guides. Sitting prominently upon the center of each ring were three-karat diamonds, to assist them to be forces for good in the world.

As Rachel and Kayla began crying and placed the rings upon their delicate tan ring fingers, they could feel the presence of their fallen sister, Gwen. They shed a tear and smiled upward. The introspective moment was interrupted when Maddy jumped up and yelled, "Jesus fucking Christ! Look at the *size* of those fuckin' things!"

An unidentified voice from the back of the room was heard shouting, "That's what *she* said!"

The entire congregation burst into laughter before Pastor Tim said with bewilderment, "Okay. Never a dull moment with this group is there? Now, if anybody here objects to these two unions, speak now or forever hold your peace."

Erick gave his wife a preemptive elbow jab in her side which caused

Maddy to give him an overly dramatic pained expression as she rubbed her "wounded" ribs.

"Okay then," Pastor Tim continued. "By the power vested in me, it is my pleasure to present to you all Adam and Rachel Anderson *and* Aaron and Kayla Anderson. You may now kiss your brides."

"We would much rather play 'Hide the Sausage,' Pastor Tim," Adam replied. Aaron then said, "Yes. Kissing is nice but 'Hide the Sausage' is much more fun. May we play *that* now?"

"Oh, shut up and kiss us!" Rachel cried out as the twin sisters grabbed their respective husbands and shoved their tongues down their throats. They released their husbands from their lips, looked at the entire congregation and yelled out, "Woooooooo!"

"Mozel Tov bitches!" Kaneko declared as she popped a cork from a bottle of Dom.

An hour later, as the newlyweds were opening their presents, an exasperated Josie yelled out, "What's with all the fuckin' weapons? This is a *baby shower* not a ninja convention!"

Lionnel wrapped his arm around his love and said to her, "Seriously, baby. With this group, is there really a difference?"

Pastor Tim and Jeremy looked on with delighted faces as they watched their dear friends laugh and joyfully cry with each unwrapped baby blanket, butcher knife, stuffed animal, throwing star, diaper bag, pepper spray, stroller, or battle axe. They burst into laughter as they heard their dear friends Erick and Maddy in the corner.

"Oh my god, this isn't right, Maddy," a near-hyperventilating Erick was saying. "This isn't *nearly* enough stuff. They aren't prepared. Okay, I'm just going to have to get my old list out and go to the big box store and pick up a few items. I mean, they only have *twelve stuffed animals* so far! They need *waaaaay* more than that. Lucy's going to have to move some of her shit from the basement. I'm going to need the room."

"Hey! Mister OCD!" Maddy yelled back. "Knock it the fuck off! These are *their* kids! It's *their* problem. Just chill the fuck out!"

Erick had not heard a word of his wife's protestations as he was mentally counting the number of diapers and baby wipes that were required to be purchased.

The giggling Pastor Tim and Jeremy looked into one another's eyes. They both held the same thought. That they were the luckiest men in the world. They were lucky to have this group of friends. They were lucky to have this church with this congregation. They were lucky to have their strong faith. And most of all, they were lucky to have the true love of one another. They smiled and leaned in for a loving kiss. The pair slightly parted their lips, allowing the delicate touching of their tongues. Jeremy opened his mouth wider. Pastor Tim felt Jeremy's tongue become intermingled with numerous small, slimy, crawling sensations. Pastor Tim opened his eyes and looked directly into the black, dead eyes of his husband. He pulled backwards and saw hundreds of maggots crawling from Jeremy's gaping mouth. He screamed and began spitting out maggots as Jessie cried out, "Oh Jesus! The evil! The pain!" and collapsed upon the floor.

Jeremy's body floated several feet into the air and began cackling sinisterly. "Well, hello everybody. So nice to see you all once again, heh, heh, heh," the Pastor's slithery voice came from Jeremy's mouth. "Oh, it is *sooooo* nice to be able to invade another's body without their permission. At any time. As long as they are unsuspecting. That is the key. That is the power that I now wield thanks to being reunited with my dark-soul mate."

His eyes then darted towards the fast-approaching Arima and Maddy. "Well, hello girls. You wanna bounce upon Daddy's knee? Aren't family reunions nice? Here. Let me provide you with another one."

The Pastor swooped down and grabbed an unsuspecting Jason Anderson by the neck, lifted him from the ground and began chewing his way through his neck until his body collapsed to the floor with a gory thud. The Pastor squealed with maniacal glee as he sucked the blood from Jason's dismembered neck and tossed it haphazardly against the large crucifix that was hanging behind the altar. Blood slowly dripped from the form of the seemingly helpless, crucified Jesus.

"There! Now he can be reunited with his insane wife, Kristy! Now perhaps all their offspring should join them. Then, on to *my* two little disappointments."

"No!" Jessie yelled out before reciting with a dark determination, "Malum tuum dolorem facit. et dolor meus es fortitudo mea (*your evil causes pain. my pain is my strength*)."

Jessie felt her body begin to absorb the intense pain caused by the Pastor's pure evil, strengthening her body ten-fold. She leapt up and grabbed Jeremy's left leg. At the same moment, the platinum blonde, Amazonian Dragenstein came lumbering forward and grabbed his right leg. The pair pulled downward until Jeremy's possessed body was on his knees between them.

"Okay Maddy," a suddenly sober Arima ordered. "Let's finish off our prick father, once and for all. And let's do it together!"

"Uh, yeah, sure," Maddy replied as she lifted two serrated daggers from the pile of baby shower gifts. "But I'm *kinda* the one that gives the orders around here, so I just want to make it clear that your order wasn't official. Okay, doesn't matter right now. We'll straighten that shit up later."

Arima and Maddy began approaching the cackling body of the possessed Jeremy. His body was writhing as he attempted to free himself from the vice-like grips of Dragenstein and Jessie. Arima and Maddy lifted their knives in unison and began their fateful downward plunge. The knives stopped in mid-air as they heard Pastor Tim cry out, "Stop!"

"Stop! Please! That's my husband! If you kill the demon, you will kill my husband! Please! There must be another way!"

A serenity fell upon Jeremy's face and his eyes returned to their normal mahogany. He looked up at his approaching love and said peacefully, "It's all okay my Timothy. I am lost. I have very little time to speak with you. He is too strong, and he will retake me at any moment. Please, Timothy. Listen to me. Either you kill me, or he will use my body to commit the most horrendous atrocities. I cannot bear that, my love. But it must be *you* that kills me. Otherwise, he will possess my soul. It must be my one true love. It must be my *soul mate*. And it must be done as we kiss. You will understand as you breathe in my dying breath."

Rosa and the other twelve members of the Coven circled the pair of lovers. Rosa said softly into Pastor Tim's ear, "It will be okay Pastor Tim. I have this. I will have his energy. Then I will give his energy to you. And you will be together forever. Please trust me." The Coven clasped one another's' hands and began concentrating. Rosa's body began to tremble and glow in a comforting light blue light.

Pastor Tim got down on his knees in front of his restrained husband as Arima handed him her dagger. He looked longingly into his beloved husband's eyes, leaned forward, and gave him the most tender kiss they had ever shared. Tears began streaming down his face the moment that he felt the stickiness of his beloved's blood flow freely between the fingers of his right hand that was clutching the dagger. The dagger that was now literally penetrating Jeremy's heart. The dagger that was now figuratively penetrating Tim's heart.

Jeremy let out one final breath and a light blue haze emerged from his mouth and effortlessly glided into that of his husband. Timothy was now truly Jeremy's one and only soul mate.

The dark purple scarred smog of the Pastor belched from Jeremy's corpse. He began morbidly cackling before saying, "No need to reach for your Holy water. I know when I'm not wanted. And I knew that it was quite unlikely that I would vanquish you all here today. This was just a warning. Just a little taste of what is to come. Oh, and girls. Daddy is *sooooo* looking forward to bringing you home. Don't worry. You are my daughters. I will take care of you. Yes. I will take care to *rip you to shreds* and consume *every little morsel* of your pathetic existences! But, until then…toodles."

The setting sun's rays beamed through the stained-glass windows creating a kaleidoscopic spotlight on the mournful form of Pastor Tim holding the corpse of his beloved husband. He looked up at the empathetic face of his dear friend Erick and said with a quiet resolve, "I now understand. I now know what I must do. But I will need your help, my friend."

———

The luxury yacht that Kaneko had purchased for this expedition lightly bobbed in the calm waters of the Atlantic Ocean. They had sailed for several days until they reached the destination that Pastor Tim had requested. Jennifer and Lucy were taking a break from piloting the vessel and sunbathing on the deck as they had decided to use this excursion for a much-needed vacation from exploding heads and oozing entrails. Henri sat above deck with his sniper rifle, scanning the horizon for any signs of trouble. Erick, Marcus, and Cliff were the only other crew members that Pastor Tim had allowed to accompany him, much to the chagrin of Maddy.

"Okay, please tell me what the fuck we are doing in the middle of the Bermuda Triangle?" a slightly annoyed and confused Erick asked his dear friend.

"Well, Jeremy told me that this is the location where my powers would be the strongest and easiest to amplify. This place holds many mysteries. And many opportunities."

"Right, right, *Jeremy* told you. C'mon Pastor Tim. I'm sorry for your tragic loss, but you need to realize that he's gone."

"Really?" Pastor Tim indignantly replied. "Really? This coming from *you*? This coming from the man whose ashes *I personally* put into an urn and who is now standing in front of me is questioning whether I have Jeremy's soul in me? That is quite rich, my friend."

"Okay. You have a point. I'm sorry Tim…um…and Jeremy. And I understand that the Bermuda Triangle is a place where weird shit happens. But how does it help *us*? What the fuck are *we* doing here?"

Pastor Tim chuckled slightly before answering. "Well, as you know, I have developed quite the ability to create Holy water. I have felt these abilities grow over the last year or so. And we know that Holy water can vanquish the dark souls forever. And you are all trying to find a way for Arima to be able to collect thousands if not millions of these dark souls into her essence all at once. And if she can do that, she can then transfer them into an inanimate object or substance to be destroyed. So, if you are successful in this, all you need is one big fucking bowl of Holy water that Arima can discharge the dark souls into. And that is what we are doing here. I am going to use the mystical powers of this location to turn every ocean and every other body of water that is connected to the oceans into Holy water."

"Tim, I've seen some crazy shit," Erick responded as Tim was tying a rope around his waist. "Hell, I've *done* some crazy shit. And I know you've gotten *really good* at the whole Holy water thing, but *this* just seems impossible!"

"We shall see, now, won't we?" Pastor Tim stated as he perched his body onto the edge of the yacht, holding a cinder block. He looked back at Erick and said with tears forming, "Goodbye my dear friend. I hope to see you soon."

"Noooooo!" Erick yelled out as he watched his friend's body plummet into the sea. Cliff and Marcus grabbed Erick by the arms before he could fling himself off the side. "No, man! The fall will kill you!" Cliff yelled at him. "Let's drop a lifeboat and you can look for him from there!"

"Fuck that!" Erick yelled back as he wriggled away from their arms and dove into the ocean.

Erick swam downward desperately searching the murky waters until his lungs painfully screamed for air. He swam back to the surface, breathed deeply, then immediately dove back down. His burning eyes scanned the watery terrain until he saw a soft blue glow coming from a reef. He swam to the light and found the serene face of Pastor Tim, his arms clinging to the cinder block. Erick's tears merged with the salt water as he embraced his deceased friend's body, trying to will him back to life.

He then felt it. He then felt the absolute love that Pastor Tim's soul possessed. The waters became clear as a soft blue mist expanded from Pastor Tim's body outward throughout the waters of the Atlantic. Then the Pacific. And the Indian. And the Antarctic. Into the connected seas, rivers, and tributaries. All over the world, the Earth's waterways were being expunged of the trash and filth that human society had corrupted it with. The seas of the world began to brilliantly shine as their pollutants were dissolved into nothingness. And it was all due to the sincere sacrifice of one faithful man. One man who had faith in a higher power. One man who had faith that that higher power was purely good. One man who had faith in his fellow man and woman. One man who had faith was able to transform the Earth's waterways from being humankinds' toilets into the most magnificent and Holiest of reservoirs. One man who had faith may have single-handedly saved humankind. Because that one man possessed pure faith in humanity.

Chapter 87
Rebel Girl

Wednesday evenings had been the group's ladies' night since Maddy's college days. The lineup had changed over the years, but the wine, appetizers, gossip, and revelry had remained intact, with a few adjustments. In the past few years, there was frequently the addition of the sacrifice of some 'Chad' just for pure amusement. It gave the group a fun activity to bond over and released some of their pent-up stress.

Some of the "sophisticated" men within their group always assumed that the ladies were relieving their stress through tickle and pillow fights in their undergarments, because Erick had told them so. As evidence, he would point to an endless amount of 80's sex/comedy romps as though they were documentaries. They were very wrong in their assumption.

Although undergarments were sometimes employed as a lure for some sadistic fucker, there was definitely no tickling. Or pillows. There could be, however, boiling water poured over a tied down, screaming worm, or acid that burned off his genitals or scalpels that sliced his flesh from his bone. On occasion, there were all three. Maddy was preparing her black duffle for that evening's escapades as her husband walked into their bedroom.

"So," Erick began sheepishly. "I was just *wonderin'*…um…that since I can't go to Pastor Tim's service tonight and hang with him and Jeremy because…um…well I just lost my friends…um…and I *really* don't have anything to do, so…um…*maybe* I could just tag along with you and the other ladies tonight?"

An amused Maddy looked up at her beloved husband as she was packing a pair of vice grips and said bluntly, "Nope. Ladies' night. You know the rules. No dudes invited. We're all upset about our losing Pastor Tim and Jeremy and believe me, we ladies are gonna take out our frustrations in style tonight. Sorry, baby, but you're just gonna have to find some other way to blow off some steam."

"Fine!" a hurt Erick yelled back. "Well maybe I'll just grab the other fellas and take them to a strip club then!"

Maddy burst out laughing at the suggestion. She knew that her husband couldn't stand strip joints. They were just so impersonal and callous to him. The men viewed the women only as sex objects and the women viewed men as nothing more than walking wallets. It was all so transactional and lacked any regard for anyone's humanity. He didn't really have anything against it. He understood that those establishments catered to people's most primal needs, and as long as no one was getting hurt, who was he to judge. But still, he was personally creeped out by the scene and never frequented them unless he was stalking some quarry or had been assigned to watch over the safety of one of the performers.

"Yeah!" Maddy retorted sarcastically through her laughter. "You do that. You go get the *'fellas'* and take them to a strip club. Fellas? Who talks like that? Anywhooo, talk about fish out of fuckin' water. The first time some chick comes up to any of you and offers you a lap dance, you're gonna blush, wet yourself and leave screaming. Especially Cliff. He won't know *what* the fuck to do without Jessie's approval. So, yeah. You do that, stud. Enjoy yourself. I think I have some extra one-dollar bills if you need them. You go and make it fuckin' rain.

"And speaking of Jessie, tonight is a big night for her. Jennifer's flying us all over to London to check out Jessie's new influencer billboards and to take some abused women to shelters where they will get new identities and be transported to someplace safe. As you know, Jess was a pretty successful influencer back before you fuckers took out the wireless internet. She was hawking everything from perfume to personal-er-we'll say massagers. Now, she's using those skills to try to deprogram some of the women who have gotten themselves caught up in the demonic, anti-democratic movement. There are so many women out there who get caught up in some guy, only to find out that he wasn't *at all* what she thought he was. They find out he's misogynistic, sexist, and often mentally or physically abusive. That's the type of evil fuckin' men that are attracted to this movement. Men who think that women are their property and that they are entitled to anything that they want. Just like my first husband. I sure as hell can't cast a stone at 'em. I had a guy brain-fuck me too. I got sucked into that quicksand and couldn't find a way out until he went too far and burned my cherished photo album. That snapped me out of it. And that's what Jess is trying to do. She's trying to reach out to women who are in bad situations and offer them an escape.

"So, she's doing television commercials, billboards, print ads and on-line shit for those few who can get the internet. And her message is so beautifully simple. It's just her perky little face saying, *You are valuable. You are important. Don't let him tell you that you aren't. Don't let him beat you down. Don't let him get you involved with his evil. Call XXX-XXX-XXXX. We can help. You are strong. You can do this. We believe in you.*

"Pretty cool, huh? She's pretty good at this shit and we wanted to be there to watch the first strong women take their first steps toward regaining their independence and dignity."

"Huh," a somewhat surprised Erick replied. "That *is* pretty cool. I just figured that you were all going to hang out at someone's apartment and have pillow fights again."

"Oh, my fucking *God!*" Maddy roared back. "How many times do I have to tell you that we don't *do* that shit? It's just the imagination of creepy old men! That shit doesn't really *happen!*"

Erick began chuckling and embraced his wife as he said softly, "I know. It's just that you're really cute when you're pissed off. Plus, I think that I've got Lionnel, Marcus, and Cliff to actually believe that shit."

At that moment, their daughter's agitated voice was heard from across the hallway. "Oh, my fucking *God*, Lionnel! How many times do I have to tell you that we don't *do* that shit? I don't care *what* my father has told you, that shit *doesn't happen!* Mom! Tell Dad to stop fucking with my boyfriend's head!"

———

The door on the private jet closed quietly and the ladies of Murder, Inc. settled in for what would be a roughly eight-hour flight to London. Jennifer's British accent came over the intercom. "Hello, ladies. Lucy and I would like to welcome you all aboard Freedom Airlines. Freedom from oppression. Freedom from evil. And tonight, freedom from all your cares and worries. I am looking forward to hearing about your exploits in London. Please prepare for takeoff. We're all about to have some fun."

"Yeah, we are," Josie stated as she looked around the room at her female friends and family members. She saw the anticipatory eyes of Jessie, LucyFur, Arima, Sam, Jamie, Alexa, Jules, Kaneko, Dragenstein, Vai, Rosa, and her mother. Their eyes began glowing intensely as she said with a diabolical smirk on her face, "Now, listen up ladies. I have something special in store for us tonight. And we have *my father* to thank for this idea."

Lucy entered the main cabin and strapped herself in as the airplane was beginning its taxi. As she listened to Josie's plan, she flashed an evil little smile as she felt a familiar primal urge. Following Josie's instructions, which were met by a fit of uncontrolled laughter by all the passengers, Lucy looked at the group and said, "Okay everybody. Since we have some time to kill, I wanted to give you all an update as to our progress. From the selfless sacrifice of Pastor Tim and Jeremy, we now have a way to destroy millions of dark souls all at once. All we have to do is have Arima absorb those dark souls, get her over the ocean or a body of water that is connected to the ocean and have her expunge them into the Holy water. They will burn up and be destroyed the moment their evil essence hits the blessed water.

"But how to get thousands of dark souls into Arima at one time? She can only absorb three, maybe four at once if she's really focused, which isn't very often. And no more than one if it's Howard. Everyone refuses to be in Arima if *he's* there. We must increase her ability thousands-fold. And I think that we've come up with a solution. Alexa has been learning at my knee and is now just as good at creating toxins as I am. Maybe better. You are so brilliant, Alexa. We have been working on a new formula along with Rod and Rosa."

"And Herbert, don't forget about him. He's the most important part," Arima interjected. "He's been coming into my soul and tweaking different herbal combinations. And we think that once we get the right recipe down, our concoction's powers can be enhanced by the scientific and spiritual manipulation of its energy by Rod and Rosa. All I will need to do is inhale, and my ability to absorb souls will be incredible! So, Maddy and her army kills them in human form, and I then absorb their dark souls and burn the bastards in the ocean of Holy water. It's gonna be the copperhead's and our father's worst nightmare. It is what they most feared. Two sisters working side by side to vanquish them. It's gonna be a helluva trip. Hey, pass those cookies, wouldja?"

———

"Now, you have fun today, but don't go *too* crazy on me, love," Jennifer lovingly said to Lucy as she was about to depart the plane in London. The pair embraced then engaged in a passionate kiss before Lucy whispered into Jennifer's ear, "You are my rock. You are my anchor that keeps me from floating away in a sea of anger."

"I know," Jennifer playfully responded. "You would be quite the nutter if it wasn't for me. Now go and have your fun. The plane will be fueled and ready for you when you all return."

As Lucy descended the plane's stairs, she looked back at her waving lover's enticing blue eyes and allowed herself a rare moment of satisfied calm.

The billboard was unveiled, and a smiling Jessie's face beamed down upon the pedestrians of London. It did not fail to garner attention. Jessie noticed that males would stop and stare at her pretty face briefly before walking on. She also noticed that females would stop and take the time to read the message on the billboard. Several wrote down the number.

"Oh, my sweetie!" Jamie exclaimed. "We are all *so proud* of you! Look at what you are doing! Look at what you have *done*! Let's go visit the first women that you have inspired!"

"Yeah, it is pretty cool, I guess," Jessie replied with a hint of arrogance. "I mean, I think there's, like, twenty-four women who we are going to get away from abusive, toxic assholes and be taken to safety.

And that's just the start. Plus, I *really* look great on that billboard. Just *look* at all the people who are paying attention to me!"

"Twenty-four, huh?" Maddy interjected as her jealous, green eyes darted at Jessie. "Yeah, that's a really cute number. Nice job. Of course, that's not *nearly* as many as *I* have helped over the years, but…"

Maddy was cut off as her daughter firmly elbowed her in the side and whispered through gritted teeth, "Mother. Shut the fuck up. Today isn't about you."

"Okay, whatevs, bitch," Maddy replied in her "hurt" voice as she once again rubbed her "wounded" ribs.

The thirteen women of Murder, Inc. entered a lavish dormitory-style holding residence. They met with each woman there and listened to every story. They heard horrendous recounts of mental abuse. Physical abuse. Rape. Captivity. Threats to their loved ones. All done to satisfy spineless men's tiny egos and indoctrinate the women into their twisted fantasies of a White, male dominated society. There was one young woman who told the story of her escape from her parents' plan for her to be forced into an insidious religious practice of genital mutilation. They witnessed the women's scars, both physical and emotional.

There were tears. And embraces. And more tears. Until finally, laughter as the women realized that they were going to be alright. Their laughter intensified after they had been invited to watch how the women of Murder, Inc. threw a party.

———

The bright flood lights came on in the operating theatre. Ten confused and naked men looked up at the stadium seats that circled above them and saw twenty-four enthralled female faces.

"What the fuck is this, bitches?" One of the skin-headed, fully bearded men yelled out. "You'd better let us out of here! You don't know who you're fucking with!"

"Oh, but we do," came Josie's playful voice over the intercom. "We know *exactly* who it is that we're dealing with. And we know *exactly* what it is that you think of *us*. You think of us as your property. As your servants. As your playthings. Now, don't worry. There is nothing to be concerned about. What would ten *big, strong men* have to fear from us *tiny little women?* We are here today to make your fantasies come to life. To give you what you so rightfully deserve. C'mon, boys. You *know* you wanna see an all-girl pillow fight, *right?*"

The operating room doors opened, and thirteen women entered. One was in a wheelchair and whispered and pointed out one of the men to her dark-haired friend before entering. The women were all wearing innocent-looking flannel footie pajamas and not-so-innocent smiles. They were also all carrying innocent-looking pillowcases.

"Slaaaaashdaaaaance!" Alexa squealed as Kaneko pushed 'play' on a CD player. As the guitar-driven beats of The Pink Spiders came pulsing through the speakers, the men realized that the pillows were far from innocent and were not filled with feathers. And they also realized why these violent women were playing a song titled "Little Razorblade."

Jamie was the first to land a blow with her blade-filled pillowcase. The razors protruded through the fabric and sliced the hysterical man's throat, nearly cutting off his swastika tattoo. Arima and Maddy were tag-teaming another screaming man. Arima was slicing through his torso with a whirlwind of blows while Maddy hit the man in his scrotum repeatedly until his slimy testicles tumbled out of his mutilated sack. They knew that he was the father of the girl who had been threatened with genital mutilation and chose him specifically for this special treatment.

Jessie sliced through a man's calves, causing him to land on his knees, then beat him repeatedly on his face until it looked like raw, pre-cooked stir-fry beef. One man was defensively flailing wildly at Alexa who skipped and giggled around him before she took the ends of her pillowcase, wrapped it around his face and violently slid it back and forth until the yelping man succumbed and fell to the floor in a bloody heap.

The platinum blonde Dragentstein looked down at the man nearest her and blew him a gentle kiss before swinging her pillowcase with all her might at the man's neck. The force of the blow decapitated him in one thrust and his head went flying toward the observation deck. A woman jumped up and grabbed the head as it was flying above her. The entire observation group exploded into cheers and bloody high-fives.

Lucy swung her pillowcase, and she heard shattering glass tubes as it made an impact on the man's skull. She began to quiver in ecstasy as she quietly watched the man's face melt off his skull as a result of her new acid.

"Great! Nice job Lucy! Way to put a wet spot in your pajamas! Now we won't be able to return them!" a blood-soaked Maddy jokingly yelled out to her dear friend as she viciously beat another anguished man with a childish enthusiasm.

"That's right, bitches!" Kaneko yelled out as her arms swung her pillowcase repeatedly against a wailing man, "Let's fuck these bastards up!"

Rosa and Vai worked over one of the remaining men on each side of his face. He shrieked in agony as he could feel the sharp blades slicing through his cheeks, nose, ears, and eyeballs. Sam ejected the blades on the feet of her wheelchair and sliced the final man's feet off. He howled in pain as he tumbled to the floor and Jules cauterized the wounds with a blowtorch.

Josie approached the writhing man and said, "Hey, are you guys gonna finish him off or what? I haven't had any fun yet, and I'm in the mood to dance." As Josie lifted her deadly pillowcase above her head, Sam said, "No. Please stop, Josie."

"Why? What the fuck, Sam?" a confused Josie asked as she forlornly lowered her case.

"Well, I have some bad news, everybody," a remorseful Sam replied. "My dear Pogo has passed away. His body just couldn't take the punishment anymore and I'm really upset by it. He made such a wonderful pincushion. And ashtray. And knife-holder. And corkboard. And the hooks I stuck in his back were just perfect for Henri's ties. So, I wanted to keep this one as my new Pogo. That will be all right, won't it?"

"Of course, it's all right! I'm *so sorry* for your loss!" a tearful Josie exclaimed as she wrapped her flannel arms around Sam's slender neck. She then wiped her tears from her eyes and yelled up at the observation seats, "Hey, ladies! Any of you wanna hold this prick down while Jules and Sam cut his limbs off?" There was the thunderous sound of forty-eight stampeding feet eagerly making their way to the operating floor's entrance as an enraptured LucyFur was lapping up blood from around the fallen corpses.

Maddy's blood-soaked form stood in the middle of the carnage with her hands proudly placed upon her hips. She flashed her mischievous smile before saying, "So. Are any of you boys in the mood for a little pillow talk, *hmmmmm*? Hey, do you guys get it? Pillow talk? Why isn't anybody laughing? That was pure fuckin' gold!"

The thirteen giddy women made their way along the darkened tarmac and approached the welcoming stairs of their private plane. Pogo II was squealing in pain as he was being dragged face down behind Sam's wheelchair, leaving a trail of blood on the harsh concrete.

Maddy was the first to enter the cabin and yelled out, "Jennifer! We're back! Let's get this fuckin' bird in the air!" She then felt a heavy liquid splash on her forehead. "What the fuck is this?" she asked as she wiped her forehead and looked at the thick, iron-scented substance on her fingertips. She then looked up and fell into a shocked silence.

"What is it?" Lucy inquired as she pushed her way through her friends to the top step.

"No, Lucy," Maddy pleaded as she placed her hands firmly on Lucy's petite shoulders. "Don't go in there, okay? Just, Just, don't."

A frantic Lucy shoved her friend to the side and stood there with the same shocked silence. Blood was dripping from the walls and ceiling of the plane's main cabin and human body parts were hanging from the backs of seats, tables, and overhead compartments. Arms, legs, internal organs, bones, and skin were strewn everywhere. The heavy stench of the massacre hung in the foreboding silence. Jennifer's semen covered, decapitated head sat on the floor next to the cockpit door. On the door it read, *It's a man's world, bitches.*

"Okay, Lucy," Maddy began in a desperate voice. "Listen. We'll find out who did this and we'll fuck them up, okay?"

"I already know who did this," Lucy replied with an eerily calm determination. "*Men* did this. Get off the plane, Maddy."

"Lucy, dammit, just listen to me, and…"

"Get off the plane, Maddy."

"Lucy, I love you. We all love you. You can't be alone right now, okay?"

"Get off the plane, Maddy."

As the remaining twelve women watched the private jet soar into the sky like a predatory bird, Josie turned to Alexa and said, "Okay Alexa. Just what *else* has she been working on?"

Chapter 88
Forty-Five

"Well, here we are," Alexa stated to the group twelve hours later. "Lucy's laboratory in the basement under the bookstore. Here's what she's been working on. He should be about ready."

A feeling of dread was hovering over all the ladies who were now joined by Erick, Marcus, Henri, Cliff, and Gregory as Alexa walked them toward a naked, screaming man in an otherwise empty sound-proof glass booth. He was standing in his own waste as he pounded on the glass frantically and screamed at them.

"So, who is *this* then?" Josie cautiously inquired as the man continued his futile pounding and began hurling his feces at the glass.

"I'm not sure," Alexa replied. "Lucy just said he was someone who had it coming. I've learned not to ask too many questions of her. She gets really agitated if I pry too hard about where she gets her test subjects. But she *does* love questions about her inventions. And their *effects*. And she said that this *new* toxin that she has created will make the world safe for women forever. That this toxin will wipe out all the males of our species. Well, except for the ones that we decide to keep locked away and use for stud in order to preserve the human race. Or at least the *females* of the human race. She said that if we failed in this war that this would be the final and definitive solution. She then got this really creepy smile on her face and said, 'Part of me *hopes* we fail. Part of me *hopes* that this will be the final solution.'

"Anyway, she calls this new one, 'Toxin T.' The 'T' stands for 'Testosterone.' It can be distributed in water supplies or can be airborne and is comprised of millions of microscopic spores. Once it is ingested by breathing it in or drinking it by a female, the toxin immediately dies. The high level of estrogen kills it and there are no effects. This would also be true of males who have higher levels of estrogen and lower levels of testosterone than normal. However, once it is ingested by a *male* with *normal* levels of testosterone and estrogen…well…then things get interesting.

"You see, these spores are attracted to higher levels of testosterone. In fact, they thrive on it. So, the spores congregate in the male testes and just…um…kinda hibernate there. For seven days the spores strengthen. And the inflicted male is highly contagious. He has no idea that there's anything wrong. There are no symptoms…yet. For seven days he is walking around infecting other males. Just by breathing near them. Or shaking their hand. At their workplace. Their schools. Their churches. Their grocery stores. Everywhere they go, they are infecting other males. Lucy said that she could take one infected male and put him in a stadium full of unaffected men and that the entire stadium would be infected within twenty minutes. Just by the men passing it from one to another. Seat by seat. Row by row. Section by section. It would spread that quickly. Kinda like when fans do the wave. Only *this* is deadly. After seven days, the spores hatch and…"

Alexa's voice trailed off as she witnessed the encased man fall on his back and begin writhing in pain. The group fell into a shocked silence as they witnessed the man's skin literally crawling. They then gasped as thousands of large black spiders tore their way through the man's skin from his head to his toes. His entire body violently shook as it was covered by the fierce arachnids that were consuming his flesh. After feasting for five minutes, the insidious spiders instantly died, leaving a half-eaten corpse.

"Yep. That's what happens. I *thought* he was about ready to hatch." Alexa stated matter-of-factly. "You see, after seven days, the spores hatch into thousands of creepy, black, carnivorous spiders. They immediately grow to about two inches in diameter, crawl throughout the body and begin eating their way out through the skin. Lucy specifically engineered them to die after five minutes of their hatching because, and I quote, 'Women have enough shit to deal with. We're not dealing with an epidemic of carnivorous spiders too.' This is the sixth and final test subject. I guess the piranhas in Maddy's old office next door are going to be happy tonight. So, this toxin is ready to be deployed. Lucy now has a weapon to virtually eliminate every male on the planet."

"Okay, guys," the ever reasonable and diplomatic Gregory interjected. "Listen, I'm sure Lucy is a little bit...um...off the rails at the moment. And for good reason. She just saw the torn apart body of her murdered love. We would *all* get a bit loopy after something horrible like that. She probably just needs some time to cool off. Maybe take out a few 'Chads.' She'll be okay. I'm sure that she doesn't intend to deploy this. I mean, my God! If she did, then she would kill *all* of *us* as well. We are her friends, and she would never do anything to harm us."

"Yeah, maybe," a suspicious Maddy stated as she walked around the glass encasement and surveyed what little remained of Test Subject Number six. "Tell me Alexa. Did she develop anything to deploy this toxin on a large scale or is she limited to just lab experiments right now?"

"Oh yeah. She could deploy it via waterways or by air on a massive scale. Fly a crop duster over a metropolitan area. Pour the liquid form into the water supply. And she already has the infection route developed. She knows just where to concentrate her efforts to spread it most efficiently. Region to region. Country to country. Continent to Continent. She said that it would take approximately nine months to wipe out eighty-six-point-three percent of the males on the planet. The remaining ones could be rounded up and kept in isolation, away from the toxin. Then, she said, we could use *them* for their seed. And target practice. She also said that it would be a blessing for any good souls who died, because they would get a fast-track to Enlightenment. The dark souls could be destroyed by Arima and others like her over time. And she said that there *would* be others like Arima. And Jessie. And Rosa. That without the heavy hand of men's persecution, women would evolve more quickly, and we could then be the stewards of this Earth as God intended. But you're right Maddy. Without the stuff in *this* room, she can't deploy it on a large scale. Maybe we're all just getting worked up over nothing."

There was a loud 'creak' as a metal door was opened then the soft 'click' of the light switch. The entire group let out an audible gasp before an unnerved Erick said, "Is it okay to get worked up *now*? Because what I'm looking at is a room full of *nothing*."

"Aw, shit," Alexa softly said as tears began to form in her blue eyes. "It's gone. It's all gone. All of it. The canisters of the gas and the aerial distribution system. Gone. All of the cannisters of the liquid toxin. Gone. All she needs is an airplane, which she has, and she could infect the entire world."

"Okay, then," Josie said with unease in her voice. "Step Numero-Uno. We find her. And we put Rod and the rest of the men on that. She may have loved you all once, but we must assume that she's completely distrustful of men right now. And that includes you guys. So, go get Rod and track her movements. She has an airplane that must land somewhere. And we have her infection route. She's very routine-oriented. She will stick to her plan.

"Step Numero-Two-O: When we find her, we will talk with her. We will get her to surrender to us. And if she *won't* come with us, then…"

Josie's statement was cut off by Maddy's mournful voice. "Don't say that, Josie. Don't *ever* say that. She is my best friend. Plus, we don't take out other women. It will be all right. She will listen to me. It *will be* all right. It *has* to be. Sweetie, I love you, but don't you *ever* finish that fucking sentence."

———

"Oh my," Rod's nasal staccato voice was heard saying as he was looking at the data that Erick had requested. "She is much too smart for this. She couldn't have remained hidden from us forever, but this is like she is wanting to be found. She has left us quite the trail of breadcrumbs to follow."

"Not exactly breadcrumbs," Lionnel replied. "But definitely, a trail. A trail of exploding heads. A trail of intestines. A trail of bodies that all lead to…what is this point on the map, Rod?"

"Well, let me see here," Rod answered as he put his pop-bottle lenses up against the screen. "Oh yes. That is the Catskill/Delaware Watershed."

"Uh, huh," Marcus replied before asking with trepidation, "And just what is the significance of *that*?"

"Well, you see," Rod answered. "That is where approximately ninety-five percent of the water comes from for New York City."

Erick, Lionnel, Jerry, Marcus, Cliff, and even Gregory let out a simultaneous "Fuuuuuuuuck."

———

"Why did those two little bitches get themselves knocked up," Maddy incredulously asked her sisterhood as they made their way through the woods surrounding the reservoir. "We could have really used Rachel and Kayla's tracking ability. This place is fucking huge! But *noooooo*! We just *had* to teach the Twins to play 'Hide the Sausage' now didn't we!' *Then* we had to tell them not to double-bag it! Dumbasses! Now we have to squirrel them away at the estate to protect them and their fucking little blessings! Those little fuckers will be blessings all right. Blessing for fucking Satan probably! Whatevs. Jessie, can't you Behold her or something? It's gonna take forever to find her here!"

"I'm sorry Maddy," Jessie answered, "But I can't. I never could with her. Her soul is neither pure good nor pure evil. Her soul is conflicted. Her soul is whatever it is required to be at any given moment. So, no. I'm sorry. I can't and…Oh! Goddamit!"

"Hey, man, what's wrong?" Arima asked her friend.

"Oh, I just broke another nail, *that's all*! How do you expect me to influence women to get out of abusive situations looking like *this*? Plus, I'm *totally* wearing the wrong shoes to stomp through the woods. And look at my blouse! Completely covered in sap! I really think that I should wait back in the bus. I'm just too…um…*important* to be out here rummaging around in the weeds."

"No, we stay together. We will do this together," came Josie's immediate and blunt order. Jessie decided that it was best not to question her leader at this particular moment.

There was a loud *CRACK* twenty yards ahead of them. "Hey, honeys," came Dragenstein's soft, petite voice. "Come this way. I just took this tree out of our way, *tee, hee.*"

"It *is* kinda nice to have an Amazonian bulldozer drag queen with us," Maddy whispered to her daughter before tripping and falling face-first into the dense brush.

"What the fuck?" Maddy yelled out as she looked down at her feet and saw the arm of a police officer sticking out of the bushes on the ground. "What's this? Number *seven* that we've found? And all men. The only surviving officer that we have found so far is that lady officer that was gagged and bound to that tree. So, we know three things. Lucy is sticking to our code to not harm women. Lucy is *not* sticking to our code of only taking out men who deserve it. And finally, we are defi-nitely going in the right direction."

The women came out of the wooded area with its sounds of rustling leaves and snapping twigs. Those sounds were replaced by the tranquil lapping of waves upon the shore. Approximately fifty yards from their position stood Lucy who was navigating a remote-controlled boat into the center of the body of water. On top of the boat rested a large metal cannister. And a small black box with a flashing red light.

"Okay guys. You approach her from here. I'm gonna circle around in the woods and try to get close to her. Just keep her talking until I can get there," Maddy instructed before her lithe frame disappeared into the timber.

"Hey Lucy," Josie said casually as she discreetly pulled an arrow from her quiver and placed it into her bow. Lucy looked up and saw Josie's dark green cat suit become increasingly visible as well as the forms of Jules, Dragenstein, Arima, Jessie, Jamie, and Alexa.

"Oh, hey guys," Lucy responded nonchalantly. "Nice to see you. Where's Sam and Maddy? They won't want to miss this."

"Oh, they're just back at the bus keeping the champagne chilled for us. We're all going to celebrate your homecoming," Josie answered calmly. "So…um…whatcha doin'? Should we just go ahead and get on the bus and get the party started? Then we can get down to the business of stopping these damned wars. C'mon. What do ya say?"

"Naw," Lucy answered dismissively. "I think that I'll stay here for a while. And after tonight, you really won't be needed to stop the wars. I'm taking care of it. Now, please just stop approaching or else, okay?"

"Well, sure, Lucy. Whatever you say," Josie replied as she obediently held up her left hand to halt the progression of her troops. "But I'm a bit confused. Or else, what? And what do you mean that you're going to end the wars tonight?"

Lucy let out an exasperated sigh and said, "Or else I hit this little button on this remote. And this little button will make that box on top of that cannister on the boat go boom. And then the liquid contents of that cannister will be spread throughout this reservoir and into New York's water system. Then, *that* water will go into the mouths of the men of New York."

Lucy then began trembling with orgasmic excitement and the cadence of her speech quickened. "And then, and then, do you know what will happen? And then the toxins that are in this water will be in the men of New York. And the men who are *visiting* New York! Yeah! And all the men of New York will die in like, seven to thirty days. And all the men who were *visiting* New York will take *my toxin* back to their homes. And *they* will spread it! Throughout the world, *my toxins* will be spread! And it will kill *all the males*! Yeah, isn't that *cool*? They will all *die*! And they will die *painfully*! They are going to be eaten from the *inside out* by *my* engineered spiders. All over the world men will be *eaten alive*! Isn't that *great*? All I have to do is push *this* little button and we will be *free* from men for *all time*, heh,heh,heh,heh,heh,heh,heh."

Josie lifted her bow and pointed it at Lucy as she said in a relaxed voice, "Lucy. You know we can't let you do that. You know our code. We don't take out innocent people. So please just put the remote down and come with us. Please, Lucy. I don't want to have to do this."

"Do *what*?" Lucy retorted angrily as her face turned from unhinged glee to maniacal intensity. "Just what are *you* going to do Josie, huh? Shoot me? I don't think so. As soon as you let that arrow fly, I'm going to press this button. You're a good shot, but you aren't *that* good. Or that quick. I'm really disappointed in you all. Maddy would understand. I wish she were here to explain it to you. She would understand because she was *mind-fucked* by the *same man* that I was! And she knows *deep down* in her soul that *all* men are that way! They are cruel! They are violent! All they want is power! All they want is to dominate others! To dominate *us*! To beat us! To rape us! To murder our loved ones and tear them limb from limb and leave them strewn about an airplane! That's *men* that did that! Not just a *few* men, either! *All* men did that because *all* men are *capable* of doing that! They destroy *everything* that they touch! They destroy this planet! They destroy our livelihoods! They destroy our bodies! And they destroy our souls! Maddy understands. I *know* that she does."

"Lucy, that isn't *true!*" Josie pleaded. "Not all men are evil! Hell, not even *most* of them are evil. Most are good, kind souls. Like Erick and Marcus and Lionnel and Henri! What about Pastor Tim and Jeremy? Look at how their selfless sacrifice might save our world! That was *men* that did that, Lucy! Now please. Put down the remote and let's just get out of here, okay? Please, Lucy. I don't want to do this."

"Yeah, well, you probably have a point," Lucy answered with a renewed tranquility. "There might be a *few* that are worth saving. Maybe they are the ones that we keep for their seed. And some might be sacrificed. Yeah, I suppose we might have to break a few eggs. But you know what they say about breaking eggs to make an omelet, right? Well, I really *love* fuckin' omelets!"

Lucy's thumb began to press down on the detonator button just as she felt a sharp pain pierce her heart through her back. Then, an arrow penetrated her right wrist, causing her to drop the detonator. Everyone gasped as the detonator tumbled from her grasp and fell to the ground. They briefly stared at it before their eyes darted toward the remote-controlled boat. There was no boom.

Lucy's lifeless body collapsed backward, knocking Maddy to the ground with it. Maddy stared into the dead eyes of her best friend, and she shook her bloody fist at the sky while screaming out to the universe, "Why? *Why* you motherfuckers? Why did I have to kill Lucy? Why did it have to come to this? Why is the world so hateful? Why is the world turning us all into heartless bastards? Why? This is it! This is the end of it all! Because if I can murder my best friend, then there's no hope for *any* of us! This war is over! And we just fucking lost. This truly is the end of it all."

A sobbing Maddy cradled and lightly rocked her dear friend's body as she began singing REM's "Why Not Smile" through her cracking voice. From their time in college, it was the song that they had always sung together during dreadful times. They would hold each other and weep and sing along with Michael's beautiful voice. At the end of the song, they would always look at one another and smile. Then laugh. Then Maddy would say, "Now get the fuck off of me!" And they would hug and laugh again. They had sung this song together countless times through countless tragedies. Maddy knew that this was the final time that she would ever sing this song because Maddy knew there could be no greater tragedy than this.

Arima's body began lightly shaking as her eyes rolled back into her head and her body elevated four feet off the ground. Her pretty ebony face looked directly into Maddy's tearful green eyes. She opened her mouth. And she joined Maddy in singing the rest of the song as she smiled widely.

Upon the song's conclusion, Lucy said through Arima, "Thank you Maddy. You were the only one who could have done this. You were the only one who could have freed me. You were the only one who loved humanity enough to sacrifice your best friend. I'm glad that I died at your hands. I'm glad that I died at the hands of the woman who I love and respect more than all others. It's okay, Maddy. You have nothing to feel guilty about. You had no choice. I gave you no choice. I gave you no choice but to send me to my Jennifer. And now, I will get the fuck off of you. For now. Win this war. I will see you on the battlefield in Enlightenment."

There was a light blue and white streak that emerged from Arima's descending body. It wistfully hovered over the astonished and grieving women for a moment before ascending into the heavens.

"Well, fuck," Maddy stated with resignation. "I guess this *isn't* the end of it all. It fuckin' sucks though. Okay. Let's get her precious body back to the bus. Let's get home. And let's find and destroy the demonic fucks who made me do this!"

Chapter 89

Oh Lord

"It looks like we both had the same idea," a drowsy Maddy stated as she saw Arima's ass sticking out of her refrigerator.

"Oh, hey, Sis," Arima replied sleepily. "Yeah, I sometimes enjoy a little midnight snack. Or one AM snack. Or three AM snack. What time is it anyway?"

"It's twelve-thirty," Maddy replied as she perched her petite born-again frame up onto the kitchen island and smiled to herself as she watched her sister rummaging through the leftovers. "So, anything in particular that you're looking for? And don't say 'tato chips. Erick is getting *really pissed* at everyone eating his 'tato chips. Except Josie. That little bitch can do whatever she wants around here."

"I dunno," Arima casually responded. "I'm kinda in the mood for something sweet."

"How 'bout some ice cream?" Maddy excitedly replied as her size-six bare feet slapped back down onto the cool linoleum floor and she opened the freezer door. "Here, let me show you something." The freezer light illuminated Maddy's ornery smile as she began removing packages of frozen dinners and vegetables from the bottom shelf and handing them to Arima. "Here. Hold this. And this. And this. And…ah… here we are. Now, Arima, I have trusted you with a lot of my secrets. But there is *no* secret that is more important than this one. I haven't told *anybody* about this, so you must keep this a secret. Underneath all this frozen healthy shit is where I keep my secret stash of butter-ripple ice cream. Erick doesn't even know about this, okay?"

"Yeah, cool," Arima replied as she handed the frozen vegetables and dinners back to her sister who began carefully placing them back into the freezer.

"Now, if you ever get in here," Maddy began instructing, "it's *very important* that you put everything back *exactly* as it was. Erick is anal-retentive as fuck. He even has an organizational system for frozen food, and he'll notice if anything has been disturbed, okay?"

"Yep. Got it," Arima answered. "So, do we need some bowls or…?"

"Fuck that," Maddy interrupted. "All we need is two spoons and we'll eat it right out of the container. Just as the good lord intended."

The pair of giggling sisters flopped their pajama-clad bottoms onto the white, plush couch cushions in the living room and eagerly opened the brand-new container of ice cream. They giggled a bit louder as their large, silver spoons dug in for their first bite.

"Oh, yeah, that's the stuff," an enraptured Arima sighed as her first taste was dribbling off her lower lip and onto her pajama collar.

"Yeah, this shit's the best!" Maddy exclaimed. "This is the flavor that my Uncle Joe and I would eat together. We would just talk and laugh and eat ice cream. I cherished those moments. Oh, shit! I just realized something!"

"What's that?" Arima inquired as another overflowing spoonful of ice cream was being excavated from its frozen container.

"I just realized that you and I haven't had a chance to really…um… talk. I mean, everything has been so fucking busy and chaotic that we haven't just been able to…um…y'know…" Maddy's voice trailed off as she looked away from Arima's inquisitive face.

"Hey, Sis, what's wrong?" Arima asked.

"Oh, fuckin' nothin'," Maddy chuckled as she wiped tears from her green eyes and embarrassingly looked back at her sister. "I'm just being a big fuckin' pussy. I can tear the fuck out of people. I can run an international hit man syndicate. Or, assassination technician syndicate, or, *whatever* the fuck Josie calls them now. I can cut people up, blow people up, dissolve them in acid, dismember them, make them watch as I feed their flesh to my piranha, and all sorts of other twisted shit. I can walk out of that room, covered in their blood, and never give them another thought. I have absolutely no emotional connection to what I've just done to another human being. None. I'm cold as fucking ice, and I *like* being that way. But when it comes to my friends, and my family, I get…well…sentimental. And it just fuckin' hit me. *I have a sister!*"

Maddy broke down in tears and physically embraced Arima for the first time. Arima hugged Maddy tightly in response and the shoulders of their respective pajama tops became saturated in their joyful tears. They each felt a strange sensation as they held each other. It was as though they had found a missing piece of themselves. Maddy's internal ember seemed to burn with a greater intensity. And Arima's inner-fortitude and ability to connect with souls seemed to be enhanced. They looked at one another, smiled, laughed, and hugged once again. For the first time, the sisters had connected emotionally. They felt their care and love for one another. They felt one another's feminine strength. They instinctively knew that their souls belonged together. And they now knew that their combined forces could never be stopped.

"Oh fuck! The ice cream!" Maddy yelled out as she pulled away from her sister and looked at the crushed and partially melted ice cream container that was between them.

They both looked down at their sugar-coated tops and broke out into hysterical laughter. "Ah, fuck it," they said in unison as they picked up their spoons and began scooping the melted ice cream from their respective tops and shoveling it into their mouths through their playful giggles. Maddy didn't even mind that four white rats had joined them to help in their clean-up efforts. They then began rapidly hurling a barrage of questions and comments toward one another. The moment one would finish, the other would begin. They had years to catch up on. They had years to make up for. And they were determined to do it all in one evening.

"So, how did you meet Erick?"

"So, how did you meet Marcus?"

"Oh my God! I loved *Cinderella* too!"

"What's your favorite color?"

"What's *your* favorite color?"

"I fuckin' asked you first!"

"Who was your first boyfriend?"

"Okay. You're stranded on a desert island, and you can only take one album with you. What album is it?"

"Really? Springsteen? Me too!"

"When did you first know you could connect with souls?"

"Who are all the people you have helped to Enlightenment?"

"You did *what*? You ate hotdogs off a burning corpse? That's so cool."

"You did *what*? You put his dark soul in tacos, ate him and then killed him by shitting him out? That's gold Arima! Fuckin' gold!"

"Who was the first person you killed?"

"Who was the *second* person you killed?"

"Who was the *third* person you killed?"

(An hour later) "Who was the *fifty-third* person you killed?"

Over two hours had passed, and the exhausted and exhilarated sisters collapsed back onto the seat cushions with feelings of newfound tranquility.

"Hey, sis," Arima stated with regret as she wiped the final remnants of butter-ripple from her chin. "I'm so sorry that you lost your best friend. Especially that way. She was a cool person. I'm sorry she's gone."

"Thanks, Arima," Maddy thoughtfully answered. "Yeah. She *was* cool. Really fucked up but cool. And, as we all now know, she isn't really gone. I mean, she is from *here*, of course, but she isn't *gone, gone*. I mean, I'll see her again when our work down here is done, and we get called back to Enlightenment. Oh, fuck. Part of me wishes that this war just goes on forever. Part of me wishes that I could stay with you and the rest of my loved ones forever. But another part of me wants it to be over. For us to beat the fuck out of these evil pricks once and for all. For us to beat the fuck out of my demonic mother and our demonic father. Then, Erick and I can move on. Back to my loved ones in Enlightenment. I feel so fucking torn. This is why I hate feeling anything."

"Hey," Arima softly answered. "There's no need to feel conflicted. What you are doing…what *we* are doing is right. And the sooner it gets done the more people we can save. We need to get this shit done as fast as possible. And listen. You can always come back into my soul whenever you want. You can visit me and Josie and everyone else whenever you want. I told you before that you have an open invitation to come into my soul. Just…um…call first, okay?"

"Okay," Maddy answered through a new bout of laughter. "Yeah, I don't wanna jump into you while you're getting busy or somethin'! Wow! It's gonna be like I have my own little personal time-share on Earth. Yeah! This could be cool! Best of both worlds! I get eternity in Enlightenment with Erick and my deceased family plus I get to visit my Earth-bound friends and family whenever I want! And the best part is that I can make fun of 'em as they get old, and their tits get all saggy and shit! Especially Sam! That's gonna be classic!"

"Well, we should probably get to bed, Sis," Arima regretfully stated. "Rod has called us all to a big meeting in the morning."

"Yeah, I suppose," Maddy responded with the same tone of regret. She never wanted this moment with her sister to end. She then thought of a way to extend it, if only for a brief time. "But first, there's one thing left to do! I have danced with *everyone* that I've ever cared about. Erick. Uncle Joe. Aunt Blair. Aunt Patty. Josie. Lucy. All my friends and family. I danced with them all. And now, my beautiful sister, I want to dance with you!"

Maddy leapt off the couch and playfully swayed her hips as she sauntered toward the entertainment center. She opened the bottom cabinet and took out a dusty cardboard box that still contained fifty-four records. It was the box of records that Erick had purchased in 2022 from Maddy's store. After all these years, every record remained in that box, in the exact order as when he had brought them home. She chuckled lightly to herself, and a single tear rolled down her slightly befreckled cheek. She looked up at the clock, smiled broadly, and exclaimed, "And I know the *perfect song* to dance to!"

She placed the forty-five on the turntable and lowered the needle. After a few seconds of crackling vinyl, Arima and Maddy were swaying, spinning, jiving, and grooving to Gary US Bonds's R&B classic, "Quarter to Three."

The song ended and the pair burst into laughter as they heard Erick's booming voice from the top of the staircase. "Hey! You two had better not be eating my 'tato chips!"

"This isn't working, Pastor," its nasal voice stated as It peered down at the dancing pair of sisters from Its unholy perch in the Realm of Perdition. "We need to end this now. We need a new strategy. She is stronger than we imagined. They both are. They have bonded and they can now combine their strength. Just as *we* have done. Our Earthbound forces are depleted. They are losing the war there. But with every human that we lose comes a new dark soul to wage war against Enlightenment. The fools are building our cosmic army for us. It is time to collect as many dark souls as we can. As many as we can get to congregate in one place. Men, women, *and* children. Collect them all. You will go to Earth and convince them, Pastor. Manipulate them one final time and convince them to commit the ultimate mortal sacrifice. Convince them to sacrifice themselves and their wives and their children. Convince them to destroy any good souls that might arise from the fallen bodies. Convince them to stand back, stand down and be ready. Ready for when we call them here. We shall do this in reverse. We shall conquer Enlightenment. Then, we shall destroy the good souls *after* they leave the Earth. Once we have conquered Enlightenment, there will be *no* place for the good souls to go. Except their own personal hell of *our* creation!"

———

"It's okay, Rod. I'll explain what's going on," an understanding Rosa stated as she looked upon her profusely sweating friend. She then leaned into his ear and whispered, "But you might want to stop staring at Jessie's chest. I think Cliff is getting pissed."

"Why are *you* so fucking perky this morning?" Erick inquired of his wife quietly. "You and Arima were up half the night."

"Yeah," Maddy responded. "I'm probably still on a sugar high from all the ice cream I ate last night."

"Ice cream? When did we get ice cream?" a confused Erick asked followed by their daughter. "Yeah! When did we get ice cream?"

"Would you two just shut the fuck up!" Maddy whisper shouted. "Rosa's about to start talking. Show some fuckin' respect!" *That was close,* Maddy thought to herself as she flashed her sister a mischievous grin.

"Madam President," Rosa respectfully began as she looked down upon Josie who was sitting to her immediate right next to her parents. Josie gave her mother a brief, haughty look. The ever-diplomatic Maddy rolled her eyes and stuck out her tongue.

"We have some very good news and some news that…well…we are confused by. Jamie has been working with Rod on keeping tabs on the most dangerous Earth-bound dark souls. These are the self-proclaimed militias, skinheads, radical militants, and their ilk. Jamie, could you please present what you and Rod are finding?"

"Yes, of course dear," the thirty-year-old, African American transsexual replied as she sauntered her mini-dressed frame up to the podium. Rod's gaze immediately went from the ceiling to Jamie's burgeoning bosom. "The Earthly forces of the Underground Autocratic Movement, also known as the demonic forces of Vetis are quite depleted. Since Gregory, Marcus, and Cliff were able to forge a partnership with the Earth's great democracies, they have been rounded up or killed off by precise military strikes. Some of these strikes have been conducted by various governments and some have been conducted by us. And, due to difficulty in being able to spread their hate-filled propaganda, they are unable to poison the minds of the weak-willed into joining their movement in large numbers as they did twenty years ago. So, the result is that the most radical and violent of their movement are now small in numbers and are clustered in various tribes. And these tribes are on the move. They are all jumping in cars, boats, and planes and heading to a dilapidated, closed resort in Florida. I have heard that it is so run down that even the rats have abandoned it. We estimate that there are approximately 10,000 people that are congregating there. This would be our best chance to wipe them out, once and for all. Then, we would need to deal with their souls. There is a problem, however. These evil men are bringing their families. Their wives and children are being brought along as well. We do not know why. So, Josie wants us to have a formidable force go to Florida and observe what they are doing. Just observe. We do not have any desire to harm the women or children. If there is an opening to take out the men, then we shall do so. But only as long as they aren't using their families as human shields. We shall leave immediately following our meeting here today."

"Thank you, Jamie," Rosa said as she retook her place behind the podium. "Okay, gang. Yes, that is confusing news. We don't know what they're up to. Maybe it's just a good-ol'-boy hootenanny. But we doubt it. They may be planning some sort of offensive. So, we'll watch them and act accordingly.

"Now, for the good news. We have done it. We have found a way to enhance Arima's ability to draw souls into herself, then expel them into the ocean of Holy water. We estimate that she will be able to absorb approximately 1,000 souls at a time."

"Wow. That's really cool," Arima replied in her customary relaxed tone. "But, like, is this gonna hurt?"

"No! That's the best part!" Rosa excitedly answered. "In fact, I think that you will find this very enjoyable. As you know, Herbert, otherwise known as The Botanist, has been entering and taking over your body and doing experiments with us. He has been working with a number of plant and herbal combinations that are designed to interact with your specific DNA. And he has found one that will work. The only drawback is that you're going to have *one hell* of a case of the munchies. He has combined various strains of cannabis with other plants and herbs. I then connected with and enhanced the spiritual energy that these herbs contain while Rod enhanced their effects on the molecular, biological level. And the result is, well, heh, heh, heh. Some *killer* fuckin' weed."

The entire room burst into a fit of laughter as Maddy sat with her arms folded, leaned over to her husband, and said, "What's with all the laughter? It wasn't *that* fuckin' funny."

"Do you wanna try some?" Rosa asked as she looked into Arima's widening eyes. Rosa had her answer.

Rod left the room and came back a few minutes later holding a five-pound bag of the most powerful stank weed known to man. "Um," Rod stammered nervously, "this is all that we have at the moment, but we'll be able to grow more soon. I hope it's enough."

"Y-y-yeah. This'll be great," a nearly hyperventilating Arima responded as Marcus loaded up a bowl for her. The entire group went into the backyard of the unassuming Brooklyn home and Marcus handed his beloved wife the pipe. "Have a nice trip, baby," Marcus lovingly said before giving her a passionate kiss.

Rosa leaned over to Maddy and said, "And since you are her sister, you share her biology. This weed will enhance *your* skills as well. Your tenacity. Your bloodlust. And it will allow you to be psychically connected with your sister. Your bodies will be acting separately, but your *souls* will be in constant communication with one another. You can coordinate your efforts that way. Still think my joke's not funny?"

Maddy smiled widely, hugged Rosa and yelled out, "Funniest fuckin' joke that I've ever heard! Hurry up, Arima. Take a hit! And don't bogart the entire fuckin' bowl! Save some for your older sis! Let's take this shit on a test-flight!"

A second pipe was loaded to ensure that Arima was unable to bogart the entire fucking bowl. The sisters looked at one another and took a long drag. As they exhaled the smoke, they both said, "Whooooaaaa!" and began giggling.

Arima floated into the sky. "Oh man, the colors," she said in a trippy voice. "So many colors. I'm going to 1,000 feet over the ocean. Stay in touch with me, Maddy."

"Will do, over and out!" Maddy responded as she was unsure as to whether she was still in the back yard or the communications director on a bomber.

"Are you okay?" a concerned Erick asked his wife.

"Oh, man, I'm more than okay." Maddy responded through her intoxicated giggles. "I just wanna fuck some motherfuckers up. I think that I'll start with that prick neighbor who always mows his lawn at six in the morning. Then that old fucker with that fuckin' yippie dog. I hate that fuckin' dog. Then…"

"Mother!" Josie interrupted. "Get it the fuck together! Control your impulses. Being high is *not* an excuse for random murders! Although you do have a point about the mowing guy. He *is* kind of a prick. But, no! He is a good soul. Annoying, yes, but still a good soul."

"Yeah, okay. Whatevs," Maddy replied in a lilted voice. "Let me just see what's going on with Arima. Soul Sister! This is Lil' Redhead! Do you copy? Over and out!"

"Yeah, I hear you," Arima responded to Maddy's soul. "But what's with the names?"

"Those are our cool code names that I just came up with. Pretty cool, huh? Over and out!"

"Yeah, that's pretty cool, I guess. Wow, Maddy. I wish you could see what *I'm* seeing. I'm floating high above the ocean, and I can literally *feel* Pastor Tim and Jeremy's spirits here. I can feel their love. They are so peaceful. And they are hungry. They are ready to feed on dark souls."

"That's really cool Soul Sister! Tell Pastor Tim and Jeremy that we love them. And please use my cool code name. Over and out!"

"I just told them, Madd…I mean Lil' Redhead. They said they love us too. I'm opening my soul now Maddy. I'm opening it up wider than it has ever been. Oh Lord, I feel so strong. So powerful. And I can feel them, Maddy. I can feel the dark souls coming to me. They are attracted to my soul."

At that moment, hundreds of dark souls which had been confined upon the Earthly plane came from all directions. There were hundreds of mystical purple streaks of dense fog converging upon Arima's body. They cackled with glee as they approached and entered Arima's soul. Then, the cackles turned to ungodly screams.

"I have hundreds of them in me, Maddy! Hundreds! I'm closing my soul now. They thought that they were attacking me. They thought that they could destroy me! But once they entered my soul, they realized that it was a trap! I can easily overpower and control them all! All they can do is try to struggle to break free. But they can't! Not unless I allow them too. And I think that I'll accommodate them right now."

Arima re-opened her soul, parted her lips and hundreds of streaks of dense smog were regurgitated out of her gaping mouth. The force of Arima's expulsion caused them to plummet into the ocean. The dark souls screeched in burning agony as the blessed ocean water tore apart their very essence. Small pieces of their being were being burned away and were immediately eaten by the aquatic wildlife. The oceans bubbled violently as the white-hot hatred of the dark souls were extinguished by the coolness of the universe's love. And Arima laughed. She laughed at the image of hundreds of sinister beings' faces being frozen in horrendous torment before letting out their final insidious gasp. The dark smog cleared from the water leaving it a shimmering blue. The ocean was nearly perfectly still, and the fair-weather puffs of clouds reflected off the water. As did the image of a bright purple aura in the shape of a thirty-year-old Jamaican American heroine.

"Oh, Lord, Maddy! That was incredible!" Arima yelled out. "I just killed off like six or seven *hundred* of those bastards. All at once. I just puked them right out of me! And I know that I can do more. I'm not done yet! I'm opening my soul again. Come to momma you bastards!"

"Um, that's really great there, Soul Sister, and a little bit gross, but I really don't want to have to keep reminding you to use my cool code name, alright? Over and out!"

An hour and countless vanquished dark souls later, Arima and

Maddy were running down the street together towards the nearest grocery store.

Erick turned to his daughter and said, "You wanna go get a pizza someplace? I get the feeling that we aren't safe around them with food tonight. And do you have any cash? Your mother and aunt are gonna max out the credit cards."

———

There was a loud squawk of feedback on the PA system, then a light buzz. Then the arrogant voice of the Pastor. "Greetings my blessed ones," the Pastor began. His adopted pale face wore a devilish smirk. He had chosen a devastatingly handsome forty-something priest to inhabit. He reveled in the ability to run his fingers through the soft, blond locks of his latest victim. His tone six-foot-four body was adorned in a purple gown and his shadow towered over his congregation in the courtyard and beyond into a vast clearing. His victim's eyes had once been a soft blue. They were now as black and cold as the heart that pumped unholy bile throughout the body.

"Yes, greetings my most holy friends. My most *patriotic* brothers and sisters. Thank you all for heeding my call. Thank you for joining me on this most momentous occasion. I am here today to tell you all that…we have won. Yes, my friends. We have won. It may not seem like it to you. It may seem as though the unholy forces of wokeness and inclusion have beaten us back. But they have not. All the news reports about our brothers being slaughtered are all lies. *We* are the victors! *We* have taken the Earth! *We* have taken the Earth from those who would deny us our rightful place! Our rightful place of dominion over the women. Over the sexual deviants. Over the dark skinned. Our rightful dominion over all the Earth's resources! Over the animals! Over the plant life! Over the oil, gold, and jewels! It is all ours! It is all *yours*! Your God-given right of dominion over *anything* that you want has been granted by our most glorious Lord!"

Tearful cheers and applause exploded from the thousands of naïve male congregants as the women and children remained in a protective, brainwashed hush. The men began chanting, "It is ours! It is ours! It is ours!" The inner circle of Murder, Inc. could only watch with trepidation as they wondered what the ending of this scene would be.

"Let's just go down there and start tearing these fuckers up!" Maddy exclaimed.

"Shaddup. You're still high," came her husband's immediate response.

"Wow," Maddy replied in a stunned tone. "*That* was a rather *blunt* response. Get it? Blunt? 'Cause of smoking pot? Get it? Why aren't you people laughing? That was pure fuckin' gold!"

"Not as gold as mine, I guess," came Rosa's catty reply.

"Would you people please be quiet?" Josie ordered. "I'm trying to hear this!"

The members of Murder, Inc. fell into an obedient silence as did the mesmerized congregation a quarter of a mile away.

"Yes, my friends, it is ours. It is *yours*," the Pastor began again as his tender ego was being pumped up by the effectiveness of his lies and manipulation upon his willfully ignorant followers. "And it is all due to *your* sacrifice. For years, *you* have been waging war against those that profess to be good and kind. They profess to care about everybody! But did they care about *you*? Did they care that *you* were preordained to rule over them? No, they did not. They just kept putting so-called human beings into positions of power over *you*! Did they care when *you* fell ill? No, they did not. They just tried to inject a vaccine of government microchips into *you*. Did they care when *you* lost your job? No, they did not. They gave *your* job to some unqualified so-called minority. They gave *your* job to someone who they said was a victim of something that *you* played no part in! Then, they made *you* feel guilty about it! They made *you* feel guilty about *your* White heritage! They made *you* feel guilty about being born the way that *you* were! They are *not* the victims! *We* are the victims! *You* are the victims! But not any longer, my brothers! For tonight, *not only* have we taken over the Earth, but *tonight* we shall begin our glorious march to the heavens! Tonight, we shall begin our journey to rule not just the Earth but *all the cosmos*! *You* have been chosen by our glorious Lord for this mission, my brothers! Join me now! Join me in this final battle to *take back* your God-given dominion over *everything*! Raise your guns into the air! Yes! Raise them high my brothers! Let me see the sun's beautiful rays *gleam* on their righteous barrels! Now place your guns against the temples of your loved ones!

Yes! Let them *feel* the cleansing strength of your steel! Now, pull the trigger and baptize them in your endless love!"

Thousands of gunshots were heard just before Jessie's anguished voice cried out, "Jesus fucking Christ! The pain! The evil! The pure *evil*! Oh, Lord! They're slaughtering their own children!"

Chapter 90
Attack of the Ghost Riders

"Why daddy?" the eight-year-old, blond-haired tyke inquired as his brilliant blue eyes stared up into the gleefully deranged eyes of his father.

"Because, son," the father said back in a trance-like tone, "This is how our lord shows us his love." *BLAM!*

The father looked down at his fallen son lying in his own brains and began cackling maniacally before placing the revolver to his own temple. *BLAM!*

A confused white and blue streak hovered over his own corpse and watched as his father killed himself. He then watched as a black smog emerged from his father's body, looked at him with flaming red eyes and swooped toward him. He begged his father's dark soul to stop as his essence was being choked out of him. Then, his blue and white streak dissipated into nothingness and the boy was gone forever.

The frantic members of Murder, Inc. watched the same scene play out over and over across the complex. *BLAM! BLAM!* Heeeee,heeeee,heeeeee, No! Please stop daddy! Please sto…"

"Oh fuck! They're not just killing their children! They're murdering their *souls* as well!" Josie screamed out. "Mom! Arima! Take a hit! Arima! Float above the complex and draw as many of those children's souls into you as you can! Mom! You, Jules, and Jessie get on the ATV's and try to attract the cult members to you. Rosa! Try to manipulate the energy of the dark souls and hold them up for as long as you can! Dragenstein! Cliff! Marcus! Dad! Get on your ATV's and try to get as many living women and children as you can to safety. Henri and Sam! Stay here and take out any fucker that tries to get to us! And Lionnel. Stay here with me and pray. We'll take care of the wounded as best we can. Now go!"

"We didn't exactly put it up to a *vote*, so I'm not sure those are *official* orders," Maddy lamented quietly as she and Arima took long drags off their pipes. "Whooooaaaa!" they said simultaneously as Arima lifted into the sky and Maddy rushed to her ATV. "Oh well, who gives a fuck. I need to kill some motherfuckin' douchebags!"

Arima hovered fifty feet off the ground and opened her soul as wide as she was able. "Hey, um, kids," she said in a hazy cadence. "Like, um, come here, ok? You'll be safe here. Come on." Her soul was bombarded by hundreds of panic-stricken blue and white streaks. Once they were inside of Arima, she could feel them cowering with each other and weeping with despair.

"Let me try something!" Jules barked out as she and the others were speeding their ATV's toward the vile resort of the weak-willed. The vein in her forehead began pulsing from her extreme level of concentration until a large clowder of feral small cats, bobcats, and panthers came running into the clearing and began zooming around from one man to the next. Smaller cats would lunge at a man's face and bite and claw him as they had dreamed of doing to toilet tissue and shoes. The larger cats bit their legs off and began eating them.

"I told them to try not to kill them!" Jules yelled at her friends. "Just take them down. If we kill them, then we'll have more dark souls to deal with!"

"Yeah! Great point, Jules!" Jessie replied before saying to herself, "Malum tuum dolorem facit. et dolor meus es fortitudo mea." Jessie felt her physical strength grow ten-fold. She zipped from one man to another in her ATV, pulling their arms from their sockets in one motion as she passed by them.

Who the fuck put them *in charge of our little group?* Maddy thought to herself as she sliced men's legs off with a broadsword as she passed them. Each time her black vinyl cat-suit was splattered with a new man's blood, she would giggle and shout out *WHACK*! Her drug-addled mind flashed back to one of Erick's 'pussy' songs. She laughed out loud and began singing Neil Sedaka's "Laughter in the Rain" as loudly as she could as she drove around swinging her bloodied sword at the bearded cult members.

Dragenstein leaped off her ATV and began violently mowing men down as though she were an all-pro pulling guard. A group of quivering men surrounded her and raised their guns. She smiled at them demurely and took off her white, chiffon dress revealing a stitched together perfectly formed muscular female. She giggled lightly, and said breathily, "I always *wanted* to be a ballerina, *tee, hee.*" She blew them a kiss then began spinning rapidly. Her engorged, steely penis looked like the whirling blade of a helicopter as it effortlessly sliced through the men's abdomens. The men screamed in agony as they felt their intestines unravel and plop onto the ground.

Cliff, Marcus, and Erick picked up screaming children and placed them onto the back of their respective ATV's. They rushed them to Lionnel and Josie who would immediately begin attending to their blood-covered bodies and their traumatized psyches. The three men would then drive once more into the heart of the carnage looking for surviving women and children.

Rosa concentrated on the energy of the dark souls. She focused on overstimulating their demented minds, causing them to be distracted and flail around in the air in confusion. But there were simply too many of them and her Coven was not there to draw strength from as they had been assigned to watch over Rachel and Kayla at the estate. After five minutes of intense manipulation of the dark souls' energy, Rosa collapsed from exhaustion at Lionnel's feet.

Arima saw the dark souls become released from Rosa's influence. She smiled to herself as she said, "Hey guys. Um, do you want your kids' souls? Just follow me." She drifted away from the land and over the Atlantic Ocean. "Okay, kids. We're going to have some fun now, okay? I'm going to take you swimming." Arima re-opened her soul and sent the hundreds of blue and white streaks into the salty water where they were immediately embraced by the love of Pastor Tim and Jeremy. The ashen souls squealed with delight as they followed the blue and white streaks of their murdered children into the inviting cool blue waves. The squeals changed from delight into anguish as soon as their dark essences hit the water and were painfully extinguished by the universe's love. "Thank you, Arima," hundreds of children said as their souls ascended from the now-tranquil water and floated into the heavens.

"Not a fuckin' time to get sentimental, Soul Sister! Over and out!" Arima heard Maddy's voice scream at her. "C'mon! Let's go say 'hi' to daddy! Over and out!"

The Pastor's blackened eyes contained an uncharacteristic gleam as he watched his two daughters approach him. Arima floated closer as Maddy's ATV cruised just beneath her. He began giggling when they finally were standing directly in front of him. They glared at him with burning hatred and readied themselves for battle.

"Oh, my darling daughters," the Pastor's slithery voice said as he peeled his new body away from his dark essence revealing a scarred, dark purple mass of smog and leaving a discarded bloody carcass on the granite floor. "Now is not the time, my dears. But just be patient. It will soon be your time. Very, *very* soon, heh, heh, heh."

His spiritual body began shifting and growing until it was in the form of a fifteen-foot part-man, part black mamba. His long, forked tongue darted out of his serpentine mouth and licked the faces of both of his offspring. He then released a sadistic laugh and disappeared into the darkest portion of the late afternoon sky.

"Uh, what the fuck was that, Soul Sister? Over and out!" a confused Maddy asked.

"Um, hey, Sis," Arima replied. "I'm standing right next to you so; I don't really think we need the cool code names or the 'over and out' at the moment. And I have no idea what the hell just happened. All that I know is that I need another hit so that I can start collecting the remaining dark souls and throw them in the ocean."

"Uh, what remaining dark souls?" Maddy asked as she watched several thousand streaks of dark smog following the same path as the serpentine Pastor into the cosmos.

"No!" Arima uncharacteristically cried out. "It isn't possible! They can't leave the Earth! They can't move on to Enlightenment or any other plane of existence! Not without me! What the hell is going on?"

"Well, Arima," a befuddled Maddy replied. "I don't know. All I know is that I just saw those fuckers leave the Earth. We did the best that we could. Let's just get with the rest of our gang and regroup and figure out what the fuck to do now. And let's do it fast. I'm fuckin' starvin'.'"

———

The representatives of Murder, Inc. looked down upon the devastation. There were thousands of men, women, and children's corpses rotting in the triple-digit Florida heat on this darkening mid-February evening.

Josie stood before her cherished friends and family and quietly tried to shake the violent images from her head and compose herself. They all had heightened anticipation as they awaited their instructions. "Hey. Are you okay?" Erick asked his beloved daughter as he placed his arm around her slender shoulders.

"Aw, fuck, Dad," Josie answered tearfully. "So much carnage. So much death. So much despair. And *why*? For *what*? For *power*? Prestige? Money? To pump up small egos? *Why*? What is *fucking wrong* with these people?

"I remember a time not so long ago when I saw everything as rainbows and butterflies and unicorns. I saw everything and everybody as having good in them. A time when I couldn't even *conceive* of the concept of pure evil. I was so stupid. So naïve. Just like so many others who were too busy checking their fucking 'likes' or swiping left or playing stupid video games or watching their fucking sports. They were too busy to see what was happening right before their eyes. They were too busy to see that millions of people were becoming brainwashed into a movement of pure evil. Hell, they fucking attacked our capitol on live TV and hardly anyone batted an eye.

"Well now, I have seen it. And so have the apathetic lemmings, many of whom have fallen victim to this. Over and over and over again I have seen it. I have seen innocent people get ripped apart. Thousands of them. For no other reason than the feelings of entitlement of a few ignorant, knuckle-dragging fucks! That's what this all boils down to. The election rigging. The threats. The physical intimidation. The attempted overthrow of our elected governments. The treatment of anyone other than people like them as less than human. The complete lack of regard or respect for their fellow man, woman, and child. They don't care about *anything* but themselves! They want what they want when they want it, and they don't give a *fuck* about how they get it. They don't care if they have to lie, steal, cheat or even murder! They just don't *fucking care*! It is all about *them*!

"And isn't a fucking mental illness either. God, how I hate that! Have you ever noticed that if a Black man shoots innocent people, he's a 'thug'?" And when it's someone from the middle east, they're a terrorist? But when it's a *White* motherfucker, they're always 'mentally ill'! Bull-shit! Hatred of other people just because of who they are isn't a mental illness! It is *bigotry*! And bigotry is pure *evil*! Which makes these *fucking bigots* pure evil! We have just seen it! They are so *fucking evil* that they would murder their own *families* just to get what they want!

"And all that they want is to feel important. To feel noticed. To feel cared about. That's what they want. But when you combine those very natural human desires with unhinged hatred and bigotry, then you get evil. And when you get enough of them, you get an evil movement. That is what Vetis and his demonic pawns have exploited. His pawns in the government and business and churches and the media. They have been working in concert to exploit these people. And they have turned people's reasonable desires into pure evil. They have turned their sense of *patriotism* into pure evil. They have turned their *faith in a higher power* into pure evil. They say that Vetis is known as 'The Tempter of the Holy'. Well, he sure as fuck is. So, this is what we are left with. Thou-sands of bodies, many of them completely innocent. Okay, fuck this. Let's get a status report. Lionnel, what are the numbers as best as you can calculate?"

Lionnel wiped his brow and approached his beloved girlfriend. He kissed her lightly upon her mauve lips before beginning.

"Okay, these are pretty rough numbers, but here it goes. There were approximately 10,000 people here today. Now, the good news is that most of these deplorable men have succeeded in driving their wives and children away from them. Probably another thing that they're pissed about. They're so toxic, that they can't get laid. Anyway, that means that about 8,000 of the people here were men. There were about five hundred women and about one thousand children."

"Okay," Josie stated. "So, what's left?"

"Well, again these are pretty raw numbers," Lionnel began again. "But it looks about like this. There are about eight hundred men that are still alive down there. Barely, but still alive. They were partially eaten by the cats or dismembered one way or another by our forces."

"Henri, Marcus, Cliff. You know what to do," Josie ordered. The three men picked up their rifles and Holy water guns and made their way back down to the killing fields. The entire group paused to listen to eight hundred popping sounds followed by shrieks of agony as each of the surviving men were shot in the head and their dark souls were extinguished by being saturated by the Holy water. Cliff said a silent prayer to his God and asked for forgiveness each time he pulled his trigger.

The three men returned and Lionnel continued. "Okay. Well, *now* there are *zero* surviving men. It looks as though Arima was able to lure about four thousand dark souls into the ocean. That means that around three thousand escaped to…um…well, wherever the hell they went.

Most of the women took their own lives as well. The ones that were indoctrinated into the cult are among the dark soul count. Those that weren't escaped into Enlightenment."

"So, how many survived?" Josie asked cautiously.

"Well," Lionnel paused before answering. "Seven."

"Seven?" Josie cried out. "Only *seven*? Oh, Jesus! How about the kids?"

"Okay," Lionnel began again. "Better numbers there. Of the thousand children, around four hundred were murdered for all time. Their bodies *and* their souls. Around six hundred were able to get to Enlightenment. And, well, we have twenty-three kids here who are alive. Some are in pretty bad shape, but they all should make it."

There was an astonished silence that hovered around the group. They simply stared at one another in a shocked stupor. No one, not even Maddy, could find any words at this sullen moment. The silence was finally broken when Maddy turned her head towards the brilliant setting sun and said, "What's that Uncle Joe? You mean right now? But it's Josie's eighteenth birthday in a few days. No, I understand. Just… just…give us a few minutes, okay?"

Chapter 91

Go Now

Come to me, Pastor, Its nasal voice was heard just before his dramatic serpentine transformation. *Come to me now before they destroy all of our beloved children. Come to me now before your daughters can do any more damage. Come to me now!*

The half-man, half-mamba spiritual form of the Pastor rose from the balcony, squealed in delight, and ascended to the darkest part of the Realm of Perdition where he found his awaiting dark-soul mate. They hissed at each other then became entwined in one another's scaley bodies. They squirmed and writhed against one another in heated ecstasy as It screamed out, "Yes, Pastor! Yes! Impregnate me! Together we can bring our demonic children from the Earth! Together we can bring them here! Together we can ready them for battle! Yes! Don't stop! I can feel them coming to me! They are entering my being! Thousands of our beautiful children are squirming within me! Yes! Yes! Yes!"

Following one final orgasmic scream, It opened itself and thousands of black snakes with copperheads emerged from her amidst a torrent of cosmic blood and demonic afterbirth. The pair held each other with morbid tenderness and giggled briefly before It said, "Now. Just one more earthly order. We must eliminate the one *true threat* to our glorious Vetis. None of *them* can destroy him. But those children can. We must have them killed before they are born."

———

The members of Murder, Inc. could only stare at each other with somber disbelief until Maddy looked at the beautiful sunset of bright orange, yellow and red. In its elegant rays she saw two forms emerge, cast in a vibrant white light.

"I'm so sorry to tell you this Buttacup," Uncle Joe began. "But it's time for you to go now. It's time for you to join us. Your work on Earth is done. It is time for both you and Erick to join the battle here."

"What's that Uncle Joe? You mean right now?" Maddy responded to her beloved Uncle.

"Yeah, fuck," Joseph answered regretfully. "Right now. We have preparations to make. It's gonna be a fuckin' bloodbath up here."

"But it's Josie's eighteenth birthday in a few days," Maddy pleaded.

"We understand that dear," Aunt Blair stated. "But the battle has now shifted from the Earth to Enlightenment. You are needed here. It is time for you to join us. It is time for you and Erick to come home, my dearest.

"No, I understand. Just…just…give us a few minutes, okay?" Maddy answered as she turned away from the forms of her cherished aunt and uncle and back towards her friends and family. Her eyes locked upon each one in turn. When her brilliant green eyes met those of her daughter, she began sobbing uncontrollably.

"I-I-I'm so sorry, sweetie. But we have to go now," Maddy's remorseful voice cried out.

"What do you mean?" Erick shouted. "No fuckin' way! Not yet! Not now! I am *not* missing my daughter's eighteenth birthday! Not happening! You just tell whoever just told you that to back the fuck off! Just a few days! That's all we need. Then…then we'll go."

"I'm sorry baby," Maddy answered as she embraced her husband. "It doesn't work like that. They need us and they need us now. We have to say our good-byes. I fucking hate this too. But we have to. We have no choice."

Erick wiped the torrent of tears from his eyes and gave his wife a smile of resignation. The pair turned toward the group and embraced each one. Sam. Jules. Jessie. Cliff. Marcus. Jamie. Rosa. Dragenstein. Henri. Lionnel. They squeezed each one as though they were pleading for them to be their anchor. Their bodies were pleading for them to never let them go.

Maddy approached her sister and hugged her tightly. She whispered into her ear, "I would rather have just a short time with my sister than to never have had a sister at all. I love you, Arima. I'll stay in touch. Please. Watch over them. Watch over them all. Watch over my daughter." Her voice then lowered to a barely audible level as she concluded with, "*You* are the one who must lead them now. I now know that it isn't just Josie's legacy to lead them from this point on. It is both yours *and* Josie's."

Josie stood expressionless as her parents' mortal bodies approached her for the final time.

"No. This can't be happening. I can't lose you again. Please. Talk to them. Stay with me. Please. Mom. Dad. I need you. Please don't leave me."

The pair embraced their sobbing daughter as Erick said, "No. You don't need us any longer. You are an adult. You are a genius. You are the best of the both of us. You will make us proud just like you have from the very day that you were born. The first time that I held you, I looked into those gorgeous green eyes and knew that you were special. Not because you were our daughter. But because you were Josie fucking Parker. You don't belong to us. You belong to the entire world. And you were brought into this world for greatness."

"Listen to your father, sweetie," Maddy added. "He's right. You are better than me. You are better than him. You are better because of the inherent compassion that you have for other people. Your father and I don't really have that. We have a sense of justice which has led us to try to protect the downtrodden. The picked-on. The bullied. The persecuted. But we don't really have compassion for them. You do. You have our sense of justice combined with a deep and genuine caring for others. And that makes you stronger than either of us. Never lose that. I know this world is fucked up. I know that true evil will never be completely extinguished. There will always be evil people and evil movements to wage war against. Greedy, self-centered people will always exist. But you understand that there is much more good in this world than evil. You've known it since you were a child. You saw goodness in your friends and teachers and stray animals. You saw goodness in everything that truly possessed it. That is special. *You* are special. I'm sorry sweetie, but we have to go now. There is a final chapter to be written and we've been called to play our part."

"But, but," Josie began stammering. "How will I know if you're going to be alright? How will I know if you've won? How will I know if you've survived?"

Maddy looked deeply into the eyes of her nearly eighteen-year-old daughter and smiled before saying, "You will know. The entire Earth will know. Your Aunt Patty has one hell of a victory concert planned. Once the music starts, you will know that it's over. And you will know that your mother and father are singing along with the angels. And you will know that we will be watching over you for all eternity. Plus, Arima said that I can use her soul as a time share, so we'll visit, okay? Goodbye my most beautiful daughter. My most *brilliant* daughter. We are so proud of you. You are our greatest accomplishment."

Josie collapsed upon her knees and screamed in anguish at the universe as her parents' bodies transformed into dust. As she was clutching her parents' empty clothes, she heard two birds singing in the distance. She wiped her tears from her eyes and winked at them as they flew away.

"Aw, fuck this shit! Let's get back home and regroup. We need to figure what, if anything, we can do at this point," Josie ordered as her five-foot-four-and a half-inch frame stood upright once again.

"Um, hey Niece Josie?" Arima stated. "Um, I think I know what we're supposed to do. I just heard from your mom. We gotta get to the estate."

Maddy's soul rushed up and hugged her Uncle Joe. Joe extended his hand to shake Erick's who was standing there with his arms folded and a look of disgust on his face.

"What the fuck's wrong with you?" Joseph bellowed out.

"Oh, he's just really pissed that we're going to miss Josie's birthday so he, um, isn't talking to you right now." An embarrassed Maddy explained.

"Listen, Erick," Joseph said as tenderly as his gruff voice would allow. "Listen. I understand. She is a special girl, your daughter. But I don't make the rules around here. I get my orders from up on high, then it's our job to bring folks back. I was just following orders."

"Maddy," Erick stated in a haughty, lilted tone. "Would you please tell your uncle that I understand that but I'm still not speaking with him at the moment."

"Oh, for fucks sake!" Joseph yelled out as his beloved wife Blair was attempting to conceal her amusement. "Listen pal! You're kinda being a douchebag right now! So just forgive me, alright? And if you don't, well, then *fuck you!*"

"Maddy," Erick began once again in the same belittling tone. "Would you please tell your uncle that use of profanity isn't really helping anything at this moment and that I'm a bit offended by his use of such vulgar language."

"Alright you two, that will be quite enough," Blair interjected with a calm bluntness. "We have far bigger things to worry about and we haven't time for this petty family squabbling. I will not stand to have a feud between Maddy's father and the man she loves. Now, both of you apologize and shake hands."

"M-my father?" a confused Maddy asked. "Why did you refer to him as that, Aunt Blair?"

"Oh, my dearest," Blair answered sweetly as she placed her hands upon Maddy's petite shoulders. "That's right. You don't know. My brother, Freddie may have been the father who raised you. And the vile Pastor and the Copperhead may have been the ones who were your biological parents on Earth. But my darling, *we* are your spiritual parents. Your soul was attracted to *our* family. And it was *your* soul that I was pregnant with when I miscarried. A miscarriage that was orches-trated by your biological parents so that she could become pregnant and carry and raise your soul. They tried to steal you from us. You see, my dearest, Joseph and I are your *spiritual* parents. You were always destined to be with us. And now you are. For all time. And we couldn't be happier."

"Well, *that's* fuckin' weird," Maddy exclaimed. "But what the fuck *else* is new? At least *this* is a *good* weird and not a fucked up weird. So, do I call you guys Mom and Dad now, or what?"

"Naw!" Joseph replied as he wiped a spiritual tear from his eye.

"That's too fuckin' awkward. Let's keep it the way it has always been. Our souls being connected means everything. Titles don't mean shit."

"Well, in that case," Maddy replied as she flashed her ornery grin, "Uncle Joe! Apologize to my husband and shake his hand! And Erick, you do the same! I'm with Aunt Blair! I'm not gonna have the two most important men in my life arguing. Now, fuckin' do it!"

Erick and Joseph looked at one another with an awkward suspicion. They extended their arms and lightly shook each other's hand while softly muttering, "Sorry." They then immediately folded their arms and looked away from one another.

"Well, *that* was fuckin' pathetic!" Maddy bellowed out angrily. "What the fuck was *that*? I'm telling you; I'm really starting to get…"

Maddy was cut off as she felt someone pinch her conjured ass and whisper into her ear, "Well, *hello*. So nice to see you again, my little red-haired toy. Are you finally ready to have some fun with me?" Howard lasciviously said as he conjured a strap-on dildo around Maddy's pelvis.

Howard then fell to the floor from the force of Erick and Joseph's fists landing on his jaw. The in-laws looked at each other, began laughing and embraced.

"I'm so sorry, Joe. I overreacted," Erick said.

"No, no," Joseph answered. "*I'm* the one that should apologize to *you*. You've been through a lot, and I could've handled that much better."

"No, no," Erick began again before being cut off by Maddy.

"Yeah, yeah, great. You're best of friends now. Can we just move on *please*? I don't know what's worse. Watching you two be pissed at each other or watching this fuckin' pukey love fest. And Howard! Why the fuck are *you* here?"

"Well," Howard replied with disgust as he rose from the misty floor, rubbing his chin, "I don't believe that I'll answer that until I receive an apology for this rude treatment!"

"Apology?" Erick roared back. "I'll give you a fuckin' apology! I'll give you an apology up your ghostly ass!"

"Well, now we're talkin'" Howard answered flirtatiously. "I've never really swung that way, but hey, any port in a storm, right?"

Howard then found himself once again on the floor following Maddy's fist landing firmly on his jaw.

"I'm telling Arima about this!" Howard yelled out as though he were a five-year-old.

"Yeah, you do that. You tell my *sister* on me," Maddy answered back just before sticking her tongue out at him. "Now, just tell us. Why the fuck are you here?"

"Oh, very well," a defeated Howard responded. "I am here to give you all some very important news. And to make our battle plans. Joe, I know you and I haven't always seen…um…eye to eye, but we need to work in tandem. They are planning their attack. It is originating from the Realm of Perdition. It will be the Pastor and his Copperheaded bitch along with a whole *shitload* of dark souls that that wretched creature has just given birth to. I propose to usher my forces against their demonic offspring. And while I am doing that, you and your family will destroy the Pastor and the Copperhead. None of the rest of us can do it. They can only be destroyed by someone who has a personal connection to them. Like, a daughter. So, my little redheaded spitfire, that is why you had to return now. You are the only one who can destroy them both. The rest of you can wound them. Weaken them. But my lovely little temptress here must be the one to put the final dagger in them. Agreed?"

"Yes, that sounds like a plan," Blair answered. "But Howard, all you will have to do is hold off their army. You won't be required to destroy them all. Just hold them off until Maddy can cut the heads off these vile serpents. Then, like all little snakes, they will go crawling back under their rocks once they have seen their leaders felled. They will lose their will to fight, because they really have no convictions about what they are fighting for. They are mindless pawns. So, Howard, you just keep them away from Enlightenment. We'll take care of the rest. And I am going to feed on the black heart of that bitch once and for all. Then, we'll see about taking out Vetis."

"Well, that's a problem and the other reason I'm here," Howard answered. "Vetis is powerful. He is too powerful even for all the blessed souls in Enlightenment. We could combine all our forces and *never* completely defeat him. Which means he is a threat to us for eternity. But there are four *new* souls who are about to come into the world that can."

Before Howard could finish his explanation, a frantic Patty burst into the area. "Hey, fuckers, what's going on?"

"Well, my dear sister," Blair began explaining. "We are in the middle of a planning session and Howard here was about to explain how Vetis can be defeated. So, as you can see, we are a bit busy here."

"*You're* busy?" Patty yelled back. "Do you know what the fuck I'm *dealing with* right now? I *finally* got the final lineup for 'Victoryfuckin-palooza' posted and do you know what happened? All these dead artists came up to me and started cussing me out because *they're* not in the lineup! So, I had to explain to them that the *asshole* who is writing this shit didn't want to speculate on when someone might pass away, so if an artist isn't dead by the time he wrote this shit in 2023, then they can't be in the lineup! Then, I had all these hip-hop cats come up to me and demand representation. So, I had to explain to *them* that this asshole author isn't well-versed in hip-hop, so he didn't include them either. But, he has quite a few Rhythm and Blues artists to represent one of the foundational musical forms of hip-hop. But did *that* make anyone happy? *Fuck no*! They *still* blame me! They're blaming me and getting all up in *my* ass instead of the *dickhead* sitting in the Midwest typing up this shit. So, excuse me for interrupting your little gabfest, but I've got stress of my own! Oh, fuck it! I gotta go make sure the light and sound crews are ready to go for whenever you pricks get off your asses and win this fuckin' war! C'mon Jacklyn, let's get the fuck out of here!"

———

"Um, hey Niece Josie?" Arima stated. "Um, I think I know what we're supposed to do. I just heard from your mom. We gotta get to the estate."

"Why? What's going on?" Josie immediately asked.

"Okay, let me try to remember everything your mom told me. She was talking really fast. Then she kept saying 'over and out,' so then I thought she was done talking but then she just kept talking. Okay. I think that I remember. They think that they can defeat the demonic souls, but they can't defeat Vetis. He's too powerful. And they're worried that he's just going to keep coming back over and over until he finally wins. But the universe has created four new souls. Four souls whose combined power can vanquish Vetis forever. And those four souls are about to be born. They will be the children of Rachel and Kayla."

"Rachel and Kayla?" a confused Josie asked. "What do you mean?

They're each only having *one* child. Rachel is having a little girl and Kayla is having a little boy."

"Uh, yeah, that's what we all thought," Arima replied. "But I guess they disguised themselves within one another for protection. And now that they're about to be born, they have split. Rachel is having *twin* girls. And Kayla is having *twin* boys. So, the Twins and the twins are each having twins. Wow. That's actually pretty cool, if you think about it. They're each having a bonus kid that they didn't plan on. It kinda reminds me of this one time when I ordered a twenty-piece chicken nugget, but when I got home, they had put *twenty-six* chicken nuggets in the box. Man, that was one of the happiest days of my life. They even gave me extra dippin' sauce. It was so cool."

"Aunt Arima!" Josie cried out to get the conversation back on track. "So, what are you telling us?"

"What was I talking about again?" Arima asked of herself before continuing. "Oh yeah. So, these four babies have the combined power to take out Vetis. The problem is the demons know this. They are sending their remaining Earthly demonic forces to the estate to murder the babies before they are born. So, my point is that we really need to get up to estate. And that if there's time that we should stop for some chicken nuggets. Y'know. If there's time."

CHAPTER 92
PURPLE RAIN

February 14, 2042. Valentine's Day. Josie was sitting outside her estate in Upper State New York watching the impending storm clouds roll in with Stellan and Paciano. They were listening to a radio broadcaster who was saying, *An unbelievable event seems to be happening all over the world. There are dark storm clouds that are forming over the entire planet. Every populated region is preparing for torrential rains and strong winds. We don't know whether this is a Biblical event or not, but I, for one, have got my arc ready, ha,ha. This segment is being brought to you by Sandler's Tire Service. A Tire for you and a tire for me. Buying new tires ensures your safety. Now, to Kip Kippering with today's sports scores.*

"Yep, laugh it up, motherfucker. You have *no idea* what type of show that you're in for," Josie dryly said to the disembodied voice. "The world's governments do, though. Gregory and Kaneko are at the United Nations right now telling them about the cosmic battle that is about to be waged. And here we are, celebrating my birthday by protecting our friends once again. Protecting them in the one place that was supposed to represent peace. This place was to be my parents' retirement home and our family's getaway home of serenity. But that's not how it will turn out. Just like every other place on the Earth, this place isn't going to be about peace. It will be tainted by bloodshed and war."

"I do not agree with you, my young friend," Stellan stated reflectively as he placed his brawny, silver-haired arm around her green vinyl-clad shoulder. "I do not agree with you at all. Yes, there will be a battle here tonight. But that battle will be waged in the *name* of peace. It will be waged to welcome four new souls into our world. Four new souls who have the power to ensure a lasting peace. This place is the *epitome* of peace. And I, for one, am proud to call it my home."

"As am I, lover," Paciano contributed as he fed his nearly two-year old, Zihad, some string beans. "I am proud to call this *my* home as well. I am proud to have worked for your parents. I am proud of our friendship with Arima and all the others from New Orleans. And I am proud to know you, Josie. I am proud to have a friend that commands such respect. A friend who is so caring. A friend who I know always has the backs of others. I am proud of you. *We* are proud of you. And we are ready to march into battle with you alongside the others."

Josie gave the married couple a long tearful embrace before saying, "Thanks guys. That means a lot to me. But I hope that you won't be going into any battle. The forces of Vetis will soon be here. Rod just sent his final recon report. They are the last truly demonic souls remaining that represent our four societal pillars. They will come together, within their respective tribes, each from a different direction. We have the assassination technicians in trees in the surrounding woods who will take out as many as they can as they approach. But there will be too many of them. Vetis's representatives within the clergy will come from the west. That is where Rosa and her Coven will meet them. His remaining pawns from the propogandist media will come from the east and will be met by Marcus, Jamie and Dragenstein. His remaining forces from what is left of the White Nationalist political party will come from the north. That is where Sam, Jerry, Jules, and her big cats will engage them in battle. And finally, his remaining forces from the business community will come from the south where they will be met by Jessie, Cliff, and Henri.

"Arima will take a hit from her killer weed and absorb their dark souls as soon as they emerge from their fallen bodies. She will then send them into the nearby pond that was blessed by Pastor Tim. I will stay at the house and protect it as best I can. If it looks like the house is going to be breached, I need you two to carry Kayla and Rachel upon your backs to the stable. Regardless, you two will assist Lionnel in the birth of the Quad. Adam, Aaron, Vai, and Alexa will be their family's last defense. I fear that it will not be an enjoyable game for those dear boys, tonight. But, no matter what, we must ensure that those infants are born, and we must ensure that they survive. You two will see to that. If it gets too…um…hairy, heh, heh. I truly didn't mean that as a joke guys. Anyway, if it gets too dangerous and the babies are born you will take them with you and Zihad. You will get away to someplace safe and never look back. You will keep them and protect them until such time as they are prepared to engage Vetis. Understand?"

"Yes, we understand perfectly," Stellan replied. "But it won't come to that. We will not need to retreat and hide with these children because you are going to be victorious on this evening or else *your* name isn't Josephine Patricia Sommers Parker. And that, my dearie, is your name. So that is just how it's going to fucking be."

The three friends burst into nervous laughter and embraced one last time. There was a flash of deep red lightning from just above them and the storm clouds turned deep crimson. Then, the rain began. A torrential rainfall of blood began to soak the Earth as the battle for Enlightenment had been engaged. Josie's pretty face was awash in blood as she looked directly up into the warring storm clouds. "Well, here we go. I love you Mom and Dad. Kick their motherfuckin' ass."

———

Maddy and Erick were nervously awaiting the warning siren. Erick paced around their conjured perfect replica of their home in Brooklyn. "Okay," Maddy stated in an effort to calm herself and her anxious husband. "Let's kill some time before we kill my bitch mother and dickhead father. How 'bout a couple rounds of real movie name to porn movie name?"

"Maddy, I'm really not in the mood at the moment," Erick answered before Maddy blurted out, "*Star Wars!*"

"Star Whores!" Erick enthusiastically responded. Maddy could only smirk as her sly manipulation put a beaming smile upon her beloved husband's face. "Okay, okay, let me see here," the easily distracted Erick retorted. "How 'bout *Dolores Claiborne.*"

"Oh, fuckin' easy!" Maddy screamed out laughing. "Clitoris Claiborne! Okay, try this one. *Field of Dreams.*"

"Well, that's a fuckin' softball," Erick scoffed. "Field of Creams! If you build it they will cum!, heh, heh, heh!"

The siren began blaring throughout the entirety of Enlightenment. Millions of blessed souls began conjuring a large white wall around their tiny portion of the vast cosmos. Howard began mobilizing his troops and stood waiting just inside their mystical fortress. He was wearing nothing but a smile and a strap on sword. Standing beside him were all the souls that Arima had helped during her time in New Orleans. The Ropers. Lillian. Herbert and Iris. Becky Peterson and her two daughters. Rachel and Kayla's sister, Gwen. Clyde Manfrengensen. Marcus's Moms and Pops. And Arima's mother Abdalla and her grandmother Louise.

Leading another contingent of warriors on the far side of the wall were the glowing spirits of Lucy Vang, Jason Anderson, and Kristy Anderson. The reunited friends held hands and smiled at one another as they waited for the onslaught to begin. They all stood in front of their amassed army of brilliant blue and white souls. They stood and stared intensely as they heard pounding at the bright white brick walls. They readied themselves as slight cracks began forming from the intense pressure of the demonic souls who were demanding to enter. The cracks grew into fissures and then, all hell broke loose.

Millions of fiendish, human sized black serpents with copper heads slithered rapidly into the awaiting warriors. Everywhere that one could see were flashes of serpents' fangs into jugulars and slashing conjured metal swords. The moment a vile serpent or a blessed soul were injured, their wound would immediately heal. Arms would grow back. Heads were replaced. Intestines would be sucked back into their caverns and the conjured body would be restored. Millions of bites and gashes resulted in nothing more than an eternal stalemate.

"Oh well, fuck!" Howard bellowed out as he was thrusting his sword/penis into a serpent's belly. "We can't kill them! And they can't kill us! All we can do is wound each other. Blair was right! We just need to hold them back so that Joe's forces can kill the leaders of this wretched movement. We need to hold them back so that they are unable to help them. Just keep slashing motherfuckers! Just hold them!"

Howard looked down at his feet and saw the white clouds that they were standing on turn jet black. They then turned into a dark red liquid. And all the spiritual blood that was being shed was being absorbed into the clouds of the cosmos until the sheer weight of the crimson, iron-scented substance tumbled out of the heavens and began drenching the entirety of the Earth.

———

Arima passionately kissed her loving husband, lit her pipe, and inhaled deeply. "Whoooaaa!" she dreamily said as her ebony body began floating above the estate. Her purple hibiscus adorned dress was immediately saturated with bloodfall and began violently whipping around as the winds suddenly went from calm to tropical storm strength. She heard light popping sounds from the surrounding woods. Her body began glowing until it was encased in a purple aura as she opened her soul and began welcoming the newly departed dark entities. She smiled to herself as the demonic spirits were attracted into her and immediately bound. All they could do was struggle as they awaited their final, tortuous fate.

Multiple "holy" men carrying guns emerged from the woods and began marching toward the main house of the estate. They stopped in their tracks, smiled at one another, and raised their rifles as they encountered thirteen handholding, black robed women standing between them and their quarry.

"Now sisters," Rosa began speaking softly. "Let us now show these abhorrent men what happens to those who betray their faith. What happens to those who betray their congregations. What happens to those who choose to gaze longingly for evil. What happens to those who betray humanity. Concentrate sisters and send your energy to me. Concentrate on the saltiest substance that you can think of. Yes! I can feel your energy flowing into me!"

Rosa's eyes turned pure white as she stared at the bemused men and said, "Now, motherfuckers! *Now* is your time to meet your lot in life! And death!"

Confused expressions were replaced by screams of agony as the men's rifles fell harmlessly to the ground. Their extremities were being turned into salt beginning at their fingers and toes. The screams grew in intensity as the transformation spread up their arms and legs and into their torsos. Their final shrieks could be heard as their salty bodies were immediately melted away by the torrent of bloody rainfall and their smoggy, purple souls were absorbed into a glowing figure floating above the house.

On the east side of the estate, Marcus, Jamie, and Dragenstein could hear the perfect broadcast-ready male voices chanting 'Kill the kids! Kill the kids! Kill the kids!' The men had spent their careers in the service of Vetis's unpatriotic, inhumane movement. They had spent endless hours, days, weeks, months, and years knowingly spreading lies and propaganda to indoctrinate the self-centered, weak-willed and willfully ignorant masses into their hate-fueled army. Now, all they could do is chant one final insipid, three-syllable phrase as they rushed toward the main house. All that they were able to do is chant from their frothing mouths. And die.

There was a high-pitched giggle before Dragenstein rushed into the throng of men and began haphazardly ripping their limbs from their bodies. Tortured screams could be heard as Marcus and Jamie joined the battle. Marcus slashed through the men's pudgy torsos with a long machete as Jamie whipped her legs up and around her body in a frenzy. With each swipe of her long, chocolate legs, the jagged heels of her stilettos sliced through yet another set of misused vocal cords.

"There's too many of them!" Marcus yelled out. "There are several over there that are getting away! I'll call Josie on my walkie!" Josie! Josie! We got most of ours, but there are about four that are running toward the house. We can't get to them in time! Get the girls out of there!"

The White Christian Nationalist movement of Vetis was mostly awash in testosterone. It was a movement by ruling white men to ensure the eternal dominion of white men. Their political careers had been advanced by an unholy alliance with demonic members of the world's clergy, media, and business leaders. They had been able to sit in their plush offices and block any attempt at humane laws designed to assist the needy. The minorities. The downtrodden. They wrapped themselves in the language of freedom, law enforcement and democracy while passing laws to censor free speech, halt the funding for any legitimate litigation of their brothers, and rig election systems. The business leaders were always available with open checkbooks. The clergy were always available to bastardize the words of Jesus Christ. And the propogandists were always available for their nightly brainwashing of the masses. All these politicians needed to do was sit back and pass the laws that would ensure their eternal dominion over others both on Earth and at the feet of Vetis. They were nothing more than pawns that had been promised everlasting power. And money. And sex. They basked in the glow of Vetis's movement on Earth while never acknowledging that Vetis held no loyalty to them. They were simply pawns. This was what these men were. And a few ignorant, power-hungry women.

Emerging from the woods in front of their more cautious male counterparts were two female Governors from Midwest states, a congresswoman from Colorado and another from Georgia. They wore evil little smiles on their deplorable, cartoonishly-made-up, and withered faces as they marched over the neatly groomed lawn toward the main house. The smiles faded as a grey, fluffy housecat sprang from a tree limb and began clawing out the eyes of one of the female governors as efficiently as a hawk.

LucyFur licked the blood from her whiskers then leapt upon the other female governor. Her razor claws tore through her collagen-injected lips before moving down and viciously chewing through her neck until it became disembodied and fell to the ground as helpless as a garden gnome.

The congresswoman from Georgia turned green as a lion being ridden by a beautiful African American woman pounced upon her and ripped her grating voice-box out of her throat in one bite. Sam chuckled to herself as she watched her paralyzed legs being sprayed with the blood of a traitor.

Before the congresswoman from Colorado could raise her sidearm, a cougar ripped her from her frequently visited vagina all the way through her body and face until its claws had snapped her geeky black glasses in half.

Jules and Jerry came bounding in on the backs of Bengal tigers accompanied by a pair of panthers. The ferocious creatures leapt from man to man, ripping their arms from their torsos and their internal organs from the bodies, leaving them laying on the ground screaming in a pool of their own blood mixed with the celestial blood that was mournfully falling from the heavens.

Two dark figures were seen scurrying toward the house as Jules yelled into her walkie, "Josie! Two got away! Get the girls out of there!"

"What the hell do we need to do this shit for?" a demonic gun manufacturer stated angrily as he watched several of his colleagues' brains get blown out by bullets from the trees. "We're getting picked off one by one! And by my own fucking guns!"

"Just keep running!" a disgraced so-called business "visionary" yelled back. "There are too many of us! They can't get us all! We have to get to that house! We have to kill those fucking babies before they are born! And I don't *mind* if a few of us get killed! Even more of that gifted baby blood for me! Then I will be powerful enough to restore the wireless internet and dominate the messages that are spread throughout the world! The people will know only what I *allow* them to know!"

The pair were gasping heavily as they exited the woods and looked toward their target. They laughed and high-fived as they saw no forces of resistance. Their arrogant guffawing stopped when they heard a female voice from behind them say, "Malum tuum dolorem facit. et dolor meus es fortitudo mea." Their silence then turned to painful screeches as a former high school football star smashed their heads together. They fell to their knees and their confused expressions looked up at a life-size glamour doll. Her shimmering blonde hair flew in a tangle of bloodied gold around her perfectly made-up face. She smiled at them and extended her hands.

"Do you like my nails?" Jessie inquired sweetly. "I had them made up just for you. I know how you sexist bastards like your women to always look like your little trophies, so I wanted to make sure to look special for you. Because I am the last woman that you will ever leer at again!"

An impressed Cliff looked on as he observed his wife's strength. His Jessie could be self-absorbed. She could be selfish. She could be arrogant. But she could also be self-determined. Caring. Merciful. Psychologically strong. And, in this moment, physically strong. Because Jessie West was not one-dimensional. Jessie West was not a stereotype. Jessie West was a woman who refused to be type-cast into a role for the amusement of men. Jessie West was a complete woman. And not one to be fucked with.

Cliff burst into uncontrollable laughter as he watched his love take her perfectly manicured nails and bury them into the jugulars of each of the squirming men. She then lifted them up by their necks. Blood was pouring down her hands to her elbows as she raised the men over her head and simply held them there. Their bodies were writhing in pain as they gasped for air from their shattered windpipes. And Jessie just held them there. She held them there and thought about how so many of her sisters throughout the ages had been held in submission. She thought about all the women who had been stifled, suppressed, abused, and oppressed. She thought about all the women whose voices had been drowned out. Whose dreams had been shattered. Whose very souls had been smothered. And she persistently held them there. She held them there until the squirming stopped. She lowered her arms and tossed the limp bodies to the side as she watched their polluted essence rise and immediately become absorbed by her elevated dear friend.

Henri emerged from the woods carrying his sniper rifle over his shoulder wearing a broad smile. "Oh my," he said to the pair. "I'm now sorry that I didn't leave a few more for you. I can never get enough of watching a strong woman in action."

"You got that right," Jessie replied before looking down at her hands and yelling out, "Goddammit Cliff! As soon as this is over, you're taking me to the salon! I've broken three nails!"

Josie put down her walkie and shouted up the stairs, "Okay everybody! We have seven of these pricks coming at us. We're not taking any chances! Stellan and Paciano! Get Rachel and Kayla on your backs and get them out to the stable! Lionnel! Go bring those babies into the world. And the rest of you guard that fucking stable as though your lives depend on it. Because it does. Now, go!"

"No, Josie," Adam stated flatly followed by his twin brother, Aaron. "No. We cannot leave you. We have been your protectors since you were born. That is why we are here. It is the game that we were brought into the world to play. And we shall continue playing until we are no longer able."

"Oh, my lovely boys," a tearful Josie replied. "You are both just so beautiful. But that is *not* why you are here. You are here to bring these new souls into the world. You are here to raise them and love them and prepare them for their future. To prepare them for their destiny. Your loyalty belongs to them and your wives. Now go. Go protect your families. Go be the nurturing protectors that all men are supposed to be."

Stellan scurried down the stairs carrying a screaming Kayla upon his back followed by Paciano and Rachel. "Fuck!" Stellan yelled out. "I think her water just broke! And all over my lovely designer shirt!"

Vai and Alexa opened the back door of the house and waved them towards the nearby stables. Adam and Aaron took one last long look upon their Josie. "Thank you, Josie," Adam said followed by Aaron's, "Yes. Thank you. Thank you for being our friend. Thank you for guiding us. And thank you for your sacrifice. You are sacrificing your safety so that we may bring our children into the world. I do not know if we will see you again. We have not seen this ending. But we have seen your compassion. And we have seen your strength. You are stronger than your father. You are stronger than your mother. Because you are Josie. You do not belong to them. You do not belong to us. You belong to the world. We love you, Josie."

"I-I love you too!" Josie blurted out as she wiped tears from her emerald green eyes. "Now get the fuck out of here, okay?"

The Twins all-white suits turned instantly to murky red as they left the house and walked out into the violent blood storm. Josie's dread-filled heart sank as she lifted her bow towards the front door. One final tear fell to the floor as she stoically awaited her fate. Alone.

———

"Where *are* those motherfuckin' cowards? Mommy? Daddy? Where aaaare yoooou? Your baby girl has a fuckin' surprise for you!" Maddy screamed out as she saw Howard's bright blue and white forces clash with copper headed, black bodied serpents on the periphery of Enlightenment. She stood at the ready holding a conjured serrated broadsword. At the end of the handle, there was a plastic male doll hanging by its neck. Her loving husband stood in his customary place directly beside her, ready to support her in any way that she needed, including murder. Directly behind her stood her Uncle Joe and Aunt Blair. They all secretly wondered if their combined might would be enough to defeat the greatest existential threat that humanity had ever known.

"C'mon bitch!" Maddy called out once again. "Are ya afraid of lil' ol' me? C'mon! Are you a *big pussy* that can't take someone on without being surrounded by your posse? Your fuckin' troops are a bit preoccupied at the moment, so you may as well come on out. We've been preparing for this since the day I came out of your musty fucking cunt, so let's do this shit! There's no one around to help you now!"

"I don't need anybody's help to slaughter you, you little whore," Its cold, nasal voice was heard as It slinked up from the misty floor. Its body was entirely serpentine, with large copper scales. It had two human arms jutting out from Its chest. Its face was surrounded by a copper, scaley hood. And Maddy could not help but notice that Its face was, for the first time in Its existence, more youthful and almost pretty.

"What the fuck Mom!" Maddy yelled out. "They got some sort of health spa in Perdition Land or whatever the fuck it's called?"

"You might call it that, you little slut." It replied haughtily. "You have no idea what the power of our glorious Vetis can bestow upon you. I have been able to suck the life force out of millions of dark souls. I have absorbed their power. Their energy. Their evil. Their beauty. I am the most powerful being in the cosmos! You and your little family stand no chance against me now. But I'm in a generous mood. Come to me, my daughter. Come and wage war by my side. Together we can rule the cosmos at the feet of Vetis. It is time for you to come home, my daughter. It is your destiny. Do this, and I will spare the rest of your family."

"Uh, well, I gotta admit that evil shit gave you quite the makeover. And I do love my family and I don't want to see them destroyed. But, how about my friends and family on Earth? What are you gonna do for them?"

"Oh, very well," It replied in an unconvincing, sweet tone. "Your precious sister, Arima, your beloved daughter, Josie and all the rest will be spared. There is an attack happening as we speak on your estate. Our forces will destroy them all on Earth and then we will permanently destroy their souls once they enter Enlightenment. Come to me now, my daughter, and I will call off the attack and spare them as well."

Its glowing red eyes glared in quiet anticipation as Maddy turned around to her family. She and Erick flashed a quick wink at one another as their eyes briefly met. She then stared into the face of her beloved Uncle Joe. She stared at the first man who had truly cared for her. He was her guide. He was her anchor. He was her hero. They looked at one another's knowing faces and silently communicated before Maddy said, "Gee, I just don't know. What do you guys think? I mean, on the one hand, I really want to kill my bitch mother. But on the other hand, I don't want anybody I love to be harmed. Gee, it's just so confusing. I feel so torn. But I guess I know what I must do. I'm not saying that it will be easy, but this is what I must do now. I'm sorry, everybody. Please forgive me."

Maddy turned to face her mother, lowered her sword, and bowed her head in reverence. "I have my answer, mother. It was really a struggle to figure it out, but I know now what I must do. Yes. I will join you." She then burst into laughter and yelled out, "Just fuckin' with ya! I'm gonna kill you muthufuckaaaa!"

Maddy leapt at the fifteen-foot serpentine figure of her mother and was immediately slapped back into the white mist on the floor by the long, black tail of a snake. "Well, my dear, I believe we have our answer," The Pastor's voice stated out of the mouth of a giant Black Mamba.

"Indeed," It answered calmly. "You know what to do. Destroy them."

The Pastor opened its jaws and struck out at Joseph while hitting Blair away with his tail. Just before his venomous fangs could impale Joseph, Erick leapt upon his head and held his jaws open. Joseph reached into the serpent's mouth and ripped out it's forked tongue causing the Pastor to rear it's scaley head back in pain. Erick looked deep into one of the Pastor's pitch-black eyes and drove a dagger into it. Erick was immediately covered in a black, sticky bile substance. "Oh, fuckin' gross! I've got demon eye cum all over me!" he yelled out as he retrieved his dagger and thrust it into the other eye, causing another geyser of demonic ejaculate.

The Pastor was whipping his body around in a frenzied attempt to free itself from Erick and Joseph, who was holding his mouth open with one hand while pulling a venom-coated fang out with his other. The Pastor let out one final high-pitched shriek as Maddy jumped on his head and sat astride him just behind her husband. The Pastor felt Maddy's broadsword penetrate the top of his skull and plunge all the way through his lower jaw. His painful squeals continued as Maddy pushed her husband off and then used the jagged edges of her blade to saw through the Pastor's head, severing it in two. The lifeless and spiritless form plopped into the white mist that was now mixed with unholy black bile.

"Well, *that* wasn't so hard!" Maddy excitedly exclaimed. "One fucker down, one to go! See Daddy? You always wanted to find out if your little girl gave good head. Did you like it, Daddy? Did you like how your little girl gave you head? Hey! Why isn't anybody laughing? That was gold! Pure fuckin' gol…"

Maddy's exclamation was cut off as It lunged down with It's jaw wide open and swallowed her daughter in one bite. Erick, Joseph, and Blair stood with their mouths agape as they watched the spiritual bulge of their fallen loved one slowly slide down the copper serpentine frame.

The moment that Maddy was encased by Its sadistic form, she felt the intense pain from Its demonic acid that was beginning to eat away at her essence. She could feel tiny pieces of herself being stripped away and being digested by the vile entity that had consumed her. Images of her life began flashing through her weakening mind. Her weekend dance and junk food parties with her beloved aunts and uncle. Her meeting her first true love. The retribution of the man who had raised her. The birth of her most precious daughter. The bonding with her newfound sister. She shed tears that were quickly absorbed by the pure evil that she was inside and knew that this was finally the end. Maddy knew that she had failed.

She then heard a familiar voice speak to her soul. "Um, hey, Sis. Or, um, I'm sorry. I mean Lil' Readhead? Whatcha doin?"

"I think I'm dying Arima," Maddy's soul meekly answered.

"No, you're not," Arima hazily replied. "Here. Just take my hand. Use my strength to fortify yours. And let's end this. Together. This was what they most feared from us. Because not only can *you* enter *my* soul at any time, but *I* can also enter *yours*. We are two souls that can become one. And once that happens, we can combine our strength. We can do *anything* together. So, stop your whining and let's get this over with. I've got the worst case of munchies right now. Hey, I just thought of somethin'. When I get here, I can conjure anything that I want right? So, like, I can conjure up an order of twenty chicken nuggets but there will be twenty-six chicken nuggets! That's gonna be so cool."

"Yes, what a fitting ending," It said snidely as it could feel It's daughter being digested into Its ungodly being. "The mother eating it's young. It is so perfect. And now you can see that all is lost for you. That little bitch was the only one who could truly destroy me. And now, I shall consume her and shit her out of me, just as she did on my grave. It is just so satisfying to have the last laugh. It is just so…"

Its arrogant diatribe was cut off as It violently flailed Its head back and hissed in agony. Maddy's broadsword came jutting out of Its copper sternum and viciously sawed its way down to Its tail. Maddy's head crowned from between the gash, covered in dark red and green ooze. She forced her head through the opening while saying to Arima's soul, "Thanks Soul Sister! I love you! See you soon! Over and out!" She crawled out of the fallen wicked serpentine body of her mother, opened her emerald green eyes, looked around with innocent amazement and let out a high pitched cry.

"What the fuck are you doing?" Erick asked his wife.

Maddy looked up at him, flashed her mischievous grin and said gleefully, "It's performance art! Since you fuckers don't get my great humor, I thought I'd use this opportunity to re-enact my birth from this fucking bitch. Pretty cool, huh? I'm even covered in goo and shit. Did anybody record this? This would be a total hit on the internet! Oh, right. Hardly anybody gets that anymore. That sucks."

Maddy looked down upon her pathetic mother's form transforming from a powerful, demonic serpent back into the withered hag from Its time on Earth. She listened to Its dying rasps and said sweetly, "Are you happy now Mommy? You always wanted me to be born again, so there ya go. Sorry about the inverse C-Section thing. Y'know, I always wondered what this moment would be like. I even had a long speech planned as I stood over your dying, bitch ass. But you know what? You're no different than all the other 'Chads' that I've taken out. You're just another piece of sadistic, narcissistic trash. And you aren't worth my fuckin' time. C'mon Uncle Joe. Let's conjure up some ice cream."

"In just a moment, Buttacup," Joseph responded. "I have a promise to keep." He strode over to the gasping form of his despised sister-in-law, reached into her chest and ripped out her barely beating, black heart. He silently walked over to his beloved wife and presented his trophy to her. Blair Sommers-Argento took his gift, smiled at him with eternal love and voraciously bit into the unholy, still-beating organ.

"Jesus Christ, Aunt Blair!" Maddy screamed out. "Gross! You coulda at least *cooked It* first!"

It laid in the white, black, red, and green mist and let out one final gasp. The entirety of Enlightenment began shaking as the millions of cowardly, demonic serpents turned away from their battle and slithered back to the Realm of Perdition. There was an explosion of brilliant purple lightning and the entirety of the cosmos turned to a majestic lavender.

From a far corner of Enlightenment came Patty's booming voice. "Wow! That was fuckin' cool Mads! Okay, Prince! Get your fuckin' ass on the stage! We've got a party to throw! And Jerry Lee, don't give me that fuckin' look!"

————

The front door exploded into splinters and seven men came rushing inside. Josie launched three arrows in quick succession into the foreheads of three of the assailants. Their dark souls immediately emerged and began swirling around her as the other four men prepared their attack.

"Arima!" Josie cried out as she ran into the adjacent living room. "Arima! Get these fuckers off of me! Where are you?" *Ah, fuck it, I'll just do it myself,* she thought to herself as she fought her way through the black smog, pulled her knife and slashed the throat of another man. The blood from the gash violently splashed on the family portrait that was hanging over the fireplace. Josie was keeping her promise that she had made to her mother two years prior. Josie was painting the walls of the estate with their blood. She picked up an axe next to the fireplace and viciously swung her petite arms, decapitating two approaching attackers with one swing. Blood erupted from the necks of the fallen men before their bodies succumbed to their final fate. Six evil souls were now swirling around her as the final intruder made his escape. The Congressman from Ohio wrestled his way off the floor and hastily made his way to the back exit.

Josie was flailing her axe in futility at the disembodied spirits as they cackled and swirled around her. Their morbid forms were then suddenly sucked away from her and out the front door. She allowed herself to catch her breath and wear a slight smile as she heard a voice from above the house say, "Hey, um, Niece Josie? Sorry about that. I had to go help your mom, I mean, Lil' Redhead, um, no, I mean, your mom for a minute. I'm just gonna take them to the holy pond. I'll be right back. I'll meet you in the stables. Hey, do you guys keep any 'tato chips or anything in the stables? Oh well, it doesn't matter. Now, what was I doing? Oh, yeah. I'll be right back."

Josie ran out the back door and found the final living demonic soul on Earth, being confronted by Alexa, Vai, and the Twins.

As the blood rained down upon them, Adam said, "you will not harm our children." "No, you won't," Aaron added. "And you are too late. All but one has been born. You can hear their cries. They are cries of innocence. They are cries of dignity. They are the cries of justice. And they are the cries of revenge. They will grow up and exact revenge upon you and all like you. The evil doers who use hate to fulfill their own wishes. The evil doers who find joy in torturing the downtrodden. You are soulless. You are demonic. And our four children shall defeat you all. We wish we had more time to play with you, but we have our family to attend to."

Adam and Aaron slowly approached the shaking man who fell to his knees and began pleading for mercy. Blood was dripping from their light blond, long strands as they looked down upon the pathetic creature that coward beneath them. They looked at one another, kicked the man over and proceeded to stomp on the man's head repeatedly with their previously all-white boots. Adam and Aaron rarely showed emotion. They did not play their games out of anger. Or hatred. They played their games out of necessity. They played their games to ensure the safety of others and to allow the downtrodden to blossom into whatever it was that they were destined to be. To allow the innocent to thrive. To allow the patriotic to lead. And to allow all genuinely kind souls to love.

This was a rare occasion of unbridled anger. As the Twins stomped on the man's face repeatedly, they shouted out, "Die! Die! Die! Die! No one threatens those that we love! No one threatens our wives! And *no one* threatens our beloved children! Go to hell *motherfucker!*"

Josie went running up to the pair, shook them and said, "Hey, hey guys. It's okay. It's over. He's dead. And I just saw Arima take his soul away. It's all over. You can stop now."

Adam looked down at the putty-like glob of flesh that was once an intact face and said in his normal, controlled tone, "Josie, did we use the term 'motherfucker' correctly?"

Josie burst into laughter and embraced the pair. The wind began picking up and there was a horrendous shriek that was heard from beyond the clouds. The roof of the stable was blown off, sending shards of wooden planks and shingles flying for miles. Josie, Adam, Aaron, Vai, and Alexa rushed into the stable and found Kayla holding her two twin children to her bosom as Lionnel was handing Rachel her newly born second child to protect. Standing over Rachel, Kayla, and their children were four Shetland ponies. They had widened their legs and stood astride over the mothers who were desperately holding their newborns. The ponies were unflinching against the onslaught of the blood hurricane as they instinctively used their undersized frames to provide shelter for the squirming infants.

"C'mon! Let's get you guys back in the house!" Josie ordered. Arima arrived just in time to be handed Kayla's baby boy. Josie then picked up one of Rachel's baby girls and wrapped her in a blue baby blanket. Adam and Aaron tenderly lifted their infant son and daughter and placed them inside of their jackets. Stellan and Paciano rushed over to the new mothers and began assisting their weary and sore frames to their feet. Trees across the estate were bowed over as the wind and bloody rainfall increased. There were flashes of copper lightning erupting all over the sky. Josie was clutching the baby girl and was nearly blown over by a final gust of wind when she saw an explosion of purple lightning. The red clouds transformed into a lush lavender and the torrential rain of blood turned to a warm purple shower.

Everyone stood in the gentle rainfall and looked upward to the sky as the lavender clouds brightened the entire Earth. "Oh my God! It's over! We've won!" an exuberant Josie shouted out as she heard Prince strum the amplified opening cords of "Purple Rain." Josie, Arima, Adam, and Aaron lifted the children in the air, laughed and began twirling them in the cleansing purple rain.

All over the Earth, people came out from their tattered shelters and looked up to the sky. They listened to the music and watched the brilliant light show in the clouds as they held hands and swayed. They watched the blood of angels and demons being washed away by the warm rainfall. They wept as they now understood that humanity had just been saved from itself. And they understood that it was now *their* duty to ensure that humanity would persevere.

Josie and Arima listened to each song that was being heard throughout the world and danced. And smiled. And embraced. And wept. And laughed. In the Purple Reign.

Epilogue 1

"Well, that was disappointing," Vetis stated with a tone of resignation. "Centuries of hard work down the drain. Ah well. It *was* entertaining, heh, heh, heh." He sat there on his throne of fire in his designated hell within the cosmos. His bright red body was covered in the shifting shadows of the millions of damned souls that he had manipulated into his servitude. His four hands were squeezing human brains that he was using to relieve his tension. The brains were not his only tension relief, however.

He looked down at the orange bulbous man's head that was bobbing from between his legs. The man's sweaty rolls of fat shook and oozed in multiple directions as his head continued its rapid vertical frenzy.

"Well, I suppose it's for the best," Vetis continued. "We'll just chalk this up as a practice run. There are so many other worlds to conquer. And we will have another shot at Enlightenment. If there's one thing that I have, it is time." Vetis then smiled broadly as yet another sadistic plan was being hatched. "Yes! Time! Of course! I am *not* done with the Earth! I can start over! I can go back in time and find fresh new souls to convert. And while these forces of so-called 'good' are spending decades battling the forces that were just defeated, they will be unaware that there is a whole *new* movement being born! A parallel movement! And this time, we will have enough forces to overpower them once and for all! And then, Enlightenment. Yes. Hey! Did anybody take this down? This shit's important!"

"O-o-of course, m-my lord," a condemned soul responded. "You will go back in time to find others to corrupt. They will, in turn, corrupt millions of others. And the two movements will run parallel to one another and overpower the forces of righteousness. It is a brilliant plan, my lord."

"Of course, it fucking is, I thought of it," Vetis dismissively replied before saying softly to himself, "as long as we don't get any trouble from those damned meddling kids." He then lifted the head of the orange man by his thinning blond hair, looked him in his tearful eyes, smiled and said, "You know, you really fucked up everything you touched on Earth, but I've gotta hand it to you. Credit where credit is due. You really can suck cock. Now get back to work."

EPILOGUE 2

The twins of the twins and the Twins were dubbed 'The Junior Quad,' and settled into their home at the estate. There were two boys and two girls, and they looked identical. Each had pure white hair and perfect, light caramel skin with the faint outline of a lightning bolt embedded into each of their tender faces. Each also had one eye that was brown and one that was blue.

Rachel and Adam named their twin daughters Sigourney and Euna. Kayla and Aaron's twin sons were named Kane and Thanatos. The children contently cooed throughout their first night in the world. The next morning, everyone noticed that they had grown substantially and were well on their way to teething. It was as though they had aged one full year overnight. Which held true on the second morning as they were now ready to be potty trained and were beginning to walk. It was determined on the third day that they had aged three years.

The puzzled parents were frantic to find an answer. "Oh my God!" Kayla screamed out on the morning of day four. "If this continues, they won't live more than three months!"

Rod was called in to work with Lionnel on various tests and Rosa was called in to tap into the children's energy. Every time she concentrated and connected her energy to theirs, she was violently overloaded and passed out, which made the children giggle.

On day five, the Junior Quad were five years old and were able to read, write and speak. Although, they only spoke as a group. Every time the children had something to say it was quadrophonic. On day ten, they were ten years old, and becoming quite mischievous. They would play games with bones that they would find in the yard of the defeated marauders and laugh when they watched violent images on the television. They also delighted in riding the Shetland ponies that had served as their protectors on the evening of their birth.

On day fifteen they were…still ten years old. The Junior Quad approached their concerned parents and explained it to them simultaneously through their four seemingly innocent voices. "Hello, mothers. Hello, fathers. We know that you are confused and worried, but there really isn't a reason to be. We have aged to ten years old, and we will remain that age for all of eternity. Unless someone strikes us down, which will be quite impossible. We are connected. We are four separate bodies connected by one soul. We think alike and speak alike. We understand what our destiny is. We have seen it. There is no reason for you to worry. All you must do is love us. And give us ice cream."

"Very well, then." Adam stated followed by Aaron. "Yes, that seems quite plausible. Oh, what fun games that we will play with our forever ten-year-olds. And yes, ice cream does sound appropriate at a time such as this."

The Twins looked down upon the displeased faces of their wives and noticed them angrily kicking their crossed legs.

"What is wrong Kayla?" Aaron asked followed by Adam's, "Yes. What is wrong Rachel?"

"Well," Rachel began in an exasperated tone. "We're thrilled to have kids and to raise them and everything, but at *some* point, we figured they'd go off to college and shit."

"Yes," Kayla added. "We obviously love them, but at what point do they go off on their own?"

The sisters were answered by four sweet voices coming from the four corners of the room. "You do not have to worry about that mothers. We can look after ourselves. We will stay with you for as long as we are needed here. But once we sense that we are needed elsewhere, we shall go. You really do not have to worry. We will be fine." The foursome then began giggling and running around the room as they were playing 'tag' with dismembered hands.

"Okay, you know what?" Rachel stated. "This is some weird shit, and we haven't been out in ages, and we need a goddam drink. So, you boys change into a clean white suit. We'll ask Arima and Josie to baby…um… child sit. Let's go out, okay?"

"Why yes," Adam enthusiastically responded. "Of course, we can go out and get you drinks!"

"Oh, my yes!" Aaron added. "You may drink as much as you would like. You always ask to play 'Hide the Sausage' when you drink alcohol. Oh, what a fun night of games we will have!"

Kayla shook her head slowly at the Twins and said, "Listen boys. We just pumped two kids out of us two weeks ago. 'Hide the Sausage' just isn't in the cards at the moment, okay?"

"Oh, alright then," a slightly disappointed Aaron replied. "But sometimes you play 'Hide the Sausage' with your mouth. Could we play that way?"

"Yeah, probably," a resigned Rachel responded before looking at her sister. They then both smiled widely and yelled out "Wooooooooo!"

———

"Oh, my fucking *God*! These kids make a fuckin' *mess*!" Josie yelled downstairs to Arima. "I know they're really smart and shit, but they'd better learn to put their fuckin' dirty clothes in a hamper. My dad always said that if the laundry isn't in the hamper, then it isn't getting done! That's why mom rarely had clean clothes to wear. She always left her shit lying all over the place. And why are their clothes covered in blood?"

Josie answered her own question when she saw a lifeless arm sticking out from underneath one of the bunkbeds. "Well," a bemused Josie voiced to herself, "I guess we know what happened to that creepy mailman. Oh well. And why are those ponies sleeping up here with them now? And where *are* the ponies? Hey, Arima! Are the ponies down there?"

"Um, no," Arima casually responded. "Hey. The pizza's here. Do ya want some? It's really good."

"Of course, I want some!" Josie angrily replied as she picked up yet another soiled shirt and threw it in the hamper. "And don't bogart it all! Save me some!"

"Uh, yeah, okay," Arima sheepishly answered. "Yeah, there's still a couple pieces left. It's really good."

"What do you mean *a couple pieces* left?" Josie yelled out as she stomped down the stairs with her sweaty, curly copper hair bouncing. "Have the JQ eaten yet? Hey, where are they?"

"Um, I dunno," Arima replied as she was attempting to discreetly place a half-eaten slice back into the cardboard box. "I thought they were upstairs with you."

"Well, fuck," Josie stated as she felt her anxiety rising. "No ponies, no JQ. Okay. No need to worry. They probably just went out for a ride. No need to worry. I'm sure they'll turn up."

An hour later, a frantic Josie greeted Rosa and Jessie at the door. "Oh my God you guys. Thanks for coming. We've looked everywhere. We have no idea where the JQ are. They couldn't have gotten far, but those ponies are pretty fast. Please, can you help us find them? Can you like Behold their souls or track their energy or something?"

"Sure, easy," Jessie replied as she placed LucyFur on the couch next to her. "Here, Rosa. Take my hand. Tap into my energy and enhance my ability to Behold them. I wanna get this done fast. There's an episode of *Seinfeld* coming on and Cliff always gets turned on by that show for some reason."

Jessie and Rosa held hands and began lightly trembling. After five minutes of concentrated effort, Jessie let go of Rosa's sweaty hand and said softly, "Aw, shit."

"What?" Josie yelled out. "What's wrong? Did you find them?"

"Yeah, we found them, alright," Jessie replied in an annoyed tone. "It looks like I'm gonna miss out on my weekly *Seinfeld* fuck."

"Well, where *are* they?" Josie desperately asked.

"Yeah," Jessie responded as Rosa was holding her shaking head in her hands unsure of whether to laugh or cry. "The question isn't *where* they are. The question is *when* they are. The little bastards can travel through time."

TO BE CONCLUDED IN "TWINFINITY: HANGING CHADS BOOK V"

Song Reference List

The author would like to thank the countless musical artists that have enhanced his entire life. In particular, the author would like to give a heartfelt thank you to the following artists for enhancing the experience of both writing and reading this book.

Cheap Trick- "Hello There"
Beastie Boys- "Sabotage"
Haley Mills- "Let's Get Together"
Bruce Springsteen- "Ghosts"
REM- "Feeling Gravity's Pull"
David Bowie- "Life on Mars"
Pink Floyd- "Hey You"
Jerry Lee Lewis- "Great Balls of Fire"
Love and Rockets- "So Alive"
Rob Zombie- "Living Dead Girl"
AC/DC- "Moneytalks"
XTC- "Dear God"
Rollins Band- "Liar"
Bob Dylan- "The Times They are A-Changin'"
My Life With the Thrill Kill Kult- "Sex on Wheelz"
White Stripes- "I Think I Smell a Rat"

Eileen Barton- "If I Knew You Were Comin' I'd've Baked a Cake"
George Harrison- "My Sweet Lord"
John Lennon- "Imagine"
10,000 Maniacs- "Candy Everybody Wants"
David Bowie & Queen- "Under Pressure"
Elvis Costello- "Radio, Radio"
Kenny Loggins- "Footloose"
Thin Lizzy- "Jailbreak"
Alice Cooper- "Our Love Will Change the World"
Bruce Springsteen- "If I Was the Priest"
David Bowie- "The Wedding Song"
Bikini Kill- "Rebel Girl"
The Pink Spiders- "Little Razorblade"
Dickie- "Forty-Five"
REM- "Why Not Smile" (Reprise)
Brian Jonestown Massacre- "Oh Lord"
Gary US Bonds- "Quarter to Three"
The Raveonettes- "Attack of the Ghostriders"
Neil Sedaka- "Laughter in the Rain"
Bessie Banks- "Go Now"
Prince- "Purple Rain"

PATTYPAZOOLA AKA VICTORYFUCKINPALOOZA

"Oh fuck!" Patty exclaimed as she witnessed the death of the Copperhead at the hands of her daughter from behind Stage One of 'Victoryfuckinpalooza.' "Maddy just ripped that cold-ass bitch in two! Fuck yeah, Mads! Prince, you got what you wanted. You wanted to set the tone for this thing. Well, you got it sweetheart. Get that tight little ass out on that stage and make some motherfuckers cry."

ACT I
Prince- "Purple Rain"
Jerry Lee Lewis- "Great Balls of Fire"
Jimi Hendrix- "All Along the Watchtower"
Freddie Mercury (Queen)- "We are the Champions"
Sam Moore & Dave Prater (Sam & Dave)- "Hold On, I'm Coming"

Joe Strummer (The Clash)- "Know Your Rights"
Ricky Nelson- "Garden Party"
 Lux Interior (The Cramps)- "Surfin' Dead"
Marvin Gaye- "What's Goin' On"
Karen Carpenter (The Carpenters)- "Top of the World"
Tom Petty- "The Waiting"

Patty rushed up to the dressing room door and anxiously knocked on it. "Okay James. Tom's just finishing up on Stage Two, then we'll have a ten-minute break, then you're on Stage One. Make 'em feel it. Make 'em feel the love and triumph. Make their heartbreak go someplace loving. Just like Boston Garden 1968. Make the Earth fuckin' stand up and take notice."

ACT II
James Brown- "I Got You (I Feel Good)"
Tony Williams, David Lynch, Herb Reed, Paul Robi, Zola Taylor (The Platters)- "Smoke Gets in Your Eyes"
Dusty Hill (ZZ Top)- "Tush"
Bill Haley- "See You Later Alligator"
Kurt Cobain (Nirvana)- "Smells Like Teen Spirit"
Stevie Ray Vaughn- "Crossfire"
Dusty Springfield- "Son of a Preacher Man"
David Cassidy- "I Think I Love You"
Whitney Houston- "I Wanna Dance With Somebody"
Sid Vicious (Sex Pistols)- "My Way"
Elvis Presley- "Good Rockin' Tonight"
Little Richard- "Rip It Up"

"Yeah, yeah, I know! I heard ya the first thousand times!" Patty yelled out to Richard Penniman. "I know, I know. You're the *real* king of rock and roll and you ain't openin' for nobody. I got it. And you got the closer in this set. Great job. Now hit the showers. Okay, where the fuck is Johnny? Oh, there you are. Didn't see you standing there in the shadows all dressed in black and shit. You ready? They are gonna freak the fuck out when you open by introducing yourself!"

ACT III
Johnny Cash- "Folsom Prison Blues"
Otis Redding- "Try a Little Tenderness"
Nilsson- "Without You"
Ritchie Valens- "Come on Let's Go"
Eddie Cochran- "C'mon Everybody"
Robbie Robertson (The Band)- "The Weight"
Ronnie Spector w/ Clarence Clemons & Danny Federici (E Street Band)- "Say Goodbye to Hollywood"
Robin & Maurice Gibb (The Bee Gees)- "Nights on Broadway"
Andy Gibb- "Shadow Dancing"
George Michael- "Faith"
Eddie Van Halen (Van Halen)- "Eruption/You Really Got Me"

"What the fuck are you guys wearing?" Patty yelled out to Johnny, Dee Dee, and Joey. "What's with the pastel leisure suits? I don't fuckin' *care* if you're trying to change your image! Get the fuck back in there and put on your ripped jeans and leather jackets! Jesus Christ! This is a fuckin' rock concert not The Flamingo!"

ACT IV
Joey, Johnny, & Dee Dee Ramone (The Ramones)- "Rock and Roll Radio"
George Jones- "White Lightnin'"
Carl Perkins- "Blue Suede Shoes"
Gene Vincent- "Be Bop a Lula"
Del Shannon- "Runaway"
Johnny Moore, Charlie Thomas, Rudy Lewis, Gene Pearson, Johnny Terry, Jimmy Lewis (The Drifters)- "Under the Boardwalk"
Sinead O'Connor- "Nothing Compares 2 U"
Tony Davis & Cliff Hall (The Spinners)- "Then Came You"
Michael Nesmith, Peter Tork, Davy Jones (The Monkees)- "Listen To the Band"
Chuck Berry- "Reelin' and a Rockin'"
Ruth Brown- "This Little Girl's Gone Rockin'"
Nina Simone- "Mississippi Goddam"

"Howard!" Patty screamed as she opened the dressing room door to make sure the next act was ready. "What the fuck are *you* doing in here? She's the 'Queen of Soul', not the queen of pegging! Get the fuck out of here! I'm so sorry about that Aretha. That little fucker has no respect."

ACT V
Aretha Franklin- "Respect"
Kim Shattuck (The Muffs)- "The Kids in America"
Janis Joplin- "Cry Baby"
Roy Orbison- "Crying"
John Phillips, Cass Elliott, Denny Doherty (The Mamas & The Papas)- "I Saw Her Again Last Night"
Patsy Cline- "Crazy"
Rick Ocasek & Benjamin Orr (The Cars)- "Magic"
Merle Haggard- "I Think I'll Just Sit Here and Drink"
John Lee Hooker- "Boom Boom"
Sam Cooke- "Cupid"
Karl & Dennis Wilson (the Beach Boys)- "Good Vibrations"
Christine McVie (Fleetwood Mac)- "Don't Stop"
Lemmy (Motorhead)- "Ace of Spades"
Bon Scott & Malcolm Young (AC/DC)- "Dirty Deeds Done Dirt Cheap"

"Oh, yeah, Jacklyn. This is the final set. Our last dance tonight," Patty said softy to her eternal wife. "But not our final dance. I'm gonna dance with you for all eternity. And I'm gonna love looking down at my Josie's smiling face as she dances with her Lionnel when "My Girl Josephine" comes on. And Joe and Blair dancing to their song. And all of Joe's friends and family singing along with Bob. Then the closing six songs. It wasn't easy to get them to agree to this, but everyone agreed that Buddy had to close the show. They all said that it just felt right. I did it, Jacklyn. I put on 'Victoryfuckinpalooza.' And *this* shit is just the beginning."

ACT VI
Donna Summer- "Last Dance"
Don & Phil Everly (The Everly Brothers)- "All I Have to do is Dream"
Bob Marley- "Three Little Birds"
Wayne Fontana & The Mindbenders - "A Groovy Kind of Love"

Fats Domino- "My Girl Josephine"
Lou Reed- "White Light / White Heat"
Marc Bolan (T. Rex)- "Cosmic Dancer"
David Bowie- "Life on Mars"
George Harrison- "My Sweet Lord"
John Lennon- "Imagine"
Buddy Holly- "Not Fade Away"

Twinfinity

Hanging Chads Book V

PROLOGUE

It was always the first thing that she noticed. The faint scent of iron as the sticky thick molasses gently dribbled off her claws and onto her awaiting tongue. She felt a slight sense of satisfaction as her furry ears positioned themselves to intensely listen to the faint exhalation of air passing through her latest victim's mouth which was now permanently formed into a silent scream. Then, the sound of the blood droplets hitting the floor. Slowly at first, like an annoying leaky faucet. *Drop....drop....drop....*then faster as the taught skin surrounding his jugular gave way completely to unleash a crimson waterfall which hit the hard wood floor as though someone had poured an entire gallon of milk upon it. She pulled her claws completely from his throat while loosening her fangs' grip from his hair. Then the familiar thud as the lifeless body succumbed to gravity completing the merciless fait accompli.

A mischievous smile forced the upward curling of the right side of her mauve lips and whiskers. *This was successful. This was liberating. This was justified,* she thought to herself as she positioned herself on the man's chest and began eagerly lapping up the blood that was gushing out of his slashed throat. She looked down upon the mess that he had created as the pool of newly released blood expanded outward like a growing hurricane churning above warm water. She heard two sets of familiar footsteps approaching. The door opened and she looked up innocently at the two pairs of frantic eyes that were staring down at her.

"Oh, *there* you are sweetie!" a relieved Jessie exclaimed as her shoes sploshed across the hardwood floor to her cherished pet. "We have been so *worried!*"

"Yup, there she is," Jules dryly stated. "And *here's* the asshole that tried to escape. Nice job, cat. You kinda made a mess, though."

"Not as much of a mess as *we're* making downstairs," Jessie playfully replied. "Oh my God! Can you believe how *loud* these pricks can scream? I mean, I thought all the *previous* fascist fuckers were loud, but this *new* batch has them beat. By a mile. And man, do they piss their pants! At least LucyFur's…um…*friend* didn't last long enough to piss everywhere. This won't be *nearly* as big of a clean-up job as ours."

The two friends could not help but let out an amused giggle as they watched LucyFur's blood-soaked face mew up at them, then return to her evening's meal. She began purring loudly as she continued her ravenous feeding.

The women's giggles turned into unbridled, full-throated laughter as they watched this blood-soaked furball's euphoric feeding. "Well," Jules observed. "At least we won't have to feed her tonight."

"What are you talking about?" Jessie shot back. She bent over her beloved pet and picked her up. A new coat of fresh blood was squeezed out of LucyFur's matted hair and saturated Jessie's designer top as she hugged the enraptured cat. "Oh, my sweetie *always* needs her nummy-num-nums, now, *don't* you?"

LucyFur's purring continued as she lovingly rubbed her drenched face against that of her "owner." The giggling and purring of the pair continued until Jessie said, "And once dinner time is over, I think I know a certain little *someone* who is going to need a B-A-T-H."

Upon hearing the ominous four letters being uttered, LucyFur shrieked with intense fear and began thrashing her paws violently into the air until Jessie was forced to let her go. The shoes of Jules and Jessie were splattered with blood as LucyFur's plump body cannonballed into the crimson pool. LucyFur looked up at Jessie with disdain, turned her back and returned to her morbid meal.

"Yeah, *that* shit's not happening," Jules replied. "And she *really* should have been named 'Maddy,' because that's one blood-lustful little bitch."

"Yeah," Jessie agreed before concluding with, "or Josie."

"Yeah," Jessie agreed before concluding with, "or Josie."

CHAPTER 93
TIME MACHINE

The four perpetual ten-year-olds were giggling uncontrollably as they began their journey to the year 1958. They were surrounded by the multi-colored flashing strobes of the universe and a kaleidoscopic mist that encased their tiny bodies. Each was wearing all-white cowboy and cowgirl outfits, complete with fringe on their respective vests, boots, skirts, chaps, and cowboy hats that covered their wispy-white shoulder-length locks. The boys had their hair parted down the middle. The girls parted their hair on the right side of their scalp. They each had light caramel skin with the faint outline of a lightning bolt embedded into each of their tender faces. Each also had one eye that was a rich brown and one that was electric blue.

On their hips, they wore double holsters. But instead of guns, which the children found distasteful and unsportsman-like, they contained knives, hatchets, and other toys that the children found amusing and useful. They rode upon the backs of their best friends and protectors. Fifteen evenings prior, these four were ushered into the world during a violent battle to save the soul of humanity both on Earth and in Enlightenment. Standing steadfast astride their respective birthmothers during the mayhem were four protective Shetland ponies. The four ponies that the children now rode into their destiny.

The first twin girl of Rachel and Adam, Sigourney, rode her pure white pony that she had named 'Snowball.' Her twin sister, Euna, rode a black pony that she had named 'Blackjack.'

Their cousins, and soulmates, were the sons of Kayla and Aaron. Kane rode a red horse that he had named 'Flame.' His twin brother, Thanatos, rode a pale green Shetland that he named…

"Snot?" Sigourney yelled out to her cousin. "What kind of name is '*Snot*'? *We* all named *our* friends something cool. Your horse's name is… um…well…it isn't very *dignified*, now, is it?"

"Hey!" Thanatos shot back. "I know we all share the same soul and when we speak to others, we usually speak as one. But we each have our *own* personalities. We each have our own *preferences*. And this is *my* horse, and *my* preference is to call him 'Snot!' Because he kinda looks like that and it's easy for me to say and it's kinda funny! Plus, he always has a runny nose. So, you name your horse how *you* want, and I'll name my horse the way that *I* want!"

"Knock it off you two! We don't have time for this silly bickering." Euna interjected. "I think that we're almost there."

"Yes, it would appear so," Kane agreed. "Look at how the mist is dissipating, and the beautiful lights are slowing down. And look there! I believe that I can see the outline of buildings and streetlights and, oh my, old cars."

"Hey! Get out of the road you crazy kids!" and enraged man yelled out his driver's side window as he swerved to miss the four riders who had suddenly emerged from the evening fog.

"We're sorry!" The Junior Quad yelled back in unison as they gallantly strode down the middle of the street of Lincoln, Nebraska on March 1, 1958. The Shetland's hoofs made uniform 'clopping' sounds upon the frigid asphalt road as the JQ turned the corner as elegantly as a well-disciplined marching band.

"We're close," Kane observed. "I can feel him. The presence of his soul is strengthening."

"Yes," Euna agreed. "I can feel him too. The first of many that Vetis will try to corrupt. The first of many that he will try to indoctrinate into his evil plans. The first of many that we must vanquish. But first, stop!"

"What? What is it?" Sigourney yelled out as the four Shetlands came to an abrupt halt in the middle of the street and three of the four rushed toward the window of a local department store.

"Oh, just look in this window, sister!" Euna excitedly shouted out. "Just look at those wonderful saddle shoes and poodle skirts!"

"Wow!" Kane added. "And look at those new records! And baseball cards! This store is awesome!"

"Do they have any chewing gum"? Thanatos inquired. "I just *love* chewing gum."

Euna squinted her eyes to block out the glare of the reflected streetlights and scanned the store before yelling out, "Yes! Yes, they do! And one of them is called 'Black Jack!' How perfect! Oh sister, can't we *please* stop and do a little shopping? They have such *wonderful* treasures here."

Sigourney slapped her forehead in frustration and said through her gritted, newly acquired permanent teeth, "No, we do *not* have time for shopping right now. Although we know *who* Vetis will target somewhere in time, we do not know exactly *when* he will arrive. All that we know is that we are somehow connected to his intentions and once he decides on his latest conquest, *we* must get to them before *he* does. Otherwise, he will have corrupted another soul that will lead a parallel fascist movement to overtake the Earth. A parallel movement to the one that our parents just helped to defeat. So, we do not have time for skirts. Or baseball cards. Or gum. Or records."

"Oh, *come on* Sigourney," Kane whined. "There's *always* time for new records! There's *always* time to discover great new music! Pleeeeease?"

"Kane, I totally understand what you are saying," Sigourney answered while attempting to remain calm. "But our *mission* is the most important thing right now. Maybe....and I do mean *maybe*...if we are successful tonight, we can go into that shop and pick up a few things. But we only have so much room in the saddlebags, so don't be greedy. Now, can we get to work?"

"Yes, of course you're right, sister," Euna conceded. "And there will be *plenty* of time to go shopping after our successful mission. And we *will* be successful. We have seen it. So, come on boys. Let's ride."

"Cool," Thanatos responded. "As long as I get some chewing gum. And some tissues. Snot's nose is really runny tonight."

The foursome approached a disheveled one-bedroom house a few blocks from the department store. With a light tug upon their reins, the ponies and their accompanying 'clopping,' stopped. "This is going to be fun. Kinda like that mailman yesterday," Sigourney whispered to her twisted little associates.

"So, what's the plan?" Thanatos inquired. "Are we just gonna go up to the door and knock?"

"Yup," Sigourney answered as her innocent face turned red and twisted into a joyfully sadistic expression.

"We gotta *do* somethin' to stop this fuckin' government," the man inside the dilapidated home said to himself as he paced around a beaten coffee table that was littered with pamphlets from the John Birch Society. "Look at what my country's become. Ever since women got the vote forty years ago, it's all gone to shit. And now even the (derogatory term omitted) *Blacks* are gettin' all uppity and demanding to have the same rights as us! The *real* Americans! They want to send their kids to *our* schools! Drink out of *our* water fountains! Go to *our* stores! No, we gotta *do* somethin' and these John Birch folks may have the right answer. If I could join them, then convince my friends and family to join them, and so on, we'd have enough people to take this country back from the skirts and the (derogatory term omitted) gays, and the (derogatory term omitted) Jews and the (derogatory terms omitted) minorities. What the fuck was Ike thinkin'? Why the hell did we defeat the Nazis, anyway? Oh sure, I get bombing the fuck out of the (derogatory term omitted) Japanese. They don't look like us, don't pray like us, don't eat like us and don't have any place on this Earth. But Hitler had the right idea. Cleanse this planet of all the vermin, so we true White Christians can live together in peace without worryin' about them takin' our money and spreading their diseases. And now Ike's the fuckin' President! He took down one of the greatest men to ever live and now he's the one pushin' to let these…these…fuckin' *rats* mingle with us! With *our* kids! Hell, *our* kids are already gettin' indoctrinated by that Goddam (derogatory term omitted) *Black* music! All those white kids gyrating around listening to the Devil's music! Hell, it won't be long before our White daughters are havin' little (derogatory term omitted) Black kids! It just makes me sick. We gotta do somethin' and we gotta do somethin' *now*, before we lose this entire generation. Before we lose our country. We gotta…now who the *hell* would be knockin' on my door at this time-a-night?"

The tall, skinny twenty-year-old man grabbed his double-barrel shotgun and yelled out, "Hey! Cantcha read? No soliciting! Now get the fuck off-a my property!"

There was a momentary silence then another light rap on the withered wooden door. "Okay, motherfucker!" the man yelled out. "You asked for it!" He threw open the door and pointed his shotgun outward. Seeing nothing as he squinted through his sight, he looked down and found four giggling, tan-skinned children looking up at him.

"What the fuck do you (derogatory term omitted) kids want? You're on the wrong side-a town. You'd better get back home to your kind… um…whatever *that* might be. I can't tell if you're a (derogatory term omitted) or a (derogatory term omitted) or a (derogatory term omitted). But it don't matter none! You don't belong here! Now get your vermin little assess off-a my porch before I blow big fuckin' holes in ya!"

"No, we belong here," the four children said in unison with sweet voices. "We were sent here to play with you. We're here to have fun with you."

Euna took a lasso from her belt and threw it around the man's neck. She pulled firmly and the confused man fell upon his face, causing his nose to shatter on the hardwood floor. "W-what the fuck?" the man screamed out as Kane took his lasso, rapidly wrapped it around the man's ankles and wrists and hog-tied him within seconds.

Euna kicked the fallen gun to the side, grabbed her end of the rope and dragged the man to the center of the living room, leaving a streak of blood and teeth on the floor. Sigourney smiled innocently, slammed the door, and approached the bound, quivering man while Thanatos retrieved a knife from his holster.

"Okay, you little bastards!" the hysterical man began shouting. "You're gonna be in big trouble! I'm gonna ki…AAAAAAAAAH!"

The man's threats were interrupted as Thanatos straddled the man's back, pulled his head upward and placed his petite, tan hand into the man's open mouth. The man's screams continued as Thanatos pulled the man's tongue out and began sawing it off with his knife. The man was shedding tears and blood of pure agony as Thanatos inquisitively looked at the severed tongue, placed it into his own mouth and began chewing.

"*BLECH!*" Thanatos exclaimed as he spit the bloody tongue across the room. "*That* doesn't taste like chewing gum."

Thanatos took his place alongside his laughing soulmates. They looked down and watched as the thrashing man was frantically trying to free himself from his bindings. They then said in their childish voices, "We understand this is confusing for you. You must be wondering what it is that you have done for us to have been summoned to play with you. And since you no longer have a tongue, you will be unable to ask your question. But we will answer it anyway. The answer to your question is that we are not here because of what you have done. We are here to prevent you from doing things that you have been *chosen* to do in the future. We are here to *prevent* you from creating another fascist movement that would be a threat to humanity. *And* we are here to have fun."

Sigourney nodded at Kane, who dutifully went in the kitchen. A few moments later, he returned with a dented electric toaster. He placed the man's bound hands into the slots of the toaster and squeezed the metal casing tightly around them. He plugged the toaster into a cracked outlet. The children looked on with delight as the man's exposed wrists began glowing orange and smoke began pouring out of the toaster.

"'Op it! Pwease 'op it!" the tortured man was screaming as he felt his hands being incinerated by the intense coils. The amused children giggled, and Euna sat astride the man's back. She took a scalpel from her holster and split the man's dirty, white T-shirt open. She then used the scalpel to carefully cut and peel off a sheet of flesh from the entirety of his back. "Oh look!" she exclaimed excitedly. "A new canvas for Auntie Alexa!"

The sweet face of Thanatos then emerged from the billowing smoke. He held his small, tan hand out which was holding a small porcelain container. He tipped his hand and began shaking salt onto the skinless back of the writhing man. His screams intensified as the salt ate into his tender flesh while his hands were turning black from being scorched by the toaster.

"I was wrong," Sigourney admitted. "This is even *more* fun than the mailman!" She then took a long piece of barbed wire and began wrapping it around the hysterical man's face. She kept pulling until the tightening wire was lodged firmly in the man's cheeks, chin, nose, ears, and eyes. Blood and puss trickled out from the edges of the barbed wire as the giggling children went skipping out of the home to their dutiful steeds. They retrieved baseball bats from each of their saddlebags and went skipping back into the house where they proceeded to mercilessly beat the man with the bats while skipping around him and whistling. The man finally let out his final breath. The four blood-soaked children held hands and looked down at their work. His body was covered with contusions and his head had been beaten into a gelatinous putty. They smiled down at him, then at each other. Their smiles then faded into looks of deep concern.

From the darkened hallway, a hulking figure appeared. The children cautiously looked up at the imposing figure that had begun lurching towards them. For the first time in their short lives the members of the Junior Quad felt confusion and fear.

"I don't know who this is," Sigourney whispered to her sister. "All I know is that he isn't supposed to be here, and we aren't supposed to play with him."

The children's anxiety immediately dissipated when the large man let out a loud belly laugh before saying, "Well, you kids sure are a part of the family alright. Very creative. And messy. Alright, now kids. Play-time's over. Let's get you four home and into your jammies. Your parents are worried sick about you. But *first*, I wonder if there are any all-night diners where we could get some ice cream?"

Chapter 94

I Put a Spell on You

"I was so fuckin' close," the demon Vetis said solemnly to his unwillingly loyal servant, Gobbo. Gobbo was picking scabs off his spindly, pale arms. His lanky, arched frame followed Vetis down the corridor of the recently arrived screaming dark souls. His black, sunken eyes looked down his hooked nose and into those of the justifiably tortured who were hanging from chains. Vetis used his long fingernails on his four hands to slice open the screaming souls' abdomens as he sauntered by them in full contemplation.

"So fucking close!" Vetis roared. "I thought it was perfect. I thought that I had chosen the right souls to convert into darkness who then, in turn, converted millions of others into our supremacist cause. So many died at their hands. So much innocent blood ran in the streets of the Earth. But then, they all went to Enlightenment, which did nothing but strengthen their numbers there. Another miscalculation. It was almost perfect. Almost. That...that...*woman* tipped the scales. The offspring of the Pastor and the Copperhead. *She* was to be the one to fight at her parents' side and usher me into domination of the Earth and Enlightenment! *She* was the key. And she turned out to be a failure. She twisted her natural tenacity and bloodlust into killing *us*! She had a special gift that inspired loyalty to those around her. And that loyalty drove them to fight even *harder* against our movement. First on Earth, then in Enlightenment. And then there was *her* daughter. And her fucking half-sister. No, the Pastor was a failure. The Copperhead was a failure. My dullard, bulbous, orange, personal cocksucker was a failure. They allowed her to tip the scales against us. So now, we must tip the scales back.

"We must find a way to overload them. They just *barely* succeeded in defeating us. But if we had just a *few more*. A *few more* willfully ignorant human assholes that we can convert. It might just be enough. So, here's the plan, Gobbo…Gobbo! Are you listening to me?"

"Of course, Master," Gobbo reverentially answered with his bald, white head bowed. "I am *always* listening to you. Please continue, Master."

"Very well, then," Vetis replied as he turned and continued his long strides down the blood-soaked cavernous hallway. "Here's the plan. We go back in time. We find *other* souls who we can convert and then, in turn, can convert others. But here's the trick. We want to convert humans who are destined to die before the great wars of the Twenty-First Century are engaged. Humans who were not available to us at that time. We will find one such human, then guide him to find others who are destined to die and convert them. We will keep them safe from harm. We will keep them away from their preordained deaths and keep them alive. We'll have them find cabins in the woods or some shit to just sit and wait and train and prepare. And breed. We'll keep them in the dark so that the only information that they have is *my* information. The only facts that they will have will be *my* facts. After several decades of sitting there and being immersed in my indoctrination, they will be *completely* insane. And ready to do *anything* that I order them to do. Then, once our original battle has commenced and is flourishing into its full-scale war, we will unleash *these* tens of thousands of converts. They will then be engaged in the battle and our adversaries will be taken off-guard. They will be surprised. And they will be overwhelmed. And there's *nothing* that that red-headed bitch will be able to do about it, heh, heh, heh. Yeah, I'm really looking forward to taking over Enlightenment and fucking that bitch up…for eternity."

———

"Where's all my fuckin' ice cream?" Maddy roared as her ass was sticking out of her freezer. She pulled her chilled copper-haired head out and swung around to look at the sheepish expression of her beloved husband, Erick.

"Um...well..." Erick began tentatively. "You see, um, well, Herbert, Jason, Clyde, Joe, Charlie, and Howard came over last night to play some cards and, um..."

"Whoooooa!" Maddy exclaimed. "*Howard?* You had *that* perverted motherfucker into our house? While I was sleeping upstairs? No, no, no, no. I don't give a fuck *how* useful he was in protecting Enlightenment! You want to have a little boys' night? Fine! But you are *not* going to have *that* twisted little fucker over and give him the opportunity to do some of his twisted little shit to my dainty spiritual ass! No fuckin' way!"

"Maddy, come on," Erick replied defensively. "I think you're overreacting just a bit, don'tcha think? Howard's really trying to fit in. I mean, he doesn't even *suggest* that we all watch porn and engage in a circle jerk anymore. That's progress, right?"

"Well, *that's* a low fuckin' bar to hit now *isn't it?*," Maddy shot back. "Oh good. I don't have to worry about stepping in cum in the morning. Gee, thanks for that. And the fact that he ever suggested that in the first place is...is...just fuckin' gross! So, do *not* invite him over *ever again*, got it?"

"Yeah, okay," Erick conceded. "So, what do you want to do today? We have all of Enlightenment to explore. I think Woody Guthrie is doing a show at the pub later. Wanna go?"

"Oh, no," Maddy countered as her five-foot-four-and-a-half-inch-frame marched toward the couch and plopped onto Erick's lap. Her intense green eyes stared into his as she continued. "You're not getting off the hook *that* easily. Now tell me. What the *fuck* happened to my ice cream?"

Erick's spiritual form began sweating as he attempted to avert his gaze from that of his eternal wife. She grabbed his chin and forced him to look at her before he began explaining. "Well, as I said, some of the fellas came over and we wanted a snack and so...um...well, what's the big fuckin' deal *anyway?* We're in Enlightenment! You can just conjure some *more* up!"

"I will *tell* you what the big fuckin' deal is!" Maddy yelled back.

"Numero-Uno: That was *my* fuckin' ice cream! Numero -Two-O: If it's *so easy* to conjure this shit, then conjure up your *own*! Numero-Three-O: Now that I know that *Howard* was over here, there's no telling *what* fucked up shit he did with *my* ice cream! And Numero-Four-O: Yeah, I can conjure up some more, but that shit takes *time* and I want my ice cream *now*! So, from now on, when you see something in the fridge or the freezer or the cabinets that is *mine* keep your *fuckin' mits* off of it! And, just in case you don't know what is *mine*, here's a little clue. I've written M-A-D-D-Y on *all* of my favorite conjured foods! Got it?"

"Yeah, fine," Erick begrudgingly agreed. "It's just that you're *really good* at conjuring up food. I mean, you really *sucked* as a cook on Earth, but you can *really* conjure up some fuckin' ice cream! I just can't seem to get the knack of it. I mean, the shit that *I* conjure up is okay, but its just never *nearly* as good as yours. So, in a way, my eating your ice cream and other snacks is *really* a *compliment* to you and your incredible gift."

Erick smiled to himself as he saw his wife's green eyes turn from intense frustration to haughty arrogance. He could always put a spell on her by playing to her oversized ego and he knew that he had bested her once again. Now, he wanted to push the envelope.

"So, how about if you conjure up some of your special ice cream and we can share it?" he asked in a child-like tone.

"Oh, okay," Maddy chuckled. "I guess I can't blame you. I *do* conjure the best fuckin' ice cream in Enlightenment. I mean, how could you resist, right? And…wait…what the fuck? Yeah, this is Lil' Red. Over and out. Come in Soul Sister. Over and out. Wazzup? Over and out."

———

Gobbo sat nervously at the feet of Vetis as he trimmed the demon's jagged toenails. "Oh, Gobbo. Perhaps I've been a bit off lately. I believe that I will give you a chance. A chance to prove your loyalty and worthiness to me. Yes, I believe I will give you the opportunity to select the one that I shall tempt into my unholy vision of world domination. Peer through time. Find someone who is destined to die before 2016. Someone who is susceptible to my manipulations. Someone that I can pervert their religion or sense of patriotism into an inhumane anti-democratic crusade. Someone who has the charisma to influence others.

But someone easy! I'm not feeling up for a challenge right now. I'm going to lay down for my nap. I expect you to have found someone by the time I awaken."

"Why, yes, Master!" Gobbo enthusiastically replied. "And thank you Master! Thank you for this grand opportunity! I will *not* disappoint you!"

"Yeah, whatever," Vetis answered through a loud yawn. "I'm tired. Just fuckin' do it. And stop kissing my ass. It's kinda creepy."

"Of course, Master," Gobbo replied before adjourning to his ice-cold corner of the universe. His tired spiritual bones let out a loud crack as he sat cross-legged on the frigid stone. He placed his boney elbows on his extended knees, shut his black eyes and concentrated. His mind began flipping the calendar and scanning all the souls that lived upon Earth in the previous nine decades. He knew that he could not go too far back into time, otherwise the chosen one would perish from old age before the great war had begun. Perhaps as early as 1950 or so, he thought to himself. Someone young enough to still be alive and relatively healthy in the year 2016. There were so many options that flashed through his brain. "No, too old," he would say to himself as he began narrowing his selections. "No charisma." "Too sensitive." "Too ugly. Vetis will want him to look the part." "Too tall." "Too fat." "Too…completely the wrong race." "Too…completely the wrong gender. Vetis has had it with trying to convert women. He says they are too headstrong. But I know that many of them are simply too empathetic and intelligent to fall for his bullshit."

What would be hours on Earth went by as Gobbo's tiring mind continued to absorb thousands of prospects from the past. "Once again, too sensitive." "Too…um…well *that* one is a maybe." "Too gallant." "Too…wait. Yes, this might be the one. Only twenty years old at this time. That would make him fifty-eight in 2016. Tall. Rugged. Already beginning to indoctrinate himself in extremist ideology. Yes. He would be an easy convert. And easy on the eyes. He would prove useful with less evolved women as well. Yes, I believe that I will go wake up…

"Master! Please wake up, my Liege! I have done it! I have found the one to hide and lead the parallel movement!"

"What the fuck?" Vetis asked drowsily as he rolled over and swung one of his four arms to knock Gobbo into the far wall. "Why are you awakening me? I still have…let's see what time is it? Yes, I still have four years to nap. What's so fuckin' important?"

"I am so sorry to disturb you, Master," Gobbo began as he picked his broken bones off the floor and approached his overlord. "But I believe that I have found him!"

"Found who?" Vetis roared back.

"Him, my Lord," a trembling Gobbo answered. "The one for you to tempt and manipulate into your parallel movement so that you can reign over both Earth and Enlightenment."

"Oh…him," Vetis answered as he wiped the sleep from his flaming red eyes. "Oh yeah, cool. So, who is it?"

"Well, Master," Gobbo began with more confidence. "I am sorry to awaken you, but I felt as though you would be quite excited to see my selection. And time is of the essence. Once you have made your selection you must go back into time and convert them before…um… before…well…before *they* get there."

"I don't wanna talk about those little bastards," Vetis replied dismissively. "Now, where and when are we going?"

"Well, Master," Gobbo answered as he stood as upright as his curved spine would allow. "We are going to Lincoln, Nebraska. Midnight, March 2, 1958."

"Those little motherfuckers," was all that Vetis could mutter as he looked down at the carnage that was to have been his latest demonic convert. The man was hog-tied, and smoke was billowing out of the toaster that was scorching his hands. The flesh from his back had been removed and was encased in salt. The man's head had been beaten to a pulp and was lying on the floor like hardened, pinkish-red play dough. "How? How the *fuck* did they get here before us?"

"Well, Master," Gobbo began nervously. "They are connected to you. The moment that you have made your decision on who to convert, they are summoned. They travel back through time, find your latest project, and dispose of them before we can arrive. They are the prophecy, Master. Perhaps you should abandon your plans and live out your hellish existence in the plane that you already dominate."

"Fuck the prophecy!" Vetis yelled out as he slapped Gobbo across the room. "No! those little fuckers will *not* best me! I will try. And try *again.*

And try *again*! For all of *eternity* if I have to! Go back to their own time. 2042. And find someone to take the fuckers out."

"B-b-but Master," Gobbo stammered. "It is quite *impossible* to kill them. We failed at our chance. They had to be murdered in their mother's womb. Now that they are born and fully developed, they are simply too *powerful*. You *know* who they are, Master. You *know* the souls that their bodies possess. I am pleading with you Master. *Please* do not fight them. For if you do, the prophecy will come true, and they will destroy all of us."

"Well, Gobbo," Vetis replied calmly as one of his four hands stroked his massive chin. "You make some good points. Yes, I know the souls that inhabit their child-like bodies. And I know that those four souls have converged into one and that they are acting in concert. And I am *very well aware* of what has been prophesized. But prophesies can be… altered. Now, what *you* do not know is just how *badly* I wish to rule over the Earth and Enlightenment, so…find someone in 2042 to kill these little pricks! And their little ponies too!"

Chapter 95

Searchin'

"Oh fuck, oh fuck, oh fuck, what are we going to do?" a sweaty Josie was stammering to herself as she nervously paced in the living room of the estate in Upper State New York. Arima, Jessie, and Rosa could only look on as Josie frantically continued. "Jesus! What is *wrong* with me? I'm the head of an international assassin freedom fighting syndicate, and I can't even keep track of four fuckin' *kids*? And what are we going to tell their *parents*? What are we going to *say* to them when they get ho…ooooooh, hey guys! You're *back* already! Sooooo, how was your evening out?"

"I don't want to talk about it!" Kayla angrily answered as she and her sister stormed into the room.

"Y'know," Rachel added, "It would be *really nice* if just *once* we could go out, have a few drinks, have a few laughs, and not *murder* someone!"

"We're sorry, ladies," a forlorn Adam stated followed, as always, by his twin brother Aaron. "Yes, we are very sorry. But that man was hurting that woman. We could not just stand by and watch that happen. And it has been days since we have been able to play our games."

"Yeah?" Rachel roared back. "But didja have to make such a *mess* of him? You *could* have just snapped his *neck* or something, but *nooooooo! You* two maniacs had to pull out your knives and carve him up like a roast beef! And now, now, my dress looks like *this!*"

Rachel opened her overcoat to reveal her sequined party dress splattered in the abusive man's blood. Kayla followed suit, revealing her own ruined dress, and the glaring pair stood in front of their husbands with their arms folded while they angrily tapped their feet.

"Oh my," Adam stated, followed immediately by his brother's, "Yes. That is quite a mess. But we told you that you were standing too close. We told you that you were in the splash zone. Nevertheless, we are sorry about your pretty dresses and will buy you new ones. Plus, we were able to get the skin from the man's back. Alexa will be so pleased with her new canvas."

"Yeah, great," Kayla replied as she rolled her eyes. "Our dresses are ruined, but your sister gets a new canvas for her art show that she's planning. What the hell is she calling her exhibition again?"

Rachel replicated her sister's eye roll and said sarcastically, "*Hanging Chads: The Lineage of our Ascension.* Whatever the hell *that's* supposed to mean. Sounds stupid. Whatevs. The night's ruined. Let's just read the kids a story and put them to bed. And while we're doing *that, you two* are going to get *rid* of that prick's body and clean the trunk of the car! Okay, where are our children? Sigourney! Euna!"

Kayla then began calling for her twin sons. "Kane! Thanatos! Come on out! Mommies are home! Do you want to hear a story before bed?"

Josie, Arima, Jessie, and Rosa just watched in awkward silence as the frustrated mothers continued calling for their children. Rosa nudged Jessie and silently mouthed, "Say something." Jessie shook her head and nudged Arima, who said in her mellow voice, "So, hey, Niece Josie. You wanna maybe tell them about the kids?"

"What *about* the kids?" Rachel and Kayla said in unison as they swung around to look into four pairs of sheepish eyes."

"Riiiiiight," Josie began through a forced chuckle. "The *kids*. Well, it's *really* kind of a funny story if you *think* about it. You see, we had ordered some pizza, and I was cleaning up their bedroom, and…oh…I found the body of the creepy mailman under one of the bunk beds, by the way. So, good news! We don't have to worry about *that* fucker anymore. Anywhoooo, as I was saying…"

Kayla and Rachel went up to Josie and stared into her green eyes and said tersely, "Josie. *Where* are our children?"

"Yep, I was just getting to that," Josie replied as she ran her hand through her sweaty, curly copper mop on the top of her head. "So, it *seems* as though *your* little guys, who are absolutely *adorable* by the way! Have I *told* you that? They are the *cutest* little children. And smart. Oh *my*, are they smart. And spirited! Yes, they have such *wonderful* spirits! Yep, you four *definitely* have just the most *wonderful* children. And *cute*! Did I mention how *cute* they…"

Kayla and Rachel took one more step towards the stammering Josie until they were inches away from her befreckled nose. They smiled innocently and said in unison, "Josie. Please stop stalling for time and tell us…" Their soft voices exploded into a shout as they concluded with, "Where the *fuck* are our children!"

"Um, 1958," Jessie's meek voice interjected.

Kayla and Rachel swung their caramel bodies to face the couch, looked down into Jessie's brilliant blue eyes and said with a forced calm through gritted teeth, "*What* did you just say?"

"Um," Jessie answered while avoiding eye contact with the twin mothers. "They're *kind* of in…um…1958. March 1, 1958, to be exact. In Lincoln, Nebraska."

Adam and Aaron watched in shocked silence as their wives approached Jessie. Kayla yelled out, "What the fuck do you *mean* they're in Lincoln, Nebraska in 1958? How the hell does *that* make any sense? Listen, I don't even know why you and Rosa are here. We left Josie and Arima in charge. And Arima and Josie are going to find our children right fucking *now*!"

"Yeah, we were just talking about how we were going to do that," Arima lazily replied as she finished the last bite of the last slice of pizza. "You see, apparently your children can travel through time, so it appears that they got on their ponies and…well…traveled through time. We're not sure why they went there and we're not quite sure how to bring them back. But one thing that we're *sure* of is that you guys are out of 'tato chips. We kinda ate them all. Sorry about that."

"*We?*" Josie yelled out. "*We* ate all the 'tato chips? Oh no. *You*, my dear auntie ate all the fucking 'tato chips. And all the *pizza*! All you had to do was watch the kids while I tidied up upstairs. But no! You had to satisfy your fucking cravings!"

"Oh my, oh my, oh my," Adam and Aaron began muttering in unison as they began nervously pacing around the living room. "Oh my, our children are missing, brother," Adam stated. Aaron replied with the same anxious cadence, "Yes. They are missing. And although they appear to be much more mature than their age, they are still children. We have not had the time to teach them how to play many of our games. Oh brother, what if our children get into trouble? What if something has happened to them?"

"Okay! Everybody just shut up and calm down!" Rosa uncharacteristically shouted out. "Listen, this isn't anybody's fault. Josie and Arima. Nobody cares about the goddam 'tato chips and pizza right now. And Adam and Aaron. Just calm down. I can feel your energy rising and I don't want to know what happens when you hit maximum capacity, so just chill the fuck out. And Rachel and Kayla. We know that your children are fine…um…at the moment. Everybody. Please just sit down and we'll explain. Then, we'll figure out how to get them back, okay?"

Kayla and Rachel threw themselves onto the couch on either side of Jessie, who gulped hard and looked down at the grey striped furball that was contently purring on her lap. LucyFur's eyes dilated, and she stared up at Rosa, as though she was enjoying the spectacle that was unfolding in front of her.

Once everybody was seated, Rosa wiped the trail of sweat from her tan forehead and began. "Okay, thanks. The only way that we're going to get through this is if we all just remain calm, think about this logically, and work together. Okay, here's what we know. The kids were in the back yard playing with cadavers when the pizza arrived. Josie was upstairs doing some housekeeping. Arima got…um…distracted by the pizza. The next thing Josie and Arima knew, the kids and their ponies had just disappeared. They looked all over the house and all over the estate for them. When they didn't turn up, they called Jessie and me to come over to help them. I tapped into Jessie's energy and enhanced it to strengthen her ability to Behold and locate their souls. We thought that it would be easy. The ponies are fast, but not *that* fast and if they were anywhere close, Jessie should have been able to locate them quickly. But she couldn't. I kept increasing her energy and Jessie began searching for their souls throughout the entire country. And, although the sensation wasn't strong enough to be their souls, Jessie would feel *something* every time she searched around Lincoln, Nebraska. She focused on that area, and I kept increasing her energy. She was *convinced* that the children were there, somewhere, but the sensation simply wasn't strong enough.

So, she focused her Beholding ability on the year *before* in that same geographical location. And the sensation got slightly stronger. Then back another year, and it was stronger yet. She kept going back until she could fully Behold their souls in Lincoln, Nebraska. March 1, 1958.

"And that is where we're at. We know *when* they are, and we know *where* they are. What we *don't* know is why they went there. Nor do we have any idea on how to bring them back. I mean, *maybe* they can find their way back themselves, but we don't know that. And they are children. Rather…um…*precocious* children who could get themselves into trouble, so we need to figure this out. Any ideas?"

"Well," Kayla began. "My *first* thought is that we *really* need to find new babysitters."

"Kayla…Rachel," Josie began pleading. "I'm *so* sorry. We had no *idea*. I *swear*, we'll find a way to bring them back. I *swear* it."

"Uh, huh," Rachel replied. "Well, you had *better*. It's *one* thing for you to have lost my pink sweater a few weeks ago. This is quite something *else*, don'tcha *think?*"

"Yes, yes, of course," Josie answered in a beleaguered tone. "I am *so sorry* that I lost your children. And I'm sorry about your sweater too, but…well, that isn't important right now. I've been racking my brain trying to think of a way to go back through time. I mean, I'm a genius, but not so much that I can just whip up a time machine! Maybe Rod could. No, he couldn't either. I mean, if we could have invented a *time machine*, we would have done it already. I have no idea. I feel so lost. I feel so sorry. I feel like a failure."

Josie put her head in her hands and began sobbing before Arima said, "Um, I might have a thought, Niece Josie."

"Y-y-yes?" Josie said as she lifted her head to peer hopefully at her aunt.

"Well, I seem to remember something that your mother told me one time. But I could have gotten it wrong. I was kinda baked. And there was so much stuff going on what with our protecting the estate here on Earth and the battle for Enlightenment and everything. And then there was the victory concert. Man, that was sweet. Remember how cool it was when we heard Prince start to play and all the blood that was pouring out of Enlightenment upon the Earth turned to a warm purple rain? Man, that was cool. And then…"

Arima was cut off by an interrupting Josie. "Aunt Arima. Could you *please* just tell us what you are thinking? You know, to find the *kids*?"

"Oh right, the kids," Arima replied casually as she reached for a half-smoked joint. "So, I think that your mom told me that there isn't anything like time in Enlightenment. All the souls that live there exist in a world that they conjure. They can make their world anything that they want it to be. And they can have their world be in any time because there *is* no time in Enlightenment as we know it here on Earth. It is a plane of existence. And they are immortal. So, there is no *use* for time.

"And we *also* know that the blessed souls of Enlightenment can return to Earth and help out with stuff, if it is for some sort of higher calling. If it is for a *pure* reason, like protection of innocents or defeating evil or shit like that. Not sure how babysitting ranks in that, though. Anyway, we saw Erick do it to battle the copperhead after Maddy's murder. And I saw Maddy's Uncle Joe do it when we defeated the Pastor on what was supposed to be me and Marcus's wedding day. And he wasn't just there is spiritual form, like Erick was. He somehow was able to conjure his body and physically intervene. I think. So, maybe they can do that for a specific period of time in order to complete a specific mission. So, I'm thinkin' that maybe Maddy could go back to 1958 and bring the kids home. Or not. I dunno. It's just something that I thought I heard her say. I wish I hadn't eaten all the 'tato chips. That sounds really good right now."

"Okay, let me get this straight," Rosa stated as the solemn Adam and Aaron wrapped their comforting arms around their despondent wives. "*If* there is no such thing as time in Enlightenment, *then* a blessed soul *may* be able to travel back to any time and any location here on Earth and they *may* be able to appear in their physical human form if it is for a righteous cause. And *if* they can do *that, then* they can make contact with the JQ and bring them home. Did I get that straight?"

"Yeah, I guess so," Arima answered. "I dunno for sure. We'd have to ask Maddy. As you all know, our souls are connected so she can inhabit my soul here on Earth at any time and I can inhabit hers in Enlightenment. I just need to give her a ringy-dingy and we can find out. Want me to contact her?"

"Oh fuck," Josie muttered under her breath as she buried her head in her hands once again. She reluctantly lifted her head, let out a deep sigh, and asked, "By chance, Aunt Arima, is there anyone *else* that you can connect with in Enlightenment, like maybe my dad?"

Arima blew out pungent smoke rings before answering. "Um, nope. I'm not soul mates with your dad. Or anyone else. Just your mom. I have to contact *her* first. Why?"

"Well," Josie replied in a resigned tone. "It's not that important and I know that my mother loves me, but she's gonna have a *field day* with this. She's *never* going to let this go and she's gonna give me shit for all eternity, I bet. But I suppose there's no other way. Yeah, go ahead and call her. And have her say 'hi' to my dad for me. Fuck. This is gonna *suuuuck.*"

CHAPTER 96
HELP!

Arima lazily slid her ass off the couch and stood in the middle of the room. She could feel the hopeful eyes of her friends and family watching as she focused on the soul of her departed half-sister. Her body floated three feet off the floor as she slipped into a trance and began trying to make contact.

"Lil' Red, this is Soul Sister. Please come in," Arima stated out loud so that the onlookers could hear. She felt her half-sister's opening soul welcoming her. As her soul floated out of her physical body toward the promise of Enlightenment, she saw wisps of colorful light swirling around her spiritual form. She smiled at the explosion of peaceful brilliance and warmth that she was being encased in. She then heard her half-sister's voice. The connection had been made. Arima's soul was now entwined with that of her half-sister, Maddy. They were once again two souls in one. They were reunited.

"Yeah, this is Lil' Red. Over and out. Come in Soul Sister. Over and out. Wazzup? Over and out."

"Yeah, hey Maddy," Arima coolly replied. "Sorry to bother you, but we have a little situation down here on Earth that we were hoping you could help us with. Oh, and you really don't have to say, 'over and out' after every sentence, okay?"

"Roger that! Over and out!" Maddy answered much more loudly

than necessary. "And please use my cool code name in future correspondence! Over and out! So, what's the sitch? Over and out!" The onlookers snickered to themselves and rolled their eyes as they heard Maddy's reply coming out of Arima's floating body.

Arima let out a deep sigh of slight frustration before answering. "Well, you see, me and Josie were babysitting the JQ so the twins and the Twins could have a night out. They were outside playing with the left-over dead bodies with their ponies when the pizza arrived. It was a combo from a new place in town. It was *really* good. You *really* need to try it the next time you visit me. I got the works on it. There was pepperoni, sausage, onions…"

Arima's fond memory of the recently enjoyed pizza was interrupted by the stern voice of Josie. "Aunt Arima! Please! Tell her about the kids!"

"Oh yeah, the kids," Arima stated before Maddy interjected. "Oh, is that my darling daughter? Over and out! Hello, sweetie! Mommy loves you! Over and out! Erick! Come here! I've got Josie on the party line through Arima's soul. Apparently, we can hear what *she* hears. Here baby, come into my soul so that *you* can hear too."

"Hi sweetie!" Erick yelled out at the same unnecessarily loud volume as his wife. "How are you? We have missed you so much! How's Lionnel? Keeping his hands to himself? He had better be or else I'm gonna have to pay him a visit!"

"Dad!" Josie yelled out. "I'm *eighteen* now, and what I do in my relationship is *none* of your business. I love you, but just leave it alone. And that's *not* why we called. Aunt Arima, *please* tell them about the kids."

"Oh yeah, *that's* why we called. Sorry Niece Josie. So, about the kids…"

Arima was once again cut off by Maddy. "Hey! Before you tell us about the sitchle boll weevil, who *else* is there, hmmmm? Didja see how I was bein' all Snoop Dogg and shit there? Pretty funny, huh? Over and out!"

Arima let out another deep sigh and answered, "Jessie, Aaron, Adam, Rachel, Kayla, and Rosa. And Maddy, I mean, um, Lil' Red, dead white women really shouldn't try to imitate Snoop. That made no sense at all."

"Yeah, whatevs. People don't get my great impersonations, either. Anywhooo, *that's* quite the murderer's row! Over and out!" Maddy responded. "Hey everybody! Nice to talk to you! So how come you got *this* fuckin' rogues gallery together? Over and out!"

"Oh my God!" Rachel screamed. "Would you *please* just ask her if she can find our kids?"

"Wait, what? Over and out!" Maddy replied before bursting out in laughter. "Are you telling me that our *genius* daughter lost your children? Hey Erick! Did you hear that? Our *genius* daughter fucked up babysitting and lost the JQ! And who did she have to call for help? Nope. Not *Ghostbusters*. Lil' ol' me! Our *genius* daughter once again needs her Mommy to bail her out. Oh sweetie, I love you, but this is gold! Pure fuckin' gold! I'm gonna give you shit about this for eternity! Over and out!"

"Oh, goddamit. I knew this was a bad idea," a red-faced Josie muttered under her breath before a frantic Kayla interjected. "Maddy, this is Kayla. *Please*, can you *help* us? Apparently, the JQ and their ponies can travel through time. They just disappeared and Jessie beheld their souls and found them in Lincoln, Nebraska on March 1, 1958. We don't know why they went there or if they're alright or if they know how to get back home. So, since there isn't anything like time in Enlightenment, we thought that maybe you could go there, make contact with them, and send them home. Can you do that? Please, *help* us! We don't know what else to do!"

There was silence on the spiritual line as Maddy sat in Enlightenment and pondered the request. She looked into the eyes of her beloved husband who smiled and nodded at her. She had heard the despair and urgency in Kayla and Rachel's voices. She understood that her response would need to be delicate and supportive. She understood that she could not fuck this up. Maddy fucked it up.

"Well," Maddy began in a contemplative tone. "I suppose I *could* go back to that date and find your kids. But I think we need to get permission or some shit before we intervene in Earthly affairs. So, I suppose I *could* ask and see if I can *do* that, but…" Maddy's voice trailed off for a moment before she roared, "But why the fuck *should* I? How is this *my* fuckin' problem? Do you know how much *paperwork* there is just to make a request like this? I'm busy! I was just about to conjure up some ice cream, which I *wouldn't* have to do if my husband and his perv friends hadn't eaten it all! Besides! I *told* you four that those fuckin' kids were going to be trouble! And *now* look who's right once again! Me! Only fifteen days after they were born and they're already running around unsupervised fucking up the space-time continuum or some shit! Nope. Not my fuckin' problem. You wanted to pump out those four little hellions, so *you* can figure out how to raise them. Otherwise, *I'm* going to be constantly interrupted every time those little fuckers get themselves into trouble. And I got shit to do! I have an eternity of lounging around with my husband and watching cool concerts from dead rock stars to do. I can't live peacefully while constantly wondering when I'm gonna get interrupted! Not fuckin' happening. Call somebody else. Over and out!"

A shocked Rachel and Kayla began angrily kicking their crossed legs before they heard another voice. It was a voice that they had not heard since the day of her death. The day that the Pastor had massacred her and many others on what was to have been Arima and Marcus's wedding day. It was the voice of an angel. It was the voice of their fallen sister, Gwen.

"Hello, Rachel. Hello, Kayla," Gwen greeted them affectionately.

"Wait, what the fuck? Over and out!" Maddy interjected. "What the fuck are *you* doing in here Gwen? I didn't invite you and there's only so much room in my soul, and it's getting fucking *crowded* in here! Over and out!"

"Maddy," Gwen began calmly as the Earthly onlookers listened in attentively. "I do not believe that you have *any* room to say *anything* right now. My sisters need help. They need *your* help. And not only have you refused to help them, but they had to listen to you lecture them. While in a time of need. Quite frankly Maddy, *you* are acting like a spoiled little bitch."

"Whoooooa, motherfucker!" Maddy shot back. "Who are you calling a bitch, *bitch*? Do you know *who the fuck* you're talking to? Do you know how many motherfuckers I've cut up in cold blood? Well, do you? Is it *my* fault that your sisters don't know how to keep track of their fuckin' kids? Erick! Are you gonna let this bitch talk to me like that? Over and out!"

"Yep, I sure am," an embarrassed Erick replied. "Because she isn't wrong. I've seen you be selfish before, but when it comes to refusing to help children just because you want some fucking *ice cream*, well, I'm sorry my love, but you are just fucking *wrong* right now. Everything that you have just said is fucking wrong. So, I would advise you to take a step back and think about what you have just said. And who you have just said it to. In all your wisdom, you have chosen this moment of great need to lecture our friends and loved ones. Those that we have battled alongside. Those that we have literally wept and bled with. And, most disappointingly to me, you have even refused to help our daughter. This is *not* a good look for you. So…whatcha gonna do there, Ace?'"

There was once again dead silence. The Earthly onlookers could almost feel Maddy's seething as Arima's connected body began glowing red. After a few moments, Arima's skin returned to its natural caramel and everyone heard a repentant Maddy say, "Oh shit. Erick, please don't be disappointed in me. And Josie. And, um, everyone. I'm sorry you guys. I guess I *am* being a bitch. Its just that…well…I haven't been up here very long, and I haven't figured out how to do what you're asking of me. So, I guess I was just lashing out because I'm kinda embarrassed that I *can't* help you. I always get defensive and arrogant when my self-confidence gets threatened. All I can think of to do is fight back. I did it my whole life against those that tried to oppress me. And then I'd go and fuck up a 'Chad' or something and then I would feel better and get my self-confidence back. But I can't do that up here. There aren't any 'Chads' up here. Well, kinda Howard, but that's beside the point. And none of that is an excuse. There *is* no excuse for refusing to help you or for what I just said. All I can say is that I'm sorry and I hope you all can forgive me. And I'm sorry that I don't have the ability to help you right now. But I know someone who *can*. I'm pretty sure that Uncle Joe has done that before. Would you like me to call for him? Um…over and out."

"Yes, Maddy," Gwen answered sweetly. "Thank you. I would go myself, but I am tied to Enlightenment. I have been tasked to be the one to approve such Earthly missions. And I most certainly will be approving this one. Also, because of my enhanced soul tracking ability, I can guide those who *will* intervene on Earth to their destination. Yes. Your Uncle Joe would be perfect. Please call for him. I will guide him, and he will find them. Together, we will bring my precious nieces and nephews back to their parents. We will bring them back to my beloved sisters."

Rachel and Kayla stopped kicking their legs, looked at one another and yelled out, "Woooooooo!" "I don't miss *that* shit," Maddy whispered to her husband as she rolled her green eyes at him.

"Okay, bye Lil' Red. Thanks for, um, *something*," Arima stated as her bare feet once again touched the hardwood flooring. Her half-sister responded with, "Okay! See ya Soul Sister! See ya everybody! We love you, Josie! Mommy and Daddy are proud of you! I'm *still* gonna give you shit though for fucking up babysitting! Maddy over and out!"

Thirty seconds later, there was a brilliant flash of light from outside the home and a joyful male voice that said, "Hey! Anyone missing some kids?"

The entire group ran out the door and looked upon the front lawn. Basking in the brilliant spiritual light of Uncle Joe were four giggling perpetual ten-year-old children on the backs of their Shetland ponies.

"Oh, thank God! Our babies are home!" Rachel and Kayla yelled out in unison. Adam ran down the stairs followed by his brother Aaron. They picked up and tightly hugged their respective children. Adam then said, "Oh my, we were so worried about you four." Aaron then contributed, "Yes. Please don't frighten us like that again children."

"We're sorry fathers, mothers," the quartet replied in unison. "But we had to go. We were called to play games with a bad man."

"Games, you say?" Adam asked followed by Aaron's, "Yes, games? Please tell us about your games, children."

Uncle Joe let out a gutteral laugh and said, "Well, if they were playing games, I sure as fuck know who lost. Man, what they did to *that* mother-fuckin' douchebag. He was hogtied and his hands were roasting in a toaster. His back had been stripped of its skin and there was salt covering it. *That* must have been unpleasant for him. And his head was *completely*, and I do mean *completely* bashed in. Yep, that was a helluva game, kids. I haven't laughed that hard in a long time. It was so nice to see you all, but the mission's finished and Gwen is calling me home. Plus, Blair's conjuring up her famous fried chicken and mashed pota-toes. I think Patty's conjuring up a half-eaten bag of chips or something. I love her, but she never could cook. Not even in Enlightenment. Oh, and I'm going to teach my niece how to do this shit. I hear she owes you one. And she'll make it right with you folks. My little buttacup always does, heh, heh, heh."

"Thank yoooooou!" came the unified response from the relieved

Earthbound members of Murder, Inc. as they watched Joseph Argento's soul dissipate into the black night.

"Let's get you four inside and you can tell us all about your games," Kayla said as tears of joy ran down her brown face. Once inside the warm home, the four blood-covered children stood in front of the entire group and said in unison, "Once again, we are sorry to have worried you. We are sorry Aunt Arima and Aunt Josie. But we have no control over when we will be called. The war with Vetis is not over. We have been born upon the Earth to vanquish him. He is trying to go back in time to corrupt other souls who will lead a parallel demonic movement upon the Earth. A parallel movement to the one that you just defeated. He believes that the two movements working together will be enough to overwhelm you. Then, he will be dominant over the Earth and will once again use his dark souls to attack Enlightenment. We are here to stop that parallel movement from happening. We are connected to his intentions. The moment that he has chosen a person to corrupt, we can sense it. We know who it is, where they are, and when they are. We will then ride our ponies to that time and place and shall destroy that person before Vetis can get to them. It will happen many times. We have seen it. Just as we have seen the final battle. We're tired. May we go to bed now?"

"Yes," Rachel said as she and her sister took each of their children by their tender hands and began leading them toward the staircase. "But *what* did you get all over your beautiful white western outfits?" Kayla asked before answering her own question. "Is that chocolate ice cream? Do you know how hard it is to get that out of white clothes?"

"We're once again sorry," the members of the JQ answered. "Yes, it is chocolate ice cream. Uncle Joe took us to an all-night diner after he found us, and it seems as though we may have spilled a bit. We are sorry. We will try to be more careful."

"Oh, its okay our darlings," Kayla answered. "We were going to have to clean the blood out of them anyway. Maybe these can be your everyday western outfits that you can play your games in, and we'll get you some new ones to keep clean for special occasions."

An exhausted Arima looked over at her equally fatigued niece and said, "You know what sounds kinda good right now?"

Thirty minutes later, Josie and Arima were basking in the calm silence of the home next to a roaring fire in the sitting room. Josie allowed her latest bite of melting chocolate ice cream to slide down her throat before earnestly saying, "I'm *never* fuckin' babysitting again. No fuckin' way. I can order hits. I can shoot people in the head with arrows. I can make battle plans to save both the Earth *and* Enlightenment. I can skin fuckers alive. But babysitting four ten-year-olds? Nope. Not my thing. Too much stress. Plus, I'm *never* calling my mother again for help. I love her and everything, but she can be *such* a pain the ass! I'm glad *I* didn't turn out like her."

A smirking Arima silently nodded and looked over at the sleeping Jessie and LucyFur on the adjacent couch. LucyFur opened her sleepy green eyes and stretched her furry grey and white round frame as far as she could. She looked at Arima, mewed politely, and jumped down onto the floor. As she made her way towards the pet door in the kitchen, she thought to herself, *Well, that was exciting. For stupid human shit. I'm hungry.*

CHAPTER 97
VAMPIRE GIRL

Lucyfur was cute and she knew it. She carried herself with the same conceited swagger that normal looking cats possessed. But LucyFur was *anything* but normal looking. Cute? Yes. But *far* from normal looking. She looked to be a mash-up of several unrelated animals in one body. Her coat was long and shaggy. It was grey and white with light streaks of rust. Her head was three times smaller than what would look normal on a nearly-completely round, rotund body which was supported by stumpy legs and enormous paws. The finishing touch on her odd appearance was a twelve-inch long full, bushy tail. She was indeed odd-looking. And cute in an odd-looking sort of way.

So, LucyFur knew that she was cute. And she knew that she was special. Her feline spiritual guide had told her so. She had been told from the time of her birth alongside her four sisters that she would be called to assist her human pets. She had been told that she would fight alongside special humans who would battle for the soul of humanity. The feline community, both on the Earth and Enlightenment, didn't particularly care about the plight of the humans on the planct. What they cared about was what the humans were *doing* to their planet. They were concerned that the human's greedy and irresponsible use of the planet's natural resources posed an existential threat to every living being on the Earth, including themselves. So, armed with this knowledge, one of their most brave souls was placed into an oddly formed kitten. A kitten that was part obese, part runt. A kitten who was told to take multiple long naps throughout the day to save her energy for more important endeavors. A kitten who took full advantage of that directive. A kitten who would be loyal to a select few humans on the planet and would assist them however she could.

First, it was Arima who had adopted her following the passing of LucyFur's first human pet. Then, LucyFur set her sights on Jessie. LucyFur did not care for Jessie much at first, so she put her through many trials and tribulations before deciding to pledge her loyalty to her. Jessie was arrogant, but also had a deep loving and caring side to her. Plus, LucyFur thoroughly enjoyed watching Jessie manipulate and dominate her husband, Cliff. LucyFur found this spectacle amusing. But the human that LucyFur *most* cared for was a woman who held the same 'who gives a fuck' attitude as every cat on the planet. This woman gave her love sparingly to others and to only those that she deemed worthy. Everyone else was a mere annoyance to navigate around. Or go through. Human emotions were not important to this woman. Loyalty was. And the promise of getting laid or fed. That was it. And this woman possessed the ability to communicate with other cats. LucyFur had found ways to communicate with Arima and Jessie. And she most *definitely* had found a way to communicate her disdain for Arima's red-headed half-sister. But she could communicate *directly* with this other woman. They could read each other's thoughts. This woman had become somewhat of a mother-figure to LucyFur. And for the first time in her short life, LucyFur experienced true love and affection for one of her pets.

LucyFur went out the kitchen pet door and made her way across the lawn and through the tall, dead brush of the estate. She stopped briefly to look at the apiary before ducking under a wooden fence and making her way through the dense woods. She crawled over leaves, twigs, branches, and the decomposing severed arms, legs, heads, and torsos of fallen marauders from just fifteen-days prior. This scene made her chuckle to herself. The trek continued for nearly four miles. She saw the lights of the small town that was near the estate. One light, in particular, drew her attention. She made her way through the nearly vacant streets and jumped upon a windowsill in front of a neon beer sign. She adjusted her focus through the bright glare and saw what she had been searching for. She saw the person that she had sensed, sitting at a run-down round wooden table alongside her wheelchair bound friend and her friend's brawny husband. She let out an innocent mew. The woman looked up to the window.

"Aw fuck, cat," Jules slurred. "What the fuck are *you* doing here?" Jules reluctantly got up from the table and opened the front door. LucyFur strutted in then stopped suddenly when the elderly female bartender yelled out, "Hey! No cats in here!"

Jules and LucyFur glared into the eyes of the barkeep until she relented and said, "Well, just this once. And if she pisses on the floor, you're cleaning it up!"

"No, I won't," Jules dryly replied as Sam and Henri burst out in a drunken laughter. Although fifty-four years old, and with one of them being in a wheelchair, it was widely known throughout the area that these two best friends were not to be trifled with. Their exploits with Murder, Inc. were spoken about in hushed tones as was their involvement with the other saviors of Enlightenment. Sam and Jules were both revered and feared in the small community. And that was exactly how they liked it.

Sam's husband, Henri, on the other hand, was simply revered. He was ten-years the junior of his beautiful wife and looked much more imposing than the women. He was tall, dark skinned, and muscular. But he also possessed a smile that could melt hearts and a boisterous laugh to accent his off-beat sense of humor.

LucyFur jumped on the round table and mewed a polite greeting to the friends before curling up on the napkins and listening intently.

"It's always so nice to come up here and get away from the city for a while," Henri stated through his thick Cameroonian accent. "The people are always so nice, and the beer is so cheap. I can get drunk on twenty dollars here, then stagger across the street to the little motel if I'm unable to make the drive back to the estate. It's perfect."

"Yeah," Sam contributed. "But I have to say those bedsprings in the motel are awfully loud. Everyone in the entire town can probably hear what we're up to and that makes me feel a bit...cheap."

"Oh, embrace your cheap side you old fuckin' prude," Jules admonished. "Ever since college, you've had a stick up your ass. And now that you're getting a steady cock up it, you're bitching? You're married to the guy. There's nothing cheap about it. Just let him spread your paralyzed legs and enjoy the ride."

"Jules," Sam retorted in her condescending tone. "Must you use such tawdry language? And just where is *your* husband tonight? Where is Jerry?"

"Oh, he decided to stay at home," Jules answered. "I like to be respectful of his being on the wagon, so I don't drink at home. But once in awhile I wanna get my fuckin' drink on. Hey! Barkeep! Didja hear that? I'm here to get my fuckin' drink on! How about another pitcher!"

"Comin' right up," the barkeep begrudgingly replied.

"And it was nice to see the twins and Twins out tonight," Henri continued. "Although they didn't stay long. I wonder why they only had one drink and left? And Kayla and Rachel did not look pleased."

"Probably not," Sam answered as she put a cigarette out on the squealing head of Pogo II who was chained under the table. "It's a rough crowd in here tonight and I saw the Twins follow that guy that was yelling at that woman at the end of the bar. My guess? There's probably a hell of a mess outside."

"Either that," Jules interjected. "Or Josie and Arima fucked up babysitting somehow. But how hard could it be to watch over four ten-year-olds? The worst thing that could happen is Arima eating all the pizza. I'm sure nothing happened and everything's fine. It's probably that first thing. I think I'll go out back and see what happened."

LucyFur internally chuckled as she thought about the hysterics from earlier in the evening. She jumped off the table and began following Jules. Once the pair reached the jukebox, LucyFur lightly swiped at Jules's ankle, then pounced on top of the jukebox.

"Yeah, alright," Jules stated as she reached into her pocket for a dollar bill. "We'll play your song." Jules inserted the crumpled dollar into the jukebox, pressed the appropriate buttons for the desired selection and went past the restrooms and out the back door.

LucyFur stood on top of the jukebox. Her fur was being illuminated by the dancing lights as "Stray Cat Strut" began booming out of the speakers. The other patrons in the bar looked over at the scene, shook their heads in drunken disbelief, and retreated back to their warming drinks.

Jules took out a flashlight and lit up the cracked concrete of the parking lot. The lot was empty with the exception of a semi with out-of-state license plates. Jules squinted her eyes to try to see the driver of the semi who was sitting silently behind the steering wheel. "Ah fuck, I hate aging," she muttered to herself as she reached into her purse and retrieved a pair of cat-eyed, black rimmed glasses. She put the glasses on in disgust and focused on the form. She saw a white man staring at her with a slight smile on his stubbled face. She flipped him off and returned to her inspection of the pavement.

Her attention was captured by something glinting on the ground. She picked it up and discovered that it was a tooth. The beam of light continued deeper into the parking lot to reveal another tooth. Then another. Then an ear. "Yep, here it is," Jules said to herself as the flashlight revealed a huge pool of drying blood surrounding a pile of extracted intestines. The bright white beam then followed a long crimson streak that abruptly ended right in front of the parked semi.

"This must have been where they were parked. Probably put him in the trunk to harvest his skin for Alexa's artwork. Wow. Those boys had *fun* with their games tonight. Good for them. They needed to get out. They were getting pretty high-strung from the pressures of fatherhood. Parents need an outlet, I guess. Now, I see the four fingers, but I wonder what they did with the thumbs?"

Jules did not have long to ponder her question as she was suddenly grabbed from behind and lifted off the ground. "Awwww, goddamit," Jules stated as she felt the man squeezing her thin frame. Her arms were pinned against her body, and she began kicking her legs as the man said, "Well, hellllllooooo there, sweetheart! Yeah, I knew these little towns would provide me with some fun! Just wait outside one of the local watering holes and wait for my entertainment to come staggering right up to me. Now, just calm down there, sweetheart. I ain't gonna hurt you none. Well, *maybe*, heh, heh, heh. You play nice with *me*, and I'll play nice with *you*. So just keep your fuckin' yap shut and let's get you outta those black jeans. Then, I'm gonna take you to the *real* party."

"Dude, you have *no idea* who you're fucking with," Jules angrily stated before the man put her on the ground, spun her around, and violently slapped her in the face. Jules wiped a slight trail of blood from her split lip and looked up intensely at her attacker. She then heard a light 'mew' from the hood of the semi. Both the would-be rapist and Jules looked at the hood and saw a small, somewhat freakish-looking cat sitting there cleaning her fur. Jules began laughing and the man slapped her again before turning his attention to the cat. "What the fuck are *you* starin' at, cat? You're not the kind of pussy that I'm lookin' for, so just get going."

LucyFur glared directly into the man's eyes as Jules continued laughing. Jules was laughing because she knew one other thing about this cat. From the moment that she was born, this kitten had an insatiable appetite for human blood.

LucyFur let out one more innocent mew. Her eyes then dilated fully. Her twitching, twelve-inch bushy tail extended like it had just been shot full of static. She let out a low growl. She then pounced upon the man's face. The man let out a pained shriek as he felt the cat's claws deeply slicing his face into ribbons. LucyFur opened her jaws, reached around the man's head, and chewed his right ear off as her razor-sharp claws continued their brutal onslaught on his face. The man fell to the ground and LucyFur immediately repositioned herself with her head over his neck. Her back claws began thrashing at his sliced-open eyes as she sunk her fangs into the man's gurgling jugular. She began purring as the man's body ended its flailing and she serenely sucked the blood from the gashed neck.

"Thanks, cat," Jules said. "I coulda taken care of it myself, but at least *one* of us gets a meal out of him. Just stay there. I think it's time to leave."

Jules went back into the bar and approached her friends. "Hey guys, I think we need to go. Anybody sober enough to get us back to the estate? LucyFur's made a bit of a mess out back. And I think I found my own ride. I'll just follow you."

"Well, I really shouldn't be driving," Henri slurred. "But I suppose if I have to. It's all backroads and I'll just pull over if there's any traffic. Let me settle the bill and I'll be right out."

Sam yanked on the heavy chain that she was holding and said, "C'mon Pogo. Get your worthless stumps out here, or else I'll drag you behind my chair...again."

The bar patrons breathed a sigh of relief as they watched this mid-fifties ebony beauty depart their bar with her grotesquely scarred pet limping behind her on his stumps.

Henri followed his beloved wife out the front door and to their awaiting sedan. He delicately lifted her from her chair, gave her a tender kiss and smile, and placed her in the passenger's seat. He carefully folded up her weaponized wheelchair and placed it in the trunk. He then picked Pogo II up, and haphazardly threw him onto the backseat before sitting behind the wheel and began patiently waiting for Jules.

Jules picked her assailant up and dragged him to the back of the trailer. She then took out her walkie-talkie. "Hey Josie, this is Jules. Pick up."

Jules only had to wait a few moments before she heard a response. "Yeah, this is Josie. Wazzup Jules?"

"Yeah, well, we're in town," Jules began. "We ran into a bit of trouble. Some guy tried to rape me, and LucyFur, um, well, LucyFur's been fed tonight. Anyway, could we use a semi and trailer? I've got one that I want to drive back to the estate. I need to get rid of this guy's body and I *really* don't want to sit next to Pogo in the back seat of the sedan. He always gets blood and snot and shit all over me. So, can we drive it up and crash there for tonight?"

"Um, sure," Josie answered. "Who all is coming?"

"It's just three of us," Jules replied. "Well, three and a *half* if you count Pogo. But we can chain him to a tree outside. Otherwise, its me, Sam, and Henri."

"Yeah, okay," Josie agreed. "Stellan and Paciano are in Atlantic City with Kaneko, so you guys can use their quarters. Hey, is there anything good in the trailer?"

"I dunno. Haven't looked," Jules responded. "Hold on a sec."

Josie could hear the creaking of the trailer's metal doors being opened through the walkie-talkie before Jules said, "Ooooooh fuck. Hey, why don't you make sure the twins and the Twins are sleeping with the JQ before we get there. I think this is something that we shouldn't bother them with right now."

The eight battered women were carefully led out of the trailer and into the welcoming warmth of the estate. Rosa and Jessie delicately washed and tended to their bruised bodies. They were put into fresh, loose clothing and invited to join the other representatives of Murder, Inc. downstairs.

The group struggled to hold back their tears as they listened to each woman recount their own harrowing story of abduction and abuse. Their anger increased as they were told that they had overheard the driver say that they were being taken to an address in Brooklyn. They were being taken there to be abused once again. Repeatedly. Until they died. For some sadistic bastard's amusement. Sam's mind kept flashing back to her own torture that she had endured. She would frequently turn to her husband and say coldly, "Kick him again." Henri would dutifully lift her paralyzed leg and thrust her six-inch stiletto into Pogo II's punished face. Sam felt little relief as she was mournfully transfixed by these women's horrific stories and shattered psyches.

Arima wept quietly and held Josie's hand. Josie said nothing. She just stared intensely with her glowering green eyes as the women told them their tales of brutality. She said nothing and just stared intensely as the sobbing women were led back upstairs to lay their sore bodies and broken minds down peacefully for the night. She said nothing and just stared intensely into the cold morbidity of the room.

Sam turned to Jules and whispered, "Do you remember in college when someone was talking to Maddy about their, um, *troubles?*"

"Yeah," Jules replied.

"Do you remember the look on her face as she listened?" Sam inquired further.

"Yeah," Jules once again replied.

"Look at Josie's face," Sam continued. "*That's* the look. She looks *just like* her mother at that age. She looks *just like* her mother as she was plotting her revenge. She looks *just like* her mother before she went out."

"Yep," Jules agreed. "Because Josie has *become* her mother. And may God help anyone who ever gets in her way."

Josie finally got up from the couch. She quietly picked up the ice cream bowls and spoons, took them to the sink, and washed them. There was a slight 'clack' as the bowls were placed in the dish drainer. Sam, Jules, Rosa, Jessie, Arima, and Henri looked on in grim silence. They knew what was about to happen. And they both welcomed it and dreaded it simultaneously.

Josie turned around from the sink and calmly walked into the living room. She lifted her head upwards. Chills ran down the group's spines as they saw a pair of intense green eyes glowing from under a mop of curly copper strands. Josie's mauve lips curled upwards into a sinister smirk as she said in a deep, devilish voice, "Ladies. Gentleman. I do believe that it's time to hold another 'Slashdance.'

Chapter 98

Dangerous Type

A solitary tear fell from Lionnel's eye and landed upon the framed photograph that he was placing into his suitcase as he listened to raucous laughter from across the hall. He solemnly stared at the picture of himself hugging his dearest friend and love on the opening night of Josie's teenage-oriented hang-out and restaurant, LOHAD. Although only four years had passed since this image was captured, to Lionnel it felt like a lifetime ago. He gazed into the brilliant emerald eyes of this hopeful young woman. She had just turned fourteen on the day the picture was taken. He was three years older than her, and although he knew her overprotective father would be disapproving, he could not help but fall in love with her.

The pair had been connected since Josie's birth. His beloved mother, Abana, had been mercilessly decapitated while babysitting himself, Josie, Adam, Aaron, Vai, and Alexa. His father, Henri, had joined the ranks of Murder, Incorporated following this tragedy and his family was immediately intertwined with that of Josie's. He had held her as she sobbed on his shoulder following her father's murder. He had performed that same sorrowful obligation following the assassination of her mother. He had stood dutifully by her side and proudly watched her ascension to the highest throne of the deadliest freedom-fighting hit-man syndicate in the world. He had shed tears with her. He had shed blood with her. He had also shared laughter.

Despite the constant violence and tragic loss that they both experienced over the past four years, there had also been plenty of tender moments between the two of them. Slow dancing while holding each other tightly. Hysterically laughing at each other as they gorged themselves on popcorn and ice cream while they watched a movie. Secretly making goofy faces at one another while she presided over assassination meetings. Picnics at the estate. Making love. He chuckled to himself as his mind recaptured the image of his love rustling under all the weaponry in her flower-adorned, 1976 yellow VW Bus to retrieve a wicker basket filled with fried chicken, ham sandwiches, and potato salad. His tears flowed more freely as he recalled the vivid image of his bare-footed, floral dress adorned lover sauntering toward the blanket that had been laid in the lush green grass. He remembered looking up at her. He remembered the feeling of his heart swelling at that moment. The brilliant sun had been shining directly behind her and her curly, copper locks glowed as though they were encased within a halo of love and tranquility. She looked like an angel. And she was. She was *his* angel.

He had fallen in love with a girl that became a young lady who was the embodiment of peace. She was free-spirited. She was intelligent. She was beautiful. She had the most wonderful sense of humor. She considered herself to be the protector of any soul that had fur. Or scales. Or wings. She spoke properly, usually, and never said harsh words toward others. She believed in human kindness. She believed in protecting the innocent. The vulnerable. The abused. The downtrodden. Despite her lofty position, she did not consider herself to be above anyone else. Everyone that Josie met loved and adored her. They instinctively knew that they were safe with her. There was no judgement from Josie. There was only caring, kindness, and genuine friendship that accompanied a beaming smile and twinkling green eyes. It had always been said about Josie that she did not belong to anyone, including her parents. It was said that Josephine Patricia Sommers Parker belonged to the world. But her *heart* belonged to *him*. And *his* heart belonged to *her*.

Lionnel lightly kissed the tips of his fingers and placed them upon the picture. He was frozen for a moment. He did not want to let go. A final tear fell upon the image as Lionnel righted himself. There was a 'click' as he closed and fastened the suitcase. He slid the bag off the bed that he and his love had shared in the Sommers-Parker home for the past two years. He prepared himself, opened the bedroom door, and trudged across the hallway. The girlish laughter and banter became louder with each step he took toward his dreaded future. There was a crack in the door. Lionnel peered in and his heart sunk even further.

"Ow! Fuck Vai!" Josie was yelling out. "Do ya have to tie the ribbon so fucking *tight*?"

"Do you *really* want your pigtails coming out halfway through the massacre?" the thirty-year-old Vai calmly asked. "I *really* don't have much time to mess with this, my dearest. I still need to dye my hair black and put my silver streak in it before I put on my dress."

"Well, um, no, I *don't* want my hair to look a mess while we're slashing these fuckers up," Josie answered. "But *fuck* man, I don't wanna be fuckin' *scalped* either! Which reminds me. Alexa! Didja want us to start keeping some scalps from the 'Chads'? It's not a big deal if you want 'em. We're *already* hanging onto large portions of their skin for you to use as your canvas. I thought maybe you'd want the scalps too. It might be cool to paint with brushes made from the human hair of these motherfuckin' douchebags. You want 'em?"

The twenty-four-year-old petite blonde beauty squealed in delight and said, "Oh my god, *yes*! I hadn't thought of that! That will *really* get me in the mood to work on my art. Oh, I just can't *wait* for everyone to see the pieces I'm working on! I think you're *really* going to love them. And I just can't *believe* that you got me a show at that gallery! It's going to be *such* a magical evening!"

"Yeah, well, I've got, um, *connections*, heh, heh, heh." Josie replied in a mischievous tone. "I made the fucker who owns the joint an offer he couldn't refuse. I mean, he isn't really a bad guy, but he's got his secrets. And I've got a flock of little birdies who just *love* to chirp!"

"I don't think your mother would approve of that, Josie," Sam mentioned as she was dolling up her fifty-four-year-old best friend, Jules, to look as close to sixteen as possible. At least in dim lighting. "Your mother only went after men who truly deserved it. This man, from what I understand, simply has a few, um, personality quirks."

"My *mother*," Josie answered with a chuckle. "God, how I love her, but I *really* don't want to talk about my *mother* right now. She was good at what she did, but she never took *full advantage* of the power that she wielded. Listen, I'm not saying we should just go around randomly harassing or killing people. All I'm saying is that the world is transactional, and we should take *full advantage* of that. I have something that *this* asshole wants, and he has something that *I* want. So, we struck a deal. No biggie. Besides! Is it *my* fault that this prick can't keep it in his pants? Is it *my* fault that he's running around cheating on his husband? No! So, *he* gets to keep his little secrets and *Alexa* gets to throw a kick-ass art show. No muss, no fuss. Everybody's happy. Hey Vai. Hand me that lipstick wouldja?"

Jules looked at herself in a hand-held mirror and said softly, "Jesus. I look ridiculous. I mean, she's had some crazy fuckin' ideas, but *this* is just twisted."

"Yeah," Sam quietly replied. "And I think that we were wrong the other night. She hasn't *become* her mother. She has *surpassed* her mother. Saving the Earth and Enlightenment has really gone to her head. She was close to snapping two years ago when Maddy was killed. She became someone different on the day of her funeral. But she was able to hold it together. She was still Josie. Just, with a bit more tenacity. And foul language. Now I think that all the tragedy and loss throughout the years combined with her newfound realization of just how much power she possesses has sent her down a dark path. She needs a wake-up call. Maybe I'll talk to Arima and Rosa about it. See if they can't talk to her. But not tonight. She's hellbent on violence tonight. And once she has violence in her mind, there's no stopping her. Just like her mother."

"Hey! What are *you two* bitches whispering about over there? Whatevs. Keep your fuckin' secrets. It's too bad Kayla and Rachel couldn't join us tonight," Josie's excited rambling continued. "If it's one thing those two hate, it's human sex traffickers. But, hey, that's what you get when you have kids. You have to be tied down constantly. Man, I'm *never* having fuckin' kids. Nope, I'm *never* going to be tied down spending my day doing laundry and picking up after some snot-nosed, screaming asshole. Then, bringing Lionnel his pipe and slippers when he gets home from work. Can you imagine? Fuck that! Naw, that's not for me. I need to be foot-loose and fancy-free to do whatever the *fuck* I want, *whenever* the fuck I want. Which reminds me. I'm kinda pissed off that Rosa and Jessie aren't here tonight. They're spending the evening trying to hone their ability to track those little hellions through time the next time that they pull that shit. Kids. What a pain in the ass. Oh, hey Jules! Can I borrow that rouge?"

Lionnel lightly rapped on the door and said, "Hey. Can I come in?"

"Oh, hey baby!" Josie screamed out. "What do ya think? Don't we look cute?"

Lionnel felt ill as he looked upon Josie, Alexa, Vai, and Jules. They were all fully dressed, except for Vai who was still wearing a robe. The others all wore short, pink, Lolita dresses complete with pigtails and white stockings. Their faces were made up in a garish combination of colors. To Lionnel, they did not look cute. They looked…

"Disgusting. No, I don't think you look cute. I think that you look like you're all five-years-old. I think that this is sick, Josie."

"Oh, my fucking *God*, Lionnel!" Josie yelled back. "Of *course*, its sick! That's the whole fuckin' *point*! These twisted fuckers get off on abusing women and children, right? So, we show up and give them a moment to live out their perv fantasy and then…and then…just look at what we have buried in these ruffles!"

Josie began excitedly digging into pockets that were hidden within the outlandish ruffles of the dresses. She began extracting knives and hatchets and throwing stars. She pressed a button on her bracelet and spikes emerged. She tapped the back of the heels on her pure white vinyl buckled shoes and blades ejected from the front of the soles.

"See?" Josie exclaimed as she bounced up and down while clapping and laughing. "These motherfuckers are not going to know *what* hit them! Just picture it! We come in all chained up looking scared and innocent and shit. Then, I hit the button on the portable CD player and…oh Lionnel! I've picked out the *perfect* fucking song to play while we're cutting these fuckers up! Anywhooo, I push play on the CD player and then…well…Slaaaaaashdaaaaance motherfuckers!"

Josie strode over to her beloved boyfriend and embraced his rigid frame. "Jesus, you're uptight," she whispered to him before saying playfully, "Y'know, if ya play your cards right, we *might* be able to use this dress for some *other* type of fun. Whatdoyasay, hmmmmmmm?"

Lionnel wiped a tear from his eye, grasped Josie's petite hands and dislodged her grip from him. He took two steps back from her and said with as much force as he could muster, "No Josie. I'm not into making love to women who look like little girls. That's sick. Josie, I'm leaving."

"Whatevs, you fuckin' prude," Josie replied dismissively as she began walking back toward her makeup table. "But I'm tellin' ya. You're missing out. I'm gonna be all *sorts* of ready when we get done with these fuckers. Oh well. I'll see ya when I get home. Have fun doin' whatever you're doin' tonight."

"No, Josie," Lionnel tried to explain. "You don't understand. I'm leaving. I'm leaving this house. I'm leaving this relationship. I'm leaving *you*."

Josie had heard the words that her beloved boyfriend had just spoken. She realized that she needed to respond delicately. Josie knew that she could not fuck this up. Josie fucked it up as she immediately bent over and clutched her ribs to protect them from her sudden onslaught of violent laughter. "Leaving me? Okay, you guys. Who put him up to this? It's not really funny, but the thought of Lionnel leaving me? C'mon. You'd *never* leave me. You *love* me. Knock this shit off. I'll see ya when I get home."

"Josie," Lionnel began again with a cold determination. "You are right. I *do* love you. So much that it hurts. Or at least I love the person that you *were*. I loved *you*, Josie. The girl who built a pet shelter and adoption agency at the age of four. The girl who smiled constantly. The girl who immediately saw the bright side of taking out the wireless internet. The girl who didn't walk but *skipped* through life. The girl that *always* had a positive outlook no matter what tragedy had befallen her. The girl who turned the site of a massacre into a safe space for teenagers of all walks of life. The girl who *everybody* loved and adored and respected. The girl that made my heart beat rapidly every time I looked into her eyes. Josie, please listen to me. My heart doesn't beat like that for you anymore. Because I am no longer looking into *your* eyes. I am looking into the eyes of your *mother*."

"Oh….you….*motherfucker*!" Josie roared. "How fucking *dare* you! I love my mother but she's all *sorts* of fucked up! I am *nothing* like her! And how *daaaare* you say that I am! You wanna leave? Then get the fuck *out* of here! What the fuck do *I* care? I can get *any* guy in this city! Hell, I can get any guy in this entire fucking *world*! Do you know how many guys would love to be the boyfriend of the girl who saved the world? Here's a hint. Fucking *all* of them! What makes *you* so fucking special, huh? Who the fuck are *you* to tell me who I should be. I'm going to be whoever the fuck I *want* to be or my name's not Josie *fucking* Parker! And *that's* my name, so *that's* how it's going to be! Now get the fuck out!"

Stunned silence fell over the room. Lionnel looked hurtfully at each of the cartoonishly painted women standing before him. He gave each of them a slight nod and dejected smile, picked up his suitcase and turned toward the door.

Lionnel!" Josie called after him. "I'm *sorry*, okay? I didn't *mean* any of that! Just come back and let's talk, okay? I *love* you! I'm just amped up for tonight, that's all! Lionnel, c'mon! Let's talk! Lionnel! Get your fucking ass back in here! That's an order!"

From down the hallway, Josie heard Lionnel respond with, "Josie, I am not one of your servants. I am your boyfriend. Well, at least I *used* to be. Good-bye Josie."

Chapter 99

Kerosene

No one in the room dared to speak. They just stood silently watching Josie. They studied her and were transfixed as Josie's face turned bright red. She then shed a single tear from her emerald eye and her bottom lip began to quiver. Within moments, her face exhibited an eerie serenity. The final transformation came, and she projected an evil little smile before saying, "Fuck him. He'll be back. He can't live without me. Let's get this show on the road. Vai, get into your dress. Don't worry about your hair. It's black enough. And where the hell is Marcus, Gregory, and Henri?"

Sam grabbed the walkie-talkie from the arm of her wheelchair and called her husband. "Hey Henri, where are you guys? We're just about ready to go."

There was static on the line, then Henri's soothing voice. "Marcus and I will be there in about five minutes. We had to stop by and pick up our special guest. And we just received a report from Rod who is overseeing our surveillance team. We're not expecting any surprises. We have hit men, um, I mean execution specialists, or whatever we're calling them, positioned outside the warehouse. The moment we go through the gate, the guards will be taken out. We'll drive into a loading dock. There are eight men inside. The men are the heads of the most prominent human traffickers operating on the Eastern seaboard.

They like to sample their, um, they like to, um, well they do stuff to their victims before shipping the orders. Um, I guess. I'm sorry. I don't know how to say this, it's just so disgusting. Sam and our special guest will wait in the van and be on standby in the event we need them. Marcus and I will lead the four of you ladies inside. You will be handcuffed and leashed. The handcuffs are breakaway, and the leashes are made of razor wire just in case you ladies want another toy to play with."

Josie walked over to Sam and grabbed the walkie-talkie from her. "Hey, Henri. Josie here. That sounds great, but where the fuck is Gregory? He's supposed to be in on this."

"No, Josie," Henri replied through the static. "He wouldn't come. He said that he is only responsible for the diplomatic end of our operations and does not want to be involved in our more violent escapades. That was the deal that he made with your mother from the start."

"Yeah?" Josie screamed back. "Well, that's fucking *insubordination*! There's nothing that I can do about it right *now*, but as soon as this shit is done, Gregory and I are going to have a little *chat* about who's in *charge* here! And it *isn't* my fucking *mother*! And if you speak to him, you *might* want to remind him that I know that his first name is 'Chad!' *That* should make the point. Just get your asses over here. We're ready to fuck some shit up."

"What the hell is wrong with *you*?" Henri yelled back. "Josie, you have *no right* to…"

"Hey, baby," Sam interrupted after she caught the walkie-talkie that Josie had flung at her. "Hold the line for a sec. Josie, I've got to use the restroom."

"Whatevs," Josie answered as her frustrated hands tightened the ribbons on her copper pigtails. "Just hurry it up."

Once inside the privacy of the restroom, Sam said, "Hey, listen. There's been a bit of drama tonight. I don't want to get into it right now. I'm sure you'll find out about it when we get home. Let's just say that I think Lionnel will be staying with us for a while. And don't tell Gregory what Josie said. She's just a bit out of sorts tonight. We'll do this job, then get Rosa and Arima on it. See you soon."

"Yeah, alright," Henri replied. "You know how much I love and respect that girl but I'm not going to take any shit from her. I told her mother that when I joined up and I am not afraid to tell the girlfriend of my son that, either. We'll be there soon."

As the black passenger van pulled around the corner and began entering the driveway of the abandoned Brooklyn warehouse, Sam looked at Henri and said, "My lord. You look so creepy with that white man's face."

Henri chuckled and said, "Yeah, I know. And I had to paint my neck and hands white to match it. But Lionnel did a wonderful job cutting the semi-driver's face off his skull. It fits me perfectly. He will be such a talented surgeon someday. I'm so proud of my boy. Hey, Josie! Do you and my son have any plans for later tonight? Sam and I are going to an all-night diner to get some burgers and shakes. You and Lionnel are more than welcome to join us if you would like."

His invitation was greeted by chilled silence. Henri looked into the rearview mirror and saw Josie's glaring green eyes staring straight ahead. Her arms were folded, and he could feel her foot violently kicking the back of his seat. He looked over to the passenger seat at Sam who looked back and silently shook her head. "Okaaaay, then," Henri said to change the subject. "It looks like we're here! Marcus, are you ready?"

"Yeah, man, I'm good to go," Marcus replied. "But, hey. If you don't mind, I think that Arima and I would love to join you guys for dinner tonight."

"Yeah, that's cool man," Henri answered. "Okay. Everybody be cool. We're coming up to the gate."

The black-clad guard checked the driver's credentials which Rod had created. The van was waived through. There was a loud 'clang' as the gate was shut behind them. The passengers in the van were completely silent as they drove toward the loading dock. The only sound that could be heard was the van's running engine and several light 'popping' sounds from behind them. The passengers looked out the rearview mirror and saw twelve guards lying on the cold concrete in pools of their own blood.

They backed into the loading dock where eight men in expensive designer suits were seated, smoking cigars, and laughing. One of the men stood up and shouted out, "The party has arrived, gentlemen!"

Sam gave her beloved husband a light kiss before she and their special guest crouched down in their respective seats so as not to be seen. The party exited the van to jubilant applause. Marcus was carrying a CD boombox and holding the leashes of the "bound" Alexa and Jules. Henri was leading Vai and Josie. "Now, *this* is gonna be a party!" One of the men exclaimed. "But, hey! There were supposed to be *eight* of these bitches. Where's the other *four*? And who is *this* guy that's with you? And what the hell happened to your *face*? You look weird."

Henri responded while trying to sound as redneck as possible. "Well, uh, sorry about that, sir. This here's my friend Marcus. You see, these bitches got a bit unruly, so I brought Marcus along to help keep 'em calm. And you can see what they did to my face. Anyway, four of 'em just couldn't be handled so we had to, um, well, let's just say they were damaged goods. But we got these 'uns all dolled up fer ya. Wanna meet 'em?"

The men's attention was immediately distracted away from Marcus and Henri as they gazed lustfully at the four women standing in front of them wearing pink Lolita dresses, white stockings, pig tails, and bright, glittered make-up. If it weren't for their height, Josie and Alexa could have passed for ten-year-olds. Vai perhaps could have been mistaken to be in her mid-teens. And fifty-four-year-old Jules could have passed for…

"That one's cute and everything, but just how old *is* she? Like, *fifty-two*? Ah well, she'll still be fun for one of our buyers. Might have to reduce the price a bit though." All eight men began laughing. Marcus and Henri also forced themselves into an overly dramatic laugh while the women stood there and "trembled." Except for Jules. She internally seethed as she detected a familiar presence.

One of the men walked up to Josie. She recoiled at the foul smell of his breath as he said to her "sweetly," "Well, aren't *you* just a precious little thing. We'll have to take *turns* with *you*. No need to have a war over a cute little piece of ass, now *is* there? What do you say, sweetheart? You ready to play some *games* with us? All *eight* of us? While your little *girl-friends* watch? Yeah, that'll be nice, *right* honey? Have your little *girl-friends* watch what's gonna happen to them *next*. Then, it'll be off to your new *masters*. And *believe* me, sweetheart. What happens to you here tonight is *nothing* compared to what your masters will do to you. I sure hope you like knives."

Josie looked up at him and smiled innocently. There was a glimmer in her emerald eyes as she said in a childish voice, "I sure do, mister. But do you know what I like more than knives?"

The man chuckled and turned around to look at his guffawing companions. "Naw. What is it that you like *more* than knives, there honey?"

Josie smiled once again and answered. "Well, I *really* like lollipops. Do any of you men have a big *lollipop* that I can suck on?"

The men's laughter exploded before the vile man replied, "Yeah sweetheart. I think we can arrange that. Why don't we see if you like *my* lollipop?"

"Okay, but can I just ask one question first before I suck on your lollipop?" Josie inquired sweetly. "I was just *wondering* if any of you are named 'Lionnel.' I *really* like that name."

The laughing men looked at each other with amused expressions. "Hey! We got a Lionnel in the house?" the man yelled out. "Lionnel! Come on out! You got a visitor!"

"No, but my names Larry!" a tall, skinny man in the back of the group shouted out gleefully.

"Close fuckin' enough!" Josie roared. "*That* fucker's *mine*! Play the fuckin' song!"

Marcus pushed 'play' on the CD player and the child-like harmonies of The Chordettes' "Lollipop" came blaring through the speakers. Before the men could react, Josie snapped her handcuffs, pressed a button on her bracelet and used the protruding metal spikes to slash the man's throat open. He began gurgling and fell to his knees as he clutched his throat to slow the flow of blood that was gushing out. Josie took the leash from around her neck, wrapped it around that of the wounded man, and began sawing back and forth with the razor wire until the head flopped backward. Josie stared into the dead eyes that were looking up at her as the blood from the severed head sprayed on her made-up face. She smiled sweetly once again, leaned down and gave the corpse a delicate kiss.

"SlaaaaaaaashDaaaaaaaaance!" Alexa squealed as she pulled a meat cleaver from one of the ruffles in her dress, pounced on the nearest man, and began ferociously hacking at his face.

The van began rocking back and forth and there was a loud rumble before the doors swung open. "W-w-what the fuck is *that?*" One of the terrified men yelled out. Lumbering toward them was the six-foot-seven-inch *Dragenstein*. She was wearing her customary Monroe-esque white dress. She approached one man and gave him a playful spin. The circulating air caused the hem of the dress to lift above her waist revealing an eighteen-inch rock-hard phallus. She paused for a moment and said in her breathy, high-pitched voice. "Sorry to be such a *drag, tee, hee.*" She then grabbed the man's shoulders and pushed him to his knees. She forced his mouth open and thrust her granite-like member into it. She moaned ecstatically as she forcefully pulled the man's head backwards and forwards, backwards and forwards, backwards and forwards until her throbbing member shot through the back of the man's skull. A stream of blood, bone, brain, and cum shot out of the dead man's head, hitting Jules on her half-exposed breasts.

"Oh, fuckin' gross," Jules lamented. "I've heard of hard enough to cut through glass, and I've heard of skull fucking, but *that* shit's ridiculous, bitch."

Dragenstein blew her a kiss, twirled, and said, "Anyone got a cigarette? *Tee, hee*" before grabbing another man by the scruff of his neck and throwing him toward Vai. Vai looked down at the man with a cool intensity and pulled two sewing needles from inside her ruffles. "My mentor, Aunt Blair, showed me how to use these. Only it *wasn't* for knitting." She then thrust the needles into the screaming man's eyes. Vai began laughing uncontrollably as she watched the blind man desperately crawling on the floor as he tried to find any type of exit from this torturous hell. Vai tapped the back heels of her shoes, causing blades to shoot out of the front of the soles. She then began to violently kick the man repeatedly in the groin until he collapsed in a pool of his own blood and vomit.

The four remaining histrionic men began running toward the back exit. Jules smirked, closed her eyes, and concentrated. From out of nowhere, thirty-eight feral cats descended upon the men from metal shelving. The men began flailing helplessly as the felines ripped at their faces.

"Hey! *Dragenstein!*" Josie yelled out. "Grab that skinny fucker and hold him down! I want him alive!"

Dragenstein pranced over to the skinny man and cautiously made her way through the misty cloud of blood and fur. "Excuse me, pussy. Excuse me, pussy. Excuse me, pussy," she said in her breathy voice until she reached her target, threw him on the ground and sat on him.

Alexa's brilliant blue eyes seemed to be glowing as she approached the bloody form of the largest of the men. "Ooooooh yeah," Alexa snarled. "I know *exactly* what I'm going to paint on *you*. And a full head of hair *too*. Perfect."

Alexa took her cleaver and buried it in the man's forehead. She pulled on his shirt, and he tumbled face first. There was a loud 'snap' as his nose was crushed against the concrete floor. Alexa giggled and sat astride on the twitching man's back. She retrieved a scalpel from her dress and used it to cut his coat and shirt open, exposing the large frame of his back.

"P-please, S-s-stop," the man pleaded before Alexa screamed out. "Hey! Shut up! And stop trembling! This is delicate work!" She carefully cut the perimeter of his back and pulled the skin from his body. She began squealing in delight and yelled out, "Oh my god! Look everybody! This is my largest canvas yet! Oh, thank you sir!"

She then took the scalpel and cut around the quivering man's hairline. She pulled on his thick, black hair and his entire scalp came free. "Oh my God! I can make so many *brushes* out of this! Oh, you *really* have been just *too kind* sir! Thaaaaaank yooooou!" Alexa concluded before playfully skipping away with her treasure.

"Okay cats, get off of them and thanks," Jules stated to her feline friends. They mewed politely up at her, licked the blood from their whiskers and retreated into the shadows of the warehouse. The two dying men laid on the concrete whimpering as blood flowed out of the myriad of deep gashes on their faces.

"So, what should we do with *these* two? Just let them bleed out?" Sam inquired as she wheeled herself towards her friends. "And, what about that skinny one?"

"Well, first things first," Josie answered in a devilish voice as her eyes were attracted to a rusty, metal can in the corner of the warehouse. She went over and picked up the five-gallon cannister and held it over the dying men. "I'm going to do to *them* what should be done to *all* of these sadistic fuckers. I want these men to suffer! I want them to *suffer* just like they make us *women* suffer! They make us suffer with their fists and their harsh words! With their tiny little pricks! And *then* do you know what they do? Oh, I'll *tell* you! They tell you that they love you and they buy you nice gifts and hold you while watching movies and make love to you and smile at you and say nice things to you and buy you flowers and shit, and then…and then…they *break up* with you! Fuckin' misogynistic, sadistic *bastards!*"

She unfastened the cap, tossed it aside and began pouring the pungent liquid contents on the pair of sex-traffickers. She giggled as she said, "Hey, Marcus. Toss me your lighter." Marcus reached into his pocket, took out his lighter and tossed it toward Josie. The lighter hit Josie directly in the hands, then bounced off and landed on the floor.

Jules leaned down to Sam and whispered, "She sure as hell can shoot arrows, but she kinda catches like a girl."

"Hey! I heard that!" Josie yelled as she picked the lighter up along with a piece of discarded paper. The flame of the lighter reflected in her emerald eyes as she gleefully lit the paper on fire and dropped it onto the two men who were saturated in kerosene. The men screamed in agonized torture and began flailing as the wicked flames consumed their bodies.

"Now, for *this* one," Josie nonchalantly continued as she sauntered over to the skinny man that *Dragenstein* was sitting on. "Sooooo, Dragalicious. Do you think you could…," Josie began to inquire before bending down and whispering into her ear.

Dragenstein giggled and said with breathy anticipation, "But *of course,* my dear." *Dragenstein* lifted the left leg of the tortured man and yanked the knee joint forward. There was a loud 'crack' as the left knee snapped in two. She continued to pull the leg back and forth, back and forth, back and forth, until the leg was ripped from the body at the joint. Blood began pouring out of the fresh wound as Josie and *Dragenstein* shared the same amused expression. The man shrieked in tormented agony as the right leg was removed in the same gruesome manner. Then the left arm at the elbow. Then the right.

"That was so fuckin' *cool!*" Josie gushed. "Now, hold his limbs over the fire to cauterize the wounds. I want to keep him alive. Sam has her Pogo and I've got my Lion…I mean, my *Larry!* Fuck *you,* Larry! Oh, but goddammit!"

"What's wrong, dear," Vai asked tenderly as the man screamed for mercy while the flames licked at his mutilated appendages.

"Well, it's just that I wish I had some hot dogs. And some ketchup," Josie regretfully answered.

"Um, Josie?" Marcus asked. "Do you think I could have my lighter back? I kinda wanna smoke this joint. Oh, and ketchup on hot dogs is doing it wrong."

Chapter 100
Beat's So Lonely

Arima and Rosa cautiously ascended the staircase that led to the third-floor party room and converted art studio of the Sommers-Parker home. They approached the metal door and heard a succession of 'Thump!' 'Aaaaaaaaaw!' 'Thump!' 'Aaaaaaaaaw!' 'Thump!' 'Aaaaaaaaaw!'

"What the hell is she *doing* in there?" Rosa asked before Arima carefully opened the door. "Um, hey Niece Josie?" Arima inquired carefully. "Um, whatcha doin?'

Josie was standing in the middle of the dance floor in her pink floral pajamas. In one hand she held a tumbler of bourbon. In the other, she was holding...

"Just playing darts with Larry," Josie answered in a slightly drunken slur. She pulled her right arm back and slung the dart toward the far wall. There was a loud 'Thump!' followed by a man wailing out 'Aaaaaaaaaw!'

Rosa and Arima looked over at the far wall and saw the quadriplegic Larry. He had hooks under his armpits that held his beaten body to the wall. He was naked except for a diaper that was leaking pungent urine and feces. His torso was dripping trails of blood from around the multiple darts that were penetrating his beaten, dark purple flesh.

"Hey everybody!" Alexa squealed as she pulled back the curtain and popped her blonde head out from her half of the third-floor space that she was using as her art studio. "I painted the dartboard on his chest! Pretty cool, huh?"

"Uh, yeah, it looks really great, Alexa," Rosa responded before turning back to Josie. "Hey Josie, could we maybe have a little chat with you?"

"Sure," Josie answered in a depressed tone. "Why not? What's the point of doing this? What's the point of doing anything? Life is just a series of heartbreaks. I may as well listen to whatever bad news *you two* are going to give me. I just have one dart left anyway. Hey. See that little hole in his left ear where he used to have an earring? Watch this shit." Josie pulled her right arm back once again and launched her final dart. It slammed perfectly into the hole in his ear, lodging it into the wall. The man screamed out, "Aaaaaaaaaw!" and Josie allowed herself a moment of quiet satisfaction before sitting on a red vinyl love seat. "Even drunk, I'm pretty good. Maybe next time Larry and I play this, I'll use my arrows. Okay. I'm here. What do *you* two want?"

"Um, Niece Josie?" Arima began sheepishly. "Well, it's just that we're a little bit worried about you. We understand that you're heartbroken over Lionnel, but…"

Arima was cut off by a belligerent Josie. "Who? Who the fuck is this *Lionnel* that you speak of? I've never *heard* of the motherfucker. Nope. The only Lionnel that *I* ever knew is fucking *dead to me* and I don't want to hear his fucking *name* ever again! Got it? Is that all? Can I get back to playing with Larry now?"

"No, you may not," Rosa answered in a stern maternal tone.

"Whoooooooa! Rosa's gonna get all *medieval* on her ass," Maddy exclaimed from her perch in Enlightenment. "Erick! Come here! I've connected with Arima's soul so that I can listen in. I can see and hear everything that *she* does. But I can't interact, because I kinda snuck into her soul and she doesn't know I'm there. Hold my hand so you can listen in too!"

"What the hell is going on *now*?" Erick replied in a disinterested tone.

"Hey! Don't use that fuckin' tone with me!" Maddy shot back. "Just hold my hand. Lionnel broke up with Josie and…"

"What?" Erick roared. "That little bastard broke my little girl's heart? I'm going to go talk to Gwen and see if she'll give me permission to haunt his ass!"

"Yeah! He totally did!" Maddy answered. "And do you know *why*? It's for the *dumbest* fuckin' reason! He said that she was becoming too much like *me*! He should *be* so fuckin' lucky to be with a girl just like me! I'm like perfect and shit!"

"Yeah, well," Erick quietly replied as he avoided his beloved wife's glowing green eyes. "You *are* kind of an acquired taste, so I *kinda* get where he's coming fr..."

"What are you babbling about?" Maddy interrupted. "Get over here and hold my hand and shut the fuck up! I wanna hear what Rosa is going to say."

"Listen, Josie," Rosa began. "We understand the pressure you've been under. I mean, my God, you've just turned eighteen and look at all the things you've had to deal with. You're the leader of an international freedom-fighting hit-man syndicate. You've just helped coordinate the salvation of both Earth and Enlightenment. You have lost so many friends and loved ones in your short life. Your parents have died, then were reborn, then left you again. The pain that you have experienced is unimaginable. We understand. But Josie, you are going down a dark path. You are becoming something that doesn't come naturally to you. You are naturally a very sweet girl who cares deeply about others. And who cares deeply about ridding the world of pure evil. And those two contradictions are battling each other. The innocent side that wants to cherish life and the dark side that must order others to commit very violent acts. Both come from the same place. Both sides want to protect the innocent. The downtrodden. But Josie, your dark side is taking over. You are becoming something that we no longer recognize. You are becoming the very thing that you have fought against. You are not becoming your mother. She always was able to keep a check on her dark side. It would come out when it was needed, then she was able to bottle it back up again. That isn't true with you. You are becoming something *more* than your mother. You are becoming your *grandmother*. You are becoming sadistic just for the sake of being sadistic. You are beginning to thrive on seeing others suffer. You are turning our syndicate into a cult of personality. A cult that is beholden only to *you*. You are losing the sweet side of yourself. You are losing that little girl who would dance around the house in a hippie dress with a flower in her hair. You are going too far. And that is why Lionnel broke up with you.

And it is why you are at risk of losing the loyalty of others as well. This is your wake-up call. Come back to us Josie. Please. Do you understand?"

Josie sat silently for a moment. Her green eyes began tearing up. The tears immediately dried and her eyes began to shimmer. "Huh," Josie said. Rosa and Arima smiled at one another. They felt that the wall had been penetrated and that the true Josie was present once again.

"Well," Josie began calmly before screaming out, "Isn't *this* just a crock of shit? Yeah! I've got a lot on my plate! And I don't need *you* two bitches or *anyone else* for that matter to tell me how to live or who I should be! Do you know who saved the Earth and Enlightenment? Me, *that's* who! This world would be consumed in the fucking flames of *Vetis* if it wasn't for me! So, yeah! Maybe people *should* bow down and kiss my fuckin' feet! And you come in here and dare *criticize* me? You fucking traitorous bitches! You want to leave me too? Then fucking *do* it! What the fuck do *I* care? Everybody that I've cared about has left me! Why should *you* two be any different? I don't *need* you! I don't *need* L-L-Lionnel…"

Josie broke down and held her tearful face in her hands as she screamed out, "Oh my fucking God, I miss him so much! Why did he *leave* me? I *need* him! Oh, goddammit, *now* what?"

The trio looked up at the door and saw Jessie rushing into the room. "Hey everybody," a breathless Jessie began. "Sorry to interrupt whatever *this* is, but I was about to go pick Jamie up from the hospital. She's being discharged after her successful sex change surgery, and I got a call on that stupid land-line phone. Anyway, it's happened again. The JQ is missing, and the twins and the Twins are besides themselves. Aaron and Adam are starting to sharpen their toys, and that's *never* good. Rosa, Arima, we need to get up to the estate and try to find those kids. Then Arima, we need you to get in touch with Maddy and see if someone can go bring them home."

Josie shook the tears from her face and the heartbreak from her soul before yelling, "Do you *see* all the shit that I have to deal with? Now, I've gotta coordinate *this* shit! Now *I'm* ultimately responsible for a bunch of little time-traveling *bastards*! And, *now* what?"

Josie was interrupted once again as Rod entered the room. "I-I'm very sorry Josie, but I have that report that you were wanting."

"Jesus Fucking Christ Rod, can't you see that I'm *busy* here?" Josie roared at him. "Fine. Give it to me. What do you have."

Josie stood up and approached the quivering Rod. His pop-bottle lenses were steaming up from all the sweat that was pouring down his face. He looked Josie squarely on her chest and began stammering. "U-um, well Josie, I have found where the reconstituted Underground Autocratic Movement is. Vetis has given them the word to stand by. He has told them that there will soon be reinforcements coming. Reinforcements that he is recruiting from the past. The new UAM is congregating now and waiting for their orders. I do not yet know who the top leaders are. They apparently have been held back in the shadows this entire time. But I will find out who they are as soon as possible. What do you want to do?"

Josie stood silently and pondered her options. Her intoxicated genius brain was clicking through the various scenarios. She then came up with her plan.

"Okay, here's what we do. Rosa and Arima. Go to the estate with Jessie and get those fuckin' kids back. Rod, give this report to Gregory and have him, Marcus, and Cliff get a meeting at the United Nations. We can't make a move without their approval. That was the deal. Then, have Sam and Jules get a group of assassination technicians together and be prepared to attack these motherfuckers. Alexa, go pick up Jamie. Larry, you just hang from the wall and bleed, you fuckin' douchebag. We'll reconvene tomorrow morning. Got it? What the fuck are you all *waiting* for? Chop, chop, motherfuckers!"

"Um, yes Josie," the stammering Rod replied as his magnified pupils stared at her chest. "R-right away."

"And, hey Rod!" Josie yelled out. "Why the fuck are you staring at my chest? You've *never* done that with me!"

"I-I'm very sorry Josie," Rod replied as he lifted his gaze from her chest to the ceiling. "It's just that I have difficulty maintaining eye contact with people I'm intimidated by."

"Yeah?" Josie countered. "I fucking *know* that. So why are you doing this to *me* now?"

"Because I am intimidated by you Josie," Rod answered in his nasal staccato. "You were always the one person in this entire world that did not intimidate me. You never judged me. From the time that you were an infant, I knew that you were special. I knew that you were somebody that I could trust. Somebody that I could be myself around. Somebody who would love me for who I was. You never judged my awkward appearance or my speech. You never judged my awkwardness. You were sweet. You were my sweet Josie. You were the *world's* sweet Josie. You aren't that person anymore. You are judgmental and becoming cruel. You never raised your voice to me or anyone. Before tonight. You yelled at me Josie. You treated me like a servant. You used to think that we were all equals. You don't believe that anymore. Power has gone to your head. And that power is corrupting you. You are now the opposite of what you have always been. You are cruel now, Josie. And I am afraid of you."

"Oh fuck," Erick whispered to his wife. "He's right. My little girl has changed. All the loss and heartbreak has corrupted her. It has corrupted her soul. If she continues on this path, she won't be allowed into Enlightenment when it is her time. The one thing that has kept me from going crazy is the thought that someday I will be able to spend eternity with my family. My *entire* family, including my little girl. But what if she isn't allowed here Maddy? What will I do? What *can* I do? I feel so powerless."

Maddy leaned over and gave her husband a light kiss on his spiritual lips. She then whispered, "You *aren't* powerless. You know *exactly* what to do. She loves you more than *anyone*. You two have a special connection. A special bond. You will know *exactly* how to reach her. Now, let's be quiet. And when Arima calls out to me, pretend that we haven't been in her this entire time. Just be cool, okay? I don't want her to rescind her invitation to use her soul as my Earthly B & B whenever I want."

The room fell into a chilled silence. Even Larry had stopped his annoying whining. Josie's face turned bright red, then softened. Her cheeks returned to their normal light pink as she said in a controlled cadence, "Thank you for your observations, Rod. Now, would you all please complete your assignments? I feel the need to be alone at the moment. Thank you. Thank you for your time tonight. I will see you all in the morning. And Arima? Please say 'Hi' to my mother for me. That will be all."

The entire group left the room in silence. Josie watched them depart. The moment the metal door was shut, she fell to her knees and began sobbing. "Oh, my lord, what have I *become*? How could I *treat* them like that? I have always been a person that attracted others to me. Now I'm the person that is driving them away. They can't stand to be around me. And I can't blame them. They are right. I've become a total bitch. And Lionnel...oh my God how I miss you. You were my rock. And I drove you away. I stopped listening to you. I ignored you. I belittled you. I took your love for me for granted. I thought that you'd always be by my side. And now you're not. Because you couldn't put up with my shit any longer and I can't blame you for that. I have to prove myself to you. I have to get you back. But to do that, I have to find *my* way back. Back to the person that I was. But *how*? Is it too late? Am I *already* too corrupted? Dad, if you can hear me, can you help? I'm so lost, and I miss you so much. I think losing you again was the final straw. You were the one who was always able to show me the way. And now you're gone. And now, I'm lost. I feel so powerless. I just wish you could hear me. I need my father right now."

The lights in the party room suddenly shut off. Josie immediately wiped the tears from her eyes and looked around in the darkness. She tightened her muscles and prepared herself for battle. She stood up in the middle of the dance floor and waited for the impending attack.

The dance lights began flickering above her curly, copper mop. The speakers began to buzz. Josie listened intently then began to laugh and twirl. She began to laugh and twirl to the song that her father used to play for her as a child. She remembered squealing with joy as her father would lift her up and spin her around the dance floor. She remembered her flowered dress floating in the breeze as she giggled in her loving father's arms. She remembered the feeling of pure joy and peace as they danced to The Fifth Dimension's, "Aquarius."

Josie began swaying to her father's music. She then felt fur rubbing around her ankles. Her cats that she had brought home from the estate, Mika, Mike, Peter, and Bill were purring and mewing up at her. Josie fell to the floor and allowed herself to be bombarded by their feline love. She rolled on the floor with her kitty friends and laughed. And squealed. And cried tears of pure joy. The fever had been broken. Josie was with her father. Josie was with her pussycats. Josie had found her way back home. And Josie's heart was once again at peace.

Chapter 101
Roadrunner

"Oh, Master! I have exciting news!" Gobbo announced joyfully as his frail, bent body sprung into Vetis's inner chamber. Vetis was sitting on his throne, twiddling his four thumbs while watching one of his remaining screaming dark souls melt away into a vat of acid. "Yes, what is it Gobbo?" He asked in a bored tone.

"I believe that I have done it, Master!" Gobbo answered with delight. "I believe that I have found a pair of assassins on 2042 Earth that can eliminate your young interlopers. They are quite skilled. They are preparing for the assassination now. They have just received a shipment from the *ACME* company and are assembling the parts as we speak!"

Vetis lifted his dark red horned head up and looked at Gobbo with hopeful eyes. "*Really?* And you think that these two can pull it off? Oh, how *wonderful* that would be. I'm so bored just waiting around for my chance to go back into time and corrupt another soul so that we can have two parallel movements to conquer the Earth and Enlightenment. I really haven't been myself since our last failure. Even the screams of these boiling souls don't cheer me up anymore.

"Yes, I could really use some good news to lift me out of this funk. I wish that I could go there myself and take care of those little bastards. I wish that I could stand my nine-foot frame in front of them and take each of them into one of my hands and squeeze them until their little fucking heads pop off! Then, I would suck their blood and absorb their souls. Oh, how I *wish* that I could do that. But I can't. I can't expose my true physical form on Earth. I would then be vulnerable to an attack from all those fucking goodie-goodies on Earth. They would all converge upon me and rip me apart and destroy me. And wouldn't they all just enjoy *that*? Destroying *me* so that *they* can live in peace throughout eternity. Those pussy fuckers. They're no fun.

"No, all I can do is whisper into the souls of mortals. I can whisper to them and turn their souls black. Then, I can direct them to do my bidding. It was wise of me to not expose all my Earthly followers during this last battle. It was wise to leave them lurking in the shadows to await my next orders. And it was wise of me to install many of them as diplomats at the United Nations. Now, we will at least know what the mortals know and what they are planning.

"But those kids…those fucking kids. Somehow, they know what my plans are. Somehow, they know who I am going to corrupt and when on the timeline that I will arrive. Then, they simply arrive a little bit before me and take out my target. Who the fuck *are* they and where did they *come* from? Oh, I am quite aware of who they are. But *how*? Who *called* for them? I guess it doesn't matter. All that matters is that they are here disrupting my plans and that makes me sad. I hate those little fuckers. Come Gobbo! Let's watch your assassins at work. If I can't destroy the little fuckers myself, I at least can get some pleasure out of watching their cute little bodies blow up. Then, it will be time to corrupt our next soul. And then, my loyal Gobbo, let the fucking fireworks start."

———

"I *told* you I felt something!" Sigourney declared arrogantly to her twin sister and twin cousins who were watching from their perch on a high ravine. A pair of men were working beneath them. One man was connecting wires to a detonator behind a large boulder. The other was digging a hole in the middle of the gravel road. "And *once again*, I was right. But we have to travel down this road to get to the time portal. And those men seem to be burying a bomb in the middle of the road. I bet they're going to blow us up when we cross that spot. What shall we do?"

"I haf a iea!" Thanatos blurted out.

"What?" Euna asked. "Would you *please* take that giant wad of gum out of your mouth so that we can understand what you're saying?"

Thanatos reached into his mouth and pulled out a giant saliva covered ball of gum. "Here, Snot. You chew on this awhile," he said as he placed the gum into the awaiting mouth of his light green colored Shetland. "I said, I have an idea! Come on! Let's go back to the house. This shouldn't take long. Then, when we return, here's what we'll do."

Kane and Euna began giggling as they listened to the plan. "Oh! that sounds like fun!" Euna declared. "Oh yes! What a fun game we shall play with them! And that will be quite easy for me to build! But we had better be careful not to soil our new white western outfits. Our parents will be cross with us," Kane contributed before the Junior Quad turned their respective ponies around and trotted back to the stables.

"Hello sirs," Euna and Sigourney innocently said as they sat astride their Shetland ponies in front of the pair of sweaty, rugged-looking men who had just completed their work. "What are you doing? Can we be of assistance to you?" The pair of twin sisters smiled sweetly and awaited the desired response.

"Huh, there's two of them now," one of the men said to the other out of the side of his mouth. "This might be easier than we thought. Let's take out these two right now, then we'll find the boys."

The other man smiled and nodded before looking up into the brown and blue eyes of the children and saying, "Well, hello there children. Yes, you *can* help us. How about you two just get down off your ponies and come over here. We got some *candy* for you."

Euna watched as the man attempted to stealthily retrieve a hunting knife from his leather bag. She then turned to her sister and quietly said, "Hmmmph. *That* isn't candy. They aren't very honest. Good thing Thanatos isn't here. He'd probably fall for that."

Sigourney nodded at her sister before turning her attention back to the grinning pair of men. "Oh, that sounds fun! We love candy! But first, let's play a game. Now, what should we play? Oh! I know! Let's play tag! You're it!"

Sigourney and Euna lightly tapped their heels into the ribs of Snowball and Blackjack and the Shetlands dutifully burst into a sprint.

"Goddammit! They're getting away!" One of the men shouted. "You chase one with the jeep! I'll chase the other on the motorcycle! We'll divide and conquer these two little bitches!"

Euna and Sigourney heard the roar of approaching engines from behind them. They gave one another a knowing nod and smile and split off from one another. Dust was flying from underneath Snowball's hooves and the tires of the motorcycle. Sigourney was laughing with glee as she would allow the motorcycle to nearly catch up to her, then would abruptly turn in another direction. She laughed louder as she would hear her pursuer yelling foul names at her and shake his fist before turning his machine around and re-engaging in the chase. Sigourney, Snowball, and the motorcycle snaked their way across a vast field of dead brush. The motorcycle inched closer to Snowball's pounding hoofs. The man flashed an evil smile and accelerated one final time to ram the galloping pony. The motorcycle was three inches from the Shetland and its giggling, white-fringed rider when Snowball suddenly turned left.

The motorcycle drove off a steep cliff. It hung suspended in the air for a moment. The man looked directly into the eyes of the reader and sorrowfully waved good-bye before plummeting to his death. There was an incredible fireball that exploded from the bottom of the ravine and the giggling twin sisters sat astride their ponies looking down at the carnage.

"Nice job," Euna said. "I hid in the woods and mine got bored and gave up just like we planned. C'mon. Let's meet up with the boys and get to the time portal. We have more games to play."

"Where the fuck is he?" the man muttered to himself as he crouched on a wooden crate that he was using as a make-shift stool. "Maybe that other one hid too and he's still looking for her." The man got up and peered around the large boulder. "Well, looks like he's gonna miss out on the fun," he said as he smiled at the four approaching riders. The man tiptoed, for some unexplained reason, around the boulder and sat back down on his crate. His sweaty hands clutched the plunger of the detonator. His heart pounded with anticipation as he heard the 'clopping' of the approaching hooves. The sound became increasingly louder. He smiled to himself and pushed down on the plunger with all his force. He heard a light clicking sound coming from under his posterior. He then heard one of the passing boys say, "Oh, I put it under his wooden crate."

The man's long, beleaguered face stared blankly ahead just before the bomb that he was sitting on exploded.

The children screamed with glee as they were showered with blood, internal organs, bone, and limbs. "Oh Kane, that was great! And what a great idea Thanatos!" Sigourney exclaimed.

"Oh, it was easy, "Kane replied as Flame trotted along. "It was a really easy bomb to build. I found the instructions in one of Aunt Lucy's trunks. So, while you two were distracting them, Thanatos and I just disconnected the bomb that they had planted in the ground and connected it to the one that I put under the crate. That was fun! But not as fun as this is going to be! Look everyone! Here come the beautiful swirling colors!"

————

"Nice job, dipshit!" Vetis roared as he backhanded Gobbo into a wall of flames. The screaming Gobbo got up and began furiously beating out the fire that had consumed him. Smoke billowed from off his ashen skin as he looked toward the floor and said regretfully, "I'm sorry master. I was so sure. But perhaps it is not too late to corrupt our targeted soul. And he will be so easy. He has already been corrupted by one of your previous minions. And he is scheduled to die long before our battle is to commence. He will be the perfect addition to your movement. Please, Master. Don't be glum. Let's go corrupt this soul."

"Oh, I suppose," a disappointed Vetis replied. "Where and when is he?"

————

"Lil' Red, this is Soul Sister. Please come in, Lil' Red." Arima was stating as her ebony frame hovered in the living room of the estate.

"Shhhhhhhh, give it a moment," Maddy whispered to her husband who was silently hiding with her in Arima's soul. "We don't want her know that we're already here or that we already know what's going on."

"Lil' Red, this is Soul Sister. We have another JQ situation. Please come in," Arima stated again as the frantic eyes of Adam, Aaron, Kayla, and Rachel looked on. Their children had explained to them that they would be going away on missions. The distraught parents knew that these missions would take their children into the past. But that knowledge did little to assuage their deep worry. Their children were gifted and formidable. But to them, they were still just children who were capable of being harmed. Kayla and Rachel sobbed on the white-coated shoulders of their respective husbands as they anxiously awaited Maddy's response.

"And *this* t-t-time, s-s-she had b-better not be a b-*bitch* about it," Kayla stammered as tears flowed from her mahogany eyes.

"What the *fuck*, man?" Maddy whispered to her husband. "*I'm* the one that's their connection in Enlightenment. *I'm* the one who sent Uncle Joe to go *get* their little brats. And *this* is the thanks I get? Fuck this."

Erick gave his wife a look. It was a look that she was familiar with. It was the look that her beloved husband would give her when he was unable to say, *Maddy, I love you. But calm the fuck down. You are once again overreacting. Get your emotions under control and listen to the situation. And don't be overly judgmental. These people have come to you for your help. And you will give it to them. And you will be gracious about it. Got it?*

All of that was said by just one brief look, so Maddy replied, "Yeah, yeah, yeah, I got it. Okay. Let's go. Hey there Soul Sister! This is Lil' Red at your service! Over and out! Wazzup? Over and out!"

There was a sigh of relief from the group in the living room as they heard Maddy's voice emitting through Arima. "Uh, yeah, hi Madd... um...I mean Lil' Red. So, the JQ's kinda missing again and we were wondering if Uncle Joe had taught you how to go back in time and get them yet? Or if there's someone else that could go? I understand that after something like that, that you spirits are really drained, so Uncle Joe probably isn't available. But could maybe you or Erick or somebody go pick them up and bring them home? Oh, and again, you don't have to yell or say, 'over and out' after every sentence, okay?"

"Roger that! Over and out!" Maddy yelled back as her husband silently shook his head in bewilderment. "Hey everybody! Nice to talk to ya again! Over and out! I'm gonna get Erick so he can hear too, okay? Over and out! Erick, come here and listen to this!"

"Oh, hey everybody," Erick greeted awkwardly. "I just got here. I haven't been listening in at *all*. What's going *on*? *I* don't have a *clue*."

Maddy looked at her husband and mouthed, *what the fuck are you doing?* Erick could only shrug back in response.

"Hey, Erick, nice to talk to you," Arima replied. "So, as I was just telling Maddy, um, I mean Lil' Red, the JQ has gone back in time again on one of their missions and the twins and the Twins are really upset. Rosa and Jessie have found them. So, do you guys think someone could go back in time and get them?"

There was silence. Erick looked at his wife. They both knew that their response would have to be delicate. They both knew that Maddy could not fuck this up. Erick took no chances and replied before his wife. "Um, hey, we still haven't been trained on that, so we won't be of any help. And Joe's still pretty tuckered out from the last time, so…"

Erick was cut off by his wife. "Uncle Joe is *what? Tuckered out?* Who the fuck talks like that, man?" She then said with a contrived sweetness, "Oh, your little *darlings* are *missing* again? Well, *of course* we would be *delighted* to help you. We know just how *precious* those little *miracles* are and we will do *everything* we can to bring them back home safely, *won't we baby?"*

"Maddy, let me handle this, please," a frustrated Erick replied. "As I was saying, we don't know how to do that yet and would probably do more harm than good. And Joe isn't an option because he's *tuckered out.* But I think that Blair and Patty could do it. I'll do all the paperwork and submit it to Gwen then go talk to them. I'm sure that they will be happy to help, okay?"

"Yes, thank you Erick," Adam stated followed by Aaron's, "Yes, thank you. You are much more civil with us than Aunt Maddy. Thank you."

"Yeah, fuckin' whatevs," Maddy replied in disgust. "We'll go find someone to help your fuckin' brats. Let's go Erick. Over and out!"

CHAPTER 102
PRECIOUS LITTLE MIRACLES

"What the *fuck* do you want?" Patty yelled out. "I've got my face buried in my wife's snatch! Then we're going to conjure up some old *Warner Brothers* cartoons and eat potato chips! Come back in an hour, or whatever the fuck an hour is up here! Now, go away! Damn. Angel pussy tastes good…like cotton candy…mmmmmmmmm."

"Patty, my dear sister," Blair answered calmly from outside the door of the conjured bedroom. "I am truly sorry to disturb you dear, but we are needed on Earth for a bit. So please wipe your mouth, get dressed, and come out."

Blair heard Patty's wife, Jacklyn, say, "It's okay, lover. We have an eternity together. Just go see what your sister wants." Blair then heard a grunt of disgust followed by her sister's booming, irritated voice. "Fine! But this had better be fuckin' important!"

Jacklyn covered her naked frame with conjured blankets as Patty threw open the bedroom door. "Alright Blair," Patty stated as she stood in the doorway wearing a sheer black robe. "You got me. What's so fuckin' important?"

"Well," the raven-haired Blair began in her customary cool tone. "It seems as though the JQ have once again traveled through time to assassinate one of Vetis's targets for manipulation. And we have been tasked with finding them and bringing them back to their distraught parents.

So please, Patty, put on something more appropriate. I don't think that you want the children to see you dressed like this."

"Alright Blair," Patty responded. "But I have a few questions first before I leave my little revved-up piece. First, why the fuck can't *Joe* go get them?"

"Because, my dear," Blair began to calmly explain, "these little adventures are quite taxing on us. Joseph just completed a mission, and he is too fatigued at the moment."

"Oh yeah?" Patty retorted. "Well, what about Maddy or her pussy husband? Why can't *they* go do it?"

"Because," Blair once again began explaining, "Maddy and Erick have not been in Enlightenment long enough. They do not yet possess the knowledge or spiritual energy required for this."

"Well, if the little fuckers can travel through time," Patty resisted, "Why can't they just find their way back when they're done doing whatever fucked up shit that they're doing? Why does *anyone* have to go get them?"

"That *is* a good question," Blair answered. "They *can* find their way back. They can travel to their destination, take care of their business, and find their way back home. But they are children. And children can become distracted or find other forms of trouble that they may not be prepared for. They are quite powerful, but we do not yet know just *how* powerful or what they might be vulnerable to. Plus, their parents are quite worried about them, just as any parent would be. They just want to know that their children are safe. Do you remember when Maddy disappeared in the year 2000 when she was twelve?"

"Yeah, I remember that," Patty answered sentimentally. "Man, was she pissed about that election. All she could talk about was having to do something about those fucking hanging chads on the Floria ballots. She just kept asking how something as insignificant as a little piece of paper could cause such significant damage. Her little mind was blown by it. She was *obsessed* by that shit."

"Yes, she was," Blair replied. "She stewed on that for hours that night, then she just disappeared. And although we knew your niece and our spiritual daughter was quite formidable, even at *that* age, we still worried about her whereabouts, didn't we?"

"Yeah," Patty conceded. "I don't think I've *ever* been so worried about someone. You called me up and said that you and Joe couldn't find her anywhere. I rushed over and we searched the entire house again. Then the neighborhood. Hell, we even called Detective Simmons to put an APB out on her. Yeah, I remember how frantic we were that night. I guess I can understand what the twins and the Twins are feeling. Alright Blair. Let's go get the little bastards. But I'm sure they're fine. Just like Maddy was. We finally found her in the one place that we had forgotten to look. In the crawlspace behind her bedroom wall. All curled up and sleeping with her blue baby blanket."

"Yes," Blair added. "And a butcher knife. If that wasn't foreshadowing, I don't know what is. She was desperately clinging to the innocence of her youth while embracing what would be her quite violent future. That moment was her crossroads and she looked so sweet and dangerous at the same time. She, Patty, was our precious little miracle. Just as the JQ are precious little miracles. Now, let's summon Gwen so that she can track them and lead us to their exact location."

"Yeah, let's go see what kind of carnage these *precious little miracles* have caused," Patty replied before asking, "just where and when are we going anyway?"

Blair looked into the blue eyes of her sister and said, "We are going to the outskirts of Phoenix, Arizona. March 29, 1972."

———

There was a brilliant flash of light followed by a dense, red fog in the middle of the Arizona desert. The skyline of downtown Phoenix was barely visible on the vast horizon. Four tan-skinned children wearing all-white western costumes emerged from the dense crimson mist riding their respective Shetland ponies.

"There's a new sheriff in town, heh, heh, heh," Sigourney stated before being interrupted by her sister, Euna. "No, like this! There's a *new* sheriff in town, heh, heh, heh."

"Neither one of you two are doing it right!" Kane yelled out to his identical twin cousins. "We have to get this right. Just think about how Aunt Maddy told us *she* said it after their battle on Highway 61. Just think about that night that Aunt Maddy came into our dreams and told us that bedtime story. It was like this. There's a new *sheriff* in town, heh, heh, heh. See? Then it'll be funny!"

"I don't think *that's* quite right either," a contemplating Sigourney replied. "Thanatos, what do *you* think? Thanatos? Hey, where the hell is he? Oh, dammit."

The trio stopped and looked behind them. Twenty yards to their rear was Thanatos. He was excitedly rushing from cactus to cactus and placing them in his mouth before yelling out, "Ow! That one doesn't taste good *either*! Ow! Nope, not *that* one. How about *this* one? Ow!"

"Thanatos!" Sigourney yelled out. "Stop putting stuff in your mouth and get back here. We're rehearsing what we're going to say to this guy when he opens the door. We must rehearse so that it'll be really funny! And we're almost up to his shack!"

"Okay," Thanatos replied as he reluctantly climbed onto the back of Snot and rejoined his male twin sibling and twin female cousins. "I don't know why you girls are rehearsing anyway. Only Kane and I can say that. Girls can't be a sheriff."

"What?" Sigourney and Euna roared back in unison. "What the hell are you *talking* about? Girls can do just *as much*, if not *more*, than boys!"

"No, you can't," Kane replied. "Girls can't be cow*boys* now, can you? You can only be cow*girls*. And cow*girls* are supposed to do stuff for the cow*boys*. You know, like do our laundry and cook for us and clean our bedroom. Stuff like that. And a cow*girl* certainly cannot be a sheriff. That is what we have learned."

Sigourney and Euna seethed before Euna bellowed out, "Just where in the hell did you learn *that*? It's 2042! Girls can do *anything* that boys can do! Anything! Including sheriff! And not only *that*, but the two of *you* can do *our* laundry and cook for *us* and clean *our* bedroom! Just like Uncle Lionnel does for Aunt Josie!

"Nope," Thanatos added. "That's not how it works. We've been watching old cow*boy* movies. And *those* things are true! And the cow*boy* is *always* the sheriff, and the cow*girl* is *always* doing the cleaning and getting the cow*boy* drinks. That's a fact!"

Euna's blue and brown eyes began glowing with rage. She shook her white, shoulder-length locks, composed herself and said, "We'll deal with this later. We're coming up to this guy's shack. Let's get off our ponies here and walk up and look in the windows. I want to see the layout before we knock on the door."

The Junior Quad were quietly giggling as they stealthily climbed onto the front porch and peered through the dusty windowpane. They held their hands over their delighted little mouths to stifle their laughter as they watched the man inside the run-down hovel.

"I *told* you, you were a fuckin' idiot Charlie!" the scruffy, skinny man was yelling at a small black and white television set with bent rabbit ears. "I *knew* I was right to get away from your fuckin' cult when I did! Murdering Hollywood stars ain't *no way* to start this race war! You gotta be more *subtle* about it. And that's just what I'm gonna do! I'm gonna get my *own* followers! Then we'll infiltrate the police. Have them plant shit on the Black Panthers. Have them go around and murder ordinary White families and pin it on the Panthers. In small town after small town, we'll get the sheriffs there on our side. We'll elect like-minded people to the city councils. Then, we'll just take out a few families, blame the Panthers, and White folks all over the country will rise up against those fuckin' (derogatory term omitted). It'll start in the small towns, then move to the big cities. There's gonna be Black blood running in the streets. Then, we'll come for the (derogatory term omitted) and the (derogatory term omitted) and the (derogatory term omitted). All I need to get started is for somebody to show me the way. Whisper in my ear. I've heard of a demon named Vetis. I'm gonna pray to him. Pray that he can show me the way. Then, I'll begin building my army. My army of cops and crooked politicians and egotistical media types. Then, my army of ordinary White folks who will be so brainwashed that they'll take to the streets and start killin' every (derogatory term omitted) that they see!

"Yep, that's how I'm gonna do it. Then, I'll be powerful. I'll have the money I deserve and the hippie pussy that I deserve. And I won't be sittin' on death row like *you've* just been sentenced to! Yep, you're gonna fry Charlie boy. Not because your ideas were bad. But because you were stupid. So, here's to you Charlie! Here's to giving me the right idea! And here's to you for teaching me the wrong way to go about it!"

The man held up a bottle of whiskey and took a big swig just before he heard a light rapping on his rotting wooden door.

"Now who the fuck can *that* be?" he asked himself as he stomped toward the door. He pulled it open and looked around. He saw nothing until he heard giggling coming from below him. He looked down and saw a quartet of snickering tan children dressed in outlandish white, fringed cowboy and cowgirl outfits. He stood confused as he listened to the children bicker amongst themselves.

"*I* want to say it!" Sigourney cried out before being interrupted by Kane. "No, we already *told* you. Cow*girls can't* say it! *I'm* gonna say it!" Thanatos pulled a cactus from the side of the porch and put it in his mouth. He then said. "Ow! No, *I'm* gonna say it with my brother! Only cow*boys* can say it!"

"What the hell are you freaky kids talkin' about?" the man said in disgust. "Say *what*? And what the fuck are you doin' here? Get back to your reservation or wherever you belong and leave me alone!"

The four children stopped their arguing, looked up at the man and said in unison with their innocent voices, "There's a new sheriff in town, heh, heh, heh."

"That wasn't right," Sigourney lamented. "That wasn't *nearly* as funny as when Aunt Maddy said it. Who is a *girl* by the way!"

"Aunt Maddy was probably just confused," Kane stated bluntly. "And it wasn't right because *you two* said it! And cow*girls* don't know how to say it because cow*girls* can't be a sheriff!"

"Oh, just stop your bickering and let's do this," Euna said as she pulled a knife from her holster and split the man's abdomen open. The man let out a tortured scream as he fell to his knees and felt his intestines begin to tumble out of his body, sploshing onto the wooden porch. Thanatos took the cactus he was holding and shoved it into the man's open mouth. Kane then took a rope and tied it firmly around the man's head and chin to secure the spiked cactus in place.

Sigourney looked at the slimy intestines laying upon the ground and said to her sister, "Hey. I think I've got an idea."

"Well, *this* is a fuckin' mess!" Patty bellowed out as her black leather-clad form appeared next to the shack.

"Yes," a bell-bottomed, T-shirt wearing Blair agreed. "I believe that we have found them. But what on God's green Earth are they doing?"

Blair and Patty walked to the front of the shack and saw a man attempting to scream out of his punctured, bloody mouth. He was lying on his back on the ground and his intestines had been pulled from his cavity. Blair and Patty's eyes followed the trail of slimy entrails until they fell upon a delightfully disgusting sight. Euna was on top of Kane who was laying on his belly and had been hog-tied by the grotesque, rancid smelling intestines. Sigourney was in the same position over the similarly situated Thanatos. The twin girls were yelling at their male cousins.

"Say it, Kane!" Euna was screaming as her sister echoed, "Yes! Say it Thanatos!"

"No, we *won't* say it! It isn't *true!*" Kane and Thanatos responded.

"Then we're going to tighten these intestines until you say it!" Euna threatened. "And it's going to hurt!"

"We *won't* say it!" Kane yelled back. "And we're going to tell our parents! You're going to be in trouble!"

"We don't care!" Sigourney screamed. "Just say it so we can go home!"

"So, what is all this then, dears?" Blair asked.

"Hi Aunt Blair! Hi Aunt Patty!" the foursome replied in their sweet voices before Sigourney began explaining. "You see, Aunties, Kane and Thanatos said that cowgirls can't be sheriffs just because we're girls. So, we tied them up with these intestines and are holding them down until they say that we *can* be sheriffs."

"Why, you sexist little pricks," Patty blurted out before Blair held up a single index finger to silence her sister. "Please Patty, let me handle this." Blair had to turn away for a moment to hide her chuckle from the children before beginning. "I see. Well, it seems to me that those are some very outdated ideas, boys. You see, girls are just as capable as boys are. Perhaps more so. There are no roles that are exclusively male or female. Men can be whatever they wish and so can women. And that goes for little girls as well. And that includes being a sheriff."

"No! That can't be true Aunt Blair!" the resistant Thanatos yelled out. "That's not what the cowboy movies taught us! Cowgirls can't be a sheriff so they can't say that they're the new sheriff in town! That's just how it is, and I won't say that they can!"

"Well, I suppose that we're in for a long wait then," Blair replied calmly. She then knelt in front of the struggling Thanatos and lifted his head until his obstinate eyes met hers. Blair lowered her voice and said coldly, "Because these two girls are going to sit on you and tighten those intestines until your little arms break. That is, unless you say that girls can be sheriff. And I believe that Patty and I may have a little chat with your parents once you are home."

Thanatos gulped hard and looked over to his twin brother. They nodded at one another then said meekly, "Girls can be sheriff."

Ten minutes (Earth time) later there was another brilliant flash of light and the demonic spirits of Vetis and Gobbo peered down at the horrific scene. Gobbo began trembling as he looked at the frozen fearful face of the fresh corpse that was being torn apart and eaten by ravenous vultures. A despondent Vetis sighed deeply and said, "Y'know. Those fuckin' kids are *really* starting to piss me off."

Following another joyful family reunion and parental consultation with Patty and Blair, Euna and Sigourney were sitting on the couch in their pajamas watching *Stan vs. Evil*. "See?" Sigourney shouted out to a long-faced Kane who was coming downstairs with a loaded laundry basket. "*This* show is on TV and *this* show has a *girl* sheriff. So there."

Euna then barked out, "Thanatos! Where are our grilled cheese sammiches?"

"Coming right up!" an apron wearing Thanatos answered. He entered the living room of the estate and presented his cousins with two plates containing jellybeans, popcorn, pretzels, and... two half-eaten grilled cheese sandwiches.

CHAPTER 103
POSITIVE BLEEDING

"How about this?' a pink-robed Jessie West excitedly asked her best friends Arima Azan and Jamie Johnson.

"Oh sweetie," Jamie responded while shaking her thick afro in disapproval. "That would be fine for a slutty New Year's party, but for the United Nations? I think you may want to tone it down a bit."

"Yeah, you're probably right," the bubbly influencer replied. "Okay, how about this?"

"Jess," Arima answered casually. "That looks just like the last one, but without the sequins. Here, let me look. I'll find you something."

Arima lazily rolled off the bed, strolled over to the closet and began digging around. "Here, try this one on."

Jessie and Jamie burst out laughing at the suggestion. "Oh, my lord!" Jamie yelled out through her chortles. "A jogging suit? For the United Nations? Ladies, please get out of my way. I know that I've only had my official lady parts for a few weeks, but whether I had a cock or a cooch, I've always known how to dress for success. Now, let's see here. What to wear to make a good impression at the United Nations. Hmmmmm. Oh, yes. Come to Momma. I'm going to have to borrow this from you dear."

Jessie and Arima could only smile and nod in approval as they looked upon the grey, pinstriped business suit with a smart white shirt and wide, black tie. Jessie enthusiastically grabbed the outfit from her friend's grasp and skipped to the bathroom.

Cliff West's jaw dropped as he saw his beautiful blonde wife strut into the living room in her form-fitting suit and four-inch black pumps. Arima plopped onto the couch next to her husband, Marcus Jefferson. They giggled at each other and proceeded to rip open a bag of corn chips. "Good, we're all here," Chadwick Gregory Davenport III, who had been advised many years earlier to go by 'Gregory' within this group, began.

He got up from his seat next to his loving wife, Rosa Alavarez, and turned to face this motley crew of a delegation. "Okay folks. We knew this day would come. We knew that the forces of evil would rear their dark heads once again and that we would have to report what we know to the United Nations. I just didn't think that it would be this soon after our incredible victory over the demonic forces of Vetis both on Earth and in Enlightenment. Enlightenment seems to be at peace and unthreatened at the moment. That isn't true here on Earth. Vetis is not going to give up. His ego won't allow it. He can't stand losing and he can't just be happy lording over his own little slice of hell in the universe. His ego has been bruised, so he will keep trying. And every time he tries, there's definitely a chance that he will succeed.

"He is now going back through time, searching for a new Earthly messiah that he can groom. A new man who was destined to die before 2016 but will now stay alive to lead a parallel movement to the one that we just defeated. Yes, my friends, we may have defeated him in the present, but he has the power to go back into time and *alter* our present. And our future. Everything that we have accomplished may be undone if he is successful.

"The Junior Quad can somehow sense when he has selected such a person, and they can go back into time and kill his target before he gets there. But we do not know if they will be capable of doing this every time. Just one mistake made by these children, and all could be lost. And he can do this for eternity. Hundreds, thousands of times. Until he finally achieves his goal. The only solution is the destruction of Vetis himself and *that* we have no idea how to do. All we can do is hope that the JQ can continue to be successful against him while we take out the small pockets of the waiting, reconstituted United Autocratic Movement in our present time. All that we can do is fight battle after battle and tread water until we figure out a way to destroy Vetis.

"We are going to the United Nations today to give them our report. That was our deal with them. All the nations of the world will support us in our endeavors as best they can, but only if we are completely transparent with them. They want to know what we are doing and why we are doing it. We must give them this report today and ask for their support to continue the battle. But I sense there might be a problem."

"Yeah," Cliff chimed in. "We're getting a funny feeling about thi…"

Cliff was abruptly cut off by his wife. "Cliff! Don't interrupt Gregory. That was rude! Now go get me a glass of wine. I need to calm my nerves after the stress of picking out this outfit."

"Um, yeah, okay, okay," Cliff stammered as Jamie and Arima rolled their eyes and made vomiting faces at each other.

"Yeah, man," Marcus then stated partially to contribute to the conversation and partially to support his spineless friend. "You see, we have actually got a meeting with the entire United Nations. Like, everybody, man. But we have been told not to bring any security with us. And that makes us nervous. So, that's why you ladies are here. Jess, you can Behold if there are any purely evil souls there. Then, Rosa, Arima, Jamie, and we dudes can do what we need to do. It's just a little strange that we can't take security and we want to be cautious."

"Correct," Cliff agreed as he handed his wife her wine. "Cliff! Now you're interrupting Marcus? When did you get to be so rude?" Jessie admonished.

"Um, sorry," the beaten-down Cliff responded as his head dipped to the floor.

Gregory looked at his emasculated friend, shook his head slightly and continued. "Yes, that is correct. So, Jessie, you will let me know if you sense pure evil and from whom in the chamber. I will then give the report that I feel is…um…appropriate for the moment. Then, we'll report back to Josie, and she can give us our orders from there. Got it?"

"Cool," Jessie replied. "It seems as though *I'm* the most important one in this little grou…"

Jessie was cut off by the ever-diplomatic Gregory. "And Cliff, you have the *most* important role of all today. You are to keep your lovely

Beholder safe. *You* are the key to this mission's success. Okay folks. The car should be here at any moment. Let's get ready."

Gregory fronted his entourage of Arima, Marcus, Jamie, and Rosa, with Jessie and Cliff to his immediate left and right. They entered the vast United Nations auditorium and Jessie immediately buckled over and dropped the note cards that she was holding. "Oh, sweet Jesus," she whispered to her attending husband. "There is a *lot* of evil here."

"Just say it, Jess. Say it and make the pain go away," a concerned Cliff quietly responded.

As UN security personnel rapidly approached the pained Jessie, she whispered to herself, "Malum tuum dolorem facit. et dolor meus es fortitudo mea. (*Your evil causes pain. my pain is my strength*)."

"Is everything alright here, miss?" one of the security personnel inquired as he was reaching for his gun. Jessie's blonde head popped up as she righted herself. Her brilliant blue eyes were glistening in the bright white light of the auditorium as she said, "Yes. Just fine. In fact…" her voice trailed off as she gave Gregory a knowing glance. "In fact, I've *never* felt stronger. I just…um…dropped my note cards. I've been instructed to um…take notes during the proceeding."

"Very well then," the security guard replied as he and the rest of the security contingent returned to their normal posts. Gregory was introduced by the Secretary of the United Nations. He cleared his throat and approached the podium. Jessie laid the notecards in front of the microphone. On them, she had written the twenty-three names of the traitorous diplomats who were in the chamber.

Gregory looked down at the cards briefly, gave Jessie a slight smile of approval and began his presentation. Just before he began speaking, he decided to present option B. "Hello esteemed dignitaries from around the world. Thank you so much for this opportunity to speak with the entire assembly. I promise not to take up too much of your valuable time, but it has been a little over a month since our glorious victory over the forces of the demonic Vetis, and we promised to keep this body updated as to the status of his threat against us. And I am very pleased to report that…everything is fine. We have not detected any threat from Vetis himself. As we all know, there will always be evil in the world. But our current assessment is that Vetis is not currently engaged in any interference here on Earth. There remain pockets of his followers, but they are currently small and pose no threat to the people or great nations of the world. Our newfound humanity and mutual cooperation are beginning to reap rewards. In every nation on the planet, we are seeing people's lives improving. This is due to our sharing of resources. The sharing of technology. Medicine. Intelligence. Agricultural techniques. Conservation of our natural resources. The list goes on and on. And this sharing is no longer dependent upon past bigoted views of those who are different from ourselves. We no longer hate one another in large numbers. We no longer harbor the desire to eliminate those that we fear. Because we no longer *fear* one another. Because the vast majority of the demonic forces that were sowing this fear, then hatred, then violence amongst us have been neutralized. Yes, my friends, it is truly a glorious time to live upon this Earth. So, I am most happy to report that all is well. We will, of course, keep this body updated and will notify you should we need to take any action. But no action is required at this time. Thank you for your time and to your selfless contributions to mankind."

Gregory could not help but notice that the first dignitaries to stand for the ovation were the twenty-three names that Jessie had written on the notecards. Gregory smiled and waved goodbye as he thought, *Good. The remaining servants of Vetis think that we're in the dark. The bad news? We're going to have to go this alone.*

The party entered the underground parking garage toward their awaiting car in silence. Cliff heard a light 'click' from behind a parked vehicle. The former high-school football star instinctively jumped in front of his unaware wife. Jessie's pin-striped business suit was covered in her husband's blood as a bullet ripped through his abdomen.

"Cliff!" Jessie cried out as five heavily armed, black-clad men emerged from behind numerous parked vehicles. Arima took a hit off her "killer weed" and began floating above the scene, awaiting the dark souls that would emerge from the soon-to-be-former-assassins. Rosa's eyes began glowing. She focused all her energy on two men who were pointing their weapons at her. Their guns exploded the moment that they depressed the trigger, sending shards of metal and bullets into their shocked faces.

Jessie kicked her high heels toward Jamie, who caught them, did a back flip, and planted the heels into the eyes of an assassin.

"Eeeeewww!" Jamie exclaimed as she wiped eye pus from her recently enhanced bosom. An enraged Jessie then used her evil-enhanced strength to rush the final two assassins. She tackled them, stood above them, and began crushing their skulls with her bare feet. When she had finished, she looked down upon her perfectly pedicured toes standing in the chunky red, pink, and white remains.

Dark purple smog emanated from the five fallen bodies. Arima opened her soul and pulled them into her essence. She bound them within herself then floated out of the garage. Her journey ended over the glistening blue waters of the New York Harbor. "See ya, assholes," Arima said flatly as she hurled the dark souls into the serenity of Pastor Tim and Jeremy's watery home. The souls screamed in anguish and dissolved the moment they hit the calm waves.

"Cliff!" Jessie screamed out as she rushed to the side of her fallen husband. "He'll be okay!" Gregory yelled. "Marcus, get him in the car, then call Lionnel. I don't trust taking him to a hospital. Not now. We'll take him to the operating room under the bookstore. And we can't wait for Arima!"

"It's okay," Marcus replied as he lifted the body of his bleeding friend. "She can float back home. She's high as a kite right now. Literally."

"Soul Sister! This is Lil' Red! Come in, Soul Sister! Over and out!" Maddy yelled at her half-sister. "Oh, yeah, hey Madd…um…I mean Lil' Red. What's up?"

"Weeeellll," Maddy began. "I just saw that you took a hit off the killer weed *without* me and I'm feeling a little bit *left out*, that's all. I mean, I *know* I'm dead and everything but it's still nice to not be *forgotten*. But that's okay. I understand how *easy* it is to forget about me. Over and out."

"Oh yeah, sorry Lil' Red," Arima responded. "Here. I'll take another hit so you can have some too. Better?"

"Oooooooh yeah," Maddy cooly answered. "That's the stuff. Ooooover and oooout."

Jessie held the head of her bloodied husband and wept as their car sped toward the Brooklyn bookstore. She sat there in shocked disbelief and prayed. She prayed that they would make it to Lionnel on time. She prayed for Cliff to have a speedy and full recovery. And she vowed to the universe that if her prayers were answered that she would *never* take his love for her for granted ever again.

Josie was sitting behind the desk in her mother's eclectically designed office beneath the bookstore talking to Rod when Gregory entered the room.

"Oh, hey Gregory!" Josie enthusiastically stated. "How did the UN presentation go? Everybody cool with supporting us?"

"Well…" Gregory began. He then paused and noticed that as Rod was speaking with Josie, his eyes were firmly planted on…her eyes. Gregory felt slightly relieved as the pressure of knowing just which Josie he was speaking with dissipated. He then presented Josie and a relaxed Rod with the details, including the injury to Cliff.

"But I'm sure he'll be okay. Lionnel has him in the operating room next door. I think it'll be fine."

"Well, that's good news," Josie responded before saying, "Soooo, you say *Lionnel's* here? Cool. Cool. Yep. That's cool. I probably shouldn't bother him while he's operating. Just, y'know. If you *happen* to see him, *maybe* just tell him I said 'Hi.' Y'know. Or don't. It doesn't matter. It's all cool. Okay, so let's do *this*. Let's get Sam and Jules ready to take out that small group in Indiana. I know they're small, but I think we want to keep the pressure on these fuc…I mean these *people*. But let's do it quietly. Bloody, of course, but quietly. We don't want to tip the diplomats off that we're up to anything. Nope. Looks like we're going to have to go this alone. In the meantime, my brilliant friend Rod and I have been discussing some tests that we can run on the JQ. We think that if we hook some electrodes up to their little brains, and Rosa taps into their energy, we might be able to collect some information about just how much power they posses and whether they can destroy Vetis. Oh, and could one of you ask Alexa when she thinks her art show will be ready? I *might* just have an idea. Yup, sooooo that's the plan. So, you say *Lionnel's* here, huh? Well, *that* doesn't matter. He's so busy. Okay. I have some work to do with Larry, so thanks you two. I truly appreciate everything that you contribute."

Josie gave Rod a large hug followed by Gregory. As Josie was embracing him, Gregory whispered into her ear, "Glad to have you back, kid." Josie whispered back, "Thanks. I'm trying. It feels good to be myself again."

Josie watched her colleagues exit the room then turned her flowered dressed form towards Larry. His battered and lacerated body was sitting pathetically on his stumps with his neck chained to an anvil.

"Okay, Larry," Josie began. "I need to run my plan by somebody. Since you can't talk because we ripped out your tongue, just nod or shake your head if you think that this will work. Okay, here it goes. Man, I'm so nervous.

"JOSIE PARKER'S PLAN TO WIN LIONNEL BACK
BY JOSIE PARKER

Numero-Uno: Um, nope. Not gonna say that. My mother says that and since Lionnel thinks that I've become too much like my mother, I think I'll go in another direction. Let's start again.

"JOSIE PARKER'S PLAN TO WIN LIONNEL BACK
BY JOSIE PARKER

Step One: Heh, heh, heh. Yeah, that's better."

CHAPTER 104

CRUSH ON YOU

"Is it me, or does it seem as though Murder, Inc. is getting increasingly female-centric?" Henri inquired of Gregory and Marcus as they were putting on their all-black outfits for the evening's mission in the dense woods of central Indiana. "I mean, it's great that they're really powerful and independent and everything, but it's starting to make me feel a bit emasculated being no more than a chauffeur. I'm a trained sniper. I have more to offer than being a cab driver. And why do you need to even be there, Gregory? You don't like getting your hands dirty. They easily could have sent one of the hitmen…um… I mean *assassination technicians* to fill in while Cliff recuperates."

"Well," Gregory began explaining. "I have been called in because Josie likes to have her most trusted members of her inner circle to run point on these operations. And as far as this organization being female-centric…well…I guess that's just something that *all* of mankind, and I do mean *man*kind, is going to have to deal with. Females are evolving at a much more rapid pace. They are evolving to use a greater amount of their brain capacity than we are. And that, my friends, is giving women great powers. My Rosa's ability to manipulate and enhance energy is just one example. Lucy's ingenuity. Maddy's fierce tenacity and ability to cultivate loyalty despite her rather, um, *interesting* personality traits. Arima's entire family lineage. Jules's ability to communicate with felines. Josie's intellect. They are evolving and becoming much more powerful than us, my friends, and *that* is something that we may as well accept if any of us want to get laid ever again."

"I think it's cool, man," a grinning Marcus contributed. "It's like being married to a superhero. Y'know, dress up in cute blue shorts and a red corset. Then tie me up with a rope and make me tell the truth and shit."

"We really don't need to know about the role-plays that you do with your wife, Marcus," Henri scolded.

"Naw, man," a chuckling Marcus countered. "We don't do *that*. It *would* be fun, though. Naw, what *we* do usually is Arima has me dress up in a fast-food restaurant uniform. And the bed is like the fast-food counter. Then, she comes in wearing something sexy and pretends to be a customer and orders a *really big* cheeseburger with *special sauce*. Then I…"

Marcus was abruptly cut off by Gregory. "Yeah, okay. We get the picture. It's a picture that I definitely never wanted in my head, but there it is. For all eternity. Now that I know that I'll go to Enlightenment and exist forever, I can thank you for always having that image emblazoned in my mind."

"You're welcome!" Marcus yelled out as he gave Gregory a firm slap on his back. "You think the ladies are ready yet? Let's go knock on their hotel room door and see if they're ready to go.

The trio of friends opened their door and gasped. Standing in front of them were the all-white suited Adam and Aaron. "Uh, hey guys," a surprised Gregory stated. "What are *you* doing here?"

"Well," Adam began explaining. "Rachel and Kayla told us that it was rude to knock on a closed door when you know someone is dressing." "Yes," Aaron contributed. "Quite rude indeed. They said that someone may be playing 'Hide the Sausage' or something and that we should not disturb them. So, we have been waiting here in the hallway until someone emerged from their room."

"Okaaaay," Gregory replied as he attempted to find the right words. "So, you have just been standing out here in the hallway? For how long?"

"Oh, about two hours," Adam replied. "Yes," Aaron added, "We have been standing here for about two hours and greeting all the other hotel guests who are staying on this floor. We say hello and offer candy to the children."

"Yes," Adam then took over. "We are quite pleasant. We smile, say hello, and offer candy to the children. But no child has taken our candy, and their parents seem quite rude. They just rush by us and go into their hotel rooms."

"Ah, shit," Henri stated as he ran his brawny hand down his face in disbelief. "Yeah, let's get you guys out of this hallway. And, *I'll* knock on the door. It's…um…okay if they're expecting you."

"Well, that is a new rule," Adam stated followed by Aaron's, "Yes, quite new. I never realized that there were so many rules for knocking on doors. We must start writing these rules down, brother."

Henri could only shake his head and whisper "Wow," to himself as he lightly rapped on the adjacent door. "Um, you ladies decent in there?"

"Yeah, we're coming. Keep your pants on," a surly Jules replied. Adam then said, "Oh, are we supposed to remove our pants? Did Rachel and Kayla come here to surprise us?" "Yes!" Aaron excitedly added. "Perhaps they have come here to play a surprise game of 'Hide the Sausage!' Oh, how fun."

"No boys, no," Marcus started explaining as Jules opened the door and said, "C'mon in."

"And leave our pants on, right?" Aaron inquired.

Jules just stared at him with a disgusted look on her face before saying, "Yeah. Why would you even *ask* that? Why are you two so *fucking weird*? Must have gotten it from your father, Jason. I always was a bit suspicious of him. Now get your asses in here. And why are you two even *here*?"

"Oh, well," Adam began. "You see, we have been unable to play our games for awhile and Rachel and Kayla said, now what was it they said exactly brother?" Aaron responded with, "They said that we needed to get out of the house and play our games because we are driving them fucking nuts. So, here we are to play games with you. Also, we were hoping to bring four of these men back to the estate alive."

"Why?" Jules asked. She immediately received a two-word response from the Twins who answered in unison, "Home schooling."

Jules shook her brunette head and said, "Yeah, I don't wanna know. Just come in."

Upon entering the room, Henri saw that his beloved wife was dressed in her all-black cat suit. "Sam, why are you dressed like that?" he inquired.

"Why do you think?" Sam answered. "I'm here on this mission. This is my mission attire. You know that. Why so surprised?"

"No, no, no," Henri replied tersely. "You are *not* going on this mission. This mission is in the dense forest. How the hell are you going to get your wheelchair down there? No, I'm sorry my love, but you simply aren't built for this mission. You are not going. You will stay here in the hotel, then we will all go out for a celebratory dinner. My decision is final. I am putting my foot down."

"I see," the quietly seething Sam replied. "Well, it must be *nice* to be able to put your foot down."

"Now, Sam, I didn't mean it like tha…" Henri was abruptly cut off by his wife. "Yes, it must be quite nice indeed. Do you know what I miss the most about losing the use of my legs? Dancing. I loved to go dancing. Me, along with Maddy, Lucy, Jules, and Kristy would go out dancing almost every weekend. I had moves. I was never one for much attention, but I just loved knowing that all eyes were on my shapely legs while I was on the dance floor. And the only time that I felt almost normal was the night of Josie's sixteenth birthday party and you lifted me from my chair, and we danced together. I almost felt normal at that moment. Almost. Then, that feeling was washed away by the tragedy of Erick being knifed in the back. By Kristy, as it turned out.

"I miss the use of my legs. But what is even worse, is that every time I look down upon them, I am reminded of the hell that I went through. The rape. The beatings. The severing of my spine which has left me in this chair permanently. It all comes back. Every time you help me put on my pants. Or pajamas. Or use the restroom. Every time you put a pair of useless shoes on my paralyzed feet, that horror comes back to me. That is why I have my new Pogo. I can put a cigarette out on his head, or stick him with a knife, or beat his sexist face with brass knuckles. Then, I feel better.

"So, I do not need you to remind me that I cannot put my foot down. I do not need you to remind me of my physical limitations. And I most *certainly* do not need you to tell me what I am capable of doing. I am a fully grown woman of fifty-four. I have been on many of these missions, and it will be *my* decision and *my* decision alone as to what missions I go on. Henri, I love you. You are the only man that I have truly loved. And you are a good man. And I understand that even the best of men can make a mistake. But you will listen to me carefully. Telling me what I cannot do because of my paralysis is a mistake that you will *never* make again. And don't worry about the forest. I'll be able to navigate through that just fine."

The temperature in the room seemed to plummet as a cold silence enveloped the space. Everyone was either looking down at the floor or up to the ceiling. The silence lasted for what seemed to be an hour until Aaron said, "Well, it appears everyone is dressed." "Yes," Adam added. "You all appear to be dressed. Is it time to play some games?"

"Yeah, let's go play some fucking games," came Henri's angry response. Everyone piled into the large van, except for Jules and Sam who entered a small trailer that was hitched to its bumper. "Where are *they* going?" Gregory asked before hearing the metal door of the trailer slam shut. "I do not know, and I do not care at the moment," Henri answered coldly as he started the engine.

"Oh, joy!" Adam yelled out followed by Aarons, "Yes! Here we go! Oh brother! We finally get to play our games! Who are we playing with Gregory?"

Gregory let out a nervous chuckle before answering. "Well, boys, we are going after a small unit of the reconstituted United Autocratic Movement. There are several small pockets of them strewn around the country. These small units were held back by Vetis. They are his reserves. And they have been told to stand down and stand by and await his reinforcements. So, these pockets are just sitting in cabins in the woods, awaiting their orders. We are going to take as many of them out as we can before they can strengthen. There are fifteen of them at this location living in three small cabins. We'll get their attention, then do what we have to do. Arima will use Rachel and Kayla to track their dark souls later and dispose of them. They can't do any harm. Not in this small of a number, anyway. Plus, I guess she's helping Josie with some other top-secret mission tonight. Otherwise, she'd be here too."

The van was parked on a narrow dirt trail about one-half mile from three small cabins that could be seen through the dense brush. Jules exited the trailer and joined the rest of the group. "So, where is Sam?"

Henri asked in an uncaring tone. "Eh, she'll be out in a while," Jules replied. "C'mon. Let's go get these bastards."

"Okay, Jules," Rosa said as the group neared makeshift alarms that consisted of tin cans that were tied together on a string about three inches off the ground. "Take my hand. Focus on Sam's paralysis. Focus all your energy on what it must be like to not be able to move. To just lay there, helpless. Focus everything that you have on that. Now, boys, go get their attention."

Adam and Aaron began shaking the strings and clanging the tin cans together. "Hello, in there!" Adam yelled out. Aaron then shouted, "Yes! Hello! We are campers and we are lost! Could you please help us? How was that brother?"

"Oh, I believe that was quite good," Adam replied as they saw fifteen heavily armed camouflaged men rush out of the cabins. "Yes, they have responded. They must believe us to be campers. Oh, what a fun joke that we have played upon them."

The fifteen scruffy bearded men raised their rifles. One of them yelled out, "Hey! Get off-a our property! There's a trail about a half-mile up that-a way! Now git! Or else yer gonna have an ass full-a lead!"

Rosa's eyes began glowing red underneath her black hood as she absorbed all the focused energy from Jules. "What the fuck is *that* bitch doin'? Oh, fuck this! Fire!" the man yelled out before screaming, "What the fuck! I can't move!" There was then a chorus of men yelling out, "No! I can't either!" Hey! Why can't I move?" "What the fuck is that witch doing to us?"

"Wow, baby," Gregory said quietly to his wife. "Remind me to never piss you off. Okay, Henri, Marcus. You know what to do. Just go slit their throats and let's get back to the hotel."

There was the roar of an engine from behind them and the amplified voice of Sam saying, "I have a better idea!" They turned their heads and saw Sam's pretty, mature face looking out of the bulletproof windshield of a mini tank. The eight-foot long by four-feet wide metal box on treads came lumbering toward the paralyzed men. "Adam! Aaron! Pick out the ones you want to keep and make it quick! We don't want Rosa to use up all her energy!"

"Oh my!" Adam yelled out. "Why this is almost like trying to decide what to buy from a candy store!" "Oh, yes! This is quite fun!" Aaron answered as the pair sauntered through the brush and approached the terrified faces of the immobilized men. "How about this one, brother?"

"No, I don't believe so," Adam answered. "How about this one?" "Oh, yes!" Aaron exclaimed. "He will be quite perfect!" The pair then retrieved large ball peen hammers from white duffle bags that they were carrying and proceeded to slam them into the knees of the chosen man until there was a loud 'CRACK!' and the tortured man fell to the ground. A second man was selected and received the same demented treatment. Then a third, and finally a fourth. The four broken men lay on the ground screaming. Their screams intensified as they felt large metal hooks being thrust into their backs and into their spinal columns. "Oh, I do believe that we have found the most perfect classroom subjects, brother," Adam proudly stated. "Yes, quite perfect," Aaron agreed. "Our children will be able to learn much from them."

"Okay, boys," Sam began ordering. "Get them out of the way. I'm going to show you what games that I can play with *my* new toy." There was a thunderous bang as a small missile was launched from the tank's turret and exploded into one of the men. The forest was showered with blood and tiny pieces of bone and flesh. This was followed by the sound of rapid machine gun fire. One of the men's bodies convulsed violently as the bullets ripped him to shreds. The engine then revved up and Sam drove the tank toward the remaining nine men. They began desperately pleading as each one in turn felt the treads of the tank crush their feet. Then crush their legs. Then crush their torso. Then crush their head. There were eruptions of blood, bones, internal organs, and eyes that streamed across the forest as Sam drove over each man in succession. Once the screaming had stopped, Sam drove over all the crushed bodies one final time leaving them looking like the most grotesque and obliterated of roadkill.

Henri walked up to the idling tank and knocked on the top hatch. The hatch opened and he saw Sam's gratified face looking up at him. "Well," he began. "I know that you cannot physically stand, but I will never allow anyone, including myself, to ever tell you what you can't do. You are the most strong and capable woman that I have ever known. You are fully capable of standing up for *yourself*. I am sorry and I love you."

"I love you too," Sam replied with a slight, uncharacteristic tear in her eye. "Now just kiss me."

"Oh, fuckin' puke! You two are making me nauseous!" Jules yelled out. "Let's get these four hooked up to the tank and drag them back into the trailer. Then, let's eat. I'm kinda craving pulled pork for some reason."

Rosa rolled off the hotel bed and trudged her bloated body over to the phone. "Oh, my God," she lamented to Sam, Jules, Gregory, Marcus, and Henri. "I don't think that I'm ever eating again. That pulled pork was so good. All drippy with barbeque sauce. And that sundae with the crushed pineapple topping was to die for. I'm going to call Josie and let her know how things went.

"Yeah, hey Josie, it's Rosa. Yeah, it went fine. Sam crushed most of them with her new mini tank. Yeah, that's a good one Josie. They must have had a crush on her. Anyway, the Twins are on their way back to the estate with four alive ones. I don't know, they just said 'home schooling.' No, I have no idea what they meant. Oh, and I spoke to Rod yesterday and he thinks that he has the electrodes ready for our tests on the JQ. So, what are you and Arima up to tonight? Well, obviously Arima wanted pizza. What else? Oh, really? Well, okay. Good luck with that. We'll be home tomorrow. Bye."

"So, what are those two doing?" Henri asked. Rosa let out a deep sigh and said, "Oh, that poor girl. She's putting her plan to get Lionnel back into motion tonight."

"Hmmmm," Henri responded. "Lionnel loved that girl very much, but he is very headstrong. Once he puts his mind to something, then that is what he is going to do. Just like medical school. He is only twenty-one and is nearly complete with his studies. He is already such a gifted surgeon. Has been since he was a teenager. But he said that he would be finished with medical school by the age of twenty-two and he is going to do just that. And he says that he doesn't love Josie anymore and that he has moved on. All that I'm saying is that Josie might be better off doing the same. But she is as headstrong as my Lionnel. So, if she is determined to try this, then she needs to be *very careful* with how she proceeds. She must be *very tactful* or else she will drive him further away. She has such a crush on that boy. I would hate to see her blow this. She *cannot* come up with some impulsive, fly-off-the-handle, hair-brained plan like her mother used to do. That *will not* work on that boy."

CHAPTER 105
MIXED UP, SHOOK UP GIRL

"Um, Niece Josie?" Arima said as she walked into Josie's bedroom. Josie had just finished putting on a psychedelic polka dotted mini-dress, white go-go boots, and sparkling make-up as she turned to her aunt.

"Yes, Aunt Arima? Have you found anything out?" an anticipatory Josie asked.

"Uh, yeah," Arima answered. "Rod has found out what movie Lionnel is going to. But do you really think that this is the best move? I mean, why don't you just try to get him to go to coffee or something?"

"Oh, Aunt Arima, I love you, but you *obviously* don't know anything about men," Josie replied while chuckling. "No, this is like a *game* and we women have to be *smart* and *savvy* so that we can win. And we *win* by making men tap into their emotions. And what is one of the *strongest* emotions? Here, let me just read you Step 1:

"JOSIE PARKER'S PLAN TO WIN LIONNEL BACK
BY JOSIE PARKER

Step 1: Make Lionnel *jealous*, heh, heh, heh."

"Oh, wow, I didn't know that *you'd* be here, Lionnel!" Josie overacted as she, a hulk of a man, Arima, and their black-clad security detail of the twelve members of Rosa's Coven casually sauntered down the line outside of a movie theater. "Wow, it's *so good* to see you. So…um…who is *this* then?"

Lionnel let out a deep sigh and said in an uninterested tone, "Josie, this is my friend from medical school, Tabitha. Tabitha, this is Josie."

"Oh, well, *hello* there Tabitha!" Josie squealed as she embraced the young African-American med student. "It is *sooooo* nice to meet you! Any friend of *Lionnel's* is a friend of mine! Oh, and this rather *large* man here is Al. Al is the starting middle linebacker for the Jets. Say 'hi' Al."

"Uh, yeah, hi," a befuddled Al said as he encased Lionnel's hand within his and shook it firmly. "I was gonna go to medical school, but then I looked at how big the books are that you have to read, so I didn't. I don't read much. I really just got through college 'cause I was a big football star and my professors were told to give me a pass so that I could keep playing."

Josie burst out into contrived laughter. "Oh my, Al! You are *sooooo* funny! Always with the quips, this one. Yes, *Al* and *I* have become *quite* the item, *haven't* we Al? Just say 'yes' Al."

"Uh, yes, I guess," the perpetually perplexed Al replied. Lionnel shook his throbbing hand to shake off the pain and shook his head to shake off the disbelief of this most transparent attempt to make him jealous. "Okay, well I'm happy for you guys. Enjoy the movie and nice to see you, I guess." Josie's eyes glowed with jealous rage as Lionnel turned his attention away from her and renewed his conversation with Tabitha.

"Okay, yeah, you too!" Josie stated loudly. "Maybe we'll see you in there!" As Josie and her deadly entourage made their way to the back of the line, Josie said quietly to Arima, "Put that little bitch on my list."

"Um, Niece Josie?" Arima sheepishly replied. "Um, I really don't think that we can put someone on the assassination list just because she's seeing a movie with Lionnel. And, you know, that seems like something that your mom would do, and you want to get away from that, so maybe we should find another way."

"You're right Auntie Arima," Josie answered. "Of course, what was I thinking? The night is young. I don't need to *kill* this bitch to win

Lionnel back. Nope, we'll just let step one play out through the evening. I'm sure by night's end, he will be *so* jealous that he'll be *begging* for me to take him back."

Al wore a dullard expression on his face as he asked, "Um, Jealous? What do you mean by jealous? What kind of date is thi…"

Al was cut off by an overexaggerated Josie yelling out, "Oh, Al! You are *soooo* funny! I haven't met *anyone* that could make me laugh like *you* can!"

"Uh, what did I say that was funny?" Al asked. "Just shut up, Al," Josie said bluntly as her copper curls popped out from behind the tall man in front of her and she peered down the line to see what affect her latest performance had on her quarry. She scowled, popped her head back behind the tall man, folded her arms and said, "I don't even think he heard me. He's too busy talking to *Taaaabiiiithaaaa*. What a pukey fuckin'…I mean what a pukey name. It's okay. Just be cool Josie, just be cool. You're a genius. This plan is genius. I'm sure it's worked like, millions of times before. Just be patient. But what the hell are they laughing about?"

Tabitha and Lionnel began laughing together after she asked, "So, why didn't you tell her that we're not together. We're just friends and we're waiting for my boyfriend to join us."

"Yeah," Lionnel answered through his laughs. "It just isn't worth the time. And she's being so *ridiculous* right now, what with this 'Al' character. I know her. They aren't a couple. She probably had Rod find out where I'd be tonight, used her connections to arrange this so-called date and is now trying to make me jealous. But it won't work. I'm over her. I'm just not ready to…um…get back out there yet."

"Uh, huh," an unconvinced and smirking Tabitha responded.

The line began moving into the theater, and Josie lost track of her prey. She had also failed to notice a second young man who had joined Lionnel and gave *Taaaaabiiiithaaaa* a warm embrace. Every few seconds, Josie would bounce her five-foot-four (and a fucking half)-inch frame as high as she could go to get a better view of the front of the line, but to no avail. She had lost him, *Taaaaaabiiiiithaaaaa,* and Tabitha's recently arrived boyfriend.

"Fuck, I mean, damn, it's dark in here," Josie whispered as she scoured the dimly lit theatre for seats. She then heard a man say, "Oh, damn. I'm sorry. My pager just went off. I'm on call at the hospital and I've got to go, but you two stay and enjoy the movie, and I'll see you back at your place, okay?"

A young man scurried past Josie who turned her attention to the direction that he had come from. She turned to her entourage and said in a wicked, deep voice, "Folks, I think I've found our seats, heh, heh, heh."

Theater patrons began relocating to other seats to find refuge from the constant barrage of "Oh, *Al*, you're so funny!" "Oh, *Al*, please hold me! I don't *like* the sight of blood! It makes me feel *woozy!*" "Oh, *Al*, I've *never* been so scared in my life! I'm *soooo* glad that *you're* here to protect lil' ol' me!" "Oh, *Al*, watch your hands there, tiger! Maybe *later!*"

Josie's frustration intensified as the heads of Lionnel and *Taaaaabiiiithaaaa* just sat motionless and continued to face the screen. There was then a bright light that was shown in Josie's face. The theater manager said sternly, "Miss, I'm going to have to ask you to quiet down or else I'm afraid that I'm going to have to ask you to leave." He then saw the intensity in her glimmering green eyes and recognized her. "I mean, I'm so sorry to disturb you, Miss Parker. I believe that I've made a mistake. Please, enjoy the movie."

"Uh, huh, that's what I *thought*," Josie said to the hastily retreating manager before thrusting her head forward between the seats of Lionnel and *Taaaaabiiiithaaaaa*. "Hey, Lionnel. You want some candy?"

"Uh, no thanks Josie. I'm just trying to watch the movie," Lionnel replied with disinterest. "Come on, man!" Josie persisted. "This is your favorite! Sorry, *Taaaaabiiiithaaaa*, but there isn't enough to share with *you*. Come on, Lionnel. Have some."

Lionnel shook his head in disgust, turned to *Taaaaaabiiiithaaaa* and said, "Come on. Let's go. I think I know how this movie is going to end."

"Okay, nice to see ya! Don't be a stranger!" a desperate Josie shouted after the departing pair.

"So, where do you want to go later?" an oblivious Al asked. "And I kinda like it when you call me 'tiger.' That was the name of my high school football team. Hey, you wanna maybe wear a cheerleader outfit?"

"Fuck off, Al. Come on everybody. Let's go. This movie sucks," a furious Josie stated as she got up from her seat and proceeded toward the exit followed by a snickering and dismayed contingent of female bodyguards.

A confused and frustrated Al sat in the center of the row of now empty seats. He was about to get up and leave when he heard a soft, female's voice say from behind him, "*I've* got a cheerleader outfit. Wanna watch me...um...*cheer?*"

"Well, *that* didn't work," a pacing Josie stated as she nervously gnawed at her fingernails. "But not to fear, Aunt Arima! That's why I have a fool-proof five step plan!"

"Please, Niece Josie," Arima pressured as she took a long drag off her joint. "Just ask him to go to coffee or something. This isn't going to work."

"Yeah, it will," a determined Josie countered. "This is *totally* going to work. What do men like to do more than anything...um...well, *almost* anything. Play the *hero*, right? So, let me read you Step 2: Play the damsel in distress by doing that thing that Aunt Blair did one time. Now give me a hit off that joint."

Lionnel was casually walking toward the apartment that he shared with his father and stepmother when he heard a woman's voice cry out, "Ow! Oh, my *ankle*! I think I've broken my *ankle!*"

Lionnel instinctively turned around and immediately slapped his forehead in frustration. Josie was sitting on the sidewalk in the middle of a spilled grocery bag holding her right ankle. "Josie, what are you doing?"

"Oh, *Lionnel*," Josie answered in a helpless voice. "Oh, it's *so good* that you're *here*! I was just walking along, and I must have caught my pretty little feet on a crack or something. Could you *please* take a look at it? I think it might be *broken!*"

Lionnel glanced up at his third-floor apartment window and saw the snickering faces of his father, Henri, and his stepmother, Sam. He rolled his eyes and shook his head in disbelief at them before saying, "Josie, you do not need my help. You have twelve security guards right over there. And why are you grocery shopping in this neighborhood anyway? Just go home Josie."

"Well, b-b-but," Josie began desperately stammering, "Yeah, I've got the Coven with me but they don't know how to fix a broken *ankle*. And, well, I *like* the grocery store on the corner and, well, hey! Don't you walk away from me Lionnel! Not in my time of need! I'm *helpless*! Oh, *I* get it! You're probably in a hurry to call *Taaaaabiiithaaaa*! Right? Well, am I *right?*"

Lionnel opened the front door of his red brick apartment building, looked back at Josie blankly and said, "No, you are not right. And your ankle isn't broken. And you've never liked that grocery store. You always said that it's impossible to find anything in there. And finally, you are about as helpless as a starving man at an all-you-can-eat buffet. Just go home Josie."

A chuckling member of Josie's security detail turned to her colleague and said quietly, "You know, for a *genius*, she *really* isn't very good at this. But I guess even being a *genius* can't overcome the broken heart and immaturity of an eighteen-year-old woman."

"Well, *this* is just starting to piss me off," Josie said to Arima as she paced rapidly on her perfectly fine ankles while literally pulling at her auburn locks. "But it's okay! Only two steps down, three to go. And I've *very cleverly* planted the seed that he can be my hero. Yeah, this time it's gonna work."

"Niece Josie," Arima responded. "It didn't work this time and it won't work the next time. Please, just ask him to go to coffee so that you two can talk. Or a pizza parlor. Or a burger joint. One with *really good* fries. And sundaes. Hey, when you call him for coffee, can I tag along?"

"No, you may *not* tag along, Aunt Arima," Josie responded gruffly. "Because asking him out for coffee isn't going to work! Don't you understand? I have to *win* him back. Talking and communicating is overrated! I need to *trick* him into falling in love with me again! Here, listen to Step 3: If Step 2 doesn't work, play the damsel in distress again by doing that *other* thing that Aunt Blair did to get Uncle Joe. Now, hand me that phone. Oh, and that joint."

Lionnel answered his avocado green rotary phone. "Hello? What is it *now*, Josie? You have a frozen water pipe that has burst, and you need me to come over and fix it? Really? Well, I don't think that's true. For starters, it's nearly seventy degrees outside, so unless your home is sitting in the middle of some supernatural polar vortex, it is impossible for your pipes to be frozen. And you have an entire department of Murder, Inc. maintenance people at your disposal. They can install alarms, booby-traps, security gates, and a million other things. Hell, they just built my stepmom a mini tank! I'm pretty sure that *they* would be able to help you more than I. *Please,* Josie. Just stop. This is over. Please don't call here again. This *isn't* going to work." As Lionnel was hanging up the phone, he heard Josie's infuriated voice shout, "Well, it worked for my Aunt Blair! Lionnel! What? You can't leave in case *Taaaabiii-ithaaaa* calls? Lionnel! Don't you *dare* hang up on…"

"Huh. Well, son of a bitch," a dismayed Josie said as she hung up her pink cordless princess phone. Her green eyes began blinking rapidly and there was a noticeable twitch on the right side of her mouth. "Okay, okay, okay, not to worry. Just need to do Step 4: Do that thing from that movie. Arima, go get me my boombox and this CD from my dad's collection upstairs. Yeah, this is going to work. Because it has to. I really don't *want* to have to do Step five. But y'know, if I have to, then I *have* to. I don't *want* to, but…"

"Niece Josie," Arima interrupted. "You are driving yourself nuts. Just call him and ask him out for coffee and…" Arima paused for a moment as Josie's effervescent eyes glared at her intensely. "Okay. I'll get the boombox and CD. But this *isn't* going to work."

Lionnel was awoken by his father's banging on his bedroom door. "Lionnel, would you please get up and take care of this?" his father demanded as Lionnel wiped the sleep from his eyes. "Take care of what?"

Henri grabbed Lionnel by the collar of his pajamas and led him to the front window. "That," Henri said sternly before storming into the kitchen. "Oh, dammit," Lionnel muttered under his breath.

He opened the front window and Peter Gabriel's "In Your Eyes" came blaring from below. Josie was standing in the middle of the street wearing a grey trench coat and holding a boombox above her head. "Hi Lionnel! I know you love this song and I'm being really romantic and shit, so just come down so we can talk, okay?"

Lionnel had known Josie since the time of her birth. They were practically raised together. They had become friends. Then they became the closest of confidants. He pined over her for years until they became an item. And finally, lovers. And throughout those eighteen years, Lionnel had never raised his voice to her. Until now. "Josie! Goddammit, stop this! This is *over!* Get it through your *thick head* and leave me the hell *alone* and go *home!* I do *not* want to see you *ever again!*

Plus, this scene has been done *before* and it has been done *better!*" Lionnel slammed the window shut and heard a crash as Josie flung the boombox against a parked car. The car's siren began blaring as Henri wrapped his arm around his son and said, "Lionnel. You need to fix this. One way or another. Great. Now all the dogs are barking. And there goes another car alarm. You need to fix this, son. If you have any feelings for her, then you need to fix this. And if you don't, well…then you *still* have to fix this so Sam and I can get some sleep!"

Josie was sobbing uncontrollably on her bed. Her heart felt as though it was being crushed by a ten-ton weight and was being ripped apart simultaneously. Except for the loss of her parents, she had never felt such excruciating emotional torment. Her pained green eyes darted between a framed picture of Lionnel and Step 5 on her list. She then looked up to her ceiling and said, "D-d-dad? I-I don't k-know if you c-can hear me o-o-or not, but I-I really n-need your h-help. P-please. If there's a-a-anything that you c-can do to reach him. Anything y-you can d-do to help him f-find his w-way back to m-me. Please. I-I love him, Dad."

She let out one final stuttered breath, wiped the tears from her eyes, reached for her pink princess phone and dialed the number. "Hey there, Kayla, it's Josie. Oh, I'm sorry. I didn't realize it was so late. Anywhoooo, since I've got you on the phone, I was just wondering if you guys would like a little break? I was hoping to take the JQ on a picnic tomorrow."

Lionnel laid his emotionally exhausted head upon his pillow. He tossed and turned for what seemed like an eternity. Frustrated, he turned his transistor radio on. From the single speaker came Jefferson Starship's "Find Your Way Back." "Aw, Jesus," he muttered to himself. "I can't listen to this tonight." He fiddled with the dial. The static stopped and out of the lone speaker came Jefferson Starship's "Find Your Way Back." "What the hell? I'll try the jazz station," Lionnel said as he twisted the dial to the left until it landed on the appropriate frequency. A cool saxophone was playing and a slightly relaxed Lionnel began drifting off to sleep. Just before he nodded off, he could hear the saxophone begin to fade. He then heard static. And finally, he heard… "Find Your Way Back" by Jefferson Starship.

Lionnel burst into laughter and held his hands over his bewildered face. "*Really*, Josie? You told your *dad* on me? Well played, Josie. And well played, Mister Parker. Fine. You win. You *both* win. I'll call her tomorrow, Mister Parker. I promise. Maybe we can get a cup of coffee somewhere and talk things out. Now, can I get to sleep?" Lionnel could only shake his head in disbelief as the cool saxophone once again could be heard coming from the solitary speaker.

CHAPTER 106
WIG WAM BAM

"Aunt Josie!" the four members of the Junior Quad squealed as they ran up to Josie's flower-adorned yellow VW Bus. "Hiya kids! Are you ready to have some fun?" Josie excitedly replied. "We sure are!" the perpetual ten-year-olds answered in unison. "What fun will we be having today?"

"Well," Josie began explaining as she pondered the right words to use. "It kinda depends. Is it possible for you guys to take people along with you into the past to an exact date and place?"

"No, it doesn't work that way, Aunt Josie," the quadrophonic voices replied. "We are called to the past when Vetis has chosen a soul to corrupt. We are called to a specific time and location. Then we get on our ponies and start riding until the pretty lights take us there. We are unable to bring anyone along with us and we have no control over where or when we are sent."

"Uh-huh, uh-huh," a contemplative Josie responded as she rubbed her delicate chin. "That's kinda what I thought. Time travel won't work. Okay, no problem. Step Five it is. So, do you want to go on a picnic? And do you kids want to play a little joke on your Uncle Lionnel?"

"Good morning, son," Henri greeted as he walked into his kitchen and rubbed the sleep from his fatigued eyes.

"Morning, Dad," Lionnel answered as he scraped the remnants of his scrambled eggs from off his plate into the waste basket.

"No coffee this morning, son?" Henri inquired. "Naw," Lionnel replied through a slight chuckle. "They've done it Dad. They've beaten me. I can't keep pushing Josie away. And her father has made it *perfectly clear* that I will never again get a good night's sleep until I patch things up with her. I still love her, Dad. I truly do. I just needed to do something extreme to try to wake her up. Try to wake up that sweet girl that I first fell in love with. But truth be told, I kinda like her darker side too. I've realized that it's necessary and that it is a part of who she is. And, despite some of her more *unorthodox* methods, I guess that I love *that* side of her too. I haven't slept in weeks since I broke up with her. That made me realize just how much she means to me. How much I need her in my life. Then, with these *latest* antics, heh, heh, heh."

Lionnel put his head in his hands and shook it for a moment in disbelief. "I mean, trying to make me jealous, and all the damsel in distress shit, and then that trick she pulled last night. Well, I found it to be *totally* immature and *completely* adorable. She proved to me just how much I mean to her, and I guess it made me fall in love with her all over again. Yep, I've officially fallen in love with Josephine Patricia Sommers Parker version 2.0. She still has that childlike innocence and hopefulness, but there's also a tenacity and dark drive to seek justice that I just must admit that I find irresistible. I love her, Dad. Everything about her. And so, I'm going to jump in the shower, bite the bullet, and invite her to go out for coffee. Just like *she* should have done weeks ago. I mean, what's with all the theatrics? Just ask me to go to coffee so we can talk things out. It's really not that complicated. But it is for her, I guess. That's the two sides of her that will always be in conflict. The sweet, innocent side that just wants to get back together with her boyfriend and the tenaciously manipulative side that comes up with stupid ways of doing that. She is *definitely* the product of both of her parents. And I guess that I wouldn't have it any other way."

Lionnel emerged from his bedroom wearing his usual attire of dark blue jeans, canvas tennis shoes, and a light blue oxford. His heart pounded with anticipation as he walked across the room toward the rotary phone. He found a note from his father that simply read, *Sam and I have a meeting this morning. Good luck. And son, FIX THIS! WE NEED OUR SLEEP!*

Lionnel chuckled to himself, took a deep breath, and lifted the receiver. A single loving tear fell upon the phone as he placed his finger into the dial. He was then interrupted by a light knocking on the door. *Who the hell could that be?* Lionnel thought to himself as he went to the door and looked out the peep hole. Seeing nothing, he started back toward the phone when he heard another light knock.

He instinctively picked up a large knife from under the phone stand, walked to the door and looked out the peep hole once again. Seeing nothing, he threw the front door open and immediately assumed a defensive posture.

"Hiya, Uncle Lionnel!" four innocent voices shouted from below him. Lionnel looked down and saw the four angelic faces of Sigourney, Euna, Kane, and Thanatos, who had a toy cowboy figure sticking out of his mouth. "Well, hi kids," a surprised Lionnel greeted. "Wow. You kids really *do* always dress up as cowboys and cowgirls don't you? Now, what are you guys doing here? Is everything alright?"

"Everything's fine, Uncle Lionnel!" the foursome answered. "We're here to play a game with you!" Sigourney and Euna then channeled their strength and tackled Lionnel at the knees causing him to fall backwards. Before he had time to react, Kane had flipped him onto his stomach, Thanatos had hog-tied him, Euna had placed a gag in his mouth, and Sigourney had placed a black burlap bag over his head.

"Okay, now lift!" Sigourney ordered as the giggling quartet hoisted the squirming Lionnel above their heads and carried him out of the apartment, down the stairs, and onto the street.

Lionnel stopped struggling and said *You've gotta be kidding me*, to himself when he heard an all-too familiar voice yell out, "Great job, kids! Now, just throw him in the back and don't crush the picnic basket."

He heard the purr of the VW engine and began lightly banging his head on the floor of the bus in amused frustration as he listened to Josie's rapid-fire attempt at an explanation. "Hiya Lionnel! I know this might be a bit *unorthodox*, and I really didn't *want* to do Step Five, but you see, there's no other *way*, 'cause the *other* steps didn't work and so I really had *no choice* but to do Step Five, you see that right? Plus, I *had* to get you back before that *Taaaabiiiithaaa* got her bitch hooks deeper into you, and of course, I know this is a bit *unusual* but drastic times call for drastic measures, right? I mean, it's not like I could just call you up and invite you for *coffee* or something. Nope, that *never* would've worked, so I *had* to do Step Five, which I really didn't *want* to do, but you left me no choice, so it's really *your* fault that I've had to do this, you see that right? Anywhoooo, there's *nothing* to worry about. We're just going up to the clearing near the estate and we're going to have a picnic! And I've made you all your favorites! Fried chicken, 'tato salad, ham sammiches, and chocolate pie! I was up all night cooking just for you. So anyway, we're just going to have a nice picnic and watch the kids play and once you *realize* that you still *love* me and you can't live *without* me and that *Taaaaabiiithaaaa* is a little bitch whore, then we'll be back together and then I'll take you home. And that's Step Five. What do you think?"

The only response that Lionnel could provide was a muffled attempt at protest. "Yep, I knew you'd like this plan!" Josie continued. "What do you kids think?"

"We think that it's a wonderful plan, Aunt Josie!" the JQ replied gleefully. "And so much fun! We hope to play this game with Uncle Lionnel again sometime."

Josie began chuckling and said, "Well, hopefully that won't be necessary, kids. But it'll always be an option. Okay! Here we are!"

The tittering children lifted the bound and gagged Lionnel out of the van and placed him on a large wool blanket in the middle of a clearing near the estate. He felt the burlap bag being lifted from his head and looked into the irresistible green eyes of his smiling love. "Hiya Lionnel," Josie softly said as she removed the gag from his mouth. "I really am sorry that I had to do this, but I *love* you and I know that you love *me*, so I *had* to do something to get your attention, and I think you'd *have* to admit that *this* was a bit of an attention grabber. And you don't have to worry about me harming *Taaabiiithaaa*. Oh sure, I've had sixteen assassination technicians following her around a bit, just in case. But that won't be necessary, right, because you and I are…"

Josie's stammering was interrupted by a smiling Lionnel tenderly saying, "Josie, just shut up and kiss me."

"Yay! We won the game!" the JQ squealed as they watched Lionnel and Josie kiss for the first time in weeks. "Aunt Josie said that if you kissed her, then we would win the game and get a special prize!"

Josie and Lionnel began laughing out loud as their foreheads touched. Josie then began untying her love and said, "That's right kids!

You all get a special prize. Each of you get to select one toy from my toy box under the back seat in the bus. You can pick out anything that you want."

"Yay!" the children yelled out as they ran into the bus and lifted the back seat up. Following five minutes of silence, Josie yelled out, "Hey! What are you kids doing? Why are you so quiet? Did you find something that you like?"

She then heard the quartet say, "It's just so beautiful Aunt Josie. All of your wonderful toys. They are all so sharp and deadly. We can play so many fun games with these. It's just too hard to choose." The tender moment then ended as Sigourney shouted out, "That one's mine!" "No, it isn't, *I* want that one!" Kane shouted back. "No, you can't have it!" Euna yelled. "Sigourney claimed it and *I'm* taking this one! And Thanatos, quit putting those poison darts in your mouth!"

"Children, please just pick something out and stop your bickering," Lionnel scolded. "Pick out the one toy that you feel most connected to and let's eat. Our lunch is getting cold."

"Sorry, Uncle Lionnel," the children replied respectfully just before they emerged from the van. "Look at what *I* got!" Kane exclaimed while proudly displaying his new broadsword. "And look at *this*!" Euna shouted as she held up a set of golden, spiked scales. "Mine is the best!" Sigourney argued as she pulled back her newly acquired bow and shot an arrow towards an apple fifty yards away.

"That's so cool, you guys," a giggling Josie stated. "But what about you, Thanatos? What is *your* prize? And *what* do you have all over your face?"

"Um," Thanatos sheepishly replied as he looked down at his shuffling white cowboy boots. "Well, I kinda found your secret stash of peanut butter cups."

A tittering Lionnel and Josie were cleaning up what remained of their lunch and watching the children gallop around the clearing on their ponies. Every so often, Lionnel would gaze into Josie's deep, green eyes and give her a slight kiss upon her tender, mauve lips which would elicit yet another childish chant from the JQ. "Aunt Josie and Uncle Lionnel sitting in a tree! K-I-S-S-I-N-G!" Lionnel then said to Josie, "Listen. I'm gonna let you off the hook. I am *not* involved with Tabitha. Not in the slightest. She's just my friend and classmate. She has had the same boyfriend for like, two years or something. *He* was the guy that had to leave the movie theatre. Okay? So, you really have no reason to be jealous of her."

"Jealous?' Josie responded incredulously. "Who the hell said I was *jealous*? You want to run around with other chicks *who are involved with someone else by the way*, well that's your deal. It's no biggie. We were broken up, so you can do whatever you want. Whatevs. *Jealous*? Please, Lionnel, don't make me laugh. I'm *far* too intellectually advanced to fall prey to something as silly as jealousy. And *nooooo* I wasn't going to kill *Taaabiiithaaaa*. Just maybe *scare* her a little, y'know, if I needed to. I mean, she really wouldn't be able to chase after you with a pair of broken legs, now, could she?"

Lionnel's eyes broadened, and his mouth dropped in shocked realization just before Josie yelled out, "Joking! I'm *joking*! Come on, man! Don't be so fuc…I mean, don't be so *gullible*! You *know* me better than that! I would *never* do that to someone just for going out with the man I love!" A relieved Lionnel failed to hear Josie finish her statement as she said under her breath, "As far as *you* know, heh, heh, heh."

"Okay, you got me," Lionnel said through his chuckles. "*That* was a good one. It's just that, man, sometimes you are so much like your mother and…well, it doesn't matter. You *aren't* your mother. You are my Josie. You are the Josie that I fell in love with, and you will *be* my Josie for the rest of our lives. But you really didn't have to go to all this trouble to get my attention. Why didn't you just call me up and…"

Lionnel's thought was interrupted by the sound of gunfire coming from a short distance away. "Shit! Get down!" Josie ordered. "Who the hell are these fuc…I mean *these* guys? Members of the UAM?"

"No, they are just more of Vetis's silly assassins," the JQ answered in unison as they led their ponies toward the safety of the rear of the bus. "We'll take care of this." The children emerged from the back of the VW as the shots continued to ring out. Their brilliant blue and brown eyes began glowing with a reserved rage as they purposefully walked through the brush toward the four assassins. "Kids! Get back here!" Lionnel shouted after them. "You're going to get shot!"

"No, we won't," the children casually replied. Josie and Lionnel looked up from their blanket in disbelief as they witnessed the children wave approaching bullets away from them with their tiny, tan hands.

The JQ continued their methodical approach, and the men continued their firing with an increased frenzy. Finally, the four children stood three feet away from the bewildered men and looked up at them. Each child placed an index finger into the barrel of a rifle. They then said in a sinisterly sweet, unified voice, "Do you *really* want to play this game with us? Do you? Doesn't Vetis understand who we *are*? Doesn't he understand what we have been brought here to *do*? Doesn't he understand that the likes of *you* cannot harm us? Do you think that you can harm us? Do you? Pull the triggers and find out."

There was a loud *BLAM!* and billowing, black smoke emerged around the four giggling children. "See?" Sigourney said in a snotty voice to the blackened men who were lying on the ground in agony. "We *told* you that you couldn't hurt us! Let's get the ponies. Now, it's *our* turn to play a game with *you*."

"Damn, baby, this really is good chocolate pie," an engorged Lionnel stated following being fed yet another bite by his cuddling girlfriend. "Where did you learn how to cook anyway? Your mother couldn't cook worth a lick."

"No, she certainly couldn't," a tittering Josie responded. "And, well, neither can I. I have a confession to make. I bought all this stuff pre-made at the grocery store this morning."

"You *didn't!*" Lionnel yelled out before playfully knocking his girl-friend onto her back and gently laying on top of her. The pair began to kiss passionately until they were interrupted by four euphoric voices.

"Uncle Lionnel! Aunt Josie! Look at us!" the JQ shouted out as they were dragging the four would-be assassins behind their ponies. The men were pleading with them to stop while their bodies were being viciously cut by thorns and their bones were being snapped apart by harsh collisions with jagged rocks. The JQ then untied the men from their horses and whispered in each pony's ear. The Shetlands reared up and began bashing the men's skulls with their heavy hoofs. The men's brains began oozing out of the fissures and spilling onto the lush green pasture. The children continued their non-stop cackles as the full weight of Snowball, Blackjack, Flame, and Snot crashed onto their heads over and over until their faces were unrecognizable puddles of pinkish, red goo.

The children looked down upon their latest late playmates and simultaneously yawned. "Aunt Josie," Kane said in a weary voice. "May we go home now? We are sleepy."

"Of course, you can," Josie replied as she and Lionnel held hands and walked toward the four mounted children. Josie and Lionnel hugged each child before Josie said, "Thank you children. Thank you for helping me play my game with Lionnel. And thank you for protecting us today."

"It's okay," Sigourney snidely answered. "It's what we do."

Lionnel and Josie watched as the forms of the JQ, and their steeds, disappeared over the horizon. "Sooooo...the *children* are gone," Josie playfully whispered into Lionnel's ear.

As Josie and Lionnel laid naked upon the blood-soaked blades of grass in between the four crushed corpses, Lionnel said, "Seriously, Josie, why didn't you just invite me to go to coffee and talk things out?" Josie rolled on top of her beau, stared at him with her intense emerald eyes, smiled demurely, and replied, "Yeah. Like *that* would've worked."

Chapter 107
School Days

"You're a fucking disappointment, Gobbo!" Vetis roared as his razor-sharp whip slashed Gobbo's tenderized demonic skin for the twentieth time. Black bile gushed from the gaping wounds as Gobbo plead for mercy. "P-please, Master! T-the children are just too powerful! Even on Earth! And they are growing stronger with each passing day! With each victory over one of our kind, they are rejuvenated further! It won't be long now until they are at full strength and are powerful enough to defeat you! Please, Master, mercy! I have done all that I can!"

Vetis tossed the dripping whip to the corner of the fiery room, sat upon his skeletal throne, and pouted. "I suppose you're right, my most faithful Gobbo. It's just that I feel it all slipping away, and that's starting to *piss me off!* We have lost almost all our dark souls here in Perdition to the failed war against Enlightenment. And there are fewer and fewer of them remining on the Earth. And those that *do* remain are destroyed by that little witch, Arima. And then there's her half-sister. The one that was to be our savior. The one that would fight alongside her copper-headed mother and Pastor father. *She* was to be the one to tip the scales in our favor. And where is she *now?* Just sitting in Enlightenment, eating her fucking ice cream happy as a fucking lark, *that's* where! Does she *care* that she has nearly destroyed me? *Nooooooooo.* Does she *care* that Perdition is practically defenseless because we have no remaining forces? *Noooooooo*. All she cares about is her *happiness*, and the *happiness* of her loved ones, that selfish little bitch.

"The only thing that is protecting us is the Great Door. Those fucking Enlightenment goodie-goodies can't get through that. They could send a million of their pure souls to storm it, and the door would remain steadfast. But if that door were ever to be opened, and just *one* of those assholes makes their way in, then not only will they have prevented us from taking over the Earth and Enlightenment, but they would be able to conquer our only refuge in this God-forsaken corner of the universe. But that would be impossible. No one would be stupid enough to open the Great Door, right Gobbo?"

"O-of course, Master," the trembling Gobbo replied as he sat at Vetis's red, calloused feet. "The Great Door is *never* to be opened. And *you* are the only one with the key. We may not have much, Master, but we will *always* have Perdition."

"I suppose you're right, Gobbo," Vetis stated in a disappointed tone. "But its just so fucking boring here! It isn't enough! *Nothing* is ever enough! I *must* conquer the Earth and I *must* conquer Enlightenment and I *must* get rid of those fucking JQ brats somehow! But how? I cannot destroy them on Earth, and I cannot lure them here. If I cannot destroy them, then I will be unable to corrupt another soul on Earth to lead my parallel movement and overwhelm the forces of Arima and that other red-headed disappointment. Oh, how I wish to hang her fucking green eyes from my lobes. It would actually look quite nice, don't you think, Gobbo?"

"Oh my, yes, *quite* nice," the submissive Gobbo answered. "Accessories are *everything* when it comes to fashion. Her green eyeballs hanging from your ears would be the *perfect* complement to your dark red flesh. I dare say, you would be *quite* the talk of the town, Master."

"Then I want *that too*!" Vetis roared. "I want that bitch's green eyes! But how? I cannot get them from her now. If I pop them out of her spiritual head, they'll just disintegrate, and she'll conjure new ones. No, I would have to take them from her human body. But that is impossible now. Yes, quite…um…impossible…um…there would be no…um…way to…Oh glory be, Gobbo! I have it! I have the answer to all our problems! This is fucking brilliant! Give Poppa Vetis a big-ol-hug, sit on my lap and listen to my ultimate plan!"

Gobbo let out a slight giggle as his frail, boney frame was encased in four six-foot long scorching hot arms. "Yes, Gobbo. This time, my plan is foolproof. Now just listen closely. This might get a bit...um...complicated. We don't *have* to get rid of those fucking JQ kids! Hell, we don't even *have* to start a parallel movement! Think about it, Gobbo. What tipped the scales towards righteousness? Give up? That red headed bitch. And what event led to that eventuality? Give up? Her first kill. It was her first kill that put her on the road to what she calls *Twisted Humanitarianism*. It was that first kill. That first taste of blood that led her down the path of revenge killings to protect the downtrodden. Then her joining and leading Murder, Inc., which eventually grew so powerful that they, along with the great democracies of the Earth, could defeat us. It was her first kill, Gobbo, that led her to her half-sister. Her *first kill*. So, if we can go back in time, and tell her first kill to not drive his sabotaged car home from the bar, then he will not die, and then I can corrupt his soul into our movement."

Gobbo reluctantly replied through a shaking voice, "B-but, Master. The four children. They will destroy every soul that you wish to corrupt before you can get to them."

"That's what's so brilliant about my plan!" Vetis yelled out as he thrust his mighty frame off the chair, hurling Gobbo's frail body across the room and into the jagged, flaming wall. "Don't you see, Gobbo? If those little fuckers aren't successful in killing this douche, and he doesn't get into his car that night, then I will have his soul to corrupt, and that little bitch will be deprived of her first kill! And if they *are* successful in killing him, then she would *still* be deprived of her first kill, because his death would not be at her hands! It's a win fucking win! Either way, *she* doesn't kill the guy and *she* doesn't start on her path of righteous killing against the oppressors, bullies, and terrorists of the world! We will have taken this bitch off the board without her even knowing it! Then, when I defeat the Earth, it will be my greatest pleasure to pop those fucking green eyes right out of her skull.

"Oh, Gobbo, I do not believe that I've ever been happier. Come. Sit back on my lap. I need to strengthen my essence to travel into the past and whisper into a man's ear. And let's watch those fucking kids and see what they're up to. They don't have *any clue* that they have just been rendered inconsequential. And get that fat, orange cocksucker in here!

He's good for relieving my...tension. Yes, Gobbo, let's watch these oblivious little fuckers enjoy their final days. Because their today is going to look *much different* tomorrow, heh, heh, heh. Huh. They *are* fucking weird. What the fuck are they *wearing*? And what the fuck are they *doing*?"

———

"Hiya Aunt Rosa! Hiya Uncle Gregory! Hiya Uncle Rod!" the Junior Quad squealed out as they were flailing their arms and clapping their hands in the living room of the estate. "Hello, children," Gregory greeted. "What on earth are you four wearing? And what are you doing?"

Kayla pushed 'pause' on the ancient DVD player and giggled as her twin sister Rachel began explaining. "Well, today is the children's first day of home schooling and we have many subjects to cover. That is why you are here today. As we are giving them their lessons, you will put electrodes on their heads and Rosa will connect with their energy to see just how powerful they are. As for what they are wearing, don't they just look *adorable*?"

Gregory, Rosa, and even the stoic Rod could not help but let out a chuckle as they looked down upon the foursome. Sigourney and Euna were wearing matching pink sweaters, pink satin jackets, pink poodle skirts with white polka dots, bobby socks, and saddle shoes. Thanatos and Kane were wearing denim dungarees that were rolled up just above their white, canvas tennis shoes, white T-shirts, and black leather jackets. Thanatos took a black comb from his back pocket, put it in his mouth, then used it to grease back his white hair.

Euna then spoke. "Yes, don't we look adorable? And we are having our first lesson of the day. This is our dance class, and we are learning how to do the hand jive. Mothers, will you please start the movie again so that we may finish our lesson?"

"Of course, dears," Kayla answered, and Sha-Na-Na's "Born to Hand Jive" came blaring out of the television speakers. The children immediately began flailing their petite arms and clapping their hands perfectly in the prescribed sequence to the song's rhythm. Upon the song's conclusion, Sigourney looked at her sibling and cousins and said, "Yep, we got it. That was easy. C'mon. Let's get dressed for our next class."

The quartet came back into the living room ten minutes later in their customary all-white, fringed western outfits. "Okay, we're ready Uncle Rod," Kane stated as they all took a seat on the couch. As Rod was sticking the electrodes onto Sigourney's forehead, she looked Rod directly in the eyes and said in her high-pitched voice, "You are a very nervous man, aren't you, Uncle Rod?" "Um, um, yes, I am, my dear. P-please don't stare at me like that." The children giggled and Rod proceeded to go down the line of tan foreheads. The electrodes were placed onto the children at the very tip of their lightning bolt birth-marks without incident until Rod reached Thanatos. "No, no," an exasperated Rod requested. "Please, Thanatos, do not put that in your...and not that one either. We must not get these wet. And, no, please Thanatos, you already had that one in your mouth."

"Thanatos!" Kane shouted. "Stop putting electrodes in your mouth! It's not healthy! Let's get this over with! I want to see what games our fathers are going to teach us later."

"Fine!" Thanatos yelled as he spit the final electrode out into Rod's awaiting, shaking hand. "Okay, now Rosa, when I tell you to, just hold onto this metal bar that is connected to the electrodes," Rod requested. "And children, please just shut your eyes for a moment and relax. Try to think of your most relaxing memory. We need to get a baseline reading. Then, as you begin your lessons, we will be able to measure the increase in your energy depending upon the subject."

"Well, we all have to think about the same thing," Sigourney stated. "So, *I* want to think about the bedtime story that Aunt Maddy told us about her shoving an arrow through a pedo's ass!"

"No!" Kane countered. "*I* want to think about Aunt Maddy's bedtime story about her blowing Aunt Vai's father's head off with fireworks!" "Yeah, that one's fun," Thanatos contributed. "But *I* want to think about Aunt Maddy's bedtime story about Aunt Blair eating a man that they cooked for a Halloween party." "Okay, let's be reasonable," Euna interjected. "Those are *all* fine stories, but don't you think that we could all agree that Aunt Maddy's *best* bedtime story was when she rigged the brakes on that man's car and his head was embedded in a tree? Won't it be relaxing to think about how she cut the brake line then feel the car speeding down the highway until it crashes?"

The four children began laughing uncontrollably before Sigourney said, "Yeah, that *will* be relaxing. Okay everybody, let's think about Aunt Maddy's first kill. But I think we're going to blow Aunt Rosa's mind."

"Very good, children. Very good," Rod complimented. "Good. You appear to be very relaxed. Now Rosa, please grab this metal bar and…" There was a violent explosion the moment Rosa touched the metal bar. Her body was flung across the room into the adjacent wall. "Rosa!" Gregory yelled out as he rushed over to the smoking body of his wife.

"I-I'm okay," Rosa said in a weary voice. "Wow. And that is when they're *relaxed*. How much energy will they have when they actually start using their little brains? I'm sorry, Rod, but this isn't going to work. They're too powerful. They overloaded my system with the slightest connection to their energy. Unless we come up with something else, I suppose we'll *never* know just how powerful they are. But I can tell you *this*. I can absorb a lot of energy. I mean, *a lot*. And for my system to be overloaded *that* easily, they *must* be at least as powerful as…a nuclear generator. At *least*."

There was a nervous silence in the room before Sigourney turned to her sister and cousins and said snottily, "I *told* you guys that we'd blow her mind." The four members of the JQ nodded before looking at Rosa and saying in their most innocent voices, "Sorry, Aunt Rosa."

"That's okay, children, it wasn't your fault," Rosa replied as her husband lifted her off the floor. Gregory then whispered into her ear, "So, you're saying that we are dealing with four ten-year-old walking nuclear power plants? What the hell happens if they ever *melt down*?" Rosa looked into her beloved husband's worried eyes and said with soft trepidation, "the apocalypse."

Thirty minutes later, Rachel, Kayla, Rod, Rosa, and Gregory stood in silent amazement as the JQ placed their final book upon the pile in front of them. "That one was easy, too," the foursome said in unison. "We have read and absorbed all the knowledge in all these books. Poetry. Literature. Algebra. Geometry. Trigonometry. Botany. Chemistry. Astronomy. World History. Civics. What will be learning about tomorrow?"

"Um," Rachel began. "I'm not *sure*. We'll have to go back to the library. Maybe some more literature. Or statistics? Theology? I don't know. I think we'll just go to the local college bookstore and buy everything that they have. *That* might kill a couple hours. But hey! Our children are like, super geniuses or something!" Rachel then looked at her sister and they both yelled out, "*Woooooooooo!*"

"Well, I certainly hope that tomorrow's books taste better than today's," Thanatos replied as their fathers, Adam and Aaron walked into the room.

"Hello children," Adam greeted followed by Aaron's, "Yes, hello. We hope that you have had a fun day of school. Now it is time for us to teach you games you can play."

"Yes, indeed," Adam added. "Games that you can play with bad men. We have four of them from our camping trip in Indiana out in the stables. Are you children ready?"

"Yay!" The children squealed as they stampeded out the back door and into the stable. They instantly began giggling and pointing at the four naked and bruised men hanging from their arms from an overhead rafter. "P-p-please, children. P-please let us down. Please h-help us," one of the beleaguered men begged.

"No, we will not!" Kane shouted out. "You are our game pieces, and we are going to have fun with you!" Adam, Aaron, and the rest of the "faculty" entered the stable. Adam and Aaron stood in between the bound, pleading men and began their lesson.

"Oh, children, this will be quite fun," Adam began. Aaron then said, "May I have a volunteer for our first game?" "Me! Me! Me! Me!" The children began yelling out with raised hands. "Hmmm, how about Euna for this first game," Adam said.

"Yay!" Euna squealed out. "That isn't right!" Thanatos shouted. "*Girls* don't get to go first! Only *boys* get to go first!" "Yeah!" Kane agreed. "One of us *boys* should go first!"

"Oh, well, we were not aware of that rule," Aaron said. "Is that correct, Kayla?"

An annoyed Kayla shook her head and said tersely, "Nope. Not even close. Thanatos, do you and Kane want to do *all* the laundry *again* this week?"

Kane and Thanatos looked at one another with defeated faces and reluctantly said, "No. Girls can go first."

"Excellent," Aaron said. "I am so glad that we cleared up that rule.

Now Euna, my brother and I are not strong enough to play this game, but perhaps you are. Do you think that you can do this?" He then bent down and whispered something into Euna's ear. Euna's excited smile widened, and she went up to the hanging 'chad.' Her blue and brown eyes began glowing just before she snapped the man's leg in two just below his knee. Her all-white cowgirl outfit became saturated with blood as she dug underneath the anguished man's tendons and muscles and pulled his jagged, broken shin bone from his lower leg. She then broke the bone in two, jumped up and thrust the bones into the wailing man's eye sockets. The whimpering man's body shook for a few moments before shuddering for a final time.

"Excellent, Euna," Adam stated followed by Aaron. "Yes, that was quite good. And remember children to always keep the bones. Do not discard them. They can be made into wonderful game pieces. Now, I believe it will be Sigourney's turn."

"Don't you *dare* say it," Sigourney said as she got up from her seat while glaring at her male cousins. "Yes, Fathers, what game shall you teach *me*?" Adam whispered something to his brother who smiled and nodded. He then bent down and whispered into Sigourney's ear. "Yeah, *I* can play *that* game," Sigourney haughtily said as she approached another pleading man. Drool and snot was running down the beaten man's face. Sigourney lowered his ropes until he fell upon his purple, broken knees. She looked deeply into his pleading eyes, smiled demurely, then began viciously biting through the flesh on his neck. Within seconds, she had chewed through his spinal column and his head popped off like a cork. The entire group was showered with blood as the head plopped onto the lap of Thanatos. "That was cool, Sigourney!" Thanatos yelled out just before he licked the blood from the severed head. "Meh, it's not bad. Needs salt," Thanatos stated flatly as he tossed the head to the side of the stable.

"That was excellent," Adam praised. Aaron then said, "Now Kane, I believe it is your turn." A snickering Kane listened intently to the whispered instructions. He pulled a step ladder from the side of the stable and placed it behind the trembling man. "You are quite lucky, sir," Kane said. "You ae going to be one of Aunt Alexa's masterpieces." His eyes began glowing and his sharpened fingernails began growing. In an instant, Kane had sliced the flesh from the screaming man's back in one sheet. Kane howled with laughter as he then cut through the back muscles and pulled them from the swaying torso. His giggling was uncontrollable as he thrust his fist all the way through the man's back and out his chest, spraying the impressed crowd with a fresh layer of fascist blood.

"Very well done, Kane," Aaron stated. "Yes, quite wonderful," Adam agreed. "Now, children, it is time to teach you our favorite game. And Thanatos, you get to go first, since you have been so patient. This is a special game that we taught your mothers just before they taught *us* a game. Oh, Rachel, Kayla. How will the children ever learn how to play 'Hide the Sausage'? That is not something that we can teach them."

"Nope, not necessary," Rachel replied sternly. "They're going to be perpetually ten years old. That is *not* a game that they will *ever* have to learn. Understand, boys?"

"I suppose so," Adam and Aaron replied in unison before tying the last man to a long, metal bench, injecting him with adrenaline, and splitting his chest open.

"What is going *on?*" Vai asked as she, Jessie, a healing Cliff, Sam, Jules, and Jamie entered the stable. "We just came up here because Josie said she has a big announcement and wants everybody here for a meeting. Arima and Marcus are on Kaneko's private jet and bringing Paciano, Stellan, and their two-year-old-son, Zihad back home. They should be here in an hour. So, we might want to clean up. This is a mess." Taking the cue, LucyFur jumped from Jessie's arms and began lapping up the fresh blood from the floor.

"We are learning how to play operation, Aunt Vai!" the JQ gleefully responded. "Would you like to play with us?"

Vai hesitated for a moment before pulling up a chair. She smiled and said, "Yes, dears. Yes, I would very much like to play. Gallbladder."

As Thanatos was pulling the screaming man's gallbladder from his slimy cavity, the children looked at one another, nodded and abruptly began exiting the stables. "Children! Where are you going?" Kayla cried out after them. As the adults watched their mounted, giggling, hand jiving children be absorbed by a swirl of colorful lights, they heard the JQ say in unison, "We are going to Madison, Wisconsin on June 7, 2017. You may want to ask Aunt Maddy to come for us this time. She may want to see this."

Chapter 108
Street Kids

"There's Aunt Maddy now!" Thanatos shouted out to his brother and cousins as the lethal quartet watched a twenty-nine-year-old Maddy Sommers crawl under a back parking lot chain link fence and disappear under a grotesquely-orange 1969 Dodge Challenger. "Let's go say 'Hi' to her!"

"You *know* we can't do that," Sigourney replied in her customary haughty tone. "That is Aunt Maddy from 2017. And she is still alive. And she won't even know who we are. Plus, we aren't to interfere with any events except for the assassination of our target. Anything other than that could disrupt the course of natural events in unpredictable ways. Let's just watch her. This is the bedtime story that she told us. Her first kill. The time when she cut the brakes on the car of the man who murdered Uncle Joe."

"Wow," Euna contributed as she was feeding Blackjack a carrot from the shadows of a nearby tree line. "Look at how quickly she did that. And how quickly she discarded her black clothes and tools into that garbage bag. It was just like her story. We all know that Aunt Maddy has a tendency to…um…*exaggerate* a bit. But not about this. Even on her first kill, she was very efficient. And very effective. We could learn much from her."

"Which leads me to a question," a pondering Kane stated. "If Aunt

Maddy was already going to kill this guy, then why were *we* summoned?" The JQ stood in contemplative silence as they watched Maddy's darkened car silently pull out from behind a dumpster, onto the street, and away from the run-down tavern. "I think that we need to watch for a while before we make a move. Something doesn't feel right. And Thanatos, quit putting old cigarettes in your mouth."

The children waited for over an hour. They watched with intensity as drunken patrons would step outside for a smoke or to slur sweet nothings into the ear of a potential conquest. The children would quietly giggle and roll their eyes at one another as they heard a steady stream of men saying, "Damn, baby, you're all grown up now aren'tcha?" "You know what would look good on you? Me!" "Wanna come over to my place and watch my new big screen? I've got some fun movies we could watch."

Their attention turned to a large, black sedan that had pulled into the parking lot and backed next to the orange monstrosity. They silently watched the man sitting behind the steering wheel. Every few seconds, there would be the tell-tale glow of a cigarette and a plume of grey smoke emerge from the open driver's side window. "There he is. There's our guy," Euna whispered as a man wearing a dirty T-shirt and jeans staggered out of the bar and began approaching the sedan.

"Are you sure? They all kinda look alike," Thanatos replied. "Yeah, I'm sure," Euna answered. "Look at all of his stupid tattoos. He has the confederate flag, swastika, the number 14, and a weird frog like image all over him. Plus, I can sense his evil. Yep, that's him alright. Hey, the guy in the car is getting out and greeting him. Let's focus our hearing on them and listen in."

"Well, well, well, if it isn't the great, grand, all-powerful *Detective Edmund Simmons*." The spindly, skin-headed man said as he walked up to the sedan. "Now, to what do I owe this great pleasure? Well, I bet I know. I bet you have a few goodies for me, don'tcha? At least you had better. I ain't goin' down for that dude's murder. You said it would be alright. You said that it would be called self-defense. But I hear the cops are looking into it. Sayin' that maybe I murdered the guy, which of course, I did. But only because you *hired* me to do it. You hired me to slap that bitch around. You hired me to lure that big oaf out of the bar.

And you hired me to shoot him when he tried to play hero. What a dumb son of a…"

The man was silenced by a fierce slap on the side of his face by Detective Simmons. "Don't you *ever* say one bad word about that man. That man *was* a hero. The world would be *lucky* to be filled with men like him. Brave. Smart. Just. He was truly a great man. And he was my best friend. I've just come from his visitation. His funeral is tomorrow. So, I will not listen to one harsh word about him, you fucking piss-ant."

"Well," the man countered. "If he was so *special*, why did you off him? Did he know a little *too much* about your business? Or maybe he was playin' around with your wife. That's it isn't it? Dipping his wick in the wrong wax."

Detective Simmons harshly slapped the man once again, causing his cheek to turn bright red. He looked down and noticed a trail of brake fluid snaking from underneath the man's Dodge Challenger and said, "Nothing like that. Joseph Angelo Argento would never mess around on his wife. Or betray his friend. Unlike me. My reasons are my own and I'm sure as hell not going to share them with you. Don't worry about the cops. I'm the lead investigator and I have ways to ensure that it'll be ruled self-defense. But just in case, and to ensure your safety from any wanna-be neighborhood vigilantes, you need to follow the plan and get out of here. I've got the briefcase with your papers. It has everything you need for your new identity, and the deed to an apartment in Brooklyn. Once there, you will find an address and key for a safety deposit box. That's when you'll get your money. That's when you will disappear. And I *never* want to see your fuckin' trashy face ever again. Understood?"

"Yeah, I understand, *Detective*." The man snidely replied. "Just remember. If the money ain't there, then I might just have to sing a little song. You got that?"

"Yeah, I'm not too worried about that," Edmund replied as he hid a slight smirk. "Just have a few final drinks with your friends, drive on home, get a good night's rest, and get your ass out of Dodge tomorrow. Just get in your car and drive to your God-forsaken destiny. Oh, and I wouldn't take this briefcase into the bar with you. You wouldn't want it to come up missing now, would you?"

"You got a point, there, *Detective*," the man said through his laughter. He took the briefcase, opened his car door, and tossed it onto the passenger seat. He slammed the door shut and said with a grin, "Now, how 'bout a twenty? A little goin' away present?"

Detective Simmons smiled, pulled a twenty-dollar-bill out and handed it to the grinning man. "Sure, sure. Here you go. It's *my pleasure* to buy you one last round. Now get the fuck away from me. I have a friend to bury."

"Let's do it now!" Thanatos said. "No, not yet," Kane urged. "There's something wrong. Let's just listen for a while longer. That detective guy is getting his phone out. Let's listen in."

"Yeah, it's Simmons. Yeah, it's done. No, he won't be a problem. This is going along just as we had planned. My heart has never felt this heavy, but you're right. It's time to light the fuse for the next generation. It's time for his niece to get her first taste of blood. Then, we'll monitor her development, and, in time, she will join our ranks. I just hate that I had to sacrifice my best friend for this. But it had to be done. We had to do something to light this first ember. And, knowing Maddy the way that I do, this will be the event that will launch her very deadly career. And this will be the event that will eventually bring her into our fold. Yeah, she cut the brake lines. He's in for a bumpy ride. No, I'm not worried about Blair. There's no way that she'll ever find out. And, she'll have *my* shoulder to cry on. I'll get her through this. Plus, she needs me to cover for Maddy. She won't be a problem. Yes, I'm sure. I don't know why you all worry about her so much. Her bark is *way* worse than her bite. She's never had the stomach to get her hands dirty. That's why she had Joe. And now, she has me. I'll check in with you after the funeral. And this asshole's autopsy."

"This doesn't make any sense," a confused Kane stated. "Aunt *Maddy* is going to kill him. We aren't needed, unless…unless…I think I know what's going on. I think that we were brought here to kill him *instead* of Aunt Maddy. And if Aunt *Maddy* doesn't kill him, then she will never tell us this bedtime story. Maybe she won't have *any* bedtime stories to tell us. The future will be altered. Vetis is very clever. But not as clever as *we* are. Okay, gang, listen up. I think that I know a way around this."

"I shouldn't do *what*?" the racist murderer screamed as he sat at the sticky bar finishing his drink. "What the hell are you yellin' about?" the bartender said. "You've had enough. Time to go. Get your drunk ass outta here. We'll see ya tomorrow."

"No, you won't, heh, heh, heh," the man slurred in response. "Hey, I'm getting the feeling that I shouldn't drive tonight. It's weird. I just had this little voice in my head tellin' me that it wasn't a good idea. It was a nice voice. A powerful voice. Anyway, I'm feelin' a bit woozy. Anybody here wanna give me a ride? We can stop off for some burgers or somethin'. My treat. I just got this feelin' that I shouldn't drive tonight. What with the cops lookin' at me and everything."

"Yeah, I can give you a ride," a rotund, overly made-up woman nearly three times his age said suggestively from the corner of the bar. "Well, hell, yeah, baby!" the tittering man responded as his intoxicated eyes peered down at what appeared to him to be a mid-twenties super model. "Yeah, *you* can give me a ride. This'll be fun. I just need to get something out of my car. I'll grab a cab and pick my car up tomorrow. Now, you just sit right there, you pretty little thing, and I'll be right back. Y'know. For that *ride*, heh, heh, heh."

The woman blushed and she felt a familiar dampness as her best prospect in years staggered out the door. The buffoonish man zigzagged over the cracked concrete toward his prized car. He was whistling and looking into his wallet. "Shit. I used my last condom the other night on that crack whore. Oh well, what do I care? If this bitch gets knocked up, then she gets knocked up. Its not like she'll ever be able to find me. Not after tonight, heh, heh, heh.

"Nope, after tonight, I'm on easy street. New name. New city. My own fancy apartment. And six figures sitting in a safety deposit box. And all I had to do was squeeze a trigger. All I had to do was get rid of another libtard. Fuckin' (derogatory term omitted) lovers. I hate those pricks. The only thing that's worse than a (derogatory term omitted) or a (derogatory term omitted) or a (derogatory term omitted) is a White man who *loves* those godless vermin. They've invaded our country. Taking over the news and the movies and the schools. Fuckin' our White women. Or turnin' our kids gay or some shit. They're a cancer. I'm *glad* I shot that son of a bitch. And I'm *really* glad to now have the money to start my *own* movement. A movement to fight against these fuckin' leftist, snowflake pricks. A movement to take our country back and put it into the hands of the *true* patriots. The *true* Americans. White Christian men. *We* are the ones who should be ruling everything! Not the (derogatory term omitted) or the (derogatory term omitted) or the (derogatory term omitted). Us! And if we have to bring this whole fuckin' democracy down to do it, well, then, so be it. Hand me the fuckin' flame thrower. Then these other so-called *people* can work for *us*. Be our slaves. Or they can fuckin' die. It's gonna be paradise on Earth. And *I'm* gonna have a front-row seat, heh, heh, heh."

The deplorable man looked up when he heard the soft voices of four children say, "You say bad things. That makes us want to play with you."

"W-w-what the fuck are you (derogatory term omitted) kids doin' on my *car*?" he screamed out as he saw four children dressed in blood-stained white western outfits sitting on top of their Shetland ponies, who in turn were standing on the roof and hood of a nightmarish-orange Dodge Challenger. The vintage metal creaked under the weight of the unwelcome passengers as the frantic man came rushing towards the car.

"Get your assess off of there!" He screamed at them. "Okay," the children replied in unison. They nudged their heels into the sides of their friends and the ponies dutifully pounced down upon the pavement. The children looked up at the approaching man and smiled innocently as he yelled out, "I'm gonna beat your fuckin' little assess! Just look at the dents! Oh, I'm gonna *kill* you little sons-a-bitches! I don't care if you're kids or not! You'll just grow up to be takers and rapists anyway! I'm gonna do the world a favor!"

"Gee," the tittering children responded as they slowly trotted away from the car. "You radical right-wing men sure are funny when you get angry. Your eyes bulge out and your white faces turn bright red. You should be careful not to get so heated. You don't want to melt now do you…snowflake? So, would you like to play a game with us? How about tag?" The four children's voices then dropped, and their faces grew dark as they finished with, "You're it."

"Snowflake? How *dare* you call me a…oh, I'm gonna play a fuckin' game with you, alright!" the man yelled as he jumped into the driver's seat and turned the ignition. "I'm gonna play roadkill! And *you're* gonna be it!"

"This is going to be fun," a giggling Sigourney said as the JQ tapped the sides of their steeds.

A lonesome tear fell down the cheek of the hopeful woman looking out the window of the bar as she heard four galloping children scream "Wooooooo!" followed by the roar of a powerful engine.

The chrome front bumper of the muscle car would come tantalizingly close to the back hooves of the Shetlands before the children would look back, stick their tongues out, laugh, and rapidly accelerate. "Wheeeee!" the exuberant children exclaimed as they guided their impossibly fast steeds along the rural road. Their blondish-white hair and bloodied, white fringe streamed straight back from the rush of the warm June air. The scene was repeated over and over through the winding curves on the outskirts of Madison. The drunken and increasingly irate driver would floor the accelerator only to once again be denied his bloodlust by a galloping and giggling cloud of dust. His anger hit a frenzied pitch and he was sweating profusely. He saw an approaching sharp curve. *Well, they're gonna* have *to slow down now,* he thought to himself as he flashed a devilish smile and slammed his foot down on the accelerator. His deafeningly loud machine was inches away from the back pounding hoofs of Snot when the road abruptly veered to the left. He watched in amazement as the laughing children's steeds effortlessly glided around the sharp corner. The RPM needle was buried in red as he desperately turned the steering wheel. There was the horrific, high-pitched sound of skidding rubber.

CHAPER 109
I Love the Sound of Breaking Glass

There was a brilliant flash of white light along the edge of a narrow highway that wound its way between the lush trees of a dense forest. The nearly full moon cast its eerie light down on two black-jeaned, black-hooded figures that had emerged from the brilliant spectacle. "Whooooa, that was *trippy*, man!" Erick exclaimed to his wife. "Is that what dropping acid is like?"

"I dunno," an annoyed Maddy replied.

"How 'bout shrooms?" Erick inquired further. "Is that what doing 'shrooms is like?"

"I dunno," Maddy answered more tersely.

"Well, how about…" Erick tried to ask again before he was abruptly cut off by an increasingly agitated Maddy. "I don't fucking *know*! I haven't *done* that shit! All I've done is smoke a little weed and then, well, I don't *even* want to talk about my little adventure with heroin. That shit nearly killed me. Now, would you like to hear all the different ways that I'm *pissed off* right now?"

"No, not really," an uninterested Erick replied following a deep sigh and eye roll.

"No, you don't?" Maddy persisted. "Well, you're fuckin' *gonna*! Here's all the reasons that I'm *really* pissed off right now! Numero-Uno: I *told* you that if we let Uncle Joe train us on how to go back to Earth through time that we would be bothered! I fucking *told* you! And guess what? I was *right*! Here we are! Numero-Two-O: I was *just about* to relax with a bowl of my delicious, conjured ice cream when Arima told me about this little escapade. So, I'm missing out on *that*! Numero-Three-O: Where the fuck *are* we exactly? Why are we standing in the middle of the fucking boondocks? Stupid fucking Gwen probably led us into the middle of nowhere on *purpose*. That's just the type of vindictive *bitch* that she is. Numero-Four-O: Here we are all dressed in our murdering finest and guess what? We can't fucking *kill* anybody! What's the point of *that*? All we can do is find the JQ and bring them home! Which leads me to Numero-Five-O: Where the fuck *are* they? Do you see the JQ? *I* sure as fuck don't see the JQ! Are we supposed to go tromping through the *fucking wilderness* to find those hell spawn brats? Well, what do you have to say, Mister?"

"Shhhhhh," Erick replied after ignoring his wife's diatribe. "I think I hear something. It sounds like...um...it sounds like...thunder." From around the sharp corner came a galloping, giggling blur of four children riding impossibly fast Shetland ponies followed by the intense roar of an engine. There was then the horrific, high-pitched sound of skidding rubber and an explosion of crumpled metal and shattering glass as the Dodge Challenger lodged itself into the trunk of a centuries-old Oak tree.

"Wow," a dismayed Maddy stated to her equally surprised husband. "That was *cool*. Is there any better sound than shattering glass? They say that when a door closes, a window opens, right? An open window with glass that you can crawl through to your next opportunity in life. *If* you have the balls to do it. Glass represents the world outside that you can look at but not touch. Not experience. You can only watch the world go by. You are safe behind the glass, but *staying* behind that glass gives you no real-life experiences. No love. No loss. No real emotional connection to anything. No impact upon the world. You're just sitting there, taking up space and resources. You're not contributing anything. You're just sponging off everybody else's hard work and experiences. It's a really sad, lonely life. But when that glass *breaks*? When it shatters, you have *no choice* but to experience the real world! You have *no choice* but to be in it!

To belong to it! Because your glass fortress has been shattered and you're exposed to the raw elements of the world, whether you want to be or not. Maybe it'll be a good thing for you. Maybe that shattering glass has given you the excuse you always needed to get out and actually live a life. And maybe that new life will be a positive for other people that you are now forced to interact with. Or maybe not. Like *this* fucker. *His* shattered glass just allowed his head to be planted into that tree. Wow, man. His head is fucking *buried*!"

"What the fuck are you talking about? Are you *sure* you don't drop acid?" a confused Erick asked before hearing the quadrophonic voices of the Junior Quad. "Hiya Aunt Maddy! Hiya Uncle Erick!" the foursome squealed.

Maddy looked upon the approaching children through her tearful effervescent eyes and yelled out, "Oh my God! Kids! It's so great to finally see you! Come here and give us a hug!" The children squealed with delight, jumped down from their ponies and launched themselves into the warm, awaiting arms of Maddy and Erick. "Oh, just let me look at you," Maddy stated through her stuttering, emotional voice. "Oh, my lord, you are all so cute! You are the *perfect* combination of your parents. It's just so great to be able to actually hold you. We've been wanting to do this since you were born, but all we could do is watch. Well, and tell you bedtime stories in your dreams. Have you heard all my bedtime stories?"

"We sure have!" the foursome responded enthusiastically. "We just *love* them!"

"Well, of course you do," Maddy retorted through her giddy chuckles as Erick rolled his eyes once again. "So, tell me. Which story is your *favorite*? Oh, I bet I know. Is it the one about me and your Uncle Erick burying that murdering fuck alive in a frigid hole? Oh! Or is it the time that I dismembered those rapists then hung their heads and torsos in that construction site? And then I said, 'Now you're hung enough for me!' Was it that one? Or how about the time I tied that prick up and cut pieces off him while dancing around? Then I cut off his dick, stuffed it into his mouth, decapitated the fucker, and hung his head on the wall. I bet it's *that* one isn't it, hmmmmm?"

"Well, not exactly, Aunt Maddy," Sigourney answered. "No, those are all great stories, but they aren't our favorite," Thanatos contributed. "I mean, *all* of your stories are *just* wonderful," Euna chimed in, "but there's *one* story that we enjoy over all others." "Yes," Kane concluded. "Our *favorite* bedtime story doesn't have *you* in it at all. The story we love the *most* is when Aunt Josie shot her first boyfriend and his father with arrows, then threw them in a pool filled with piranha. *That* one is our favorite!"

"What the *fuck* are you little bastards talking about?" an agitated Maddy roared. "That fuckin' story *suuuuucks*! And those piranhas were *mine*! She *stole* them, the thieving little bitch! Plus, she made a joke at the end of it that referenced porn, and children should *not* be exposed to that. I just can't believe that my daughter would tell you about that. That's just wrong." Maddy's tone then changed to a contrived, innocent manipulation as she looked down upon their tender faces and said, "Come on kids. I *know* that one of *my* stories is probably your favorite. It's okay. Just tell me, then we can all go home. It's okay. Take your time to think about it. I can wait. I have *all* the time in the world. Literally."

Euna, sensing the need for diplomacy replied, "Well, I suppose that if we were to choose one of *your* stories, Aunt Maddy, then it would be *this* one." The other three children nodded emphatically in agreement while awaiting their opportunity to change the subject.

"What do you mean *this* one? *You* killed this guy. *I* didn't. What are you talking about?" Maddy asked while wearing a confused expression upon her slightly befreckled face. "Don't you recognize the car, Aunt Maddy?" Sigourney asked.

Maddy walked across the highway with her husband while staring at the twisted metal. The front end was completely wrapped around the tree and the smoking engine block had crushed the driver's feet, legs, and torso into the back seat. Blood dripped from the bark that encased his obliterated head. Maddy reached over the jagged metal and gently stroked what remained of the victim's shaved scalp and said softly, "Oh…my…God. I'm in Madison. It's June 7, 2017. This is one of the saddest nights of my life."

"Who *is* this?" a concerned Erick asked. "This," Maddy quietly replied, "is the man who murdered Uncle Joe. This is the man who destroyed my family for a time. This is the man whose brakes I cut. This is the first man that forced me to kill him."

Erick put his arm around his beloved wife, and she laid her copper locks upon his shoulder. He felt his black hoodie become saturated in her tears and said tenderly, "Are you okay?"

Maddy responded by bouncing into the middle of the highway while clapping her hands and laughing. "Okay? Are you fucking *kidding* me? I've never *seen* this before! I knew that I caused him to crash his car, but I never had the opportunity to *see* what I did! And just *look* at it! It's fucking *beautiful!* Look at his body! It doesn't even *exist* anymore! It's just a bunch of mush! And his head is fucking *pulverized!* And look at all the beautiful blood on the pavement and clear up in the tree! Oh my God! Do you know what I'm thinking about? I'm thinking about his final thoughts. Can you *imagine?* Can you *imagine* knowing that in a split-second you're going to fucking crash into a tree? Can you *imagine* knowing that in a split-second your entire body is going to be destroyed? The thought of all the *pain* that you're going to experience just before you fucking *die?* Can you *imagine?* Okay? Fuck yeah, I'm okay! This is fucking awesome!

"But wait," Maddy said in a more reserved tone as she turned her attention to the beaming smiles of the JQ. "If *I* killed him, which I did, then why are *you* four here? Why were *you* called? I had it handled."

"Well," Kane began explaining. "It seems as though Vetis is trying to be a bit cute with time and future events. He used his influential powers to tell this man to not drive his car home tonight. And, if he *hadn't* driven home, then he would not die, and you would not have had your first kill. And if you *didn't* have your first kill, then perhaps you don't go on to your career as a vigilante serial killer and freedom fighter. And you would not have connected with your half-sister, Aunt Arima. And if you *don't* do any of that, then perhaps Vetis would not have been defeated in the year 2042. You were the key to it all, Aunt Maddy, and Vetis tried to make you irrelevant."

"Yes," Euna contributed. "And *we* were called because this bad man was to be Vetis's next soul to darken. So, *we* were to kill him. But we realized what was happening. We realized that if *we* killed this man instead of *you* killing him, then Vetis would succeed in his plan. So, we had to *make sure* that the man drove his car tonight. That is all we had to do. Make sure he drives his car with the cut brakes. And that was quite simple. We just played 'Tag' with him. He was 'it'."

"Yes!" Sigourney exclaimed. "And it was fun! We had such fun allowing him to almost catch us then speed up until…" "BOOM!" a giggling Thanatos yelled out. "So, you see Aunt Maddy, you still killed him. There will be no record of our being here. As far as your 2017 self knows, he died completely at *your* hands. As will so many others now from this point on. And then, we will hear all your wonderful bedtime stories."

"Huh," a chin stroking Maddy said as she pondered what she had just heard. "Well, *that* was a pretty fucked up thing to do. That Vetis is a real prick. We really need to find a way to destroy him once and for all, so I don't have to worry about being bothered while eating my ice cream."

"Oh, we have a plan, Aunt Maddy," the quartet stated in unison. "And you are going to play a very important part in it."

"Whaaaat?" Maddy answered dismissively. "No, no, no. This is *Earth's* problem. When I said 'we' I really meant 'you.' I've got shit to do. Just have Arima tell me when you've got it done."

"Well, *I'll* listen to your plan, kids. Why are *you* always the one that people plan with?" an incredulous Erick asked. "I mean, I've killed people *too*! I've planned the murder of a *bunch* of fuckers! In a lot of *fun ways* too! Jamming toy soldiers up that pedo's ass, for example. Remember *that* one? Or, how about when I had to infiltrate the brown-shirts? Sure, I didn't *kill* them, but I had to infiltrate them so that you *could*. Or, how about the guy that almost killed you and our unborn child? I ripped *that* fucker's heart right out of his chest! Why don't *I* get a bit more respect for *my* contributions in saving the world?"

Maddy looked into the hurt eyes of her beloved husband. She knew that she had to find the right words to soothe his bruised ego. She knew that she could not fuck this up. Maddy fucked it up. "Well, because I'm the *star* of this book series, duh. *That* was a stupid fuckin' question."

"Well, you *used* to be the star," an offended Erick countered. "You *used* to be the focal point of this story. But now, the *main* story lines involve our daughter and the JQ. Face it, you're nothing more than a *secondary* character now."

Erick immediately looked down to hide his knowing grin from his enraged wife. *This is so easy,* he thought to himself just before he heard Maddy shout out, "You motherfucker! *Secondary* character? *Secondary* character? Oh, I'm no fucking *secondary* character! I was, and still *am,* the *star* of this half-baked shit! If it wasn't for *me*, Josie and the JQ and Arima and all the *rest* of these fuckin' poseurs wouldn't even have a story to *be* in! I'm the fuckin' star and will *continue* to be the fuckin' star or else my name isn't Maddy *fuckin'* Sommers! And *that's* my name, so *that's* just how it's going to be! Okay kids, you got my attention. It's time that I shatter my own pane of glass, stop watching this shit, and get back in the game. So, what's your plan. And just whisper it to me. Your Uncle Erick doesn't need to know. He's just a *secondary* character, anyway."

"Maddy, come on. Don't be like that," Erick pleaded. "I didn't mean anything by it. Come on. Please let me hear the plan."

"Well, I don't know," Maddy responded in her "hurt" voice while staring down at her shuffling feet. "If it was your goal to hurt my feelings tonight, well, congratulations sir. You have accomplished that. I hope that you feel proud of yourself."

"Maddy, I didn't mean to hurt your feelings," a back peddling Erick answered. "What is it that you want? What can I say to make you feel better?"

"Well," Maddy's lilting voice responded. "I *suppose* that I *might* feel better if you were to retract that horrible *lie* that you just told and admit that *I'm* the star of these books. That *might* make me feel better."

Erick let out a deep sigh, shook his hung head in disbelief and said in a defeated voice, "Fine. I'm sorry that I said that. You are the star. Are you happy now?"

"Yep, sure am!" Maddy cheerfully replied. "You know, one of the things that I love about you is that you know when to admit that you're wrong. Okay kids, how about that plan? And speak up so that your Uncle Erick can hear it too."

A swirling bright white light emerged from the tree line next to the highway as sirens could be heard approaching from the distance. Just before Maddy, Erick, and the JQ entered, they heard a soft, feminine voice say, "Please, Maddy. Please don't go just yet. Just give us a moment." A blonde-haired woman and bald man emerged from the glare of the kaleidoscope. Their eyes were filled with tears as they rushed towards the children.

"Oh, fuckin' Gwen," Maddy muttered to her husband. "She's such a fuckin' softie." Maddy then turned to the figures who were embracing the children as they sat upon their ponies. "But make it fuckin' fast, bitch! We gotta get out of here before the cops show up. I can't be seen here."

"Who are you?" the JQ asked in unison. The chuckling woman wiped tears from her blue eyes and said, "Well, my dears, I am your Grandmother Kristy Anderson. And this is your Grandfather Jason Anderson. We are the parents of your fathers, Adam and Aaron and of your Aunt Alexa and Aunt Vai. We have been pleading with the powers in Enlightenment to allow us to come here and hold you just one time. I have done some very stupid and destructive things in my life, and my penance was to never be able to be in contact with my loved ones. Until now. Thank you, Maddy. Thank you for forgiving me and allowing this visit."

"You did *what?*" a shocked Erick asked. "*You* set this up? I'm so *proud* of you right now."

"Yeah, yeah, yeah," Maddy stated as she looked away from the group. "It's not a big thing. I just thought that they might want to meet their grandkids, that's all. Nothing to make a big deal over."

Erick lifted his wife's head up with his index finger and looked into her tearful eyes. He smiled at her and gave her a slight nod. Maddy let out a relieved chuckle and yelled out, "Oh my God Kristy, I've missed you so much!" The pair of reunited friends embraced tightly as Maddy continued. "And of *course*, I forgive you. I mean, I stole your kids and drove you away. What *else* could you do but allow yourself to be possessed by my bitch mother and murder me?"

"Oh, I've missed you too," the joyful Kristy replied. "But I'm still sorry that I murdered you. And Erick! I really shouldn't have stabbed him in the back. My beef was with you, not him."

"It's okay," Maddy answered which prompted Erick to say, "Um, no it's not. She fucking stabbed me."

"Just get over it!" Maddy ordered before taking Kristy and Jason by their hands and leading them back to a bewildered JQ. "Listen to me, kids. These are your grandparents. And they are wonderful people. They are my friends. You can trust them, and you can love them. Just as I do."

As the figures dissipated into the bright, swirling light, there was the sound of tires screeching to a halt over the shattered glass on the pavement. "That really *is* a great fuckin' sound," Maddy said as they were carried away to the estate in 2042.

Chapter 110

Anything You Can Do (I Can Do Better)

"Well, everybody's here except for the JQ and I guess we can't get started until they get back and we know that they're safe," Josie stated as she looked upon the multiple faces of her friends and most trusted members of Murder, Inc. on this cooling June evening. Each were seated in folding chairs in a cleared pasture behind the estate in pre-assigned groups. Everyone then gasped as they noticed a bright white light explode from behind them.

"Oh my God, is it them?" Rachel cried out. The group then began chuckling as they heard pounding on the front door of the estate and a demanding woman's voice shouting, "Hey motherfuckers! Anyone home? We have your fuckin' kids!"

"Yeah, it's them," Josie stated as she rolled her eyes. The group got up from their seats and rushed to the front of the house where they found Erick, Maddy, Kristy, Jason, and the JQ on their ponies. "Oh, thank God!" Kayla yelled out as she and her twin sister rushed to their respective children.

Tears of joy were plentiful as the group embraced one another in this unexpected reunion. "We're sorry that we snapped your neck, Mother," Adam stated followed by Adam's, "Yes, quite sorry. We did not enjoy playing that game." "Oh, just shut up and come here!" Kristy exclaimed as she and her husband Jason were enveloped in the embrace of Adam, Aaron, Alexa, and Vai.

"Dad!" Josie squealed as she launched herself into her father's awaiting arms. "Uh, what the fuck am I, chopped liver?" an annoyed Maddy said. Josie looked at her near-mirror image, sauntered up to her and said softly, "Hello, Mom. It's great to see you. Thanks for helping with this." Erick took the opportunity to approach Lionnel. "Helloooo, Lionnel," Erick said nonchalantly. "Um, h-hello sir, I mean, M-Mr. Parker, I mean sir," a nervous Lionnel replied. "Soooo," Erick continued. "I hear that you've been listening to some Jefferson Starship." Lionnel let out a nervous chuckle and replied, "Yes sir. It's a new discovery for me. And one that I found to be...um...inspirational." Erick wiped a tear from his eye, approached the nervous young man and hugged him tightly. He then whispered into his ear, "I love you like a son, Lionnel, but don't you *ever* break my Josie's heart again, do you understand?" "P-perfectly, sir," Lionnel replied before they were joined in a group hug by Maddy and Josie.

Kristy and Jason made the rounds as they were introduced to everybody by the uncharacteristically emotional Sam and Jules. Maddy approached the rightfully suspicious Rachel and Kayla and said, "So, here ya go. Here's your fuckin' brats. So, just try to keep track of them from now on, okay? I have shit to do, and I don't even *like* these little fuckers, so just leave me out of it from now on."

The JQ then said in their unified, innocent voices, "That isn't true Aunt Maddy. You like us. Love us even. That is why you tell us bedtime stories every night."

"What the fuck are you four talking about?" Maddy yelled out, garnering the attention of the entire group. "Bedtime stories? Me? Fuckin' kids and their imaginations. Listen kids, I've got nothing against you *personally*, it's just that I *told* your parents that you four would be a fuckin' *nightmare* and look at all the *shit* that you've caused." She then looked over to her husband who gave her a single look. It was just the two of them silently communicating with one another as Erick's look said, *Maddy, you don't have to be right all the time and you don't have to be tough all the time. Let down your guard and allow yourself to express the love that you have in your heart for these children.* Maddy chuckled, nodded, and said, "Oh, fuck it! Come here you four! I love you all so much! And you can call me whenever you need me, okay? If you need anything at all, just let Arima know, and I'll be here for you. I'll be like your lil' redheaded guardian in the sky!"

"And we will be *your* guardian here on Earth, Aunt Maddy," the JQ replied. "Should we tell them about our plan now? Your mission will not be over, and you cannot go back to Enlightenment until we tell them."

"What plan?" Josie inquired. "Oh, just a little something that me and the kids have cooked up," Maddy answered haughtily. "And since we have the entire murderer's row here, I guess its as good a time as any."

"Okay, but *I* have a plan to announce *first*," Josie stated bluntly. "Uh, well, I'm sure you do," Maddy countered. "But since *I* am the slight elder here, and *my* plan is probably a bit more *important*, then *I* think that *I* should go first." "Mother," Josie's stern voice replied as she pasted a fake smile upon her youthful face. "Once again, and for the *last time*, I am in charge of Murder, Inc. and *I* am leading this meeting. So, *I* will call on *you* at the appropriate time. Thank you for your understanding. I'm glad that's settled."

"Why, you ungrateful little bit..." Maddy attempted to counter before she felt her husband's warm hand clasp her mouth. Erick then said, "That will be fine, dear. You just let us know when it's time for her to speak. And take your time. I'm enjoying being here with you."

"This is fucking ridiculous," an annoyed Maddy stated to her husband as she angrily kicked her crossed leg with her arms tightly folded. "How come I have to go second? Oh, I bet *I* know. It's because I'm now a *secondary* character, right?" "Just let it go and shut up," an annoyed Erick answered before Josie got up and stood in front of her assembly.

"Thank you all for being here," Josie began as her flowered summer dress waved subtly in the cooling breeze. "And thank you for your continued support for our organization. I know that I've been a bit... um...out of sorts lately. But I'm back on my game and ready to lead this entire group with the respect, dignity, and empathy that you all deserve. Now, to our little plan.

"As we all know the Underground Autocratic Movement, or UAM, still has some fighters hiding out in various rural areas in this country. There are a handful of pockets throughout the world, actually, but we will target the members in *this* country first. The world takes its cues from America. So, if we complete the eradication of them *here*, other countries should follow suit. Well, once we get rid of a few turncoat foreign dignitaries, that is. But that's another discussion for another time. This country can be a shining beacon for all the world, or it can be a toxic, hate-fueled cesspool that drags *everyone* down into darkness. We've done much to turn the tide, but our battle is not yet over. My friends, we *will* turn this country into the humanitarian shining beacon that all *true* freedom and peace-loving patriots aspire for it to be. And we will do it by doing to them what they wish to do to us. We're going to rip these fascists apart and crush them once and for all.

"I have divided the country into five quadrants. Each of you will lead groups of Assassination Technicians to flush the traitors out and destroy them. Alexa has been producing a stockpile of Lucy's toxins that you will have at your disposal along with your other customary…um… toys. The specific locations and assignments are in the packets that I have given you. Here are the teams. Quadrant One will be Jessie, Cliff, and…um…LucyFur, I guess. Quadrant Two will be Sam and Henri. Quadrant Three will be Kayla and Rachel. Yes, ladies, it's time for you two to get back in the game." Rachel and Kayla looked at one another, smiled and yelled out, "Wooooooo!"

"Oh, for fuck sakes, that's annoying," Maddy muttered under her breath before being jabbed in her ribs by her husband's elbow.

"Quadrant Four will be Rosa and Dragenstein. And finally, Quadrant Five will be Vai and The Twins. It's time for you boys to start playing your games again. Go there, kill them in any way you find most appropriate and enjoyable. But bring at least one of them back alive from each quadrant. I want a few that we will interrogate. We'll dispose of them after we obtain all the information that we can from them. As for everybody else, Gregory and Marcus will fly Aunt Arima to each quadrant as the missions are completed so that she can absorb and destroy their dark souls. Kaneko, Stellan, and Paciano will remain here and care for Zihad and the JQ. And Rod, Lionnel, and I will work on the most important part. None of this will end as long as there is pure evil in the universe that is influencing humanity. As long as Vetis exists, he will continue to whisper into the ears of the willfully ignorant and continue to build hate-filled, self-absorbed armies of dutiful dullards. We must find a way to destroy him, and that is what we are working on right now. How we on Earth can reach and destroy him in The Realm of Perdition. We don't know how to do that yet, but we're working on it."

"Well, good luck with *that*," Maddy stated in an arrogant tone. "Mother, do you have something to say?" Josie asked as her intense, green eyes glared at Maddy. "Well, I was just *thinkin'*," Maddy coyly responded. "That it would be *great* if someone *here* had a plan for that. But, y'know, it really doesn't seem to be that *important*, seeing as how *I* have to go *second* and everything, so I guess I'll just keep it to myself."

"Mother," and increasingly frustrated Josie replied. "If you would like to share your plan with us, now would be the time." "Oh, I dunno if I'm in the *mood* now," Maddy replied as she looked up into the starry night while twiddling her thumbs. "I mean, I *was* in the mood, but seeing as how your plan seems to be *primary*, I guess my *secondary* plan just isn't all that important."

"Oh, Jesus Christ!" Erick bellowed to his wife. "Would you just get the fuck up there and tell them what the JQ's plan is?" "Fine! I will!" Maddy snapped back. "But not until our *genius* daughter admits that this is the most important part of the plan!" Erick looked at his proud daughter with pleading eyes before Josie finally broke down and said in a cold, tense voice, "Fine, Mother. Your plan is the most important part of this. Are you happy now?"

"Yep, sure am!" Maddy exclaimed as she jumped up from her seat and bounded to the front of the dismayed but amused group. "Thanks dear for the introduction and thanks for admitting when you're wrong. You may be a genius, but there's nothing that can replace good old-fashioned experience. Oh, please don't sit in my chair, dear. I think there's one towards the back. Yep, right over there. Thank you for your consideration. Okay gang, here's the deal. There are two parts to this. One battle will be waged on the Earth and the other will be waged in the Universe. And when the smoke clears, that fucker Vetis is going to wish that he had *never* fucked with humanity, heh, heh, heh."

There was nervous silence as Maddy took a bow following her overly animated presentation and gestured to her daughter to come to the front. "The floor is now yours, dear," Maddy said in a conceited tone with her nose in the air. "Thank you, Mom. Really, thank you," Josie said as she reassumed her position in front of the group. "Wow. Well, that's the plan then. Kaneko, we're going to need a lot of your luck to rub off on us for this to work. Okay, a few final thoughts. This operation will take a few months. We will have to sacrifice a bit and be away from each other for long periods of time and I just want to express right now how much I love you all and will miss you. We also need to have this completed by Alexa's art show. We will use her incredible art as a final celebration of our victory. When will you be ready, Alexa?"

"Well," the bubbly blonde began. "At the pace that I'm working, I'm looking at February 14 of next year, 2043." Josie chuckled and said, "February 14th. Valentine's Day. My birthday. My parents' anniversary. Of course. It's perfect Alexa. Thank you. Okay folks, that's it. Let's have these fascist, demonic assholes all wrapped up in a bow by next Valentine's Day. Oh! But that's not the most *important* part!" Josie squealed. "*Some* of you may have *noticed* that I arrived here with a certain *handsome man* on my shoulder. So, no need for rumors. That's right! Lionnel and I are back together! Isn't that great?"

The entire group stood and gave the couple a standing ovation more from relief than actual adulation. Marcus whispered to Arima, "How exactly is that the most important part? I mean, it's nice and everything, but saving the world and the universe seems a bit more important." "Yeah, I know," Arima calmy answered. "But teenage girls, y'know. What are you gonna do? Hey, did you see how our weed is doing in the back garden? This is gonna be a fun summer."

A bright white swirling light appeared just behind the seats of Erick and Maddy. "Aw, shit, we have to go," a somber Erick muttered. Following tearful hugs good-bye, the forms of Erick, Jason, and Kristy walked into the vortex. Just before following them in, Maddy grabbed her daughter and said, "Listen. I know that I can be a bit…um…*difficult* sometimes, but just know that I love you and I am proud of you, okay?" "Okay, Mom. I love you too," Josie replied in her choked up voice.

"Damn, this never gets easier," Josie said through a forced smile as the reflection of the white vortex disappeared from her tears. "But that's our reality. And at least we know that our loved ones are still with us. Alright, let's shake this off. I think we need to have some fun before we call it a night. Kaneko, would you please bring out the libations? Stellan and Paciano, could you grab the snacks? And Adam and Aaron, would you please bring out our entertainment for the evening?"

With each awkward step that they took as they were being led by a heavy chain by the Twins, Pogo II and Larry shrieked in pain. Wooden "feet" had been nailed to their stumps where their knees once were, causing intense misery with every forced step. Holes had been drilled into what remained of their arms and serrated kitchen knives had been lodged into the tender wounds. Their soiled diapers leaked urine and excrement as the screaming pair were lifted by the Twins and placed into a large playpen. Rachel and Kayla placed mouthguards over what teeth the pair had remaining, for safety reasons one would assume, looked at each other and yelled out, "Woooooo!" Sam and Josie wore lascivious little grins as they approached their trembling, tortured mini gladiators. Sam looked down and said, "Okay, Pogo II. This is your chance. Despite your torture of innocent women over the years, I am giving you this chance to redeem yourself. If you win this match, I'll stop putting cigarettes on your head for a while and I'll change your diaper more than once a week. Now, get in there and kill this bastard!"

"Huh," Josie snorted before turning to her Larry. "Well, Larry, you are *just* as much of a dickwad as Pogo over there. But if *you* win, I'll have *your* diaper changed *daily* and I'll stop using your *chest* as a dart board. Pretty good deal, huh? Now cut this little prick up!"

Josie took her place at the side of the cartoon-adorned "ring" next to Lionnel who looked straight up to the sky while trying to pretend this wasn't happening. "Hey!" Josie yelled out. "They aren't doing anything! Zap 'em!"

"Alright Josie," Adam said as he pressed a button on a remote causing Pogo's shock collar to rip electricity into his neck. "Yes, alright. What a fun game you have chosen," Aaron said as he pressed his button causing Larry to squeal in agony. The pair of reluctant warriors stared at each other for a moment then began flailing their arms.

"Oh, wow," Jules said in amazement. "Look at how fast they can twirl their little arms." "Yeah, my Pogo's going to kick his ass," Sam cooly replied. "No, he won't," Josie retorted followed by the pair going back and forth with, "Yes, he will," "No, he won't", "Yes, he will," "No, he...oh shit! Lionnel look at *this*!"

Larry had managed to bowl Pogo over with a butt of his shaved, scarred head and was now straddling his face. Pogo was choking on the pungent feces that he was being smeared with and was dripping into his open, screaming mouth. The entire group, including Lionnel, burst out into uncontrolled laughter. "Okay, this is pretty messed up, Josie," Lionnel said through his howls. "But I have to admit, that's pretty funny. Especially for a pair of deplorables like them. Come on Pogo! Are gonna take that shit? I mean, literally! Are you gonna take that shit? Get up!" "Hey!" Josie yelled out. "Whose side are you on anyway?" "Oh yeah, sorry," Lionnel said. "I kinda forgot whose was whose. Fascists all look the same to me. Come on Larry! Stab him in the eye!"

"Eat shit and die!" Jamie yelled while Dragenstein said in her Monroe-esque voice, "You know, it seems like only yesterday that I snapped Larry's limbs off and now look at him. I'm so proud." A red-faced Cliff turned to his beloved Jessie and whispered, "Oh man, I'm going to hell just for being here. Are you *sure* you can't behold any evil in this group?" Jessie's brilliant blue eyes remained locked on the vile carnage as she replied, "Nope. Not one bit. No evil here. Just vengeance. And popcorn. Hand me the popcorn, Cliff."

The group's laughter became louder as Pogo spun out from underneath Larry, bounced upon his wooden "feet" and slashed the entirety of Larry's face from his forehead to his chin with his left "arm." "That's my Pogo!" Sam yelled out. "That's cheating! Where's the ref?" Josie screamed as she jumped to her bare feet. "Oh man," Marcus said to Arima. "Is this really happening right now, or am I tripping balls?" "I dunno," his wife answered through her haze. "Looks real. But I'm pretty baked right now so…hey pass me those brownies, wouldja? They're nice and gooey, just how I like them."

An ashamed Rosa and Gregory looked upon the scene while trying to conceal their amusement. "Well, she had to find *some* sort of outlet," Rosa said to her husband. "I guess this is better than those power trips that she went on." A shocked but entertained Gregory could only smile and nod as his eyes were transfixed upon the comedically horrific scene.

Larry struggled to see out of his left eye as blood poured into it from his forehead. He grimaced, then plunged one of his knives into Pogo's thigh. They both lost their balance and tumbled backwards. The laughter continued as the pair rolled about on the blood, urine, and excrement-soaked padding of the playpen. "Oh, Jesus Christ, this is funny!" Henri bellowed. "Look at them! They look like a pair of fucked up turtles!" "Come on! Get up!" Jerry yelled out before the entire group began enthusiastically clapping and chanting, "Fight! Fight! Fight! Fight!"

Josie once again yelled out, "Zap them!" Their tiny bodies convulsed as the electricity shot through their torsos and what was left of their extremities. "Shit! That didn't work!" Josie screamed. "Zap 'em again!" Following six more painful electrocutions, the pair of trimmed, blood-ied, and filth-covered combatants continued thrashing about on the mattress in vain. "Shit!" Josie screamed. "They can't get up! Someone go pick them up or roll them over or something!"

"No, no, no," Rod responded. "I'm sorry Josie, but that would be interference and the rules state that no one from outside the playpen can interfere." "Well, shit," Sam muttered. "What do we do in the event of a tie?" Rod looked over the rules that Josie had scribbled out just before the match and showed them to Jules. "Yeah, okay. I've got this," Jules said as she focused her attention on a nearby grove of trees. Two majestic white tigers came strutting out of the wooded area and approached the playpen. The group looked on in anticipatory silence as the tigers lunged down and bit the heads off the weeping and pleading sex traffickers. Blood from the severed necks sprayed the enthralled onlookers while the small, headless bodies continued to convulse. The satisfied felines licked their whiskers and gave a nod to Jules before lumbering back to their home. *Wow, that was cool*, LucyFur thought to herself as she lapped blood splatter from Jessie's face. "I win!" Kaneko yelled out to Stellan and Paciano. "Pay up bitches! I had my money on it being a tie and their heads being eaten by tigers. Don't know why, but that was my bet." "Yes, you did. We thought you were insane. How did you even know that was a possibility? Here's your ten dollars, dearie," Stellan said as he begrudgingly handed the money over.

"Well, so much for Pogo II and Larry, but rules are rules. Not exactly what I had planned, but it was still fun, right?" a cheerful Josie stated. The entire captivated audience stood up, cheered, whistled, and applauded as they watched the battered, headless bodies shudder one final time and come to a rest. Josie looked at the blood and filth covered playpen, turned to Lionnel, and said, "Do you think we could clean that up and get a couple bucks out of it at a yard sale?" Lionnel looked at his love and solemnly shook his head. "Well, *that* sucks," a disappointed

Josie replied. "Stupid Pogo and Larry. That was a perfectly good playpen. The JQ only used it for like four days and now its ruined!"

"Oh, my fucking *God*, that was *funny!*" Maddy shout-whispered to her husband. "I thought we weren't supposed to say anything?" Erick asked. "Oh," Maddy answered, "Arima's so baked right now, she has *no idea* that we've entered her soul. Besides, what a fun way to spend an evening! You know, I'm pretty good at torturing people, but I have to admit, our daughter can do it better. I'm so proud of her."

Chapter 111
Walk Unafraid

It was always the first thing that she noticed. The faint scent of iron as the sticky thick molasses gently dribbled off her claws and onto her awaiting tongue. She felt a slight sense of satisfaction as her furry ears positioned themselves to intensely listen to the faint exhalation of air passing through her latest victim's mouth which was now permanently formed into a silent scream. Then, the sound of the blood droplets hitting the floor. Slowly at first, like an annoying leaky faucet. *Drop....drop....drop....*then faster as the taught skin surrounding his jugular gave way completely to unleash a crimson waterfall which hit the hard wood floor as though someone had poured an entire gallon of milk upon it. She pulled her claws completely from his throat while loosening her fangs' grip from his hair. Then the familiar thud as the lifeless body succumbed to gravity completing the merciless fait accompli.

A mischievous smile forced the upward curling of the right side of her mauve lips and whiskers. *This was successful. This was liberating. This was justified,* she thought to herself as she positioned herself on the man's chest and began eagerly lapping up the blood that was gushing out of his slashed throat. She looked down upon the mess that he had created as the pool of newly released blood expanded outward like a growing hurricane churning above warm water. She heard two sets of familiar footsteps approaching. The door opened and she looked up innocently at the two pairs of frantic eyes that were staring down at her.

"Oh, *there* you are sweetie!" a relieved Jessie exclaimed as her shoes sploshed across the hardwood floor to her cherished pet. "We have been so *worried*!"

"Yup, there she is," Jules dryly stated. "And *here's* the asshole that tried to escape. Nice job, cat. You kinda made a mess, though."

"Not as much of a mess as *we're* making downstairs," Jessie playfully replied. "Oh my God! Can you believe how *loud* these pricks can scream? I mean, I thought all the *previous* fascist fuckers were loud, but this *new* batch has them beat. By a mile. And man, do they piss their pants! At least LucyFur's…um…*friend* didn't last long enough to piss everywhere. This won't be *nearly* as big of a clean-up job as ours."

The two friends could not help but let out an amused giggle as they watched LucyFur's blood-soaked face mew up at them, then return to her evening's meal. She began purring loudly as she continued her ravenous feeding.

The women's giggles turned into unbridled, full-throated laughter as they watched this blood-soaked furball's euphoric feeding. "Well," Jules observed. "At least we won't have to feed her tonight."

"What are you talking about?" Jessie shot back. She bent over her beloved pet and picked her up. A new coat of fresh blood was squeezed out of LucyFur's matted hair and saturated Jessie's designer top as she hugged the enraptured cat. "Oh, my sweetie *always* needs her nummy-num-nums, now, *don't* you?"

LucyFur's purring continued as she lovingly rubbed her drenched face against that of her "owner." The pair giggled and purred until Jessie said, "And once dinner time is over, I think I know a certain little *someone* who is going to need a B-A-T-H."

Upon hearing the ominous four letters being uttered, LucyFur shrieked with intense fear and began thrashing her paws violently into the air until Jessie was forced to let her go. The shoes of Jules and Jessie were splattered with blood as LucyFur's plump body cannonballed into the crimson pool. LucyFur looked up at Jessie with disdain, turned her back and returned to her morbid meal.

"Yeah, *that* shit's not happening," Jules replied. "And she *really* should have been named 'Maddy,' because that's one blood-lustful little bitch."

"Yeah," Jessie agreed before concluding with, "or Josie."

"Yeah, she's really fucking those three up downstairs," Jules stated. "And making a mess all over the hard-wood floors of the living room in this beautiful estate. And on Christmas, no less. It's kind of a shame. Well, one down, one to go. I'll go check and see if Sam has found the other one. Then we really need to figure out how those two escaped from the stable. Josie really shouldn't have let all the assassination technicians off for Christmas, but oh well. I'll see you in a while after we find that other asshole. Don't let Josie have all the fun."

Jessie entered the living room and found the rest of the inner circle of Murder, Inc. sitting around three bloodied, urine-soaked men tightly bound to chairs. "Oh, you *really* want to screw with me?" Josie was screaming as she glanced up at the blood-stained portrait of her parents hanging over the fireplace. "Do you *know* who I am? Do you *know* who my parents are? Do you *know* what I'm capable of? I know that Vetis has been whispering his plans to you. We know that he has to keep you somewhat updated as to his progress so that you'll stay in the fold. We found you in your little hidey-holes. We exterminated the rest of you vermin in your camps, and we have allowed you five to keep breathing for one reason and one reason only! Information! So, you *will* tell me everything that Vetis has told you and I will allow you to keep on living. For awhile anyway. Or you can keep your mouths shut and watch as I take tiny pieces off of each of your bodies! Oh, hey Jess. Have you guys found the escapees yet?"

"Yeah," Jessie answered as she kneaded the back of LucyFur's soaked neck. "LucyFur took out one of them upstairs. It's kind of a mess. Jules is looking to see if Sam has found the other one. Don't worry. He couldn't have gotten far. Not with the big cats roaming around."

"I don't like Sam out there by herself," Henri muttered to Gregory who whispered back, "She's fine. Have you learned nothing? I'm telling you, if you say one overprotective word to her, you're going to be in the doghouse."

"Okay, nice work, Jess," Josie cheerfully replied before giving the rest of the group a dark glare. "But *someone* in this group needs some additional training on tying knots. Those two were tied up *way* too loosely. But I'll deal with that later."

Lionnel looked sheepishly up at his beloved girlfriend and stammered, "Um, I-I'm sorry Josie. That was *my* fault. I used the wrong type of rope on those two. I swear they were bound up tight, but I ran out of the good rope and thought that the thinner stuff would do the trick. I was wrong. They were able to wriggle out of it. I'm so sorry."

Josie cocked her copper-topped head and looked at her boyfriend for a moment before grasping him around his neck and declaring, "Oh, that's okay baby! Mistakes happen! Okay, now back to you three." Josie's brilliant green eyes darted at the three trembling but defiant men. She raised her knife and sauntered over to the man in the middle and said sweetly, "*C'mon* now handsome. You don't *really* want to die like *this*, do you? And for *what*? A *traitor*? For someone who is a *traitor* to all of humanity? Don't you understand that this is all about *him*? Don't you understand that he doesn't *care* about you? That you're just a *pawn* to help him gain *power*? And he doesn't even want power because he thinks that he can make things *better* for people. He only wants power to soothe his *tender little ego*. We just kicked his *ass*, and now its all about vengeance. Because his *tiny little antichrist ego* is bruised. Well, sweetie, our little group here kinda wrote the *book* on vengeance. He may be a demon, but we have righteousness on our side. And righteousness will *always* defeat pure evil. *Always*. We defeated him once and we will do it again. In glorious fashion. That's going to happen with or without your help. So, waddayasay? How's about you just open that pretty little mouth of yours and tell us what we want to know. Then, we'll all just relax and have a nice Christmas. Okay, sweetie?"

The beaten man smiled at Josie as though he was in a trance and said, "That ain't true bitch. Vetis is the chosen one. He has been anointed by God to save this world from your kind. He's come to save the world from all the (derogatory term omitted) and (derogatory term omitted) and (derogatory term omitted). And all of you who love those Godless scum. He will rise to power with our help, and the Earth will be ruled by the *true* patriots. The *truly* blessed. And even if you kill us, our souls will still be here to help him. You *can't* kill us. He has promised us immortality."

"Wow. You poor, brainwashed bastard," Arima stated. "That isn't true at all. We can kill your physical body and I can destroy your black soul. Easily. And I will. Hey, are there any more of those Christmas tree cookies left? You know, the white ones with the green frosting and sprinkles? Those were so good."

"No, sorry Aunt Arima," Josie answered. "You and Marcus ate all those last night. I think there's still some fudge though. Okay, now where were we? Oh yeah. So, you *see* sweetie, we *can* kill you. There will be no victory for you and there will be no immortality. Just excruciating pain and suffering. So, just be a *good* little fascist bigot and tell us what we want to know, alright?"

The unblinking man continued to stare straight ahead with the same plastic smile before saying, "I ain't telling you shit. Now get the fuck away from me, bitch." He then spat blood and saliva into Josie's befreckled face.

"Well," Josie said calmly as she wiped her face with her hand. "I guess it's a good thing that all my vaccinations are up to date because there's no *telling* what kind of *diseases* you knuckle draggers are carrying." She then shot her effervescent glare at the white-suited Twins while her mauve lips twisted upward into a mischievous little smile. "Okay. I tried to be nice. Boys, do you want to play with your Christmas gifts?"

"Oh, my yes, thank you Josie," Adam replied followed by Aaron's, "Yes. We love our gifts. Thank you so much." The quivering man watched as the Twins went behind his chair and approached the Christmas tree. He heard the rustling of paper, boxes, and Styrofoam padding. He gulped hard and broke out of his indoctrinated stupor as he heard the high-pitched whirring of two drills. It was the last sound that he ever heard. Arima floated above the floor, absorbed the recently released dark soul, and placed it into a large piece of fudge. She and Marcus giggled as they bit into the rich, dark chocolate. "Yeah, he'll be totally flushed away in a couple hours," a satisfied Arima stated. "And man, is he delicious."

LucyFur suddenly jumped down from Jessie's lap and ran out of the pet door in the kitchen. "What the hell is *her* problem?" Jerry asked. "I don't know," Henri replied. "But I think that we'd better go check on our wives."

This shit's starting to piss me off, Jules thought to herself as she trudged through the pure white snow toward a shed on the outskirts of the estate. *But this has to be where they're at. There's bare footprints. And Sam's tread marks.* Jules raised her sword and cautiously opened the creaking, wooden door. She saw the back of Sam's treaded wheelchair. "Sam! What the fuck, man! Did you take care of this fucker or what?" Jules shouted out as she walked toward the wheelchair. She dropped her sword and gasped as she found Sam staring at the ceiling. There was a slight trail of blood coming from her ebony lips and a pitchfork coming from her chest.

"Oh, Jesus Christ, Sam!" a pained Jules screamed out as she fell to her knees and clutched her dear friend's face. Sam's eyes drifted slowly and focused on the beautiful face of one of her best friends. They had known one another since their freshman year of college. Despite their differing personalities and constant bickering, they truly loved one another. They loved one another as deeply as they loved the rest of their tight-knit clan from those days. Lucy. Kristy. Maddy. They had shared countless triumphs and tragedies. The pair were sadly destined to share one final tragedy together on this night. Sam forced a smile and said through a bloody gurgle, "Y-you owe me th-three dollars. P-put it in the swear j-jar, heh. L-look out. B-b-behind you."

The entire group of Henri, Jerry, Josie, Lionnel, Rachel, Kayla, Alexa, Adam, Aaron, Stellan, Paciano, Jessie, Arima, Marcus, Cliff, Jamie, Gregory, Rosa, and Kaneko followed Lucyfur's tracks to the shed. They flung the door open. Henri fell to his knees and let out an anguished scream as the remaining members of Murder, Inc's. inner circle saw two black panthers, two white tigers, two lions, and Lucyfur feasting upon the decapitated body of the final escapee. Streaming tears froze onto their traumatized faces as they also saw the corpses of two best friends holding one another in a final embrace. Sam had been impaled by a pitchfork. Jules's throat had been slashed open.

LucyFur left her feast, jumped upon the wheelchair, let out a mournful mew and lovingly licked the face of Jules. She then pounced down, looked at the big cats and said to them, *My friends, we have just lost one of our true friends on this Earth. And now, ladies and gentlemen of my pride, I am here to declare that there is a new sheriff in town.* The panthers, tigers, and lions looked at one another mournfully, let out tortured cries, and crouched reverentially at the oversized feet of LucyFur.

"You motherfuckers!" Josie roared as the group re-entered the living room with the bodies of their fallen friends. "I'm not fucking around anymore! Give me that fucking drill!" Adam quickly handed Josie the drill while Aaron forced one of the trembling men's mouths open. There was the shriek of the drill's motor followed by a morbid grinding sound as Josie thrust the drill all the way into the violently shaking man's mouth and out the back of his head. Blood and skull shrapnel pelted the cold bodies of Sam and Jules who had been delicately laid on a table next to the Christmas tree.

Josie tossed the bloodied drill onto the couch and grabbed another of the Twins' presents. She approached the final fear-stricken man and said in a deep growl, "Okay, motherfucker. Show and tell time. I *really* wouldn't fuck with me right now."

"Okay, okay, okay, I'll tell you!" the hyperventilating man yelled out. "I'll tell you everything! I know what Vetis has planned! I'll tell you! P-p-please just don't hurt me!"

Following the man's hysterical confession, Josie's glowing green eyes fell upon the tiny bodies of the JQ. "Hey, kids!" Josie bellowed. "That shit gonna be a problem for you?" "No, Aunt Josie," came the unified voices of Sigourney, Euna, Kane, and Thanatos. "Good," Josie stated before turning her burning emerald eyes once more to the trembling man.

She lifted the axe that she had been holding and began smashing it relentlessly into the man's body. She was wielding the axe with an unbridled fury and deep gashes were cut into the man's legs, neck, and torso. She wore a demented smile on her blood-spattered face as she lopped off each of his arms with one blow each. A river of blood was flowing out of the screaming man's multiple wounds. His agony finally stopped as Josie buried the axe between the man's treacherous eyes.

A physically and mentally drained Josie dropped the axe and looked around the room. The tinsel, ornaments, and needles of the Christmas tree were dripping blood and skin fragments. Henri and Jerry were holding one another while sobbing uncontrollably. Her Lionnel was rocking in a ball in the corner while muttering, "It's all my fault. It's all my fault. It's all my fault." Everyone was embracing one another as their faces were covered with anguish and tears.

Josie reached deep inside herself and said a private prayer to her mother. "Jesus Mom, what am I supposed to do now?" She closed her eyes and listened to her heart. She then righted her spine, looked at Arima and said, "Aunt Arima, put their fucking dark souls in the Christmas turkey. We're gonna fuckin' roast them. They're going to burn for hours. Then, we're *all* going to enjoy them for our Christmas dinner. And they're going to burn again in our stomach acid. Something good just *has* to come out of this."

"O-okay Niece Josie," Arima stammered before she lifted off the floor. Her eyes rolled back into her head. She opened her mouth. The only voice that could possibly bring any sense of comfort to Murder, Inc. in this moment came out. "Oh, Jesus, you guys," a remorseful Maddy stated through Arima. "I am so sorry for your loss. Henri, Jesus what you must be going through. I'm so sorry. And Jerry. You loved Jules so much. I'm so sorry. Lionnel. Pick yourself up. This wasn't your fault. This wasn't anybody's fault except for Vetis. His narcissistic evil has taken two more loved ones from you. But never again. We got this. The plans are in the works up here. And please take just a little comfort in knowing that I now have my final two best friends alongside me. Please don't worry about them. They are with me and Erick and will stay here until they learn how to conjure their own homes. And Henri, I know this isn't much consolation, but Sam can walk again. And man, is she pissed."

Chapter 112

We Go Together

"Finally, we have a plan that will work, Gobbo!" Vetis roared with self-satisfaction. "Finally, we will get rid of that pesky fucking JQ and proceed with our domination over the Earth and Enlightenment! Finally, we will be able to move out of this dreary Realm of Perdition. It's so fucking depressing that this is the only place in the universe that I am safe since my defeat. Which was *rigged* by the way! I did *not* lose my war! They *cheated*! Anyway, I hate being secluded here. All these horrible souls milling about. I need fresh blood to conquer and dominate! I need fresh minions to worship at my feet! Perdition is not enough! It has never been enough! Plus, I hate what that slithery, copper headed bitch did to the place while I put her in charge up here. I mean, what's with all the tapestries everywhere? In a world of fire? In a world filled with dark souls? It just looks ridiculous. An embarrassment, really. Gobbo, get one of the enslaved to take down the tapestries. And have them paint all the walls black. I want to leave this place just as I discovered it. Dark and menacing. And more skulls! Why did that bitch take down all the skulls? That will look nice. Then, my loyal Gobbo, once I am the ruler of the universe, you shall be granted dominion over this dreadful place and all the few remaining dark souls that reside here. Then, you can decorate it however you like. But for right now, I want it dark and menacing! Got it?"

"W-why Yes, Master," the groveling Gobbo replied. "Of course. I will get someone on it right away. Have you had a chance to look at my suggestions, Master? Are you ready to choose our four warriors from Earth's past to eliminate the Junior Quad?"

"Yes, I have made my choices, Gobbo," Vetis sneered back. "And it doesn't matter when or where they are. I have no other use for them than to destroy those fucking brats. And it was quite the masterful plan on my part. They are too powerful together. But separately? Heh, heh, heh. Separately they can be defeated as long as I find the right assassins. And I have. Four of the most ruthless child-murderers ever to walk the Earth. They are vile. They are evil. They are perfect. All I have to do is send my signal that they are the next that I will attempt to convert. Send the signal about all four of them. Then, the despised JQ will have no choice but to separate and try to defeat them one on one. Which they won't be able to do! They draw their strength from one another! Without their soul mates, they are nothing more than ten-year-old children. They are no more menacing or threatening than kids running around on a playground. And the beautiful part, Gobbo? They won't see it coming! They will still think that they are invulnerable! Then, my hand-picked assassins will carve those little fuckers up. I hope they do it nice and slow. This is a moment that I wish to savor. All of that is correct, right Gobbo?"

"Why, yes, Master," Gobbo replied. "It was all in your daily briefing. I do wish that you would take the time to read that, Master. And, well, actually, this plan was *my* pla…"

Vetis slapped Gobbo across the room and roared at him. "*Your* plan? Were you about to say that this was *your* plan? Were you about to take credit from your *Master*? And fuck your daily briefing. It's boring. And there's too many big words. That's what I have you for. To give me the information that I need to make decisions. Now, whose plan was this exactly, Gobbo?"

"I-it most certainly *was* your plan, Master," Gobbo meekly replied as he lifted his boney frame from off the cold stone floor. "It was *your* plan to separate them, thereby eliminating their ability to draw strength from one another, thereby eliminating their powers. It was *your* plan to falsely identify these four child-murdering assassins as your next to be indoctrinated, thereby luring the separate members of the JQ to their ghastly fate. And it has *always* been *your* plan to eliminate the JQ so that you may conquer the universe without having to go through the Great Door. You can do all of this while commanding your troops from the safety of your throne in Perdition. Because, if you were to go out the Great Door, your physical form would be vulnerable upon the Earth. And, as imposing as your physical form is, Master, going through the Great Door is a risk that someone as great as you should never be exposed to. This was *your* plan, Master. And I am in awe of it."

"Of course you fucking are," Vetis answered with a tone of self-satisfaction. "Everyone should be in awe of me. And they will be. The entire population of Earth will cower at the very mention of my name by my hand-picked dictators. All the goodie-goodies in Enlightenment will *beg* me for the privilege of serving me. Everyone, Gobbo. It makes me feel warm and fuzzy. Now, hand me those names. Allow me to concentrate on each one. Then, let's watch Sigourney, Euna, Kane, and Thanatos be sent back to the hell from whence they were summoned. This is going to be fun."

"Hey! This isn't fun!" Sigourney screamed out. "Let me out of this cage!" A tall man emerged from the shadows of a dingy basement in the year 1897 wearing a tattered cowboy hat and a haggard smile. The sound of sharpening knives being rubbed against one another created a high-pitched squeak. The man looked at the confined ten-year-old girl. His eyes traversed her entire tiny body. He savored every aspect of her. Her white, fringed cowboy hat resting upon her nearly pure-white strands. Her caramel face with a birthmark resembling a lightning bolt that streaked between one brown eye and one blue. Her little white cowgirl shirt, fringed vest, and long skirt. He began laughing as he peered down upon the tassels on her white cowboy boots.

"Oh, my dear," he began with a lascivious sneer. "I had a dream about you. A dream of a little girl dressed all in white. A very *powerful* little girl whose powers would be stripped from her. A little girl who would provide me with my latest and greatest feast. It was such a wonderful dream. And now, my dream has come true. Here you are. My little delicacy. All locked up in my little cage. Just waiting to have tiny ribbons of your flesh sliced off, battered, and deep fried. Oh, I'm going to feast on you for weeks, little girl. And with each bite, I will listen to your pleas. I will chew your flesh and laugh as you beg me to stop. It will be so satisfying to get rid of one more bitch from this world. One less bitch to look down upon me. One less bitch to tell me what to do. One less bitch who would deny me. Yes, you will just grow up to be a little bitch, just like *all* the women that I have encountered. I have travelled from town to town getting rid of little bitches just like you. But *you* will be my favorite. Because I was told in my dream that getting rid of *you* in a most unpleasant manner would grant me powers. And immortality. And I have no reason to doubt that. Because *you* were in that dream. And now, here you are. And now, I am going to prepare my first taste. Stick your arm out of the bars, little girl. Let me have a taste."

Sigourney folded her arms defiantly, tilted her head and said in a snotty tone, "No. I don't want to. I don't *want* to play this game. You are a very bad man. I understand why Vetis chose you. So, I don't *want* to play this game. I have another game in mind. But, if you do me one favor, perhaps I *will* play this game with you."

The man bent over laughing, nearly dropping his knives before saying, "What is it my little treat? What is the favor that you are asking of me?"

"Just look deeply into my eyes," Sigourney answered in a sweet voice. "Look deeply into my eyes and if after doing that you still want to carve me up and eat me, then I'll play your game."

"Sure, why the hell not?" the chortling man replied. He bent down so that his eyes were directly in front of hers. His smile turned to painful shock as Sigourney's eyes began glowing. He fell to his knees and began screaming in agony.

"That's what I thought," Sigourney stated bluntly as she pulled the iron bars apart, stepped out of the cage and looked down upon the tortured man. "Do you know what you are experiencing? You are experiencing all the innocent souls who died at your hands. You are experiencing their conquest of you. They are all inside of you. They are tearing you apart from the inside out. Are you enjoying my game?"

The man's tortured screams continued as tiny, glistening hands began ripping their way out of the man's flesh. There was the echoing laughter of female children as their souls tore through his chest, legs, arms, and back. His internal organs flopped onto the dirt basement floor and blood flowed freely from wide lacerations in his entire body before the hysterical man looked up and peered into the intense eyes of his executioner one final time.

There was a clopping sound that came down the basement stairs. Sigourney climbed upon the back of Snowball. She opened her mouth. The dying, disgusting man then heard the voices of four distinct children saying in unison…

"Hey! Let me out of these shackles!" Kane demanded in German as he stared at the approaching Nazi scientist in 1941. "This is uncomfortable!"

"Oh, my special little friend," the evil, nearly hyperventilating scientist said as he snapped rubber gloves around his wrists. "Oh, how I have waited for you. A child such as yourself. I have dissected and studied so many children over these past several years. I have been looking for the secret powers of the human mind and body. Secrets that I believe that only the untarnished minds and bodies of children possess. Secrets that I can harvest and develop into a master race for my Fuhrer. Secrets that I can use to help him dominate the world. I must admit, I have become a bit despondent. I have studied over one-thousand children, but no secrets have been revealed to me. At first, I thought that it was because I was dissecting the wrong children. Vermin children. So, we started our breeding program. We created children that were spawned from the most healthy and pure of our race. I had great hopes as I sliced their wriggling little bodies open. But they held no secrets for me either. I was actually about to report that my research was a failure when *it* happened.

"I dreamed of you last night, my little friend. I dreamed of a little child, all dressed in a white American West outfit. A child who held the secrets of not only humankind, but secrets of the universe! This morning when I woke up, I of course thought that it was just my subconscious playing cruel tricks on me. Then, I checked my traps in the forest where the local children like to play. And I found *you* all wrapped up in a tidy metal package. So, here we are, my young friend. *You* will be responsible for unlocking our secrets. And *you* will be responsible for the glorious victory of the Third Reich! It will be my *great honor* to cut you open. To listen to your screams as I inspect each of your organs. To listen to your incoherent ramblings as I slice little pieces of your brain from out of your precious little skull. I would *like* to say that I'm sorry that you must remain awake for this ordeal, but I'm *not*, heh, heh, heh."

"Well, okay then," Kane responded casually from his position laying on the cold, metal operating table as the man bent over his head with a scalpel. As he was leaning forward, the maniacal scientist's eyes briefly locked onto the glowing eyes of Kane. His sly smile immediately transformed into shocked horror. He fell upon his knees and clutched his anguished eyes with his hands. Kane lifted his arms and legs, snapping his iron restraints. As the shrieking man continued to clutch his face, Kane whistled. The forty-inch-high Flame came bursting through the door and trotted to his friend's side. Kane climbed upon his faithful steed and looked down upon the tortured man.

"Do you know what you are experiencing?" Kane inquired with his sweet voice. "You are experiencing the horrors of war. War that you have contributed to. You are experiencing images of blown-apart bodies. And you are experiencing the pain that each of the innocent victims of war feel just before their passing."

Kane continued to look on as pieces of the scientist's body were being blown off him as though micro bombs were carpeting his flesh. Geysers of blood and pieces of bone shrapnel were violently showering the laboratory. Just before the man let out his final anguished breath, this murderer of the innocent heard the voices of four distinct children saying in unison…

"You better let me out if you know what's good for you!" the chair-bound Thanatos shouted to the pinstripe-suited gangster standing in the dark corner in front of multiple bottles. "Yeah, that's not happening kid," the gangster stated as he came from out of the shadows and stood in front of the young cowboy under a single overhead lightbulb. "I don't know why the competition keeps sending you kids around to snoop on me. I enjoy killing kids as much as I enjoy killing anyone else. You know what I love, kid? I love my booze. I love *selling* my booze in my speakeasy. I love getting broads drunk. But what I *really* love is that look on someone's face just as that bullet hits them right between the eyes. Man, woman, kid. It doesn't matter. I love that look of fear and pain. I love the look of *death*. Now, how about you tell me who sent you? Maybe I'll make it painless for you."

"No, I don't think so," Thanatos answered. "Hey! What's in those bottles back there? Does it taste good?"

"Still trying to get information, huh?" the wise guy said through a respected chuckle. "Well, you've got balls, I'll give you that. I guess you're not going to tell me, so I guess I'll just have to put one between your eyes. I gotta get going anyway. I have new showgirls to audition." The gangster pulled a revolver from his jacket, pointed it at Thanatos and stared directly into his latest victim's shining eyes. The man's body was suddenly thrown backwards against the wall of bottles as a barrage of bullet holes ripped through his flesh.

"Well, that was easy," Thanatos stated as he flicked his wrist and broke the ropes. Thanatos whistled and the pale green form of Snot came barreling into the liquor cellar. Thanatos climbed upon his friend and had him trot over to the remaining bottles on the shattered shelves. "What's this? Gin?" he shouted out before taking a huge swig from the bottle. "Blech! What's this? Whiskey? Blech! What's this? Vodka? Blech! What's (hic) this (hic)? Rum? Oh, I don't feel so well."

Thanatos looked down upon the riddled man as he gasped for breath. Blood flowed out of countless bullet holes on his body and face as Thanatos said, "Do you know what you're experiencing? You are experiencing your favorite thing. You are experiencing the pain of everyone that you have murdered. You are experiencing death. *Your* death and *their* deaths. All of them, combined into one painful experience. Thanatos then smiled and opened his mouth. The last thing that the dying criminal heard were the voices of four distinct children saying in unison…

"Hey! This isn't funny! Let me out!" Euna screamed to the dark, towering figure in the attic of a townhouse in 1963. She looked around the space from her chair that she was tied to and saw soiled stuffed animals and toys strewn everywhere. The insane, giggling man approached her and said, "Oh good. You're awake. Oh, thank you for coming to my door and asking for candy. Thank you so much. It is a pleasure to have you here."

"Yeah, well it's not *my* pleasure so let me go!" Euna ordered. "Oh no, no, no. I can't *do* that. I can't *do* that," the giddy man answered. "Oh no, no, no. You are my new *toy*. I need to play with you. And you look so… so…healthy. I must *play* with you. Oh, how I have played with so *many* children. It is so fun. But I haven't been able to play for such a long time. Not since I was defrocked. Oh, how I found so *many* wonderful play-mates at my churches. So many trusting families that just let me play with their precious children. Even after it was revealed what I and so many others like me had done, those families continued to go to that church and trust another. Then another. Then another. It was so *easy* to move from church to church and find my toys. Fun, cute little toys who I would play my games with. But that was taken away from me. I haven't had anyone to play with in so long. It has been so sad for me just watching all these toys that I long to play with walk past my house every day. Why, there's the Jacob's little boy. He just started kindergarten. I just love to watch him walk in his tight little jeans and I dream of playing with him. Then there's the eight-year-old girl of the Robinson's. She looks so cute in her little dresses. Oh, the games that I wish to play with her. She could be my little dolly. But I can't. No one comes to my house. I was about to hang myself, until last night.

"Last night I was awoken by the most wonderful dream. I dreamed of a tanned-skinned little girl dressed in an adorable cowgirl costume. I dreamed of playing cowgirl and Indian with her. I dreamed of tying her up and doing things to her. I dreamed of her cries as I made her do things in my teepee. Her wonderful, innocent cries! I heard the doorbell ring, and I woke up. And there you were. So cute. So eager to feast upon my poisoned candy. So ready to be played with. So ready to be kissed."

The perverted former priest bent down to kiss Euna's tan lips. He smiled as he locked his eyes upon hers. Euna's brown and blue eyes began radiating. The man shrieked, ended his attempted debauchery, and fell into the fetal position on the floor. Euna shrugged and the ropes that were binding her snapped in half. She whistled and the clomping of hooves came bounding up the attic stairs. Euna looked down upon the whimpering man as she climbed upon the back of Blackjack.

"Do you know what you are experiencing?" Euna asked in her inno-cent voice. "You are experiencing the emptiness that all your victims experienced. You did not just cause physical trauma, which was horrible enough. You caused never-ending emotional and psychological trauma. That is what you are now experiencing. The feelings of famine that ravaged their souls every moment of every day from what you did to them. Those horrible things that you put them through caused them to feel guilt. Shame. Embarrassment. For the rest of their lives, they were empty of any feelings of joy. Happiness. Love. Trust. Their souls were incapable of being nourished. For their entire lives they were emotionally famished."

Euna watched as the man's body and face began to sink in. His eyes began bulging out and his tongue hung from his gasping mouth. His bones became visible just under the thin layer of now ashen-grey skin. He lifted his head slightly, looked at Euna with his sunken in, emaciated eyes and listened as the voices of four distinct children said in unison, "Silly Vetis. We do not *have* to be physically together in order to be connected. We are *always* together. We will *always* have our love of each other and the love of good souls to strengthen us. We cannot be destroyed. We are invulnerable. We are immortal. And we have been called here once again to rid this world of evil men like you. We possess the souls of the Four Horsemen of the Apocalypse. But not an apocalypse of the Earth. An apocalypse of the *evil* upon the Earth. Thank you for playing with us. It has been fun. We have to go home now. Our parents are probably worried, and we don't want to be grounded. Plus, it's dinner time and it's taco night. Good-bye."

"Stupid Gobbo! What kind of stupid fucking idea was that?" Vetis screamed as he repeatedly slapped Gobbo's face mercilessly. He tossed Gobbo's limp frame to the floor, stroked his crimson chin with one of his four hands and said, "So be it. I now know what I must do. I should have done this long ago. They are powerful, yes. But I am a demon. I contain all the evil in the universe. I must do this personally. I must go to Earth in my physical form. And I will use each of my four arms to rip each one of those little bastards apart. Here Gobbo. Here is the key to the Great Door. You will guard it with your very existence until my return. And I *will* return. With the four tiny heads of the four horsemen. *And* the heads of their little ponies *too*."

Chapter 113

Across the Universe

Vetis let out a deep sigh as Gobbo placed the iron key into the Great Door. There was a loud THUNK as the locks disengaged allowing the vast iron hinges to squeak open. "Gobbo," Vetis said sternly. "You let me back in as soon as you hear me knocking on this door. You know that my time on Earth is limited. If I stay too long, then I will be trapped there in my physical form and I will be vulnerable. Yes, as powerful as I might be, I could actually perish upon the Earth. But that won't be a problem. I'm going to vanquish the fucking JQ once and for all. And I'm going to enjoy every moment of it."

Vetis righted his nine-foot, crimson red frame with false bravado and stepped outside the safety of Perdition and into the cosmos. He mournfully looked up at the obscenely large gold letters that spelled VETIS hanging over the door, then gulped as he heard the Great Door slam shut. He chuckled nervously and concentrated on the glowing blue ball that was orbiting a bright yellow star. He concentrated further, trying to pick up the essence of his unsuspecting quarry. He smiled as he felt the sensation being emanated from the souls of Sigourney, Euna, Kane, and Thanatos. He took one step forward with his massive, clawed right foot.

A dense, dark red fog appeared in a clearing near the Sommers-Parker estate in upper New York State. Vetis emerged from the sinister shroud. He threw his horned head back defiantly, roared, flexed his four biceps, and looked down where he saw the smiling faces of Arima, Jessie, Jamie, Rosa, Vai, Adam, Aaron, Kayla, and Rachel. They were standing around a long, pure white hearse wearing knowing smirks with their coated arms casually folded. He heard giggling coming from around his feet. His fiery eyes looked down further and he saw the mischievously grinning Junior Quad looking up at him while sitting on their faithful Shetlands. Vetis's heart began beating rapidly as he watched the children's brown and blue eyes begin to eerily glow. He could feel his blood pressure rise as he heard the seemingly innocent voices of the four children say in unison, "Hello Vetis. We have been expecting you. We have seen this day. Thank you for coming. Thank you for coming to play with us. We are going to have great fun with you."

The hyperventilating Vetis clutched his fear-stricken heart and declared, "Oh fuck this! Maybe just ruling Perdition isn't so bad after all! I'm outta here! Fuck you guys!" Vetis's massive frame disappeared back into the dark red fog as the children mocked the retreating spineless bully. "Vetis!" the children shouted after him. "Come back! You are so big and powerful. We are just children. What's the matter? You can't fight your own fights? You have to hide behind your demonic army? Come on back, Vetis! You big pussy!" The final thing that Vetis heard as his massive, wilted frame re-entered the cosmos was the deriding laughter of four ten-year-olds followed by an admonishment by their mothers for using the word 'pussy.' Lava tears of embarrassment streamed down his disgraced red face as he approached the promised sanctuary of the Great Door.

There was a violent pounding upon the Great Door as a booming voice yelled out, "Hey Gobbo! Let me in!"

"Y-yes?" Gobbo replied with trepidation. "W-who is it?"

"Who the fuck (*clink*) do you *think* it is? The fuckin' (*clink*) pizza guy? Let me in!"

The iron key was heard being inserted into the lock. There was a loud THUNK as the locks were once again disengaged. Gobbo pulled the door open and gasped at the sight that stood in the doorway in front of him. A joyful, black tear fell from one of his yellowed eyes as he bowed at the feet of the five intense women who stood confidently in front of the backdrop of the kaleidoscopic universe.

Lucy was dressed in an all-black cat suit holding a conjured box of test tubes and other "science shit" that the rest of her friends did not care to understand. Next to her stood Kristy in a flowing yellow sundress holding a freshly conjured bundt cake. Jules stood to the far left of the group wearing conjured faded blue jeans, black boots, and a black leather biker jacket. Sam was proudly standing on her tone, caramel legs that were enveloped in a tight, pin-striped pencil skirt that accented the rest of her business attire which included a bulging designer purse. Gobbo looked up at the figure that was standing in the middle. She slowly lifted her head, allowing her piercing green eyes to meet his. Her slender mauve lips curled up in a mischievous smile as she removed the black hood from her copper bangs. Maddy Sommers let out a low, devilish laugh and clutched her right hand around a pair of well-worn brass knuckles before saying, "Took you long enough. We've got shit (*clink*) to do!" Maddy looked behind her college friends at the rest of her beloved entourage. "Come on everybody! Let's get to work! It's going to take awhile to conjure this fucking (*clink*) place into shape! And what the fuck (*clink*) is that fucking (*clink*) clinking sound?"

Sam wore a haughty smile as she retrieved a large glass jar from her purse. "This," she began explaining, "is the source of that clinking sound. This is our new swear jar. Every time somebody swears, a good deed that they must perform will be deposited into it. And, I must say my old friend, you've already racked up quite a tab. You see, Maddy, not everybody is comfortable with foul language, and we want this to be a place where everybody can live throughout eternity in blissful comfort."

"Fuck (*clink*) that!" Maddy roared back. "No fuckin' (*clink*) way! That isn't heaven! That's fuckin' (*clink*) hell!"

Sam chuckled, patted Maddy on her auburn head and proceeded to lead the group into Perdition. "Okay now everybody," Sam began as she pulled a large notebook from her bag. "As you will see from my schematics of Perdition, everybody has an exact equal amount of space to use to conjure your homes. And Jules, could you please keep your space tidy this time? We *really* don't want a repeat of your college closet. Now, the diner and ice cream shop that Uncle Joe and Aunt Blair requested will be in *that* area over there. And the rock club where Aunt

Patty and Jacklyn will book musicians to play will be *here*. Now, Herbert, or Mister Botanist. Could you and your lovely wife, Iris, and your adorable daughter begin sprucing up the place? These rocks are just so depressing. And let's get rid of those skulls hanging all over."

"It will be our pleasure," Herbert answered as he held hands with his family and closed his beady eyes. Throughout Perdition, exotic plants and flowers began growing and blossoming out of the jagged, fiery stone. Fresh blades of lush green grass covered the entire surface, and a stream of clear, blue water replaced the flowing lava in the river. In a matter of moments, morbid darkness had been replaced by an explosion of colorful life.

"Very, very nice," Sam stated to the proud Botanist. "Now, Louise, Abdalla, and Gwen, this area over *here* will be your spiritual amplification center where we can all go to reach out to our loved ones on Earth. And Clyde Manfre…um…Manfren… Manfrengensen, this area over *here* will be your vintage clothing and jewelry shop. But please. No more bullet holes. Please conjure fresh vintage clothing, okay? Thank you. Sean, Charlie, and Rosetta, this area over *here* will be your karaoke bar. And believe me, we ladies are going to get a *lot* of use out of that!"

"Wh-what about *my* request?" a hesitant voice stated from behind the group. "I don't suppose you have anything in that notebook for *me*, do you?" Sam let out a deep sigh, rolled her brown eyes and hastily flipped through the notebook. "Yes, here it is," Sam replied with resignation. "Okay, do you see that dark path between those jagged rocks? Just go between there, then keep walking until you run into a wall. Then turn left and keep walking. There will be a very narrow rock passageway. Cross that, then keep walking. Turn left at the fried chicken stand. Keep walking. You will eventually come to a completely barren area. That is where you may conjure your pegatorium, Howard."

"Oh, thank you!" Howard exclaimed as he embraced Sam's frame. "And you are welcome to visit anytime you like, my dear. We could have some…*ahem*…fun together."

"Gross. Get the fuck (*clink*) off of me," came Sam's terse reply before continuing. "Let's keep moving, people. Now, Abana and I will be conjuring a Complaint Center in *this* location. We believe that Henri will be pleased that both of his deceased wives will be working together to process any infractions of our rules. And helping us will be Marcus's parents, Lillian, Mr. and Mrs. Roper, and Amanda Denhart. Erick, Jason, and the rest of you men can conjure your sports bar in *this* location."

"I didn't ask for a fuckin' (*clink*) sports bar," Erick whispered to his increasingly annoyed wife who had her arms tightly folded while impatiently tapping her size six left foot. "Shit, (*clink*) that jar's really fuckin' (*clink*) sensitive."

"Okay, may *I* now ask a question?" Maddy inquired in a lilting voice as she tilted her head slightly to the side. "Why, of course you may, Maddy," Sam replied. "But please make it quick. I have much more to go over."

"Oh, *this* won't take very long," Maddy replied as she innocently batted her copper eyelashes at her overbearing friend. "I just have *one* question. And that question is…" Maddy's voice trailed off for a moment before she got into Sam's face and screamed, "Who the *fuck* (*clink*) put *you* in charge? *I'm* the one that the JQ had make contact with Gobbo! *I'm* the one that convinced him to let us in as soon as Vetis hit the bricks to try to kill the JQ! *I'm* the one that promised him that he and the rest of the dark souls would be allowed to live here in peace as long as they played nicely with us! *I'm* the one that promised them no more torture and a chance for redemption of their black fuckin' (*clink*) souls! Is this fuckin' (*clink*) place called 'Samville?' Fuck (*clink*) no, it isn't! It's called 'Maddyville!'"

"Maddyville?" Erick inquired of his wife. "Where the fuck (*clink*) did you come up with 'Maddyville?'"

"Well," Maddy began excitedly explaining. "I figured that we needed a new cool name for our new home in the universe. I mean, we can't keep calling it 'Perdition' now, can we? That's fuckin' (*clink*) depressing. And I just thought since *I'm* going to be the mayor, then it should be called 'Maddyville.' Pretty cool, huh?"

"No, it isn't cool," her beloved husband responded dryly. "And who said that *you* were going to be mayor? What, are you just going to self-appoint yourself and surround yourself with a bunch of feckless yes-men who will mindlessly do your bidding, then disparage anyone that has even the *slightest* disagreement with you? And then, claim that everybody's out to get you and everything's rigged against you so that you will be an all-powerful martyr for all eternity? Was *that* your brilliant fucking (*clink*) plan?"

"Well, yeah, kinda," an embarrassed Maddy answered as she looked down upon her shuffling feet. Erick took his admonished wife into his arms, lifted her head with his index finger and said softly, "You don't *need* to be in charge. You don't *need* to be in control of everything. Just look around you. You are surrounded by the kindest souls in the universe. You can finally let your guard down and allow yourself to completely trust others. You don't have to be prepared for battle anymore. We can just live together in peace. We will *all* play our part, and we will run this place *together*."

"Buuuuut," Maddy tentatively began asking in her "hurt" voice. "Can I still run the group meetings? I've always been *really good* at that."

"Of course you may, my love," Erick answered before Lucy interrupted. "Hey! I've got an idea for a really cool name! How about 'Mel?'

Erick and Maddy looked at Lucy for a moment before simultaneously saying, "No." Erick's face then beamed with a huge smile as he said, "I think I have it! I think that I have our cool new name for this place! How about 'Unison?'"

The entire group cheered and applauded the suggestion with one notable exception who muttered under her breath, "It's *okay*, I guess, but it doesn't have the same ring as 'Maddyville.'"

She then perked up and said, "Okay fine. I'll run the meetings, but rules will be made by a vote of everyone living in Unison. Erick, Uncle Joe, Aunt Blair, and Aunt Patty will be my consiglieres."

"But...but...wait...you're still putting yourself in cha..." Erick attempted to interject before being sharply elbowed in the ribs by Lucy. "Do you really think that you're going to get a better deal than this? Just let her have it. Besides, it's not like there's a rules enforcement mechanism. Just do whatever you want."

Maddy glared at the disruptive pair before continuing. "Lucy, Jules, and Kristy will be in charge of rules enforcement."

"Yay! This will be fun!" Lucy yelled out. She then intensely looked Erick in his brown eyes and said, "You'd *better* be good. *I'm* going to be a hardass. And you *know* that I distrust men, even you. So don't fuck (*clink*) with me." Erick could do nothing but shake his head in amazement and laugh to himself at the absurdity of the situation. *Wow*, he thought to himself. *The more things change, the more they stay the same. Nothing's going to change their world.*

"And Sam," Maddy continued, "can be in charge of organizing shit (*clink*) and processing the fuckin' (*clink*) complaints. And there's *one* fuckin' (*clink*) complaint I'm going to take care of right fucking (*clink*) now! Come on Erick! Let's go behind those trees in our new forest!"

The group stood in silence and awkwardly stared up at the brilliant stars as they listened to the tell-tale sounds of passion coming from the grove of trees. Maddy emerged from the forest as she was pulling her pants up, strode over to Sam and said, "We don't really need these fuckin' (*clink*) things to prevent pregnancy or diseases, but they sure as fuck (*clink*) come in handy to get rid of fuckin' (*clink*) swear jars! And there's a helluva (*clink*) lot more where this came from, so don't try me, bitch (*clink*)!" Maddy then threw a used condom into the jar. All the glowing good deeds that had been collected disappeared as they were covered in Erick's spiritual seed. "Fine!" Sam yelled out before slamming the jar to the ground, causing it to disappear. "Just watch your language! It's not ladylike!"

"What fuckin' ever," Maddy replied dismissively. She then paused for a moment and listened for a clinking sound that never came. Satisfied, she began again. "Okay, now that *that's* settled, Gobbo, go round up your dark souls. We're about to have our first *official* meeting in Unison!"

Erick could only hold his bewildered head in his hands as he heard his wife's triumphant voice shout out, "Here ye! Here ye! Here ye! There's a new sheriff in town, heh, heh, heh."

Chapter 114

Long White Cadillac

"Awwwww, this is the life," a finally serene Maddy slurred as she stretched her petite, bikini-clad frame out on the lounge chair next to their newly conjured swimming pool. "Just hanging around, sipping on conjured tropical cocktails, taking a dip in the pool. Yeah, this is the life. I never thought that eternal bliss would be so..." Maddy halted in mid-sentence and turned her fierce green eyes towards the bushes that had suddenly began thrashing about. "Howard!" She yelled out. "You had *better not* be perving on us and jerking off in the bushes! What is it with guys who jerk off into plants? I mean, what the fuck did the plant do to deserve being covered in some freak's jizz? And what's erotic about that anyway? I mean peaches, sure, that makes sense. They kinda look the part. But innocent house plants? That's just wrong."

As Maddy was completing her somewhat coherent diatribe, the thrashing in the bushes intensified. "Oh fuck, I shouldn't have mentioned peaches," Maddy regretfully stated. "Howard! Get your ass out of there you fuckin' perv!"

"I'll handle this," the pale green-skinned Iris stated. She flicked her wrist and vines from the bushes wrapped around the waist of their quarry and lifted him into the air.

"I-I'm sorry, Maddy," a nervously excited Howard began mumbling as he gripped his engorged penis in his right hand. "But you ladies all look so…um…look so…um…*sexy* in those bikinis. You, and Sam, and Iris, and Jules, and Kristy, yes, *especially* Kristy and…and…" Howard's exclamation ended as he shot his climax several feet, cannonballing perfectly into Maddy's Mai Tai.

"Motherfucker!" Maddy screamed in disbelief as she wiped the splashed goo from her left eye. "Get the fuck out of here! And you are *soooo* fucking banned from the pool area! For all eternity! I have decreed it! Go back to your pegatorium and do weird shit with a dark soul!"

"I-I'm sorry, Maddy," Howard said as he slinked off toward his dark hole. A black, viciously scarred form carrying a round tray approached the pool-side table and said, "Here. I have conjured a fresh drink for you Maddy."

"That's *Mrs.* Sommers to you, you fucking creep. Thanks for the drink," Maddy replied. "Of course, Mrs. Sommers. My mistake and my apologies," the dark spirit of Detective Edmund Simmons answered before turning his attention to the rest of the group. "Would anyone else care for anything from the bar?"

"Naw, get the fuck out of here, you fuckin' douchebag traitor," Joseph Argento replied in a surly tone. Blair whispered something into her husband's ear. Joseph then said, "Wait. Come back here and drop that tray." Detective Simmons reluctantly returned to the table of anxious observers. Joseph lifted his brawny frame from his chair, looked his former best friend in the eye and struck him squarely under his chin. Edmund's demonic teeth flew out of his mouth in a stream of black bile. "*Now* you can go, asshole," Joseph stated. He picked up the dislodged teeth, placed them in a napkin, and handed them to his adoring wife.

"Okaaaay then," Maddy said. "I guess *that* little feud is going to last awhile. Well, let's change the subject. Hey, Aunt Patty! Who did you get to play the opening night of the newly conjured LOHAD? I bet it's somebody really cool, right?"

"Hey! I have a question!" Erick interjected. "I get that you wanted to replicate the club you had on Earth but what's the point of having the 'No Drugs! No Guns! No Assholes!' sign? I mean, we're in paradise. *Our* paradise. There isn't any of that shit up here."

"Oh yeah, there is," came Patty's immediate and terse reply. "There are *definitely* assholes up here. Assholes that would wear a conjured

Barry Manilow T-shirt into *my* fuckin' club! And that shit ain't happening! Got it?"

"Yeah, I got it," Erick replied softly as his wife pursed her lips tightly to keep herself from laughing. "Okay, now back to the question Mads asked," Patty continued. "So, I've reached out to all kinds of cool artists. And do you know what they told me? That the club wasn't big enough, and that they don't want to go slumming, and they don't want to travel all across the universe just to play a forty-five-minute set and blah, blah, blah. Fuckin' prima donnas. But I found two fucked up, don't give a shit motherfuckers to play a double bill! Lux Interior and Mojo Nixon! How fuckin' cool is *that* going to be?"

"Wow," the entire group stated in unison before Maddy exclaimed, "Hold on a minute! I think Arima's trying to get ahold of me! Yeah, Soul Sister, this is Lil' Red! I can hear you fine! Over and out!"

"Okay, hey Mad…I mean Lil' Red? I mean, you really don't have to yell so loud and say, 'over and out' after every sentence, okay?" Arima said.

"Yep! Copy that, Soul Sister! Over and out! So, what's the sitch? Is Vetis dead yet? Over and out!"

"Um, no," Arima answered. "He came down here, took one look at the JQ and split. I'm sure he's on his way back there. I'm not sure how long it takes to travel through the universe, but he should be there at any time."

"Figures. Fuckin' pussy," Maddy muttered. Arima responded, "Um, hey Lil' Red? Maybe you shouldn't say 'pussy' around the JQ anymore. They just got in trouble for using that word and they spilled that they heard it from you, so Kayla and Rachel are kinda pissed right now."

"What's with all the fuckin' language police, anyway? Over and out!" Maddy yelled as she glanced over at the haughty face of Sam. "Oh fuck you, Sam. Like you think you know everything," Maddy stated before turning her attention back to Arima. "Yep, okay, Soul Sister! We kinda figured he would puss…um…I mean that he'd back down! That's cool! We're all set up here for when he shows up! We're almost done conjuring our little slice of heaven! All we have to do is not let him in the Great Door, then his time will run out, and he'll be sucked right back to the last place on Earth that he'd been, and his physical form will be trapped there! Then the JQ can fuck him up! Over and out! Oh! And one more fuckin' thing! You need to have a talk with your perv friend! Do you know what he just did? He was looking at us women and jerking off in the bushes and blew his fuckin' wad right into my drink! That shit isn't cool, Soul Sister! You need to set him straight, or I will, got it? Over and out!"

"Yeah, okay Lil' Red. I'll have a talk with him," a slightly embarrassed Arima replied. Maddy then said, "Oh, and just one more thing! Is my lovely daughter there? I want to say hi to Josie! Over and out!"

"Naw," Arima answered. "She took Lionnel to Bermuda for a few days. His friend Tabitha has been calling him wanting him to come over and help her study and Josie's getting really jealous and pissed about it. She said that if she doesn't get him away from that little skank that she's going to cut her head off and that would piss Lionnel off, so she doesn't want to do that."

"Huh," Maddy replied. "Well, I can't see as I blame her. Chicks gotta protect her property. If that little whore doesn't back down, then she'll leave Josie no choice. Well, okay then! Keep me updated Soul Sister! Hug everybody for us and we'll talk soon! Well, maybe not Rachel and Kayla if they're being uptight little bitches, but hug everybody else! Maddy out!"

Maddy settled back into her lounge chair just as there was a frenzied pounding at the Great Door. "Gobbo!" Maddy ordered. "Get your sniveling ass over here! It's showtime!"

Maddy, Gobbo and the rest of the group got up from their pool side seats and approached the Great Door while snickering.

"Gobbo!" Vetis roared. "Let me in! Shit didn't work out!"

"Whooooo iiiis iiiit?" an exaggeratedly high female voice responded followed by giggling.

"Who is it?" Vetis yelled back. "Who the fuck do you *think* it is? The pizza guy? It's Vetis! Let me in!"

The female voice lowered and replied through her chuckles, "Vetis isn't here, man." Vetis fumed as he heard uncontrolled laughter coming from the other side of the Great Door. He then looked up and noticed that the grand golden letters that had spelled out his name had been removed. In their place, in bright yellow, red, green, blue, pink, and purple, it read 'UNISON.'

"What the hell is going on in there?" Vetis screamed out. "Gobbo!

Stop fucking around and open this door, right now Goddammit!" Vetis heard the slight creak of hinges as the rectangular peep hole in the Great Door was being opened. Vetis's dark red eyes peered into the opening. He then gasped at what he saw. Peering back at him were a pair of glowing green eyes. "Hey, hey, hey, what the fuck are *you* doing in there, bitch?" Vetis began stammering. "Gobbo! Kill this bitch now and let me in!"

"Oh, I'm sorry, Vetis," Maddy coolly replied. "But you *see*, Gobbo and the *rest* of the dark souls got tired of putting up with your shit. So, they invited us to come over and…um…redecorate. And that is what we have done. And I know that Gobbo told you that the Junior Quad could be destroyed if you separated them, but that was a little fib. Actually, he didn't lie to you completely. All the *accurate* information was in your daily briefing. There's really no excuse for not having read those. And… Hey! Don't drop that! Do you know how long it took me to conjure that fucking thing? Jesus, take a little pride in your work, wouldja? Sorry about that. These fucking dark souls don't give a fuck about anything. Anywhoooo, where was I?

"Oh yeah. And I'm not the *only* one here from Enlightenment. I've brought a *whole group* of Pure Souls with me. Sorry, but you're just going to have to face it. This place is under new management. And we have called it 'Unison.' Why? Because we are so much stronger when we work together as a group than when we work against one another individually. You know when you're in a conversation and everybody's talking over one another and everybody eventually gets pissed and not one fucking thing is accomplished by it? See, that's the world that *you* tried to create. A world where everybody is suspicious of one another and hates one another then wants to actually kill one another. But through your defeat, people have realized that they have much more in common than they have differences. They have realized that hating one another doesn't do anything to benefit *anybody*. They have learned that by working together, that *everybody* has a chance to live a long, happy life both on Earth and in Enlightenment. Yes, Vetis, they have learned to work in Unison."

"That's not *actually* why I thought of it," Erick whispered up to his wife. "I just thought it sounded cool at the time and it was better than 'Maddyville' and it kinda played into how the JQ always speak in unison and shit like that. I didn't think about any of *that* stuff until you started your little speech."

"Shut up, Erick! I'm on a roll here! And it is *not* cooler than 'Maddyville'!" Maddy shot back before glaring once again into the forlorn eyes of a spineless demon. "So, you see, Vetis, you *really* aren't welcome here. In fact, a vile piece of shit like you isn't welcome *anywhere* where there are good, decent people. They have rejected you. Oh, and your tiny little army of twenty-three UN dignitaries that you think will lead a new war on Earth? Well, don't worry about *them*. My *daughter* is going to take care of *them* really soon. Too bad you won't be around to see it. But, if you're lucky, maybe they'll let you *hang around* for a while and watch the grand finale of our sordid little tale. So, I'm sorry, but we can't let you in. Plus, the place is still a *bit* of a mess and we *really* aren't prepared to entertain. But, hey! Thanks *so much* for stopping by! It means the *world* to us! Seriously. It *literally* means the world to us! Okay, then! Safe travels! Byeeeeee!"

Vetis roared in frustration as the peephole door slammed shut and he once again was forced to listen to the howls of mocking laughter. "Motherfucker!" Vetis screamed. "Oh shit! I can feel it! I'm being pulled back! Gobbo! Gobbo, please! Come on little buddy! Let me in! I'll do anything! You can rule Perdition! Anything! Please Gobbo- Noooooooooo!" Gobbo could not help but smile as he heard the voice of his eternal oppressor finally fade out of his tormented life. "Fuck him," Gobbo defiantly stated.

"Hey!" Maddy yelled out. "Watch your fuckin' language! There's kids around! Jesus Christ, were you raised by heathens or something? Show some fuckin' class!" Gobbo then wondered if he had made the right decision.

"So, why are *we* here exactly?" Vai asked her friends as they were sitting around folding tables next to the long, white hearse playing cards and watching the delighted faces of the Junior Quad. The foursome was prancing around the field on their ponies playing polo. They were using dismembered legs as mallets and a decapitated head as the ball that had been provided by their fathers. "Goooooooaaaaal!" Sigourney shouted out. "See? We *girls* are better than you *boys* at *everything*. Even *polo*," Euna snottily stated. "That's not true!" Kane shouted out followed by

Thanatos. "Yeah, that's not true! We let you win! You cheated! We're better!"

"Boys!" their mother, Kayla scolded. "You did *not* let them win! They won fair and square. Now apologize to them! Or do you want yet *another* week on laundry duty?"

"No Ma'am," the boys answered meekly as they hung their heads. "We're sorry. You won fair and square."

"And girls," Rachel added. "It really isn't polite to rub the noses of your opponents in your victory. It is unsportsmanlike. Now, you two apologize for that. Or do you want to do dishes for the next month?"

"No, Ma'am," the girls replied. "We're sorry we pointed out to you that we girls are better than you boys at everything, including polo, and that we are the stronger sex and..."

They were suddenly cut off by their mother. "Girls! That is *not* an apology! Try again, or so help me, you will *both* find yourselves so grounded that you couldn't fly even if you're in an airplane!"

Sigourney and Euna let out a deep sigh, looked at one another and said, "Okay. We're sorry that we are better than you."

"Nope. Try again," a frustrated Rachel said as she began walking towards her all-powerful daughters. "Okay, okay, sheesh," Sigourney stated. Both girls then said, "We're sorry that we were poor sports and sore winners, and we won't do it again."

"That's better," a satisfied Rachel said as she walked back to the group. "So, anyway, what was the question again?" a tripping Arima asked. "Oh yeah. Why are we here? Well, Maddy's taken over Perdition and locked Vetis out, so he'll end up being trapped back here so the JQ can take him out and...oh yeah. Why *are* we here?"

"We are here, dearies," Jamie answered, "Just in case our little gladiators need some backup."

"We won't!" came the children's unified voices from the field as they continued to bat the head around with the dismembered legs. The group began chuckling before Rosa said, "Well, Jess, Arima, and I are here for a specific purpose. Arima just smoked some of her 'Killer Weed.' That will allow her to absorb the dark soul of Vetis. But instead of destroying him, I am going to manipulate his energy while he is in Arima. I am going to bind him in his own evil energy. Then, Arima will release his bound soul, Jess will recite her incantation and his great evil will give her great strength. His evil soul will perish as soon as it is transformed into Jess's permanent strength. Vetis will be no longer. And Jess will never feel the pain of evil again. And she will *always* be able to kick its ass."

"Oh, how fun," Adam stated followed by Aaron. "Yes, quite fun, indeed. Plus, we need to assist in putting the pieces of the body in the hearse. Oh, what fun Alexa will have playing with his body parts. But they will be quite heavy. I wonder if we will need more help."

At that moment, an out of breath Dragenstein came running into the field. Her white, chiffon dress was blowing up, exposing her large phallus and she was carrying her size eighteen white pumps. "Oh my, that was quite a trek. Have I missed anything?" she asked in her breathy voice. "No," Vai answered. "What the hell are *you* doing here? I thought you were on a drag tour. And would it kill you to wear some underwear? I mean, its really chilly out here."

"Teehee," Dragenstein tittered as she demurely covered her mouth. "Sorry about that. It's just that undergarments are so restrictive, and I tend to run a bit warm blooded. And I just *couldn't* miss this! I just *couldn't* miss the grand finale!"

"This isn't the grand finale," the trailing Kaneko stated as she picked up Vai's hand of cards and looked at them. "Gin! I win again! Nope, this isn't the grand finale. There will be blood, but not enough of it. Plus, if you've been counting the chapters, we're only on the twenty-second chapter of this book. There's always twenty-three. Always. So, this isn't the grand finale. But it sure as hell is going to be fun, right kids?"

"It sure will, Aunt Kaneko!" the enthralled children responded before Euna yelled out "Goooooaaaal! That's twelve to nothing boys!"

"Awwww shit, here he comes," Jessie stated as she buckled over in intense pain and chanted, "Malum tuum dolorem facit. et dolor meus es fortitudo mea, (*your evil causes pain. my pain is my strength*). Okay that's better. I'm ready."

A dark red cloud oozed from out of nowhere in the clearing. The nine-foot-tall, horned-headed, four-armed Vetis threw his head back and roared once again. "Okay, you little bastards. I'm back. Earlier I just thought I'd let you off the hook, but I've changed my mind. I'm going to destroy you."

"That's not true! You are lying!" the JQ replied in unison. "You are frightened of us. You know the power that we wield. You were forced to come back to us because Aunt Maddy has moved into your home, and you have nowhere else to go. You do not wish to play with us, but we wish to play with you."

"But not just yet!" Thanatos said before yelling out, "Goooooaaaaal!" "Hey!" Sigourney yelled. "That doesn't count! We weren't paying attention!" "It does so count!" Kane yelled back.

Vetis stood and watched the children in confused disbelief as there was a barrage of, "No it doesn't!", "Yes, it does!", "No, it doesn't!", "Yes, it does!"

Finally, Vai ended the verbal and pointless stalemate when she said, "Children, would you please stop your bickering and take care of Vetis?"

"Oh yeah, him," Thanatos answered. "Bring it on, you little fuckers. I can take anything that you throw at me," Vetis growled with fake confidence.

"Okay," The four children stated before casually looking at Vetis's knees. Their eyes glowed for a moment and Vetis's kneecaps exploded. Vetis screamed in anguish as he watched his dark red flesh and black bones fly across the field in a stream of black blood. He fell to the ground, lifted his four arms, and began concentrating on the four cute blonde heads that were bobbing towards him.

"What is he *doing?*" Kane asked. "I think he's trying to blow up our heads," Euna answered. "Really, is that what you are doing?" Sigourney asked of the desperate demon. "That's silly. You can't blow up our heads. You have no power over us. We know that you can blow up dark souls and the bodies of humans. But you cannot blow *us* up. Here, let us show you how to do it. Thanatos, would you like to do the honors?"

"Sure would," Thanatos stated. His eyes began glowing as he focused on the four-foot-long abdomen of the legless creature. Vetis let out a tortured wail as his internal organs exploded out of his frame, showering the onlookers with black blood and squishy, slimy intestines.

"Huh," Vai whispered to Rosa as she threw a piece of gooey flesh off her head. "It kinda *seems* to be enough blood for a grand finale." "Nope," was all the enthralled Rosa could say in response as she chewed her popcorn.

"How, how are you *doing* this to me?" the hysterical Vetis exclaimed as the JQ were binding his arms to the saddles of their Shetlands with leftover intestines. "This isn't supposed to happen to me! I am all-powerful! I control *everything*! I *am* everything! I can do *anything* that I want! I *never* have to face consequences!"

"No, you are *not* all-powerful," the children said in unison as they climbed upon the backs of their friends. "You are pure *evil*. You may be able to get your way by bullying and lying to others for a while, but eventually your debt will have to be paid. Eventually your evil deeds will catch up to you. Eventually you will be vulnerable. And eventually, *we* will be called. We are the four horsemen of the apocalypse, and we were sent here to help the human race extinguish pure evil. The pure evil that you possess and plant into the hearts of others. We are going to destroy you now. You are *not* all-powerful. You are nothing but a big pussy. HYAW!"

Upon hearing their cue, Snowball, Blackjack, Flame, and Snot began galloping at full speed in different directions, ripping Vetis's four arms from his body. Rivers of black blood flowed out of the gaping sockets as the children trotted back to the suffering body.

"Don't forget to save the head, children," Adam reminded followed by Aaron's, "Yes. Please save the head. Alexa would like to play with it."

"Okay fathers," the children replied. They began to giggle uncontrollably as their eyes glowed again. Vetis pleaded for mercy as he could feel razor-sharp slashes cutting through his throat. His screams turned to pathetic gurgles as the slashes penetrated ever deeper until his head was completely removed from his torso. The red, horned face of Vetis was frozen in an expression of eternal shock and fear as the remaining blood flowed out of his neck and pooled around his impotent horns.

"Got him!" Arima yelled out as she floated several feet above the scene. "And I have him bound in his own evil," Rosa answered. "Jess, are you ready?" "Fuck yeah. Give him to me," Jessie answered. Arima released the dark, bound soul of Vetis into the awaiting soul of her dear friend. Jessie could feel the anguish that Vetis was experiencing as his evil was being transformed and consumed by her feminine strength. Jessie flexed her muscles, smiled, walked over to the fragmented torso of their enemy, and carried it to the hearse with one arm.

The members of the Junior Quad were giggling and whispering to one another. "What are you four talking about?" Kayla asked. The four looked at her and said in unison, "We were just trying to make sure we remembered the joke that Aunt Maddy wanted us to tell after his arms were ripped off him. We are supposed to say, 'Well, I guess he won't be grabbing any more pussy with *those*.' Then we're supposed to say, 'Funny, right?'"

"That's enough!" Rachel yelled out. "That is now the *third time* that you have used the P-word!"

"But Mothers," the JQ began pleading. "Aunt Maddy said that it would be funny."

"Well, it *isn't* funny!" Rachel countered. "It is *not* funny to hear those filthy words coming out of the mouths of children! We are going to go home and wash your mouths out with soap! Then, you are going to bed early and you are grounded for a week! Do you four understand?"

"Yes, Ma'am," the four despondent children replied as they began placing the slimy remnants of Vetis into the back of the long, white, Cadillac.

Maddy and Erick silently departed from their observation perch in Arima's soul. Maddy turned to her beloved husband and said, "What the fuck is *wrong* with those uptight bitches? That was gold! Pure fucking gold! Sure, I could have delivered it *better*, but having kids say that? That was funny as fuck! I *told* you we never should have let the Twins get involved with those two. Nope. They've been nothing but trouble."

The only reply that a beaten down Erick could provide was, "Okay. You're right. I'll go conjure up the ice cream."

Chapter 115

If You Want Blood (You've Got It)

The air temperature outside the estate was beginning to plummet in the early evening of February 13th, 2043. Inside the cozy home, two increasingly frustrated mothers were frantically trying to get ready before their departure to an art gallery in Brooklyn. "For the last time children," Rachel was saying sternly as she applied glittery makeup to her ebony face, "You are *not* going to the art show tonight!"

"But why not?" the four pleading voices answered in unison. "We'll be good. We promise."

Kayla put her hair dryer down and looked into the seemingly innocent eyes of Sigourney, Euna, Kane, and Thanatos. "Because, children, we will be up very late, well past your bedtimes. Now please leave us alone and let us get ready. Go with Kaneko and get your dinner. Then, I'm sure she can teach you some fun games to play. Or do we need to have yet *another* week without TV?"

"Yeah, c'mon kiddos," Kaneko enthusiastically stated. "I've got four frozen cheese pizzas in the oven. And each of you gets your own. Then, I'm going to teach you all how to play poker. You do have piggie banks, don't you?"

"Okay," the children said in a resigned tone as they sorrowfully began trudging out of the room. "But we're *not* happy about it."

"Oh, and children," Rachel added. "No time travel or murdering tonight, understand? Just stay at home and play games with Kaneko, got it?"

"Yeah, we got it," the disappointed children replied. "You don't have to worry about us time traveling anymore. It isn't necessary now that Vetis is dead. Okay, mothers. Have a nice evening. We'll just go eat our pizzas and be good."

Kaneko left with the tikes. Rachel and Kayla heard their pattering footsteps descend the stairs. The twin sisters looked at one another, smiled and let out a loud "Woooooooo!"

"Oh, this is going to be so much fun tonight," Rachel said. "You bet," Kayla answered. "I just can't *wait* to see what the guests think about Alexa's artwork. Oh, I hope it goes over well. She has worked so hard on it these past few months." "Don't worry, my dear sister," Rachel replied. "I'm just sure that tonight will be a *hit!*" The pair looked at one another and once again yelled out, "Wooooooooo!"

Josie was firmly gripping Lionnel's hand as she excitedly opened the door to the art gallery. The pair were immediately stopped by a brick-wall of a man. "Sorry folks," the man stated in a dullard tone. "I have to check your IDs before you can come in."

"Al!" Josie exclaimed. "You *know* who we are! And what the hell are *you* doing here anyway?"

"Well," the six-foot-six-inch behemoth began explaining. "Alexa said that if I worked security tonight, she'd dress up in her cheerleader outfit for me and um…make me cheerful. So, here I am."

"Okay, first off, gross," Josie replied as she shook her curly copper locks in disbelief. "Secondly, you will *not* be working door security tonight. We have the Twins and the twins for that. How about you go into the kitchen, hmmmmm? You can be…um…food security. Your job is to keep Aunt Arima from the…" Josie's voice trailed off as she saw Arima in the corner popping something into her mouth. "Aunt Arima!" Josie yelled. "*Please* don't eat all the hors d'oeuvres! Those are for our guests!"

"Oh, hey, Niece Josie," Arima calmly answered. "Yeah, sorry about that, but these little bacon wrapped ones are just so good." "Aunt Arima," Josie said as she sauntered over to her aunt wearing an amused look on her youthful face. "*That* isn't bacon." She then leaned over and whispered something into her ear. Arima clutched her mouth and dashed into the nearby restroom.

"Okay, everybody," Josie announced to the gathering of her murderer's row. "Let's get ready. And remember, Alexa has been waiting for this night for months, so let's all just have a good time and make this an enjoyable and memorable evening for everyone. Okay?"

There was raucous applause and backslapping before the group assumed their positions for the event. A few minutes later, the hands on the clock struck twelve. The date was now February 14th. Valentines Day. "Happy nineteenth birthday, baby," Lionnel whispered into his love's ear. He shed a slight tear as he looked upon the five-foot and four-and-a-half-inch frame of his fiancée that was draped in a full, flowing red gown. "I hope you get everything that you have ever wished for tonight." "Oh, Lionnel," Josie purred. "You have *already* given me everything that I want. And more. Come on. Let's let them in."

"Welcome everybody!" Josie exclaimed as she unlocked the door and hung a sign that read, 'No Guns! No Drugs! No Assholes!' on the outside window. "Please, won't you come in and join us on this most special evening."

Twenty-three male dignitaries from all over the world began making their way through the entrance. They were stopped and thoroughly patted down by the all-white suited Adam and Aaron before handing their invitation to the awaiting Kayla and Rachel. The twin sisters would look carefully at each golden ticket which read,

Welcome to Alexa's premiere art show, Hanging Chads: The Lineage of our Ascension. Tonight you will be greeted by an explosion of artistic delights. And tonight, will mark the first evening of unison between the servants of Vetis and the members of Murder, Inc. Tonight, all debts will be settled, and we will become one in harmony. We are pleased that you have joined us. And we are pleased to join you. Welcome and enjoy the show.

Each dignitary let out a slight impressed gasp as they looked upon the artwork on the walls that were painted upon odd-looking canvases.

There were nearly photographic renditions of treasured faces from the lives of the Argento, Azar, and Sommers families. Henri, Gregory, Jerry, Marcus, and Cliff wore all black tuxedoes with red bow ties as they circulated around the room carrying trays of hors d'oeuvres. They would approach the dignitaries and say, "Would you care to try our bacon surprise? They really are to die for." More than one dignitary commented on how tasty the treat was while also noticing its unique texture. Rosa, Jessie, Jamie, Vai, and Dragenstein wore tight black knee-length dresses with red scarves around their necks. As they circulated throughout the party, they offered glasses of a thick, dark black liqueur. "Hmmmm, tastes a bit like licorice," they would frequently say following their first sip.

"What the hell are you looking for?" Lionnel asked Josie as she nervously peered out the front window. "Oh, um, nothing," Josie anxiously replied. She suddenly felt at ease as the front door opened for a final time and a young Black woman entered the gallery. "Oh, *hellooooo* there, Tabitha!" Josie squealed as she ran up and hugged the unsuspecting guest. "Um, Hi," Tabitha responded. "I was a little surprised by getting this invitation. I mean, I'm not sure what this gathering is about or this whole Vetis thing, but I'm glad to be here."

Lionnel looked confused as he watched his beaming Josie say in her overly friendly voice, "Oh, I wouldn't want *you* to miss *this*. Please just accept this as *my apology*. I know that I've been acting a *tiny bit* immature about your friendship with my Lionnel here, and I just wanted to make it up to you. Here, *please* let me show you around." Josie gave the perplexed Lionnel a mischievous wink as she locked her arm around Tabitha's and began leading her down the row of artwork that had been meticulously painted with brushes made from human hair on canvasses of skin.

"Now *this* painting is of my Great Grandparents, Hank and Betty Sommers standing in front of their new Buick. I never got the chance to meet them, nor did my mother, as they died in a car accident several years before she was born. They were leaving a key party, and he was drunk and *SMASH*! I heard they were nice, though. Now this is Charlie and Rosetta who taught my dad how to sing. Well, kind of, heh, heh, heh. And this is Robbie. He was a transexual friend of my parents who died at the hands of two rapists. And these two bloody torsos hanging in this construction site are what was left of them after my mother got ahold of them. Pretty cool, huh?

"*This* is a beautiful portrait of my grandfather, Freddie. Look how proud he looks. This portrait was painted from a picture taken just a few days before he passed away from cancer. My mom said that she had never seen him so calm and proud of himself after he left his wife. And here she is! This is my so-called bitch grandmother and biological grandfather, the Pastor. See how intricately painted the snake scales are on their faces? Alexa's just so talented. Come to find out, they weren't just *servants* of the demon Vetis, which I know you don't know about. They were *actually* his *children*. That's why they're snake-like. His Earthly offspring are always serpentine in some way or another. So, my mom is *actually* the product of incest between a demonic brother and sister. I know, gross right? Explains a lot about her, I guess.

"And speaking of the Pastor, here is a portrait of his *other* child, my Aunt Arima, surrounded by her mother, Abdalla, and her grandmother, Louise. Look at how they're glowing behind her. This is one of my favorites. And here is Aunt Arima's most handsome husband, Marcus, with his Moms and Pops. He loved them so, and he still goes to New Orleans to visit them at their gravesite at least once a year. He's right over there carrying that tray of bacon-wrapped hors d'oeuvres. You should try one. They're to *die* for! Anywhooo, *this* picture might be a bit confusing. I know its just bloody teeth on the pavement, but these are the teeth that my Great-Uncle Joe knocked out of the Pastor's mouth and took home as a present to my Great Aunt Blair.

"Now, this is Clyde Manfrengensen, Aunt Arima's boss at the morgue she and Marcus worked at. And these are the spirits of the most wonderful couple, Mr. and Mrs. Roper, who helped Aunt Arima before they ascended into Enlightenment. And speaking of Enlightenment, this is Herbert, also known as the Botanist, with his green wife, Iris. Look at the explosion of colors of all the flowers surrounding them! Alexa said it took her *hours* to mix the bloo…um…the *paint* to get the colors on this one right.

"Oh wow, memories. This really large canvass is a before and after. This is a bloody rendition of my Great Aunt Patty's club LOHAD the night she and everybody in the club were executed. See the detail of the bullet holes in Sean's flesh? He was my mom's manager at the bookstore that my mom owned. And the next picture is the kids-only club and diner that I turned it into following that tragedy. Oh, the fun games we played in that basement, let me tell ya. Oh! This is *also* one of my favorites! This is my first boyfriend being eaten alive by piranha! See how the calm, blue water in the pool is turning into a violent red? Yeah, I planned it that way. It's like, symbolic or something.

"What's next? Oh! These fine-looking ladies are my mom's best friends that she met in college. This is Sam, Jules, Lucy, and Kristy. We just lost Sam and Jules recently and we're still struggling to get over that. I pray that you never have to learn what it is like to lose a loved one. Especially a parent, like I've had to do. Okay, sorry. Let's not get all teary-eyed and lift our spirits a bit. This is a really cool painting of Larry, Pogo, and Pogo II. They were rapists and murderers that we kept around for our um…amusement. See all the little holes in Larry's chest? Yeah, I used to use him as a dart board. He was so fun. I kinda miss him. Now, *this* handsome couple is Stellan and Paciano, our friends and care-takers at our estate. And this is Kaneko, the luckiest woman to have ever lived.

"Now *here*, we have Adam and Aaron with their respective brides Rachel and Kayla. Look at the detail of the dripping blood on their smiling faces. They are always so happy when they get to play their games. You met them at the front door and don't worry. They wouldn't harm a fly. Well, unless I tell them to. Alexa said that she kept trying to paint a portrait of their children, but the image would disappear off the fle…um *canvass* as soon as she finished.

"This portrait is of Aunt Arima's best friends, Jamie, Cliff, and Jessie. Oh, and LucyFur is on Jessie's lap. She's kinda nuts. Don't piss her off. She's around here, somewhere. And this is Rosa with her coven. They were rescued by my dad from a bunch of white-supremacist dicks who enslaved them. Big mistake on their part. Rosa and her group have taken out *hundreds* of these assholes since. And this is Rosa's husband Gregory giving a speech at the UN. That's where all of tonight's guests are from. They're *actually* servants of Vetis and we're…um…joining them tonight. And finally, this *last* portrait is of my dad's friends, Pastor Tim and Jeremy. Their souls now live in the oceans of our world and their love for each other, and all humankind, has blessed every body of water upon the Earth. Whew. Man, that was a lot of work."

Tabitha, Josie, and Lionnel came to the end of the presentation and were standing by a wall that was draped in a long, red velour curtain. "Um," Tabitha began inquiring. "These are really great. And I'm really happy that you seem to have settled with these Vetis people and everything, but why aren't there any portraits of your parents? The show just seems to be a bit, um, incomplete."

"Oh, don't worry about *that*," Josie demurely said as the smiling Alexa joined her and took her hand. "We have *one more piece* to show everybody. And I *do believe* that its about time." Josie and Alexa stood behind a podium that was positioned in front of the large red curtain. "Here ye! Here ye! Here ye!" Josie boomed. The entire group turned their attention to her and fell into a bemused silence.

"Once again," Josie began, "thank you all for coming here. Thank you for allowing us to join with you on this glorious evening. And thank you *Taaaabiiiithaaaa* for joining us as well. You are our *most* special guest. You see, *I* know that *you* know everybody here. Because *I* know that *you* have been placed on this Earth to lead Vetis's next attack. But you aren't just a *servant* of Vetis, now, are you? No, you are *much more* special than that. I would like to now present our *final* piece of the exhibit. I love *all* this work, but *this* one is *by far* my favorite. I like to call this one...," Josie dramatically paused for a moment, looked directly at Tabitha with her jealous, green eyes, smiled wickedly, and concluded in a demented growl, "Who's Your Daddy?"

"Hit it Rod!" The goggle-lensed Rod slicked back his greasy hair and pulled on a wide, golden rope. There was a loud gasp as the crimson curtain succumbed to gravity and pooled on the floor. Josie's petite, mauve lips curled up in a morbid smile as she watched Tabitha's eyes begin to stream tears. Hanging on the wall was the violently dismembered body of Vetis. His torso had been split open, and all his internal organs had been rearranged in the cavity in a 'Peace' symbol. His long, black tongue hung out of his decapitated head that was lodged on the end of his erect penis. Alexa had lettered "DICKHEAD" on his forehead beneath his sawed-off horns. Streaks of black blood drizzled over the entire piece, making it look like Pollack had obscenely bastardized a demented work of Picasso. The four arms of Vetis had been screwed into the wall and were jutting out toward the aghast audience. Each of their hands were turned upward and held a large gold frame containing a painted canvass made of human flesh.

The arm on the far left held the portrait of the beaming faces of Uncle Joe, Aunt Blair, and Aunt Patty holding a smiling, three-year old, copper headed girl. The arm on the far right held the portrait of a proud and tearful Erick Parker cradling his daughter for the first time in the hospital. The arm on the bottom of the piece held the portrait of a flower-dressed and barefoot Josie embracing her husband-to-be, Lionnel. And jutting out from the chest cavity in the middle of the grisly peace sign was the fourth arm. It held the largest painting depicting a young, auburn-haired woman wearing a black hoody, and a devilish smile. The intense gaze of the brilliant green eyes of Madeline Ruth Sommers penetrated the dark souls in attendance causing them to shiver in fear.

"You know, *Taaaabiiithaaa*, Josie began again. "It's *one* thing to try to turn our world into a demonic, fucking hell-hole. But it's quite *another* to try to steal my *boyfriend* to do it! Fuck *you*, you skanky little snake!" Josie reached behind the podium, took out a sword and decapitated Tabitha with one stroke. A geyser of black blood-bile serpents came shooting out of Tabitha's gaping hole. Her body began to wilt and deflate until it was a pile of flaccid skin lying upon the white-tiled floor.

"Huh," a blank-looking Lionnel said. "I really thought that that she was just my friend." "Eh," Josie responded with a shrug. "Don't worry about it. We'll talk about it later." Alexa then shouted out, "Slaaaaaash-daaaaance!" Rod pressed a button on a remote and AC/DC's "If You Want Blood (You've Got It)" came thundering through the speakers embedded in the ceiling.

On cue, the jubilant members of Murder, Inc. sprang into action. Dragenstein ripped the arms off the nearest dignitary in one violent motion. She then began spinning the screaming man in a tight circle, sending streams of blood around the room as though he were a lawn sprinkler from hell.

Rachel, Kayla, Adam, and Aaron grabbed conveniently hidden axes and began chopping at the tops of the skulls of four others. They shrieked in agony as they fell to the floor with their blood and skull fragments showering the ceiling and artwork on the wall. Rosa slashed a throat, forced the gurgling man to his knees, pulled his head back violently, and released a torrent of blood which came shooting out of his gaping wound. Jessie grabbed a man by his neck, and thrust upwards, liberating his head and spinal column from his body. Blood gushed out of the man's sliced open back, creating a crimson, iron-scented mess all over the previously white tile.

An outside police cruiser stopped suddenly, and the driver started to exit the vehicle after he had seen sheets of blood spraying the inside window of the gallery. His partner grabbed the rookie by the arm and pulled him back into the cruiser. "Huh-uh," the experienced officer said. "That's a party being thrown by Murder, Inc. We don't get involved. Just keep driving."

The carnage was incomprehensible as the gleefully demented members rid the remaining forces of Vetis from the Earth. The skin and future canvass of each corpse was carefully cut away and removed by the meticulous Lionnel as his loving fiancée looked on. Josie's glimmering green eyes reflected the torrent of blood being unleashed within the hall. Cliff and Al, who had been relieved from food security, took turns beating a dignitary's face repeatedly until it resembled ground beef that had been mixed with pink play dough, put into a blender, poured into a cocktail glass, and garnished with a tomato. Gregory held one man down while Henri and Marcus used a two-man tree saw to viciously saw through his quivering abdomen. Intestines and organs came tumbling out of the exposed cavity and laid in a pool of depraved justice.

The smiling Vai quietly directed the slaughter as axes, knives, and machetes were being whirled around in a frenzy. Blood geysers intermingled with tiny pieces of bone shrapnel splashed upon the walls, ceiling, and floor with each subsequent blow. The joyfully exhausted group finally ceased their frantic spree and looked around with expressions of satisfaction as the ecstatic LucyFur was rolling around in the thick blood while purring. The ceiling was raining blood as the grotesque droplets succumbed to gravity and splashed upon the saturated floor and festive faces of the party's hosts. The walls had been transformed into scarlet waterfalls. Every inch of every surface of the space was covered in a two-inch thick paste of blood, brain, skin, tendons, and bone as though the entirety of a meat packing plant had exploded within the tight confines.

"This is what we saw as children, brother," Aaron stated followed by Aaron's, "Yes indeed. This was our vision. This is the final game that we saw Josie play. This is her grand finale."

The images of Alexa's beautiful artwork were barely visible behind the thick coat of dripping blood that was being absorbed by the flesh canvass. Every inch of every surface was completely covered in the dark crimson goo. With one exception. At the end of the room, being held up by the dismembered arm of a cowardly demon, was a pair of proud, glowering green eyes that had remained untouched as they overlooked the deliciously vicious events of the evening.

The blood-soaked form of Arima floated above the group. She exhaled deeply and the trapped dark souls of the dignitaries were released from her soul and into the blessed punchbowl of black liqueur which had been made from the flesh and bile of Vetis. As had been the 'Bacon Surprise.' The group exploded into laughter as Josie let out a satisfied breath and said, "Wow. The owner of this place is gonna be *really* pissed. This is a fuckin' *mess*! Somebody wanna call the clean-up crew? Nice job everyone! I've *never* been so proud of you! Let's go find some pizza! I'm fuckin' starvin'!"

As the cleaned-up and newly clothed group were preparing to depart out the back exit, Lionnel took Josie into his arms and embraced her. Their loving bodies were pressed against one another tightly. Lionnel looked at Josie directly in her sparkling green eyes and chuckled. He wiped a tear from his eye, gazed down at their joined abdomens and said, "Hey. I think that I just felt Erika Ruth kick." The pair began laughing with one another after Josie said, "Yeah. My dad's gonna be *really* pissed about *that*. But he'll get over it. He's going to love being a grandpa."

Epilogue

"Hey! Hey, wake up!" Erick cried out to his screaming wife. Maddy woke up saturated in her own sweat and found herself lying in her bed being gently shaken by her loving husband.

"Whoa, you musta *really* had a bad dream. Are you okay?" a concerned Erick stated softly to his beloved wife.

"Yeah. I was just dreaming about all the shit that has happened. Y'know, all the 'Chads' that I fucked up or killed back when I was a vigilante serial killer. Then, our getting involved with Murder, Inc. and taking out the Underground Autocratic Movement. Then finding out that the demon Vetis was really the one who was trying to conquer the Earth and Enlightenment, led by my real father, the Pastor, and my evil bitch mother. So, then we had to team up with my half-sister Arima and our daughter Josie and a bunch of other people and spirits to rid the cosmos of all the dark souls. Then chasing the twins of the twins and the Twins throughout time. Y'know. Same old, same old. I was just dreaming about all the shit we had to do to save the Earth and Enlightenment. What's for breakfast? I'm fuckin' starvin'!"

"Wow," Erick replied in wonderment. "That really *was* a helluva dream. But who is Chad? And Arima? And Vetis? *What* twins? And how was your bitch mother involved in this dream exactly? I'm sorry Maddy, but I have *no idea* what you're talking about."

"Wait, what?" the half-asleep Maddy exclaimed as she sat upright in the bed. "Are you telling me that all that shit that I just said was all a *dream*? None of that shit *happened*? That we're just a married couple with a daughter who has never been serial killers or had to battle the forces of true evil to save the cosmos? Is *that* what you're telling me? Don't you dare *Dallas* this shit! Don't you fuckin' *dare* tell me that this was all a dream!"

Erick began chuckling as he hugged his barely awake wife and said mischievously, "Naw. All that shit happened. I just wanted to fuck with ya...grandma."

"You motherfucker!" Were the last words that Erick heard his beloved wife scream as he ran out of the room laughing hysterically while Van Halen's version of "Happy Trails" boomed out of their conjured CD player.

THE END...um...Probably

Song Reference List

The author would like to thank the countless musical artists that have enhanced his entire life. In particular, the author would like to give a heartfelt thank you to the following artists for enhancing the experience of both writing and reading this book.

And thank you, dear reader, for your interest in and support of my work. Whether I have had the privilege of personally meeting you or not, please know that you have my eternal gratitude. I look forward to the time when my work will allow our hearts and minds to meet again. Bless you all.

-Evan

Cracker- "Time Machine"
Screaming Jay Hawkins- "I Put a Spell on You"
The Coasters- "Searchin'"
The Beatles- "Help!"
Jonathan Richman- "Vampire Girl"
Stray Cats- "Stray Cat Strut"
The Cars- "Dangerous Type"
Miranda Lambert- "Kerosene"
The Chordettes- "Lollipop"

Charlie Sexton- "Beat's So Lonely"
The Fifth Dimension- "Aquarius / Let the Sunshine In"
The Modern Lovers- "Roadrunner"
Todd Snider- "Precious Little Miracles"
Urge Overkill- "Positive Bleeding"
Bruce Springsteen- "Crush on You"
Mink DeVille- "Mixed Up, Shook Up Girl"
Peter Gabriel- "In Your Eyes"
Jefferson Starship- "Find Your Way Back"
Sweet- "Wig Wam Bam"
Chuck Berry- "School Days"
Sha-Na-Na- "Born to Hand Jive"
Elton John- "Street Kids"
Nick Lowe- "I Love the Sound of Breaking Glass"
Ethel Merman & Ray Middleton- "Anything You Can Do (I Can Do Better)"
REM – "Walk Unafraid"
Olivia Newton-John & John Travolta- "We Go Together"
David Bowie- "Across the Universe"
The Blasters- "Long White Cadillac"
AC/DC- "If You Want Blood (You've Got It)"
Van Halen- "Happy Trails"